A.S. by<del>tt</del> <del>is a</del>
novelist, <del>...</del> <del>...</del> <del>...</del> er
books include *Pos<del>...</del>* <del>...</del> <del>...</del> on the
Booker Prize in 1990, and the qu<del>a</del>rtet of *The
Virgin in the Garden*, *Still Life*, *Babel Tower*
and *A Whistling Woman*. She was appointed
DBE in 1999.

ALSO BY A.S. BYATT

Fiction

The Shadow of the Sun
The Game
The Virgin in the Garden
Still Life
Sugar and Other Stories
Angels and Insects
The Matisse Stories
The Djinn in the Nightingale's Eye
Babel Tower
The Biographer's Tale
A Whistling Woman
Elementals
The Children's Book

Non-fiction

Degrees of Freedom: The Novels of Iris Murdoch
Unruly Times: Wordsworth and Coleridge
Passion of the Mind: Selected Writings
Imagining Characters: Six Conversations about Woman Writers (with Ingês Sodré)
On Histories and Stories

A.S. BYATT

Possession

A Romance

VINTAGE BOOKS
London

Published by Vintage 2009

2 4 6 8 10 9 7 5 3 1

First published by Chatto & Windus Ltd, 1990

Vintage
Random House, 20 Vauxhall Bridge Road,
London, SW1V 2SA

www.vintage-books.co.uk

Addresses for companies within The Random House Group Limited
can be found at: www.randomhouse.co.uk/offices.htm

The Random House Group Limited Reg. No. 954009

A CIP catalogue record for this book
is available from the British Library

ISBN 9780099535157

The Random House Group Limited supports The Forest
Stewardship Council (FSC), the leading international forest
certification organisation. All our titles that are printed on
Greenpeace approved FSC certified paper carry the FSC logo.
Our paper procurement policy can be found at
www.rbooks.co.uk/environment

Printed and bound in Great Britain by
CPI Bookmarque, Croydon CR0 4TD

FOR ISOBEL ARMSTRONG

ACKNOWLEDGEMENTS

Acknowledgements are due to the following for permission to quote copyright material: The Coop UTOPIA S.R.L., Rome, for an extract from an essay by Silvia Vegetti Finzi entitled 'Melusina, Malia e Fobia del Femminile' (used here in translation) in *Melusina. Mito e Leggende di Una Donna Serpente*, 1986; the Hogarth Press and the Institute of Psycho-Analysis for an excerpt from *An Outline of Psychoanalysis* by Sigmund Freud in Vol. XXIII of the *Standard Edition of the Complete Psychological Works of Sigmund Freud*, translated by James Strachey; Routledge, Chapman & Hall Ltd for an excerpt from *Totem and Taboo* by Sigmund Freud, also translated by James Strachey and included in Vol. XIII of the *Standard Edition*; A. P. Watt Ltd on behalf of the Executors of the Estate of Robert Graves for the poem 'She Tells Her Love While Half Asleep', and two excerpts from the poem 'Sick Love' from *Collected Poems 1975* by Robert Graves; *Écrits: A Selection*, by Jacques Lacan, translated by Alan Sheridan, Tavistock Publications, 1977 and Routledge, 1989.

When a writer calls his work a Romance, it need hardly be observed that he wishes to claim a certain latitude, both as to its fashion and material, which he would not have felt himself entitled to assume, had he professed to be writing a Novel. The latter form of composition is presumed to aim at a very minute fidelity, not merely to the possible, but to the probable and ordinary course of man's experience. The former – while as a work of art, it must rigidly subject itself to laws, and while it sins unpardonably so far as it may swerve aside from the truth of the human heart – has fairly a right to present that truth under circumstances, to a great extent, of the writer's own choosing or creation... The point of view in which this tale comes under the Romantic definition lies in the attempt to connect a bygone time with the very present that is flitting away from us.

Nathaniel Hawthorne, Preface to
The House of the Seven Gables

And if at whiles the bubble, blown too thin,
Seem nigh on bursting, – if you nearly see
The real world through the false, – what *do* you see?
Is the old so ruined? You find you're in a flock
O' the youthful, earnest, passionate – genius, beauty,
Rank and wealth also, if you care for these:
And all depose their natural rights, hail you,
(That's me, sir) as their mate and yoke-fellow,
Participate in Sludgehood – nay, grow mine,
I veritably possess them – ...

And all this might be, may be, and with good help
Of a little lying shall be: so Sludge lies!
Why, he's at worst your poet who sings how Greeks
That never were, in Troy which never was,
Did this or the other impossible great thing!...

But why do I mount to poets? Take plain prose –
Dealers in common sense, set these at work,
What can they do without their helpful lies?
Each states the law and fact and face o' the thing
Just as he'd have them, finds what he thinks fit,
Is blind to what missuits him, just records

What makes his case out, quite ignores the rest.
It's a History of the World, the Lizard Age,
The Early Indians, the Old Country War,
Jerome Napoleon, whatsoever you please.
All as the author wants it. Such a scribe
You pay and praise for putting life in stones,
Fire into fog, making the past your world.
There's plenty of|'How did you contrive to grasp
The thread which led you through this labyrinth?
How build such solid fabric out of air?
How on so slight foundation found this tale,
Biography, narrative?' or, in other words,
'How many lies did it require to make
The portly truth you here present us with?'

      Robert Browning, from 'Mr Sludge. "the Medium"'

CHAPTER ONE

These things are there. The garden and the tree
The serpent at its root, the fruit of gold
The woman in the shadow of the boughs
The running water and the grassy space.
They are and were there. At the old world's rim,
In the Hesperidean grove, the fruit
Glowed golden on eternal boughs, and there
The dragon Ladon crisped his jewelled crest
Scraped a gold claw and sharped a silver tooth
And dozed and waited through eternity
Until the tricksy hero Herakles
Came to his dispossession and the theft.

> Randolph Henry Ash, from
> *The Garden of Proserpina*, 1861

The book was thick and black and covered with dust. Its boards were bowed and creaking; it had been maltreated in its own time. Its spine was missing, or rather protruded from amongst the leaves like a bulky marker. It was bandaged about and about with dirty white tape, tied in a neat bow. The librarian handed it to Roland Michell, who was sitting waiting for it in the Reading Room of the London Library. It had been exhumed from Locked Safe no. 5 where it usually stood between *Pranks of Priapus* and *The Grecian Way of Love*. It was ten in the morning, one day in September 1986. Roland had the small single table he liked best, behind a square pillar, with the clock over the fireplace nevertheless in full view. To his right was a high sunny window, through which you could see the high green leaves of St James's Square.

The London Library was Roland's favourite place. It was shabby but civilised, alive with history but inhabited also by living poets and thinkers who could be found squatting on the slotted metal floors of the stacks, or arguing pleasantly at the turning of the stair. Here Carlyle had come, here George Eliot had progressed through the bookshelves. Roland saw her black silk skirts, her velvet trains, sweeping compressed between the Fathers of the Church, and heard her firm foot ring on metal among the German poets. Here Randolph Henry Ash had come, cramming his elastic mind and memory with unconsidered trifles from History and Topography, from the felicitous alphabetical conjunctions of Science and Miscellaneous – Dancing, Deaf and Dumb, Death, Dentistry, Devil and Demonology, Distribution, Dogs, Domestic Servants, Dreams. In his day, works on Evolution had been catalogued under Pre-Adamite Man. Roland had only recently discovered that the London Library possessed Ash's own copy of Vico's *Principj di Scienza Nuova*. Ash's books were most regrettably scattered across Europe and America. By far the largest single gathering was of course in the Stant Collection at Robert Dale Owen University in New Mexico, where Mortimer Cropper worked on his monumental edition of the *Complete Correspondence of Randolph Henry Ash*. That was no problem nowadays, books travelled the aether like light and sound. But it was just possible that Ash's own Vico had marginalia missed even by the indefatigable Cropper. And Roland was looking for sources for Ash's *Garden of Proserpina*. And there was a pleasure to be had from reading the sentences Ash had read, touched with his fingers, scanned with his eyes.

It was immediately clear that the book had been undisturbed for a very long time, perhaps even since it had been laid to rest. The librarian fetched a checked duster, and wiped away the dust, a black, thick, tenacious Victorian dust, a dust composed of smoke and fog particles accumulated before the Clean Air Acts. Roland undid the bindings. The book sprang apart, like a box, disgorging leaf after leaf of faded paper, blue, cream, grey, covered with rusty writing, the brown scratches of a steel nib. Roland recognised the handwriting with a shock of excitement. They appeared to be notes on Vico, written on the backs of book-bills and letters. The librarian observed that it didn't look as though they had been touched before. Their edges, beyond the pages, were dyed soot-black, giving the impression of the borders of mourning cards. They coincided precisely with their present positions, edge of page and edge of stain.

Roland asked if it was in order for him to study these jottings. He gave his credentials; he was part-time research assistant to Professor Blackadder, who had been editing Ash's *Complete Works* since 1951. The librarian tiptoed away to telephone: whilst he was gone, the dead leaves continued a kind of rustling and shifting, enlivened by their release. Ash had put them there. The librarian came back and said 'yes', it was quite in order, as long as Roland was very careful not to disturb the sequence of the interleaved fragments until they had been listed and described. The Librarian would be glad to know of any important discoveries Mr Michell might make.

All this was over by 10.30. For the next half-hour Roland worked haphazardly, moving backwards and forwards in the Vico, half-looking for Proserpina, half-reading Ash's notes, which was not easy, since they were written in various languages, in Ash's annotating hand, which was reduced to a minute near-printing, not immediately identifiable as the same as his more generous poetic or letter-writing hand.

At 11.00 he found what he thought was the relevant passage in Vico. Vico had looked for historical fact in the poetic metaphors of myth and legend; this piecing together was his 'new science'. His Proserpine was the corn, the origin of commerce and community. Randolph Henry Ash's Proserpine had been seen as a Victorian reflection of religious doubt, a meditation on the myths of Resurrection. Lord Leighton had painted her, distraught and floating, a golden figure in a tunnel of darkness. Blackadder had a belief that she represented, for Randolph Ash, a personification of History itself in its early mythical days. (Ash had also written a poem about Gibbon and one about the Venerable Bede, historians of greatly differing kinds. Blackadder had written an article on R. H. Ash and relative historiography.)

Roland compared Ash's text with the translation, and copied parts onto an index card. He had two boxes of these, tomato-red and an intense grassy green, with springy plastic hinges that popped in the library silence.

'Ears of grain were called apples of gold, which must have been the first gold in the world while metallic gold was unknown ... So the golden apple which Hercules first brought back or gathered from Hesperia must have been grain; and the Gallic Hercules with links of this gold, that issue from his mouth, chains men by the ears: something which will later be discovered as a myth concerning the fields. Hence Hercules remained the Deity to propitiate in order to find treasures, whose god was Dis (identical with Pluto) who carries off Proserpine (another name for Ceres or grain) to the underworld described by the poets, according to whom its first name was Styx, its second the land of the dead, its third the depth of furrows ... It was of this golden apple that Virgil, most learned in heroic antiquities, made the golden bough Aeneas carries into the Inferno or Underworld.'

Randolph Henry Ash's Proserpina, 'gold-skinned in the gloom', was also 'grain-golden'. Also 'bound with golden links' which might have been jewellery or chains. Roland wrote neat cross-references under the headings of grain, apples, chain, treasure. Folded into the page of Vico on which the passage appeared was a bill for candles on the back of which Ash had written: 'The individual appears for an instant, joins the community of thought, modifies it and dies; but the species, that dies not, reaps the fruit of his ephemeral existence.' Roland copied this out and made another card, on which he interrogated himself.

'*Query*? Is this a quotation or is it Ash himself? Is Proserpina the Species? A very C19 idea. Or is she the individual? When did he put these papers in here? Are they pre- or post-*The Origin of Species*? Not conclusive anyway – he cd have been interested in Development generally ...'

That was 11.15. The clock ticked, motes of dust danced in sunlight, Roland meditated on the tiresome and bewitching endlessness of the quest for knowledge. Here he sat, recuperating a dead man's reading, timing his exploration by the library clock and the faint constriction of his belly. (Coffee is not to be had in the London Library.) He would have to show all this new treasure-trove to Blackadder, who would be both elated and grumpy, who would anyway be pleased that it was locked away in Safe 5 and not spirited away to Robert Dale Owen University in Harmony City, with so much else. He was reluctant to tell

Blackadder. He enjoyed possessing his knowledge on his own. Proserpina was between pages 288 and 289. Under page 300 lay two folded complete sheets of writing paper. Roland opened these delicately. They were both letters in Ash's flowing hand, both headed with his Great Russell Street address and dated, June 21st. No year. Both began 'Dear Madam', and both were unsigned. One was considerably shorter than the other.

Dear Madam,

Since our extraordinary conversation I have thought of nothing else. It has not often been given to me as a poet, it is perhaps not often given to human beings, to find such ready sympathy, such wit and judgment together. I write with a strong sense of the necessity of continuing our ~~intere~~ talk, and without premeditation, ~~under the impression that you were indeed as much struck as I was by our quite extraordinary~~ to ask if it would be possible for me to call on you, perhaps one day next week. I feel, I know with a certainty that cannot be the result of folly or misapprehension, that you and I must speak again. I know you go out in company very little, and was the more fortunate that dear Crabb managed to entice you to his breakfast table. To think that amongst the babble of undergraduate humour and through all Crabb's well-wrought anecdotes, even including the Bust, we were able to say so much, that was significant, simply to each other. ~~I cannot surely be alone in feeling~~

The second one ran:

Dear Madam,

Since our pleasant and unexpected conversation I have thought of little else. Is there any way in which it can be resumed, more privately and at more leisure? I know you go out in company very little, and was the more fortunate that dear Crabb managed to entice you to his breakfast table. How much I owe to his continuing good health, that he should feel able and eager, at eighty-two years of age, to entertain poets and undergraduates and mathematical professors and political thinkers so early in the day, and to tell the anecdote of the Bust with his habitual fervour without too much delaying the advent of buttered toast.

Did you not find it as strange as I did, that we should so immediately understand each other so well? For we did understand each other uncommonly well, did we not? Or is this perhaps a product of the over-excited brain of a middle-aged and somewhat disparaged poet, when he finds that his ignored,

his arcane, his deviously perspicuous meanings, which he thought not
*meanings, since no one appeared able to understand them, had after all one
clear-eyed and amused reader and judge? What you said of Alexander Selkirk's
monologue, the good sense you made of the ramblings of my John Bunyan,
your understanding of the passion of Iñez de Castro . . . gruesomely* resurrecta
. . . but that is enough of my egoistical mutter, and of those of my personae,
who are not, as you so rightly remarked, my masks. *I would not have you
think that I do not recognise the superiority of your own fine ear and finer
taste. I am convinced that you must undertake that grand Fairy Topic — you
will make something highly strange and original of it. In connection with that,
I wonder if you have thought of Vico's history of the primitive races — of his
idea that the ancient gods and later heroes are personifications of the fates and
aspirations of the people rising in figures from the common mind? Something
here might be made of your Fairy's legendary rootedness in veritable castles
and genuine agricultural reform — one of the queerest aspects of her story, to a
modern mind. But I run on again; assuredly you have determined on your own
best ways of presenting the topic, you who are so wise and learned in your
retirement.*

*I cannot but feel, though it may be an illusion induced by the delectable
drug of* understanding, ~~that you must in some way share my eagerness that
further conversation could be mutually profitable that we must meet. I cannot~~
*do not think I ~~am~~ can be mistaken in my belief that our meeting was also
~~important~~ interesting to you, and that however much you may value your
seclusion*

*I know that you came only to honour dear Crabb, at a small informal party,
because he had been of assistance to your illustrious Father, and valued his
work at a time when it meant a great deal to him. But you did come out, so
I may hope that you can be induced to vary your quiet days with*

I am sure you understand

Roland was first profoundly shocked by these writings, and
then, in his scholarly capacity, thrilled. His mind busied itself
automatically with dating and placing this unachieved dialogue
with an unidentified woman. There was no year on the letters,
but they must necessarily come after the publication of Ash's
dramatic poems, *Gods, Men and Heroes*, which had appeared in
1856 and had not, contrary to Ash's hopes and perhaps expectations, found favour with the reviewers, who had declared his
verses obscure, his tastes perverse and his people extravagant and

improbable. 'The Solitary Thoughts of Alexander Selkirk' was one of those poems, the musings of the castaway sailor on his island. So was 'The Tinker's Grace', purporting to be Bunyan's prison musings on Divine Grace, and so was Pedro of Portugal's rapt and bizarre declaration of love, in 1356, for the embalmed corpse of his murdered wife, Iñez de Castro, who swayed beside him on his travels, leather-brown and skeletal, crowned with lace and gold circlet, hung about with chains of diamonds and pearls, her bone-fingers fantastically ringed. Ash liked his characters at or over the edge of madness, constructing systems of belief and survival from the fragments of experience available to them. It would be possible, Roland thought, to identify the breakfast party, which must have been one of Crabb Robinson's later efforts to provide stimulating conversation for the students of the new London University.

Crabb Robinson's papers were kept in Dr Williams's Library in Gordon Square, originally designed as University Hall, supported by Robinson as a place in which lay students could experience collegiate university life. It would, it must, be easy to check in Robinson's diary an occasion on which Ash had breakfasted at 30 Russell Square with a professor of mathematics, a political thinker (Bagehot?) and a reclusive lady who knew about, who wrote, or proposed to write, poetry.

He had no idea who she might be. Christina Rossetti? He thought not. He was not sure that Miss Rossetti would have approved of Ash's theology, or of his sexual psychology. He could not identify the Fairy Topic, either, and this gave him a not uncommon sensation of his own huge ignorance, a grey mist, in which floated or could be discerned odd glimpses of solid objects, odd bits of glitter of domes or shadows of roofs in the gloom.

Had the correspondence continued? If it had, where was it, what jewels of information about Ash's 'ignored, arcane, deviously perspicuous meanings' might not be revealed by it? Scholarship might have to reassess all sorts of certainties. On the other hand, had the correspondence ever in fact started? Or had Ash finally floundered in his inability to express his sense of urgency? It was this urgency above all that moved and shocked Roland. He thought he knew Ash fairly well, as well as anyone might

7

know a man whose life seemed to be all in his mind, who lived a quiet and exemplary married life for forty years, whose correspondence was voluminous indeed, but guarded, courteous and not of the most lively. Roland liked that in Randolph Henry Ash. He was excited by the ferocious vitality and darting breadth of reference of the work, and secretly, personally, he was rather pleased that all this had been achieved out of so peaceable, so unruffled a private existence.

He read the letters again. Had a final draft been posted? Or had the impulse died or been rebuffed? Roland was seized by a strange and uncharacteristic impulse of his own. It was suddenly quite impossible to put these living words back into page 300 of Vico and return them to Safe 5. He looked about him: no one was looking: he slipped the letters between the leaves of his own copy of the Oxford Selected Ash, which he was never without. Then he returned to the Vico annotations, transferring the most interesting methodically to his card index, until the clanging bell descended the stairwell, signifying the end of study. He had forgotten about his lunch.

When he left, with his green and tomato boxes heaped on his Selected Ash, they nodded affably from behind the issue desk. They were used to him. There were notices about mutilation of volumes, about theft, with which he quite failed to associate himself. He left the building as usual, his battered and bulging briefcase under his arm. He climbed on a 14 bus in Piccadilly, and went upstairs, clutching his booty. Between Piccadilly and Putney, where he lived in the basement of a decaying Victorian house, he progressed through his usual states of somnolence, sick juddering wakefulness, and increasing worry about Val.

CHAPTER TWO

> A man is the history of his breaths and thoughts, acts, atoms and
> wounds, love, indifference and dislike; also of his race and nation,
> the soil that fed him and his forebears, the stones and sands of his
> familiar places, long-silenced battles and struggles of conscience,
> of the smiles of girls and the slow utterance of old women, of
> accidents and the gradual action of inexorable law, of all this and
> something else too, a single flame which in every way obeys the
> laws that pertain to Fire itself, and yet is lit and put out from one
> moment to the next, and can never be relumed in the whole waste
> of time to come.

So Randolph Henry Ash, *ca* 1840, when he was writing *Ragnarök*,
a poem in twelve books, which some saw as a Christianising of
the Norse myth and some trounced as atheistic and diabolically
despairing. It mattered to Randolph Ash what a man was, though
he could, without undue disturbance, have written that general
pantechnicon of a sentence using other terms, phrases and rhythms
and have come in the end to the same satisfactory evasive metaphor. Or so Roland thought, trained in the post-structuralist
deconstruction of the subject. If he had been asked what Roland
Michell was, he would have had to give a very different answer.

In 1986 he was twenty-nine, a graduate of Prince Albert College,
London (1978) and a PhD of the same university (1985). His
doctoral dissertation was entitled *History, Historians and Poetry?
A Study of the Presentation of Historical 'Evidence' in the Poems of
Randolph Henry Ash*. He had written it under the supervision of
James Blackadder, which had been a discouraging experience.
Blackadder was discouraged and liked to discourage others. (He

was also a stringent scholar.) Roland was now employed, part-time, in what was known as Blackadder's 'Ash Factory' (why not Ashram?, Val had said) which operated from the British Museum, to which Ash's wife, Ellen, had given many of the manuscripts of his poems, when he died. The Ash Factory was funded by a small grant from London University and a much larger one from the Newsome Foundation in Albuquerque, a charitable Trust of which Mortimer Cropper was a Trustee. This might appear to indicate that Blackadder and Cropper worked harmoniously together on behalf of Ash. This would be a misconception. Blackadder believed Cropper to have designs on those manu-scripts lodged with, but not owned by, the British Library, and to be worming his way into the confidence and goodwill of the owners by displays of munificence and helpfulness. Blackadder, a Scot, believed British writings should stay in Britain and be studied by the British. It may seem odd to begin a description of Roland Michell with an excursus into the complicated relations of Blackadder, Cropper and Ash, but it was in these terms that Roland most frequently thought of himself. When he did not think in terms of Val.

He thought of himself as a latecomer. He had arrived too late for things that were still in the air but vanished, the whole ferment and brightness and journeyings and youth of the 1960s, the blissful dawn of what he and his contemporaries saw as a pretty blank day. Through the psychedelic years he was a schoolboy in a depressed Lancashire cotton town, untouched alike by Liverpool noise and London turmoil. His father was a minor official in the County Council. His mother was a disappointed English gradu-ate. He thought of himself as though he were an application form, for a job, a degree, a life, but when he thought of his mother, the adjective would not be expurgated. She was disappointed. In herself, in his father, in him. The wrath of her disappointment had been the instrument of his education, which had taken place in a perpetual rush from site to site of a hastily amalgamated three-school comprehensive, the Aneurin Bevan school, combining Glasdale Old Grammar School, St Thomas à Becket's C of E Secondary School and the Clothiers' Guild Technical Modern School. His mother had drunk too much stout, 'gone up the school', and had him transferred from metal work to Latin, from Civic Studies to French; she had paid a maths coach with the earnings of a paper-round she had sent him out on. And so he had acquired an old-fashioned classical education, with gaps where teachers had been made redundant or classroom chaos had reigned. He had done what was hoped of him, always, had four As at A Level, a First, a PhD. He was now essentially unemployed, scraping a living on part-time tutoring, dogsbodying for Black-adder and some restaurant dishwashing. In the expansive 1960s he would have advanced rapidly and involuntarily, but now he saw himself as a failure and felt vaguely responsible for this.

He was a small man, with very soft, startling black hair and small regular features. Val called him Mole, which he disliked. He had never told her so.

He lived with Val, whom he had met at a Freshers' tea party in the Student Union when he was eighteen. He believed now, though this belief may have been a mythic smoothing of his memory, that Val was the first person his undergraduate self had spoken to, socially that was, not officially. He had liked the look of her, he remembered, a soft, brown uncertain look. She had been standing on her own, holding a teacup in front of her, not looking about her, but rather fixedly out of the window, as though she expected no one to approach and invited no one. She projected a sort of calm, a lack of strife, and so he went over to join her. And since then they had never not been together. They signed up for the same courses and joined the same societies; they sat together in seminars and went together to the National Film Theatre; they had sex together and moved together into a one-roomed flat in their second year. They lived frugally off a diet of porridge and lentils and beans and yogurt; they drank a little beer, making it spin out; they shared book-buying; they were both entirely confined to their grants, which did not go far in London, and could not be supplemented with holiday earnings, for these had vanished with the oil crisis. Val had been, Roland was sure, partly responsible for his First. (Along with his mother and Randolph Henry Ash.) She simply expected it of him, she made him always say what he thought, she argued points, she worried constantly about whether she was, whether they both were, working hard enough. They quarrelled hardly at all and when they did it was almost always because Roland expressed concern about Val's reserve with the world in general, her refusal to advance opinions in class, and later, even to him. In the early days she had had lots of quiet opinions, he remembered, which she had offered him, shyly slyly, couched as a kind of invitation or bait. There had been poems she had liked. Once she had sat up naked in his dark digs and recited Robert Graves:

> She tells her love while half asleep,
>   In the dark hours,
>   With half-words whispered low:
> As Earth stirs in her winter sleep
>   And puts out grass and flowers
>   Despite the snow,   .
>   Despite the falling snow.

She had a rough voice gentled, between London and Liverpool, as the group voice was. When Roland began to speak, after this, she put a hand over his mouth, which was as well, for he had nothing to say. Later, Roland noticed, as he himself had his successes, Val said less and less, and when she argued, offered him increasingly his own ideas, sometimes the reverse side of the knitting, but essentially his. She even wrote her Required Essay on 'Male Ventriloquism: The Women of Randolph Henry Ash'. Roland did not want this. When he suggested that she should strike out on her own, make herself noticed, speak up, she accused him of 'taunting' her. When he asked, what did she mean, 'taunting', she resorted, as she always did when they argued, to silence. Since silence was also Roland's only form of aggression they would continue in this way for days, or, one terrible time when Roland directly criticised 'Male Ventriloquism', for weeks. And then the fraught silence would modulate into conciliatory monosyllable, and back to their peaceful co-existence. When Finals came, Roland did steadily and predictably well. Val's papers were bland and minimal, in large confident handwriting, well laid-out. 'Male Ventriloquism' was judged to be good work and discounted by the examiners as probably largely by Roland, which was doubly unjust, since he had refused to look at it, and did not agree with its central proposition, which was that

Randolph Henry Ash neither liked nor understood women, that his female speakers were constructs of his own fear and aggression, that even the poem-cycle, *Ask to Embla*, was the work, not of love but of narcissism, the poet addressing his Anima. (No biographical critic had ever satisfactorily identified Embla.) Val did very badly. Roland had supposed she had expected this, but it became dreadfully obvious that she had not. There were tears, night-long, choked, whimpering tears, and the first tantrum.

Val left him for the first time since they had set up house, and went briefly 'home'. Home was Croydon, where she lived with her divorced mother in a council flat, supported by social security, supplemented occasionally by haphazard maintenance payments from her father, who was in the Merchant Navy and had not been seen since Val was five. Val had never, during their time together, proposed to Roland that they visit her mother, though Roland had twice taken her to Glasdale, where she had helped his father wash up, and had taken his mother's jeering deflation of their way of life in her stride, telling him, 'Don't worry, Mole. I've seen it all before. Only mine drinks. If you lit a match in our kitchen, it'd go up with a roar.'

When Val was gone, Roland realised, with a shock like a religious conversion, that he did not want their way of life to go on. He rolled over, and spread his loosened limbs in the bed, he opened windows, he went to the Tate Gallery alone and looked at the dissolving blue and gold air of Turner's Norham Castle. He cooked a pheasant for his rival in the departmental rat-race, Fergus Wolff, which was exciting and civilised, although the pheasant was tough and full of shot. He made plans, which were not plans, but visions of solitary activity and free watchfulness, things he had never had. After a week, Val came back, tearful and shaky, and declared that she meant at least to earn her living, and would take a course in shorthand-typing. 'At least you want me,' she told Roland, her face damp and glistening. 'I don't know why you should want me, I'm no good, but you do.' 'Of course I do,' Roland had said. 'Of course.'

When his DES grant ran out, Val became the breadwinner, whilst he finished his PhD. She acquired an IBM golfball typewriter and did academic typing at home in the evenings and various well-paid temping jobs during the day. She worked in the City and in teaching hospitals, in shipping firms and art galleries. She resisted pressure to specialise. She would not be drawn out to talk about her work, to which she almost never referred without the adjective 'menial'. 'I must do just a few more menial things before I go to bed' or, more oddly, 'I was nearly run over on my menial way this morning.' Her voice acquired a jeering note, not unfamiliar to Roland, who wondered for the first time what his mother had been like *before* her disappointment, which in her case was his father and to some extent himself. The typewriter clashed and harried him at night, never rhythmical enough to be ignored.

There were now two Vals. One sat silently at home in old jeans and unevenly hanging long crêpey shirts, splashed with murky black and purple flowers. This one had lustreless brown hair, very straight, hanging about a pale, underground face. Just sometimes, this one had crimson nails, left over from the other, who wore a tight black skirt and a black jacket with padded shoulders over a pink silk shirt and was carefully made up with pink and brown eyeshadow, brushed blusher along the cheekbone and plummy lips. This mournfully bright menial Val wore high heels and a black beret. She had beautiful ankles, invisible under the domestic jeans. Her hair was rolled into a passable pageboy and sometimes tied with a black ribbon. She stopped short of perfume. She was not constructed to be attractive. Roland half wished that she was, that a merchant banker would take her out to dinner, or a shady solicitor to the Playboy Club. He hated himself for these demeaning fantasies, and was reasonably afraid that she might suspect he nourished them.

If he could get a job, it might be easier to initiate some change. He made applications and was regularly turned down. When one came up in his own department there were 600 applications. Roland was interviewed, out of courtesy he decided, but the job went to Fergus Wolff, whose track record was less consistent, who could be brilliant or bathetic, but never dull and right, who was loved by his teachers whom he exasperated and entranced, where Roland excited no emotion more passionate than solid approbation. Fergus was also in the right field, which was literary theory. Val was more indignant than Roland about this event, and her indignation upset him as much as his own failure, for he liked Fergus and wanted to be able to go on liking him. Val found one of her insisting words for Fergus too, one which was askew and inaccurate. 'That pretentious blond bombshell' she said of him. 'That pretentious sexpot.' She liked to use sexist wolf-whistle words as a kind of boomerang. This embarrassed Roland, since Fergus transcended any such terminology; he was indeed blond, and he was indeed sexually very successful, and that was an end to it. He came to no more meals, and Roland feared Fergus thought this was a function of his, Roland's, resentment.

When he got home that evening he could smell that Val was in a mood. The basement was full of the sharp warmth of frying onions, which meant she was cooking something complicated. When she was not in a mood, when she was apathetic, she opened tins or boiled eggs, or at most dressed an avocado. When she was either very cheerful or very angry, she cooked. She stood at the sink, chopping courgettes and aubergines, when he came in, and did not look up, so he surmised that the mood was bad. He put down his bag quietly. They had a cavernous basement room which they had painted apricot and white, to cheer it up; it was furnished with a double divan, two very old arm-chairs with curvaceous rolled arms and head-rests, plum and plushy and dusty, a second-hand stained-oak office desk, where Roland worked, and a newer varnished beech desk, where the typewriter sat. These were back to back on the long side-walls each with their Habitat anglepoise, Roland's black, Val's rose-pink. On the back wall were bookcases, made of bricks and planks, sagging under standard texts, most of them jointly owned, some duplicated. They had put up various posters; a British Museum poster from the *Koran*, intricate and geometric, a Tate advertisement for a Turner exhibition.

Roland possessed three images of Randolph Henry Ash. One, a photograph of the death mask which was one of the central pieces in the Stant Collection of Harmony City, stood on his desk. There was a puzzle about how this bleak, broad-browed carved head had come into existence, since there also existed a photograph of the poet in his last sleep, still patriarchally bearded. Who had shaved him, when? Roland had wondered, and

Mortimer Cropper had asked in his biography, *The Great Ventriloquist*, without finding an answer. His other two portraits were photographic copies, made to order, of the two portraits of Ash in the National Portrait Gallery. Val had banished these to the dark of the hall. She said she did not want him staring at her, she wanted a bit of her life to herself, without having to share it with Randolph Ash.

In the dark hall the pictures were difficult to see. One was by Manet and one was by G. F. Watts. The Manet had been painted when the painter was in England in 1867, and had some things in common with his portrait of Zola. He had shown Ash, whom he had met previously in Paris, sitting at his desk, in a three-quarters profile, in a carved mahogany chair. Behind him was a kind of triptych with ferny foliage, to the left and right, enclosing a watery space in which rosy and silver fish shone between pondweeds. The effect was partly to set the poet amongst the roots of a wood or forest, until, as Mortimer Cropper had pointed out, one realised that the background was one of those compartmentalised Wardian cases, in which the Victorians grew plants in controlled environments, or created self-sustaining ponds, in order to study the physiology of plants and fishes. Manet's Ash was dark, powerful, with deepset eyes under a strong brow, a vigorous beard and a look of confident private amusement. He looked watchful and intelligent, not ready to move in a hurry. In front of him on his desk were disposed various objects, an elegant and masterly still life to complement the strong head and the ambivalent natural growths. There was a heap of rough geological specimens, including two almost spherical stones, a little like cannon balls, one black and one a sulphurous yellow, some ammonites and trilobites, a large crystal ball, a green glass inkwell, the articulated skeleton of a cat, a heap of books, two of which could be seen to be the *Divina Commedia* and *Faust*, and an hourglass in a wooden frame. Of these, the inkwell, the crystal ball, the hourglass, the two named books and two of the others, which had been painstakingly identified as *Quixote* and Lyell's *Geology*, were now in the Stant Collection, where a room had been arranged, Wardian cases and all, to resemble the Manet setting. The chair had also been collected, and the desk itself.

The portrait by Watts was mistier and less authoritative. It had been painted in 1876 and showed an older and more ethereal poet, his head rising, as is common with Watts's portraits, from a vague dark column of a body into a spiritual light. There was a background but it had darkened. In the original portrait it could be vaguely made out as a kind of craggy wild place; in this photographic reproduction it was no more than thickenings and glimmerings in the black. The important features of this image were the eyes, which were large and gleaming, and the beard, a riverful of silvers and creams, whites and blue-greys, channels and forks resembling da Vinci's turbulences, the apparent source of light. Even in the photograph, it shone. These pictures, Roland considered, seemed somehow more real as well as more austere, because they were photographs. Less full of life, the life of the paint, but more realistic, in the modern sense, according to modern expectations. They were a bit the worse for wear; the flat was not clean and was damp. But he had no money to renew them.

At the end of the room the window opened onto a little yard, with steps to the garden, which was visible between railings in the upper third of their window. Their flat was described as a garden flat when they came to see it, which was the only occasion on which they were asked to come into the garden, into which they were later told they had no right of entry. They were not even allowed to attempt to grow things in tubs in their black area, for reasons vague but peremptory, put forward by their landlady, an octogenarian Mrs Irving, who inhabited the three floors above them in a rank civet fug amongst unnumbered cats, and who kept the garden as bright and wholesome and well-ordered as her living-room was sparse and decomposing. She had enticed them in like an old witch, Val said, by talking volubly to them in the garden about the quietness of the place, giving them each a small, gold, furry apricot from the espaliered trees along the curving brick wall. The garden was long, thin, bowery, with sunny spots of grass, surrounded by little box hedges, its air full of roses, swarthy damask, thick ivory, floating pink, its borders restraining fantastic striped and spotted lilies, curling bronze and gold, bold and hot and rich. And forbidden. But they did not know that in the beginning, as Mrs Irving expatiated in her

17

cracked and gracious voice on the high brick wall which dated from the Civil War, and earlier still, which had formed one boundary of General Fairfax's lands when Putney was a separate village, when Cromwell's Trained Bands assembled there, when the Putney Debates on liberty of conscience were held in St Mary's Church on the bridge. Randolph Henry Ash had written a poem purporting to be spoken by a Digger in Putney. He had even come there to look at the river at low tide, it was in Ellen Ash's Journal, they had brought a picnic of chicken and parsley pie. That fact, and the conjunction of Marvell's patron, Fairfax, with the existence of the walled garden of fruit and flowers were enough to tempt Roland and Val into the garden flat, with its prohibited view.

In spring their window was lit from above by the yellow glow of a thick row of bright daffodils. Tendrils of Virginia creeper crept down as far as the window-frame, and progressed on little circular suckers across the glass, at huge vegetable speed. Swathes of jasmine, loose from a prolifically flowering specimen on the edge of the house, occasionally fell over their railing, with their sweet scent, before Mrs Irving, clothed in her gardening gear of wellingtons and apron over the seated and threadbare tweed suit in which she had first enticed them in, came and bound these back. Roland had once asked her if he could help in the garden, in exchange for the right to sit there sometimes. He had been told that he didn't know the first thing about it, that the young were all the same, destructive and careless, that Mrs Irving set a value on her privacy. 'You would think,' said Val, 'that the cats would do the garden no good.' That was before they found the patches of damp on their own kitchen and bathroom ceilings, which, when touched with a finger, smelled unmistakably of cat-piss. The cats too, were under prohibition, confined to quarters. Roland thought they ought to look for somewhere else, but held back from proposing it, because he was not the breadwinner, and because he didn't want to do anything so decisive, in terms of himself and Val.

Val put before him grilled marinated lamb, ratatouille and hot Greek bread. He said, 'Shall I get a bottle of wine?' and Val said, disagreeably and truthfully, 'You should have thought of that some time back; it'll all go cold.' They ate at a card-table, which they unfolded and folded again, after.

'I made an amazing discovery today,' he told her.

'Oh?'

'I was in the London Library. They've got R. H. Ash's Vico. His own copy. They keep it in the safe. I had it brought up and it was absolutely bursting at the seams with his own notes, all tucked in, on the backs of bills and things. And I'm ninety per cent sure no one had looked at them, ever, not since he put them there, because all the edges were black and the lines coincided . . .'

'How interesting.' Flatly.

'It might change the face of scholarship. It *could*. They let me read them, they didn't take it away. I'm sure no one knew it was all there.'

'I expect they didn't.'

'I'll have to tell Blackadder. He'll want to see how important it is, make sure Cropper hasn't been there . . .'

'I expect he will, yes.'

It was a bad mood.

'I'm sorry, Val, I'm sorry to bore you. It does look exciting.'

'That depends what turns you on. We all have our little pleasures of different kinds, I suppose.'

'I can write it up. An article. A solid discovery. Make me a better job prospect.'

'There aren't any jobs.' She added, 'And if there are, they go to Fergus Wolff.'

He knew his Val: he had watched her honourably try to prevent herself from adding that last remark.

'If you really think what I do is so unimportant . . .'

'You do what turns you on,' said Val. 'Everyone does, if they're lucky, if there is anything that turns them on. You have this thing about this dead man. Who had a thing about dead people. That's OK but not everyone is very bothered about all that. I see some things, from my menial vantage point. Last week, when I was in that ceramics export place, I found some photographs under a file in my boss's desk. Things being done to little boys. With chains and gags and – dirt – This week, ever so efficiently filing records for this surgeon, I just happened to come across a sixteen-year-old who had his leg off last year – they're fitting him with an artificial one, it takes months, they're incredibly slow – and it's started up for certain now in his other leg, he doesn't know, but I know, I know lots of things. None of them fit together, none of them makes any sense. There was a man who went off to Amsterdam to buy some diamonds, I helped his secretary book his ticket, first class, and his limousine, smooth as clockwork, and as he's walking along a canal admiring the housefronts someone stabs him in the back, destroys a kidney, gangrene sets in, now he's dead. Just like that. Chaps like those use my menial services, here today, gone tomorrow. Randolph Henry Ash wrote long ago. Forgive me if I don't care what he wrote in his Vico.'

'Oh, Val, such horrible things, you never say – '

'Oh, it's all very *interesting*, my menial keyhole observations, make no mistake. Just it doesn't make sense and it leaves me nowhere. I suppose I envy you, piecing together old Ash's world-picture. Only where does that leave *you*, old Mole? What's *your* world-picture? And how are you ever going to afford to get us away from dripping cat-piss and being *on top of each other*?'

Something had upset her, Roland reasonably deduced. Something that had caused her to use the phrase 'turn you on' several times, which was uncharacteristic. Perhaps someone had grabbed her. Or had not done so. No, that was unworthy. Anger and petulance *did* turn her on, he knew. He knew more than was quite good for him about Val. He went across and stroked the nape of her neck, and she sniffed and stiffened and then relaxed. After a bit, they moved over to the bed.

He had not told her, and could not tell her, about his secret theft. Late that night, he looked at the letters again, in the bathroom. 'Dear Madam, Since our extraordinary conversation, I have thought of nothing else.' 'Dear Madam, Since our pleasant and unexpected conversation I have thought of little else.' Urgent, unfinished. Shocking. Roland had never been much interested in Randolph Henry Ash's vanished body; he did not spend time visiting his house in Russell Street, or sitting where he had sat, on stone garden seats; that was Cropper's style. What Roland liked was his knowledge of the movements of Ash's mind, stalked through the twists and turns of his syntax, suddenly sharp and clear in an unexpected epithet. But these dead letters troubled him, physically even, because they were only beginnings. He did not imagine Randolph Henry Ash, his pen moving rapidly across the paper, but he did have the thought of the pads of the long-dead fingers which had held and folded these half-covered sheets, before preserving them in the book, instead of jettisoning them. *Who*? He must try to find out.

CHAPTER THREE

In this dim place
The creeping Nidhogg, with his sooty scales
Gnaws at the great Tree's root, and makes his nest,
Curled in the knotted maze on which he feeds

R. H. Ash, *Ragnarök* III

Roland went to Bloomsbury on his bicycle next morning, setting off very early when Val was still applying her workaday face. He went weaving perilously through and through the stinking five-mile worm of traffic across Putney Bridge, along the Embankment, through Parliament Square. He had no office in his old college, but inhabited an office on sufferance, for his few hours' part-time teaching. Here, in an empty silence, he unpacked his bicycle panniers and went up to the pantry where the bulk of the Xerox squatted amongst unsavoury tea-towels beside a tea-stained sink. Whilst the machine warmed up, in the din and hum of the extractor fan, he took out his two letters and read them again. Then he spread them face down, to be scryed on the black glass, under which the rods of green light floated and passed. And the machine spat out, hot and chemical-scented, spectrograms of those writings, black-rimmed by imaged empty space as the originals were edged by a century's dust. He was honest: he wrote his debt in the departmental notebook on the draining board. Roland Michell, 2 sheets, 10p. He was dishonest. He now had a fair copy and could slip the letters back unremarked into the London Library Vico. But he did not want to. He felt they were his. He had always slightly despised those enchanted by things touched by the great: Balzac's ornate walking-stick, Robert Louis

Stevenson's flageolet, a black lace mantilla once worn by George Eliot. Mortimer Cropper was in the habit of drawing Randolph Henry Ash's large gold watch from an inner fob pocket, and arranging his time by Ash's timepiece. Roland's Xeroxes were cleaner and clearer than the faded coppery-grey script of the originals; indeed the copy-ink had a black and gleaming freshness, the machine's rollers must have been newly inked. But he wanted the originals.

When Dr Williams's library opened he presented himself and asked to see the manuscript of Crabb Robinson's monumental Diary. He had been there before, but had to use Blackadder's name, to remind them, though he had no idea of showing Blackadder what he had found, not yet at least, not until his own curiosity was satisfied and the papers restored.

He started reading in 1856, the year of publication of *Gods, Men and Heroes*, which Crabb Robinson, indefatigable, had read and commented on.

JUNE 4 Read several dramatic poems from Randolph Ash's new book. I noted particularly those purporting to be spoken by Augustine of Hippo, the ninth-century Saxon monk, Gotteschalk, and 'Neighbour Pliable' from *Pilgrim's Progress*. Also a singular evocation of Franz Mesmer and the young Mozart playing their glass harmonica at the court of the Archduke in Vienna, full of sounds and strange airs, excellently conceived and embodied. This Gotteschalk, a precursor of Luther, even to renouncing his Vows, might be thought in his intransigent predestinarian vision to figure some of the later Evangelicals of our day, and Neighbour Pliable perhaps a satire upon those like myself, who believe that Christianity does not consist in the idolatrous presence of the Deity in a piece of bread, nor yet in the five points of metaphysic faith. As is his wont, Ash treats Pliable, with whom he might be supposed to sympathise, with more apparent spleen than he directs towards his monstrous monk whose ravings have a certain real sublimity. It is difficult to know where to *have* Randolph Ash. I fear he will never become a popular poet. His evocation of the Black Forest in 'Gotteschalk' is very fine, but how many of the public are prepared to endure his theological strictures to come to it? He convolutes and wreathes his melodies with such a forcing of rhyme and such a thicket of peculiar and ill-founded analogies, that his meaning is hard to discern. When I read Ash, I think of the younger Coleridge, reciting with gusto his epigram upon Donne:

> With Donne whose muse on dromedary trots
> Wreathe iron pokers into true-love knots.

This passage was already well known to Ash scholars and had been extensively quoted. Roland liked Crabb Robinson, a man of indefatigable good will, intellectual curiosity, delight in literature and learning, and yet full of self-deprecation.

'I early found that I had not the literary ability to give me such a place among English authors as I should have desired; but I thought that I had an opportunity of gaining a knowledge of many of the distinguished men of the age, and that I might do some good by keeping a record of my interviews with them.' He had known them all, two whole generations, Wordsworth, Coleridge, de Quincey, Lamb; Mme de Staël, Goethe, Schiller; Carlyle, G. H. Lewes, Tennyson, Clough, Bagehot. Roland read through 1857 and embarked on 1858. In the February of that year Robinson wrote:

> Were this my last hour (and that of an octogenarian cannot be far off) I would thank God for permitting me to behold so much of the excellence conferred on individuals. Of women, I saw the type of her heroic greatness in Mrs Siddons; of her fascinations, in Mrs Jordan and Mlle Mars; I listened with rapture to the dreamy monologues of Coleridge – 'that old man eloquent'; I travelled with Wordsworth, the greatest of our lyrico-philosophical poets; I relished the wit and pathos of Charles Lamb; I conversed freely with Goethe at his own table, beyond all competition the supreme genius of his age and country. He acknowledges his obligations only to Shakespeare, Spinoza and Linnaeus, as Wordsworth, when he resolved to be a poet, feared competition only with Chaucer, Spenser, Shakespeare and Milton.

In June, Roland found what he had been looking for.

> My breakfast party went off very well indeed, as far as talk was concerned. I had with me Bagehot, Ash, Mrs Jameson, Professor Spear, Miss LaMotte and her friend Miss Glover, the last somewhat taciturn. Ash had never met Miss LaMotte, who indeed came out exceptionally to please me and to speak of her dear

Father, whose *Mythologies* I have had some hand in bringing before the English public. Discussion of poetry was animated, especially of Dante's incomparable genius, but also of the genius of Shakespeare in his poems, especially the playfulness of his young works, which Ash particularly admires. Miss LaMotte spoke more forcefully than I would have expected: she is surprisingly handsome when animated. We discussed also the so-called 'spiritual' manifestations, about which Lady Byron wrote to me with great feeling. There was talk of Mrs Stowe's claim to have conversed with the spirit of Charlotte Brontë. Miss Glover, in one of her few interventions, said warmly that she believed such things could and did happen. Ash said he would require foolproof experimental conviction and did not imagine it would be forthcoming. Bagehot said that Ash's presentation of Mesmer's belief in spiritual influences showed he was less rigorously confined by positive science than he now claimed to be. Ash replied that the historical imagination required a kind of poetic belief in the mental universe of his characters and that this was so strong with him, that he was in danger of having no beliefs of his own at all. All appealed to Miss LaMotte on the question of the rapping spirits; she declined to express an opinion, answering only with a Monna Lisa smile.

Roland copied out this passage and read on, but could find no further reference to Miss LaMotte, though Ash was a fairly frequent host and guest. Robinson paid tribute to Mrs Ash's excellent housekeeping, and lamented that she had never become the Mother she was ideally suited to be. He did not appear to have noticed any extraordinary knowledge of Ash's poetry in either Miss LaMotte or Miss Glover. Perhaps the conversation, 'pleasant and unexpected' or alternatively 'extraordinary' had taken place elsewhere or on another occasion. Crabb Robinson's records looked odd transcribed in Roland's own rather cramped script, less confident, less homogeneously part of a life. Roland knew that statistically he was almost bound to have corrupted this text in some way, if only by inadequate transcription. Mortimer Cropper's graduate students were made to transcribe passages – usually from Randolph Henry Ash – transcribe again their own transcriptions, type them up, and then scan them for errors with a severe editorial eye. There was never an error-free text, Cropper said. He kept up this humbling exercise, even in the days of effortless photocopying. There was no such professional method about Blackadder, who nevertheless noticed and corrected a plethora of errors, accompanying this correction with a steady series of disparaging comments on the declining standard of English education. In his day, he said, students were grounded in spelling and had learned poetry and the Bible by heart. An odd phrase, by heart, he would add, as though poems were stored in the bloodstream. ' "Felt along the heart" as Wordsworth said,' Blackadder said. But in the best English tradition he did not consider it his business to equip his deficient students with tools they had not got. They must muddle through in a fog of grumble and contempt.

Roland went to the British Museum in search of Blackadder. He had not made up his mind what to say to him, so spent time establishing a position in the Reading Room, under the high dome, which, however high, held, he felt, insufficient oxygen for all the diligent readers, so that they lay somnolent like flames dying in Humphry Davy's bell-jar as their sustenance was consumed. It was afternoon – the morning had gone on Crabb Robinson – which meant that all the ample, high, soft-blue leather desks along the spokes of the great wheel that radiated from the Superintendent's desk, ensphered by the Catalogue, were taken, and he had to be content with one of the minimal flat triangular ends of the late-come segments inserted between these spokes. These inserts were ghost-desks, secondary desks, stammering desks, DD GG OO. He found a place at the end of AA (for Ash) near the door. In his first pleasure at being admitted to this inner circle of learning he had compared it to Dante's Paradiso, in which the saints and patriarchs and virgins sat in orderly ranks in a circular formation, a huge rose, and also the leaves of a huge volume, once scattered through the universe, now gathered. The gilt lettering on the soft-blue leather added to the mediaeval imagining.

In which case, the Ash factory, hutched in the bowels of the building was the Inferno. There was a way down, on iron rungs, from the Reading Room, and a way out, through a high locked portal, which brought you up into the sunless Egyptian necropolis, amongst blind staring pharaohs, crouching scribes, minor sphinxes and empty mummy-cases. The Ash factory was a hot place of metal cabinets and glass cells containing the clatter of typewriters, gloomily lit by neon tubes. Micro-readers glowed green in its gloom. It smelled occasionally sulphurous, when the photocopiers short-circuited. It was even beset by wailings and odd shrieks. The whole of the lower regions of the British Museum reeks of tom-cat. The creatures work their way in through gratings and airbricks, prowl and are harried and occasionally stealthily fed.

Blackadder sat amongst the apparent chaos and actual order of his great edition, sifting a drift of small paper slips in a valley between cliffs of furred-edged index cards and bulging mottled files. Behind him flitted his clerical assistant, pale Paola, her long colourless hair bound in a rubber band, her huge glasses moth-like, her finger-tips dusty grey pads. In an inner room, beyond the typewriter cubicle, was a small cavern constructed of filing cabinets, inhabited by Dr Beatrice Nest, almost bricked in by the boxes containing the diary and correspondence of Ellen Ash.

Blackadder was fifty-four and had come to editing Ash out of pique. He was the son and grandson of Scottish schoolmasters. His grandfather recited poetry on firelight evenings: *Marmion*, *Childe Harold*, *Ragnarök*. His father sent him to Downing College in Cambridge to study under F. R. Leavis. Leavis did to Blackadder what he did to serious students; he showed him the terrible, the magnificent importance and urgency of English literature and simultaneously deprived him of any confidence in his own capacity to contribute to, or change it. The young Blackadder wrote poems, imagined Dr Leavis's comments on them, and burned them. He devised an essay style of Spartan brevity, equivocation and impenetrability. His fate was decided by a seminar on dating. The Cambridge room was crowded, the floor full, the chair-arms perched on. The lean and agile don, in his open-necked shirt, stood on the window-sill and tugged at the casement to let in fresh air, cold Cambridge light. The dating handout contained a troubadour lyric, a piece of dramatic Jacobean verse, some satirical couplets, a blank verse meditation on volcanic mud and a love-sonnet. Blackadder, schooled by his grandfather, saw immediately that all these poems were by Randolph Henry Ash, examples of his ventriloquism, of his unwieldy range. He himself had two choices: to state his knowledge, or to allow the seminar to proceed, with Leavis enticing unfortunate undergraduates into making wrong identifications, and then proceeding to demonstrate his own analytic brilliance in distinguishing fake from authenticity, Victorian alienation from the voice of true feeling. Blackadder chose silence, and Ash was duly exposed and found wanting. Blackadder felt that he had somehow betrayed Randolph Henry Ash, though he might more justly have been thought to have betrayed himself, his grandfather, or possibly Dr Leavis. He compensated. He wrote his PhD on *Conscious Argument and Unconscious Bias: a Source of Tension in the Dramatic Poems of Randolph Henry Ash*. He became an expert on Ash in Ash's most unfashionable days. He had been talked into editing the *Complete Poems and Plays* as early as 1959, with the blessing of the present Lord Ash, an elderly Methodist peer who was a descendant of a remote cousin of Ash himself and heir to the ownership of the unsold manuscripts. He had in those days of innocence seen the Edition as a finite task that would lead on to other things.

He had research assistants, in fluctuating numbers, whom he despatched like Noah's doves and ravens into the libraries of the world, clutching numbered slips of paper, like cloakroom tickets or luncheon vouchers, each containing a query, a half-line of possible quotation, a proper name to be located. The hub of a Roman chariot, tracked through Gibbon's footnotes. 'The dangerous dreamed melon of the sage' which turned out to come from the dream of Descartes. Ash had been interested in everything. Arab astronomy and African transport systems, angels and oakapples, hydraulics and the guillotine, druids, and the grande armée, catharists and printers' devils, ectoplasm and solar mythology, the last meals of frozen mastodons and the true nature of manna. The footnotes engulfed and swallowed the text. They were ugly and ungainly, but necessary, Blackadder thought, as they sprang up like the heads of the Hydra, two to solve in the place of one solved.

He thought often, in his dim place, of how a man becomes his job. What would he be now if he had become, say, a civil servant allotting housing finance, or a policeman, poring over bits of hair and skin and thumbball prints? (This was a very Ash-like speculation.) What would knowledge be, collected for its own sake, for his own sake, that was, for James Blackadder, with no reference to the pickings, digestion and leavings of Randolph Henry Ash?

There were times when Blackadder allowed himself to see clearly that he would end his working life, that was to say his conscious thinking life, in this task, that all his thoughts would have been another man's thoughts, all his work another man's work. And then he thought it did not perhaps matter so greatly. He did after all find Ash fascinating, even after all these years. It was a pleasant subordination, if he was a subordinate. He believed Mortimer Cropper thought himself the lord and owner of Ash, but he, Blackadder, knew his place better.

He had once seen a naturalist on the television who seemed to him to be an analogue of himself. This man went out with a pouch and gathered up owl-pellets, which he labelled, and later, took apart with forceps, bathed in glass beakers of various cleansing fluids, ordering and rearranging the orts and fragments of the owl's compressed package of bone, tooth and fur, in order to reconstitute the dead shrew or slow-worm which had run, died, and made its way through owl-gut. He was pleased with this image and momentarily considered making a poem out of it. Then he discovered Ash had been beforehand with him. He had described an archaeologist:

> Finding out ancient battles from the shards
> Of shattered blades or mashed and splintered bones,
> Or broken brain-pans, as the curate reads
> The death of vole or slow-worm in the dried
> Packets the tidy owl ejects, cast out
> By white death floating by on softest sails
> The bloody hook curved in the downy ruff . . .

Then Blackadder could not think whether he had noticed the screen naturalist because his mind was primed with Ash's image, or whether it had worked independently.

Roland emerged from tunnels of shelving into Blackadder's icily lit domain. Paola smiled at him and Blackadder frowned. Blackadder was a grey man, with a grey skin and iron-grey hair, which he wore rather long, because he was proud that it was still so thick. His clothes, tweed jacket, cord trousers, were respectable, well-worn and dusty, like everything else down there. He had a good ironic smile when he smiled, which was very infrequently.

Roland said, 'I think I've made a discovery.' ·

'It will probably turn out to have been discovered twenty times already. What is it?'

'I went to read his Vico and it's still crammed with his manuscript notes, bursting with them, between every page. In the London Library.'

'Cropper will have been through it with a toothcomb.'

'I don't think so. I *truly* don't think so. All the dust is *set* in black rims, it reaches the edges of the paper. No one's touched it for a long, long time. I guess not ever. I read some.'

'Useful?'

'Oh, very. Enormously.'

Blackadder, reluctant to show excitement, began to clip together bits of paper. 'I'd better have a look,' he said. 'I'd better see for myself. I'll get over there. You didn't disturb anything?'

'Oh no. Oh no. That is, a lot of the papers simply flew out when the book was opened, but we put them back in place, I think.'

'I don't understand it. I thought Cropper was ubiquitous. You'd better keep this absolutely hush-hush, you understand, or it'll all be winging its way across the Atlantic, whilst the London Library replaces its carpets and installs a coffee machine and Cropper sends us another of his nice helpful smiley-regretful Faxes, offering access to the Stant Collection and every possible assistance with microfilm. You haven't said anything to anyone?'

'Only the Librarian.'

'I'll get over there. Patriotism will have to do instead of funding. Stop the drain.'

'They wouldn't – '

'I wouldn't trust anyone, faced with Cropper's cheque-book, not further than I could see.'

Blackadder was struggling into his overcoat, a shabby British Warm. Roland had given up all thought, in any case not very realistic, of discussing the purloined letters with Blackadder. He did, however, ask, 'Can you tell me anything about a writer called LaMotte?'

'Isidore LaMotte. *Mythologies*, 1832. *Mythologies indigènes de la Bretagne et de la Grande Bretagne*. Also *Mythologies françaises*. A great scholarly compendium of folklore and legends. Suffused by a kind of fashionable search for the Key to All Mythologies but also with Breton national identity and culture. Ash would almost certainly have read them, but I've no recollection of any precise use he made of them ...'

'There was a Miss LaMotte ...'

'Oh, the daughter. She wrote religious poems, didn't she? A gloomy little booklet called *Last Things*. And children's stories. *Tales Told in November*. Things that go bump in the night. And an epic which they say is unreadable.'

'I think the feminists are interested in her,' said Paola.

'They would be,' said Blackadder. 'They haven't any time for Randolph Ash. All they want is to read Ellen's endless journal once our friend in there has actually managed to bring it to the light of day. They think Randolph Ash suppressed Ellen's writing and fed off her imagination. They'd have a hard time proving that, I think, if they were interested in proof, which I'm not sure they are. They *know* what there is to find before they've seen it. All they've got to go on is that she spent a lot of time lying on the sofa, and that's hardly unusual for a lady in her time and circumstances. Their real problem – and Beatrice's – is that Ellen Ash is *dull*. No Jane Carlyle, more's the pity. Poor old Beatrice began by wanting to show how self-denying and supportive Ellen Ash was and she messed around looking up every recipe for gooseberry jam and every jaunt to Broadstairs for *twenty-five years*, can you believe it, and woke up to find that no one wanted self-denial and dedication any more, they wanted proof that Ellen was raging with rebellion and pain and untapped talent. Poor Beatrice. One publication to her name, and a slim book called *Helpmeets* without irony doesn't go down well with today's feminists. One little anthology in 1950 of wise, witty and tender sayings from the female companions of the great. D. Wordsworth, J. Carlyle, E. Tennyson, Ellen Ash. But the Women's Studies people can't get their hands on all that stuff to publish as long as poor old Bea is still the official editor. She doesn't know what's hit her.'

Roland did not want to hear another long speech from Blackadder about Beatrice Nest's long-delayed edition of Ellen Ash. There was a note that came into Blackadder's voice when he got onto the subject of Beatrice, a jarring, snarling note, that put Roland in mind of hounds baying. (He had never heard hounds baying except on the television.) The idea of Cropper produced a furtive, conspiratorial look in the scholar.

Roland did not offer to accompany Blackadder to the London Library. He went off to look for coffee. After that he could pursue Miss LaMotte, who now had an identity of sorts, through the Catalogue, like any other dead soul.

He emerged amongst the Egyptian heavyweights and saw, between two huge stone legs, something rapid and white and golden that turned out to be Fergus Wolff, also heading for coffee. Fergus was very tall, with brassy hair cut long on top and short at the back, in the 1980s version of the 1930s, over a dazzling white heavy sweater and loose black trousers like a Japanese martial artist. He smiled at Roland, a pleased, voracious smile, with bright blue eyes and a long mouth terribly full of strong white teeth. He was older than Roland, a child of the Sixties who had temporarily dropped out, opted for freedom and Parisian revolutions, sitting at the feet of Barthes and Foucault, before coming back to dazzle Prince Albert College. He was pleasant enough in general, though most people who met him formed the vaguest of ideas that he might be dangerous in some unspecified way. Roland liked Fergus because Fergus seemed to like him.

Fergus was writing a deconstructive account of Balzac's *Chef-d'Oeuvre Inconnu*. Roland had ceased to be surprised that an English Department was sponsoring the study of French books. There seemed to be nothing else nowadays, and in any case Roland did not want to be thought insular. His own French, owing to his mother's passionate interference with his education, was good. Fergus sprawled in the cafeteria banquette and said the challenge was to deconstruct something that had apparently already deconstructed itself, since the book was about a painting that turned out to be nothing but a chaotic mass of brush-strokes. Roland listened politely and said,

'Do you know anything about a Miss LaMotte who wrote children's stories and religious poetry in the 1850s or thereabouts?'

Fergus laughed rather a long time at this, and said tersely, 'I should.'

'Who was she?'

'Christabel LaMotte. Daughter of Isidore, the mythographer. *Last Things. Tales Told in November.* An epic called *The Fairy Melusina.* Very bizarre. Do you know about Melusina? She was a fairy who married a mortal to gain a soul, and made a pact that he would never spy on her on Saturdays, and for years he never did, and they had six sons, all with strange defects – odd ears, giant tusks, a catshead growing out of one cheek, three eyes, that sort of thing. One was called Geoffroy à la Grande Dent and one was called Horrible. She built castles, real ones that still exist, in Poitou. And in the end, of course, he looked through the keyhole – or made one in her steel door with his sword-point according to one version – and there she was in a great marble bath disporting herself. And from the waist down she was a fish or a serpent, Rabelais says an 'andouille', a kind of huge sausage, the symbolism is obvious, and she beat the water with her muscular tail. And he said nothing and she did nothing until Geoffroy, the tough son, took exception to his brother Fromont taking refuge in a monastery, and when he wouldn't come out, he piled up brushwood and burned the whole thing down, monks and Fromont and all. And when this was reported, Raimondin (he was the original knight, the husband) said, "This is all your fault, I should never have married a horrible snake." And then she reproached him and turned into a dragon, and flew away round the battlements making a terrible noise and battering the stones. Oh, before that she gave him strict injunctions to be sure to kill Horrible or he would destroy them all, which was duly done. And she comes back to the Counts of Lusignan to foretell deaths – she is a kind of Dame Blanche, or Fata Bianca. There are all sorts of symbolic and mythological and psychoanalytic interpretations, you can imagine. Christabel LaMotte wrote this long and very convoluted poem about Melusina's story in the 1860s and it was published at the beginning of the 1870s. It's an odd affair – tragedy and romance and symbolism rampant all over it, a kind of dream-world full of strange beasts and hidden meanings and a really weird sexuality or sensuality. The feminists are crazy about it. They say it expresses women's impotent desire. It wasn't much read until they rediscovered it – Virginia Woolf knew it, she adduced it as an image of the essential androgyny of the creative mind – but the new feminists see Melusina in her bath as a symbol of self-sufficient female sexuality needing no poor males. I like it, it's disturbing. It keeps changing focus. From very precise description of the scaly tail to cosmic battles.'

'That's very useful. I'll look it up.'

'Why do you want to know?'

'I came across a reference in Randolph Ash. There's a reference to almost everything in Randolph Ash, sooner or later. Why did I make you laugh?'

'I became an involuntary expert on Christabel LaMotte. There are two people in the world who know all that is known about Christabel LaMotte. One is Professor Leonora Stern, in Tallahassee. And the other is Dr Maud Bailey in Lincoln University. I met them both at that Paris conference on sexuality and textuality I went to. If you remember. I don't think they like men. Nevertheless I had a brief affair with the redoubtable Maud. In Paris and then here.'

He stopped and frowned to himself. He opened his mouth to say more and then closed it again. He said after a time,

'She – Maud – runs a Women's Resource Centre in Lincoln. They've got quite a lot of Christabel's unpublished papers there. If you want anything out of the way, there's where to look.'

'I might. Thanks. What is she like? Will she eat me?'

'She thicks men's blood with cold,' said Fergus with a lot of undecodable feeling.

CHAPTER FOUR

> The Thicket is Thorny
> Up snakes the glassy Tower
> Here is no sweet Dovecote
> Nor plump Lady's Bower
>
> The wind whistles sourly
> Through that Sharp land
> At the black casement
> He sees her white hand
>
> He hears the foul Old One
> Call quavering there
> Rapunzel Rapunzel
> Let down your Hair
>
> Filaments Glosses
> Run trembling down
> Gold torrent loosened
> From a gold Crown
>
> The black claws go clutching
> Hand over hand
> What Pain goes shrilling
> Through every strand!
>
> Silent he watches
> The humped One rise
> With tears of anguish
> In his own eyes
>
> Christabel LaMotte

When Roland arrived in Lincoln he was already irritated by having to take the train. It would have been cheaper to have taken the coach, if longer, but Dr Bailey had sent a curt postcard telling him it would be best for her to meet him off the noon train; the campus was some way out of town, it would be best that way. On the train, however, it was possible to try to catch up on what there was to know about Christabel LaMotte. His college library had provided two books. One was very slim and ladylike, written in 1947 and entitled *White Linen* after one of Christabel's lyrics. The other was a fat collection of feminist essays, mostly American, published in 1977: *Herself Herself Involve, LaMotte's Strategies of Evasion.*

Veronica Honiton provided some biographical information. Christabel's grandparents, Jean-Baptiste and Emilie LaMotte, had fled to England in the Terror of 1793 and had settled there, choosing not to return after the fall of Bonaparte. Isidore, born in 1801, had gone to Cambridge, and toyed with writing poetry, before becoming a serious historian and mythographer

much influenced by German researches on folk-tales and the origins of biblical narrative, but staunch in his own mystical Breton brand of Christianity. His mother, Emilie, was an older sister of the republican and anticlerical historian, also a folklore enthusiast, Raoul de Kercoz, who still maintained the family manor of Kernemet. In 1823 Isidore married Miss Arabel Gumpert, daughter of Canon Rupert Gumpert of St Paul's, whose firm religious faith was a powerful steadying influence on Christabel's childhood. There were two daughters of the marriage, Sophie, born in 1830, who became the wife of Sir George Bailey, of Seal Close, in the Lincolnshire Wolds, and Christabel, born in 1825, who lived with her parents until in 1853 a small independence, left her by a maiden aunt, Antoinette de Kercoz, enabled her to set up house in Richmond in Surrey, with a young woman friend whom she had met at a lecture of Ruskin's.

Miss Blanche Glover, like Christabel, had artistic ambitions, and painted large canvases in oil, none of which have survived, as well as carving the skilful and mysterious wood engravings which illustrate Christabel's delightful, if slightly disquieting, *Tales for Innocents*, and *Tales Told in November*, and her religious lyrics, *Orisons*. It is believed to be Miss Glover who first encouraged Christabel to embark on the grandiose and obscure epic poem, *The Fairy Melusina*, a retelling of the old tale of the magical half-woman, half-snake. The rifts of the *The Fairy Melusina* are

36

heavily overloaded with ore; during the Pre-Raphaelite Period it was admired by certain critics, including Swinburne, who called it, 'a quiet, muscular serpent of a tale, with more vigour and venom than is at all usual in the efforts of the female pen, but without narrative thrust; rather, as was Coleridge's Serpent who figured the Imagination, with its tail stuffed in its own mouth.' It is now deservedly forgotten. Christabel's reputation, modest but secure, rests on the restrained and delicate lyrics, products of a fine sensibility, a somewhat sombre temperament, and a troubled but steadfast Christian faith.

Miss Glover was unfortunately drowned in the Thames in 1861. The death seems to have had a distressing effect on Christabel, who returned eventually to her family, living with her sister Sophie for the rest of her quiet and uneventful life. After *Melusina* she appears to have written no more poetry, and retreated further and further into voluntary silence. She died in 1890 aged sixty-five.

Veronica Honiton's comments on Christabel's poetry concentrated sweetly on her 'domestic mysticism', which she compared to George Herbert's celebration of the servant who 'sweeps a room as for Thy laws'.

> I like things clean about me
> Starched and gophered frill
> What is done exactly
> Cannot be done ill
>
> The house is ready spotless
> Waiting for the Guest
> Who will see our white linen
> At its very best
> Who will take it and fold it
> And lay us to rest.

Thirty years later the feminists saw Christabel LaMotte as distraught and enraged. They wrote on 'Ariachne's Broken Woof: Art as Discarded Spinning in the Poems of LaMotte.' Or 'Melusina and the Daemonic Double: Good Mother, Bad Serpent.' 'A Docile Rage: Christabel LaMotte's Ambivalent Domesticity.' 'White Gloves: Blanche Glover: occluded Lesbian sexuality in LaMotte.' There was an essay by Maud Bailey herself on 'Melusina, Builder of Cities: a Subversive Female Cosmogony.' Roland knew he should tackle this piece first, but was inhibited by its formidable length and density. He started 'Ariachne's Broken Woof' which elegantly dissected one of Christabel's insect poems, of which there were apparently many.

> From so blotched and cramped a creature
> Painfully teased out
> With ugly fingers, filaments of wonder
> Bright snares about
> Lost buzzing things, an order fine and bright
> Geometry threading water, catching light.

It was hard to concentrate. The Midlands went flatly past, a biscuit factory, a metal box company, fields, hedges, ditches, pleasant and unremarkable. Miss Honiton's book contained, as a frontispiece, the first image he had seen of Christabel, a brownish, very early photograph, veiled under a crackling, protective translucent page. She was dressed in a large triangular mantle and a small bonnet, frilled inside its rim, tied with a large bow under her chin. Her clothes were more prominent than she was, she retreated into them, her head, perhaps quizzically, perhaps considering itself 'birdlike', held on one side. She had pale crimped hair over her temples, and her lips were parted to reveal large, even teeth. The picture gave no clear impression of anyone in particular; it was generic Victorian lady, specific shy poetess.

At first he did not identify Maud Bailey, and he himself was not in any way remarkable, so that they were almost the last pair at the wicket gate. She would be hard to miss, if not to recognise. She was tall, tall enough to meet Fergus Wolff's eyes on the level, much taller than Roland. She was dressed with unusual coherence for an academic, Roland thought, rejecting several other ways of describing her green and white length, a long pine-green tunic over a pine-green skirt, a white silk shirt inside the tunic and long softly white stockings inside long shining green shoes. Through the stockings veiled flesh diffused a pink gold, almost. He could not see her hair, which was wound tightly into a turban of peacock-feathered painted silk, low on her brow. Her brows and lashes were blond; he observed so much. She had a clean, milky skin, unpainted lips, clearcut features, largely composed. She did not smile. She acknowledged him and tried to take his bag, which he refused to allow. She drove an immaculately glossy green Beetle.

'I was intrigued by your question,' she said, as they drove off. 'I'm glad you made the effort to come. I hope it will be worth it.' Her voice was deliberately blurred patrician; a kind of flattened Sloane. She smelled of something ferny and sharp. Roland didn't like her voice.

'It may be a wild-goose chase. It's almost nothing really.'

'We'll see.'

Lincoln University was white-tiled towers, variegated with violet tiles and orange tiles and from time to time acid-green tiles. In high winds, Dr Bailey said, these blew off and were a real hazard to walkers. There were often high winds. The campus was fenny-flat, laid out like a kind of chess-board, redeemed by an imaginative water-gardener who had made a maze of channels and pools, randomly flowing across and around the rectangular grid. They were now clogged with fallen leaves, amongst which Koi carp pushed blunt pearly noses. The University dated from the opulent heyday of expansion and was now slightly grubby and tatty, mortared cracks grinning between the white oblongs under their urban plaque.

The wind stirred the silk fringes of Dr Bailey's too-rich headgear. It ruffled Roland's black fur. He pushed his hands in his pockets and stepped a little behind her as she strode. No one else seemed to be about, although it was term. He asked Dr Bailey, where were the students and she told him that today, Wednesday, was a non-teaching day, reserved for sports and study.

'They all disappear. We don't know where. As if by magic. Some of them are in the library. Most aren't. I don't know where they go.'

The wind ruffled the dark water; orange leaves made its surface jagged and sloppy at once.

She lived at the top of Tennyson Tower – 'It was that or Maid Marian,' she remarked, as they swung its glass door, her voice distantly scornful. 'The Alderman who funded it wanted it all called after Sherwood folk. Here is the English Department and the Arts Faculty Office and History of Art and also Women's Studies. Not our Resource Centre. That's in the Library. I'll take you. Would you care for coffee?'

They went up in a paternoster lift which cranked regularly past its otherwise vacant portals. These doorless lifts unnerved Roland; she stepped in precisely and was lifted above him before he dared follow, so that he was already clambering onto the pedestal she occupied when he lunged forward and up, almost too late. She did not remark on this. The walls of the paternoster were mirror-tiled, bronze-lit; she flashed at him from wall to wall, hotly. Out again she came precisely; he tripped on this threshold too, the floor lifting beneath him.

Her room was glass-walled on one side, and lined floor to ceiling with books on the others. The books were arranged rationally, thematically, alphabetically, and dust-free; this last was the only sign of housekeeping in that austere place. The beautiful thing in that room was Maud Bailey herself, who went down on one knee very gracefully to plug in a kettle, and produced from a cupboard two blue and white Japanese mugs.

'Take a seat,' she said crisply, indicating a low upholstered bright blue chair where students no doubt sat to have their work handed back. She handed him walnut-coloured Nescafé. She had not taken off the headdress. 'Now, how can I be of help to you?' she said, taking her own seat behind the barrier of the desk. Roland meditated strategies of evasion of his own. He had vaguely imagined, before meeting her, that he might be able to show her Xeroxes of the purloined letters. Now he knew he could not. Her voice lacked warmth. He said.

'I am working on Randolph Henry Ash. As I wrote to you. It's just come to my attention that he might have corresponded with Christabel LaMotte. I don't know if you have any knowledge of such a correspondence? They certainly met.'

'When?'

He handed her a copy of his transcript of Crabb Robinson's Journal.

'That might be mentioned in Blanche Glover's diary. We've got one of her diaries in the Resource Centre. It covers that period – she began it when they moved to Richmond. The papers we have in our Archive are essentially the contents of Christabel's desk when she died – she expressed a wish that they should be sent to one of her nieces, May Bailey, "in the hope that she may come to care about poetry".'

'And did she?'

'Not as far as I know. She married a cousin and went off to Norfolk and had ten children and ran a large household. I'm descended from her – she was my great-great-grandmother, which makes me Christabel's great-great-great-niece. I persuaded my father to let us lodge the papers in the Archive when I came here. There isn't a lot of material, but it's important. Manuscripts of the Tales, lots of undated lyrics on random little slips of paper, and of course all the revisions of *Melusina*, which she rewrote at least eight times, always changing it. And a commonplace book, and a few letters from friends, and this one diary of Blanche Glover's, just for three years. I don't know if we once had more – no care was taken of them, I'm sorry to say – none has come to light.'

'And LaMotte. Did she keep a journal?'

'Not as far as we know. Almost certainly not. She wrote to one of her nieces advising against it. It's a rather good letter. "If you can order your Thoughts and shape them into Art, good: if you can live in the obligations and affections of Daily Life, good. But do not get into the habit of morbid Self-examination. Nothing so unfits a woman for producing good work, or for living usefully. The Lord will take care of the second of these – opportunities will be found. The first is a matter of Will."'

'I'm not sure about that.'

'It's an interesting view of it. That's late – 1886. Art as will. Not a fashionable view for a woman. Or maybe for anyone.'

'Do you have her letters?'

'Not many. A few family ones – admonitions like that, recipes for bread-baking and wine-making, complaints. Others exist, not many from the Richmond period, one or two from visits she made to Brittany; she had family there, as maybe you know. She doesn't seem to have had intimate friends, except Miss Glover, and they didn't need to correspond, since they shared their house. The letters haven't been edited – Leonora Stern's trying to get something together, but there's little to go on. I suspect Sir

George Bailey at Seal Court may have something but he's not willing to let anyone look. He threatened Leonora with a shotgun. I thought it might be better if she went there – she's from Tallahassee, as you no doubt know – rather than myself, since there's an unfortunate history of litigation and unpleasantness between the Seal Court family and the Norfolk one. But Leonora's approaches had a most unfortunate effect. Most unfortunate. Yes. Well. And how did you come to form the opinion that Randolph Henry Ash was interested in LaMotte?'

'I found an unfinished draft of a letter to an unidentified woman in a book of his. I thought it might be her. It mentioned Crabb Robinson. He said she understood his poems.'

'That doesn't sound very probable. I wouldn't have thought his poems would appeal to her. All that cosmic masculinity. That nasty anti-feminist poem about the medium, what was it, *Mummy Possest*? All that ponderous obfuscation. Everything she wasn't.'

Roland considered the pale incisive mouth with a kind of hopelessness. He wished he had not come. The hostility towards Ash somehow included himself, at least in his own eyes. Maud Bailey went on: 'I've checked my card index – I'm working on a full-length study of *Melusina* – I've only found one reference to Ash. It's from a note to William Rossetti – the MS is in Tallahassee – about a poem he published for her.

' "In these dim November days I resemble nothing more than that poor Creature of RHA's Fantasy, immured in her terrible *In-Pace*, quieted perforce and longing for her Quietus. It takes a Masculine Courage to find pleasure in constructing Dungeons for Innocents in his Fancy, and a Female Patience to endure them in sober fact." '

'That's a reference to Ash's *Incarcerated Sorceress*?'

'Of course.' Impatiently.

'When was it written?'

'1869. I think. Yes. Vivid but not much help.'

'Hostile if anything.'

'Exactly.'

Roland sipped his coffee. Maud Bailey reinserted the card into its place in her file. She said, looking into the box,

'You must know Fergus Wolff, he must be at your college, I think.'

'Oh yes. It was Fergus who suggested I should ask you about LaMotte.'

A pause. The fingers moved busily, tidying.

'I know Fergus. I met him at a Conference, in Paris.'

A little less crisp, the voice, a little less elderly-authoritative, he thought unkindly.

'He told me,' said Roland, neutrally, watching for a sign of her consciousness of what Fergus might have said, of how he might have spoken. She compressed her lips and stood up.

'I'll take you to the Resource Centre.'

The Lincoln Library could not have been more different from the Ash Factory. It was a skeletal affair in a glass box, with brilliant doors opening in glass and tubular walls, like a box of toys or a giant ConstructoKit. There were dinging metal shelves and footfall-deadening felt carpets, pied-piper red and yellow, like the paint on the stair-rails and lifts. In summer it must have been bright and baking, but in wet autumn slate-grey sky lay like another box against its repeating panes, in which lines of little round lights were reflected, like Tinkerbell's fairylights in her Never-Never-Land. The Women's Archive was housed in a high-walled fish-tank. Maud Bailey settled Roland into a tubular chair at a pale oak table, like a recalcitrant nursery-school child, and put before him various boxes. *Melusina* I. *Melusina* II. *Melusina* III and IV. *Melusina Unassigned. Breton Poems. Poems of Devotion. Misc Lyrics. Blanche.* In this box she showed him a long thick green book, a little like an accounts book, with sombre marbled endpapers:

A Journal of Our Home-Life.
In Our House in Richmond

Blanche Glover

Commenced on the day of our setting up house.

May 1st May Day 1858

Roland took it up respectfully. It did not have for him the

magnetic feel of the two letters which were folded into his pocket, but it represented the tease of curiosity.

He was worried about his Day Return ticket. He was worried about Maud's limited patience. The journal was written in an excited and pretty hand, in short rushes. He skimmed it. Carpets, curtains, the pleasures of retirement, 'Today we engaged a Cook-general', a new way to stew rhubarb, a painting of the infant Hermes and his mother, and yes, Crabb Robinson's breakfast.

'Here it is.'

'Good. I'll leave you. I'll fetch you when the Library shuts. You've got a couple of hours.'

'Thank you.'

We went out to breakfast with Mr Robinson, a pleasant but prosy old gentleman who told us a complicated tale of a bust of Wieland, retrieved by himself from unworthy oblivion, to the great delight of Goethe and other literary eminences. Not much of interest was said, and certainly not by shadowy me, though that is as I would have it. Present were Mrs Jameson, Mr Bagehot, Ash the poet, without Mrs Ash, who was indisposed, and some younger members of the London University. The Princess was much admired and rightly. She spoke great good sense to Mr Ash, whose poetry I cannot like, though she professed to like it greatly, which naturally flattered him. He lacks, in my view, the lyrical flow and intensity of Alfred Tennyson, and I doubt his seriousness. His poem about Mesmer is a great puzzle to me, as I cannot tell with any certainty *what* is his attitude to Animal Magnetism, whether mocking or endorsing, and this is so with other of his work, so that often one is led to wonder whether there is not a great pother of talk about nothing much. For my part, I endured a long disquisition on the Tractarians from a young and opinionated university liberal. He would have been much surpris'd to know my true Opinion on these matters, but I did not chuse to let him be so much familiar, I kept mum, and smiled and nodded as best I might, keeping my Thoughts to myself. But I was almost glad when Mr Robinson decided to tell the company at large of his Italian journeyings with Wordsworth, who desired to be back at home with every step they made, and could only with the utmost difficulty be persuaded to look about him.

I too desired to be at home, and was glad when we were able

to close our own dear front door behind us, and be gathered in to the silence of our little parlour.

A home is a great thing, as I had not courage to say to Mr Robinson, if it is certainly one's *own home*, as our little house is. When I think of my previous existence – of all I thought I could reasonably expect of the rest of my life, an allowed place at the extreme corner of someone's drawing-room carpet, a Servant's garret or no better, I give thanks for every little thing, which is unspeakably dear to me. We had a late luncheon, cold fowl and a salad got up by Liza, walked in the Park in the afternoon, worked, and in the evening had a dish of warm milk and white bread, sprinkled with sugar, quite as Wordsworth himself might have done. We played and sang together, and read aloud a little of the *Faerie Queene*. Our days weave together the simple pleasures of daily life, which we should never take for granted, and the higher pleasures of Art and Thought which we may now taste as we please, with none to forbid or criticise. Surely Richmond is Beulah, I said to the Princess, who said it was only to be hoped no wicked Fairy envied us our pleasant lot.

Nothing further, for three and a half weeks, except simple meals, walks and readings, music and Blanche's plans for paintings. Then Roland found a sentence which could have been something or nothing. Nothing if you were not looking carefully.

I have been wondering whether to attempt, in oils, a subject from Malory, the imprisoning of Merlin, maybe, by the damsel Nimue, or the solitary Maid of Astolat. My brain is filled full of vague images, but no clear vision of one necessary thing. I have sketched oak trees in Richmond Park all week – all my lines are too light for the thick solidity of their girth. What draws us to *make pretty* what should express Brute Power? Nimue or the Lily Maid would require a model and the Princess can hardly be asked for so much of her time, though I hope she may think the time spent on 'Christabel before Sir Leoline' was not wholly wasted. I paint so thinly, as though my work were unlit stained glass that requires a flood of light from beyond and behind to illuminate and enliven it, and there is no beyond and behind. Oh I want *Force*. She has hung 'Christabel' in her bedroom where it catches the morning sun and shows up my imperfections. She is much exercised about a long letter which arrived today, which she did not show me, but smiled over, and caught up and folded away.

There was nothing at all, except Roland's own need and concern, to suggest that the long letter might be his own letter. It could have been any letter. Had there been more? Three weeks later he found another meaningful/meaningless sentence.

Liza and I have been busy with our apple-and-quince jelly; the kitchen is veiled and festooned in dripping jelly-muslin, ingeniously caught up amongst the legs of inverted chairs, like spider-webs. Liza burned her tongue, testing whether it would set or not, and being too greedy to taste or anxious to please. (Liza *is* greedy. I am sure she consumes bread and fruit in the middle of the night. Coming down to breakfast I find raw, slanting cuts *I* never made on the loaf in the crock.) The Princess did not help us this year. She was getting her Literary Letter ready to post, though she denied this, and said she was hurrying to finish the *Glass Coffin* for the book of tales. I believe she is writing fewer poems. Certainly she does not show me them, of an evening, as we were used to do. All this correspondence is detrimental to her true gifts. She is in no real need of epistolary adulation. She knows her own worth. I only wish I were as sure of mine.

Two weeks later:

Letters, letters, letters. Not for me. I am not meant to see or know. I am no blind mouldiwarp, my Lady, nor no well-trained lady's maid to turn my head and not see what is stated not to concern me. You need not hurry them away to lie in your sewing-basket or run upstairs to fold them under your handkerchiefs. I am no Sneak, no watcher, no Governess. A governess is what I am most surely not. From that fate you rescued me, and you shall never, for one moment, one little moment, suppose me ungrateful or making claims.

Two weeks later:

So now we have a Prowler. Something is ranging and snuffing round our small retreat, trying the shutters and huffing and puffing inside the door. In old days they put mountain ash berries and a cast horseshoe over the lintel to frighten away the Fairy Folk. I shall nail some up now, to show, to prevent passage, if I may. Dog Tray is nervous of prowlers. His hackles go up on his shoulders, as a wolf's would, when he hears the Hunter. He gnashes the empty air. How very small, how very safe, is a threatened dwelling. How large the locks seem, how appalling would be their forcing and splintering.

Two weeks later:

Where is our frankness of intercourse? Where the small, unspeakable things we used to share in quiet harmony? This Peeping Tom has put his eye to the nick or cranny in our walls and peers shamelessly in. She laughs and says he means no harm, and is incapable of seeing the essential things we know and keep safe, and so it is, so it must be, so it must always be. But it amuses her to hear him lolloping and panting round our solid walls, she thinks he will always be Tame, as he is now. I cannot claim to know better, I know nothing, I never have known very much, but I fear for her. I asked her how much writing she had lately done, and she laughed, and said she was learning so much, so very much, and when it was all learned she should have new matter to write about and many new things to say. And she kissed me, and called me her dear Blanche, and said I knew she was a good girl, and very strong, and not foolish. I said we were all, all foolish, and in need of divine strength to help us out when we were weak. She said she had never so much felt its presence, its immediacy, as lately. I went up to my bedchamber and prayed, as I have not prayed – from desolation – since I prayed to leave Mrs Teape's house and thought I should never be answered. The candle flame ran huge shadows like grasping fingers across the ceiling in the draught. I could put some such running, grasping lines of light and shadow around Nimue and Merlin. She came in to me as I knelt there and raised me up, and said we *must never quarrel* and that she would never, ever, give me cause to doubt her, and I must not suppose she could. I am sure she meant what she said. She was agitated; there were a few tears. We were quiet together, in our special ways, for a long time.

Next day:

The Wolf is Gone from the Door. Dog Tray's hearth is his own. I have begun on the Lily Maid of Astolat, which suddenly seemed best.

This writing ended, indeed the book ended, abruptly, not even at the end of the year. Roland wondered if there were other diaries. He put little slips of paper in the entries that made up his fragile narrative or non-narrative. There was no evidence to connect the Prowler with the letter-writer, or the letter-writer with Randolph Henry Ash, and yet he felt a powerful conviction that all three were one and the same. If they were, would not Blanche have said so? He must ask Maud Bailey about the Prowler, yet how could he do so without coming clean in some way – about his own interest in the matter? And exposing himself to that censorious and supercilious gaze?

Maud Bailey put her head round the door.

'Library's closing. Did you find anything?'

'I think so. It may be all in my own head. There are things I need to ask someone, you. Is it permitted to photocopy the manuscript? I simply haven't had time to copy out what I've found. I – '

'You seem to have had a profitable afternoon.' Drily. Then, as a concession, 'Exciting, even.'

'I don't *know*. The whole thing is a wild-goose chase.'

'If I can help – ' said Maud, having packed away Blanche's pages into their box. 'I shall be only too happy. Let's have coffee. There's an SCR Coffee place in the Women's Studies block.'

'Am I allowed in?'

'Naturally,' said the frigid voice.

They sat down at a low table in the corner, under a poster for the Campus Crèche and facing posters for the Pregnancy Advisory Service – 'A woman has a right to decide about her own body. We put women first' – and a Feminist Revue: Come and see the Sorcieres, the Vamps, the daughters of Kali and the Fatae Morganae. We'll make your blood run cold and make you laugh on the Sinister side of your face at Women's Wit and Wickedness. The room was largely uninhabited: a group of women in jeans were laughing in the opposite corner, and two girls were in earnest conversation by the window, pink spiky heads leaning together. Maud Bailey's excessive elegance was even odder in this context. She was a most untouchable woman; Roland, who had desperately decided to gamble on showing her the Xeroxes of the letters, who wanted secrecy and privacy, was forced to lean forward in a kind of pseudo-intimacy and speak low.

'You know this Prowler Blanche Glover got so worried about? Is anything known about him? The wolf at the door?'

'Nothing certain. I think Leonora Stern has made a tentative identification with a young Mr Thomas Hearst of Richmond who liked to come and play the oboe with the ladies. They were both accomplished pianists. There do exist two or three letters from Christabel to Hearst – she even sent him a few poems in one, which he kept, fortunately for us. He married someone else in 1860 and drops out of the picture. Blanche may have made up the prowling. She had a vivid imagination.'

'And was jealous.'

'Of course.'

'And the literary letters she refers to? Is it known who they were from? Or if they were connected to the "prowler"?'

'Not as far as I know. She had abundant letters from people like Coventry Patmore who admired her "sweet simplicity" and "noble resignation". Lots of people wrote. It could have been anyone. You think it's R. H. Ash?'

'No. I just. I think I'd better show you what I have.'

He brought out the photocopies of his two letters. Whilst she was unfolding them, he said,

'I should explain. I found these. I haven't shown them to anyone else. No one knows they exist.'

She was reading. 'Why?'

'I don't know. I kept them to myself. I don't know why.'

She finished reading.

'Well,' she said, 'the dates fit. You could make up a whole story. On no real evidence. It would change all sorts of things. LaMotte scholarship. Even ideas about *Melusina*. That Fairy Topic. It's *intriguing*.'

'Isn't it? It would change Ash scholarship, too. His letters are really rather boring, correct and distant really – this is quite different.'

'Where are the originals?'

Roland hesitated. He needed help. He needed to speak.

'I took them,' he said. 'I found them in a book and I took them. I didn't think about it, I just took them.'

'*Why*?' Stern but much more animated. 'Why did you?'

'Because they were alive. They seemed *urgent* – I felt I had to do something. It was an impulse. Quick as a flash. I meant to put them back. I will. Next week. I just haven't, yet. I don't think they're *mine*, or anything. But they aren't Cropper's or Blackadder's or Lord Ash's, either. They seemed private. I'm not explaining very well.'

'No. I suppose they might represent a considerable academic scoop. For you.'

'Well, I wanted to be the one who does the work,' Roland began innocently, and then saw how he had been insulted. 'Wait a minute – it wasn't like *that* at all, not like that. It was something *personal*. You wouldn't know. I'm an old-fashioned textual critic, not a biographer – I don't go in for this sort of – it wasn't *profit* – I'll put them back next week – I wanted them to be a secret. Private. And to do the work.'

She blushed. Red blood stained the ivory.

'I'm sorry. I don't know why I should be; it was quite a reasonable assumption and I can't begin to imagine how anyone would *dare* to whip two manuscripts like that out of sight – I'd never have the nerve. But I do see you weren't thinking in these terms. I do really.'

'I just wanted to know what happened next.'

'I can't let you xerox Blanche's diary – the spine won't stand it – but you can copy it out. And go on hunting through those boxes. Who knows what you'll find. No one was hunting for Randolph Henry Ash, after all. Can I book you a guest room until tomorrow?'

Roland thought. A guest room seemed infinitely attractive; a quiet place where he could sleep without Val, and think about Ash, and take himself at his own pace. A guest room would cost money he hadn't got. Also there was the Day Return.

'I have a Day Return ticket.'

'We could change that.'

'I'd rather not. I am an unemployed postgraduate. I haven't got the money.'

Now she was wine-red. 'I hadn't thought. You'd better come back to my place. I've got a spare bed. It's still better than buying another ticket now you're here – I'll cook supper – and tomorrow you can look at the rest of the Archive. It would be no trouble.'

He looked at the shiny black trace of the faded brown writing. He said, 'All right.'

Maud lived on the ground floor of a red-brick Georgian house on the outskirts of Lincoln. She had two large rooms, and a kitchen and bathroom constructed from what had been a warren of smaller domestic offices; her own front door had once been the tradesmen's entrance. The University owned the house; the upper floors were university flats. The kitchen, quarry-tiled, looked out onto a courtyard paved in red brick with various evergreen shrubs in tubs.

Maud's living room was not what might have been expected of a Victorian scholar. It was bright white, paint, lamps and dining-table; the carpet was a Berber off-white. The things in this room were brilliantly coloured in every colour, peacock, crimson, sunflower, deep rose, nothing pale or pastel. Alcoves beside the fireplace held a collection of spotlit glass, bottles, flasks, paper-weights. Roland felt wakeful and misplaced, as though he was in an art gallery or a surgeon's waiting-room. Maud went away to make supper, refusing offers of help, and Roland called the Putney flat where there was no reply. Maud came through with a drink and said, 'Why don't you read *Tales for Innocents*? I've got a first edition.'

The book was scuffed green leather, with faintly Gothic lettering. Roland sat on Maud's huge white sofa, by the wood fire and turned the pages.

Now there was once a Queen, who might have been thought to have everything she could desire in the world, but had set her heart on a strange silent bird a traveller had told of, which lived in the snowy mountains, nested only once, raised its gold and silver chick, sang once only, and then faded like snow in the lowlands.

There was once a poor shoemaker who had three fine strong sons and two pretty daughters and a third, who could do nothing well, who shivered plates and tangled her spinning, who curdled milk, could not get butter to come, nor set a fire so that smoke did not pour into the room, a useless, hopeless, dreaming daughter, to whom her mother would often say that she should try to fend for herself in the wild wood, and then she would know the value of listening to advice, and of doing things properly. And this filled the perverse daughter with a great desire to go even a little way into the wild wood, where there were no plates and no stitching, but might well be a need of such things as she knew she had it in herself to perform.

He looked at the woodcuts, which were described on the title page as 'Illustrations by B.G.' A female figure with a scarfed head, flying apron and great wooden shoes, standing in a clearing surrounded by dark pine trees full of white eyes among their crossing arms of needles. Another figure wrapped in what appeared to be netting hung with little bells, beat netted fists against a cottage door whilst squashed, lumpen faces leered behind upper windows. A little house, surrounded by the same black trees, at the foot of which, his chops on the whited steps, his sinuous length curved around its corner in a dragon-clasp, the long wolf lay, whose hairs were cut in harmony with the incisive feathering of the trees.

Maud Bailey gave him potted shrimps, omelette and green salad, some Bleu de Bresse and a bowl of sharp apples. They talked about *Tales for Innocents*, which, Maud said, were mostly rather frightening tales derived from Grimm and Tieck, with an emphasis on animals and insubordination. They looked together at the one about the woman who had said she would give anything for a child, of any kind, even a hedgehog, and had duly given birth to a monster, half-hedgehog, half-boy. Blanche had drawn the hedgehog-child in a Victorian high chair at a Victorian table; behind it were dark panes of cupboard glass, before it a huge intruding hand, pointing to its dish. Its face was blunt and furred and screwed up as though about to burst into tears. Its prickles were round its ugly head like spined rays of a halo, and descended its neckless shoulders, criss-crossing, to meet the incongruity of a starched, frilled collar. It had blunt little claws on its stubby hands. Roland asked Maud what the critics made of this. Maud said that Leonora Stern believed it represented Victorian women's fear, or any woman's fear, of giving birth to a monstrosity. It was related to Frankenstein, the product of Mary Shelley's labour pains and horror of birth.

'Do you think that?'

'It's an old story, it's in Grimm, the hedgehog sits on a black cock in a high tree and plays the bagpipes and tricks people. I think you can understand things about Christabel from the way she wrote her version. I think she simply disliked children – the way many maiden aunts must have done, in those days.'

'Blanche is sorry for the hedgehog.'

'Is she?' Maud examined the little picture. 'Yes, you're right. Christabel isn't. It becomes a very resourceful swineherd – multiplies its pigs on forest acorns – and ends up with a lot of triumphant slaughter and roast pork and crackling. Hard for modern children to stomach who grieve for the Gadarene swine. Christabel makes it into a force of nature. It likes winning, against the odds. In the end it wins a King's daughter who is expected to burn its hedgehog-skin at night, and does so, and finds herself clasping a beautiful Prince, all singed and soot-black. Christabel says, "And if he regretted his armoury of spines and his quick wild wits, history does not relate, for we must go no further, having reached the happy end."'

'I like that.'

'So do I.'

'Did you start work on her because of the family connection?'

'Possibly. I think not. I knew one little poem by her, when I was very small, and it became a kind of touchstone. The Baileys aren't very proud of Christabel, you know. They aren't literary. I'm a sport. My Norfolk grandmother told me too much education spoilt a girl for a good wife. And then the Norfolk Baileys don't speak to the Lincolnshire Baileys. The Lincolnshire ones lost all their sons in the First World War, except one invalid one, and became rather impoverished, and the Norfolk Baileys hung on to a lot of the money. Sophie LaMotte married a *Lincolnshire* Bailey. So I didn't grow up with the idea that I had a poet in the family, by marriage of course. Two Derby winners and an uncle who made a record ascent of the Eiger, that's the sort of thing that *mattered*.'

'What was the little poem?'

'The one about the Cumaean Sibyl. It was in a little book I

once got for Christmas called *Ghosts and Other Weird Creatures*. I'll show you.'

He read

> *Who are you?*
> Here on a high shelf
> In webbed flask I
> Hook up my folded self
> Bat-leather dry.

> *Who were you?*
> The gold god goaded me
> Sang shrieking sang high
> His heat corroded me
> Not mine his cry.

> *What do you see?*
> I saw the firmament
> Steady the sky
> I saw the cerement
> Close Caesar's eye.

> *What do you hope?*
> Desire is a dowsed fire
> True love a lie
> To a dusty shelf we aspire
> I crave to die.

'It's a very sad poem.'

'Young girls are sad. They like to be; it makes them feel strong. The Sibyl was safe in her jar, no one could touch her, she wanted to die. I didn't know what a Sibyl was. I just liked the rhythm. Anyway, when I started my work on thresholds it came back to me and so did she.

'I wrote a paper on Victorian women's imagination of space. *Marginal Beings and Liminal Poetry*. About agoraphobia and claustrophobia and the paradoxical desire to be let out into unconfined space, the wild moorland, the open ground, and at the same time to be closed into tighter and tighter impenetrable small spaces – like Emily Dickinson's voluntary confinement, like the Sibyl's jar.'

'Like Ash's Sorceress in her *In-Pace*.'

'That's different. He's punishing her for her beauty and what he thought of as her wickedness.'

'No, he isn't. He's writing about the people, including herself, who thought she *ought* to be punished because of her beauty and wickedness. She colluded with their judgment. He doesn't. He leaves it to our intelligence.'

A disputatious look crossed Maud's face, but all she said was,

'And you? Why do you work on Ash?'

'My mother liked him. She read English. I grew up on his idea of Sir Walter Ralegh, and his Agincourt poem and Offa on the Dyke. And then *Ragnarök.*' He hesitated. 'They were what stayed alive, when I'd been taught and examined everything else.'

Maud smiled then. 'Exactly. That's it. What could survive our education.'

She made him up a bed on the high white divan in her living-room – not a heap of sleeping-bags and blankets but a real bed, with laundered sheets and pillows in emerald green cotton cases. And a white down quilt, tumbled out of a concealed drawer beneath. She found him a new toothbrush in its unbroken wrap, and said,

'It's a pity about Sir George. Being such a curmudgeon. Who knows what he's got? Have you ever seen Seal Court? Victorian Gothic at its most tracery-like, pinnacles and lancets, deep in a dell. We could drive out there. If you think you've got time. I very rarely feel any curiosity about Christabel's life – it's funny – I even feel a sort of squeamishness about things she might have touched, or places she might have been – it's the *language* that matters, isn't it, it's what went on in her mind – '

'Exactly – '

'I've never bothered much about Blanche's Prowler and that sort of thing – it didn't seem to matter who it was, only that she thought something existed – but you've stirred something up –'

'Look,' he said. He fetched the envelope out of his case. 'I brought them with me. After all, what else could I do with them? They're faded but ... '

Since our extraordinary conversation I have thought of nothing else ... I feel,

*I know with a certainty that cannot be the product of folly or misapprehension,
that you and I must speak again —*

'I see,' she said. 'They're alive.'

'They don't have ends.'

'No. They're beginnings. Would you like to see where she
lived? And ended, indeed?'

He was visited by a memory of a cat-pissed ceiling, of a room
with no view.

'Why not? Since I'm here.'

'You go in the bathroom first. Please.'

'Thank you. For everything. Good night.'

He moved gingerly inside the bathroom, which was not a place
to sit and read or to lie and soak, but a chill green glassy place,
glittering with cleanness, huge dark green stoppered jars on water-
green thick glass shelves, a floor tiled in glass tiles into whose
brief and illusory depths one might peer, a shimmering shower
curtain like a glass waterfall, a blind to match, over the window,
full of watery lights. Maud's great green-trellised towels were
systematically folded on a towel-heater. Not a speck of talcum
powder, not a smear of soap, on any surface. He saw his face in
the glaucous basin as he cleaned his teeth. He thought of his home
bathroom, full of old underwear, open pots of eyepaint, dangling
shirts and stockings, sticky bottles of hair conditioner and tubes
of shaving foam.

Later, Maud stood in there, turning her long body under the hot
hiss of the shower. Her mind was full of an image of a huge,
unmade, stained and rumpled bed, its sheets pulled into standing
peaks here and there, like the surface of whipped egg-white.
Whenever she thought of Fergus Wolff, this empty battlefield
was what she saw. Beyond it lay, if she had chosen to conjure
them up, unwashed coffee cups, trousers lying where they had
been stepped out of, heaped dusty papers ring-stained with wine-
glasses, a carpet full of dust and ashes, the smell of socks and other
smells. Freud was right, Maud thought, vigorously rubbing her
white legs, desire lies on the other side of repugnance. The Paris
conference where she had met Fergus had been on Gender and

the Autonomous Text. She had talked about thresholds and he had given an authoritative paper on 'The Potent Castrato: the phallogocentric structuration of Balzac's hermaphrodite hero/ines'. The drift of his argument appeared to be feminist. The thrust of his presentation was somehow mocking and subversive. He flirted with self-parody. He expected Maud to come into his bed. 'We two are the most intelligent people here, you know. You are the most beautiful thing I have ever seen or dreamed about. I want you, I need you, can't you feel it, it's irresistible.' Why it had been irresistible, Maud was not rationally sure. But he had been right. Then the arguments had begun. Maud shivered.

She slipped on her nightdress, long-sleeved and practical, and loosed from her shower-cap all her yellow hair. She brushed fiercely, supporting the fall, and considered her perfectly regular features in the mirror. A beautiful woman, Simone Weil said, seeing herself in the mirror, knows 'This is I.' An ugly woman, with equal certainty, 'This is not I.' Maud knew this neat division represented an over-simplification. The doll-mask she saw had nothing to do with her, nothing. The feminists had divined that, who once, when she rose to speak at a meeting, had hissed and cat-called, assuming her crowning glory to be the seductive and marketable product of an inhumanely tested bottle. She had worn it almost shaved in her early teaching days, a vulnerable stubble on a white and shivering scalp. Fergus had divined how afraid she was of the doll-mask and had dealt with it in his own way, daring her to let it all hang out, quoting Yeats at her in his Irish voice.

> Never shall a young man
> Thrown into despair
> By those great honey-coloured
> Ramparts at your ear
> Love you for yourself alone
> And not your yellow hair.

'You should be ashamed to believe that,' said Fergus, 'and you so wise and clever about every other thing, my dear.' 'I don't,' Maud had said, 'believe that or care.' So he had dared her to grow it, and she had grown it, from eyebrow to ear to nape to the length of the neck to the shoulders. The growing had lasted the affair, almost exactly; when they parted, the long queue knocked on her spine. Now, for pride, she would not crop it, she would not so much mark the occasion, but instead wore it always inside some sort of covering, hidden away.

Roland felt buoyed up by the height of Maud's great divan. The room smelled of the ghost of wine and a hint of cinnamon. He lay in his white and emerald nest under the shaded light of a heavy brass lamp, green above, creamy inside. There was an incapable sleeper somewhere in his mind, a sleeper bruised and tossing on heaped feather mattresses, the Real Princess, suffering the muffled pea. Blanche Glover called Christabel the Princess. Maud Bailey was a thin-skinned Princess. He was an intruder into their female fastnesses. Like Randolph Henry Ash. He opened *Tales for Innocents* and read:

<h1 style="text-align:center">The
GLASS COFFIN</h1>

There was once a little tailor, a good and unremarkable man, who happened to be journeying through a forest, in search of work perhaps, for in those days men travelled great distances to make a meagre living, and the services of a fine craftsman, like our hero, were less in demand than cheap and cobbling hasty work that fitted ill and lasted only briefly. He believed he should come across someone who should want his skills – he was an incurable optimist, and imagined a fortunate meeting around every corner, though how that should come about was hard to see, as he advanced farther and farther into the dark, dense trees, where even the moonlight was split into dull little needles of bluish light on the moss, not enough to see by. But he did come upon the little house that was waiting for him, in a clearing in the depths, and was cheered by the lines of yellow light he could see between and under the shutters. He knocked boldly on the door of this house, and there was a rustling, and creaking, and the door opened a tiny crack, and there stood a little man, with a face as grey as morning ashes, and a long woolly beard the same colour.

'I am a traveller lost in the woods,' said the little tailor, 'and a master craftsman, seeking work, if any is to be found.'

'I have no need for a master craftsman,' said the little grey man. 'And I am afraid of thieves. You cannot come in here.'

'If I were a thief I could have forced my way in, or crept secretly in,' said the little tailor. 'I am an honest tailor in need of help.'

Now behind the little man stood a great grey dog, as tall as he was, with red eyes and hot breath. And at first this beast had made a low girning, growling sound, but now he hushed his threatening, and waved his tail slowly, and the little grey man said,

'Otto is of the opinion that you are honest. You may have a bed for the night in return for an honest evening's work, for help with cooking and cleaning and what must be prepared in my simple home.'

So the tailor was let in, and there was a strange household. In a rocking chair stood a brilliantly coloured cockerel and his pure white wife. In the fire-corner stood a black-and-white goat, with knobby little horns and eyes like yellow glass, and on the hearth lay a very large cat, a multi-coloured, mazy-patterned brindled cat, that looked up at the little tailor with eyes like cold green jewels, with black slits for pupils. And behind the dining table was a delicate dun cow, with milky breath and a warm wet nose and enormous soft brown eyes. 'Good morning,' said the tailor, to this company, for he believed in good manners, and the creatures were surveying him in a judging and intelligent way.

'Food and drink you will find in the kitchen,' said the little grey man. 'Make us a fit supper and we will eat together.'

So the little tailor turned to, and prepared a splendid pie, from flour and meat and onions he found there and decorated its top with beautifully formed pastry leaves and flowers, for he was a craftsman, even if he could not exercise his own craft. And whilst it was cooking he looked about him, and brought hay to the cow and goat, golden corn to the cock and hen, milk to the cat and bones and meat from his cooking to the great grey dog. And when the tailor and the little grey man were consuming the pie, whose warm smell filled the little house, the little grey man said,

'Otto was right, you are a good and honest man, and you care for all the creatures in this place, leaving no one unattended and nothing undone. I shall give you a gift for your kindness. Which of these things will you have?'

And he laid before the tailor three things. The first was a little purse of soft leather, which clinked a little as he put it down. The second was a cooking pot, black outside, polished and gleaming inside, solid and commodious. And the third was a little glass key, wrought into fantastic fragile shape, and glittering with all the colours of the rainbow. And the tailor looked at the watching animals for advice, and they all stared benignly back. And he thought to himself, 'I know about such gifts from forest people. It may be that the first is a purse which is never empty, and the second a pot which provides a wholesome meal whenever you demand one in the right way. I have heard of such things and met men who have been paid from such purses and eaten from such pots. But a glass key I never saw or heard of and cannot imagine what use it might be; it would shiver in any lock.' But he desired the little glass key, because he was a craftsman, and could see that it had taken masterly skill to blow all these delicate wards and barrel, and because he did not have any idea about what it was or might do, and curiosity is a great power in men's lives. So he said to the little man, 'I will take the pretty glass key.' And the little man answered, 'You have chosen not with prudence, but with daring. The key is the key to an adventure, if you will go in search of it.'

'Why not?' replied the tailor. 'Since there is no use for my craft in this wild place, and since I have not chosen prudently.'

Then the animals came closer with their warm, milky breaths that smelled sweetly of hay and the summer, and their mild comforting gaze that was not human, and the dog lay with his heavy head on the tailor's foot, and the brindled cat sat on the arm of his chair.

'You must go out of this house,' said the little grey man, 'and call to the West Wind, and show her your key, when she comes, and let her carry you where she will, without struggle or alarm. If you fight or question she will toss you on the thorns and it will go ill with you before you come out of there. If she will take you, you will be set down in a bare heath, on a great stone, which is made of granite and is the gate to your adventure, though it will seem to have been fixed and unmoving since the making of the world. On this stone you must lay a feather from the tail of the cockerel here, which he will willingly give you, and the door will be opened to you. You must descend without fear, or hesitation, and descend further, and still descend; you will find that your glass key will shed light on your way if you hold it before you. In time you will come to a stone vestibule, with two doors leading to branching passages you must not follow, and a low curtained door leading on and downwards. You must not touch this curtain with your hand, but must lay on it the milk-white feather which the hen will give you, and the curtain will be opened silently, by unseen hands, and the doors beyond it will lie open, and you may come into the hall where you shall find what you shall find.'

'Well, I will adventure,' said the little tailor, 'though I have great fear of the dark places under the earth, where there is no light of day and what is above is dense and heavy.' So the cock and the hen allowed him to take a glistening burnished black and emerald feather and a soft creamy-white feather, and he bade them all good-bye and went into the clearing, and called to the West Wind, holding up his key.

And that was a delightful and most alarming sensation, when the long, airy arms of the West Wind reached down through the trees and caught him up, and the leaves were all shivering and clattering and trembling with her passing, and the straws danced before the house and the dust rose and flew about in little earth-fountains. The trees grabbed at him with twiggy fingers as he rose up through them, lurching this way and that in the gusts, and then he felt himself held against the invisible rushing breast of the long Wind, as she hurled moaning along the sky. He rested his face against his airy pillow, and did not cry out or struggle, and the sighing song of the West Wind, full of fine rain and glancing sunshine, streaming clouds and driven starlight, netted him around and around.

She put him down as the little grey man had foretold on a huge grey granite stone, pitted and scarred and bald. He heard her whisking and wailing on her way, and he bent down and laid the cock-feather on the stone, and behold with a heavy groaning and grinding the huge stone swung up in the air and down in the earth, as though on a pivot or balance, disturbing waves of soil and heather like thick sea-water, and showing a dark, dank passage under the heather-roots and the knotty roots of the gorse. So in he went, bravely enough, thinking all the time of the thickness of rock and peat and earth over his head, and the air in that place was chill and damp and the ground underfoot was moist and sodden. He bethought him of his little key and held it up bravely before him, and it put out a little sparkling light that illumined a step at a time, silvery-pale. So he came down to the vestibule, where the three doors were, and under the sills of the two great doors light shone, warm and enticing, and the third was behind a musty leather curtain. He touched this leather, just brushing it with the tip of his soft henfeather, and it was drawn away in angular folds like bat-wings, and beyond a little dark door lay open into a tiny hole, into which he thought he might just manage to put his shoulders. Then truly he was afraid, for his small grey friend had said nothing of this narrow little place, and he thought if he put his head in he might never come out alive.

So he looked behind himself and saw that the passage he had just come down was one of many, all wrinkled and wormy and dripping and tangled with roots, and he thought he could never find his way back so he must perforce push on and see what lay in store. It took all the courage he had to thrust his head and shoulders into the mouth of that entrance, but he closed his eyes and twisted and turned and after a time tumbled out into a great stone chamber, lit with a soft light of its own that dimmed the glitter of his shining key. It was a miracle he thought, that the glass had not shivered in that tight struggle, but it was as clear and brittle as ever. So he looked about him, and saw three things. The first was a heap of glass bottles and flasks, all of them covered with dust and cobwebs. The second was a glass dome, the size of a man, and a little taller than our hero. And the third was a shining glass coffin, lying on a rich velvet pall on a gilded trestle. And from all these things the soft light proceeded, like the glimmering of pearls in the depth of water, like the phosphorescent light that moves of itself on the night surface of southern seas, or shines round the heaving shoals, milky-white over their silver darts, in our own dark Channel.

Well, he thought, one or all of these is my adventure. He looked at the bottles, which were many colours, red and green and blue and smoky topaz, and contained wisps and rinsings of nothing much, a sigh of smoke in one, a rocking of spirituous liquid in another. All were corked and sealed, and he was too circumspect to break the seals till he saw better where he was and what was to do.

He moved on to the dome, which you must imagine like the magic covers you have seen in your drawing-room under which dwell all sorts of brilliant little birds, as natural as life on their branches, or flights of mysterious moths and butterflies. Or maybe you have seen a crystal ball containing a tiny house which you can shake to produce a brilliant snowstorm? This dome contained a whole castle, set in a beautiful park, with trees and terraces and gardens, fishpools and climbing roses, and bright banners hanging limp in its many turrets. It was a brave and beautiful place, with innumerable windows and twisting staircases and a lawn and a swing in a tree and everything you could desire in a spacious and desirable residence, only that it was all still and tiny enough to need a magnifying glass to see the intricacies of its carvings and appurtenances. The little tailor, as I have told you, was first and foremost a craftsman, and he stared in wonder at this beautiful model and could not begin to imagine what fine tools or instruments had carved and wrought it. He dusted it a little, to marvel better, and then moved on to the glass coffin.

Have you remarked, where a fast-flowing stream comes to a little fall, how the racing water becomes glassy smooth and under it the long fine threads of the water-weed are drawn along in its still-seeming race, trembling a little, but stretched out in the flow? So under the surface of the thick glass lay a mass of long gold threads, filling in the whole cavity of the box with their turns and tumbles, so that at first the little tailor thought he had come upon a box full of spun gold, to make cloth of gold. But then between the fronds he saw a face, the most beautiful face he could have dreamed of or imagined, a still white face, with long gold lashes on pale cheeks, and a perfect pale mouth. Her gold hair lay round her like a mantle, but where its strands crossed her face they stirred a little with her breathing, so that the tailor knew she was alive. And he knew – it is always so, after all – that the true adventure was the release of this sleeper, who would then be his grateful bride. But she was so beautiful and peaceful that he was half-loath to disturb her. He wondered how she had come there, and how long she had been there, and what her voice would be like, and a thousand other ridiculous things, whilst she breathed in and out, ruffling the gold threads of hair.

And then he saw, in the side of the smooth box, which had no visible cleft or split, but was whole like a green ice egg, a tiny keyhole. And he knew that this was the keyhole for his wondrous delicate key, and with a little sigh he put it in and waited for what should ensue. And the little key slipped into the keyhole and melted, as it seemed into the glass body of the casket, so for a moment the whole surface was perfectly closed and smooth. And then, in a very orderly way, and with a strange bell-like tinkling, the coffin broke into a collection of long icicle splinters, that rang and vanished as they touched the earth. And the sleeper opened her eyes, which were as blue as periwinkle, or the summer sky, and the little tailor, because he knew this was what he must do, bent and kissed the perfect cheek.

'You must be the one,' said the young woman, 'You must be the one I have been waiting for, who must release me from enchantment. You must be the Prince.'

'Ah no,' said our hero, 'there you are mistaken. I am no more –
and indeed no less – than a fine craftsman, a tailor, in search of
work for my hands, honest work, to keep me alive.'

Then the young woman laughed merrily, her voice strength-
ening after what must have been years of silence, and the whole
strange cellar rang with that laughter, and the glass fragments
tinkled like broken bells.

'You shall have enough and more than enough, to keep you
alive forever, if you help me out of this dark place,' she said. 'Do
you see that beautiful castle locked in glass?'

'Indeed I do, and marvel at the craft with which it was made.'

'That was no carver's or miniaturist's craft, but black magic,
for that was the castle in which I lived, and the forests and
meadows round it were mine, where I roamed freely, with my
beloved brother, until the black artist came one night seeking
shelter from foul weather. For you must know that I had a
twin brother, as beautiful as the day, and gentle as a fawn, and
wholesome as new bread and butter, whose company pleased me
so much, as mine also pleased him, that we swore an oath never
to marry but to live forever peacefully in the castle, and hunt and
play together the livelong day. But when this stranger knocked,
in a howling gale, with his wet hat and cloak pouring rainwater
and his smiling mouth, my brother invited him in eagerly, and
gave him meat and wine, and a bed for the night, and sang with
him, and played cards, and sat by the fire, talking of the wide
world and its adventures. As I was not pleased with this, and
indeed a little sorrowful that my brother should take pleasure in
another's company, I went to bed early and lay listening to the
West Wind howling round the turrets and after a while fell into
an uneasy slumber. From this I was wakened by a strange, very
beautiful twanging music, coming from all about me. I sat up,
and tried to see what this might be or mean, and saw the door of
my chamber slowly open and he, the stranger, came striding in,
dry now, with black curly hair and a dangerous smiling face. I
tried to move, but could not, it was as though a band gripped my
body, and another band was tied about my face. He told me that
he meant me no harm, but was a magician, who had made the
music play around me, and wished to have my hand in marriage
and live in my castle, with me and my brother, in peace hereafter.
And I said – for I was permitted to answer – that I had no desire
for marriage, but wished to live unwed and happy with my dear
brother and no other. So he answered that that might not be, that

he would have me whether I would or no, and that my brother was of his opinion in this matter. We shall see that, said I, and he answered unabashed, with the invisible instruments twanging and humming and jangling all over the room, "You may see it, but you must not speak about this or anything that has passed here, for I have silenced you as surely as if I had cut out your tongue."

'Next day I tried to warn my brother, and it was as the black artist had said. When I opened my mouth to speak on this topic it was as though my lips were sewn together with great stitches in the flesh, and my tongue would not move in my mouth. Yet I might ask to have the salt passed, or discourse of the evil weather, and so my brother, to my great chagrin, noticed nothing, but set out blithely to go hunting with his new friend, leaving me at home to sit by the hearth, and to feel silent anguish at what might ensue. All day I sat so, and in the late afternoon, when the shadows were long on the castle lawns and the last rays of the sun were brassy and chill, I knew with certainty that something terrible had happened, and ran out of the castle, and away to the dark woods. And out of the dark woods came the black man, leading his horse on one arm, and on the other a tall grey hound with the saddest face I have ever seen on any creature. He told me my brother had suddenly gone away, and would return no more for a great and uncertain length of time and had left me, and the castle, in charge of him, the dark magician. He told me this gaily, as if it did not much matter whether I believed it or no. I said I would by no means submit to such injustice and was glad to hear my own voice steady and confident, for I feared my lips might again be sewn into silence. When I spoke great tears fell from the eyes of the grey hound, more and more, heavier and heavier. And I knew in some sort, I think, that the animal was my brother, in this meek and helpless form. Then I was angry, and said he should never come into my house, nor come near me, with my good will. And he said that I had perceived correctly, that he might do nothing without my goodwill which he would strive to gain, if I would allow it. And I said, this should never be, and he must never hope for it. Then he became angry, and threatened that he would silence me forever, if I would not agree. I said that without my dear brother I had little care where I was, and no one I wished to speak to. Then he said I should see whether that was so after a hundred years in a glass coffin. He made a few passes and the castle diminished and shrank, as you see it now, and he made a pass or two more and it was walled with glass as you see. And my people, the men and maidservants who came running, he confined as you see, each in a glass bottle, and finally closed me into the glass coffin in which you found me. And now, if you will have me, we will hasten from this place, before the magician returns, as he does from time to time, to see if I have relented.'

'Of course I will have you,' said the little tailor, 'for you are my promised marvel, released with my vanished glass key, and I love you dearly already. Though why you should have me, simply because I opened the glass case, is less clear to me altogether, and when, and if, you are restored to your rightful place, and your home and lands and people are again your own, I trust you will feel free to reconsider the matter, and remain, if you will, alone and unwed. For me, it is enough to have seen the extraordinary gold web of your hair, and to have touched that whitest and most delicate cheek with my lips.' And you may ask yourselves, my dear and most innocent readers, whether he spoke there with more gentleness or cunning, since the lady set such store on giving herself of her own free will, and since also the castle with its gardens, though now measurable with pins and fine stitches and thumbnails and thimbles, were lordly and handsome enough for any man to wish to spend his days there. The beautiful lady then blushed, a warm and rosy colour in her white cheeks, and was heard to murmur that the spell was as the spell was, that a kiss received after the successful disintegration of the glass casket, was a promise, as kisses are, whether received voluntarily or involuntarily. Whilst they were thus disputing, politely, the moral niceties of their interesting situation, a rushing sound was heard, and a melodious twanging, and the lady became very agitated, and said the black magician was on his way. And our hero in his turn, felt despondent and fearful, for his little grey mentor had given him no instructions for this eventuality. Still, he thought, I must do what I can to protect the lady, to whom I owe so much, and whom I have certainly, for better, for worse, released from sleep and silence. He carried no weapon save his own sharp needles and scissors, but it occurred to him that he could make do with the slivers of glass from the broken sarcophagus. So he took up the longest and sharpest, wrapping its hilt round in his leather apron, and waited.

The black artist appeared on the threshold, wrapped in a swirling black cloak, smiling most ferociously, and the little tailor quaked and held up his splinter, thinking his foe would be bound to meet it magically, or freeze his hand in motion as he struck. But the other merely advanced, and when he came up, put out a hand to touch the lady, whereupon our hero struck with all his might at his heart, and the glass splinter entered deeply and he fell to the ground. And behold, he shrivelled and withered under their eyes, and became a small handful of grey dust and glass powder. Then the lady wept a little, and said that the tailor had now twice saved her, and was in every way worthy of her hand. And she clapped her hands together, and suddenly they all rose in the air, man, woman, house, glass flasks, heap of dust, and found themselves out on a cold hillside where stood the original little grey man with Otto the hound. And you, my sagacious readers, will have perceived and understood that Otto was the very same hound into which the young brother of the lady of the coffin had been transformed. So she fell upon his grey hairy neck, weeping bright tears. And when her tears mixed with the salty tears that fell down the great beast's cheek, the spell was released, and he stood before her, a golden-haired young man in hunting-costume. And they embraced, for a long time, with full hearts. Meanwhile the little tailor, aided by the little grey man, had stroked the glass case containing the castle with the two feathers from the cock and hen, and with a strange rushing and rumbling the castle appeared as it must always have been, with noble staircases and innumerable doors. Then the little tailor and the little grey man uncorked the bottles and flasks and the liquids and smokes flowed sighing out of the necks of them, and formed themselves into men and women, butler and forester, cook and parlourmaid, all mightily bewildered to find themselves where they were. Then the lady told her brother that the little tailor had rescued her from her sleep and had killed the black artist and had won her hand in marriage. And the young man said that the tailor had offered him kindness, and should live with them both in the castle and be happy ever after. And so it was, and they did live happily ever after. The young man and his sister went hunting in the wild woods, and the little tailor, whose inclination did not lie that way, stayed by the hearth and was merry with them in the evenings. Only one thing was missing. A craftsman is nothing without the exercise of his craft. So he ordered to be brought to him the finest silk cloth and brilliant threads, and made for pleasure what he had once needed to make for harsh necessity.

CHAPTER FIVE

The ploughman, turning sullen clods may see
(Air whistling in his brain that rose in sighs
From belly griped by famine) the soil work
And work, to extrude a demon, with knobbed brow
And golden eyes, that opens a brown mouth
To promise — not the dream of avarice —
But pots of gold to buy the pots of pulse
Of which, no more, he dreams. So she may feel
Whisk past her skirt and scamper, hairy feet
Of an old gentle godling, who leaves tracks
In the warm ashes, or whose grincing voice
Laughs even in the cradle, saying 'Love me,
Rock me, and find your treasure, never fear.
The old gods keep their gifts to give their own.'
From such small demons, what harm might they fear?

R. H. Ash, from *The Incarcerated Sorceress*

The wolds of Lincolnshire are a small surprise. Tennyson grew up in one of their tight twisting valleys. From them he made the cornfields of immortal Camelot.

On either side the river lie
Long fields of barley and of rye
That clothe the wold and meet the sky.

Roland saw immediately that the word 'meet' was precise and surprising, not vague. They drove over the plain, up the rolling road, out of the valley. The valleys are deep and narrow, some wooded, some grassy, some ploughed. The ridges run sharply across the sky, always bare. The rest of the large, sleepy county is marsh or fen or flat farmed plain. These slightly rolling hills appear to be folded out of the surface of the earth, but that is not the case; they are part of a dissected tableland. The villages are buried in the valleys, at the end of blind funnels. The green car went busily along the ridgeway, which was patterned with roads and paths like the branches of spines. Roland, who was urban, noted colours: dark ploughed earth, with white chalk in the furrows; a pewter sky, with chalk-white clouds. Maud noticed good rides and unmended gates, and badly crunched hedgerows, gnashed by machine-teeth.

'Down on the left,' she said. 'Seal Court. In the hollow.'

A carpet of treetops, not homogeneous, and a glimpse of battlements, a round turret, another turn, and a sort of keep, perhaps.

'The land's private, of course. We can go down into the village. Christabel's buried there. In St Etheldreda's churchyard. The village is called Croysant le Wold; it's a lost village, more or less – there are a lot of lost villages scattered round the feet of these hills, no more than a grange and a church still standing. I don't think the Croysant church is in use nowadays. Christabel thought Croysant was derived from Croyance, meaning belief, and Saint – but it was one of those inaccurate guessing nineteenth-century etymologies. They say it really came from Croissant, meaning crescent, because there's a bend in the valley and the river there. She liked St Etheldreda, who was a Virgin Queen, although she was twice married – she became Abbess of Ely and founded a great House, and was buried in the odour of sanctity –'

Roland was not very interested in St Etheldreda. This morning Maud seemed again remote and patronising. They descended the switchback road and turned off in the valley towards the church, which stood in its walled graveyard, solid, square-towered. Outside its gate a battered estate-car was parked; Maud drew up at a distance, and together they walked in. The earth was wet. Blackening beech leaves, from a tree near the gate, clogged the path through the little graveyard, which was overgrown with damp, dun hay. Flanking the heavy stone porch were two large yews, heavy-shadowed. Maud, sensible in trench-coat and wellingtons, her head still scarfed, strode up to the wrought-iron gate across the porch, which was bolted and padlocked. Water, containing a brilliant green sediment, dripped from a gutter onto the stone, leaving a sinuous stain.

'The Baileys are *in* the church,' said Maud. 'But Christabel's out on the edge, in the wind and the rain, where she wanted to be. Over here.'

They clambered over tussocks and humps. They put their feet in the rabbit-runs between the dead. There was a shoulder-high stone wall, rooted with ivy-leaved toadflax. Christabel's tombstone leaned over at a slight angle. It was made of local limestone, not marble, and roughened by weather. Someone had cleaned the lettering, not very recently.

Here lie the mortal remains of
Christabel Madeleine LaMotte
Elder daughter of Isidore LaMotte
Historian
And of his beloved wife
Arabel LaMotte
Only sister of Sophie, Lady Bailey
Wife of Sir George Bailey of Seal Court
Croysant le Wold

Born January 3rd 1825
Laid to rest May 8th 1890

After mortal trouble
Let me lie still
Where the wind drives and the clouds stream
Over the hill
Where grass's thousand thirsty mouths
Sup up their fill
Of the slow dew and the sharp rain
Of the mantling snow dissolv'd again
At Heaven's sweet will.

Someone, again not recently, had sheared the hay from the grave, which was surrounded by a low and crumbling stone rim, thrust apart by couch grass and thorny trails of bramble. On the grassy mound lay the ghost of a large, indeed opulent bouquet, held together by bridal wires, now rusted amongst the mop heads of dead chrysanthemums and carnations, the skeletal leaves of long-faded roses. A green satin ribbon, water-stained and earth-stained, held these fragments together; there was a card tied to this, on which was palely visible in typewriting

> For Christabel
> From the women of Tallahassee
> Who truly honour you
> Who keep your memory green
> And continue your work
> 'The stones I shaped endure.'
> *Melusina*, XII, 325

'Leonora was here,' said Maud. 'In the summer. When Sir George threatened her with a shotgun.'

'She had a go at the weeds perhaps,' said Roland, who felt threatened by damp and melancholy.

'Leonora would be very shocked at the state of this graveyard,' said Maud. 'She would not find it romantic. I think it's all right. A slow return to nature and oblivion.'

'Did Christabel write that poem?'

'It's one of her quieter efforts. You see it's not ascribed. The tombstone mentions her father's profession, and doesn't say a word about her own.'

Roland felt briefly guilty of the oppressions of mankind. He said mildly,

'It's the poem that sticks in the memory. Rather sinister.'

'As though the grass were supping up Christabel.'

'Well, it was, I suppose.'

They looked at the grass. It lay damply, in decaying tufts.

'Let's walk up the hill,' said Maud. 'We can look down on Seal Court from a distance. She must have come this way often enough, she was a diligent churchgoer.'

From behind the church a ploughed field slanted up to the uncompromising skyline. Silhouetted against the grey sky, on the top, was a figure Roland at first took for a seated monarch by Henry Moore, enthroned and crowned. Then it inclined its head and struggled fiercely with arms pointing earthwards, and Roland caught glints of silver and reconstituted it as a person in a wheelchair, possibly in difficulty.

'Look!' he said to Maud.

Maud stared upwards.

'Perhaps they're in trouble.'

'Someone must be with them or they wouldn't have got up there,' said Maud reasonably.

'Perhaps,' said Roland, setting off nevertheless, his town shoes thickening with mud as he climbed, his hair ruffling. He was in good health, owing to the cycling perhaps, despite carbon monoxide and lead in London streets.

In the wheelchair was a woman, wearing a deep-crowned, wide-brimmed green felt hat, obscuring her face, and a paisley silk scarf at the throat of a caped loden coat. The chair had spun out of the central track along the ridge and was now skewed at the precipitous edge of what would be a steep and stony career. Leather-gloved hands strove with the huge hoops. Leather boots, beautifully soft and polished, rested placidly on the shifting step. There was, Roland saw, a huge flint embedded in the mud under the back of the wheel, preventing all attempts at manoeuvre or reversal.

'Can I help?'

'Oh,' on a long stressed sigh. 'Oh, thank you. I do s-seem to be b-bogged down.' The voice was hesitant, old and patrician. 'S-such a b-bother. So so h-h-h-h-*helpless*. If you please –'

'There's a stone. Under the wheel. Wait. Hold on.'

He had to kneel down in the muddy track, damaging his trousers, reminding him of playground agonies; he gripped, tugged, balanced.

'Is the chair stable?' he said. 'I seem to be tipping you.'

'It's d-designed for s-stability. I have the brakes on.'

The full real anxiety of the position slowly came over Roland. Any wrong move, and she would have been over. He inserted his hands into the mud, and scrabbled. He found a not very effective twig and scraped. He used another flint as a primitive lever and finally fell back, clasping the offending object in both hands, damaging the haunches of his trousers too.

'There,' he said. 'Like dentistry. It's out.'

'I am very grateful.'

'You were in a bit of a fix. You must have skidded over it one way and then it tipped back and put up this sort of tooth, like a ratchet, look.' He became aware that she was trembling. 'No, wait a minute, let's get the chair back on the track. I'm afraid my hands are muddy.'

He was out of breath by the time he had canted her back, ground her round, settled the chair on the rough track again. Its wheels dripped mud. She turned her face up to him then. It was large and moony, stained with the brown coins of age, thick with ropes and soft pockets of flesh under the chin. The eyes, huge and pale brown, were swimming. From under the smooth, pulled-back grey hair at the sides of the hat, trickled large drops of sweat.

'Thank you,' she said. 'I had got myself in a very foolish position. I might well have gone over. F-foolhardy, my husband would say. I sh–should s–stay on the level ground. My dependence annoys me.'

'Of course,' said Roland. 'Of course it must. You were all right really. Someone must have come.'

'Just as well you did. Are you out walking?'

'I'm visiting. Out with a friend.' Where was Maud? 'Marvellous air. You can see so far.'

'That's why I come up here. The dog is meant to stay with me, but he never does. My husband likes to poke about in the woods. Where are you walking?'

'I don't know. My friend knows. Shall I walk with you, a little?'

'I don't feel very well. My h–hands are shaky. If you would be good enough to come to – the foot of the track, down the wold, my husband –'

'Of course, of course.'

Maud came up. She looked neat and clean in her Burberry and wellingtons.

'We got the chair out,' Roland told her. 'It was jammed on a stone. I'm just going to walk down the hill with this lady – her husband's there – she's had rather a shock –'

'Of course,' said Maud.

They progressed, all three, Roland behind the chair, down the track. The land over the hill was thickly wooded. Through trees Roland saw again, more leisurely, a turret, a battlement, white in the gloom.

'Seal Court,' he said to Maud.

'Yes.'

'Romantic,' he offered.

'Dark and damp,' said the lady in the wheelchair.

'It must have cost a fortune to build,' said Maud.

'And to maintain;' said the lady in the wheelchair. Her leather hands danced a little in her lap, but her voice was steadying.

'I suppose so,' said Roland.

'You are interested in old houses?'

'Not exactly,' said Roland. 'We wanted to see that one.'

'Why?'

Maud's boot sliced into his ankle. He suppressed an exclamation of pain. A very dirty Labrador appeared, out of the woodland.

'Ah, Much,' said the lady. 'There you are. Useless great lump. Useless. Where's your master? Tracking badgers?'

The dog measured its blond belly in the mud, agitating its stern.

'Tell me your names,' said the lady in the wheelchair. Maud said quickly,

'This is Dr Michell. From London University. I teach at Lincoln University. My name's Bailey. Maud Bailey.'

'My name is Bailey too. Joan Bailey. I live at Seal Court. Are you a relation?'

'I am a Norfolk Bailey. A relation far back. Not very close. The families haven't kept up –'

Maud sounded repressive and cold.

'How interesting. Ah, here is George. George dear, I have had an adventure and been rescued by a knight. I was entrenched on the top of Eagle's Piece, with a huge stone under my wheel and the only way out seemed to be over the edge, *most* humiliating. And then Mr Michell here came along, and this young woman, whose name is Bailey.'

'I told you to keep to the centre of the track.'

Sir George was small and wet and bristling. He had laced leather boots with polished rounded calves, like greaves. He had a many-pocketed shooting jacket, brown, with a flat brown tweed cap. He barked. Roland took him for a caricature and bristled vestigially with class irritation. Such people, in his and Val's world, were not quite real but still walked the earth. Maud too saw him as a type; in her case he represented the restriction and boredom of countless childhood country weekends of shooting and tramping and sporting conversation. Rejected and evaded. He was not carrying a gun. Water stained his shoulders, shone on his footwear, stood in drops on the furry ribs of the socks between his breeches and his boots. He considered his wife.

'You're never content, are you?' he said. 'I push you up the hill and then you're not content to take it steady on the track, oh no. Any harm done?'

'I do feel a bit shaken. Mr Michell came in time.'

'Well, you weren't to expect that.' He advanced on Roland, his hand held out. 'I'm very grateful. My name's Bailey. The idiot dog is meant to stay with Joan, but he will not, he will go off on his own little expeditions in the gorse. I expect you think I should have stayed up there, ha?'

Roland demurred, touching his forthright hand, stepping back.

'So I should. So I should. I'm a selfish old blighter. There are badgers, though, Joanie. Not that I should say so, encourage trespassers, wildlifers, terrifying the poor brutes out of their wits. The old Japanese juniper's in good fettle, too, you'll be glad to know. Quite recovered.'

He advanced on Maud.

'Afternoon. My name's Bailey.'

'She knows,' said his wife. 'So's her name, I told you, she's one of the Norfolk Baileys.'

'Is that so? They aren't seen about here very often. Less than badgers, I'd say. What brings you here?'

'I work in Lincoln.'

'You do, do you?' He did not ask at what. He considered his wife with some intensity of observation.

'You look clammy, Joan. You aren't a good colour. We should get you home.'

'I should like to ask Mr Michell and Miss Bailey to c-come to t-tea if they would. Mr Michell needs a wash. They are interested in Seal Court.'

'Seal Court isn't interesting,' said Sir George. 'It isn't open to the public, you know. It's in a bad way. My fault, indirectly. Lack of funds. Coming down round our ears.'

'They won't mind that. They're young.' Lady Bailey's large

face took on a set expression. 'I should like to ask them. For courtesy.'

Maud's face flamed. Roland saw what was going on. She wanted proudly to disclaim any interest in penetrating Seal Court: she wanted to go there, because of Christabel, because, he guessed, Leonora Stern had been turned away: she felt, he assumed, dishonest in not saying straight out why she had an interest in going.

'I should be very glad of a brief chance to wash,' he said. 'If it's not too much trouble.'

They drove in convoy round behind the great house, on a sopping weed-infested gravel drive, and pulled up in the stable-yard, where Roland helped Sir George to disembark the wheelchair and Lady Bailey. The short day was darkening; the back door swung in heavily under a Gothic porch over which a rose, now leafless, was trained. Above, rows of dark windows, with carved Gothic frames, were dark and blank. The door had been elongated to remove steps, so that the wheelchair could go in. They progressed along dark stone corridors, past various pantries and flights of steps, arriving eventually in what later turned out to have been the servants' hall and was now superficially, and partially, converted for modern living.

At one end of this dim room was an open fireplace, in which a few huge logs still smouldered in a bed of white ash; on either side of this were two heavy, curved and padded armchairs, covered in velvet, a dark charcoal colour, patterned with dark purple flowers, a kind of glamorised *fin-de-siècle* bindweed. The floor was covered with large red and white vinyl tiles, rubbed in ridges that betrayed the presence of flagstones underneath. Under the window was a heavy table, thick-legged and partly covered with an oilcloth patterned in faintly tartan checks. At the other end of the room, which later proved to lead out to the kitchen and other domestic offices, was a small two-barred electric fire. There were other, slightly threadbare chairs, and a collection of extremely glossy, lively pot plants, in glazed bowls. Maud was worried by the lighting, which Sir George turned on – a dim standard lamp by the fire, a slightly happier lamp, made from a Chinese vase, on the table. The walls were whitewashed, and bore various pictures of horses, dogs and badgers, oils, water-colours, tinted photos, framed glossy prints. By the fire was a huge basket, obviously Much's bed, lined with a stiff and hair-strewn navy blanket. Large areas of the room were simply empty. Sir George drew the curtains, and motioned Roland and Maud to sit down by the fire, in the velvet chairs. Then he wheeled his wife out. Roland did not feel able to ask if he could help. He had expected a butler or some obsequious manservant, at the least a maid or companion, to welcome them into a room shining with silver and silk carpets. Maud, inured to poor heating and the threadbare, was still a little disturbed by the degree of discomfort represented by the sad lighting. She put her hand down and called Much, who came and pressed his body, trembling and filthy, against her legs, between her and the sinking fire.

Sir George came back and built up his fire with new logs, hissing and singing.

'Joan is making tea. I'm afraid we don't have too many comforts or luxuries here. We live only on the ground floor, of course. I had the kitchen made over for Joan. Every possible aid. Doors and ramps. All that could be done. I know it's not much. This house was built to be run by a pack of servants. Two old folk – we echo in it. But I keep up the woods. And Joan's garden. There's a Victorian water garden too, you know. She likes that.'

'I've read about that,' said Maud cautiously.

'Have you now? Keep up with family things, do you?'

'In a way. I have particular family interests.'

'What relation are you to Tommy Bailey then? That was a great horse of his, Hans Andersen, that was a horse with character and guts.'

'He was my great-uncle. I used to ride one of Hans Andersen's less successful descendants. A pig-headed brute who could jump himself out of anything, like a cat, but didn't always choose to, and didn't always take me with him. Called Copenhagen.'

They talked about horses and a little about the Norfolk Baileys. Roland watched Maud making noises which he sensed came naturally, and sensed too that she would never make in the Women's Studies building. From the kitchen a bell struck.

'That's the tea. I'll go and fetch it. And Joan.'

It came in an exquisite Spode tea service, with a silver sugar-bowl and a plateful of hot buttered toast with Gentleman's Relish or honey, on a large melamine tray designed, Roland saw, to slot into the arms of the wheelchair. Lady Bailey poured. Sir George quizzed Maud about dead cousins, long-dead horses, and the state of the trees on the Norfolk estate. Joan Bailey said to Roland,

'George's great-great-grandfather planted all this woodland, you know. Partly for timber, partly because he loved trees. He tried to get everything to grow that he could. The rarer the tree, the more of a challenge. George keeps it up. He keeps them alive. They're not fast conifers, they're mixed woodland, some of those rare trees are very old. Woods are diminishing in this part of the world. And hedges too. We've lost acres and acres of woodland to fast grain farming. George goes up and down protecting his trees. Like some old goblin. Somebody has to have a sense of the history of things.'

'Do you know,' said Sir George, 'that up to the eighteenth century the major industry in this part of the world was rabbit-warrening? The land wasn't fit for much else, sandy, full of gorse. Lovely silver skins they had; they went off to be hats in London and up North. Fed 'em in the winter, let 'em forage in the summer, neighbours complained but they flourished. Alternated with sheep in places. Vanished, along with much else. They found ways to make sheep cheaper, and corn too, and the rabbits died out. Trees going the same way now.'

Roland could think of no intelligent comments about rabbits, but Maud replied with statistics about Fenland warrens and a description of an old warrener's tower on the Norfolk Baileys' estate. Sir George poured more tea. Lady Bailey said,

'And what do you do in London, Mr Michell?'

'I'm a university research student. I do some teaching. I'm working for an edition of Randolph Henry Ash.'

'He wrote a good poem we learned at school,' said Sir George. 'Never had any use for poetry myself, but I used to like that one. "The Hunter". Do you know that poem? About a stone-age chappie setting snares and sharpening flints and talking to his dog and snuffing the weather in the air. You got a real sense of *danger* from that poem. Funny way to spend your life, though, studying another chap's versifying. We had a sort of poet in this house once. I expect you'd think nothing to her. Terrible sentimental stuff about God and Death and the dew and fairies. Nauseating.'

'Christabel LaMotte,' said Maud.

'Just so. Funny old bird. Lately we get people round asking if we've got any of her stuff. I send them packing. We keep ourselves to ourselves, Joan and I. There was a frightful nosy American in the summer who just turned up out of the blue and told us how honoured we must be, having the old bat's relics up here. Covered with paint and jangling jewellery, a real mess, she was. Wouldn't go when I asked her politely. Had to wave the gun at her. Wanted to sit in Joan's winter garden. To remember Christabel. Such rot. Now a *real* poet, like your Randolph Henry Ash, that'd be something different, you'd be reasonably pleased to have someone like that in the family. Lord Tennyson was a bit of a soppy old thing too, on the whole, though he wrote some not bad things about Lincolnshire dialect. Not a patch on Mabel Peacock though. She really could hear Lincolnshire speech. Marvellous story about a hedgehog. Th'otchin 'at wasn't niver suited wi' nowt. Listen to this then. "Fra fo'st off he was werrittin' an witterin' an sissin an spittin perpetiwel." That's real history that is, words that are vanishing daily, fewer and fewer people learning them, all full of *Dallas* and *Dynasty* and the Beatles jingle jangle.'

'Mr Michell and Miss Bailey will think you are a frightful old stick, George. They *like* good poetry.'

'They don't like Christabel LaMotte.'

'Ah, but I do,' said Maud. 'It was Christabel who wrote the description I read of the Seal Court winter garden. In a letter. She made me see it, and the different evergreens, and the red berries and the dogwood and the sheltered bench and the silvery fish in the little pool ... Even under the ice she could see them suspended –'

'We had an old tom cat who used to take the fish –'

'We restocked –'

'I'd love to see the winter garden. I'm writing about Christabel LaMotte.'

'Ah,' said Lady Bailey. 'A biography. How interesting.'

'I don't see,' said Sir George, 'that there'd be much to put in a biography. She didn't *do* anything. Just lived up there in the east wing and poured out all this stuff about fairies. It wasn't a *life*.'

'As a matter of fact, it isn't a biography. It's a critical study. But of course she interests me. We went to look at her grave.'

This was the wrong thing to say. Sir George's face darkened. His brows, which were sandy, drew down over his plummy nose.

'That unspeakable female who came here – she had the impudence to hector me – to read me a lecture – on the state of that grave. Said its condition was shocking. A national monument. Not *her* national monument I told her, and she shouldn't come poking her nose in where it wasn't wanted. She asked to borrow some shears. That was when I got the gun out. So she went and bought some in Lincoln and came back the next day and got down on her knees and cleaned it all up. The Vicar saw her. He comes over once a month, you know, and says Evensong in the church. She sat and listened in the back pew. Brought a huge bouquet. Affectation.'

'We saw –'

'You don't have to shout at Miss Bailey, George,' said his wife. 'She's not responsible for all that. There's no reason why she shouldn't be interested in Christabel. I think you should show these young people Christabel's room. If they want to see. It's all locked away, you know, Mr Michell, and has been for generations. I don't know what sort of a state it's in, but I believe some of her things are still there. The family has occupied less and less of this house since the World Wars, every generation a little less – Christabel's room was in the east wing that's been closed since 1918, except for use as some kind of a glory-hole. And we, of course, live in a very small part of the building, and only downstairs, because of my disability. We do try to have general repairs done. The roof's sound, and there's a carpenter who sees to the floors. But no one's touched that room to my knowledge, since I came here as a bride in 1929. Then we lived in all this central portion. But the east wing was – not out of bounds exactly – but not used.'

'You wouldn't see much,' said Sir George. 'You'd need a torch. No electricity, in that part of the house. Only on the ground floor corridors.'

Roland felt a strange pricking at the base of his neck. Through the carved window he saw the wet branches of the evergreens, darker on the dark. And the dim light in the gravel drive.

'It would be marvellous just to have a look –'

'We should be very grateful.'

'Well,' said Sir George, 'Why not? Since it's all in the family. Follow me.'

He gathered up a powerful modern storm-lantern and turned to his wife. 'We'll bring you back any treasure we find, dear. If you wait.'

They walked and walked, at first along tiled and bleakly lit corridors under electric lighting, and then along dusty carpets in dark shuttered places, and up a stone staircase and then further up a winding wooden stair, cloudy with dark dust. Maud and Roland neither looked nor spoke to each other. The little door was heavily panelled and had a heavy latch. They went in behind Sir George, who waved his huge cone of light around the dark, cramped, circular space, illuminating a semi-circular bay window, a roof carved with veined arches and mock-mediaeval ivy-leaves, felt-textured with dust, a box-bed with curtains still hanging, showing a dull red under their pall of particles, a fantastically carved black wooden desk, covered with beading and scrolls, and bunches of grapes and pomegranates and lilies, something that might have been either a low chair or a prie-dieu, heaps of cloth, an old trunk, two band boxes, a sudden row of staring tiny white faces, one, two, three, propped against a pillow. Roland drew his breath in minor shock: Maud said, 'Oh, the *dolls*' – and Sir George brought his light back from a blank mirror entwined with gilded roses and focussed it on the three rigid figures, semi-recumbent under a dusty counterpane, in a substantial if miniature four-poster bed.

They had china faces, and little kid-leather arms. One had fine gold silken hair, faded and grey with the dust. One had a kind of bunched white nightcap, in white dimity edged with lace. One had black hair, pulled back in a circular bun. They all stared with blue glassy eyes, filled with dust, but still glittering.

'She wrote a series of poems about the dolls,' said Maud, in a kind of dreadful whisper. 'They were ostensibly for children, like the *Tales for Innocents*. But not really.'

Roland turned his eyes back to the shadowy desk. He did not feel the presence of the dead poet in the room, but he did have a vague excited sense that any of these containers – the desk, the trunks, the hat-boxes, might contain some treasure like the faded letters in his own breast-pocket. Some clue, some scribbled note, some words of response. Only that was nonsense, they would not be here, they would be wherever Randolph Henry Ash had put them, if they had ever been written.

'Do you know,' Roland said, turning to Sir George, 'whether there were papers? Is there anything left in that desk? Anything of hers?'

'That was cleared, I suppose, at her death,' said Sir George.

'May we at least look?' said Roland, imagining perhaps a hidden drawer, and at the same time uncomfortably aware of the laundry lists in *Northanger Abbey*. Sir George obligingly moved the light across to the desk, restoring the little faces to the dark in which they had lain. Roland lifted the lid on a bare casket. There were empty arched pigeonholes at the back, fretted and carved, and two empty little drawers. He felt unable to tap and tug at the framework. He felt unable to urge the unbuckling of the trunk. He felt as though he was prying, and as though he was being uselessly urged on by some violent emotion of curiosity – not greed, curiosity, more fundamental even than sex, the desire for knowledge. He felt suddenly angry with Maud, who was standing stock still, in the dark, not moving a finger to help him, not urging, as she with her emotional advantage might well have done, further exploration of hidden treasures or pathetic dead caskets. Sir George said, 'And what in particular might you expect to find?' Roland did not know the answer. Then, behind him, chill and clear, Maud spoke a kind of incantation.

> Dolly keeps a Secret
> Safer than a Friend
> Dolly's Silent Sympathy
> Lasts without end.
>
> Friends may betray us
> Love may Decay
> Dolly's Discretion
> Outlasts our Day.
>
> Could Dolly tell of us?
> Her wax lips are sealed.
> Much has she meditated
> Much – ah – concealed.

Dolly ever sleepless
Watches above
The shreds and relics
Of our lost Love
Which her small fingers
Never may move.

Dolly is harmless.
We who did harm
Shall become chill as she
Who now are warm
She mocks Eternity
With her sly charm.

Sir George swung the light back onto the dolls' cot.

'Very good,' he said. 'Fantastic memory you've got. Never could learn anything by heart myself. Barring Kipling and the Lincolnshire bits that amuse me, that is. What is it all about though?'

'It sounds, in here, like a treasure-hunt clue,' said Maud, still with a strained clarity. 'As though Dolly is hiding something.'

'What might she be hiding?' said Sir George.

'Almost anything,' said Roland, suddenly wanting to put him off the trail. 'Keepsakes.' He could feel Maud calculating.

'Somebody's children must have had those dolls out,' said their owner plausibly, 'since 1890.'

Maud knelt down in the dust. 'May I?' He turned the light down on her; there she was, her face bending into shadow, as though Latour had painted its waxiness. She reached into the cot and plucked out the blonde doll by the waist; her gown was pink silk, with little rosebuds round its neckline and tiny pearl buttons. She handed this creature to Roland, who took it as he might have done a kitten, cradling it in the crook of his elbow, and adding to it, in turn, the nightcapped one, in tiny white pleats and broderie anglaise, and the dark-headed one, severe in dark peacock. They lay along his arm, their tiny heads heavy, their tiny limbs trailing, rather horrid, a little deathly. Maud took out the pillow, untucked the counterpane, folded away three fine woollen blankets and a crocheted shawl, and then lifted out one feather mattress and another, and a straw palliasse. She reached in under this, into the wooden box beneath it, prised up a hinged board and brought out a package, wrapped in fine white linen, tied with tape, about and about and about, like a mummy.

There was a silence. Maud stood there, holding on. Roland took a step forward. He knew, he knew, what was wrapped away there.

'Probably dolls' clothes,' said Maud.

'Have a look,' said Sir George. 'You seemed to know where to find it. I bet you've got a shrewd guess what's in it. Open up.'

Maud plucked with pale neat lamplit fingers at the old knots, which were, she discovered, faintly covered with sealing wax.

'Do you want a penknife?' said Sir George.

'We shouldn't – cut –' said Maud. Roland itched to help. She worked. The tapes fell away and the linen, many-layered, was turned back. Inside were two parcels, wrapped in oiled silk, and tied with black ribbon. Maud pulled at the ribbon too. The old silk squeaked and slipped. There they were, open letters, two bundles, neat as folded handkerchiefs. Roland did step forward. Maud picked up the top letter on each pile. Miss Christabel LaMotte, Bethany, Mount Ararat Road, Richmond, Surrey. Brown, spidery decisive, known, the hand. And, much smaller, more violet, Randolph Henry Ash Esqre, 29, Russell Square, London. Roland said, 'So he did send it.'

Maud said,

'It's both sides. It's everything. It was always there . . .'

Sir George said, 'And what exactly have you got there? And how did you know to go for the dolls' bed?'

Maud said, her voice high-edged and clear, 'I didn't know. I just thought of the poem, standing there, and then it seemed clear. It was sheer luck.'

Roland said, 'We thought there might have been a correspondence. I found – a bit of a letter – in London. So I came to see Dr Bailey. That's all there is to it. This could be –' he was about to say 'terribly' and held back – 'quite important.' It could change the face of scholarship, he nearly said, and held back again, driven by some instinct of cunning reserve. 'It makes a great difference to our research work, to both our projects. It wasn't known they knew each other.'

'Hm,' said Sir George. 'Give those parcels to me. Thanks. I think we should go back down now and show these to Joan. And see if they're anything or nothing. Unless you want to stay and open everything else?' He circled the round walls with his spotlight, revealing a skewed print of Lord Leighton's Proserpina, and a cross-stitched sampler, impossible to read under the dust.

'Not now,' said Maud.

'Not immediately,' said Roland.

'You may never come back,' said Sir George, more threatening than joking apparently, from behind his lance of light, turning through the door. So they progressed back again, Sir George clutching the letters, Maud the opened cocoon of linen and silk, and Roland the three dolls, out of some vague fancy that it was cruel to leave them in the dark.

Lady Bailey was quite excited. They all sat round the fireplace. Sir George put the letters into his wife's lap, and she turned them over and over, under the greedy eyes of the two scholars. Roland told his half-truth about his bit of a letter, not saying when or where he had come across it. 'Was it a love letter, then?' Lady Bailey asked, innocent and direct, and Roland said, 'Oh no' and then added, 'but excited, you know, as though it was important. It was a draft of a first letter. It was important enough to make me come up here to ask Dr Bailey about Christabel LaMotte.' He wanted to ask and ask. The date, for God's sake, on the top letter from Ash, was it the *same*, why were they all together, how long does it go on, – how did she answer, what about Blanche and the Prowler ...

'Now what would be the right way to proceed?' said Sir George slowly, and deliberately pompously. 'In your view, young man? In yours, Miss Bailey?'

'Someone should read them –' said Maud. 'Oh –'

'And you naturally think *you* should read them,' said Sir George.

'I – we – should like to, very much. Of course.'

'So would that American, no doubt.'

'Of course she would. If she knew they were there.'

'Shall you tell her?'

He watched Maud hesitate, his fierce blue eyes shrewd in the firelight.

'Probably not. Not yet, anyway.'

'You'd like the first crack?'

Maud's face flamed, 'Of course. Anyone would. In my – in our position . . .'

'Why shouldn't they read them, George?' Joan Bailey enquired, drawing the first letter out of its envelope, looking casually down at it, not avid, barely curious.

'For one thing, I believe in letting dead bones lie still. Why stir up scandals about our silly fairy poetess? Poor old thing, let her sleep decently.'

'We aren't *looking* for scandals,' said Roland. 'I don't suppose there is any scandal. I just hope – he told her what he was thinking about poetry – and history – and things like that. It was one of his most fertile periods – he wasn't a great letter-writer – too polite – he said she understood him in the letter I – I – saw – he said –'

'For *another* thing, Joanie, what do we really know about these two? How do we know they're the proper people to have sight of these – documents? There's two days' reading in that heap, easy. I'm not letting them out of my hands, am I?'

'They could come here,' said Lady Bailey.

'It's a bit more than two days,' said Maud.

'You see,' said Sir George.

'Lady Bailey,' said Roland. 'What I saw was the first draft of the first letter. Is that it? What does it say?'

She put on reading glasses, round in her pleasant large face. She read out:

Dear Miss LaMotte,

It was a great pleasure to talk to you at dear Crabb's breakfast party. Your perception and wisdom stood out through the babble of undergraduate wit, and even surpassed our host's account of the finding of Wieland's bust. May I hope that you too enjoyed our talk – and may I have the pleasure of calling on you? I know you live very quietly, but I would be very quiet – I only want to discuss Dante and Shakespeare and Wordsworth and Coleridge and Goethe and Schiller and Webster and Ford and Sir Thomas Browne et hoc genus omne, not forgetting of course, Christabel LaMotte and the ambitious Fairy

Project. Do answer this. You know, I think, how much a positive answer would give pleasure to

> *Yours very sincerely*
> *Randolph Henry Ash*

'And the answer?' said Roland. 'The answer? I'm sorry – I'm *so* curious – I've been wondering *if* she answered, and if so, what she said.'

Lady Bailey drew out the top letter of the other sheaf, almost teasingly, like an actress announcing on television the award for the Best Actress of the Year.

Dear Mr Ash,

No truly – I do not Tease – how should I demean you or myself so – or you demean Yourself to think it. I live circumscribed and self-communing – 'tis best so – not like a Princess in a thicket, by no means, but more like a very fat and self-satisfied Spider in the centre of her shining Web, if you will forgive me the slightly disagreeable Analogy. Arachne is a lady I am greatly sympathetic to, an honest craftswoman, who makes perfect patterns, but is a little inclined to take unorthodox snaps at visiting or trespassing strangers, not perceiving the distinction between the two, it may be, often until too late. Truly I make but a stammering companion, I have no graces, and as for the wit you may have perceived in me when we met, you saw, you must have seen, only the glimmerings and glister of your own brilliance refracted from the lumpen surface of a dead Moon. I am a creature of my Pen, Mr Ash, my Pen is the best of me, and I enclose a Poem, in earnest of my great goodwill towards you. Now would you not rather have a Poem, however imperfect, than a plate of cucumber sandwiches, however even, however delicately salted, however exquisitely fine-cut? You know you would, and so would I. The Spider in the poem however, is not my Silken Self, but an altogether more Savage and businesslike sister. You cannot but admire their facile diligence? Would Poems came as naturally as Silk Thread. I write Nonsense, but if you care to write again, you shall have a sober essay on the Everlasting Nay, or Schleiermacher's Veil of Illusion, or the Milk of Paradise, or What you Will.

> *Yours to command in some things*
> *Christabel LaMotte*

Lady Bailey's reading was slow and halting; words were miscast; she stumbled over *hoc genus omne* and Arachne. It was like frosted glass between them, Roland and Maud, and the true lineaments of the prose and the feelings of Ash and LaMotte. Sir George appeared to find the reading more than satisfactory. He looked at his watch.

'We've just time to do what I always do with Dick Francis; spoil the suspense by peeking at the end. Then I think we'll put these away until I've had time to consider my position. Take advice. Yes. Ask around a little. You'd have to be getting back, anyway, wouldn't you?'

He was not asking. He looked indulgently at his wife.

'Go on Joanie. Give us the end of it.'

She peered at the texts. She said, 'She appears to have asked for her letters back. His is an answer to that.

Dear Randolph,

All is indeed at an end. And I am glad, yes, glad with all my heart. And you too, you are very sure, are you not? One last thing — I should like my letters to be returned — all my letters without fail — not because I do not trust your honour, but because they are mine, now, because they are no longer yours. You understand me, in this at least, I know.

Christabel

My dear,

Here are your letters, as you request. They are all accounted for. Two I have burned and there may be — indeed there are — others which should immediately meet the same fate. But, as long as they are in my hands, I cannot bring myself to destroy any more, or anything written by you. These letters are the letters of a wonderful poet and that truth shines steady through the very shifting and alternating feelings with which I look at them in so far as they concern me, that is in so far as they are mine. Which within half an hour they will not be, for I have them packaged and ready to be delivered into your hands to do with as you shall see fit. You should burn them, I think, and yet, if Abelard had destroyed Eloisa's marvellous constant words, if the Portuguese Nun had kept silent, how much the poorer should we not be, how much less wise? I think you will destroy them; you are a ruthless woman; how ruthless I am yet to know and am just beginning to discern. Nevertheless if there is anything I can do for you in the way of friendship, now or in the future, I hope you will not hesitate to call upon me.

I shall forget nothing of what has passed. I have not a forgetting nature. (Forgiving is no longer the question, between us, is it?) You may rest assured

I shall retain every least word, written or spoken, and all other things too, in the hard wax of my stubborn memory. Every little thing, do you mark, everything. If you burn these, they shall have an afterlife in my memory, as long as I shall live, like the after-trace of a spent rocket on the gazing retina. I cannot believe that you will burn them. I cannot believe that you will not. I know you will not tell me what you have decided, and I must cease scribbling on, anticipating, despite myself, your never-to-be anticipated answer, always in the past, a shock, a change, most frequently a delight.

I had hoped we could be friends. My good sense knows you are right in your stark decision, and yet I regret my good friend. If you are ever in trouble – but I have said that once already, and you know it. Go in peace. Write well.

Yours to command in some things
R. H. A.

'You were wrong about the scandal,' said Sir George to Roland, with a complicated mixture of satisfaction and accusation. Roland felt a huge irritability mounting inside himself, mild though he knew himself to be, compounded of distress at hearing Lady Bailey's faded voice stammer across Randolph Henry Ash's prose, which sang in his head, reconstituted, and also of frustration because he could not seize and explore these folded paper time-bombs.

'We don't *know* until we've read it all, do we?' he retorted, creaky with self-restraint.

'But it might put a cat among the pigeons.'

'Not *exactly*. The importance is literary –'

Analogies raced through Maud's mind and were rejected as too inflammatory. It's as though you'd found – Jane Austen's love letters?

'You know, if you read the collected letters of any writer – if you read her biography – you will always get a sense that there's something missing, something biographers don't have access to, the real thing, the crucial thing, the thing that really mattered to the poet herself. There are always letters that were destroyed. *The* letters, usually. These may be those letters, in Christabel's life. He – Ash – obviously thought they were. He says so.'

'How exciting,' said Joan Bailey. 'How very exciting.'

'I must take advice,' said Sir George, stubborn and suspicious.

'So you shall, my dear,' said his wife. 'But you must remember that Miss Bailey was clever enough to *find* your treasure. And Mr Michell.'

'If, at any time, sir – you would consider giving me – us – access to the correspondence – we could tell you what was there – what its significance to scholarship was – whether an edition might be possible. I have seen enough already to know that my work on Christabel must be seriously altered in the light of what you have in these letters – I wouldn't be happy going on without taking them into account – and that must be true of Dr Michell's work on Ash too, just as true.'

'Oh yes,' said Roland. 'It might change the whole line of my thought.'

Sir George looked from one to the other.

'That may be so. That may well be so. But are you the *best people* – to trust with the reading? –'

'Once it is generally known,' said Roland, 'that these letters exist, everyone will be at your door. Everyone.'

Maud, who was afraid of exactly this possibility, glowered whitely at him. But Sir George, as Roland had calculated, was more alarmed at the thought of pilgrimages of Leonora Sterns than aware of the possibilities of Cropper and Blackadder.

'That won't do at all –'

'We could catalogue them for you. With a description. Transcribe – with your permission – some –'

'Not so fast. I shall take advice. That's all I can say. That's fair.'

'Please,' said Maud, 'let us know, at least, what conclusion you come to.'

'Of course we will,' said Joan Bailey. 'Of course we will.'

Her capable hands stacked those dry leaves in her lap, ordering, squaring.

Driving back in the dark, Roland and Maud communicated in brief businesslike bursts, their imaginations hugely busy elsewhere.

'We both had the same instinct. To play it down.' Maud.

'They must be worth a fortune.' Roland.

'If Mortimer Cropper knew they were there –'

'They'd be in Harmony City tomorrow.'

'Sir George would be a lot richer. He could mend that house.'

'I've no idea *how much* richer. I don't know anything about money. Perhaps we should tell Blackadder. Perhaps they ought to be in the British Library. They must be some sort of national heritage.'

'They're love letters.'

'It seems so, certainly.'

'Perhaps Sir George will get advised to see Blackadder. Or Cropper.'

'We must pray not Cropper. Not yet.'

'If he gets advised to come to the University, he may simply get sent to me.'

'If he gets advised to go to Sotheby's, the letters'll vanish, into America or somewhere else, or Blackadder'll get them if we're lucky. I don't know why I think that'd be so bad. I don't know why I feel so *possessive* about the damned things. They're not mine.'

'It's because we found them. And because – because they're private.'

'But we don't want him just to put them into a cupboard?'

'How can we, now we know they're there?'

'Do you think we might agree – a kind of pact? That if one of us finds out any more, he or she tells the other and no one else? Because they concern both poets equally – and there are so many other possible interests involved . . .'

'Leonora –'

'If you tell her, it's halfway to Cropper and Blackadder – and they have much more punch than she has, I suppose.'

'It makes sense. Let's hope he consults Lincoln University and they send him to me.'

'I feel faint with curiosity.'

'Let's hope he makes his mind up soon.'

But it was to be some considerable time before any more was heard of the letters or of Sir George.

CHAPTER SIX

His taste, that was his passion, brought him then
To bourgeois parlours, grey and grim back rooms,
All redolent of Patriarchal teas,
Pacing behind a lustrous, smiling Jew,
All decorous, 'twixt brute mahogany,
Meuble or chest, and solid table, clothed
Smug in its Sabbath calm, in indigo,
Faded maroon and bistre cotton stripes –
He'd see, perhaps, extracted one by one,
From three times locked, but plumply vulgar drawers
From satchels soft of oriental silk,
To spread in ordered and in matched array,
So tenderly unmuffled and revealed
The immemorial amethystine blue
Of twenty ancient Damascene glazed tiles
As bright as heaven's courts, as subtle-hued
As living sheen upon the peacock's neck.
And then his soul was satisfied, and then
He tasted honey, then in those dead lights
Alive again, he knew *his* life, and gave
His gold, to gaze and gaze ...

> R.H. Ash, *The Great Collector*.

The bathroom was a long narrow rectangle, space-saving, coloured like sugared almonds. The fitments were a strong pink,
tinged with a dusky greyish tone. The tiled floor was a greyish
violet. With little bunches of ghostly Madonna lilies – they were
of Italian design – on certain tiles, not all. These tiles extended
halfway up the walls, where they met a paisley vinyl paper

crawling with busy suckered globules, octopods, sea-slugs, in very bright purple and pink. There were toning ceramic fitments, in dusty pink pottery, a lavatory-paper holder, a tissue-holder, a toothmug on a plate like those huge African lip-decorations, a scallop-shell holding pristine ovoids of purple and pink soap. The slatted, wipe-clean vinyl blind represented a pink dawn, with rose-tinged bulbous cumuli. The candlewick bath-mat, with its hide-like rubber backing, was lavender-coloured and so was the candlewick crescent snugly clutching the lavatory pedestal and so was the candlewick mob-cap cushioned protector worn by the lavatory lid. On the top of this, alert for house-sounds, and urgently concentrating, perched Professor Mortimer P. Cropper. It was 3.00 a.m. He was arranging a thick wad of paper, a black rubber torch, and a kind of rigid matt black box, just the size to fit on his knee without bumping the walls.

This was not his milieu. He enjoyed in part the spice of the incongruous and the prohibited. He wore a long black silk dressing-gown, with crimson revers, over black silk pyjamas, crimson-piped, with a monogram on his breast-pocket. His slippers, mole-black velvet, were embroidered in gold thread with a female head surrounded by shooting rays or shaken hair. These had been made in London, to his specification. The figure was sculpted on the portico of the oldest part of Robert Dale Owen University, the Harmonia Museum, named after the ancient Alexandrian academy, that 'bird-coop of the muses'. She represented Mnemosyne, Mother of the Muses, though few now recognised her without prompting, and she was most often taken, by those with a smattering of education, as the Medusa. She appeared also, not too ostentatiously, at the head of Professor Cropper's letters. She did not appear on his signet ring, an imposing onyx with the impression of a winged horse, which had once belonged to Randolph Henry Ash, and now reposed on the pink washbasin where Cropper had just washed his hands.

His face in the mirror was fine and precise, his silver hair most exquisitely and severely cut, his half-glasses gold-rimmed, his mouth pursed, but pursed in American, more generous than English pursing, ready for broader vowels and less mincing sounds. His body was long and lean and trim; he had American hips, ready for a neat belt and the faraway ghost of a gunbelt.

He pulled a string and the bathroom heater fizzed into slow action. He pushed down a switch on his black box, which also fizzed a little, and glowed briefly with light. He switched on his torch and balanced it in the washbasin, illuminating his work. He switched off the light, working flaps and switches in a practised darkroom way. Out of the envelope, with delicate finger and thumb, he drew a letter. An old letter, whose folds he pressed skilfully flat before inserting it into his box, closing the lid, locking, switching.

He was greatly attached to his black box, a device he had invented and perfected in the 1950s, and was now reluctant to abandon in favour of newer or slicker machines since it had served him well over the decades. He was adept at acquiring invitations into the most unlikely houses where some relic of Ash's hand might be found; once there he had come to the conclusion that it was necessary to make some record, privately, for himself, of what he found, in case the owner subsequently proved reluctant to sell, or even to allow copies to be made, as had been known, once or twice, most detrimentally to the cause of scholarship. There were cases where his clandestine pictures were the only record, anywhere in the world, of documents that had vanished without trace. He did not think that would be the case here; he was reasonably sanguine that Mrs Daisy Wapshott would part with her defunct husband's inherited treasure once she knew what size of cheque might be exchanged for it – a modest figure would do perfectly well, he was of the opinion. But odd things had happened in other cases, and if she dug her heels in, he would not have another chance. Tomorrow he would be back in his comfortable hotel in Piccadilly.

The letters were not much. They were written to Daisy Wapshott's husband's mother who appeared to have been called Sophia, and appeared to have been Randolph Henry's godchild. He could check who she was, later. He had been told about Mrs Wapshott by a nosy bookseller of his acquaintance who 'did' local auction sales and told Cropper of anything interesting. Mrs Wapshott had not brought the letters to the sale; she had been helping out with teas; but had told Mr Biggs about what were always called 'Grummer's tree-letters from that there poet'. And Mr Biggs had mentioned them in a P.S. to Cropper. And Cropper had spent six months tempting Mrs Wapshott, with tentative queries and finally the information that he 'just happened to be passing by ...' This was not quite so. He had passed from Piccadilly to the outskirts of Preston, specifically and specially. And here he was, amongst the candlewick, with the four little messages.

Dear Sophia,

Thank you for your letter and for your very accomplished drawings of ducks and drakes. As I am an old man, with no children or grandchildren of my own, you must forgive me if I write to you as I should to any dear friend who had sent me something pretty that I shall treasure. How well-observed was your upended duckling, busy among the roots and grubs in the pond-bottom.

I cannot draw so well as you, but I think gifts should be reciprocated, so here is a lopsided version of my namesake, the mighty Ash. It is a common and magical tree – not as the mountain ash is magical, but because our Norse forefathers once believed it held the world together, rooted in the underworld and touching Heaven. It is good for spearhafts and possible for climbing. Its buds, as Lord Tennyson observed, are black.

I hope you will not mind me calling you Sophia and not Sophy. Sophia means wisdom, the heavenly Wisdom that kept things in order before Adam and Eve foolishly sinned in the garden. You will no doubt grow up to be very wise – but now is your playing-time, and your time for delighting with ducks your elderly admirer

Randolph Henry Ash

This effusion had a rarity value. It was the only letter written to a child that Mortimer Cropper knew to be in existence. Ash in general had a reputation for impatience with children. (He was not known to be tolerant of his wife's nephews and nieces, against whom he was heavily protected.) This would entail a subtle adjustment. Cropper photographed the other letters, which were accompanied by drawings of a Plane, a Cedar, and a Walnut, and put his ear to the bathroom door to hear if Mrs Wapshott, or her fat little terrier, were stirring. In fact, after a moment, he ascertained that both were snoring, on different notes. He tiptoed back across the landing, squeaking once on the linoleum, into his frilled box of a guest-room, where, on a glass-topped, kidney-shaped dressing-table, doubly skirted in puce satin and white net, he had placed Randolph Ash's pocket-watch in a heart-shaped dish, decorated with gardenias.

He breakfasted in the morning with Daisy Wapshott, a comfortable bosomy lady in a crêpe-de-chine dress and a pink angora cardigan, who waited on him, despite his protestations, with a huge plate of ham and eggs, mushrooms and tomatoes, sausages and baked beans. He ate triangular toasts, and marmalade from a cut-glass dish with a swinging lid and a scallop shell spoon. He drank strong tea from a silver pot under a teacosy embroidered to resemble a nesting hen. He abominated tea. He was a black coffee drinker. He congratulated Mrs Wapshott on her tea. From the windows of his own elegant house he could have seen a formal garden, and beyond it the sages and junipers of the mesa, and the mountain heads rising out of the desert into a clear sky. Here he saw a strip of lawn, along which ran plastic fencing separating it from identical strips on each side.

'I spent a very comfortable night,' he told Mrs Wapshott. 'I am extremely grateful to you.'

'I'm glad you found my Rodney's letters of interest, Professor. He inherited them from his Mum. Who'd come down in the world, if he was to be believed. I never met his family. I married him in the War. Met him fire-fighting. I was a lady's maid in them days, Professor, and he was a gentleman, anyone could see. But he never had no inclination for any kind of work, really. We kept the shop – general haberdashery – to tell the truth, I did all the work, and he just smiled at the customers, half shame-faced. I never knew exactly where he got them letters. His Mum gave them to him – she said he might be the literary one and they were letters from a famous poet. He did show them to the Vicar, who said he didn't think they was of much interest. I did say as I'd never part with them, Professor. They aren't much, really, just letters to a kid about trees.'

'In Harmony City,' said Mortimer Cropper, 'in the Stant Collection in the University there, I have the largest and finest collection of Randolph Henry Ash's correspondence anywhere in the world. It is my aim to know as far as possible everything he did – everyone who mattered to him – every little pre-occupation he had. These small letters of yours, Mrs Wapshott, are not much, maybe, on their own. But in the global perspective they add lustre, they add detail, they bring the whole man just that little bit more back to life. I hope you will entrust them to the Stant Collection, Mrs Wapshott. Then they will be preserved forever in the finest conditions and purified air, controlled temperature and limited access, only to accredited scholars in the field.'

'My husband wanted them to go to Katy. Our daughter. In case she was the literary one. That's her bedroom you're sleeping in, Professor. She's been left home now ever such a long time – she's got a son and daughter of her own – but I keep her room just so, for her to come back to, if things get on top of her. She appreciates that. She was a teacher before the children. She did teach English. She often expressed an interest in Grummer's tree letters. That's what we always called them. Grummer's tree letters. I couldn't possibly think of letting you have them without so much as asking her. They're hers, in a sort of way – in trust, if you see what I mean.'

'Of course you should consult her. You should say we would naturally give you an advantageous price for these documents. When you speak to her you should mention that. We have very ample funds, Mrs Wapshott.'

'Very ample funds,' she repeated after him, vaguely. He was aware that she thought it would be ill-bred to ask him what sort of price he might offer, and that suited him very well, that gave him room to manoeuvre, as he calculated that the richest dreams of her modest avarice would be unlikely to reach the sort of sum he would willingly pay on the open market. He was rarely wrong in these cases. He could most frequently foretell to a dollar what some country curate or school librarian might suppose he could demand, both before and after professional advice.

'I shall have to think about it,' she said, troubled, but implicated. 'I shall have to see what's best.'

'There's no hurry,' he assured her, finishing his toast, wiping his fingers on his damask napkin. 'Only one thing – if anyone else should approach you about these documents, it would be kind if you remembered I showed an interest first. We all have our little academic courtesies, but some of us are quite prepared to go behind each other's backs. I should like your assurance that you will do nothing with these short letters without consulting me first. If you feel able to give it. I can also assure you that you will find it to your advantage to consult me.'

'I wouldn't think of it. Not getting in touch, that is. If anyone were to. Which I'm sure they won't, no one ever has, in all these years up to now, up till your arrival, Professor.'

Neighbours put their heads out of the windows when he drew away from the front of the little house. His car was a long black Mercedes, of the kind more normally seen driving dignitaries in countries behind the Iron Curtain, a swift funereal car. He knew that in England it was overstated, unlike his tweed jacket. He did not care. It was beautiful and powerful, and he had a flamboyant side to his nature.

As he floated down the motorway he thought of his next ports of call. There was a sale at Sotheby's, with an autograph album with a quatrain by Ash, and his signature. He must also spend a few days in the British Museum. His face contracted with distaste at the thought of James Blackadder. He must also – a matter which he also regarded with more distaste than pleasure – take Beatrice out to lunch. If there was one matter in the world he regretted more than any other it was Beatrice's lien, her semi-exclusive propriety in Ellen Ash's Journal. Had he himself and his team of research assistants had proper access to that work, much of it would be in print by now, annotated, indexed, ready to be cross-referred and to illuminate his own findings. But Beatrice, with what he saw as a truly English costiveness and dilettantism, continued to sit and shuffle and *wonder* about meanings and facts, getting nowhere at all, and apparently quite comfortable, like the obstructive sheep in *Alice Through the Looking-Glass*. He had a whole notebook full of queries to check, when he could, when she gave him access. Every time he came across the Atlantic he had such a notebook. It was his firmly held belief – not one he ever questioned intellectually or experienced as other than a sensuous lack, a knowledge of something missing from his essential comfort – that Ellen Ash's papers should be in the Stant Collection.

Now and then Mortimer Cropper toyed with the idea of writing an autobiography. He had also considered writing a family history. History, writing, infect after a time a man's sense of himself, and Mortimer Cropper, fluently documenting every last item of the days of Randolph Henry Ash, his goings-out and his comings-in, his dinner engagements, his walking-tours, his excessive sympathy with servants, his impatience with lionising, had naturally perhaps felt his own identity at times, at the very best times, as insubstantial, leached into this matter-of-writing, stuff-of-record. He was an important man. He wielded power: power of appointment, power of disappointment, power of the cheque book, power of Thoth and the Mercurial access to the Arcana of the Stant Collection. He tended his body, the outward man, with a fastidiousness that he would have bestowed on the inner man too, if he had known who he was, if he did not feel the whole thing to be thickly veiled. He only thought of this intermittently when, as now, he was encased in smooth black solitude and on the move.

MY EARLY LIFE

I knew what I should become at a very early stage in my growth, in the Treasure Cabinet of my lovely parental home in Chixauga, New Mexico – not far from where Robert Dale Owen University is so beautifully situated.

Everblest House is full of beautiful and strange things collected by my grandfather and great-grandfather, all of them museum-pieces of the most excellent quality, though garnered in with no guiding principle other than their rarity, or special associative interest with some great figure or other from the past. We had a fine mahogany music-stand that was built for Jefferson himself according to his own ingenious mechanical directions as to hinges and angling. We had a bust (of Wieland) that had once belonged to the genial diarist and acquaintance of many great mèn, Crabb Robinson, who had himself rescued it, with discerning eye, from the oblivion of a glory-hole. We had a theodolite used by Swedenborg and a hymn book of Charles Wesley as well as an ingeniously designed new hoe employed by Robert Owen in his pioneering days in New Harmony. We had a striking-clock, presented by Lafayette to Benjamin Franklin and a walking stick of Honoré de Balzac's, encrusted with jewels in a somewhat opulent and tasteless way. My grandfather used to compare this *parvenu* ostentation with the true dignity and simplicity of Owen's hoe. Since the hoe was in pristine condition there is some uncertainty as to whether it was an object of such utility as my grandfather imagined, but the sentiment does him honour all the same. We also had many *objets de vertu*, including fine collections of Sèvres porcelain, *pâte tendre*, Venetian glass and oriental tiles. The majority of these pieces – the European objects – were collected by my grandfather, a patient searcher-out of unconsidered trifles, a wanderer on four continents, who returned always with new treasures to the gleaming white house fronting the *mesa*. The high glass-fronted cases in the Treasure Cabinet were of his own design, a harmonious blend of the simplicity of the early utilitarian furniture of the idealistic settlers from whom he was descended, and the crude but powerful Hispanic work of the people among whom they had tried to build.

My father, who suffered from what would now be called periods of clinical depression – which effectively prevented him from pursuing any profession although he had graduated *summa cum laude* in Divinity from Harvard – amused himself from time to time by allowing me to examine these treasures, to the cataloguing of which he devoted his more lucid days, somewhat unsuccessfully, since he could never establish any guiding principle as to how they should be ordered. (Mere chronology, of fabrication or of acquisition, would have been the simplest, but his mind did not tend to simplicity.) 'Here, Morty, my boy,' he would say to me, 'here is History to hold in your hand.' I was particularly taken by the collection of portrait sketches and signed photographs of eminent nineteenth-century figures – drawings by Richmond and Watts, photographs by Julia Margaret Cameron – which had mostly been presented to, or solicited by my great-grandmother, Priscilla Penn Cropper. Those very fine portraits – unequalled, I believe, as a single collection, by any other in the world – now form the nucleus of the portrait section of the Stant Collection at Robert Dale Owen University, of which I have the honour to be the Chairman. In those days, they were my child-hood companions, and my imagination animated their solemn features and made them smile kindly. I was enthralled by the craggy features of Carlyle, enchanted by the sweetness of Elizabeth Gaskell, in awe of the heavy, solemn thoughtfulness of George Eliot and lightened in spirit by the saintly unworldliness of Emerson. I was a frail child, educated mostly at home by my dear Ninny, my governess, and later by a tutor, a Harvard man, recommended to my father as a poet who would gain by this employment a safe basis for writing a great work. His name was Hollingdale, Arthur Hollingdale; he early claimed to detect considerable literary talent in my youthful compositions, and thus encouraged me to turn my mind that way. He attempted to interest me in modern writing – he was, I recall, enthusiastic about Ezra Pound – but my own tastes and aptitudes were already formed, my passion was for the past. I do not think Mr Hollingdale ever wrote his great work. He found our desert solitude not to his liking, took in a poetic way to drinking tequila, and finally departed, with no regret on either side.

In my family's possession was one letter – one very significant letter – addressed by Randolph Henry Ash to my great-grand-mother, Priscilla Penn Cropper, *née* Priscilla Penn. This ancestress was a most forceful, and so to say *eccentric* personality, a native of Maine, a daughter of devoted Abolitionists, who had housed runaway slaves and had participated in the ferment of new ideas and lifestyles then to be found in the New England States. She was a fervent speaker for the Emancipation of Women, and was also, as was common with those doughty fighters for human rights, involved in other movements. She was a firm believer in mesmeric healing, from which she claimed to have benefited greatly, and she was also very much involved in the spiritualist experiments of those days, which blossomed so freely in the United States, after the Fox Sisters heard their first 'raps'; she entertained the visionary Andrew Wilson, author of the *Univer-coelum*, or Key to the Universe, who in her house (then in New York) conversed with the spirits of Swedenborg, Descartes and Bacon. I should perhaps add that though she did not disclaim any kinship with the Pennsylvania Penns, the Quakers, my own researches do not indicate that there was any solid connection. She went down to history, maybe unfairly when we consider her versatility and inventiveness, as the creator of Priscilla Penn's Regenerating Powders, a patent medicine which I devoutly believe killed no one, and may have saved some at least of the thousands of lives claimed by my ancestress, if only through a *placebo* effect. The Powders, imaginatively marketed, made Priscilla's fortune, and Priscilla's fortune erected Everblest House. Everblest House comes as a considerable surprise to visiting stran-gers, being an exact replica of a Palladian mansion in Mississippi, lost during the War between the States by my paternal great-great-grandfather, Mortimer D. Cropper. It was his son, Sharman M. Cropper, who rode North in those troubled days in search of a living and was, so family legend runs, transfixed by the sight of my great-grandmother addressing an open-air meeting on the

Fourierist principles of Harmony and the duty to prosecute a search for free passion and pleasure. Whether from passion or opportunism I do not know, he attached himself to her following and thus came in 1868 to New Mexico when a group of them attempted to found a phalanstery. Some of them had previously formed part of what we would now call splinter groups from the model communities and rectangular villages built unsuccessfully by Robert Owen and his son, Robert Dale Owen, author of *The Debateable Land Between This World and the Next*.

The project of the phalanstery, less austere than Owen's villages, failed because the magic number of 1620 inhabitants, representing all possible variants on all possible passions of both sexes, was never attained, and also because among the enthusiasts there was no one who was skilled in agriculture or knew anything about desert conditions. My great-grandfather, a Southern gentleman, also an entrepreneur in a personal way, bided his time and proposed to my great-grandmother a rebuilding of the Paradise of his lost youth according to the rational and harmonic principles of her way of life – basing their happiness on the attainable pleasures of family life (with servants, though of course without slaves) without repining for the enthusiastic group-love that had proved so divisive and so unmanageable. Accordingly, the proceeds of the Regenerating Powders were put into the erection of the lovely house which I and my mother still inhabit, and my great-grandfather turned to collecting.

There are many portraits of Priscilla Penn Cropper in existence; she was obviously a person of considerable beauty and ample charms. During the 1860s and 1870s her house was a centre for spiritualist research, in which, with her customary enthusiasm, she attempted to involve the thinking men of the whole civilised world. It must have been one of these attempts that elicited the letter from Randolph Henry Ash which for some mysterious reason excited me so and gave rise to my life's absorbing interest. I have never, despite my most diligent enquiries, been able to come across the letter she must have written to him, and the fear is constant that she may have destroyed it. I do not know why this one of the many treasures in our possession moved me most. God moves in a mysterious way – it may even be that Randolph Henry's rebuff to my ancestress's interest gave rise to my wish to show that we were, after all, worthy to understand, and, so to speak, to entertain him. Certainly I felt, when my father first handed me the handwritten pages, preserved in tissue, to see if I could decipher them, something akin to the thrill of Keats's stout Cortez, silent on his peak in Darien. And when I had touched the letter, I felt, in Tennyson's words, that the dead man had touched me from the past: I have made my life among 'Those fallen leaves which keep their green/The noble letters of the dead.'

Our Cabinet of Treasures has an ingenious little cupola with a windowed dome of plain, not many-coloured glass, which can be shaded by half-blinds or wholly shuttered by the turning of a handle. On that day, unusually, my father had opened, not only the shutters but the green blinds through which a soft safe light is slowly filtered, so the room was full of sunbeams. In that sunlit hush was conceived the germ of the idea that gave rise to the Stant Collection which adorns the Harmonia Museum of Robert Dale Owen University, of which my ancestor Sharman Cropper was an illustrious co-founder, and to which the Regenerative Powders contributed their fertilising mite.

I give in full my great-grandmother's letter. It now stands, in its proper place in Volume IX of my edition of the Collected Letters (No. 1207, p. 883) and an excerpt from it is included in the footnotes to *Mummy Possest*, RHA's spiritualist poem, in the edition of the Complete Works, proceeding surely, if regrettably slowly for enthusiasts, under the overall editorial direction of James Blackadder of the University of London. I do not accept Professor Blackadder's identification of my ancestress with the grossly credulous fictional Mrs Eckleburg in that poem. There are far too many striking points of dissimilarity, which I have detailed in my article on the subject 'A case of mis-identification' (*PMLA*, LXXI, Winter 1959, pp. 174–80), to which I refer the curious.

Dear Mrs Cropper

I thank you for your communication to me about your experience with the planchette. *You were right in supposing that I might feel some interest in anything at all that came from the pen of Samuel Taylor Coleridge. I must also feel, I shall tell you directly, considerable abhorrence at the thought of that bright spirit, having made his painful way out of our weary and oppressive earthly life, being constrained to heave mahogany tables, or float partially embodied, through firelit drawing-rooms, or turn his liberated Intelligence to the scrawling of such painful and inane nonsense as you have sent to me. Should he not now feed in peace on honeydew and drink the milk of Paradise?*

I am not jesting, Madam. I have attended attempted exhibitions of the kind of manifestations you allude to – nihil humanum a me alienum puto, *I may say, as all of my profession should say – and I think the likeliest explanation is a combination of bald fraud and a kind of communal hysteria, a miasma or creeping mist of spiritual anxiety and febrile agitation, that plagues our polite society and titillates our tea-party talk. A speculative temperament might find the cause of this miasma in the increasing materialism of our society, and in the rigorous questioning – both natural and inevitable, given the present state of our intellectual Development – of our historical religious narratives. All is indeed uncertainty in that field, and the historian and the man of science alike make inroads on our simple faith. Even if the end result of our strenuous inquisitions be to strengthen that faith, it will not, quite properly, happen with ease, or in our time, maybe. This is not to say that the* Nostrums *thrown up to gratify a queasy public hunger for certainties or solidities are either sanative or solidly based.*

The Historian and the Man of Science alike may be said to traffic with the dead. Cuvier has imparted flesh and motion and appetites to the defunct Megatherium, whilst the living ears of MM Michelet and Renan, of Mr Carlyle and the Brothers Grimm, have heard the bloodless cries of the vanished and given them voices. I myself, with the aid of the imagination, have worked a little in that line, have ventriloquised, have lent my voice to, and mixt my life with, those past voices and lives whose resuscitation in our own lives as warnings, as examples, as the life of the past persisting *in us, is the business of every thinking man and woman. But there are ways and ways, as you must well know, and some are tried and tested, and others are fraught with danger and disappointment. What is read and understood and contemplated and intellectually grasped is our own, madam, to live and work with. A lifetime's study will not make accessible to us more than a fragment of our own ancestral past, let alone the aeons before our race was formed. But that fragment we must thoroughly* possess *and hand on. Hoc opus, hic labor est. There is, I am tempted to assert, no easy way, no short cut: we are, in attempting those, like Bunyan's Ignorance who found a path to Hell at the very gate of the City of Heaven.*

Think what you do, Madam, in attempting to address them, the dear and terrible dead, directly. *What wisdom in all this waste of time have they imparted? That Granny has left her new brooch in the grandfather clock, or that an ancient Aunt resents, from beyond the bourn, the imposition of an infant coffin upon her own in the family Vault. Or as your S. T. C. solemnly assures you, that there is 'eternal bliss for they who deserve such and a time of correction for they who do not' in the Beyond. (He who never misplaced a pronoun in seven languages.) It needs no ghost, Madam, come from the grave, to tell us this.*

That there may be wandering spirits I grant you, earth-bubbles, exhalations, creatures of the air, who occasionally cross our usual currents of apprehension, proceeding on their own unseen errands. That agonised reminiscence of some kind in some mental form does inhere in some terrible places there is some evidence. There are indeed more things in heaven and earth than are dreamed of in our philosophy. But they will be found out I believe, not through rappings or tappings or palpable handlings or Mr Home floating round and round the chandelier with his arms stiffly upheld, nor yet through the scribblings of your planchette, *but through long and patient contemplation of the intricate workings of dead minds and live organisms, through wisdom that looks before and after, through the microscope and the spectroscope and not through the interrogation of earth-obsessed spectres and revenants. I have known a good soul and a clear mind, quite unhinged by such meddling, and to no good end, indeed to a bad one.*

I have written at such length because I do not wish you to think I take your kind thoughts of me frivolously or in a spirit of unthinking bellicose denigration, as some might say. I do have deep-rooted con-victions – and a certain amount of apposite experience of my own, which precludes my receiving your communication – your spirit *com-munication – with any great interest or pleasure. I must ask you to send no more such writings. But for* yourself, *and for your disinterested pursuit of truth, I do of course feel great respect and enthusiasm. Your fight on behalf of your Sex is noble, and must succeed, sooner or later. I hope to hear more of that in the future, and beg to remain*

> *Yours most sincerely*
> *R. H. Ash*

The transcription of this letter always marked, in Mortimer Cropper's autobiographical sketches, a high point, from which they tailed off rapidly into banal childhood memories or a mere scholarly cataloguing of his subsequent relations with Randolph Henry Ash – almost, he sometimes brushed the thought, as though he had no existence, no separate existence of his own after that first contact with the paper's electric rustle and the ink's energetic black looping. It was as though his unfinished scripts were driven by a desire to reach and include the letter, the perusal of the letter, the point of recognition, and then lost their drive and tension, shuddered to a stop. There was a sentence he often appended, for no very good reason, about the involving of this early memory with the ancestral smell of his grandmother's excellent *pot-pourri* imported to that desert, rose-petals and essential refreshing oils, sandalwood and musk. He was aware also, without wishing in any way to examine this awareness, that his reluctance, or incapacity, to continue in this mode of writing was to do with some prohibition set on writing about his mother, with whom he shared his American domestic life and to whom he wrote, every day when he was abroad, long and affectionate letters. All of us have things in our lives which we know in this brief, useful allusive way, and neglect deliberately to explore. Mrs Cropper sat in the desert and made it blossom and flower by power of will and money. In his dreams of her Professor Cropper always lost his sense of proportion, so that she loomed large as his capacious entrance hall, or stood hugely and severely astride his paddock. She expected much of him, and he had not failed her, but feared to fail.

He arrived, reasonably satisfied, at Barrett's Hotel, which he had chosen partly for its comfort, but more because American writers, visiting Ash, had stayed there in the past. A heap of letters was waiting there for him, including one from his mother, and a note from Blackadder saying that he saw no reason to emend his note on *Ask to Embla III* in the light of Cropper's discoveries about the Icelandic landscape. There was also a catalogue from Christie's, where a sale of Victoriana included a needlecase traditionally believed to have belonged to Ellen Ash, and a ring, once owned by an American widow in Venice, which was said to contain, in its crystal cavity, a few of Ash's hairs. The Stant Collection contained several consecutive clippings from that great mane, in its faded darkness, its later grizzled mix, and its final post-mortem silver, now the brightest, the most enduring. The Ash Museum in Ash's Bloomsbury house would perhaps bid, and Cropper himself would certainly bid, and the needlecase and the curl of hair would be enshrined in the hexagonal glass room at the very centre of the Stant Collection, where Ash's relics and those of his wife, family and acquaintances accumulated in the still, regulated air. Cropper sat by a leaping fire in a high leather chair in the bar and read his letters and was briefly visited by a vision of his white temple shining in the desert sun, enclosing cool courts, high staircases and a kind of glass honeycomb of silent cells, radiating carrels and mounting interlinked storage and study rooms, their frames gleaming and gilded, enclosing shafts and pillars of light, within which, cocooned in gilded shuttles, the scholars rose and descended, in purposeful quiet.

When he had made his purchases he would, he thought, take Beatrice Nest out to lunch. He would also, he supposed, see Blackadder. He had expected Blackadder to say something dismissive about his Icelandic observations. Blackadder, to his knowledge, had not stepped outside the British Isles for many years, except to attend international conferences on Victorian poetry, all of which took place in identical seminar rooms reached by car from identical hotels. He, Cropper, on the other hand, had early begun to trace the journeyings of Randolph Ash – not consecutively, but as the chances presented themselves, so that his first expedition had been to the North Yorkshire Moors and coast where Ash had enjoyed a solitary walking-tour, combined with amateur marine biologising, in 1859. Cropper had repeated this tour in 1949, searching out pubs and rock-formations, Roman roads and pearly becks, staying in Robin Hood's Bay and drinking warm disagreeable brown beer, eating unspeakable neck-of-mutton stews and pieces of braised offal which had turned his stomach. Later he had followed Ash to Amsterdam and the Hague, and had walked in Ash's tracks in Iceland, contemplating geysers, seething circles of hot mud and those two poems inspired by Icelandic literature, *Ragnarök*, the epic of Victorian doubt and despair, and the sequence of poems, *Ask to Embla*, the mysterious love lyrics, published in 1872 but certainly written much earlier, possibly even during his courtship of Ellen Best, daughter of the Dean of Calverley, whom he had loved for fifteen years before she, or her family, would consent to the marriage, which had taken place in 1848. It was certainly typical of Blackadder's snail-like progress with the Edition that he should just have got round to considering Mortimer Cropper's Icelandic observations made in the 1960s. Cropper had published his biography – *The Great Ventriloquist* – in 1969, taking his title from one of Ash's teasing monologues of self-revelation or self-parody. Before doing so he had undertaken all Ash's major journeys, visiting Venice, Naples, the Alps, the Black Forest and the Breton coast. One of his last ventures had been the reconstruction of the wedding journey of Randolph and Ellen Ash in the summer of 1848. They had crossed the Channel in a storm in a packet-boat, and proceeded to Paris in a carriage (Cropper had followed their route in a car) and had taken the railway from Paris to Lyon, where they had travelled down the Rhône by boat to Aix-en-Provence. Their journey had taken place in lashing rain. Cropper, ever resourceful, had negotiated a passage on a cargo-boat, carrying timber, smelling of resin and oil, and had been lucky with the weather, bright sun on the yellow water, burning the skin on his long wiry forearms. He had settled in Ash's hotel in Aix and had done the Ashes' excursions, culminating in a visit to the Fontaine de Vaucluse, where the poet, Petrarch, had lived in solitude for sixteen years, contemplating his ideal love for Laure de Sade. The profit of this journey could be seen in Cropper's account of the Fountain in *The Great Ventriloquist*.

So on a clear June day in 1848 the poet and his new bride made their way along the shady river bank to the cavern which shelters the source of the Sorgue, a sight awesome and sublime enough to satisfy even the most romantic traveller and how much more impressive when conjoined with the memory of the great courtly lover, Petrarch, living out there the days of his devotion and the horror of learning of his mistress's death of the plague.

The baked river banks are slippery now with use, and the northern traveller must shuffle towards his goal amongst crowds of tourists, yapping French dogs, paddling children and candy floss sellers, solicited by hideous souvenirs and mass-produced 'craft' articles. The river has been tamed by weirs and pipes, though the guide-book tells us it can rise and flood the whole cavern and surrounding countryside. The literary pilgrim should persist: he will be rewarded by a vision of green water and louring rocks which can in the nature of things have changed very little since our travellers came to see it.

The water rises very swiftly inside the cavern, fed by an underground river of some power, and by the confluence of the rainfall collected from the plateau of Vaucluse and the stony sides of the Mont Ventoux, Petrarch's Windy Mount, as Randolph put it in a letter. He must have been put in mind, at the sight of this majestic stream, of Coleridge's sacred river, and perhaps of the Fountain of the Muses, given the association with Petrarch, a poet to whom he was greatly attached and whose sonnets to Laura are thought to have influenced the poems to Embla. In front of the cavern, which is fringed with fig-trees and fantastic roots, several white rocks rise among the surface of the fast-flowing stream, which seeps away into a mat of flowing green weeds, which could have well been painted by Millais or Holman Hunt. Ellen remarked on the beauty of these 'chiare, fresche e dolci acque'. Randolph, in a charming gesture, lifted his new wife and carried her across the water, to perch her, like a presiding mermaid, or water-goddess, on a throne-like white stone, dividing the stream. We may imagine her sitting there, smiling demurely under her bonnet, holding her skirts away from the wet, whilst Randolph contemplated his possession, so unlike Petrarch's, of the lady he had worshipped from afar, through so many hindrances and difficulties, for almost as long as the earlier poet's sixteen-year sojourn of hopeless devotion in this very spot.

Ash always maintained, unlike many of his contemporaries, notably Professor Gabriele Rossetti, father of the poet, that Petrarch's Laura and Dante's Beatrice, along with Fiametta, Selvaggia, and other objects of Platonic courtly affection, were real live women, chaste but loved in the flesh, before their deaths, and not allegories of the politics of Italy, or the government of the Church, or even of their creators' souls. Petrarch saw Laure de Sade in Avignon in 1327 and fell immediately in love with her, and loved her steadily, despite her fidelity to Hugo de Sade. Ash wrote indignantly to Ruskin that it was a misunderstanding of the poetic imagination and of the nature of love to suppose that it could be so abstracted into allegory, could not in verity spring from 'the human warmth of an individual embodied soul in all its purity and mortal vitality'. His own poetry, he added, began and ended with 'such incarnate truths, such unrepeated unique lives'.

Given this sympathy with Petrarchan adoration, it is not surprising that he should have waited so devotedly on what may be called the Christian scruples or caprices of Ellen Best and her father. In the early days of their acquaintance Ellen was a high-minded devout young girl with a fragile and delicate beauty, if we are to believe her family and Ash himself. As I have shown, the Dean's anxieties about Ash's capacity to support a wife had some foundation, and were supported by Ellen's own very real religious anxieties about the doubtful tendencies of *Ragnarök*. Such letters as have survived of their courtship – pitifully few, no doubt owing to the officious ministrations of Ellen's sister, Patience, after her death – suggest that she was not flirting with him, and that her affections were not, nevertheless, deeply engaged. But she was, by the time she accepted Randolph's hand, in the difficult position of seeing her younger sisters, Patience and Faith, making advantageous and happy marriages whilst she remained a spinster.

All this raises the question of the feelings of the ardent poet-lover, now aged thirty-four, for his innocent bride, now no young girl, but a mature thirty-six-year-old aunt, devoted to her nephews and nieces. Was his innocence as great as hers? How had he endured, the twentieth-century mind suspiciously asks, the privations of his long wait? It is well-known that many eminent Victorians turned in their doubleness for relief to the garish creatures of the Victorian underworld, the joking, painted temptresses who created so much noise and nuisance at Piccadilly Circus, the lost seamstresses, flowersellers and Fallen Women who died under the arches, begged from Mayhew or were rescued, if they were lucky, by Angela Burdett-Coutts and Charles Dickens. Ash's poetry, for Victorian poetry, is knowledgeable about sexual *mores* and indeed about sensuality. His Renaissance noblemen are convincingly fleshly, his Rubens a connoisseur of the solid human form, the speaker of the *Embla* poems a real as well as an ideal lover. Could such a man have remained happy with a purely Platonic desire? Did Ellen Best's prim delicacy, a little past its flowering, hide an unexpected ardour of response? Perhaps it did. There is no record of any early peccadillo on Randolph's part, let alone any later one – he was always, as far as we can tell, the *preux chevalier*. What did they see in each other, those two, alone and self-absorbed, as he put his hands round her comfortable waist and lifted her to her stony throne? Had they come from a night of bliss? Ellen wrote home that her husband was 'exquisitely considerate in all things', which we can read how we choose.

There is another explanation, to which I personally incline. It depends on two powerful and equally, nowadays, unfashionable forces, the idealisation of the Poets of Courtesy, on which we have touched, and the theory of sublimation elaborated by Sigmund Freud. Quite simply, Randolph Henry Ash wrote, during the courtship years:

28,369 lines of verse, including one twelve-book epic, 35 dramatic monologues covering History from its dimmest origins to modern theological and geological controversy, 125 lyrics and three verse dramas, *Cromwell, St Bartholomew's Eve* and *Cassandra*, unsuccessfully performed at Drury Lane. He worked with dedication, far into the night. He was happy, for he saw his Ellen as a fount of purity, a vision of girlish grace, breathing an air infinitely more refined than the blood-soaked, plague-ridden scenes of his imagination, the tousled beds of the Borgias or 'the sulphurous mud of the extinguished earth' in *Ragnarök*. No sense visited him that he was less a man for this chaste waiting, this active solitude. He would work, and would win her, and so it happened indeed. If later poems, such as 'The Fountain Sealed' or 'A Painted Lady', with its image of beauty fixed forever on the canvas and fading in the face – if these later poems suggest that Randolph later came to count the cost of his long apprenticeship to love, this does not invalidate my case. Nor do these poems help us in our speculations about the feelings of the newly-wed couple on that sunny day outside the dark cave of the Fountain of Vaucluse.

Mortimer Cropper went up to his pleasant suite of rooms and re-read his photographed letters. He telephoned Beatrice Nest. Her voice had a thick woollen quality; she demurred, as she always did, putting up a flurry of slow half-objections, and then agreed, as she always did. He had learned that flattering Miss Nest produced no good results, but that making her feel guilty did.

'I have one or two very precise queries that only you can answer ... I have saved this especially for you ... any other time would be extremely inconvenient, though naturally I would change to oblige you ... my dear Beatrice if you cannot come, I *must* make other arrangements, I have no desire to inconvenience you in your busy life ...' It took a long time. Since the conclusion was foregone, it ought not to have done.

He opened his locked case, putting away Randolph Ash's letters to his godchild, or anyway the stolen images, and drew out those other photographs of which he had a large and varied collection – as far as it was possible to vary, in flesh or tone or angle or close detail, so essentially simple an activity, a pre-occupation. He had his own ways of sublimation.

CHAPTER SEVEN

> Men may be martyred
> Any where
> In desert, cathedral
> Or Public Square.
> In no Rush of Action
> This is *our* doom
> To Drag a Long Life out
> In a Dark Room.
>
> Christabel LaMotte

If people thought of Beatrice Nest – and not many did, not very often – it was her external presence, not her inner life that engaged their imagination. She was indisputably solid, and nevertheless amorphous, a woman of wide and abundant flesh, sedentary swelling hips, a mass of bosom, above which spread a cheerful-shaped face, crowned by a kind of angora hat, or thick wool-skein of crimped white hair, woven and tucked into a roll from which lost strands trailed and wandered in all directions. If they thought of her harder, those few people who knew her – Cropper, Blackadder, Roland, Lord Ash – they might add a metaphoric identity. Cropper, it has been noted, thought of her in terms of Carroll's obstructive white sheep. Blackadder, in bad moods, thought of her as one of those puffed white spiders, bleached by the dark, feeling along the threads of her trap from her central lair. The feminists who had from time to time sought access to the Journal saw her as some kind of guardian octopus, an ocean Fafnir, curled torpidly round her hoard, putting up opaque screens of ink or watery smoke to obscure her whereabouts. There had once been those who knew Beatrice – notably, possibly uniquely, Professor Bengt Bengtsson. She had been Professor Bengtsson's student in London from 1938–41, a troubled time, during which male undergraduates had become soldiers, bombs had fallen and food had been scarce. Some women during that time had experienced an unexpected frivolity and freedom. Beatrice had experienced Professor Bengtsson. He ruled the English Department of Prince Albert College. His main love was the Eddas and ancient Norse mythology. Beatrice studied these things. She studied philology, Anglo-Saxon, Runes, mediaeval Latin. She read Masefield and Christina Rossetti and de la Mare. Bengtsson said she should read *Ragnarök* – R. H. Ash was no mean scholar for his time, and was thought to be a precursor of modern poetry. Bengtsson was tall and gangling and bearded; he had fierce eyes and more animated energy than could be employed in instructing young ladies in the niceties of Nordic roots. He did not, however, direct that energy towards the souls, let alone the flesh, of the young ladies, but abused it daily in the bar of the Arundel Arms, in the company of his peers. In the mornings he was bone-pale and glittering under his blond thatch. In the afternoons he was ruddy and slurred and breathed beer in his stuffy office. Beatrice read *Ragnarök* and *Ask to Embla*. She took a First and fell in love with Randolph Henry Ash. Such loves were once not uncommon. 'There are poets', Beatrice wrote in her Finals paper, 'whose love poems seem to be concerned neither with praise nor with blame of some distant lady, but with true conversation between men and women. Such is John Donne, though he may also revile the whole sex in certain moods. Such might have been Meredith if circumstances had been happier. A brief attempt to think of other "love" poets who expect reciprocity of intelligence, must persuade us of the pre-eminence of Randolph Henry Ash, whose "Ask and Embla" poems present every phase of intimacy, opposition and failure of communication, but always convince the reader of the real thinking and feeling presence of her to whom they are addressed.'

Beatrice hated writing. The only word she was proud of in this correct and dull disquisition was 'conversation', which she had chosen in preference to the more obvious 'dialogue'. For such *conversation* Beatrice would have given everything, in those days.

Reading those poems, she obscurely knew, offered her a painful and as it seemed illicit glimpse of a combination of civilised talk and raw passion which everyone must surely want, and yet which no one, as she looked round her small world, her serious Methodist parents, Mrs Bengtsson running her University Women's Tea Club, her fellow-students agonising over invitations to dance and whist – no one seemed to have.

> We two remake our world by naming it
> Together, knowing what words mean for us
> And for the others for whom current coin
> Is cold speech – but *we* say, the tree, the pool,
> And see the fire in air, the sun, our sun,
> Anybody's sun, the world's sun, but here, now
> Particularly our sun . . .

Ash told her and she heard him. She did not expect to hear such things from anybody else; nor did she. She told Professor Bengtsson that she wished to write her doctoral dissertation on *Ask to Embla*. He was very doubtful about this. It was uncertain ground, a kind of morass, like Shakespeare's sonnets. What Contribution to Knowledge did she hope to make, could she be sure of making? The only safe PhD in Professor Bengtsson's view was an Edition, and he really would not recommend R. H. Ash. He had a friend, however, who knew Lord Ash, who had deposited the Ash papers in the British Museum. It was known that Ellen Ash had kept a journal. Editing that might be a suitable undertaking – something certainly new, modestly useful, manageable and related to Ash. When she had completed that task, Miss Nest would be excellently situated to branch out. . .

So it had been. Miss Nest had settled uneasily in front of the boxes of papers – letters, laundry lists, receipt-books, the volumes of the daily journal and other slimmer books of more private occasional writing. What had she hoped for? Some intimacy with the author of the poems, with that fine mind and passionate nature.

Tonight Randolph read aloud to me from Dante's sonnets in his *Vita Nuova*. They are truly beautiful. Randolph pointed out the truly masculine energy and vigour of Dante's Italian, and the spiritual power of his understanding of love. I do not think we will ever tire of these poems of genius.

Randolph read aloud to his wife daily, when they were in the same house. The young Beatrice Nest did try to imagine the dramatic effect of these readings, but was not helped by the vague adjectival enthusiasm of Ellen Ash. There was a sweetness, a blanket dutiful pleasure in her responses to things that Beatrice at first did not like, and later, immersed in her subject, came to take for granted. By then she had discovered other, less bland, tones of voice.

I can never say enough in praise of Randolph's unvarying goodness and forbearance with my feebleness and inadequacies.

That, or something like that, recurred like the regular tolling of a bell throughout these pages. As is common with extended acquaintance with any task, topic or human being, Beatrice had an initial period of clear observation and detached personal judgment, during which she thought she saw that Ellen Ash was rambling and dull. And then she became implicated, began to share Ellen's long days of prostration in darkened rooms, to worry about the effect of mildew on damask roses long withered, and the doubts of oppressed curates. This life became important to her; a kind of defensiveness rose up in her when Blackadder suggested Ellen was not the most suitable partner for a man so intensely curious about all possible forms of life. She became aware of the mystery of privacy, which Ellen, for all her expansive ordinary eloquence, was protecting, it could be said.

There was no PhD in all this. One might have been discovered by the feminist movement, or by some linguistic researcher into euphemism and indirect statement. But Miss Nest had been brought up to look for Influences and Irony and there was little of either here.

Professor Bengtsson suggested she compare the wifely qualities of Ellen Ash with those of Jane Carlyle, Lady Tennyson and Mrs Humphry Ward. You must publish, Miss Nest, said Professor Bengtsson, glittering in matutinal icy determination. I cannot give you work, Miss Nest, without evidence of your suitability, said Professor Bengtsson, and Miss Nest wrote, in two years, a small book, *Helpmeets*, about the daily lives of wives of genius. Professor Bengtsson offered her an assistant lectureship. This was a great pleasure and terror to her; on the whole more pleasure than terror. She discussed with students, mostly female, swing-skirted and lipsticked in the Fifties, mini-skirted and trailing Indian cotton in the Sixties, black-lipped under Pre-Raphaelite hairbushes in the Seventies, smelling of baby lotion, of Blue Grass, of cannabis, of musk, of unadulterated feminist sweat, the shape of the sonnet through the ages, the nature of the lyric, the changing image of women. Those were the good days. Of the bad days, which were to come later, before she took early retirement, she did not care to think. She never crossed the threshold, now, of her old college. (Professor Bengtsson had retired in 1970 and died in 1978.)

She had a minimal private life. She lived, in 1986, and had lived for many years, in a tiny house in Mortlake. Here occasionally she had entertained groups of students, less and less frequently as she sensed her growing irrelevance to the deliberations of her department, as Bengtsson was succeeded by Blackadder. No one had come there since 1972. Before that there had been parties with coffee, cakes, a bottle of sweet white wine, and discussion. Those girls in the 1950s and 1960s had thought of her as motherly. Later generations had assumed she was lesbian, even, ideologically, that she was a repressed and unregenerate lesbian. In fact her thoughts about her own sexuality were dominated entirely by her sense of the massive, unacceptable bulk of her breasts. These, in her youth, she had flattened uncorseted under tunic dresses and liberty bodices, allowing them freely to develop their own muscles, as the best medical advice then suggested, stretching and sagging them, in the event, irremediably. Another woman might have flaunted them, might have carried them proudly before her, moulded grandly about a cleavage. Beatrice Nest bundled them into a drooping, grandmotherly bust-bodice and stretched over them hand-knitted jumpers decorated with lines of little tear-drop shaped holes, which gaped a little, pouted a little, over her contours. In bed at night she felt them fall heavily sideways over the broad case of her ribs. In her cubbyhole with Ellen Ash she felt their living weight in all its woolly warmth, brush against the rim of her table. She imagined herself grotesquely swollen, looked modestly down and met no one's eye. It was to these heavy rounds that she owed her reputation for motherliness, a rapid stereotypic reading which also read her round face and pink cheeks as benign. When she was past a certain age, what had been read as benign was read, equally arbitrarily, as threatening and repressive. Beatrice was surprised by certain changes in her colleagues and students. And then, finally, accepting.

On the day of Mortimer Cropper's proposed luncheon, she was visited by Roland Michell.

'Am I disturbing you, Beatrice?'

Beatrice smiled automatically.

'No, not particularly. I was just thinking.'

'I've come up against something – I wondered if you could help. Do you happen to know if Ellen Ash says anything anywhere about Christabel LaMotte?'

'I don't *remember* anything.' Beatrice sat smiling, as though her lack of memory clinched the matter. 'I don't think so, no.'

'Is there any way of checking?'

'I could look at my card index.'

'I'd be very grateful.'

'What sort of thing are we looking for?'

Roland experienced a not uncommon desire to poke, prod or startle Beatrice, who sat monumentally still, with the same fussy little smile on her face.

'Just anything really. I came across some evidence that Ash was interested in LaMotte. I just wondered.'

'I could look at my card index. Professor Cropper is coming at lunchtime.'

'How long is he here this time?'

'I don't know. He didn't say. He said he was coming on from Christie's.'

'Could I see your card index, Beatrice?'

'Oh, I don't know, it's all a bit of a muddle, I have my own *system*, you know, Roland, for recording things, I think I'd better look myself, I can better understand my own hieroglyphics.'

She put on her reading glasses, which dangled over her embarrassment on a gilt-beaded chain. Now she could not see Roland at all, a state of affairs she marginally preferred, since she saw all male members of her quondam department as persecutors, and was unaware that Roland's own position there was precarious, that he hardly qualified as a full-blooded departmental male. She began to move things across her desk, a heavy wooden-handled knitting bag, several greying parcels of unopened books. There was a whole barbican of index boxes, thick with dust and scuffed with age, which she ruffled in interminably, talking to herself.

'No, that one's chronological, no, that's only the reading habits, no, that one's to do with the running of the house. Where's the master-box now? It's not complete for all notebooks you must understand. I've indexed some but not all, there is so much, I've had to divide it chronologically and under headings, here's the Calverley family, that won't do ... now this might be it ...

'Nothing under LaMotte. No, wait a minute. Here. A cross-reference. We need the reading box. It's very theological, the reading box. It appears –' she drew out a dog-eared yellowing card, the ink blurring into its fuzzy surface – 'it appears she read *The Fairy Melusina*, in 1872.'

She replaced the card in its box, and settled back in her chair, looking across at Roland with the same obfuscating comfortable smile. Roland felt that the notebooks might be bristling with unrecorded observations about Christabel LaMotte that had slipped between Beatrice's web of categories. He said doggedly,

'Do you think I could *see* what she said? It might be –' he rejected 'important' – 'it might be of interest to me. I've never read *Melusina*. There seems to be a revival of interest in it.'

'I tried once or twice in the old days. It's terribly long-winded and impenetrable. Gothic, you know, Victorian Gothic, a bit *gruesome*, in places for a lady's poem ...'

'Beatrice – could I just cast my eyes over what Mrs Ash said?'

'I'll just see.' Beatrice rose from her table. She put her head into the metal dark of a khaki filing-cabinet inside which the yearly volumes of the Journal lay. Roland observed her huge haunches under herring-bone tweed. 'Did I say 1872?' Beatrice called from inside her echoing box. Reluctantly she produced the volume, leather-bound, with marbled end-papers in crimson and violet. She began to turn the pages, holding the text up, between Roland and herself.

'Here,' she finally pronounced. 'November 1872. Here she begins it.' She began to read aloud.

'Today I embarked on the *Fairy Melusina*, which I bought for myself in Hatchard's on Monday. What shall I find there? So far I have read the rather long preamble which I found a little pedantic. I then came on to the knight Raimondin and his encounter with the shining lady at the Fontaine de Soif which I liked better. Miss LaMotte has an unquestionable gift for making the flesh creep.'

'Beatrice —'

'Is this the sort of thing you were —?'

'Beatrice, could I possibly read that for myself, to make notes on it?'

'You can't take it out of the office.'

'Perhaps I could perch at the corner of your table. Would I be terribly in your way?'

'I suppose not, no,' said Beatrice. 'You could have that chair if I lifted that heap of books off it —'

'Let me do that —'

'And you could sit opposite me then, if I cleaned that corner of my table —'

'So I could. Thank you.'

They were engaged in space clearing when Mortimer Cropper appeared in the doorway, making everything appear dingier in comparison to his suave elegance.

'Miss Nest. How pleasant to see you again. I trust I'm not too early. I could always come back again . . .'

Beatrice was flustered. A heap of papers sighed sideways and fanned out on the floor.

'Oh dear. I *was* ready, Professor, I was quite ready, only Mr Michell wanted to enquire . . . wanted to know . . .'

Cropper had detached Miss Nest's shapeless mackintosh from its hook and was holding it for her.

'Glad to see you, Michell. Making progress? What did you want to know?'

His clearcut face was composed of pure curiosity.

'Just checking on Ash's reading of some poems.'

'Ah yes. Which poems?'

'Roland was enquiring about Christabel LaMotte. I couldn't *remember* anything . . . but there turned out to be a minor reference . . . you may sit there whilst I have lunch with Professor Cropper, Roland, if you try not to disturb the order of things on my desk, if you *promise* not to take anything out of here . . .'

'You need help, Miss Nest. Your task is too huge.'

'Oh no. I do *much* better alone. I should not know what to do with help.'

'Christabel LaMotte,' said Cropper, musing. 'There's a photograph in the Stant Collection. Very pale. Not sure if it was the effect of near-albinism or a defect in the printing. Probably the latter. Was Ash, do you think, interested in her?'

'Only very marginally. I'm just checking. Routinely.'

When Cropper had shepherded his charge out, Roland settled at his table corner and turned the pages of Randolph Ash's wife's journal.

Still engaged in reading *Melusina*. An impressive achievement.

Have reached Book VI of *Melusina*. Its aspirations to cosmic reflection might be thought to sit uneasily with its Fairytale nature.

Still reading *Melusina*. What diligence, what confidence went to its contriving. Miss LaMotte despite a lifetime's residence in this country, remains essentially *French* in her way of seeing the world. Though there is nothing to which one can take exception in this beautiful and daring poem, in its morals indeed.

And then, several pages later, a surprising and uncharacteristic outburst.

Today I laid down *Melusina* having come trembling to the end of this marvellous work. What shall I say of it? It is truly original, although the general public may have trouble in recognising its genius, because it makes no concession to vulgar frailties of imagination, and because its virtues are so far removed in some ways at least from those expected of the weaker sex. Here is no swooning sentiment, no timid purity, no softly gloved lady-like *patting* of the reader's sensibility, but lively imagination, but force and vigour. How shall I characterise it? It is like a huge, intricately embroidered tapestry in a shadowed stone hall, on which all sorts of strange birds and beasts and elves and demons creep in and out of thickets of thorny trees and occasional blossoming glades. Fine patches of gold stand out in the gloom, sunlight and starlight, the sparkle of jewels or human hair or serpents' scales. Firelight flickers, fountains catch light. All the elements are in perpetual motion, fire consuming, water running, air alive and the earth turning ... I was put in mind of the tapestried hunts in *The Franklin's Tale* or in *The Faerie Queene*, where the observer sees the woven vision come alive under his wondering eyes, so that pictured swords draw real blood, and the wind sighs in pictured trees.

And what shall I say of the scene in which the husband, a man of insufficient faith, bores his peephole and observes his *Siren-spouse* at play in her vat of waters? I should have said, if I was asked, that this scene was best left to the imagination, as Coleridge left Geraldine – 'a sight to dream of, not to tell.' But Miss LaMotte tells abundantly, though her description might be a little *strong* for some stomachs, especially maidenly English ones, who will be looking for fairy winsomeness.

She is beautiful and terrible and tragic, the Fairy Melusina, inhuman in the last resort.

> The sinuous muscle of her monster tail
> Beating the lambent bath to diamond-fine
> Refracting lines of spray, a dancing veil
> Of heavier water on the breathless air
>
> How lovely-white her skin her Lord well knew,
> The tracery of blue veins across the snow...
> But could not see the beauty in the sheen
> Of argent scale and slate-blue coiling fin ...

Perhaps the most surprising touch is that the snake or fish is beautiful.

Roland gave up any idea of having lunch himself to copy out this passage, mostly because he wanted to give it to Maud Bailey, who *must* be excited at this contemporary female enthusiasm for her admired text, but also because he felt that extravagant admiration of this sort, from Ash's wife for a woman whom he was already thinking of as Ash's mistress, was perhaps unexpected. Having copied it out, he turned the pages idly.

My recent reading has caused me for some reason to remember myself as I was when a young girl, reading high Romances and seeing myself simultaneously as the object of all knights' devotion – an unspotted Guenevere – and as the author of the Tale. I wanted to be a Poet and a Poem, and now am neither, but the mistress of a very small household, consisting of an elderly poet (set in his ways, which are amiable and gentle and give *no* cause for anxiety), myself, and the servants who are not unmanageable. I see daily how Patience and Faith are both worn down and hagged with the daily care of their broods and yet shine with the flow of love and unstinted concern for their young. They are now grandmothers as well as mothers, doted on and doting. I myself have come to find of late a kind of creeping insidious vigour come upon me (after the unspeakable years of migraine headache and nervous prostration). I wake feeling, indeed, rather spry, and look about for things to occupy myself with. I remember at sixty the lively ambitions of the young girl in the Deanery, who seems like someone else, as I watch her in my imagination dancing in her moony muslin, or having her hand kissed by a gentleman in a boat.

I hit on something I believe when I wrote that I meant to be a Poet and a Poem. It may be that this is the desire of all reading women, as opposed to reading men, who wish to be poets and heroes, but might see the inditing of poetry in our peaceful age, as a sufficiently heroic act. No one wishes a man to be a Poem. That young girl in her muslin was a poem; cousin Ned wrote an execrable sonnet about the chaste sweetness of her face and the intuitive goodness shining in her walk. But I now think – it might have been better, might it not, to have held on to the desire to be a Poet? I could *never* write as well as Randolph, but then no one can or could, and so it was perhaps not worth considering as an objection to doing something.

Perhaps if I had made his life more difficult, he would have written less, or less freely. I cannot claim to be the midwife to genius, but if I have not *facilitated*, I have at least not, as many women might have done, *prevented*. This is a very small virtue to claim, a very negative achievement to hang my whole life on. Randolph, if he were to read this, would laugh me out of such morbid questioning, would tell me it is never too late, would cram his huge imagination into the snail-shell space of my tiny new accession of energy and tell me what is to be done. But he shan't see this, and I will find a way – to be a very little more – there now I'm crying, as that girl might have cried. Enough.

Roland slid out of the Ash factory and went home before Cropper or Blackadder could return from lunch and ask him any awkward questions. He was annoyed with himself for creating a situation in which Cropper could discover Christabel's name. Nothing was wasted on that sharp noticing mind.

The Putney basement was silent, sensuously entangled with the BM basement by its feline reek. Winter was darkly coming, and dark stains and some slow form of creeping life had appeared on the walls. It was hard to heat. There was no central heating, and Roland and Val had supplemented their one gas fire with paraffin stoves, so that the smell of petrol mingled with the smells of cat and mild mould. It was a cold petrol smell, not a burning one, and there was no smell of cooking, no burning onion nor warm curry powder. Val must be out. They could not afford to keep the hall stove lit in her absence. Roland, without taking his coat off, went to find a match. The wick was behind a cranky hinged door in the chimney, made of a transparent horny substance, smoke-stained and crackling. Roland turned the key, extruded a little wick and set it flaring with a low boom; he hastily closed the aperture, producing a steady blue inverted crescent of flame. There was something ancient and magical about the colour, a clear blue, touched with green and dense with purple.

There was a little heap of letters in the hall. Two for Val, one self-addressed. Three for him: a request for a library book, a card acknowledging receipt of an article sent to a learned journal, and a handwritten letter that was unfamiliar.

Dear Dr Michell,

I hope you will not have taken our silence for rudeness, or something worse. My husband has been making the inquiries he spoke of. He has consulted his solicitor, the Vicar, and our dear friend Jane Anstey who is a retired Deputy County Librarian. None of these had any very clear advice. Miss Anstey spoke very highly of Dr Bailey's work and of the archive she looks after. She feels it would be entirely proper to allow Dr Bailey to read our treasure trove and give a preliminary opinion on it — especially as it was she who found it. I am writing to you too, since you were present at the finding, and expressed an interest in Randolph Henry Ash. Would you care to come and examine the papers with Dr Bailey, or if you would find this time-consuming suggest someone to come in your place? I appreciate that this would be more difficult for you, coming from London, than for Dr Bailey who lives conveniently near Croysant le Wold. I would offer to accommodate you for a few days – though this has its difficulties, since we are as you will remember, confined to the ground floor, and the old house is woefully cold in winter. What do you think? How long do you imagine you will need to take stock of our find? Would a week be sufficient? We have visitors over Christmas but none over the New Year if you would care to make a foray to the Lincolnshire Wolds at that time.

I am still grateful for your gentlemanly and practical assistance on that field-edge. Let me know how you think it best to proceed.

Yours sincerely
Joan Bailey.

Roland felt several things at once. Primary elation – a kind of vision of the bundle of dead letters come to rushing life like some huge warm eagle stirring. Irritation at the primacy Maud Bailey seemed to have assumed in the affair which had begun with the discovery of his purloined letter. Practical, calculating anxiety – how to accept the half-invitation to stay without revealing his own extreme poverty, which might make him appear an inadequately weighty person to be entrusted with the letter-reading. Fear of Val. Fear of Maud Bailey. Anxiety about Cropper and Blackadder and even Beatrice Nest. He wondered exactly why Lady Bailey had thought or suggested, he might want to suggest someone else to read the letters – fun, folly, or an edge of uncertainty about himself? How friendly was her gratitude? Did Maud want him there to read the letters?

Above his head at street level, he saw an angled aileron of a scarlet Porsche, its jaunty fin more or less at the upper edge of his window frame. A pair of very soft, clean glistening black shoes appeared, followed by impeccably creased matt charcoal pin-striped light woollen legs, followed by the beautifully cut lower hem of a jacket, its black vent revealing a scarlet silk lining, its open front revealing a flat muscular stomach under a finely-striped red and white shirt. Val's legs followed, in powder-blue stockings and saxe-blue shoes, under the limp hem of a crêpey mustard-coloured dress, printed with blue moony flowers. The four feet advanced and retreated, retreated and advanced, the male feet insisting towards the basement stairs, the female feet resisting, parrying. Roland opened the door and went into the area, fired mostly by what always got him, pure curiosity as to what the top half looked like.

The shoulders and chest were as expected; the tie was knitted red and black silk. The face was oval. There were horn-rimmed glasses under a modified 1920s haircut, very short back and sides, moderately long over the brow, black.

'Hi,' said Roland.

'Oh,' said Val. 'I thought you were in the Museum. This is Euan MacIntyre.'

Euan MacIntyre leaned over and gravely extended a hand downwards. There was something powerful about him, Pluto delivering Persephone at the gate of the underworld.

'I brought Val home. She wasn't feeling very well. I thought she should lie down.'

His voice was clear and ringing, not Scots, full of what Roland might inaccurately have called toffee-nosed sounds, or plummy sounds, sounds he had spent his childhood learning to imitate derisorily, hooting, curtailed, drawling, chipping sounds that prickled his non-existent hackles with class hostility. He was obviously waiting to be asked in, with an ease which in earlier novels might have proclaimed the true gentleman, but to Roland and probably to Val suggested nosiness and their own shame. Val drifted slowly and faintly towards Roland.

'I'll be all right. Thank you for the lift.'

'Any time.' He turned to Roland. 'I hope we meet again.'

'Yes,' said Roland vaguely, backing down below Val's descent. The Porsche sped away.

'He fancies me,' said Val.

'Where did he spring from?'

'I've been typing things for him. Last Wills and Testaments. Deeds of Covenant. Opinions on this and that. He's a solicitor. Bloss, Bloom, Trompett and MacIntyre. Respectable, not sharp, very successful. Office full of photographs of horses. He owns a leg of one, he says. He asked me to go to Newmarket.'

'What did you say?'

'Would you mind what I said?'

'It would do you good to have a day out,' Roland said, and wished he hadn't.

'Listen to yourself. It would do you a lot of good. How repellently *patronising*.'

'Well, I've got no right to stop you, Val.'

'I told him you wouldn't like it.'

'Oh Val —'

'I should have told him you couldn't care less. I should have gone.'

'I can't see why you didn't go.'

'Oh if you can't *see* —'

'What has happened to us?'

'Too much confinement, too little money, too much anxiety and too young. You want to get rid of me.'

'You *know* that isn't true. You *know*. I love you, Val. I just don't give you a very good time.'

'I love you too. I'm sorry I'm so short-tempered and suspicious.'

She waited. He took hold of her. It was will and calculation, not desire. There were two ways out of this, a row, or making love, and the second was more conducive to eventual dinner and a peaceful evening's work and the eventual broaching of the Lincolnshire project.

'It's suppertime,' said Val faintly.

Roland looked at his watch.

'No it isn't. Anyway, there's only ourselves to please. We used to do things spontaneously, remember. Pay no attention to clocks. We ought to put ourselves first, now and then.'

They undressed and cuddled together for cold comfort. At first Roland thought it was not going to work after all. There are certain things that cannot be done only on will power. The thought of the warm feathers of his letter-eagle produced a stirring. Val said, 'I don't want anyone but you, not really,' and it almost subsided again. He lit on an image, a woman in a library, a woman not naked but voluminously clothed, concealed in rustling silk and petticoats, fingers folded over the place where the tight black silk bodice met the springing skirts, a woman whose face was sweet and sad, a stiff bonnet framing loops of thick hair. Ellen Ash, constructed from Richmond's sketch, reproduced in Cropper's *Great Ventriloquist*. All Richmond's women have a generic mouth, firm and fine and generous and serious, variable yet related to some ideal type. The mental vision of this woman, half-fantasy, half-photogravure, was efficacious. They comforted each other. Later he would be able to think of a way to ask about Lincoln without saying exactly where he was going or why.

CHAPTER EIGHT

All day snow fell
Snow fell all night
My silent lintel
Silted white
Inside a Creature –
Feathered – Bright –
With snowy Feature
Eyes of Light
Propounds – Delight.
                    C. LaMotte

They faced each other over the packages in the library. It was bitterly cold; Roland felt as though he should never be warm again, and thought with longing of articles of clothing he had never had occasion to wear; knitted mittens, long johns, balaclava. Maud had driven out early and had arrived, keen and tense, before breakfast was over, well-wrapped in tweed jacket and Aran wool sweater, with the bright hair, visible last night at dinner in the Baileys' chilly hall, again wholly swallowed by a green silk knotted scarf. The library was stony and imposing, with thickets of carved foliage in its vaulted roof and a huge stone fireplace, swept and empty, with the Bailey arms, a solid tower and a small clump of trees, carved on its mantel. Gothic windows opened onto a frosty lawn; these were partly clear glass in leaded panes and partly richly stained Kelmscott glass, depicting, in central medallions, the building of a golden keep on a green hill, fortified and bedizened with banners, entered, in the central medallion, by a procession of knights and ladies on horseback. Along the top of the window ran a luxuriating rose tree, bearing both white and red flowers and blood red fruit together. Round the sides vines were rampant, carrying huge purple grape bunches on gilded stems amongst curling tendrils and veined spreading leaves. The books, behind glass, were leather-backed, orderly, apparently immobile and untouched.

There was a table in the middle, leather-topped and heavy, ink-stained and scratched, with two leather-seated armchairs. The leather had been red and was now brown and powdery, of the kind that leaves rusty traces on the clothes of those who sit there. In the centre of the table was an inkstand, with an empty silver pen tray, tarnished, and greenish glass vessels, containing dried black powder.

Joan Bailey, wheeling round the table, had laid the packages on it.

'I hope you'll be comfortable. Do let me know if you need anything else. I would light the fire for you, but the chimneys haven't been swept for generations – I'm afraid you'd suffocate with smoke, or else we'd set the whole house on fire. Are you warm enough?'

Maud, animated, assured her that they were. There was a faint flash of colour in her ivory cheeks. As though the cold brought out her proper life, as though she were at home in it.

'Then I'll leave you to it. I long to see how you get on. I'll make coffee at eleven. I'll bring it to you.'

There was a frostiness between the two of them when Maud brought out her proposals for the way they should proceed. She had decided that they should each read the letters of the poet who interested them, and that they should agree conventions of recording their observations on index cards according to a system she was already using in the Women's Resource Centre. Roland objected to this, partly because he felt he was being hustled, partly because he had a vision, which he now saw was ridiculous and romantic, of their two heads bent together over the manuscripts, following the story, sharing, he had supposed, the emotion. He pointed out that by Maud's system they would lose any sense of the development of the narrative and Maud retorted robustly that they lived in a time which valued narrative uncertainty, that they could cross-refer later, and that anyway they had so little *time*, and what concerned her was primarily Christabel LaMotte. Roland agreed, since the time constraint was indeed crucial. So they worked for some time in silence, interrupted only by Lady Bailey bearing a thermos of coffee, and the odd request for information.

'Tell me,' said Roland, 'did Blanche wear glasses?'

'I don't know.'

'There's a reference here to the glittering surfaces of her gaze. I'm sure it says surfaces in the plural.'

'She could have had glasses, or he could have been comparing her to a dragonfly or some other insect. He seems to have read Christabel's insect poems. People were obsessed with insects at that time.'

'What did she really look like, Blanche?'

'No one really knows for certain. I imagine her very pale, but that's only because of her name.'

At first Roland worked with the kind of concentrated curiosity with which he read anything at all by Randolph Ash. This curiosity was a kind of predictive familiarity; he knew the workings of the other man's mind, he had read what he had read, he was possessed of his characteristic habits of syntax and stress. His mind could leap ahead and hear the rhythm of the unread as though he were the writer, hearing in his brain the ghost-rhythms of the as yet unwritten.

But with this reading, after a time – a very short time – the habitual pleasures of recognition and foresight gave way to a mounting sense of stress. This was primarily because the writer of the letters was himself under stress, confused by the object and recipient of his attentions. He found it difficult to fix this creature in his scheme of things. He asked for clarification and was answered, it appeared, with riddles. Roland, not in possession of the other side of the correspondence, could not even tell what riddles, and looked up increasingly at the perplexing woman on the other side of the table, who with silent industry and irritating deliberation was making minutely neat notes on her little fans of cards, pinning them together with silver hooks and pins, frowning.

Letters, Roland discovered, are a form of narrative that envisages no outcome, no closure. His time was a time of the dominance of narrative theories. Letters tell no story, because they do not know, from line to line, where they are going. If Maud had been less coldly hostile he would have pointed this out to her – as a matter of general interest – but she did not look up or meet his eye.

Letters, finally, exclude not only the reader as co-writer, or predictor, or guesser, but they exclude the reader as reader, they are written, if they are true letters, for *a* reader. Roland had another thought; none of Randolph Henry Ash's other correspondence had this quality. All was urbane, considerate, often witty, sometimes wise – but written wholly without *urgent* interest in the recipients, whether they were his publisher, his literary allies and rivals, or even – in the notes which survived – his wife. Who had destroyed much. She had written:

> Who can endure to think of greedy hands furrowing through Dickens's desk for his private papers, for these records of personal sentiment that were his and his only – not meant for public consumption – though now those who will not reread his marvellous books with true care will *sup up* his *so-called* Life in his Letters.

The truth was, Roland thought uneasily, these letters, these busy passionate letters, had never been written for him to read – as *Ragnarök* had, as *Mummy Possest* had, as the Lazarus poem had. They had been written for Christabel LaMotte.

… your intelligence, your marvellous quick wit, – so that I may write to you as I write when I am alone, when I write my true writing, which is for everyone and no one – so that in me which has never addressed any private creature, feels at home with you. I say 'at home' – what extraordinary folly – when you take pleasure in making me feel most unheimlich, *as the Germans have it, least of all at home, but always on edge, always apprehensive of failure, always certain that I cannot appreciate your next striking thought or glancing shaft of wit. But poets don't want homes, – do they? – they are not creatures of hearths and firedogs, but of heaths and ranging hounds. Now tell me – do you suppose what I just wrote is the truth or a lie? You know, all poetry may be a cry of generalised love, for this, or that, or the universe – which must be loved in its particularity, not its generality, but for its universal*

131

life in every minute particular. I have always supposed it to be a cry of unsatisfied love – my dear – and so it may be indeed – for satisfaction may surfeit it and so it may die. I know many poets who write only when in an exalted state of mind which they compare to being in love, when they do not simply state, that they are in love, that they seek love – for this fresh damsel, or that lively young woman – in order to find a fresh metaphor, or a new bright vision of things in themselves. And to tell you the truth, I have always believed I cd diagnose this state of being in love, which they regard as most particular, as inspired by item, one pair of black eyes or indifferent blue, item, one graceful attitude of body or mind, item, one female history of some twenty-two years from, shall we say, 1821–1844 – I have always believed this in love to be something of the most abstract masking itself under the particular forms of both lover and beloved. And Poet, who assumes and informs both. I wd have told you – no, I do tell you – friendship is rarer, more idiosyncratic, more individual and in every way more durable than this Love.

Without this excitement they cannot have their Lyric Verse, and so they get it by any convenient means – and with absolute sincerity – but the Poems are not for the young lady, the young lady is for the Poems.

You see the fork I have impaled myself on – Nevertheless I reiterate – because you will not bridle at my strictures on either manly devotion to a female ideal – or on the duplicity of Poets – but will look at it with your own Poet's eye – askance and most wisely – I write to you as I write when I am alone, with that in me – how else to put it? you will know, I trust you you know, – with that which makes, which is the Maker.

I should add, that my poems do not, I think, spring from the Lyric Impulse – but from something restless and myriad-minded and partial and observing and analytic and curious, my dear, which is more like the mind of the prose master, Balzac, whom, being a Frenchwoman, and blessedly less hedged about with virtuous prohibitions than English female gentility, you know and understand. What makes me a Poet, and not a novelist – is to do with the singing of the Language itself. For the difference between poets and novelists is this – that the former write for the life of the language – and the latter write for the betterment of the world.

And you for the revelation to mere humans of some strange unguessed-at other world, is that not so? The City of Is, the reverse of Par-is, the towers in the water not the air, the drowned roses and flying fish and other paradoxical elementals – you see – I come to know you – I shall feel my way into your thought – as a hand into a glove – to steal your own metaphor and torture it cruelly. But if you wish – you may keep your gloves clean and scented and *folded away — you may — only write to me, write to me, I love to see the hop and skip and sudden starts of your ink — . . .*

Roland looked up at his partner or opponent. She seemed to be getting on with an enviable certainty and speed. Fine frown-lines fanned her brow.

The stained glass worked to defamiliarise her. It divided her into cold, brightly coloured fires. One cheek moved in and out of a pool of grape-violet as she worked. Her brow flowered green and gold. Rose-red and berry-red stained her pale neck and chin and mouth. Eyelids were purple-shadowed. The green silk of her scarf glittered with turreted purple ridges. Dust danced in a shadowy halo round her shifting head, black motes in straw gold, invisible solid matter appearing like pinholes in a sheet of solid colour. He spoke and she turned through a rainbow, her pale skin threading the various lights.

'I'm sorry to interrupt — I just wondered — do you know about the City of Is? I.S. I.S?'

She shook off her concentration as a dog shakes off water.

'It's a Breton legend. It was drowned in the sea for its wickedness. It was ruled by Queen Dahud, the sorceress, daughter of King Gradlond. The women there were transparent, according to some versions. Christabel wrote a poem.'

'May I look?'

'A quick glance. I'm using this book.'

She pushed it across the table.

Tallahassee Women Poets. Christabel LaMotte: a Selection of Narrative and Lyric Poems, ed. Leonora Stern. The Sapphic Press, Boston. The purple cover bore a white linear image of two mediaeval women, bending to embrace each other across a fountain in a square basin. They both wore veiled headdresses, heavy girdles and long plaits.

He scanned *The Drowned City*. This had a prefatory note by Leonora Stern.

In this poem, as in 'The Standing Stones', LaMotte drew on her native Breton mythology, which she had known from childhood. The theme was of particular interest to a woman writer, as it might be said to reflect a cultural conflict between two types of

133

civilisation, the Indo-european patriarchy of Gradlond and the more primitive, instinctive, earthy paganism of his sorceress daughter, Dahud, who remains immersed when he has taken his liberating leap to dry land at Quimper. The women's world of the underwater city is the obverse of the male-dominated technological industrial world of Paris or Par-is, as the Bretons have it. They say that Is will come to the surface when Paris is drowned for its sins.

LaMotte's attitude to Dahud's so-called crimes is interesting. Her father, Isidore LaMotte, in his Breton Myths and Legends, does not hesitate to refer to Dahud's 'perversions' though without specifying. Nor does LaMotte specify . . .

He flicked across the pages of the text.

> There are none blush on earth, y-wis
> As do dames of the Town of Is.
> The red blood runs beneath their skin
> And feels its way and flows within,
> And men can see, as through a glass
> Each twisty turn, each crossing pass
> Of threaded vein and artery
> From heart to throat, from mouth to eye.
> This spun-glass skin, like spider-thread
> Is silver water, woven with red.
> For their excessive wickedness
> In days of old, was this distress
> Come on them, of transparency
> And openness to every eye.
> But still they're proud, their haughty brows
> Circled with gold. . . .
>
> Deep in the silence of drowned Is
> Beneath the wavering precipice
> The church-spire in the thickened green
> Points to the trembling surface sheen
> From which descends, a glossy cone
> A mirror-spire that mocks its own.
> Between these two the mackerel sails
> As did the swallow in the vales
> Of summer air, and he too sees
> His mirrored self amongst the trees

That hang to meet themselves, for here,
All things are doubled, and the clear
Thick element is doubled too
Finite and limited the view
As though the world of roofs and rocks
Were stored inside a glassy box.
And damned and drowned transparent things
Hold silent commerce . . .

This drowned world lies beneath a skin
Of moving water, as within
The glassy surface of their frown
The ladies' grieving passions drown
And can be seen to ebb and flow
In crimson as the currents go
Amongst the bladderwrack and stones
Amongst the delicate white bones.

And so they worked on, against the clock, cold and excited, until Lady Bailey came to offer them supper.

When Maud drove home, that first evening, the weather was already changing for the worse. Clouds were darkly gathering; she could see, through the trees, a full moon which, because of some trick of the thickening air, seemed both far away and somehow condensed, an object round and small and dull. She drove through the park, much of which had been planted by that earlier Sir George who had married Christabel's sister Sophie, and had had a passion for trees, trees from all parts of the distant earth, Persian plum, Turkey oak, Himalayan pine, Caucasian walnut and the Judas tree. He had had his generation's expansive sense of time – he had inherited hundred-year-old oaks and beeches and had planted spreads of woodland, rides and coppices he would never see. Huge rugged trunks came silently past the little green car in the encroaching dark, rearing themselves suddenly monstrous in the changing white beam of the headlight. There was a kind of cracking of cold in the woods all round, a tightening of texture, a clamping together that Maud had experienced in her own warm limbs as she went out into the courtyard and cold ran into her constricted throat and pulled tight something she thought of poetically as the heartstrings.

Down these rides Christabel had come, wilful and perhaps spiritually driven, urging her little pony-cart on to the ritualist eucharist of the Reverend Mossman. Maud had not found Christabel an easy companion all day. She responded to threats with increasing organisation. Pin, categorise, learn. Out here it felt different. The mental pony-cart bowled along, with its veiled passenger. The trees went up, solid. A kind of elemental clanging accompanied the disappearance of each into the dark. They were old, they were grey and green and stiff. Women, not trees, were Maud's true pastoral concern. Her idea of these primeval creatures included her generation's sense of their imminent withering and dying, under the drip of acid rain, or in the invisible polluted gusts of the wind. She was visited by a sudden vision of them dancing, golden-green, in a bright spring a hundred years ago, flexible saplings, tossed and resilient. This thickened forest, her own humming metal car, her prying curiosity about whatever had been Christabel's life, seemed suddenly to be the ghostly things, feeding on, living through, the young vitality of the past. Between the trees the ground was black with the shining, sagging wet rounds of dead leaves; in front of her, the same black leaves spread like stains on the humping surface of the tarmac. A creature ran out into her path; its eyes were half-spheres filled with dull red fire, refracted, sparkling and then gone. She swerved, and nearly hit a thick oak stump. Ambiguous wet drops or flakes – which? – materialised briefly on the windscreen. Maud was inside, and the outside was alive and separate.

Her flat, with its unambiguous bright cleanliness, seemed unusually welcoming, apart from the presence of two letters, caught in the lips of the letterbox. She tugged these free, and went round, closing curtains, putting on many lights. The letters too were threatening. One was blue and one was the kind of tradesman's brown with which all universities have replaced their milled white crested missives in the new austerity. The blue one was from Leonora Stern. The other said it was from Prince Albert College; she would have supposed it was from Roland, but he was here. She had been not very polite to him. Even bossy. The whole business had put her on edge. Why could she do nothing with ease and grace except work alone, inside these walls and curtains, her bright safe box? Christabel, defending Christabel, redefined and alarmed Maud.

Here is a Riddle, Sir, an old Riddle, an easy Riddle — hardly worth your thinking about — a fragile Riddle, in white and Gold with life in the middle of it. There is a gold, soft cushion, whose gloss you may only paradoxically imagine with your eyes closed tight — see it feelingly, let it slip through your mind's fingers. And this gold cushion is enclosed in its own crystalline casket, a casket translucent and endless in its circularity, for there are no sharp corners to it, no protrusions, only a milky moonstone clarity that deceives. And these are wrapped in silk, fine as thistledown, tough as steel, and the silk lies inside Alabaster, which you may think of as a funerary Urn — only with no inscription, for there are as yet no Ashes — and no pediment, and no nodding poppies engraved, nor yet no lid you may lift to peep in for all is sealed and smooth. There may come a day when you may lift the lid with impunity — or rather, when it may be lifted from within — for that way, life may come — whereas your way — you will discover — only Congealing and Mortality.

An Egg, Sir, is the answer, as you perspicuously read from the beginning, an Egg, a perfect O, a living Stone, doorless and windowless, whose life may slumber on till she be Waked — or find she has Wings to spread — which is not so here — oh no —

An Egg is my answer. What is the Riddle?

I am my own riddle. Oh, Sir, you must not kindly seek to ameliorate or steal away my solitude. It is a thing we women are taught to dread — oh the terrible tower, oh the thickets round it — no companionable Nest — but a donjon.

But they have lied to us you know, in this, as in so much else. The Donjon may frown and threaten — but it keeps us very safe — within its confines we are free in a way you, who have freedom to range the world, do not need to imagine. I do not advise imagining it — but do me the justice of believing — not imputing mendacious protestation — my Solitude is my Treasure, the best thing I have. I hesitate to go out. If you opened the little gate, I would not hop away — but oh how I sing in my gold cage —

Shattering an Egg is unworthy of you, no Pass time for men. Think what you would have in your hand if you put forth your Giant strength and crushed the solid stone. Something slippery and cold and unthinkably disagreeable.

Maud felt reluctant to open Leonora's letter, which had an imperious and accusing air. So she opened instead the brown one and saw it was worse, it was from Fergus Wolff, with whom she had had no communication for over a year. Certain handwriting can turn the stomach, after one, after five, after twenty-five years. Fergus's was, like much male writing, cramped, but with characteristic little flourishes. Maud's stomach turned, the vision of the tormented bed rose again in her mind's eye. She put a hand to her hair.

Dear Maud, never forgotten, as I hope I'm not either, quite. How are things in damp old Lincolnshire? Do the fens make you melancholy? How is Christabel? Would you be pleased to hear I have decided to give a paper on Christabel at the York conference on metaphor? I thought I'd lecture on

    The Queen of the Castle: What is kept in the Keep?

    How does that strike you? Do I have your imprimatur? Might I even hope to be able to consult your archive?

    I should deal with contrasting and conflicting metaphors for the fairy Melusine's castle-building activities. There's a very good piece by Jacques Le Goff on 'Melusine Défricheuse'; according to the new historians she's a kind of earth spirit or local goddess of foison or minor Ceres. But then you could adopt a Lacanian model of the image of the keep – Lacan says, 'the formation of the ego is symbolised in dreams by a fortress or stadium [any stadiums in Christabel?] – surrounded by marshes and rubbish-tips – dividing it into two opposite fields of contest where the subject flounders in quest of the lofty, remote inner castle whose form symbolises the id in a quite startling way.' I could complicate this with a few more real and imaginary castles – and a loving and respectful reference to your own seminal work on the limen and the liminal. What do you think? Will it wash? Will I be torn by Maenads?

    I was inspired to write partly by the excitement of this project, partly because my spies tell me that you and Roland Michell (a dull but honourable contemporary of mine) have been discovering something or other together. My chief spy – a young woman who is not best pleased by the turn of events – tells me you are spending the New Year together, investigating connections. I am naturally consumed by curiosity. Perhaps I will come and consult your archive. I do wonder what you make of young Michell. Don't eat him, dear Maud. He isn't in your class. Academically, that is, he isn't, as you may have discovered by now.

    Whereas you and I could have had the most delectable talk about towers above and under water, serpent tails and flying fish. Did you read Lacan on flying fish and vesicle persecution? I miss you from time to time, you know.

You weren't wholly nice or fair to me. Nor I to you, you will say – but when are we ever? You are so severe with male shortcomings.

Please give me the go-ahead on my siege-paper.

Much love as always
Fergus

Dear Maud,

I find it odd that I haven't heard from you for maybe two months now – I trust all is well with you, and that your silence indicates only that your work is going well and absorbing all your attention. I worry about you when you are silent – I know you haven't been happy – I think of you with great love as you progress –

When I last wrote I mentioned I might write something on water and milk and amniotic fluid in Melusina – why is water always seen as the female? – we've discussed this – I want to write a big piece on the undines and nixies and melusinas – women perceived as dangerous – what do you think? I could extend it to the Drowned City – With special reference to non-genital imagery for female sexuality – we need to get away from the cunt as well as from the phallus – the drowned women in the city might represent the totality of the female body as an erogenous zone if the circumambient fluid were seen as an undifferentiated eroticism, and this might be possible to connect to the erotic totality of the woman/dragon stirring the waters of the large marble bath, or submerging her person in it as LaM. tellingly describes her. What do you think, Maud?

Would you be prepared to give a paper at the Australian meeting of the Sapphic society in 1988? I had in mind that we would devote that session entirely to the study of the female erotic in nineteenth-century poetry and the strategies and subterfuges through which it had to present or dis-cover itself. You might have extended your thinking about liminality and the dissolution of boundaries. Or you might wish to be more rigorous in your exploration of LaMotte's lesbian sexuality as the empowering force behind her work. (I accept that her inhibitions made her characteristically devious and secretive – but you do not give her sufficient credit for the strength with which she does nevertheless obliquely speak out.)

I think so often of the brief time we had together in the summer. I think of our long tramps on the Wolds and late hours in the library, and scoops of real American ice-cream by your fireside. You are so thoughtful and gentle – you made me feel I am crashing around in your fragile surroundings, clumsily *knocking down little screens and room dividers you have set up around your English privacy – but you aren't happy, are you, Maud? There is an emptiness in your life.*

It would do you good to come out here and experience the hectic storm and stress of American Women's Studies. I could find you a post as soon as you wanted it, no problem. Think about it.

In the interim, go and leave my love at Her grave – use the shears if you've time, or inclination – it made my blood boil to see how she was neglected. Put some more flowers down in my name – for the grass to drink – I found her resting-place unbearably moving. I wish I thought she could have foreseen she was to be loved as she should be loved –

And I send you all my love – and wait for an answer this time

Your
Leonora

This letter posed and shelved a moral problem: when and how much was it wise or honourable to tell Leonora about the discovery? She would not particularly like it. She did not like R. H. Ash. Still less would she like being put in the position of not having known about it, if she continued to write confident papers on Christabel's sexuality. She would feel betrayed and sisterhood would be betrayed.

As for Fergus. As for Fergus. He had a habit which Maud was not experienced enough to recognise as a common one in ex-lovers of giving little tugs at the carefully severed spider-threads or puppet-strings which had once tied her to him. She was annoyed at his proposal for a siege-paper, without knowing how much it was manufactured *ad hoc* to annoy her. She was also annoyed by his arcane reference to Lacan and flying-fish and vesicle persecution. She decided to track this down – method was her defence against anxiety – and duly found it.

I remember the dream of one of my patients, whose aggressive drives took the form of obsessive phantasies; in the dream he saw himself driving a car, accompanied by a woman with whom he was having a rather difficult affair, pursued by a flying fish, whose skin was so transparent that one could see the horizontal liquid level through the body, an image of vesicle persecution of great anatomical clarity . . .

The tormented bed rose again in her mind's eye, like old whipped eggs, like dirty snow.

Fergus Wolff appeared to be slightly jealous of Roland Michell. It was clever, if obvious, to describe him to Maud as 'not in your class'. Even if she noticed the transparency of this device, the label would stick. And she *knew* Roland was not in her class. She should have been less ungracious. He was a gentle and unthreatening being. Meek, she thought drowsily, turning out the light. Meek.

The next day, when she drove out towards Seal Court, the wolds were blanched with snow. It was not snowing, though the sky was heavy with it, an even pewter, weighing on the airy white hills that rolled up to meet it, so that the world seemed reversed here too, dark water above circling cloud. Sir George's trees were all fantastically hung with ice and furbelows. She parked just outside the stable yard on an impulse and decided to walk to the winter garden, built for Sophie Bailey and much loved by Christabel LaMotte. She would see it as it had been meant to be seen, and store the memory to be shared with Leonora. She trod crunchingly around the kitchen-garden wall and up a yew alley, festooned with snow, to where the overlapping, thick evergreens – holly, rhododendron, bay – enclosed a kind of trefoil-shaped space at the heart of which was the pool where Christabel had seen the frozen gold and silver fish, put there to provide flashes of colour in the gloom – *the darting genii of the place*, Christabel had said. There was a stone seat, with its rounded snow-cushion which she did not disturb. The quiet was absolute. It was beginning to snow again. Maud bowed her head with the self-consciousness of such a gesture, and thought of Christabel, standing here, looking at this frozen surface, darkly glowing under blown traces of snow.

> And in the pool two fishes play
> Argent and gules they shine alway
> Against the green against the grey
> They flash upon a summer's day
>
> And in the depth of wintry night
> They slumber open-eyed and bright
> Silver and red, a shadowed light
> Ice-veiled and steadily upright

> A paradox of chilly fire
> Of life in death, of quenched desire
> That has no force, e'en to respire
> Suspended until frost retire –

Were there fish? Maud crouched on the rim of the pool, her briefcase standing in snow beside her, and scraped with an elegant gloved hand at the snow on the ice. The ice was ridged and bubbly and impure. Whatever was beneath it could not be seen. She moved her hand in little circles, polishing, and saw, ghostly and pale in the metal-dark surface a woman's face, her own, barred like the moon under mackerel clouds, wavering up at her. Were there fish? She leaned forward. A figure loomed black on the white, a hand touched her arm with a huge banging, an unexpected electric shock. It was meek Roland. Maud screamed. And screamed a second time, and scrambled to her feet, furious.

They glared at each other.

'I'm sorry –'.⎫
'I'm sorry –'⎭

'I thought you were overbalancing –'

'I didn't know anyone was there.'

'I shocked you.'

'I embarrassed you –'

'It doesn't matter –'⎫
'It doesn't matter –'⎭

'I followed your footsteps.'

'I came to look at the winter garden.'

'Lady Bailey was worried you might have had an accident.'

'The snow wasn't that deep.'

'It's still snowing.'

'Shall we go in?'

'I didn't want to disturb you.'

'It doesn't matter.'

'Are there fish?'

'All you can see is imperfections and reflections.'

The work time that followed was a taciturn time. They bent their heads diligently – what they read will be discovered later – and looked up at each other almost sullenly. Snow fell. And fell. The white lawn rose to meet the library window. Lady Bailey came with coffee, silently rolling, into a room still with cold and full of a kind of grey clarity.

Lunch was sausages and mashed potatoes and buttery peppery mashed swede. It was eaten round the blazing log-fire, on knees, backs to the slatey white-flecked window. Sir George said,

'Hadn't you better be getting back to Lincoln, Miss B.? You don't have snow-chains, I suppose. The English don't. Anyone'd think the English'd never seen snow, the way they go on when it comes down.'

'I think Dr Bailey should stay here, George,' said his wife. 'I don't think it's safe for her to go even *trying* to thread her way through the wolds, in this. We can make her bed up in Mildred's old nursery. I can lend her some things. I think we should get the bed made up and get some hot water bottles in it now. Don't you think so, Dr Bailey?'

Maud said she couldn't and Lady Bailey said she must, and Maud said she shouldn't have set out and Lady Bailey said nonsense, and Maud said it was an imposition and Sir George said that whatever the rights and wrongs of it, Joanie was right and he would go up and see to Mildred's bed. Roland said he would help, and Maud said by no means, and Sir George and Maud went away upstairs to find sheets, whilst Lady Bailey filled a kettle. She had taken to Roland, whom she addressed as Roland, whilst she still addressed Maud as Dr Bailey. She looked up at him on the way across the kitchen, the brown coins on her face intensified by the fire.

'I hope that pleases you. I hope you'll be pleased to have her here. I hope you haven't had some tiff, or something.'

'Tiff?'

'You and your young woman. Girl friend. Whatever.'

'Oh no. That is, no tiff, and she isn't –'

'Isn't?'

'My – girl friend. I hardly know her. It was – is – purely professional. Because of Ash and LaMotte. I've got a girl friend in London. Her name's Val.'

Lady Bailey showed no interest in Val.

'She's a beautiful girl, Dr Bailey. Stand-offish or shy, maybe both. What my mother used to call a chilly mortal. She was a Yorkshirewoman, my mother. Not County. Not a lady.'

Roland smiled at her.

'I used to share a governess with some cousins of George's. To be company for them. I used to exercise their ponies, whilst they were away at school. Rosemary and Marigold Bailey. Not unlike your Maud. That's how I met George, who decided to marry me. George gets what he's set his mind on, as you see. That's how I took to hunting too. And ended up under a horse under a hedge when I was thirty-five and now as you see.'

'I see. Romantic. And terrible. I'm sorry.'

'I don't do too badly. George is a miracle. Hand me those bottles. Thank you.'

She filled them with a steady hand. Everything was designed for her ease; the kettle, the kettle-rest, the place to park and steady the chair.

'I want you both to be comfortable. George is so ashamed of the way we live – skimping and saving – the house and grounds *eat* money, just preventing deterioration and decay. He doesn't like people to come and see how things are. But I do love having someone to talk to. I like to see you working away in there. I hope it's proving useful. You don't say much about it. I hope you aren't *frozen* in that great draughty room . . .'

'A little bit. But I love it, it's a lovely room . . . But it would be worth it if it was twice as cold. It doesn't seem possible to say anything about the work yet. Later. I shall never forget reading these letters in that lovely room . . .'

Maud's bedroom – Mildred's old nursery – was at the opposite end of the long corridor that housed Roland's little guest bedroom and a majestic Gothic bathroom. No one explained who Mildred was or had been; her nursery had a beautifully carved stone fireplace, and deeply recessed windows in the same style. There was a high wooden bed with a rather bulky mattress of horsehair and ticking: Roland, coming in with his arms full of hot water bottles, was reminded as once before of the Real Princess and the pea. Sir George appeared with one of those circular copper dishes which contain a fat stamen of an electric fire, which he directed at the bed. Locked cupboards revealed blankets and a heap of 1930s children's dishes and toys, oilskin mats with Old King Cole on them, a nightlight with a butterfly, a heavy dish with an image of the Tower of London and a faded beefeater. Another cupboard revealed a library of Charlotte M. Yonge and Angela Brazil. Sir George, embarrassed, reappeared with a sugar-pink winceyette nightdress and a rather splendid peacock-blue kimono embroidered with a Chinese dragon and a flock of butterflies in silver and gold.

'My wife hopes you'll find these comfortable. Also I have a new toothbrush.'

'You are very kind. I feel so foolish,' said Maud.

'Another time might have been better with hindsight,' said Sir George. He called them, with pleasure, to the window.

'Look at it though. Look at the trees, and the weight of it on the wold.'

It was falling with great steadiness, through a still atmosphere; it was silent and swallowing; distinctions of ledges and contours were vanishing on the hills and the trees were heavy with capes and blankets glittering softly, curved and simple. Everything had closed in on the house in the hollow, which seemed to be filling. Urns on the lawn were white-crowned and slowly sinking, or so it seemed, in the deepening layers.

'You won't get out tomorrow, either,' he said. 'Not without a snow plough, which the Council may get round to sending if it lets up enough to make it worth it. Hope I've got enough dog food to go on with.'

In the afternoon they read steadily and with more surprise. They dined with the Baileys by the kitchen fire on pieces of frozen cod and chips and a rather good jam rolypoly pudding. They had agreed without real discussion to fend off questions about the letters for the time being. 'Well, are they worth anything, or nothing much in your view?' Sir George asked. Roland said he knew nothing about the value, but the letters had some interest certainly. Lady Bailey changed the subject to hunting, which she discussed with Maud and her husband, leaving Roland to an inner ear full of verbal ghosts and the rattle of his spoon.

★

They went upstairs early, leaving their hosts to their ground-floor domain, now patchily warm, unlike the great staircase and the long corridor where they were to sleep. Cold air seemed to pour down the stone steps like silky snow. The corridor was tiled, in peacock and bronze, depicting formal lilies and pomegranates now thickly softened with pale dust. Over these had been laid long, wrinkling, canvas-like carpets – 'drugget?' said Roland's word-obsessed mind, which had met this word in the poems of R. H. Ash where someone – an escaping priest – had 'tiptoed on drugget and scuttled on stone' before being surprised by the lady of the house. These runners were pale and yellowish; here and there, where a recent foot had slipped, they had wiped away the dust-veil from the gleam of the tiles.

At the top of the staircase Maud turned decisively to him and inclined her head with formality.

'Well, good night, then,' she said. Her fine mouth was set. Roland had vaguely supposed that they might, or should, discuss progress now they were together, compare notes and discoveries. It was almost an academic duty, though he was, in fact, tired, by emotion and the cold. Maud's arms were full of files, clasped against her like a breastplate. There was an automatic wariness in her look which he found offensive. He said, 'Good night, then,' and turned away towards his own end of the corridor. He heard her behind him tap away into the dark. The corridor was badly lit; there were what he assumed to be inoperative gas-mantels and two miserable 60-watt lights with saloon-bar coolie metal covers. It was then that he realised that he would have been glad to have discussed the bathroom with her. He assumed it would be polite to wait for her to go first. It was so cold in the corridor that he intensely disliked going up and down it – or standing about in it – in his pyjamas. He decided to give her a good three-quarters of an hour – plenty of time for any female ablutions that could take place in near-ice. In the interim he would read Randolph Henry Ash. He would read, not his notes on the letters, but the battle of Thor and the Frost Giants in *Ragnarök*. His room was bitterly cold. He made himself a nest of old eiderdowns and counterpanes, all covered with blue splashy roses, and sat down to wait.

*

When he came along the corridor in the silence, he thought he had been clever. The heavy, latched door was dark inside its stone arch. There was no sound of plashing or flushing. He was then seized with doubt as to whether the bathroom was in fact empty – how could any sound penetrate that solid oak? He did not want to rattle a locked door and embarrass both her and himself. So he went down on one knee on the putative drugget and put his eye to the huge keyhole which glinted at him and disconcertingly vanished as the door swung back and he smelled wet, freshness, steam in cold air. She nearly fell over him there; she put out a hand to steady herself on his shoulder and he threw up a hand and clasped a narrow haunch under the silk of the kimono.

And there it was, what Randolph Henry Ash had called the *kick galvanic*, the stunning blow like that emitted by the Moray eel from under its boulders to unsuspecting marine explorers. Roland got somehow on his feet, briefly clutching the silk and letting it go as though it stung. Her hands were pink and slightly damp; the fringes of the pale hair were damp too. It was down, he saw, the hair, running all over her shoulders and neck, swinging across her face, which he meekly supposed would be furious and saw, when he looked, was simply frightened. Did she simply *emit* the electric shock, he wondered, or did she also feel it? His body knew perfectly well that she felt it. He did not trust his body.

'I was looking if there was a light. So as not to disturb you if you were in there.'

'I see.'

The blue silk collar was dampish too. The whole thing appeared in this half-light to be running with water, all the runnels of silk twisted about her body by the fiercely efficient knot in which she had tied her sash. Below the silk hem were the ruffled mundane edge of pink winceyette and slippered sharp feet.

'I waited some time for *you* to use the bathroom,' she said, conciliatory.

'So did I.'

'No harm done,' she said.

'No.'

She held out her wet hand. He took it and felt its chill, and the subsidence of something.

'Good night, then,' she said.

'Good night.'

He went into the bathroom. Behind him, the long Chinese dragon wavered palely away, on its aquamarine ground, along the shifting carpets, and the pale hair gleamed coldly above it.

Inside the bathroom small patches of vapour clung to the basin, small traces of water, and one long wet footprint on the carpet inside showed she had been there. The bathroom was cavernous, built somehow under eaves, which sloped away, leaving a kind of bunker beneath them, in which were heaped maybe thirty or forty ewers and washbasins of an earlier day, dotted with crimson rosebuds, festooned with honeysuckle, splattered with huge bouquets of delphiniums and phlox. The bath stood monumental and deep in the very centre of the room, rising on clawed lion-feet, a kind of marbly sarcophagus, crowned with huge brass taps. It was far too cold to contemplate running water into this, which would in any case have taken forever to fill. Roland was sure that even the fastidious Maud would not have attempted it; to judge from her wet footprints on the cork bath mat she had washed thoroughly at the basin. The basin and the lavatory, which stood enthroned on its own pedestal at the dark end of the room, were English and floral and entranced Roland, whose experience had included nothing like them. Both were glazed and fired over a riotous abundance of English flowers whose tangled and rambling clusters and little intense patches seemed wholly random and natural, with no discernible repeating pattern. In the basin, as he filled it, under the hazy surface of the water, lay dog-roses, buttercups, poppies and harebells, a bank in reverse, resembling Titania's if not Charles Darwin's tangled bank. The lavatory was slightly more formalised than the washbasin – diminishing garlands and scattered nosegays swirled down its cascades over lines of maidenhair ferns. The seat was majestic, squared mahogany. It seemed sacrilegious to use anything so beautiful for its proper purpose. Roland assumed that Maud had seen such fittings before and was uninhibited by their splendour. He washed himself, rapid and trembling, above winking poppy-heads and blue cornflowers, and on the stained-glass window the ice crackled and set again. There was a gilt mirror over the washbasin in which he imagined Maud examining her perfection;

his own furry darkness was only a shadow on it. He was rather sorry for Maud. He had quite decided that she wouldn't have been able to see the romance of the bathroom as he could.

Back in his bedroom he looked out of the window into the night. Yesterday's dark enclosing trees were soft and shining white; across the space of his window snowflakes fell into the square of light and became visible. He should have shut his curtains against the cold but could not so much close out the strangeness outside. He put out the light and watched it all go grey – many greys, silver, pewter, lead – in the suddenly visible moonlight, in which the snowfall was both thicker, more animated and slower. He put on his sweater and socks and climbed into his narrow bed and curled himself into a ball as he had done last night. The snow fell. He woke in the small hours from a dream of great violence and beauty which went back in part to his primitive infant fear of something coming up the lavatory bend and striking at him. In his dream he was hopelessly entwined and entangled with an apparently endless twisted rope of bright cloth and running water, decorated with wreaths and garlands and tossed sprays of every kind of flower, real and artificial, embroidered or painted, under which something clutched or evaded, reached out or slid away. When he touched it, it was not there; when he tried to lift an arm or a leg it prevented him, gripping, coiling. He had the microscopic eye of the dreamer of great dreams; he could linger over a cornflower or inspect a dog-rose or lose his sense of shape in the intricacies of a maidenhair fern. The thing smelled dank in his dream and yet also rich and warm, a smell of hay and honey and the promise of summer. Something struggled to get out, and as he moved across the floor of the room he was dreaming, its ever more intricate train flowed after it, impeding yet increasing its length and circling folds. His mind said, 'It is wringing wet' in his mother's voice, censorious yet concerned for it, and noted that 'wringing' appeared to be a pun; it appeared to be wringing its veiled hands as it struggled with its wrappings. His mind said a line of poetry – 'Despite the snow, despite the falling snow' – and his whole soul was distressed not to be able to remember the great importance of that line, which he had heard, where? when?

CHAPTER NINE

The Threshold

The old woman bade the Childe farewell, courteously enough, if curtly, and set him on his way to the frontier, telling him to keep boldly on along the track, deviating neither to right nor left, though creatures might call and beckon to him enticingly, and wonderful lights might be seen from time to time, for this was enchanted country. He might see meadows or fountains, but he must keep his stony way, she told him, apparently with no great faith in his strength of purpose. But the Childe said he wished to come to the place his father had told him of, and that he wished to be faithful and true in all things and that she need not fear. 'As to that,' said the crone, 'it is all one to me whether the whiteladies pick your fingers or whether the sluggish goblins of the grimpen dispute your little toes between them. I have lived too long to care much for the outcome of one quest or another: cleaned white bones are as good as a burnished princeling in a mailcoat to my old eyes. If you come you will come; if not, I shall see the whiteladies' flickering fire on the heath.' 'I thank you nevertheless for your courtesy,' said the punctilious Childe, to which she said, 'Courtesy is too fine a name for it. Be off with you before I fall into a teasing frame of mind.' He did not like to think how that frame of mind might be, so he pricked his good horse with his spurs and rode out onto the stony track with a clatter.

He had a thwarting day of it. The heath and moor were criss-crossed with little tracks, dusty and twisting between the heather and the bracken and the little juniper trees with their clinging roots. There was not one way but many, all athwart each other like the cracks on a crazy jug, and he followed first one and then the other, choosing the straightest and stoniest and finding himself always under the hot-sun at another crossing just like the one he had just left. After a time he decided to go with the sun behind him always – at least this led to consistency of proceeding – though it must be told that when he decided this he had only the haziest idea, dear readers, of where the sun had been at the beginning of the venture. So it often is in this life. We become consistent and orderly too late, on insufficient grounds, and perhaps in the wrong direction. So it was with the poor Childe, for at dusk he found himself apparently back at the place where he had set out from. He had seen neither whiteladies nor grimpen goblins, though he had heard singing at the end of straight sandy paths he had avoided, and had seen creatures crash and spring briefly far away in seas of bracken and moorland herbs. He thought he recognised the twisted thorn trees, and might indeed have done so; there they stood in their triangle, as they had done at dawn; but of the old crone's little hut there was no sign. The sun was going down fast, over the edge of the plain; he pricked forward a little, hoping he might be mistaken, and saw before him, a little on his way, an avenue of standing stones, which he had no memory of seeing before, though they were, to say the least of it, hard to miss, even in the greying light. At the end of the avenue was a building, or structure, with huge gateposts and a heavy roofing stone and a stone to mark a threshold. And beyond, the growing dark. And out of this dark, towards him, stepped three most beautiful ladies, walking proudly between the stones, and each bearing before her on a silken cushion a square casket. And he marvelled much that even in the gloaming he had not been aware of their coming, and was wary of them, for he said to himself in his mind, 'It may be that these are the bonecracking whiteladies of whom the old woman spoke so lightly, come to turn me from my path as the light of the world fails.' Certainly they were creatures of the evening for each seemed to create her own light as she walked, a haze of shimmering, and glittering and fluctuating light, most lovely to behold.

And the first came in a golden glow, putting out gold-slippered feet from under a dress rich and stiff with cloth of gold and all manner of silk embroidery. And the cushion she bore was tissue of gold and the chased box shone like the vanishing sun herself with rich gold chasing and fretwork.

The second was bright with silver like the light of the moon, and her slippered feet were like slivers of moonlight, and all over the silvery gown shone crescents and luminous rounds of argent light, and she was bathed in a cool but intense brilliance, which most beautifully embellished the polished surface of the silver casket she bore on cloth of silver, with its threads like needles of pure white light.

And the third was dull behind these two, and had a subdued lustre, like that of armour burnished and used, like that of the undersides of high clouds hiding the true light that suffuses their steely grey with a borrowed brilliance. Her dress was alive with slow lights like still water under the stars but in the shadow of great trees, and her slippered feet were softly velvet, and her hair, unlike that of the others, was caught back under a masking veil. And the first two smiled at the Childe as they came out of the stone shadows in their brilliant pools of glimmering light. Only the third cast down her eyes, modestly, and he could see that her lips were pale, and that her eyelids were heavy and smoky dark and threaded with violet veinings and her lashes were like the feathery plumes of moths on her colourless cheeks.

And they spoke to him, it seemed, with one voice, which had in it three tones, a clear clarion, a reedy oboe, a whispering low flute.

'You may go no further this way,' said they, 'for this is the edge of things, here, and beyond is another country. But you may choose, if you will, one of us to be your guide, and venture further. Or you may turn back if you will, without dishonour, and trust yourself again to the plain.'

And he answered them courteously that they should speak on, for he had not come so far and so wearily simply in order to turn back. Moreover he was charged by his father with a mission, which he might not reveal in that place. 'It is known to us already,' said the three damsels. 'We have waited long for you.'

'How am I to know, then,' asked the Childe, greatly daring, and in tones of the most humble respect, 'that you are not those whiteladies of whom they speak with such fear and honour in the villages I have come through?'

Then they laughed, high, low, clear and whispering, and said they doubted much whether honour was so very apparent when those were spoken of; however there was much superstition and misbelief, as to the whiteladies, among the common people, to which he should perhaps not give too much credence.

'As for ourselves,' said they, 'you must take us as you find us, and judge of us as you see us, what we are, or what we may be to you, as all men must, who have a high courage and a clear vision.'

Then said he, not knowing before he spoke that he had made up his mind to venture, but as if some voice spoke through him,

'I will assay.'

'Choose now,' they said then, 'and choose wisely, for extremes of bliss and misery stand in your choice.'

Then passed they before him, each in her turn, each in her own little cage of light, as though, it might be, she were a candle and cast the beams of her glory a little distance, through the walls of a lanthorn. And as they passed, each sang, and to her song unseen instruments twangled and made delicious moan. And the last rays of the bloody sun showed the standing stones grey on a grey heaven.

First came the gold lady, stepping proudly, and on her head a queenly crown of gold, a filigree turret of lambent sunny gleams and glistering wires above crisping gold curls as heavy with riches as the golden fleece itself. She held out her gold box bravely before her and it struck out such rays that his eyes were briefly dazzled with it and he was forced to look down at the grey heather.

And she sang:

> Mine the bright earth
> Mine the corn
> Mine the gold throne
> To which you're born
> Lie in my lap
> Tumbled with flowers
> And reign over
> Earth's tall towers

And he could have stretched out his hands and warmed them, in that cold gloaming, at all the fire and brilliance that shook from her as she passed. And he thought she offered happiness, but said, natheless,

'I shall see all, before I speak.'

Then came the silver lady, with a white crescent burning palely on her pale brow, and she was all hung about with spangled silver veiling that kept up a perpetual shimmering motion around her, so that she seemed a walking fountain, or an orchard of blossom in moonlight, which might in the day have been ruddy and hot for bee kisses, but at night lies open, all white to the cool, secret light that blesses it without withering or ripening.

And she sang:

> Mine the long night
> The secret place
> Where lovers meet
> In long embrace
> In purple dark
> In silvered kiss
> Forget the world
> And grasp your bliss

And he thought she knew his secret soul, and would have stretched out his arms to her in longing, for she made him see in his mind's eye a closed casement in a high turret, and a private curtained bed where he would be most himself. For it was himself, surely, she offered him, as the other offered the sunlit earth. And he turned from the gold lady and would have taken the silver, but caution, or curiosity, restrained him, for he thought he would still see what the dim last might offer, compared to her two sweet sisters.

And she came, almost creeping, not dancing nor striding, but moving imperceptibly like a shadow across his vision, in a still pool of soft light. And her garments did not sparkle or glitter but hung all in long pale folds, fluted like carved marble, with deep violet shadows, at the heart of which, too, was soft light. And her face was cast down in shadows, for she looked not at him, but at the dull lead casket, as pale as might be, and seemingly without hinge or keyhole, that lay cradled before her. And around her brow was a coronet of white poppies and on her feet were silent silken slippers like spider webs, and her music was single, a piping not of this earth, not merry, not sad, but calling, calling.

And she sang:

> Not in the flesh
> Not in the fire
> Not in action
> Is heart's desire
> But come away
> For last is best
> I alone tender
> The Herb of Rest

And then the heart of the Childe was wrung indeed, for it was the Herb of Rest which his father so desired him to bring home, to end, as only that might, his long agony. And the Childe's heart rebelled a little, for he was loth to abandon the rich brightness of the golden dame, or the lovely clarity of the silver one, for the softness and quiet and downcast eyes of this half-invisible third. And you know, and I know, do we not, dear children, that he must always choose this last, and the leaden casket, for wisdom in all tales tells us this, and the last sister is always the true choice, is she not? But let us have a moment's true sorrow for the silver blisses the Childe would have preferred, and the sunlit flowery earth which is my own secret preference, and then let us decorously follow as we must, as he takes up the soft hand of the third, as his fate and the will of his father decree, and says, half-musing, 'I will come with you.'

And one day we will write it otherwise, that he would not come, that he stayed, or chose the sparkling ones, or went out again onto the moors to live free of fate, if such can be. But you must know now, that it turned out as it must turn out, must you not? Such is the power of necessity in tales.

Well, she took his hand softly, and the touch of her cool fingers was the kiss of moths, or cool linen after a hard day's work, and she turned her face towards him and lifted up those eyelids and looked at him and then he saw her eyes. What can I say of her eyes, save that he looked into them and was lost and no more saw the heath, nor the other two bright creatures turning and turning in their cages of light, nor yet his own trusty steed who had come with him prancing and saddle-sore to the known world's end? If I were to attempt this description – but no, I cannot – yet I must, for I am your chronicler, bound to recount to you, what? Imagine then twin pools at midnight, lit by no external shining, but from deep within, some glimmer, some promise, lucid through sloe-black deep after deep after deep. Imagine then, when she turned her head slightly, a black not after all bluish, like those black plums, but very faintly brown, the slightly hot black of panther-skin, still, waiting, out of the gleam of the moon.

'I will come with you,' said the Childe, a second time, and she said softly enough, inclining her head in what might have been a dutiful way, 'Come then.'

And she drew him on, over and under the threshold of the standing stones, and his horse called out in alarm, but he stepped on unhearing. And although the stones seemed simple enough in the midst of the moor, which seemed vaguely to stretch on behind as it had before, he found it was no such thing, for beyond the lintel was a descending track, winding and winding, between banks of sweetly scented flowers he had never seen or dreamed of, blowing soft dust at him from their huge throats, and lit by a light neither of day nor of night, neither of sun nor of moon, neither bright nor shadowy, but the even perpetual unchanging light of that kingdom . . .

Christabel LaMotte

CHAPTER TEN

The Correspondence

Dear Miss LaMotte,

I do not know whether to be more encouraged or cast down by your letter.
The essential point in it is 'if you care to write again', for by that permission
you encourage me more than by your wish not to be ·seen – which I must
respect – you cast me down. And you send a poem, and observe wisely that
poems are worth all the cucumber-sandwiches in the world. So they are indeed –
and yours most particularly – but you may imagine the perversity of the poetic
imagination and its desire to feed on imagined cucumber-sandwiches, which,
since they are positively not to be had, it pictures to itself as a form of English
manna – oh the perfect green circles – oh the delicate hint of salt – oh the
fresh pale butter – oh, above all, the soft white crumbs and golden crust of the
new bread – and thus, as in all aspects of life, the indefatigable fancy idealises
what could be snapped up and swallowed in a moment's restrained greed, in
sober fact.

But you must know that I am happy to forgo the sandwiches, dreamed or
soberly chewed, for your delightful poem – which as you say, has a note of
savagery proper to the habits of true spiders as they have lately been observed.
Do you wish to extend your metaphor of entrapment or enticement to Art? I
have read other of your poems of Insect Life, and marvelled at the way they
combined the brilliance and fragility of those winged things – or creeping –
with something too of the biting and snapping and devouring that may be seen
under a microscope. It would be a brave poet indeed who would undertake a
true description of the Queen Bee – or Wasp – or Ant – as we now know
them to be – having for centuries supposed these centres of communal worship
and activity to be Male Rulers – I somehow imagine you do not share your

Sex's revulsion at such life-forms — or what I imagine to be a common revulsion —

I have in my head a kind of project of a long poem on insect life of my own. Not lyric, like yours, but a dramatised monologue such as those I have already written on Mesmer or Alexander Selkirk or Neighbour Pliable — I do not know if you know these poems and shall be glad to send them to you if you do not. I find I am at ease with other imagined minds — bringing to life, restoring in some sense to vitality, the whole vanished men of other times, hair, teeth, fingernails, porringer, bench, wineskin, church, temple, synagogue and the incessant weaving labour of the marvellous brain inside the skull — making its patterns, its most particular sense of what it sees and learns and believes. It seems important that these other lives of mine should span many centuries and as many places as my limited imagination can touch. For all I am is a nineteenth-century gentleman plumb in the midst of smoky London — and what is peculiar to him is to know just how much stretches away from his vanishing pin-point of observation — before and around and after — whilst all the time he is what he is, with his whiskered visage and his shelves full of Plato and Feuerbach, St Augustine and John Stuart Mill.

I run on, and have not communicated to you the subject of my insect-poem, which is to be the short and miraculous — and on the whole tragic — life of Swammerdam, who discovered in Holland the optic glass which revealed to us the endless reaches and ceaseless turmoil of the infinitely small just as the great Galileo turned his optic tube on the majestic motions of the planets and beyond them the silent spheres of the infinitely great. Are you acquainted with his story? May I send you my version when I have worked it out? If it comes to good? (As I know it will for it is so full of tiny particular facts and objects in the observation of which the animation of the human mind inheres — and you will ask — my mind or his? — and I do not know, to tell the truth. He invented marvellous tiny instruments for peering and prying into the essence of insect life, and all made of fine ivory, as less destructive and harmful than harsh metal — Lilliputian needles he made, before Lilliput was thought of — faery needles. And I have merely words — and the dead husks of other men's words — but I shall bring it off — you need not believe me yet, but you shall see.)

Now — you say I may have an essay on the Everlasting Nay — or on Schleiermacher's Veil of Illusion or the Milk of Paradise — or what I will. What prodigality — how am I to chuse? I think I will not have the Everlasting Nay, but remain still in hope of eventual cool green circles — to go with the milk of Paradise and a modicum of Bohea — and I want from you not illusion *but truth. So perhaps you will tell me more about your Fairy Project — if it may be spoken of without hurting your thinking — There are times when to speak — or to write — is helpful, and times when it is most nugatory — if you would rather not pursue our conversation I shall understand. But I hope for a letter in answer to all my rambling nonsense — which I hope has given no offence to one I hope to know better*

Yours very truly
R. H. Ash

Dear Mr Ash,

I am ashamed to think that what you may reasonably have taken for coyness — or even churlishness — in myself should have produced such a generous and sparkling mixture of wit and information from you. Thank you. If all persons to whom I refused mere vegetable aliment were so to regale me with intellectual nourishment I should remain obdurate in the matter of sandwiches till all eternity — but most petitioners are content with one denial — And that is truly for the best, for we live so very quietly, we two solitary ladies, and run our little household — we have our sweet daily rhythms which are not disturbed, and our circumscribed little independence — on account of being wholly unremarkable — your delicacy will see how it is — I speak soberly for once — we neither call nor receive callers — we met, you and I, because Crabb Robinson was a friend of my dear father — as whose friend was he not? I did not feel it in my power to refuse a request in that name — and yet I was sorry — for I do not go out into society — the lady protests too much, you will say — but she was moved by your green circular visions of contentment, and did wish, briefly, that it was in her power to give a more satisfactory answer. But it would have been regretted, it would — not only by me, but also by yourself.

I was greatly flattered by your good opinion of my little poem. I am uncertain as to how to answer your question on entrapment or enticement as qualities of Art — of Ariachne's art they may be — and by extension of merely fragile or glistening female productions — but not surely of your own great works. I was quite shocked that you might suppose I did not know the Poem on Mesmer — or that on Selkirk on his terrible island, face to face with an unrelenting Sun and an apparently unresponsive Creator — or that too on Neighbour Pliable, and his religious versatility or tergiversations. I should have told a small Fib — and said I knew them not — for the grace of receiving them at their Author's hands — but one must keep truth — in small things as in great — and this was no small thing. You are to know that we have all your volumes, ranged forbiddingly side by side — and that they are often opened and often discussed in this little house as in the great world. You are to know too — or maybe you are not — how should I say this, to you with whom my acquaintance is so recent — and yet if not to you, to whom — and I have just written, one must keep truth, and this is so central a truth — you are to know then, after all, for I must take my courage in my hands — that your great poem Ragnarök was the occasion of quite the worst crisis in the life of my simple religious faith, that I have ever experienced, or hope to experience. It was not that anywhere in that poem you attacked the Christian religion — which indeed was not made mention of with complete Poetic Propriety — and moreover you speak never, in your poetry, with your own voice, or from your own heart directly. (That you question is clear — the creator of Pliable, of Lazarus, of the heretic Pelagius is as wise as the serpent about all the most subtle and searching questionings and probings of the Grounds of our Belief that in our time have been most persistently and unremittingly explored. You know the 'ambages and sinuosities' of the Critical Philosophy, as your Augustine says of your Pelage — for whom I have a weakness, for was he not a Breton, as I in part am, and did he not wish sinful men and women to be nobler and freer than they were? ...) I digress wildly from Ragnarök and its pagan Day of Judgment and its pagan interpretation of the mystery of the Resurrection, and the New Heaven and the New Earth. It seemed to me you were saying 'Such Tales men tell and have told — they do not differ, save in emphasis, here and there.' Or even 'Men tell what they Desire shall be or might be, not what it is divinely, transcendently decreed Must Be and Is.' It seemed to me you made Holy Scripture no more than another Wonder Tale — by dint of such writing, such force of imagining. I confuse myself, I shall not go on, I ask your pardon if what I have said appears incomprehensible to you. I doubted and I admitted Doubts I have had to live with since. Enough of that.

I did not mean to write all this. Can you doubt that I shall be delighted to receive your Swammerdam — if, as you come to the end of it, you should still have an inclination to make a copy and send it here. — I cannot promise intelligent criticism — but you cannot be in need of that — a receptive and a Thoughtful reading you are assured of. I was most interested in what you tell me of his discovery of the microscope — and his ivory needles for examining the minuter Forms of Life. We in this house have done a little work with microscopes and glasses — but We have a very womanly reluctance to take life — you will find no pinned and chloroformed collection Here — only a few upturned Jars housing temporary guests — a large House-spider — and a Moth in chrysalis form — a voracious Worm with many legs which we have been wholly unable to identify and which is Possessed of a Restless Demon — or hatred of Jar-panopticons.

I send two more Poems. They form part of a series on Psyche — in modern form — that poor doubting Girl — who took Heavenly Love for a Serpent.

I have not answered yr question about my Fairy Poem. I am deeply flattered — and no less deeply alarmed — that you remember it so — for I spoke — or affected to speak — idly on the matter, as about something which might be pleasant to Toy with — or pretty to investigate — one of these unoccupied days —

Whereas in verity — I have it in my head to write an epic — or if not an epic, still a Saga or Lay or great mythical Poem — and how can a poor breathless woman with no staying-power and only a Lunar Learning confess such an ambition to the author of the Ragnarök? But I have the most curious certainty that you are to be trusted in this matter — that you will not mock — nor deluge the fairy of the fountain with Cold Water.

Enough. The Poems are enclosed. I have many more on the subject of metamorphosis — one of the problems of our time — and all Times, rightly known. Dear Sir — forgive my excited prolixity — and send, when you may, if you will, your Swammerdam to edify

Your sincere well-wisher
C. LaMotte.

[*Enclosed*]

Metamorphosis

Does the ruffled Silken Flyer
Pause to recall how She — began —
Her soft cramped crawling Origins —
               Does man
In all his puffed and sparking Glory
Cast back a Thought
To the Speck of Flesh the Story
Began with, from Naught?

But both, in their Creator's terrible keen sight
Lay curled and known through timeless Day and Night
He Form and Life at once and always — Gave
Is still their Animator and their Grave —

Psyche

In ancient Tales — the Creatures — helpful were
To taxed and fearful Humans in despair.
The World was One for those Men, which now is
A dissonant Congeries.

The Nation of the Spinster Ants
Their help to sorrowing *Psyche* brought
Whom cruel *Venus* set to sort
The mingled grains and seeds of plants.

They brought their feeling Sympathy
To human Task and Trouble.
They brought their Social Huswifery
To Venus – taunting – Muddle –
They sorted – cleaned – and ordered
What lay in – feckless – Heap
That Psyche – all incapable –
Her tryst – with Love – might keep.

Think not – that Man's Approval
Anticipated Kiss
Is Guerdon of our Merit
Or Order's Warrant – Is

The Ants toil for no Master
Sufficient to their Need
The daily commerce of the Nest
The storage of their Seed
They meet – and exchange Messages –
But none to none – bows down
They – like God's thoughts – speak each to each –
Without – external – crown

Dear Miss LaMotte,

How generous of you, after all, to write so promptly and so fully. I hope my answer is not too precipitate – I would not for the world, harass you importunately – but there was so much of interest in what you said that I should like to set my thoughts down whilst they are fresh and clear. Your poems are delightful and original – if we were face to face I should hazard a guess or two at the deeper reaches of riddling allegory in the Psyche – which I have not the courage or effrontery to set down in black and white. You begin so meekly, with your cast-down princess and useful creatures – and end quite the opposite, with a moral dispensation – from what? is the difficulty – from monarchy – or the Love of Man – or Eros as opposed to Agape – or the malignity of Venus? Is the social affection of the anthill truly a better thing than the love of men and women? Well, you are to be the judge – the poem is yours and a fine one – and there is enough evidence in human history of topless towers set on fire for a passionate whim – or poor souls enslaved by loveless unions imposed by parental will and the dictates of lineage – or friends slaying each other – Eros is a bad and fickle little godhead – and I have quite talked myself round to your way of thinking, Miss LaMotte, without still wholly knowing what that is.

Now I have given your poems the priority which is their due, I must tell you that I have been in some distress to think that my poem had occasioned doubt in you. A secure faith – a true prayerfulness – is a beautiful and a true thing – however we must nowadays construe it – and not to be disturbed by the meanderings and queryings of the finite brain of R. H. Ash or any other puzzled student of our Century. Ragnarök was written in all honesty in the days when I did not myself question Biblical certainties – or the faith handed down by my fathers and theirs before them. It was read differently by some – the lady who was to become my wife was included in these readers – and I was at the time startled and surprised that my Poem should have been construed as any kind of infidelity – for I meant it rather as a reassertion of the Universal Truth of the living presence of Allfather (under whatever Name) and of the hope of Resurrection from whatever whelming disaster in whatever form. When Odin, disguised as the Wanderer, Gangrader, in my Poem, asks the Giant Wafthrudnir what was the word whispered by the Father of the gods in the ear of his dead son, Baldur on his funeral pyre – the young man I was – most devoutly – meant the word to be – Resurrection. And he, that young poet, who is and is not myself, saw no difficulty in supposing that the dead Norse God of Light might prefigure – or figure – the dead Son of the God Who is the Father of Christendom. But, as you perceived, this is a two-handed engine, a slicing weapon that cuts both ways, this of figuration – to say that the Truth of the Tale is in the meaning, that the Tale but symbolises an eternal verity, is one step on the road to the parity of all tales ... And the existence of the same Truths in all Religions is a great argument both for and against the paramount Truthfulness of One.

Now – I must make confession. I have written and destroyed an earlier answer to your letter in which – not disingenuously – I urged you to hold fast by your faith – not to involve yourself in the 'ambages and sinuosities' of the Critical Philosophy – and wrote, what may not be nonsense, that women's minds, more intuitive and purer and less beset with torsions and stresses than those of mere males – may hold on to truths securely that we men may lose by much questioning, much of that mechanical futility; 'A man may be in as just possession of truth as of a City, and yet be forced to surrender it' – this was the wise saying of Sir Thomas Browne — and I would not be instrumental in demanding the keys of that city from you in pursuit of a false claim.

But I thought — and I was right in thinking, was I not? — that you would not be best pleased to be exempted from argument by an appeal to your superior Intuition and an abandoning of the field by me?

I do not know why — or how — but I do know wholeheartedly that it is so — so I cannot prevaricate with you, and worse, cannot leave decently undiscussed matters of such import. So you will have remarked — you so sharply intelligent — that I have nowhere in this letter claimed that I now hold the simple or innocent views of the young Poet of Ragnarök. And if I tell you what views I do hold — what you will think of me? Will you continue to communicate your thoughts to me? I do not know — I only know that I am under some compulsion of truthfulness.

I am not become any kind of an Atheist, nor yet positivist, at least, not as to the extreme religious position of those who make a religion out of Humanity — for although I wish my fellow men well, and find them endlessly interesting, yet there are more things in Heaven and Earth than were created for their, that is our, benefit. The impulses to religion might be the need to trust — or the capacity for wonder — and my own religious feelings have always been inspired more by the latter. I find it hard to shift without the Creator — the more we see and understand, the more amazement there is in this strangely interrelated Heap of things — which is yet not disordered. But I go too fast. And I cannot, I must not, burden you with a complete confession of what are in any case a very confused, very incoherent, indeed inchoate set of ideas, perceptions, half-truths, useful fictions, struggled for and not possessed.

The truth is — my dear Miss LaMotte — that we live in an old world — a tired world — a world that has gone on piling up speculation and observations until truths that might have been graspable in the bright Dayspring of human morning — by the young Plotinus or the ecstatic John on Patmos — are now obscured by palimpsest on palimpsest, by thick horny growths over that clear vision — as moulting serpents, before they burst forth with their new flexible-brilliant skins, are blinded by the crusts of their old one — or, we might say, as the lovely lines of faith that sprung up in the aspiring towers of the ancient minsters and abbeys are both worn away by time and grime, softly shrouded by the smutty accretions of our industrial cities, our wealth, our discoveries themselves, our Progress. Now, I cannot believe, being no Manichee, that He, the Creator, if he exists, did not make us and our world that which we are. He made us curious, did he not? — he made us questioning — and the Scribe of Genesis did well to locate the source of all our misery in that greed *for knowledge which has also been our greatest spur – in some sense – to good. To good and evil. We have more of both those, I must believe, than our primitive parents.*

Now, my great question is, has He withdrawn Himself from our vision so that by diligence of our own matured minds we might find out His Ways – now so far away from us – or have we by sin, or by some necessary thickening of our skins before the new stages of the metamorphosis – have we reached some stage which necessitates our consciousness of our ignorance and distance – and is this necessity health or sickness?

I was in Ragnarök – where Odin, the Almighty, becomes a mere wandering Questioner in Middle-Earth – and is necessarily destroyed with all his works on the last battlefield at the end of the last terrible Winter – I was feeling towards some such question – unknowing –

And then there is the whole question of what kind of Truth may be conveyed in a wonder-tale, as you rightly named it – but I trespass terribly on your patience – which may by now be at an end with me – I may have put myself beyond the pale of your keen and discerning attention –

And I have not answered what you said of your Epic. Well – if you still care for my views – as why should you? You are a Poet and in the end must care only for your own views – why not an Epic? Why not a mythic drama in twelve books? I can see no reason in Nature why a woman might not write such a poem as well as a man – if she but set her mind to it.

Does this sound brusque? It is because it distresses me that you should even – with your gifts – suppose an apology of any kind was needed for the Project –

I am very well aware that an Apology is needed for my tone throughout this letter, which I shall not re-read, for it is out of my power to recast it again. So it comes to you rough, unhouseled, unannealed – and I shall wait – resigned but anxious – to see if you feel any response is possible –

Yours,
R. H. Ash

Dear Mr Ash,

If I held Silence – too long – forgive me. I deliberated indeed not whether but what – I might Reply – since you do me the honour – I had almost writ, the painful honour – but indeed it is not – that is not so – of trusting me with your true opinions. I am no Miss in an evangelical novel to fly into a fine frenzy of – elevated – Rebuff or Rebuttal at expressions of honest doubt – and am partially in accord with you – Doubt, doubt is endemic to our life in this world at this time. I do not Dispute your vision of our historical Situation –

we are far from the Source of Light – and we know Things – that make a Simple Faith – hard to hold, hard to grasp, hard to wrestle.

You write much – of the Creator – whom you do not name Father – save in yr Norse analogy. But of the true tale of the Son you say wondrous little – and yet that lies at the Centre of our living faith – the Life and Death of God made man, our true Friend and Saviour, the model of our conduct, and our hope, in his Rising from the Dead, of a future life for all of us, without which the failing and manifest injustice of our earthly span would be an intolerable mockery. But I write – like a Sermon-Preacher – which we Women are not – it is Decreed – fitted to be – and tell you no more than you must have endlessly – in your wisdom – already cogitated.

And yet – could we have conceived that Sublime Model, that Supreme Sacrifice – if it were not so?

I could adduce against you – the Evidence of your own Lazarus-poem – whose riddling title you must some day expound to me in its mystery. Déjà-vu or the Second Sight – indeed. How are we to take that? My friend – my companion and I have lately become interested in psychic phenomena – we have attended some local lectures on unusual States of Mind – and Spirit manifestations – we have even been bold enough to sit in at a seance conducted by a Mrs Lees – Now Mrs Lees is convinced that the phenomena of Déjà-Vu – whereby the experient is convinced that a present experience is only a Repetition of what has already, perhaps frequently – been lived through before – is Evidence of some circularity of inhuman time – of Another Adjacent World where things eternally are with no change or decay. And that the well-attested Phenomena of Second Sight – the gift of pre-Vision, or foretelling or prophecy – is another Dipping into that forever refreshed Continuum. So – in this view yr poem wd seem to be suggesting that dead Lazarus moved in and out of Eternity again – 'from Time to Time' as you wrote in that poem – if I understand you – and now sees Time – from the perspective of Eternity. It is a conceit worthy of you – and now I come to know you better – his risen vision of the miraculous Nature of the Minute Particulars of Life – the Goat's yellow barred Eye – the bread on the Platter with the scaly Fishes waiting for the oven – all these are to you the essence of living, – and it is only to your perplexed narrator that the living-dead man's gaze appears Indifferent – for truly he sees all to have value – All –

Before I met Mrs Lees – I took your Second Sight more generally – as a Prefiguring of that Second Coming we await – little grains of sand shall be sifted and counted, as the hairs on our heads, in the eye of the dead man –

The Son of God speaks not in your poem. But the Roman Scribe who tells the tale – he the census-taker, the collector of minor facts – is he not amazed despite his own inclinations – despite his Prosaic mental habits of officialdom – by the effect of the presence of the Man on that small community of believers – who are cheerfully ready to Die for Him – and as ready to live in penury – 'tis all one to thee' he writes, puzzled – but we are not puzzled – for He has oped to them the Door of Eternity and they have glimpsed the light within – that illuminates the loaves and fishes – is not that so?

Or am I too Simple? Was He – so loved, so absent, so cruelly dead – merely Man?

You have most dramatically presented the Love of Him, – the Need of his Comfort – now Absent – among the women of Lazarus' household – the ceaselessly active Martha and the visionary Mary, each in her way aware of what His Presence once meant – though Martha sees it as household decorum – and Mary sees it as Lost Light – and Lazarus sees – only what he sees – momently –

Oh what a puzzle. Now I come to the end of my clumsy apprentice adumbration of your masterly monologue – have I described the liveliness of Living Truth – or the dramatisation merely – of faith – of Need?

Will you say what you mean? Are you like the Apostle, all things to all men? Where – where have I led – myself?

Tell me – He Lives – for you

Well, my dear Miss Lamotte, I am tied to the stake and I must stay the course – though in other respects dissimilar enough from Macbeth. I was first relieved to have your letter, and to see that I was not judged excommunicado – and then, on better judgment making, I weighed it for some time, turning it this way and that in case it should after all speak Brimstone and Ashes to me.

And when I came to open it, there was such generosity of spirit, such fervent faith and such subtlety of understanding of what I had written – I mean not only my dubious letter, but my poem on Lazarus. You know how it is, being yourself a poet – one writes such and such a narrative, and thinks as one goes along – here's a good touch – this concept modifies that – will it not be too obvious to the generality? – too thick an impasto of the Obvious – one has almost a disgust at the too-apparent meaning – and then the general public gets hold of it, and pronounces it at the same time too heartily simple and too loftily incomprehensible – and it is clear only that whatever one had hoped to convey is lost in mists of impenetrability – and slowly it loses its life – in one's own mind, as much as in its readers'.

And then you come along – with a dash of apparently effortless and casual wisdom – and resuscitate the whole thing – even to your own doubtful question at the end – did He do this – did Lazarus live – did He, the God-man, truly resurrect the dead before Himself triumphing over Death – or was it all only the product, as Feuerbach believes, of human Desire embodying itself in a Tale –?

You ask me – tell me – He Lives – for you –

Lives – yes – but How? How? Do I truly believe that this Man stept into the charnel house where Lazarus was already corrupt and bade him stand and walk?

Do I truly believe that all this is only figments of hopes and dreams and garbled folklore, embellished for the credulous by simple people?

We live in an age of scientific history – we sift our evidence – we know somewhat about eyewitness accounts and how far it is prudent to entrust ourselves to them – and of what this living-dead-man (I speak of Lazarus, not of his Saviour) saw, or reported or thought, or assured his loving family of what lay beyond the terrible bourn – not a word.

So if I construct a fictive eye-witness account – a credible plausible account – am I lending life to truth with my fiction – or verisimilitude to a colossal Lie with my feverish imagination? Do I do as they did, the evangelists, reconstructing the events of the Story in after-time? Or do I do as false prophets do and puff air into simulacra? Am I a Sorcerer – like Macbeth's witches – mixing truth and lies in incandescent shapes? Or am I a kind of very minor scribe of a prophetic Book – telling such truth as in me lies, with aid of such fiction as I acknowledge mine, as Prospero acknowledged Caliban – I nowhere claim my poor bullet-headed brute of a Roman censor as other than mine, a clay mouth to whistle through.

No answer, you will say, your head on one side, considering me, like a wise bird, sharply, and judging me as a prevaricator.

Do you know – the only life I am sure of is the life of the Imagination. Whatever the absolute Truth – or Untruth — of that old life-in-death — Poetry can make that man live for the length of the faith you or any other choose to give to him. I do not claim to bestow Life as He did – on Lazarus – but maybe as Elisha did – who lay on the dead body – and breathed life into it –

Or as the Poet of the Gospel did — for he was Poet, whatever else — Poet, whether scientific historian or no.

Do you touch at my meaning? When I write I know. Remember that miraculous saying of the boy Keats – I am certain of nothing, but the holiness of the Heart's affections and the truth of Imagination –

Now I am not saying — Beauty is Truth, Truth Beauty, or any such quibble. I am saying that without the Maker's imagination nothing can live for us — whether alive or dead, or once alive and now dead, or waiting to be brought to life —

Oh, I have tried to tell you my truth — and have written only dreary quibbles about poetry. But you know – I do believe you know –

Tell me you know — and that it is not simple – or simply to be rejected — there is a truth of Imagination.

Dear Mr Ash,

MacBeth was a Sorcerer – had he not born of woman not put an end to him – with his sharp sword – think you not that good King James – with his pious Daemonologie – would not have desiderated his Burning?

Yet in our time you may sit quietly there and plead – oh but I am a mere poet – if I urge that we receive Truth only through the Life – or Liveliness of Lies – there's no harm in that – since we all take in both with our mother-milk – Indissoluble – it is the human case –

He said – I am the Truth and the Life – what of that, Sir? Was that an approximate statement? Or a Poetic adumbration? Well – was it? It rings – through eternity – I AM –

Not that I will not grant you – now I climb down from my preaching-place, my unattainable pulpit – that there are Truths of your sort. Who that judges does not know – that Lear's agony — and the Duke of Gloster's pain — are true – tho' those men never lived – or never lived so – you will tell me that they lived indeed in some sort – and that he – W.S. – sage sorcerer prophet – brought them again to huge Life – so much so that no Actor – could do his part therein, but must leave it to the studium of you and me to flesh it out.

But what a Poet might be in those days of Giants, which were also the days of the aforesaid King James and his Daemonologie – and not only of his Daemonologie – but of his commissioning of the Word of God in English – so writ then to aftertime that every word of it rings with faith and truth – and has accrued more, of faith at least – through the centuries – until our own faithlessness –

What a poet was then – seer, daemon, force of nature, the Word – is not what he is now in our time of material thickening —

It may be that your diligent — reconstitution — like the restoration of old Frescoes with new colours — is our way to the Truth — a discreet patching. Would you acknowledge my simile?

We went to hear another lecture on the recent Spiritual Manifestations, given by a most respectable Quaker – who began with a predisposition to believe in the life of the Spirit – but with no vulgar desire to be shocked or startled. Himself an Englishman he characterised the English – in a manner not wholly alien to the style of the poet Ash. We have undergone – this good man said – a double process of Induration. Trade – and Protestant abjuration of spiritual relations – have been mutually doing the work of internal petrification and ossification upon us. We are grossly materialist – and nothing will satisfy us but material proofs – as we call them – of spiritual facts – and so the spirits have deigned to speak to us in these crude ways – of rapping – and rustling – and musical hummings – such as once were not needed – when our Faith was alight and alive in us –

He said too the English are particularly indurate by reason of our denser atmosphere, less electrical and magnetic in its character than that of the Americans – who are conspicuously more nervous and excitable than we are – with more genius for social schemes – more belief in the betterment of Human Nature – whose Minds, like their Institutions – have shot up with a rapidity of growth resembling that of tropical jungles – and have in consequence greater openness and receptivity. They had the Fox Sisters and the first rapping messages – they the Revelations of Andrew Jackson Davis and his Univercoelum, they fostered the genius of D.D. Home.

Whereas our 'telluric conditions' (do you savour the phrase as I do?) are less favourable to the transmission of spiritual impressions.

I know not what is your opinion of these matters – with which Society is now so universally busy – that it has stirred the quiet backwaters of our Richmond river-front – ?

This letter is not a worthy answer to your inspiring remarks on Keats and poetic truth, or your self-exposition as a prophet-sorcerer. It is not written at White Heat – as others have been – but I must plead that I am not well – that we are not well – both my dear friend and I have been somewhat afflicted with a slight feaver and consequent lowness of spirits. I have spent today in a darkened Room – and feel the benefit of that – but am still weak.

In such a situation fancies easily abuse the mind. I had half made up my mind to plead – no more such letters – leave me quiet with my simple faith – leave me aside from the Rush of your intellect and power of writing – or I am a Lost Soul – Sir – I am threatened in that Autonomy for which I have so struggled. Now I have indeed, in a Winding and Roundabout Way – made such a plea – by presenting the thing itself as a hypothetical designation of what I might say. So whether I might – or Do – so plead – I leave to your generous judgment.

Dear Miss LaMotte,

You do not forbid me to write again. Thank you. You do not even reproach me strongly with equivocation and dabbling with arcane powers. Thank you also for that. And enough — for the time being — of these harsh subjects.

I was most distressed to hear that you were ill. I cannot think that this mild Spring weather — or my letters, so full of goodwill, however else intrusive — could affect you so uncomfortably — and so am reduced to suspecting the oratory of your inspired Quaker — whose telluric conditions of magnetic inertia, whose observation of Induration — I enjoy quite as much as you could have hoped. May he invoke a force that will, indeed 'strike flat the thick rotundities o'th'earth'. There is a masterly lack of logic in accusing an Age of Materialism and then invoking a wholly material spirituality — is there not?

I did not know you walked out so readily or so frequently. I had quite envisaged you barricaded behind your pretty front door — which I imagine, because I am never content without using my imagination, quite embowered in roses and clematis. What should you say if I were to evince a strong desire to hear your reasonable Quaker for myself? You may forbid me cucumber sandwiches, but not spiritual sustenance.

No — do not be anxious — I would do no such thing — I would not risk our friendship —

As for the rappings and tappings — I have not, so far, been much interested in them. I am not, as some are, whether for religious or for sceptical reasons, convinced that they are nothing — the kind of nothing that emanates from human weakness and gullibility and the strong desire to believe in the loving presence of those lost and much missed, which we must all have felt at times. I like to credit Paracelsus, who tells us that there are minor spirits doomed to inhabit the regions of the air who wander the earth perpetually and whom we might, from time to time, exceptionally, hear or see, when the wind, or the trick of the light, is right. (I believe too that Fraud is a possible and probable explanation for much. I am more ready to believe in D.D. Home's prestigious skills than in any pre-eminent spiritual opening to him.)

It occurs to me — speaking of Paracelsus — that your Fairy Melusine was just such a Spirit in his books — do you know the passage? You must — but I transcribe it because it is of such interest — and to ask if this is the shape of your interest in the Fairy — or is it her more beneficent castle-building propensities that have interested you — as I remember you said?

The Melusinas are daughters of kings, desperate through their sins. Satan bore them away and transformed them into spectres, into evil spirits, into horrible revenants and frightful monsters. It is thought they live without rational souls in fantastic bodies, that they are nourished by the mere elements, and at the final Judgment will pass away with these, unless they may be married to a man. In this case, by virtue of this union, they may die a natural death, as they may have lived a natural life, in their marriage. Of these spectres it is believed that they abound in deserts, in forests, in ruins and tombs, in empty vaults, and by the shores of the sea ...

Now please tell me, how does your work go? I have most egoistically – and at your generous urging – elaborated on my Ragnarök and on my Déjà-Vu – but of the Melusina – despite some suggestion that you might not be averse to writing of her – nothing. And yet she it was who caused this correspondence to be opened. I remember, I think; every small word of our one conversation – I remember your face – turned aside a little – but decisive – I remember your speaking with such feeling – of the Life of Language – do you remember that phrase? I began so ordinary-polite – you said – you hoped to write a long poem on the subject of Melusina – and your eye partly defied me to find fault with this project – as though I could or would – and I asked – was the poem to be in Spenserian stanzas or blank verse or in some other metre – and suddenly you spoke – of the power of verse and the Life of the Language – and quite forgot to look shy or apologetic, but looked, forgive me, magnificent – it is a moment I shall not easily forget while this machine is to me –

Now – I hope you will write to say that you and of course Miss Glover – are well-recovered, and able to bear the light of this bright Spring again. I do not so much hope to hear that you are venturing forth to more lectures on the Marvellous – for I am not convinced of their beneficence – but if Quakers and table-turners may have sight of you – maybe one day I may hope – for another discussion of rhyme – if not for the sliced green planisphere –

Dear Mr Ash,

I write to you from an unhappy House – and must be brief – for I have an Invalid dependent upon me – my poor Blanche – quite racked with hideous headaches – and nausea – quite prostrated – and unable to pursue the work which is her life. She is engaged on a large painting of Merlin and Vivien – at the moment of the latter's triumph when she sings the Charm which puts him in her power, to sleep through time. We are very hopeful of this work – 'tis all veiled suggestion and local intensity – but she is too ill and cannot go on. I am not in much better case myself – but I make tisanes, which I find *efficacious – and wet handkerchiefs – and do what I may.*

The other members of the household – the servant Jane, my little Dog Tray and Monsignor Dorato the canary, are of no help. Jane is a clumsy nurse – though diligent – and Dog Tray trundles to and fro looking – not commiserating – but reproachful that we do not accompany him to the park, or hurl interesting sticks for him –

So this letter will not be long.

It does me so much Good – that you should write to me of the Melusina – quite as though she were a decided thing – only waiting the accomplishment. I will tell you how the project began – quite back in the mists of time – when I was a child at my dear father's knee – and he was compiling his Mythologie Française – of which great task I had only an inkling and a wild surmise – I did not know what it might be, his magnum opus as he jokingly said – but I did know, that I had a Papa who told better Tales than any other Papa – or Mama – or nursemaid – that could possibly be imagined. Now, he was in the habit of talking to me some of the time – when his tale-telling fit was upon him – as though he were the Ancient Mariner (a much-loved early acquaintance of Mine, through Him) himself – But some of the time he would talk as though I were a fellow-worker in the field, a fellow-scholar, erudite and speculative – and he would talk in three or four languages – for he thought in French – and English – and Latin – and of course in Breton. (He did not like to think in German for reasons I shall make clear, though he could and did when occasion arose.) He told me the tale of Mélusine – often and often – for the reason, he said, that the very existence of a truly French mythology was dubious – but that if such a thing might be found – the Fairy Mélusine was indisputably one of its eminences and bright stars – My dear father had hoped to do for the French what the Brothers Grimm did for the German people – recount the true pre-history of the race through the witness of folktale and legend – discover our oldest thoughts as Baron Cuvier spliced together the Megatherium from a few indicative bones and hypothetic ligatures – and his own Wit and powers of Inference. But whereas Germany and Scandinavia have those rich myths and legends from which you drew your Ragnarök – we French have a few local demons and a few rational tales of trickery in villages – and the Matter of Bretagne which is also the matter of Britain – and the Druids of whom my dear Parent made much – and the menhirs and the Dolmens – but no dwarves and elves – as even the English have – We have the Dames Blanches – the Fate Bianche – I translate – whiteladies – amongst whom my father said Melusina might be numbered, in some of her aspects – for she appears – to warn of Death –

I wish you might have known my father. His conversation would have delighted you. There was nothing he did not know — in his chosen field — and nothing he knew that was to him Dead Knowledge — but all alive and brilliant and full of import for our lives — He had always so sad a face — thin and lined and always pale. I thought he was sad for the lack of French mythology — piecing together what he said — but he was sad, I think, to be exiled — and to have no native home — he whose paramount preoccupation — was just the Lares and Penates of the home Hearth.

My sister Sophie took no interest in these matters. She liked things women like — pretty things — she was no reader — it irked her, that we lived secluded — as it irked my mother — who had supposed that a Frenchman was always a galant — a Man of the World — or so I believe she supposed — for they were ill-matched. My pen runs away with me — I have had little sleep these last three nights — you will think my thoughts are all over the place — how can I be supposing you want my life-history in place of my Melusina-epic? Yet they are so intertwined — and I trust you —

He wore — at first simply for reading — and then always — little round steel-rimmed glasses. I think of these Cold Circles — as the most friendly, the most comfortable and comforting appearance possible — his eyes behind them were underwater Eyes — sad and large and full of veiled friendliness. I wished to become his Amanuensis — and to this end persuaded him to teach me Greek and Latin, French and Breton, also German — which he did willingly — not to that end — but because he was proud of the speed and economy with which I learned —

Enough of my Papa. I have sadly missed him lately — I think because I have been putting off my epic — and for Reasons —

Yr citation from Paracelsus was of course familiar to me. And with your usual quickness you have seen that I am interested in other visions of the fairy Melusine — who has two aspects — an Unnatural Monster — and a most proud and loving and handy woman. Now there is an odd word — but no other seems to suffice — all she touched was well done — her palaces squarely built and the stones set on rightly, her fields full of wholesome corn — according to one legend my father discovered she even brought Beans to Poitou — the true haricots — which shows she lived on into the seventeenth century — for Beans he proves, were not grown before that date. Think you not — she was not only Ghoul — but a kind of goddess of Foison — a French Ceres, it might be, or turning to your own mythology, the Lady Holda — or Freya of the Spring — or Iduna of the Golden Apples — ?

Her Progeny it is true all had something of the monstrous about them. Not only Geoffroy à la Grande Dent – or Boar's Tusk – but others who became kings in Cyprus and Armenia – had ears like jug-handles – or uneven eyes –

And the Infant Horrible, with three Eyes, whose death she urgently required at Raimondin's hand, at the moment of her metamorphosis – what are we to make of him?

I would write, if I undertook it – a little from Melusina's – own – vision. Not, as you might, in the First Person – as inhabiting her skin – but seeing her as an unfortunate Creature – of Power and Frailty – always in Fear of returning to the Ranging of the Air – the not-eternal – but finally-annihilated – Air –

I am called. I cannot write more. I must make haste to seal this – which I fear is a Plaintive Screed – a Convalescent Muttering – I am called again – I must close. Believe me yours most truly

Dear Miss LaMotte,

I trust all is now well in your household, and that work – on the Merlin and Vivien – and on the increasingly fascinating Melusina – continues apace. As for myself – I have now nearly finished my poem on Swammerdam – I have a rough blocked-out version of the whole – I know what is in and what is never so regretfully eternally abandoned – and when I have tidied up a multitude of imperfections – I shall make you my first fair copy.

I was entranced and moved by your brief portrait of your father – whose prodigious scholarship I have always admired and whose works I have read and reread most frequently. What better Father could a poet have? I was emboldened by your mention of the Ancient Mariner to wonder – was it he who named you and was that for Coleridge's heroine of his unfinished poem? I have not had occasion to tell you – though I tell all I meet, with the regularity with which dear Crabb tells his tale of retrieving Wieland's bust – I once met Coleridge, I was once taken to Highgate – when I was very young and green – and had the chance of hearing the Angelic – (and mildly self-important) voice speak on and on – of the existence of angels and the longevity of yew-trees, and the suspension of Life in Winter (the banal and the truly profound thick and fast upon each other here) and premonitions and the Duties of Man (not Rights) and how Napoleon's Spies had been hot on his heels in Italy on his return from Malta – and on true Dreams and Lying Dreams. And more, I think. Nothing on Christabel.

I was so young and green, I worried inordinately that I had no chance, in all this spate of brilliant monologue, to interpose my own voice – to be heard to be able to think in that company – to be remarked. I do not know what I should have said if I could have spoken. Very likely something futile or silly – some erudite and pointless questioning of his doctrine of the Trinity, or some crude wish to be told the end of the poem Christabel. I cannot bear not to know the end of a tale. I will read the most trivial things – once commenced – only out of a feverish greed to be able to swallow the ending – sweet or sour – and to be done with what I need never have embarked on. Are you in my case? Or are you a more discriminating reader? Do you lay aside the unprofitable? Do you have any privileged insight into the possible ending of the great S.T.C.'s Tale of Christabel? – which teases so, for it is like the very best tales, impossible to predict how it may come out – and yet it must – but we shall never know – its secret sleeps with its lethargic and inconsequential author – who cares not for our irritable quandary –

I partly see your meaning about Melusina – but hesitate to write thoughts of mine which may distort your thinking – either by causing you annoyance at my imperceptiveness – or worse by muddling the bright tracks of your own ideas.

What is so peculiarly marvellous about the Melusina myth, you seem to be saying, is that it is both wild and strange and ghastly and full of the daemonic – and it is at the same time solid as earthly tales – the best of them – are solid – depicting the life of households and the planning of societies, the introduction of husbandry and the love of any mother for her children.

Now – I am greatly daring, and I trust you not to fly out at me scornfully if I am wrong – I see in the gifts you show already in your writings such mastery of both these contradictory elements – that the Story may appear to be made for you, to await indeed – You – to tell it.

Both in your wonder-tales and in your fine lyrics – you have a most precise eye and ear for the matter of fact and the detailed – for household linen for instance, for the fine manipulations of delicate sewing – for actions like Milking – which make a mere man see the world of little domestic acts as a paradisal revelation –

But you are never content to leave it there ... your world is haunted by voiceless shapes ... and wandering Passions ... and little fluttering Fears ... more sinister than any conventional Bat or Broomstick-witch.

As if to say – you have the power to render the secure keep of Lusignan – as it might be in the lives of the lords, ladies and peasants in the brilliant colours of a Book of Hours – and yet you can render also – the Voices of the Air – the Wailing – the Siren Song – the Inhuman Grief that cries down the avenues of the years –

What will you be thinking of me now? I told you — I cannot think of anything without imagining it, without giving it shape in my mind's eye and ear. So, as I said, I have the clearest mental vision of yr unseen Porch, overarched with Clematis — one of those delightful deep-blue violet ones — and little clambering roses. I have also the clearest vision of your parlour — with its two peaceful Human inhabitants employed — I will not say at netting, but perhaps at reading — aloud, some work of Shakespeare or Sir Thomas Malory — and Monsignor Dorato all lemony plumes in a filigree dome — and your little dog — now of what kind is he? if I were to hazard a guess I would say perhaps a King Charles Spaniel — yes, I see him now, unfortunately clearly, with one chocolate ear and one white and a feathery tail — and yet he is maybe no such thing — but a small hound — a milk-white fine creature such as Sir Thos Wyatt's ladies kept in their mysterious chamber. I have no vision of Jane at all — but that may come. I do have the clearest olfactory ghost of yr tisanes — though they hesitate between verveine and lime and raspberry-leaves, which my own dear mother found most efficacious in case of headache and lassitude.

But I have no right, however I may extend my imagining gaze on harmless chairs and wallcoverings — I have no right to extend my unfortunate curiosity to your work, your writing. You will accuse me of trying to write your Melusina, but it is not so — it is only my unfortunate propensity to try to make concrete in my brain how you would do it — and the truly exciting possibilities open up before me — like vistas of long rides in sun-dappled shade in the mysterious forest of Brocéliande — I think — so, she will do it — so, she would enter the project. And yet I know your work is nothing if not truly original — my speculations are an impertinence. What can I say? I have never before been tempted to discuss the intricacies of my own writing — or his own — with any other poet — I have always gone on in a solitary and self-sufficient way — but with you I felt from the first that it must be the true things or nothing — there was no middle way. So I speak to you — or not speak, write to you, write written speech — a strange mixture of kinds — I speak to you as I might speak to all those who most possess my thoughts — to Shakespeare, to Thomas Browne, to John Donne, to John Keats — and find myself unpardonably lending you, who are alive, my voice, as I habitually lend it to those dead men — Which is much as to say — here is an author of Monologues — trying clumsily to construct a Dialogue — and encroaching on both halves of it. Forgive me.

Now if this were a true dialogue — but that is entirely as you may wish it to be.

Dear Mr Ash,

Have you truly Weighed — what you ask of me? Not the Gracile Accommodation of my Muse to your promptings — for that wd be resisted to the Death of the Immortal — which cannot Be — only Dissipation in Air. But you Overwhelm my small diligence — with Pelion piled on Ossa of Thought and fancy — and if indeed I sit down to answer all as it should be answered — there is the morning quite gone — and what has become either of the setting of the junket or of the Fairy Melusina?

Yet do not on that account cease to write to me — if I skimp a little on the Fairy-cakes — and write you a truncated and scanty answer — and procrastinate — not unfruitfully — one more day for the Melusina — all may be botched together somehow.

You say you cannot imagine Jane. Well — I will tell you, this much — she has a Sweet Tooth — a very sweet tooth. It is beyond her powers to let be a set of little milk-jellies — or delicious macaroons — or brandy-snaps — in the Larder — without abstracting one insignificant exemplar here — or indenting a Spoon there and leaving traces of her gourmandise. So it is with my sad Self and the inditing of letters. I will not do it I say, until this is quite done — or that embarked on — but in my mind runs an answer to this that or the other — and I say to myself — if this argument were disposed of (if just that sweetmeat were tasted and slid down) my mind would be my own again, without agitation —

No, but how ungracious to quibble. I was just asserting — I am no Creature of your thought, nor in danger of becoming so — we are both safe in that regard. As for the Chairs and wall-coverings — imagine away — think what you will — and I shall from time to time write a small Clue — so that you may be the more thoroughly confounded. I will say nothing as to clematis and roses — but we have a very fine Hawthorn — just now tressed and heavy with pink and creamy blooms and alive with that almond smell — so sweet — too sweet — that the sense aches at it. I will not say where this Tree is — nor how young or old, large or small — so you will be imagining it not as it is indeed — Paradisal and Dangerous — you know the May must never be brought into the house.

Now I must discipline myself — and address my wandering wits to your momentous questions — or we are swallowed up, both of us, in frippery imaginations, and vain speculations.

I too have seen S.T.C. I was but an infant — his pudgy Hand rested on my golden curls — his Voice remarked on their flaxen paleness — he said — or

I have since by thinking created his voice saying – for I too, like you, must be imagining, I cannot let things alone – I believe he said 'It is a beautiful name and will I trust not be a name of ill omen.' Now this is all the Clue I have to the end of the poem of Christabel *– that its heroine was destined for tribulation – which is not hard to see – though how she might obtain Happiness thereafter is harder, if not Impossible.*

Now I must change my habitual Tone wholly. Now I must write stringently and not fly about distracting you with flappings of tinsel or demoiselle-flickering. What nonsense in you to pretend to fear, or to fear truly perhaps, that I could be anything but wholly gratified by what you say of the Melusina *and of my own powers of writing – of what I might do. You have read my thoughts – or made clear to me what were my predispositions – not in an intrusive way – but with true insight. She is indeed – my Melusine – just such a combination of the orderly and humane with the unnatural and the Wild – as you suggest – the hearth-foundress and the destroying Demon. (And female, which you do not remark on.)*

I had not known you were a reader of such childish things as Tales Told in November. *Those were my Father's tales, above all – and told – only – in those dark months to which they belong. He used to say that those collectors or researchers who went to Brittany in the summer months – when the sea smiles sometimes, and the mist lifts from the granite so that it almost shines – might never come by what they looked for. The true tales were only told on dark nights – after Toussaint, All Saints, had passed. And the November Tales were the worst – of revenants, of demons, of portents, of the Prince of the Powers of the Air. And of the Ankou – who drove a terrible chariot, – a creaking groaning grinding sort of a conveyance anyone might hear behind him on a lonely heath on a dark night – full of dead bones, it might be, heaped and dangling. And the Driver was a Man of Bones – under his huge hat you saw only his hollow Orbits – he was not, you must know, Death, but Death's Servitor – come with his Scythe – whose blade faced not inward for harvesting but outward – for what? (I can hear my father's voice on a dark evening, asking – for what? And if I tell it to you somewhat flatly – why – it is because the days lengthen, and outside a thrush sings and sings in my foamy May – and all this is Out of Time.) If we are still writing letters to each other in November – as why should we? and why should we not? – I can a tale unfold – and shall – quite in my father's manner. After November came the gentler tales of the Birth of Our Lord – you will remember it is a Breton belief that on that holy day the Beasts talk in the Stalls and Byres – but no man may hear what they say, those sage and innocent creatures – on pain of Death –*

Now mark — you must write no more of your interest in my work as a possible Intrusion. You do not seem aware, Mr Ash, for all your knowledge of the great world I do not frequent, of the usual response which the productions of the Female Pen — let alone as in our case, the hypothetick *productions — are greeted with. The best we may hope is — oh, it is excellently done — for* a woman. *And then there are Subjects we may not treat — things we may not know. I do not say but that there must be — and is — some essential difference between the Scope and Power of men and our own limited consciousness and possibly weaker apprehension. But I do maintain, as stoutly, that the delimitations are at present, all* wrongly drawn *— We are not mere candle-holders to virtuous thoughts — mere chalices of Purity — we think and feel, aye and read — which seems not to shock you in us, in me, though I have concealed from many the extent of my — vicarious — knowledge of human vagaries. Now — if there is a reason for my persistence in this correspondence — it is this very unawareness in you — real or assumed — of what a woman must be supposed to be capable of. This is to me — like a strong Bush, well-rooted is to the grasp of one falling down a precipice — here I hold — here I am stayed —*

I will tell you a Tale — no I will not neither, it does not bear thinking on — and yet I will, as an instance of trust *— towards You.*

I sent some of my smaller poems — a little sheaf — selected with trembling — to a great Poet — who shall be nameless, I cannot write his name — asking — Are These Poems? Have I — a Voice? He replied with courteous promptness — that they were pretty things — not quite regular *— and not always well-regulated by a proper sense of decorum — but he would encourage me, moderately — they would do well enough to give me an interest in life until I had — I quote him exactly — 'sweeter and weightier responsibilities'. Now how should I be brought by this judgment to desire those — Mr Ash — how? You understood my very phrase — the* Life of Language. *You understand — in my life Three — and Three alone have glimpsed — that the need to set down words — what I see, so — but words too, words mostly — words have been all my life, all my life — this need is like the Spider's need who carries before her a huge Burden of Silk which she* must *spin out — the silk is her life, her home, her safety — her food and drink too — and if it is attacked or pulled down, why, what can she do but make more, spin afresh, design anew — you will say she is patient — so she is — she may also be Savage — it is her Nature — she* Must *— or die of Surfeit — do you understand me?*

I can write no more at this time. My heart is too full — I have said too much — if I overlook these sheets, my courage will fail me — so they shall go all uncorrected as they are, with their imperfections on their heads – God bless you and keep you.

Christabel LaMotte

My dear Friend,

I may call myself your friend, may I not? For my true thoughts have spent more time in your company than in anyone else's, these last two or three months, and where my thoughts are, there am I, in truth, – even if, like the May, only a threshold-presence, by decree. I write to you now in haste – not to answer your last most generous letter – but to impart a vision, before the strangeness of it fades. An answer you shall and must have – but this I must tell you of, before I lose my courage. Are you curious? I hope so.

First I must confess my vision occurred in a ride in Richmond Park. And why must I confess this? May a poet and a gentleman not ride out with friends wherever he pleases? I was invited to take exercise with friends in the Park, and felt a vague unease as though its woody plantations and green spaces were girdled with an unspoken spell of prohibition – as your Cottage is – as Shalott was to the knights – as the woods of sleep are in the tale, with their sharp briar hedges. Now on the level of tales, you know, all prohibitions are made only to be broken, must be broken – as is indeed instanced in your own Melusina with striking ill-luck to the disobedient knight. It may be even that I might not have come to ride in the park if it had not had the definite glitter and glamour of the enclosed and barred. Though I must add, as a true nineteenth-century gentleman, I did not feel it was within my right to saunter past the clematis and roses, or the foamy May-tree, as I might so easily and casually have done – pavements are free places. I will not exchange my imagined rose-bower for reality until I am invited to step inside it – which may be never. So – I rode within the pale of the Park – and thought of those who dwelt so close to its iron gateways – and fancied that at every turn I might see a half-familiar shawl or bonnet whisk out of sight like one of yr own whiteladies – And I felt a little irritation with the good Quaker gentleman whose stolid telluric conditions have so much more confidence-inspiring virtue than the poetic morality of R. H. Ash –

Now, as all good knights in all good tales do – I was riding along, a little apart, and musing to myself. I was making my way along a grassy ride in what you might well have supposed to be an enchanted stillness. In other parts of the park, Spring had been busy – we disturbed a family of rabbits in the new bracken, which rose in strong little involuted fronds, like new-born serpents, somewhere between the feathered and the scaly — There were hosts of black ravens, very busy and important, striding about and stabbing at the roots of things with their blue-black triangular beaks. And larks rising, and spiders throwing out their gleaming geometrical Traps and staggering butterflies and the unevenly speeding blue darts of the dragonflies. And a kestrel riding the air-currents in superlative ease with its gaze concentrated on the bright earth.

So — I went on, on my own — deeper and deeper into the silent Tunnel of the Ride — not so sure of where I was and yet not anxious either, not concerned about my companions nor even about the nearness of — certain friends. The trees were beech, and the buds, just breaking, fiercely brilliant, and the new, the renewed light on them — intermittent diamond — but the depths were dark, a silent Nave. And no birds sang, or I heard none, no woodpecker tapped, no thrush whistled or hopped. And I listened to the increasing Quiet — and my horse went softly on the beech-mast — which was wet after rain — not crackling, a little sodden, not wet enough to plash. And I had the sensation, common enough, at least to me, that I was moving out of time, that the way, narrow and dark-dappled, stretched away indifferently before and behind, and that I was who I had been and what I would become — all at once, all wound in one — and I moved onward indifferently, since it was all one, whether I came or went, or remained still. Now to me such moments are poetry. Do not misunderstand me — I do not mean missishly 'poetical' — but the source of the driving force of the lines — And when I write lines I mean the lines of verse indeed, but also some lines of life which run indifferently through us — from Origin to Finish. Ah, how can I tell you? And to whom but you could I even begin to describe such indescribable — such obscurely untouchable things? Imagine an abstract sketch such as a drawing-master might make to correct your perspective for you — a fan or tunnel of lines, narrowing not to blindness, not to Nought, but to the Vanishing point, to Infinity. And then imagine these Lines embodied in the soft bright leaves and the pale light and the blue moving over it — and the tall trunks with their grey soft hide diminishing — and the very furrows in the ground — such a unique carpet of such browns and sooty blacks and peat and amber and ash — all distinct and all one — all leading on and yet stationary ... I cannot say ... I trust you know already ...

In the distance there appeared to be a Pool. It lay across my path — a brown pool — deep in colour, uncertain in depth — reflecting the canopy in its dark unbroken surface. I looked at it and looked away, and when I looked back it contained a Creature. I must suppose this Creature to have come there by some minor magic for it had certainly not been there before, and could hardly have walked there, for the surface remained still and unbroken.

Now the Creature was a small hound, milky-white in colour, with a finely-pointed little head and black intelligent eyes. It lay — or couched would be better — it was like the sphinx, *couchant* — half-above and half-below the water, so that its shoulders and haunches were licked and divided by a fine hairline of surface, and its limbs, below the surface, gleamed through flowing green and amber. Its delicate forefeet were stretched before it and its fine tail curled round about. It was as still as though it was made of marble, and this not for only one or two moments but for some considerable time.

Round its neck it wore a series of spherical silver bells on a silver chain — not miniature tinkling bells, but large bells, akin to gulls' eggs, or even bantam eggs.

My horse and I stopped and stared. And the creature, stone-still always, stared back, with comfortable confidence, and a look, somehow, of command.

I was for a period of several moments wholly undecided as to whether this manifestation were a reality, or a hallucination, or what? Had it come from another time? It lay there so improbably, half-submerged, a veritable *Canis aquaticus*, a water-spirit emerging, or an earth-spirit half-submerged.

I could not for the life of me press on or make it give way or move or vanish. I stared, it stared. It seemed to me a solid Poem, and you came into my mind, and your little dog and your unearthly creatures walking the earth. There also came into my mind several poems of Sir Thos Wyatt — hunting poems for the most part, but where the creatures of the Chase are denizens of the Court Chamber. *Noli me tangere*, the beast seemed to proclaim haughtily, and indeed I could not and did not advance upon it, but returned to time and daylight and the time-keeping of daily chatter, as best I might.

Now I write it out — it may seem no great matter to you — or to anyone who may read this account of it. And yet it was. It was a sign. I thought of Elizabeth in the days of her youth hunting in that same park with just such small hounds — a Virgin Huntress — an implacable Artemis — and I fancied I saw her fierce face in its whiteness and the deer running from her. (The full-fed ones I passed cropped the turf contentedly enough, or watched me like statues and snuffed the air of my passing.) Did you know that the Wild Hunt used sometimes, after passing through a homestead, to leave a little dog in the hearth which would be frighted with the right charm but otherwise stayed a year, eating the sustenance of the house, until the Huntsmen came again?

I shall write no more on this topic. I have made myself foolish enough and put my dignity wholly in your hands — with as much trust as you expressed *towards me in your never-to-be-forgotten last letter, which, as I said in opening, shall have its answer.*

Let me have your view of my apparition –

Swammerdam needs a touch or two more. He was a queer intellect and a lost soul – despised and rejected like so many great men – the circumstances of his life almost perfectly coincident with the great preoccupations – nay obsessions – of his nature. Think, my dear friend, of the variousness and the shape-shifting and the infinite extensibility of the human spirit – that can at one time inhabit a stuffy Dutch Cabinet of Curiosities – and dissect a microscopic heart – and contemplate a visionary water-hound in the brightest English air and leafiness – and tramp about Galilee considering the lilies of those fields with Renan, and pry unforgivably and in fantasy into the secrets of the unseen room where your head is bent over your paper – and you smile at your work – for by this time Melusina is embarked on and the knight comes to the encounter by the Fountain of Thirst –

My dear Friend,

If I address you So – it is for the Last Time as well as for the First. We have rushed down a Slope – I at least have Rushed – where we might have descended more circumspectly – or Not at All even. It has been borne in upon me that there are dangers in our continued conversation. I fear I lack delicacy in saying so – I see no good way out indeed – I reproach you with nothing – not myself neither – unless with an indiscreet confessional – and of what then – that I loved my father, and was set upon writing an epic?

But the world would not look well upon such letters – between a woman living in a shared solitude as I do – and a man – even if that man were a great and wise poet –

There are those who care for what the world – and his wife – may say. There are those who are hurt by his bad opinion. It is pointed out to me, quite rightly – that if I am jealous of my freedom to live as I do – and manage my own affairs – and work my work – I must be more than usually careful to remain sufficiently respectable in the eyes of the world and his wife – to evade his bad opinions – and consequent niggling restrictions on my freedom of movement.

I would not impugn your delicacy in any thing – or your judgment – or your good faith.

Do you not think it would be better – if we were to cease to correspond?

I shall be your well-wisher always

Christabel LaMotte

My dear Friend,

Your letter came as a shock to me – as you must, of course, have foreseen, from its complete contrast with its predecessor, and with the good faith and trust that had grown and subsisted (I thought) between us. I asked myself – what had I done to alarm you so – and answered myself that I had transgressed the bounds of your delineated privacy in coming to Richmond, and not only in coming, but in writing, as I did, of what I had seen. I could urge you to take that as a whimsical exaggeration of a curious phaenomenon – though it was not – if I thought truly, upon reflection, that that was the cause of the matter. But it is not – or if it was, after the tone of your letter, it no longer is.

I will confess, I was at first not only shocked, but angry, that you should write so. But too much was at stake – including the delicacy and good judgment and good faith you kindly attribute to me – for me to write back in anger. So I thought long and hard about our correspondence, and about your predicament, as you choose to describe it – of a woman 'jealous of her freedom to live as she does'. I have no designs on your freedom, I wanted to retort – much the opposite, indeed, I respect and honour and admire that freedom and the product of it, your work, your words, your web of language. I know to my own cost the unhappiness that lack of freedom can bring to women – the undesirability, the painfulness, the waste, of the common restrictions placed upon them. I thought of you most truly as a fine poet and my friend.

But – forgive me this necessary failure in delicacy – one thing your letter does is to define us fair and square in relation to each other as a man and a woman. Now, as long as this was not done, we might have gone on forever, simply conversing – with a hint of harmless gallantry, courtly devotion perhaps – but mostly with a surely not illicit desire to speak of the art, or craft, we both profess. I thought this freedom was one you claimed for yourself. What has caused you to retreat so behind a palisade of prickling conventions?

Can anything be retrieved?

I would make two observations here. The first is that you do not by any means utter a firm resolution that we must write no more letters. You write in the interrogative mood – and moreover with a deference to my opinion that is either mere feminine deprecation (most mal à propos?) or a true reflection of your state of mind – a not complete certainty of closure in this matter.

No – my dear Miss LaMotte – I do not (on the evidence you have offered) think it would be better if we were to cease to correspond. It would not be better for me – I should be almost infinitely a loser, and without any gratifying moral certainty that I had done a right or noble thing in renouncing a correspondence that gave me intense delight – and freedom – and harmed no one.

I do not think it would be better for you — but I am not wholly aware of your circumstances — I am open to conviction.

I said, I would make two observations. This was the first. The second is, that you write — do I go too far — as though your letter was in part dictated by the views of some other person or persons. I say this most tentatively — but it is very striking — some other voice *speaks in your lines — do I divine truly? Now, this may be the voice of someone with much greater claims on your loyalty and attention than I may put forward — but you must be very sure that such a person sees truly and not with a vision distracted by other considerations. I cannot find a tone to write to you that does not veer towards the hectoring or the plaintive. I do not know — so quickly have you become part of my life — how I should do without you.*

I should like still to send you Swammerdam. May I do that, at least?

> *Yours to command*
> *Randolph Ash*

My dear Friend

How shall I answer you? I have been abrupt *and* ungracious *— from fear of Infirmity of Purpose, and because I am a voice — a voice that would be still and small — crying plaintively out of a* Whirlwind *— which I may not in Honesty describe to you. I owe you an Explanation — and yet I Must Not — and yet I* must *— or stand convicted of hideous Ingratitude as well as lesser vices.*

But Truly Sir it will not do. The — precious — *letters — are too much and too little — and above all and first, I should say, compromising.*

What a cold sad word. It is His word — the World's word — and her word too, that prude, his Wife. But it entails freedom.

I will expatiate — on freedom and injustice.

The injustice is — that I require my freedom — from you — who respect it so fully. That was a noble saying of yours about freedom — how can I turn from

I will put in Evidence a brief History. A History of little nameless unremembered acts. Of this our Bethany cottage — which was named for a reason. Now to you and in your marvellous Poem — Bethany is the Place where the master called his dead friend to resurrection beforetimes and particularly.

But to us Females, it was a place wherein we neither served nor were served — poor Martha was cumbered with much serving — and was sharp with her sister Mary who sat at His Feet and heard His Word and chose the one thing needful. Now I believe rather, with George Herbert, that 'Who sweeps a room as for Thy laws – Makes that and the action fine.' We formed a Project – my dear Companion and myself – to make ourselves a Bethany where the work of all kinds was carried on in the Spirit of Love and His Laws. We met, you are to know, at one of Mr Ruskin's marvellous lectures on the dignity of handicraft and individual work. We were Two – who wished to live the Life of the Mind – to make good things. We saw after thought that if we put together the pittances we possessed – and could come by by giving drawing lessons – or by selling Wonder Tales or even Poems – we might make ourselves a life in which drudgery was Artful – was sacred as Mr Ruskin believes is possible – and it was shared, for no Master (save Him Who is Lord of All and visited the true Bethany.) We were to Renounce. Not the lives that then encompassed us – cramped Daughterly Devotion to a worldly mother – nor the genteel Slavery of governessing – those were no loss – those were gleefully fled and opposition staunchly met. But we were to renounce the outside World – and the usual female Hopes (and with them the usual Female Fears) in exchange for – dare I say Art – a daily duty of crafting – from exquisite curtains to Mystical Paintings, from biscuits with sugar roses to the Epic of Melusina. It was a Sealed Pact – I say no more of that. It was a chosen way of life – in which, you must believe, I have been wondrously happy – and not alone in being so.

(And the Letters we have written are with me such an Addiction, I want to ask – have you ever seen Mr Ruskin demonstrate the Art of Nature in the depicting a veined Stone in a water-glass? So jewel-bright his colours, so fine his pen and brush, so exact his description of why we must see what is truly there – but I must not run on – it is right that we should cease –)

I have chosen a Way – dear Friend – I must hold to it. Think of me if you will as the Lady of Shalott – with a Narrower Wisdom – who chooses not the Gulp of outside Air and the chilly river-journey deathwards – but who chooses to watch diligently the bright colours of her Web – to ply an industrious shuttle – to make – something – to close the Shutters and the Peephole too –

You will say, you are no threat to That. You will argue – rationally. There are things we have not said to each other beyond the – One – you so starkly – Defined.

I know in my Intrinsic Self – the Threat is there.

Be patient. Be generous. Forgive

Your friend
Christabel LaMotte

My dear Friend

These last letters have been like Noah's Ravens – they have sped out over the waste waters, across the turgid Thames in these rainy days – and have not returned or brought back any sign of life. I was most hopeful of the latest-despatched, with Swammerdam *with the ink barely dry on him*. I thought you must certainly see that you had in some sense *called him up* – that without your fine perceptions, without your intricate sense of minute inhuman lives, he would have presented an altogether grosser semblance, not so articulate on his dry bones. No other Poem of mine has ever in the slightest been written for a particular Reader – only for myself, or some half-conceived Alter Ego. Now, *you* are not that – it is your difference, your otherness to which I address myself – fascinated, intrigued. And now my vanity – and something more – my sense of Human Friendship – is hurt that you cannot – for it is nonsense to say that you *dare* not – even acknowledge my poem.

If I have offended you by calling your last long ago letter contradictory (which it was) or timid (which it was) then you must forgive me. You may well ask why I am so tenacious in continuing writing to one who has declared herself unable to maintain a friendship (which she also declared to be valuable to herself) and remains resolute in silence, in rejection. A lover might indeed in all honour accept such a congé – but a peaceable, a valued friend? It is not as though I ever breathed – or scribbled or scratched – the faintest hint of any improper attention – no 'if things were otherwise, ah well then . . .' no 'Your eyes, which I know to be bright, may peruse . . .' – no – all was straightforward from my honest thoughts *which are closer to my essential self than any such nonsensical gallantry* – and this you cannot support?

And why am I so tenacious? I hardly know myself. For the sake of future Swammerdams, it may be – for I see that I had insensibly come to perceive you – mock not – as some sort of Muse.

Could the Lady of Shalott have written Melusina in her barred and moated Tower?

Well, you will say, you are too busy writing the poetry itself, to require employment as a Muse. I had not thought the two were incompatible – indeed they might even be thought to be complementary. But you are adamant.

Do not be misled by my mocking tone. It is all that seems to come. I shall hope against hope – that this letter is the Dove which will return with the hoped-for Olive-Branch. If not, I shall cease to bother you.

Ever yours most truly
R. H. Ash

Dear Mr Ash,

This is not the first time this letter has been embarked on. I know neither how to start nor how to proceed. A Circumstance has arisen – no, I know no longer how to write, neither, for how could a circumstance arise, or what appearance might such a creature – bear?

Dear Sir – your Letters have not reached me – for a Reason. Not your Raven-ous letters – nor yet, to my infinite loss – your Poem.

I fear – I know indeed, with all but ocular proof positive – they have been Taken.

Today I happened – to run a little faster to greet the Postman. There was almost a papery – Tussle. I snatched. To my shame – to our shame – we – snatched.

I ask you – I beg you – I have told you the Truth – do not condemn. My honour was being guarded – and if I do not exactly share the conception of Honour which prompted the zealous carefulness – I must be grateful, I must, I am.

~~But to stoop to Theft~~

Oh, Sir, I am torn by contrary emotions. I am grateful, as I have said. But I must be very angry to have been so deceived – and angry on your behalf – for though I might have thought it best – not to answer those letters – no one else had the right to interfere with them – whatever the motive.

I cannot find them. They are torn to shreds, I am told. And Swammerdam with them. How shall that be forgiven? And yet – how may it not?

This house – so happy once – is full of weeping and wailing and Black Headache like a Painful Pall – Dog Tray slinks to and fro – Monsignor Dorato is silenced – and I – I pace up and down – I ask myself to whom, I may turn – and think of you my Friend, the unwitting cause of so much Woe –

It is all misapprehension, I know.

I no longer know what was right and wrong about the Original Step – to discontinue the writing –

If it was to safeguard – domestic harmony – that is now most thoroughly jangled, out of tune and harsh.

Oh, dear friend – I am so very angry – I see strange fiery flashes before my drowned eyes –

I dare not write more. I cannot be sure that any further communication of yours will reach me – intact – or at all –

Your Poem is lost.

And shall I give up – so? I who have fought for my Autonomy against Family and Society? No, I will not. In the known risk of appearing –

Inconsequential, Tergiversatory, infirm of purpose and feminine – *I ask you –
is it possible for you to walk in Richmond Park – when shall I say – you will
be occupied – any day the next three days at about eleven in the morning. You
will urge that the Weather is inclement. These last few days have been fearful.
The Water has been so high – with each high Tide the Thames advances and
runs in over foreshore and quay wall – climbing* that, *with watery ferocity –
and laughing and slapping its way across the cobbled pavements on the bank –
invading people's gardens, paying no attention to wicket-gates or wooden
fence – but creeping sinuously – and bubbling up – brown and strong – bringing
with it a trail of such things – cotton waste, feathers, soaking garments, dead
small creatures – overtopping pansy and Forget-me-nots – and aspiring to early
Hollyhock. But I shall be there. I shall step out with Dog Tray – he at least
will thank me wholeheartedly – in solid boots and armed with an umbrella –
I shall enter by the Richmond Hill gate of the Park – and perambulate near
there – if you should chuse to come.*

I have an Apology to make that I wish to make in Person.

Here is your Olive-branch. Will you receive it?

Oh, the lost poem –

Your true friend

My dear friend,

*I hope you got safe home. I watched till you were out of sight – two
determined little booted feet and four loping grey clawed ones setting up small
fountains as you went, without once looking back. You at least did not do so –
but Dog Tray once or twice twisted his grey head, I hope regretfully. How
could you deliberately mislead me so? There was I, looking diligently about
me for a King Charles Spaniel, or a milky sharp small hound – and there
were you, quite overwhelmed and half-hidden by a huge gaunt grey creature
out of some Irish fairytale or Northern saga of wolf-hunting. What else have
you so mischievously misrepresented to me? My idea of yr Bethany House
revises itself daily now – eaves shift, windows laugh and lengthen, hedges
advance and retreat – it is all a perpetual shape-shifting and adjustment –
nowhere constant. Ah, but I saw your face, even if only in flashes under the
dripping brim of a bonnet and the arching shadow of that huge and most
purposeful umbrella. And I held your hand – at the beginning and the end –
it rested in mine, with trust, I hope and believe.*

*What a walk, in what a wind, never-to-be-forgotten. The clashing together
of our umbrella-spines as we leaned to speak, and their hopeless tangling; the*

rush of air carrying our words away; the torn green leaves flying past, and on the brow of the hill the deer running and running against that labouring mounting mass of leaden cloud. Why do I tell you this, who saw it with me? To share the words too, as we shared the blast and the sudden silence when the wind briefly dropped. It was very much your world we walked in, your watery empire, with the meadows all drowned as the city of Is, and the trees all growing down from their roots as well as up — and the clouds swirling indifferently in both aerial and aquatic foliage —

What else can I say? I am copying Swammerdam for you again — a problematic labour as I keep discovering small defects, some of which I mend and some of which merely make me anxious. You shall have him next week. Next week we shall walk again, shall we not, now it is very clear to you that I am no ogre, but only a mild and somewhat apprehensive gentleman?

And did you find — as I did — how curious, as well as very natural, it was that we should be so shy with each other, when in a papery way we knew each other so much better? I feel I have always known you, and yet I search for polite phrases and conventional enquiries — you are more mysterious in your presence (as I suppose most of us may be) than you seem to be in ink and scribbled symbols. (Perhaps we all are so. I cannot tell.)

I will not write more now. I have addressed this, as requested, to the Richmond Poste Restante. I do not wholly like this subterfuge — I do not like the imputed shady dealing of such a step — I find it inhibiting. Nor can you, with your quick moral discernment and yr proud sense of yr own moral autonomy, find it at all easy. Can we not think of something better? Will the urgency diminish? I am in your hands, but unquiet. Let me know, if you are able, that you have received this first waiting-letter. Let me know how you are, and that we may meet again soon. My respects to Dog Tray —

My dear Friend,

Your letter came safely. Your word of — subterfuge — hit home. I will think — there are Veils and Whirligigs of hindrances — I will think — and hope I may come up with more than — a headache.

I shall not easily forget our shining progress across the wet earth. Nor any Word you said — not the most courteous Nothing — nor yet the moments snatched to speak Truth and Justice about the Future Life. I hope you may be convinced that Mrs Lees' seances are worthy of your serious consideration. They bring such unspeakable Comfort — to the deeply grieving. Last week a Mrs Tompkins held her dead infant on her knees for upward of ten minutes — his very weight, she said, his very curling fingers and toes — how can mother-love be mistaken? The Father too, was able to touch the soft curls of this briefly-returned being. There was too, glancing unearthly light – and a ghost of a sweet perfume.

It is most true as you say, that embodied – I had almost writ confrontation – conversation – unsettles the Letters. I know not – what to write. My pen is reluctant. I am overawed by your voice – in truth – by Presence – however taken. Shall we see each other again? Will it do good or harm? Dog Tray – who sends his respects – knows it will do good – and I know nothing – so let it be Tuesday – if you come not, I will look in the Poste Restante, where I stand beside seamen's wives, and fashionable Creatures, and a dour Tradesman whose face creases to thunder when nothing is produced for him.

I long for Swammerdam.

> Your true friend

My dear,

I was about to begin in this vein – 'how can I apologise?' and so forth – 'a moment's madness' then I thought I might circumvent the whole happening, deny that Magnets rush towards each other, and deny it so steadily, the lie might become a kind of saving fiction that held a kind of truth. But the Laws of Nature deserve as much respect as any other, and there are human laws as strong as the magnetic field of iron and lodestone – if I deviate into lying, to you to whom I have never lied – I am lost.

I shall see you – as you were the moment before the madness – until the day I die. Your little face, with its pale candour, turned to me – and your hand out – in the watery sunshine, between the great trees. And I could have taken your hand – or not taken your hand – could I not? Either? But now only the one. Never have I felt such a concentration of my whole Being – on one object, in one place, at one time – a blessed eternity of momentariness that went on forever, it seemed. I felt you call me, though your voice said something different, something about the rainbow spectrum – but the whole of you, the depth of you called to me and I had to answer – and not with words – this wordless call. Now is this only my madness? With you in my arms (I tremble as I remember it to write it) I was sure it was not.

Now, away from you, I do not know what you think or feel.

But I must speak. I must say to you what is in my mind. The unforgivable embrace was no sudden impulse – no momentary excitation – but came from what is deepest in me, and I think also what is best. I must tell you – ever since that first meeting, I have known you were my fate, however from time to time I may have disguised that knowledge from myself.

I have dreamed nightly of your face and walked the streets of my daily life with the rhythms of your writing singing in my silent brain. I have called you my Muse, and so you are, or might be, a messenger from some urgent place of the spirit where essential poetry sings and sings. I could call you, with even greater truth — my Love — there, it is said — for I most certainly love you and in all ways possible to man and most fiercely. It is a love for which there is no place in this world — a love my diminished reason tells me can and will do neither of us any good, a love I tried to hide cunningly from, to protect you from, with all the ingenuity at my command. (Except complete silence, you will rightly say, which was out of my power.) We are rational nineteenth-century beings, we might leave the coup de foudre to the weavers of Romances — but I have certain evidence that you know what I speak of, that you acknowledged, however momently (that infinite moment) that at least what I claim is true.

And now, I write to ask, what are we to do? How shall this be the end, that is in its very nature a beginning? I know fully that this letter will cross one from you which will say, wisely and rightly, that we must meet no more, no more see one another — that even the letters, that space of freedom, must be put an end to. And the plot which holds us, the conventions which bind us, declare that I must, as a gentleman, acquiesce in that requirement, at least for a time, and hope that Fate, or the plotter who watches over our steps will decree some further meeting, some accidental re-opening . . .

But, my Dear, I cannot do this. It goes against nature — not my own particularly, but Dame Nature herself — who this morning smiles at me in and through you, so that everything is alight — from the anemones on my desk to the motes of dust in the beam of sunlight through the window, to the words on the page in front of me (John Donne) with you, with you, with you. I am happy — as I have never been happy — who should be writing to you in who can say what agony of mind full of guilt and horrified withdrawal. I see your quizzical little mouth and I reread your riddling words about the Ants and Spiders — and I smile, to think you are all the time there, poised and watchful — and something more, that I know of, whether you will or no . . .

What do I ask? you will enquire in your precise and yet mocking way — cutting down my protestations to precise proposals. I do not know — how can I know? I only cast myself upon your mercy, not to be cut off, not scanted with a single famished kiss, not yet, not now. Can we not find a small space, for a limited time — in which to marvel that we have found each other?

Do you remember — no, of course you must remember — how we saw the Rainbow, from the brow of our hill, under our clump of trees — where light suffused the watery drops in the indrowned air — and the Flood was stayed — and we — we stood under the arch of it, as though the whole Earth were ours, by new Covenant — And from foot to distant foot of the rainbow is one bright, joined curve, though it shifts with our changing vision.

What a convoluted Missive, to lie and gather dust, maybe forever, in the Poste Restante. I shall walk, from time to time, in the Park, and wait even, under those same Trees — and trust you will forgive — and a little more

Your R.H.A.

Oh Sir — things flicker and shift, they are indeed all spangle and sparks and flashes. I have sat by my fireside all this long evening — on my safe stool — turning my burning cheeks towards the Aspirations of the flame and the caving-in, the ruddy mutter, the crumbling of the consumed coals to — where am I leading myself — to lifeless dust — Sir.

And then — out there — when the Rainbow stood out on the dark air over a drowning world — no Lightning struck those Trees, nor trickled along their Wooden Limbs to earth — yet flame licked, flame enfolded, flame looped veins — burned up and utterly consumed —

> Struck trees die black
> Fire in the Air
> Leaves not a Wrack
> of bone or hair —

Our first Parents hid under such strong circling trees, I believe — but the Eye saw them — who had incautiously eaten knowledge which was death to them —

If the world shall not be drowned with water a second time — it is certain how we shall perish — it is told us —

And you also — in Ragnarök — matched Wordsworth's fleet waters of a drowning world — with — the tongues of Surtur's flames that lapped the shores — Of all the earth and drunk its solid crust — And spat it molten gold on the red heaven —

And after that — a rain — of Ash —

> Ash the sheltering World-Tree, Ash the deadly Rain
> So Dust to Dust and Ash to Ash again —

I see whole bevies of shooting stars — like gold arrows before my darkening eyes — they presage Headache — but before the black — and burning — I have a small light space to say — oh what? I cannot let you burn me up. I cannot.

194

I should go up — not with the orderly peace of my beloved hearth *here — with its miniature caverns of delight, its hot temporary jewel-gardens with their palisadoes and promontories — no — I shall go up — like Straw on a Dry Day — a rushing wind — a tremor on the air — a smell of burning — a blown smoke — and a deal of white fine powder that holds its spillikin shape only an infinitesimal moment and then is random specks — oh no I cannot —*

You see, Sir, I say nothing of Honour, nor of Morality — though they are weighty matters — I go to the Core, which renders much disquisition on these matters superfluous. The core is my solitude, my solitude that is threatened, that you threaten, without which I am nothing — so how may honour, how may morality speak to me?

I read your Mind, my dear Mr Ash. You will argue now for a monitored and carefully limited *combustion — a fire-grate with bars and formal boundaries and brassy finials — ne progredietur ultra —*

But I say — your glowing salamander *is a Firedrake. And there will be — Conflagration —*

Before Migraine-headaches there is a moment of madness. This has extended from the burning in the clearing — until this minute — and now speaks.

No mere human can stand in a fire and not be consumed.

Not that I have not dreamed of walking in the furnace — as Shadrach, Meshach and Abednego —

But we latter-day Reasonable Beings have not the miracle-working Passion of the old believers —

I have known — Incandescence — and must decline to sample it further.

The headache proceeds apace. Half my head — is merely a gourd full of pain —

Jane will post this so it goes now. Forgive its faults. And forgive me.

Christabel

My dear,

What am I to make of your missive — I had almost writ missile — which as I foretold has crossed mine — but which as I had not the courage to foretell is not a cool denial but a most heated *riddling, to take up your metaphor? You are a true poet — when you are agitated, or discomposed, or unusually interested in any matter — you express your ideas in metaphor. So what am I to make of all this scintillation? I will tell you — a Pyre from which you, my Phoenix, shall fly up renewed and unchanged — the gold more burnished, the eye brighter — semper eadem.*

And is it an effect of Love — to set beside each of us, like a manifest emanation some mythic monstrous and inhuman self? So that it becomes easy and natural for you to write as a Creature of the burning fiery furnace, a hearth-salamander turned Firedrake of the air, and easy and natural for you to see me in both mythic readings at once of my pliable name — the World-Tree consumed to its papery remnants. You feel — as I feel — elemental in this force. All creation rushed round us out there — earth, air, fire, water, and there we were, I beg you to remember, warm and human and safe, in the circle of the trees, in each other's arms, under the arch of the sky.

The most important thing to make clear to you is this. I make no threat to your solitude. How should I? How may I? Is not your blessed desire to be alone the only thing which makes possible what would else in very truth harm someone?

This agreed — may we not, in some circumscribed way — briefly, perhaps, probably — though it is Love's Nature to know itself eternal — and in confined spaces too — may we not steal some — I almost wrote small, but it will never be that — some great happiness? We must come to grief and regret anyway — and I for one would rather regret the reality than its phantasm, knowledge than hope, the deed than the hesitation, true life and not mere sickly potentialities. All of which casuistry is only to say, my very dear, come back to the Park, let me touch your hand again, let us walk in our decorous storm together. There may well come a moment when this will be impossible, for many good reasons — but you know, and feel, as I know and feel that this moment of impossibility is not yet, is not now?

I am reluctant to take my pen from the paper and fold up this letter — for as long as I write to you, I have the illusion that we are in touch, that is, blessed. Did you know, speaking of dragons as we were, and of conflagration and intemperate burning — that the Chinese dragon, who in Mandarin is Lung — is a creature not of the fiery, but exclusively of the watery element? And thus a cousin of your mysterious Melusina in her marble tub? Which is to say, there may be cooler dragons, who may take more temperate pleasures. He appears, blue and winding, on Chinese dishes, with a sprinkling mane and accompanied by what I once took to be little flakes of fire, and now know to be curlings of water.

What a page of prose to lie like some bomb in the Poste Restante. I am become, in the last two days, a restless Anarchist.

I shall wait under the trees — from day to day, at your time — and look out for a woman like a steady upright flame and a grey hound poured along the ground like smoke —

I know you will come. *All along, what I have known, has been. It is not a state of affairs I normally experience, nor one I ever required – but I am an honest man, and recognise what is, when it is ... So you will come. (Not peremptory but quiet, this knowing –)*

Your R.H.A.

Dear Sir

I am too proud – to say I knew, I should not have come – and yet came. I acknowledge my Acts – of which all that trepidant walk was one – from Mount Ararat Road to the Tempting Knoll – with Dog Tray circling and growling – He loves you not, Sir – and the end of that sentence could be – 'and nor do I' as well as the more expected ending 'whatever I may feel'. Were you happy I came? Were we godlike as you promised? Two earnest pacers, pointing diligent toes in the dust. Did you remark – setting Electrical Powers and Galvanic Impulses aside for the moment – how shy we are one with another? Mere acquaintances, if not on paper. We pass the time of day – and the Time of the Universe has a brief stop at our fingers' touch – who are we? who? – would you not rather have the freedom of the white page? Is it alas too late? Is our primaeval innocence gone?

No – I am out – I am out of my Tower and my Wits. I have my cottage to myself for a few brief hours – Tuesday afternoon – ca 1.00 p.m. – should you care to reconnoitre the humdrum truth of your imagined Bower – of – ? Will you take Tea?

Oh, I regret much. Much. And there are things that must be said – soon now – and will find their moment.

I am sad, sir, today – low and sad – sad that we went walking, yet sad too, that we are not walking still. And that is all I can write, for the Muse has forsaken me – as she may mockingly forsake all Women, who dally with Her – and then – Love –

Your Christabel

My Dear

So now I may think of you in truth – in your little Parlour – presiding over the flowering little cups – with Monsignor Dorato prinking and trilling, not, as I had hypothesised, in a Florentine palazzo but in a very Taj Mahal of burning brass wires. And over the mantel, Christabel before Sir Leoline – *yourself caught like a statue with coloured light striking garishly across you and an equally frigid Dog Tray. Who ranged, busily seeking, with his hackles like porpentine quills and his soft grey lip wrinkled in a snarl – truly, as you* say, he at least does not love me, and once or twice threatened my composed attention to the excellent seed cake, and rattled cup and saucer. And no porch with tumbling flowers – all vanishing froth and fantasy – but stiff tall Roses like a thicket of sentinels.

I think your house did not love me, and I should not have come.

And it is true, as you said, across the whole hearth, that I too have a house, which we have not described or even spoken of. And that I have a wife. You asked me to speak of her and I was speechless. I know not how you construed that – I grant it was your absolute right to ask – and yet I could not answer. (Though I knew you must ask.)

I have a wife, and I love her. Not as I love you. Now, I have sat for half-an-hour, having written those bleak little sentences, and quite unable to go on. There are good reasons – I cannot discuss them, but they are good, if not absolutely adequately good – why my love for you need not hurt her. I know this must sound bald and lame. It must, most probably, be what many men, philandering men, have said before me – I do not know – I am inexperienced in these matters and never thought to find myself writing such a letter. I find I can say no more, only aver that I believe what I have said to be true and hope that I shall not lose you by this necessary uncouthness. To discuss this any further would be the most certain way to betray her. I should feel the same if the question were ever to arise of discussing you – with anyone at all. Even the implicit analogy is distressing – you must feel it. What you are is yours – what we have – if anything – is ours.

Please destroy this letter – whatever you do or have done with the rest – because in itself it constitutes such a betrayal.

I hope the Muse has not indeed forsaken you – even briefly, even for so long as a Teatime. I am writing a lyric poem – most intransigent – about Firedrakes and Chinese Lung dragons – a conjuration, it might rightly be called. It is to do with you – as everything I do these days, or think, or breathe, or see is to do with you – but it is not addressed to you – those poems are to come.

If any answer comes to this plain letter – I shall know both that you are generous indeed, and that our small space is ours – for our short time – until the moment of impossibility makes itself known –

Your R.H.A.

My dear Sir,

Yr plainness and yr reticence can do you nothing but Honour – if that might be thought to be pertinent in this – Pandora's Box – we have opened – or wet

Outdoors we have ventured into. I find I can write no more – indeed and indeed my Head Hurts – and matters in this House – of which I shall not speak, from something the same motives of I hope honour – enfin, they do not go well. Can you be in the park on Thursday. I have matters to impart that I would rather speak.

Ever, C.

My dear

    My Phoenix is temporarily a woebegone and even bedraggled bird – speaking uncharacteristically small and meek – and even from moment to moment deferential. This will not do – this may not be – I will renounce all, all my heart's happiness, I say – to see you brighten and flare as you were wont. I would do all in my power that you might sparkle in your sphere as ever before – even renounce my so-much-insisted-upon claim on you. So tell me – not that you are sad, but why you are so, and truthfully, and I will take it upon me to mend what's ill, if it lies in my power. Now write back to me as you may, and come again on Tuesday.

Always, R.H.A.

Dearest Sir,

    In faith I know not why I am so sad. No – I know – it is that you take me out of myself and give me back – diminished – I am wet eyes – and touched hands – and lips am I too – a very present – famished – fragment of a woman – who has not her desire in truth – and yet has desire superabundantly – ah – this is painful –

    And you say – so kind you are – 'I love you. I love you.' – and I believe – but who is she – who is 'you'? Is she – fine fair hair and – whatever yearns so – I was once something else – something alone and better – I was sufficient unto my self – and now I range – busily seeking with continual change. I might be less discontented if my daily Life were happy, but it is become a brittle tissue of silence and needle-sharp reproach punctuating. I stare proudly – and seem most ignorant where I am most sharply knowing – and known – but this costs – it is not easy – it is not good.

    I read yr John Donne.

> *But we, by a love so much refined,*
> *That ourselves know not what it is,*
> *Inter-assured of the mind,*
> *Care less, eyes, lips, and hands to miss.*

This is a fine phrase — 'inter-assured of the mind'. Do you believe it is possible *to find such* — *safe mooring* — *in the howling gale?*

And I have now a new word in my vocabulary, much hated, to which I am enslaved — it goes 'And if —' ' And if —' And if we had time and space to be together — as we have allowed ourselves to wish to be — then we would be free together — whereas now — caged?

My dear,

The true exercise of freedom is — cannily and wisely and with grace — to move inside what space confines — and not seek to know what lies beyond and cannot be touched or tasted. But we are human — and to be human is to desire to know what may be known by any means. And it is easier to miss lips hands and eyes when they are grown a little familiar and are not at all to be explored, the unknown calling. 'And if' we had a week — or two — what would we not make of it? And maybe we shall. We are resourceful and intelligent persons.

I would not for the whole world diminish you. I know it is usual in these circumstances to protest — 'I love you for yourself alone' — 'I love you essentially' — and as you imply, my dearest, to mean by 'you essentially' — lips hands and eyes. But you must know — we do know — that it is not so — dearest, I love your soul and with that your poetry — the grammar and stopping and hurrying syntax of your quick thought — quite as much essentially you as Cleopatra's hopping was essentially hers to delight Antony — more essentially, in that while all lips hands and eyes resemble each other somewhat (though yours are enchanting and also magnetic) — your thought clothed with your words is uniquely you, came with you, would vanish if you vanished —

The journey I spoke of is not finally decided on. Tugwell finds himself greatly involved in his work at home — and though the project was long ago decided upon for when the weather should be clement — to be civilised these days requires an intelligent interest in the minuter forms of life and the monstrous permanent forms of the planet — it now hangs fire. And I who was all enthusiasm — now hang fire — hang upon fire — for how should I willingly go so far from Richmond?

Until Tuesday then

P.S. Swammerdam is almost ready once more.

Dearest Sir,

My dubious Muse is back. I send you (unperfected) what She has dictated.

> *The grassy knoll*
> *Shivers in His embrace*
> *His muscles – roll*
> *About – about – His Face*
> *Smiles hot and gold*
> *Over the small hill's brow*
> *And every fold*
> *Contracts and stiffens – now*
> *He gathers strength*
> *His glistering length*
> *Grips, grips: the stones*
> *Cry out like bones*
> *Constricted – earth – in pain*
> *Cries out – again –*
> *He grips and smiles –*

My very dear,

I write in haste – I fear your answer – I know not whether to depart or no – I will stay, for you – unless this small chance you spoke of prove a true possibility. Yet how may that be? How could you satisfactorily explain such a step? How can I not nevertheless hope?

I do not wish to do irreparable damage to your life. I have so much rational understanding left to me, as to beg you – against my own desires, my own hope, my own true love – to think before and after. If by any kind of ingenuity it may be done satisfactorily so that you may afterwards live as you wish – well then – if it may – this is not matter for writing. I shall be in the Church at noon tomorrow.

I send my love now and always.

Dear Sir,

It is done. BY FIAT. I spoke Thunder – and said – so it shall be – and there will be no questions now – or ever – and to this absolute Proposition I have – like all Tyrants – meek acquiescence.

No more Harm can be done by this than has already been done – not by your will – though a little by mine – for I was (and am) angry.

CHAPTER ELEVEN

Swammerdam

Bend nearer, Brother, if you please. I fear
I trouble you. It will not be for long.
I thank you now, before my voice, or eyes,
Or weak wit fail, that you have sat with me
Here in this bare white cell, with the domed roof
As chalky-plain as any egg's inside.
I shall be hatched tonight. Into what clear
And empty space of quiet, she best knows,
The holy anchoress of Germany
Who charged you with my care, and speaks to God
For my poor soul, my small soul, briefly housed
In this shrunk shelly membrane that He sees,
Who holds, like any smiling Boy, this shell
In his bright palm, and with His instrument
Of Grace, pricks in his path, for infinite Light
To enter through his pinhole, and seek out
What must be sucked to him, an inchoate slop
Or embryonic Angel's fledgling wings.

I have not much to leave. Once I had much,
Or thought it much, but men thought otherwise.
Well-nigh three thousand winged or creeping things
Lively in death, injected by my Art,
Lovingly entered, opened and displayed –
The types of Nature's Bible, ranged in ranks
To show the secrets of her cunning hand.
No matter now. Write – if you please – I leave
My manuscripts and pens to my sole friend,
The Frenchman, the incomparable Thévenot,

Who values, like a true philosopher
The findings of a once courageous mind.
He should have had my microscopes and screws –
The copper helper with his rigid arms
We called Homunculus, who gripped the lens
Steadier than human hands, and offered up
Fragments of gauze, or drops of ichor, to
The piercing eyes of Men, who dared to probe
Secrets beyond their frame's unaided scope.
·But these are gone, to buy the bread and milk
This curdled stomach can no more ingest.
I must die in his debt. He is my friend
And will forgive me. Write that hope. Then write
For her, for Antoinette de Bourignon
(Who spoke to me, when I despaired, of God's
Timeless and spaceless point of Infinite Love)
That, trusting her and Him, I turn my face
To the bare wall, and leave this world of things
For the No-thing she shewed me, when I came
Halting to Germany, to seek her out.
Now sign it, Swammerdam, and write the date,
March, 1680, and then write my age
His forty-third year. His small time's end. His *time* –
Who saw Infinity through countless cracks
In the blank skin of things, and died of it.

Think you, a man's life grows a certain shape
As out of ant's egg antworm must proceed
And out of antworm wrapped in bands must come
The monstrous female or the winged drone
Or hurrying worker, each in its degree?
I am a small man, closed in a small space,
Expert in smallness, in the smallest things,
The inconsiderable and overlooked,
The curious and the ephemeral.
I like your small cell, Brother. Poverty,
Whiteness, a window, water, and your hand
Steadying the beaker at my cracking lips.
Thank you. It is enough.
                    Where I was born
Was a small space too, not like this, not bare,
A brilliant dusty hutch of mysteries,
A cabinet of curiosities.

What did my eyes first light on? There was scarce
Space for a crib between the treasure-chests,
The subtle-stoppered jars and hanging silks,
Feathers and bones and stones and empty gourds
Heaped pêle-mêle o'er the tables and the chairs.
A tray of moonstones spilled into a bowl
Of squat stone scarabs and small painted eyes
Of alien godlings winked from dusty shelves.
A mermaid swam in a hermetic jar
With bony fingers scraping her glass walls
And stiff hair streaming from her shrunken head.
Her dry brown breasts were like mahogany,
Her nether parts, coiled and confined, were dull,
Like ancient varnish, but her teeth were white.
And there was too a cockatrice's egg,
An ivory-coloured sphere, or almost sphere,
That balanced on a Roman drinking-cup
Jostling a mummy-cat, still wrapped around
With pitch-dark bandages from head to foot,
Sand-dried, but not unlike the swaddling-bands
My infant limbs were held in, I assume.

And your hands, will they? presently will fold
This husk here in its shroud and close my eyes,
Weakened by so much straining over motes
And specks of living matter, eyes that oped
In innocent lustre on that teasing heap
Of prizes reaped round the terrestrial globe
By resolute captains of the proud Dutch ships
That slip their anchors here in Amsterdam,
Sail out of mist and squalls, ride with the wind
To burning lands beneath a copper sun
Or never-melted mountains of green ice
Or hot dark secret places in the steam
Of equatorial forests, where the sun
Strikes far above the canopy, where men
And other creatures never see her light
Save as a casual winking lance that runs
A silver shaft between green dark and dark.

I had a project, as a tiny boy

To make a catalogue of all this pelf,
Range it, create an order, render it,
You might say, human-sized, by typing it
According to the use we made of it
Or meanings we saw in it. I would part
Medicine from myth, for instance, amulets
(Pure superstition) from the minerals –
Rose-quartz, quicksilver, we could grind to heal
Agues or tropic fever. Living things
Should have their own affined taxonomy,
Insect with insect, dusty bird with bird,
And all the eggs, from monstrous ostrich-globe
To chains of soft-shelled snakes' eggs, catalogued,
Measured with calipers and well set out
Gainst taffeta curtains, in curved wooden cups:

My father had a pothecary's shop
And seemed well-pleased at first to have a son
With such precocious yearnings of the mind.
He was ambitious for me. In his thoughts
He saw me doing human good, admired
By men, humble in God's eyes, eloquent
For truth and justice. When he saw that I
Was not the lawyer-son his hopes embraced
He fixed on a physician. 'Who can mend
Man's ailing frame, succours his soul too,' said
My father, a devout and worldly man,
'And keeps himself in bread and meat and wine.
Since fallen man must ail, the doctor's care
Is ever-wanted, this side of the grave.'
But I had other leanings. Did they come
From scrupulous intellect, or glamorous spell
Cast by my infant nursery's denizens?
It seemed to me that true anatomy
Began not in the human heart and hands
But in the simpler tissues, primal forms,
Of tiny things that crept or coiled or flew.
The clue to life lay in the blind white worm
That eats away the complex flesh of men,
Is eaten by the farmyard bird who makes
A succulent dinner for another man
And so completes the circle. Life is One

I thought, and rational anatomy
Begins at the foot o' the ladder, on the rung
Nearest the fertile heat of Mother Earth.

Was it for that, or was it that my Soul
Had been possessed, in that dark Cabinet
By the black spider, big as a man's fist,
Tangible demon, in her sooty hair,
Or by the coal-black Moths of Barbary
Pierced through their frail dark wings, and crucified
With pins, for our amusement?

                          These were strange
And yet were forms of life, as I was too
(With a soul superadded, understood)
And kin to me, or so I thought, when young.
For all seemed fashioned from the self-same stuff,
Mythic gold yolk and glassy albumen   .
Of ancient Egypt's fabled Mundane Egg,
Laid in the Void by sable-plumaged Night.
From which sprang Eros, all in feathered light
Who fecundated Chaos, wherein formed
Germens of all that lives and moves on Earth.
The Orphic fables in their riddling wit
Pointed us there, perhaps, towards a truth.

I sought to know the origins of life.
I thought it lawful knowledge. Did not God
Who made my hands and eyes, lend me the skill
To make my patient copper mannikin
Who held the lenses, variously curved
Steady above the living particles
I learned to scry and then to magnify
Successively in an expanding scale
Of diminution or of magnitude,
Until I saw successive plans and links
Of dizzying order and complexity?
I could anatomise a mayfly's eye,
Could so arrange the cornea of a gnat
That I could peer through that at New Church Tower,
And see it upside down and multiplied,
Like many pinpoints, where no Angels danced.
A moth's wing scaly like a coat of mail,
The sharp hooked claws upon the legs of flies –

I saw a new world in this world of ours –
A world of miracle, a world of truth
Monstrous and swarming with unguessed-at life.

That glass of water you hold to my lips,
Had I my lenses, would reveal to us
Not limpid clarity as we suppose –
Pure water – but a seething, striving horde
Of animalcules lashing dragon-tails
Propelled by springs and coils and hairlike fronds
Like whales athwart the oceans of the globe.
The optic lens is like a slicing sword.
It multiplies the world, or it divides –
We see the many in the one, as here,
We see the segments of what once seemed smooth,
Rough pits and craters on a lady's skin,
Or fur and scales along her gleaming hair.

The more the Many were revealed to me
The more I pressed my hunt to find the One –
Prima Materia, Nature's shifting shape
Still constant in her metamorphoses.

I found her Law in the successive Forms
Of ant and butterfly, beetle and bee.
I first discerned the pattern of the growth
From egg to simple grub, from grub encased,
Shrinking in part, in other putting forth
New organs in its sleep, until it stir,
Split and disgorge the tattered silk, which fast
Trembles and stiffens and then takes the air
Unfurled in splendour, tawny, sapphire blue,
Eyed like the peacock, tiger-barred, or marked
Between its wings with dark death's eyeless head.

Within the crystal circle of the lens
My horny thumbs were elephantine pads.
I fashioned me a surgeon's armoury –
Skewers and swords, scalpels and teasing hooks –
Not out of steel, but softest ivory,
Sharpened and turned beyond our vision's range,
Lances and lancets, that the naked eye
Could not discern, beneath the lens's stare.

With these I probed the creatures' very life
And source of life, of generation.
Their commonwealths are not as we supposed.
Lay out the ant-hill's Lord, the beehive's King
The centre of the patterns that they weave
Fetching and carrying, hurrying to feed,
Construct and guard their world, the pinnacle
Or apex of the social hierarchy –
Lay out this creature on the optic disk,
Lay bare the seat of generation
The organs where the new lives lie and grow,
Where the eggs take their form. She is no King
But a vast Mother, on whose monstrous flanks
Climb smaller sisters, hurrying to tend
Her progeny, to help with her travail,
Carry her nectar and give up their lives
If needs be, to save hers, for she is Queen,
The necessary Centre of the Brood.

It was these eyes first saw the Ovaries,
These hands that drew them, and this fading mind
Discerned the law of Metamorphosis
And wrote it down to show indifferent men.
I had no honour of it. Not at Home –
My father cast me bankrupt in the street –
Nor 'mongst my peers in Medicine. When, by Want
Driven to sell my library of slides,
My demonstrations and experiments,
I found no Buyer, nor no man of Science,
Philosopher or Doctor, who would take
My images of Truth, my elegant
Visions of life, and give them hope to last.
And so I came to penury and beg
For sops of bread and milk and scraps of meat
Scattered with maggots of the self-same flies
I marked the breeding of.

Great Galileo with his optic tube
A century ago, displaced this Earth
From apprehension's Centre, and made out
The planets' swimming circles and the Sun
And beyond that, motion of infinite space
Sphere upon sphere, in which our spinning world

Green grass and yellow desert, mountains white
And whelming depths of bluest sea, is but
A speck in a kind of star-broth, rightly seen.
They would have burned him for his saying so,
Save that the sage, in fear of God and strong
In hope of life, gainsaid his own surmise,
Submitted him to doctors of the Church
Who deal in other truths and mysteries.

It was one step, I say, to displace Man
From the just centre of the sum of things –
But quite another step to strike at God
Who made us as we are, so fearfully
And wonderfully made our intellects,
Our tireless quest to *know*, but also made
Our finitude, within His Mystery,
His soft, dark, infinite space, wherein we rest
When all our questions finish and our brain
Dies into weeping, as my own taxed mind
Died in dissecting the Ephemera.
I found their forms, those dancing specks of life,
The one-day flies, I gave my years to them,
Who live one day's space, never know the night.

I ask myself, did Galileo know
Fear, when he saw the gleaming globes in space,
Like unto mine, whose lens revealed to me –
Not the chill glory of Heaven's Infinite –
But all the swarming, all the seething motes
The basilisks, the armoured cockatrice,
We cannot see, but are in their degrees –
Why not? – to their own apprehension –
I dare not speak it – why not microcosms
As much as Man, poor man, whose ruffled pride
Cannot abide the Infinite's questioning
From smallest as from greatest?

[*Desunt cetera.*]

CHAPTER TWELVE

What is a House? So strong – so square
Making a Warmth inside the Winds
We walk with lowered eyelids there
And silent go – behind the blinds

Yet hearts may tap like loaded bombs
Yet brains may shrill in carpet-hush
And windows fly from silent rooms
And walls break outwards – with a rush –

Christabel LaMotte

They stood on the pavement and looked up at the carved letters over the porch: BETHANY. It was a sunny day in April. They were awkward with each other, standing at a distance. The house was spick and span, three storeys high, with sash windows. Prettily sprigged curtains hung on carved wooden rings from a brass rail. Inside the front window a maidenhair fern stood in a large Minton pot. On the front door, painted a deep Delft blue, hung a sinuous brass dolphin door-knocker. There were buds on the roses and a sea of forget-me-nots at their feet. There was a frieze of bricks with moulded sunflowers between storeys. Every brick breathed fresh air; they had been stripped and drenched with blow-torch and high-speed jet, so that the house lay revealed beneath its original skin.

'It's a good restoration job,' said Maud. 'It makes you feel funny. A simulacrum.'

'Like a fibre-glass copy of the sphinx.'

'Exactly. You can just see a very Victorian fireplace in there. I can't tell if it's an original or a vamped-up one from a demolition lot.'

They looked up at the bland or blind face of Bethany.

'It would have been sootier. It would have looked older. When it was younger.'

'A postmodern quotation –'

There was a porch now, with the first tendrils of a very new clematis advancing up it, a porch of new white wooden arches, a miniature bower.

Out of here she had come, stepping rapidly, in a swirl of determined black skirts, lips tight with determination, hands compressed on her reticule, eyes wide with fear, with hope, wild, how? Had he come down the road from St Matthias' Church, in his tall hat and his frock coat? Had she, the other, peered through her rimmed glasses from an upper window, her eyes blurring?

'I've never been much interested in places – or things – with associations –'

'Nor I. I'm a textual scholar. I rather deplore the modern feminist attitude to private lives.'

'If you're going to be stringently analytical,' Roland said, 'don't you have to?'

'You can be psychoanalytic without being *personal* –' Maud said. Roland did not challenge her. It was he who had suggested they came to Richmond to discuss what to do next, and now they were here, the sight of the little house was indeed disturbing. He suggested that they went into the church at the end of the road, a huge Victorian barn, containing modern glass-walled galleries and a quiet coffee bar. The church was full of children's activities, prancing and bedizened clowns, fairies and ballerinas, easels and scraping violins and piping recorders. They settled in the coffee bar, in a reminiscent patch of stained-glass light.

Nothing had been heard from Sir George since they had despatched their fervent thank-yous in January. Maud had taught a difficult term. Roland had applied for jobs – one in Hong Kong, one in Barcelona, one in Amsterdam. He had little hope of these – he had once seen a copy of Blackadder's standard reference for him, lying around in the Ash factory, which praised his diligence and thoroughness and caution, making him sound thoroughly dull. They had agreed, Roland and Maud, to say nothing to anyone, and to do nothing until they either heard from Sir George or saw each other again.

Roland had said to Maud, on that last cold day in Lincoln, that it looked as though perhaps Christabel had contemplated accompanying Randolph on his natural history expedition to North Yorkshire in June 1859. This had seemed obvious to him; he had not taken into account Maud's complete lack of knowledge of R. H. Ash's movements. He elaborated. Ash had been gone for a month, travelling alone, walking along shores and cliffs, studying geology and marine life. He was to have been accompanied by Francis Tugwell, the clergyman author of *Anemones of the British Coast*, but illness had prevented Mr Tugwell from coming. Critics ascribed to this studious month, Roland told Maud, a shift in the subject-matter of Ash's poetry, from history to natural-history, so to speak. Roland himself did not subscribe to this view. It was part of a general intellectual movement at the time. *The Origin of Species* was published in 1859. Ash's friend Michelet, the great historian, had at this time taken to nature study and had written four books related to the four elements – *La Mer* (water), *La Montagne* (earth), *L'Oiseau* (air), and *L'Insecte* (fire, since insects lived in the hot underneath). Ash's 'natural' poems were like these, or like Turner's late great paintings of elemental light.

Ash had written to his wife, most days, if not every day, during this tour. The letters were in Cropper's edition; Maud and Roland had brought photocopies to their meeting.

My dearest Ellen,

I and my tall basket of specimen jars arrived in one piece in Robin Hood's Bay – though much bruised and dirtied from the shaking of the train and the continuous rain of smuts and live sparks from the engine, most particularly in the tunnels. The Pickering-Grosmont line travels through the Newtondale Gorge – a cleft formed during the Ice Age – where the engine produces, amongst romantically desolate moorland, a sublime volanic eruption of its own, due to the steepness of the gradient. It put me in mind of Milton's Satan, winging his black way throught the asphaltic fumes of Chaos – and of Lyell's solid, patient yet inspired work on the raising of the hills and the carving of the valleys by ice. I heard curlews, making their peremptory, desolate sound, and saw what I like to believe was an eagle, though it was probably no such thing – at all events, a hovering predator, floating on the invisible element. Strange narrow-chested sheep bound away, scattering stones, and swaying their woolly integument in the air like banks of weed in the sea-water – heavy and slow – They stare from crags – I was about to write inhumanly – but that goes without saying – they have a look almost daemonic and inimical, for domesticated animals. You would be interested by their eyes – yellow with a black bar of a pupil – horizontal, not vertical – which gives them their odd look.

The train is a modern successor to a successful horse-drawn railway designed and built by George Stephenson himself. I should almost have preferred that more decorous conveyance to the snorting firedragon who ruined my travelling-shirt (no, I shall not send it home, my landlady, a Mrs Cammish, is an excellent laundress and starcher, I am assured.).

Here everything seems primaeval – the formations of the rocks, the heaving and tossing of the full sea, the people with their fishing boats (called cobles in the local speech) which I imagine are not much changed from the primitive if versatile little craft of the early Viking invaders. Here on the shore of the German Ocean I feel the presence of those Northern Lands across its cold grey-green wastes – very different from the close civilised fields of France across the Channel – Even the air is somehow both ancient and fresh – fresh with salt and heather and a kind of absolute biting cleanness, resembling the taste of the water here, which has bubbled deliciously from perforated limestone, and is more surprising than wine – after the turgid Thames.

But you will be thinking I have no regret for my warm house and library and smoking-jacket and desk, and for the company of my dear wife. I think of you steadily and with steady love – of which you need no assurance. Are you well? Are you able to go about and to read without headache? Write and tell me of all your doings. I shall write more, and you shall see that I am become a diligent anatomist of simple life-forms – a vocation, more satisfying at the moment, than the recording of human convulsions.

JUNE 15

I have been diligently reading at Lyell in my long evenings, when I have done with my dissection, which I try to do whilst the light is good, between coming in from the walks and dining. I have abandoned the tall specimen-jars for a series of plain yellow pie dishes which sit about on all the available surfaces of my dining-room, containing Eolis pellucida, Doris billomellata, Aplysia *and several varieties of polyps – Tubularian, Plumularian, Sertularian – exquisite little Aeolides and some compound Ascidians. It is hard indeed, Ellen, not to imagine that some Intelligence did not design and construct these perfectly lovely and marvellously functioning creatures – and yet it is hard also not to believe the weight of evidence for the Development Theory, for the changes wrought in all things, over unimaginable Time, by the gradual action of ordinary causes.*

Tell me, were you indeed able, or well enough, to hear Professor Huxley's paper on 'The Persistent Types of Animal Life'? He must argue, like Darwin, against repeated acts of Creation in the setting of a distinct species on the face of the earth – but rather for the gradual modification of existing species. Were you able to make any notes? They would be of the greatest value – in assuaging curiosity at least – to your enthusiastic amateur husband.

Today I walked down the cliffs from Scarborough to see the awesome Flamborough Head, where so many have met terrible deaths, in the race of water and the powerful currents – which you can almost see and hear, chuckling beneath the slap of the high waves even on a good smiling day, as this was. The cliffs are chalky-white and carved and faceted and sliced by the elements into fantastic shapes – which the superstitious might take for Divine sculptures, or petrified ancient giants. One stands out to sea – raising an impotent or menacing stump – like a bandaged member eaten by some white leprosy. There were two Rocks known as the King and Queen – of which the latter only is still standing. Lyell describes the whole of this coast as subject to gradual dilapidation and writes of the waste of Flamborough, wch is being decomposed by the salt spray, the process, lower down the coast, being facilitated by the throwing out of many springs from the argillaceous beds.

It occurs to me to think – if salt water and fresh water may so patiently – and with such inevitable blind causation – give form to these white marble caves and churches and inhuman Figures by sculpting with chisel, or by moulding with the pressure of the threads of water growing to a head in the spring, and cutting fine channels with droplets and the thrust of gravity –

If this mineral force can create such forms as stalactites and stalagmites – why may not the channels of the ear or the vesicles of the heart – over millennia – respond to pressure and direction –?

How may what is born, is formed by gradual causes, transmit this form to its offspring – transmit the type – tho the individual may fail? This if I mistake not, is not known. I may cut off a sprig of a tree – and grow a whole tree – roots and crown and all from that – and how may that be? How does the twig-slip know to form root and branch?

We are a Faustian generation, my dear — we seek to know what we are maybe not designed (if we are designed) to be able to know.

Lyell tells us also of many villages on this coast which have been engulfed by the waters — such are Auburn, Hartburn and Hyde as well as Aldbrough which has moved inland. I have not been able to find that there are myths or legends connected with these melancholy vanished communities — as I believe there are, for instance, in Brittany — but fishermen have found relics of houses and churches out on sandbanks in the midst of the sea ... However, if there is no drowned city of Is to torment my nights with underwater bells calling, I have found a homely English sprite, a Hob, who inhabits a Hole, called naturally a Hob Hole. This genial Hob cures the whooping cough (known in this part of the world as the kink-cough.) This Hob Hole is a cave in the cliff near the village of Kettleness — which fell into the sea, one dark December night in 1829, sliding downwards all of a smooth piece.

You will be beginning to think I am in danger of drowning, or being engulfed in brine and sand. A wave whipped away a net I had left carelessly by my side when feeling in a deep pool on Filey Brigg for a recalcitrant Polyp — but I am unscathed, apart from a few honourable scratches from barnacle-crusts and infant mussels. I shall be restored to you in two weeks time — with all my dead wonders of the deep —

'Mortimer Cropper claims to have traced every step of that holiday,' Roland told Maud. ' "The long tramp to Pickering along the Roman Road must have made the Poet as footsore as it made me, though his keen eye must have remarked even more to please and interest him than I could see in these later times ..." '

'He didn't imagine Ash had a companion?'

'No. Would you, reading those letters?'

'No. They read exactly like the letters of a solitary husband on holiday, talking to his wife of an empty evening. Unless it's significant that he never says "Wish you were here" or even "I wish you could see" — that's all a textual critic could make of it. Apart from the obvious reference to drowned Is which we knew he already knew about. Think about it — if you were a man in the excited state of the writer of the Christabel letters — could you sit down every evening and write to *your wife* — in front of Christabel, it would have to have been? Could you produce these — travelogues?'

'If I thought I *must* – for her sake – Ellen's – I might.'

'It would require quite horrible self-control and duplicity. And they look such peaceable letters –'

'They do seem to be reassuring her – from time to time –'

'We would read that in, though, once we supposed –'

'And Christabel? Is anything known about her in June 1859?'

'There's nothing at all in the Archive. Nothing until Blanche dies in 1860. Do you think –?'

'What *happened* to Blanche?'

'She drowned herself. She jumped from the bridge, at Putney – with her clothes wetted and her pockets full of big round stones. To make sure. She's on record as admiring the heroism of Mary Wollstonecraft's suicide attempt from the same bridge. She obviously noted that Wollstonecraft found it hard to sink, because of her clothes floating.'

'Maud – is it known *why*?'

'Not really. She left a note saying that she couldn't pay her debts and that she was a "superfluous person", "of no utility" in this world. She hadn't a penny in the bank. The coroner diagnosed a temporary female imbalance of the mind. "Women are known for strong and irrational alterations of temperament," he said.'

'Women are. Feminists use that argument about car accidents and exams –'

'Don't get distracted. I take your point. The thing is – scholars have always assumed Christabel was *there* – she gave evidence saying she'd been "away from home at that time" – I've always assumed that meant a day or a week or two at the most –'

'What time of year did Blanche die?'

'June 1860. For a year before that we've nothing about Christabel – nothing but the Lincolnshire letters, that is. And some fragments of *Melusina*, we think, and a few fairy tales she sent to *Home Notes* including – wait a minute – one about a Hob who cures whooping-cough. Not that that *proves* anything.'

'He could have told her that story.'

'She could have read it elsewhere. Do you think she did?'

'No. Do you think she went to Yorkshire?'

'Yes. But how can it be proved? Or disproved?'

'We could try Ellen's journal. Do you think you could

approach Beatrice Nest? Without saying why, or connecting it with me?'

'That shouldn't be difficult.'

A troupe of infant ghouls, white-sheeted and livid-green faced, gambolled into the coffee room, and cried out for more juice, more juice, more juice. A child in a leotard and warpaint pranced beside them, the lines of his body more than apparent, a savage putto. 'What would Christabel have thought?' Roland asked Maud, who said:

'She invented enough goblins. She knew well enough what we are. She doesn't seem to have been hampered by respectability.'

'Poor Blanche.'

'She came here – to this church – before she made up her mind to jump. She knew the Vicar. "He suffers me as he suffers many maiden ladies with imagined pain. His Church is full of women, who may not speak there, who may embroider little stools but must not presume to offer sacred paintings –"'

'Poor Blanche.'

'Hullo?'

'May I speak to Roland Michell?'

'He's not here. I don't know where he is.'

'Could I leave a message?'

'If I see him, I can give him one. I don't always see him. He doesn't always read messages. Who's speaking?'

'My name is Maud Bailey. I just wanted him to know I'll be in the British Library tomorrow. To see Dr Nest.'

'Maud Bailey.'

'Yes. I wanted to talk to him first, if possible – in case anyone – it's rather delicate – I just wanted him to *know* – so he could make arrangements. Are you still there?'

'Maud Bailey.'

'That's what I said. Hullo? Are you there? Who cut us off? Damn.'

'Val?'

'What?'

'Is anything wrong?'

'No. Not particularly.'

'You're behaving as though something is.'

'Am I? How am I behaving? It makes a change for you to notice I'm behaving at all.'

'You haven't said anything all evening.'

'That's not unusual.'

'No. But there are *ways* of not saying anything –'

'Forget about it. It's not worth bothering about.'

'All right. I'll forget.'

'I shall be out late tomorrow. That should suit you.'

'I can work late in the BM. No problem.'

'You'll enjoy that. There was a *message* for you. People seem to think I'm an eternal secretary, just taking down messages.'

'A message?'

'Very *de haut en bas*. Your friend Maud Bailey. She'll be in the Museum tomorrow. I don't recollect the details.'

'What did you say to her?'

'Now I've got you all worried. I didn't *say* anything. I put the phone down.'

'Oh Val.'

'Oh Val, Oh Val, Oh Val. That's all you ever say. I'm going to bed now. I must turn in for my long day tomorrow. A huge income-tax fraud, isn't that exciting?'

'Does Maud say I should ... or shouldn't ... did she mention Beatrice Nest?'

'I don't recollect, I told you. I shouldn't think so. Fancy her being in London, Maud Bailey ...'

If he had had it in him to raise his voice, to shout Don't be so ridiculous, and mean it, things might never have come to this?

If there had been more than one bed in the flat he could have used his natural defence, which was self-enfolded inattention. He was stiff with keeping to himself on the edge of the mattress.

'It's not what you seem to think.'

'I don't think anything. It's not my place to think anything. I'm not told anything. I don't share anything, so I don't think anything. I'm a superfluous person. Never mind.'

And if this was in some terrible sense, *not Val*, where was she, lost, transmuted, in abeyance, what should he, what could he do? How was he responsible for this lost Val?

Maud and Beatrice began badly, partly because they found each other physically unsympathetic, Beatrice like an incoherent bale of knitting-wool and Maud poised and pointed and sharp. Maud had constructed a sort of questionnaire about Victorian wives, under headings, and worked her way slowly round to the question, which did interest her, of the nature of the reason for Ellen's writing.

'I'm very keen to know if the wives of these so-called great men –'

'He *was* a great man, in my opinion –'

'Yes. If their wives were content to rest in their husbands' glory or felt that they themselves might have achieved something if conditions had been favourable. So many of them wrote journals, often work, secret work, of very high quality. Look at Dorothy Wordsworth's marvellous prose – if she had supposed she could be a writer – instead of a sister – what might she not have done? What I want to ask is – why did Ellen write her journal? Was it to please her husband?'

'Oh no.'

'Did she show it to him?'

'Oh no. I don't think so. She never says so.'

'Do you think she wrote it for publication, in any form?'

'That's a harder question. I think she knew it might be read. There are several sharp comments in it about contemporary biographical habits – rummaging in Dickens's desk before he was fairly buried and that sort of thing – the usual Victorian comments. She knew he was a great poet and she must have known they would come – the scavengers – sooner or later if she didn't burn it. And she didn't burn it. She burned a lot of letters, you know. Mortimer Cropper thinks Patience and Faith burned them, but I think it was Ellen. Some are buried with her.'

'Why do you think she wrote the journal, Dr Nest? In order to have someone to talk to? As an examination of conscience? Out of a sense of duty? Why?'

'I do have a theory. It's far-fetched, I think.'

'What is your theory?'

'I think she wrote it to baffle. Yes. To baffle.'

They stared at each other. Maud said,

'To baffle whom? His biographers?'

'Just to baffle.'

Maud waited. Beatrice described helplessly, her true experience:

'When I started on it, I thought, what a nice dull woman. And then I got the sense of things flittering and flickering behind all that solid – oh, I think of it as *panelling*. And then I got to think – I was being led on – to imagine the flittering flickering things – and that really it was all just as stolid and dull as anything. I thought I was making it all up, that she could have said something interesting – how shall I put it – intriguing – once in a while – but she *absolutely wasn't going to*. It could be an occupational hazard of editing a dull journal, couldn't it? Imagining that the author was deliberately baffling me?'

Maud looked back at Beatrice, baffled. She saw the outline of stalwart strapping under the so-soft speckled wool of Beatrice's bolster-like front. The wool was basically powder-blue. It was hugely vulnerable. Beatrice dropped her voice.

'I expect you think I've very little to show for all these years of work on these papers. Twenty-five years to be precise, and sliding past at increasing speed. I've felt very conscious of that – that slowness – with the increasing interest shown by – your sort of scholar – people with ideas about Ellen Ash and her work. All I had was a sort of sympathy for the – helpmeet aspect of her – and to be truthful, Dr Bailey, a real admiration for him, for Randolph Ash. *They* said it would be better to – to do this task which presented itself so to speak and seemed appropriate to my – my sex – my capacities as they were thought to be, whatever they were. A good feminist in *those* days, Dr Bailey, would have insisted on being allowed to work on the Ask and Embla poems.'

'Being allowed?'

'Oh. I see. Yes. On *working* on the Ask and Embla poems.' She hesitated. Then: 'I don't think you can imagine, Miss Bailey, how it was then. We were dependent and excluded persons. In my early days – indeed until the late 1960s – women were *not permitted* to enter the main Senior Common Room at Prince Albert College. We had our own which was small and slightly *pretty*.

Everything was decided in the pub – everything of import – where we were not invited and did not wish to go. I hate smoke and the smell of beer. But should not therefore be excluded from discussing departmental policy. We were grateful for employment. We thought it was bad being young and – in some cases, not in mine – attractive – but it was worse when we grew older. There is an age at which, I profoundly believe, one becomes a *witch*, in such situations, Dr Bailey – through simple ageing – as always happened in history – and there are *witch-hunts* –

'You will think I am mad. I am trying to excuse twenty-five years' delay – with – personalities – You would have produced an edition twenty years ago. The truth is also, I wasn't sure it was right. If she would have liked what I was doing.'

Maud felt a heat of fellow-feeling, unexpected and powerful.

'Can't you give up? Do your own work?'

'I feel responsible. To myself, all those years. To *her*.'

'Could I see the journal? I'm particularly interested in 1859. I read his letters to her. The Yorkshire ones. Did she get to Huxley's lecture?'

Was this too blatant? Apparently not. Beatrice raised herself slowly and extracted the volume from a grey steel cabinet. She clasped it for a moment defensively.

'A Professor Stern came. From Tallahassee. She wanted to know – to know – to find out about Ellen Ash's sexual relations – with him – or anyone. I told her there was nothing of that kind in this journal. She said there must be – in the metaphors – in the omissions. We were not taught to do scholarship by studying primarily what was omitted, Dr Bailey. No doubt you find me naive.'

'No. I occasionally find Leonora Stern naive. No, that's the wrong word. Single-minded and zealous. And she may have been right. Maybe what you find baffling is a systematic omission –'

Beatrice thought. '*That* I may grant. Something is omitted. I fail to see why it must be presumed to be – that kind of thing.'

This dogged and flushed minor defiance struck another chord of fellow-feeling in Maud, who edged her chair closer and looked into the rumpled weary face. Maud thought of Leonora's ferocity, of Fergus's wicked playfulness, of the whole tenor and endeavour of twentieth-century literary scholarship, of a bed like dirty egg-white.

'I agree, Dr Nest. In fact I do agree. The whole of our scholarship – the whole of our thought – we question everything except the centrality of sexuality – Unfortunately feminism can hardly avoid privileging such matters. I sometimes wish I had embarked on geology myself.'

Beatrice Nest smiled and handed over the journal.

Ellen Ash's Journal

JUNE 4TH 1859

The house is echoing and silent without my dear Randolph. I am full of projects for improvements in his comfort to be effected whilst he is away. The study curtains and those in his dressing-room must come down and be beaten out thoroughly on the line. I am in doubts as to the wisdom of attempting to *wash* the upper ones. The drawing-room pair I attempted have never been the same, either as to lustre or as to the 'hang' of their folds. I shall set Bertha to a diligent beating and brushing and see what can be done. Bertha has been somewhat sluggish of late; she comes slowly when called and leaves tasks not rounded-off (the silver candlesticks, for instance, which have streaks of tarnish under the rims or the buttons on R's nightshirt, which are still deficient). I wonder if something is amiss with Bertha. After the uncertainties and dilapidations – and yes, violence and destruction – wrought by her predecessors I had hoped that Bertha would continue to be the half-invisible busy birdlike presence she commenced with so successfully. Is she unhappy or unwell? Both I fear but do not wish to think. Tomorrow I will ask her directly. She would be surprised if she knew what courage, and of what variable kinds (as to the disturbance of both her comfortable goings-on and my own) this requires of me. I lack my mother's force of character. I lack many things in which my dear mother was both proficient and naturally greatly endowed.

Above all, when my dear one is away, I miss our hours of quiet reading to each other of an evening. I wondered whether to go on with our study of Petrarch, where he left off, and decided against it; it loses too much without his beautiful voice bringing to life the ancient passion of the Italian. I read a chapter or two of Lyell's *Principles of Geology* in order to share with him his enthusiasm for his study, and was equally charmed by the intellectual gravity of Lyell's vision and chilled by his idea of the aeons of inhuman time that went to the making of earth's crust – which is still, if he is to be believed, perpetually in process of making. And where may hide what came and loved our clay? as the Poet asked finely. I do not – unlike the Reverend Mr Baulk – feel that this newly-perceived ancient state of things impinges on our settled faith in any decisive way. Perhaps I am unimaginative or too instinctive or intuitive in my trust. If the Tale of Noah's Deluge turns out to be a fine poetic invention, shall I, the wife of a great poet, thereby cease to pay attention to its message about the universal punishment of sin? If the exemplary Life and mysteriously joyful Death of that greatest and only truly good Man were to be thought of as inventions that would be differently threatening.

And yet, to live in a time which has created a *climate* of such questioning ... surely, after all, Herbert Baulk has cause for anxiety. He tells me I should not trouble my intellect with questions which my intuition (which he qualifies as womanly, virtuous, pure and so on and so on) can distinguish to be vain. He tells me I *know* that my Redeemer liveth, and looks eagerly for my assent to his proposition as though my assent provides him with strength also. Well, I assent. I do assent. I do know that my Redeemer liveth. But I should be grateful on earth if Herbert Baulk could respectably resolve his intellectual doubts so that our prayers could be full of honest praise and robust faith in a watchful Providence, rather than darkly *riddling*, as at present.

It is late for me to be writing this. I should not work so late if I was not alone – apart from the servants – in the house. I shall shut this book and betake myself to my pillow to fortify myself for the curtain-battle and the questioning of Bertha.

JUNE 6TH

This day brings a letter from Patience, who begs to stay here overnight with her brood, on the way to her seaside summer in Etretat. I must make her welcome – and indeed I shall be more than glad to exchange views and news of many dear ones unfortunately distant. But it is not a good time to receive any visit, with half the furnishings dismantled and a thorough inventory and washing of the china embarked on and not carried through, and some of the chairs under covers, and others being stitched by the useful Mr Beale. He discovered between the arm and the deep cushion of Randolph's study chair (the green leather tub chair) two guineas, the lost bill for candles which caused such a dispute, and the penwiper presented by the Ladies of St Swithin's church (and how they could have thought that anyone could have brought himself to sully all that fine work with ink blotches is beyond my comprehension). The chandelier is down and all its crystals are being carefully cleaned and polished. And into this more or less regulated disorder are to *rush* Enid, George, Arthur and Dora, who are as dangerous to crystal teardrops in their exaggerated carefulness as in any wanton playfulness. And yet they must come, of course. I have written to say so. Shall I retrieve or send away the chandelier? I dine in my study on broth and a slice of bread.

JUNE 7TH

A letter from Randolph. He is well and pursuing his studies profitably. We shall have much to discuss on his return. I have had a sore throat and violent attacks of sneezing – maybe from all the dust aroused by the cleaning efforts – and retired to my couch for the afternoon, behind closed curtains, where I dozed only fitfully, not well. Tomorrow I must rouse myself to receive Patience. Bertha has made up beds for the children in the old Nursery. I have still not asked her if anything ails her – but she is if anything more sullen and more lethargic than she was a week ago.

JUNE 9TH

How fortunate that the Master of this house is absent, for it has in the last twenty-four hours been converted into a veritable Pandemonium. George and Arthur are sturdy little creatures, for which we must always be grateful, and the dear girls – in repose – have an air of great sweetness with their soft pale skins and large unclouded eyes. Patience refers to them as my angels – and so they are, they are, but the city of Pandemonium was peopled by *fallen angels*, and all four of my exquisite nephews and nieces have a great propensity to *fall* just where it is most inopportune, dragging down cloths, scattering posies, and in Georgie's case cannoning, just as I feared, into the china bowl containing the crystal drops from the chandelier which rattled like pebbles underwater. Patience's nursemaid is not a great disciplinarian though she is excellent and perpetual at kissing and cuddling. Patience smiles benignly and says she declares Grace loves the dear infants truly, which I am sure is the case.

I told Patience she looked blooming, which is not exactly so, but I hope God will forgive me a small white lie. I was a little shocked at the changes in her – a fading of lustre from the hair, a lining of her dear tired face, a loss of that trimness of figure in which she used so to delight. She declares frequently that she is well and happy, but complains also of shortness of breath, lumbar pains, incessant toothaches and headaches, and other insidious ailments which have persisted – strengthened their attack, she says – since her last lying-in. She says Barnabas is the most *considerate* husband a woman could have, in this situation. He is much occupied with his theological writings – he is not of Herbert Baulk's persuasion at all – and has hopes, Patience tells me, of a Deanery before too long.

JUNE IOTH

Patience and I have had time for much private conversation, both over dinner and because the bevy of cherubs flew out to Regent's Park for some air. We had a sharp-sweet reminiscing talk about the old days in the Close, and how we ran in the orchard and dreamed of being women. We talked quite girlishly of old fans and stockings and the pain of oppressive bonnets during long sermons and of the trials dear Mamma must have borne, giving birth to fifteen infants, of whom we four girl children only survived.

Patience with her customary acuteness observed immediately that something ailed Bertha, and made a shrewd guess as to what it might be. I said I should speak to Bertha, and had indeed been waiting for an opportune moment to do so. Patience said it could only harm Bertha and the household if it waited too long. Patience has a strong sense that it is contaminating to continue in the presence of sin. I said I felt we were enjoined to love the sinner, and Patience retorted that this did not entail cohabiting with the visible proof of the sin, unchastised. We remembered Mamma's fortitude in such situations, and how she felt it to be her duty to inflict chastisement herself on erring young women. I remember one in particular, poor Thyrza Collitt, running screaming from room to room and Mamma whirling after her with upraised arm. I shall never forget that screaming. I shall never beat any servant of mine, and nor, whatever she says, will Patience, though she claims Barnabas believes it to be, in certain judiciously selected circumstances, a salutary proceeding. I do not believe my dearest Randolph would ever consider applying his hand – or anything else – to any young person in our employment. I must ask Bertha to go, before he returns; it is my duty.

My dear husband writes at length; he is well and his researches flourish. I have packed all my descriptions of my busy days into his long letter, which is posted and have no time nor inclination to note here more than those things which it is not fitting he should be troubled with. There are flaws in two of the crystal teardrops – one large one from the central crown, and a less significant one from the peripheral circle. What shall I do? I am convinced – no, that is unjust – I have a propensity to suspect – that the accidental kicking of the crystal-bath by Arthur and Georgie has shattered these two. I have said nothing to dearest R about these beaverings; I mean to surprise him with a home newly gleaming and radiant. I could attempt to replace the flawed droplets – but am convinced that could never be done in the time and would moreover be costly. I do not like to think of the thing hanging there with these cracks and chasms apparent in its surface.

I have spoken to Bertha. It is as I thought and Patience said. She cannot be brought to say who is the responsible man – but denied strenuously, in a great burst of weeping, that he could possibly be required to take care of her, either by marrying, or in any other way. She expressed no penitence, but also no defiance, asking me only over and over 'What can I do?' to which I have no sufficient answer. 'It all continues on whatever I will,' she strangely said. I said I should write to her mother, and she pleaded with me not to do so – 'it would break her heart and set her obdurately against me forever,' she said. Where will she go? What home can she have? What should I, in Christian charity, do for her? I do not want to trouble Randolph's work with these matters, and yet am not empowered to do much for Bertha without his assent. There is also the dreadful problem of the *replacement* to be thought of, with all the fears of drunkenness, theft, breakages and moral corruption which go with such choices. Some ladies I know seek servants far afield and in country places – Cockney *knowingness* is a thing I find difficult to confront or command as I should.

Patience says the servant classes are naturally ungrateful, lacking education. At times like this – when they must be encountered and judged and enquired into – I am led to wonder why they do not rather feel hatred? That hatred is what some do feel I am convinced. And I do not see how a true Christian can find a world of master and man to be 'natural' – *He* came even to the least, and perhaps more urgently to the least – to the mean, to the poor – in goods or spirit.

If Randolph were here I could discuss this with him. Perhaps it is as well he is not – it belongs to my sphere of influence and responsibility.

JUNE

Patience and her brood departed this morning for Dover, all smiles and fluttering handkerchiefs. I hope they had a smooth crossing. I hope they enjoy to the full their seaside pleasures. Another letter is come from Randolph, just as they had set off, full (the letter that is) of sea air and breezes and other delightful free forces. London is brassy hot and heavy – I think we may have a storm. It is unnaturally quiet and sultry. I have resolved to consult Herbert Baulk about Bertha. I felt a headache coming on, and a sense of being flustered by the sudden silence and emptiness of my house again. I retired to my room and slept for two hours, waking somewhat refreshed, though with a vestigial headache.

JUNE

Herbert Baulk came and stayed to take tea and talk. I proposed a game of chess – because I thought it might distract him from a too vehement expression of his doubts and certainties, and because I enjoy these miniature campaigns. He was pleased to tell me that I played very well for a lady – I was content to accept this, since I won handsomely.

I asked him about Bertha. He told me of an institution that makes very handsome provision for women in her position to be brought to bed and if at all possible re-established in a useful trade. He said he would inquire if she might be accepted – I was bold enough to engage myself – that is, my dearest Randolph – to contribute to her keep until her lying-in, if that might aid in securing a bed for her. He is told the dormitories are kept spotlessly clean by the exertions of the inmates themselves, and that the food is plain but nourishing, and cooked by the women themselves in the same way.

I slept badly and as a result had a strange fragmented dream in which I was playing chess with Herbert Baulk, who had decreed that *my Queen* could move only one square, as his King did. I knew there was injustice here but could not in my dreaming folly realise that this was to do with the existence of *my King* who sat rather large and red on the back line and seemed to be incapacitated. I could see the moves She should have made, like errors in a complicated pattern of knitting or lace – but she must only lumpishly shuffle back and forth, one square at a time. Mr Baulk (always in my dream) said calmly, 'You see I told you you could not win,' and I saw it was so, but was unreasonably agitated and desirous above all of moving my Queen freely across the diagonals. It is odd, when I think of it, that in chess the female may make the large runs and cross freely in all ways – in life it is much otherwise.

Mr Baulk came again in the afternoon and spoke eloquently and at length about the wickedness of imputing fraudulent motives to the New Testament miracles, most especially that of the resurrection of Lazarus. He said inquiries were going on promisingly as to the institution for Bertha. I have not told her of it, lest her hopes be raised only to be dashed. She goes slowly and dully enough about her work, with a puffed face.

A surprise! A small package came, containing a gift from my beloved Randolph, with a poem, all for me. He has been to Whitby, a fishing-town, where, he writes, the local people have a highly-developed art of polishing and carving jet which is cast up on their beaches and made by them into useful buttons and also decorative objects and jewellery. He sends me a most exquisite brooch, carved with a wreath of Roses of Yorkshire – all with their thorny twigs entwined and leafage – it is both artistic and wonderfully truthful. It is blacker than soot, and yet every way you turn its facets, it sparkles with light and a kind of angry energy of its own – one of the qualities of jet is that if rubbed it will attract light bodies, as in animal magnetism. It is a form of *lignite*, R. writes, obviously delighted with the substance, an *organic stone*, like coal, of course. I have some jet beads, and have seen many of course, but never any to match this for depth of darkness or brilliance of sheen.

I transcribe his poem here, for it is worth more to me than the
lovely gift itself. ~~Despite all~~ We have been so happy in our life
together, even our separations contribute to the trust and deep
affection that is between us.

> I love a paradox and so I send
> White Yorkshire roses carved in sombre jet
> Their summer frailty fixed here without end
> A life in death but not funereal yet
>
> As ancient forests in their black deaths warm
> Our modern hearths with primal vanished light
> So may our love, safe in your heart from harm
> Shine on, when we are grey, and make us bright.

JUNE

Not a good day. I told Bertha she must go, and that Herbert
Baulk would arrange for her to be received at the Magdalen
Home if she consented to it. She answered me not a word but
stared and stared, breathing very heavily, and a dark plum-red in
colour, as though she was unable to take in what I was saying. I
repeated that Mr Baulk had been very kind, and that she was very
fortunate, and all I heard was this fierce sighing or panting breath,
somehow filling my little sitting-room. I dismissed her, saying I
expected an answer when she had thought over the offer; I should
have added that I expected her to be away by the end of next
week, but could not. What will become of her?

The mail brought a whole heap of letters of the kind we are
increasingly in receipt of – inclosing poems or parts of poems,
pressed flowers for 'his' Bible or Shakespeare, requests for auto-
graphs, recommendations (impertinent) for *his* reading, and
humble or sometimes peremptory requests for him to read Epic
Poems or treatises or even novels, which their authors believe
may interest him, or may be helped by *his* recommendation. I
answer those gently enough, wishing them well, and saying how
very busy He is – which is quite true. How do they expect him
to continue to 'astonish and delight' them with 'his recondite
ideas', as one put it, if they do not leave him free time to pursue
his reading and intricate thought? Among these letters was one
requesting an interview with *me personally* in a matter of great
importance, the writer said, to me myself. This too is not unusual –
many, especially young women – appeal to *me* in order to come
into close quarters with my dear one. I replied civilly that I did

not grant personal interviews to strangers as too many were requested, but that if the writer had anything very particular to communicate I would beg her in the first instance to write to me with some indication of the matter in question. We shall see if this produces anything or nothing, pertinence, or, as I suspect, something vague and crazed.

JUNE

A worse day. The headache seized me and I lay all day in a darkened bedroom, betwixt asleep and wake. There are many bodily sensations that are indescribable yet immediately recognisable, as is the smell of baking bread or that of metal polish, which could never be conveyed to one who had no previous experience of them. Such is the way in which the preliminary dizziness or vanishing incapacitates the body and intimates the headache to come. It is curiously impossible – once entered into this state – to imagine ever issuing out of it – so that the Patience required to endure it seems to be a total eternal patience. Towards evening it lifted a little.

Another letter from the mysterious and urgent lady. A matter of life and death, she writes. She is well-educated, and if hysterical, not *frantically* so. I put the letter by, feeling too low in spirits to decide about it. The headache introduces one to a curious twilight deathly world in which life and death seem no great matter.

JUNE

Worse still. Dr Pimlott came and prescribed laudanum, which I found some relief in. During the afternoon there was a hammering at the door, and a distracted Bertha let in a strange lady who demanded to see me. I was at that time up, and sipping broth. I told her she might come back when I was recovered and she accepted this postponement briskly and nervously. I took more laudanum and went back into my dark room. No writer has written well enough of the Bliss of sleep. Coleridge wrote of the pains of sleep, and Macbeth speaks of a sleep foregone – but not of the bliss of relaxing one's grip of the world and warmly and motionlessly moving into another. Folded in by curtains, closed in by the warmth of blankets, without weight, it seems –

JUNE

Half a bad day, and half, as may happen, a good clear day, one might say, renewed. The furniture-cleaning has gone on well during my somnolent absence and all that – the arm-chairs, the table covers, the lamps, the screen – seems also renewed.

My importunate visitor came and we talked some time. That matter is now I hope quite at an end and wholly cleared up.

JUNE

A Poet is not a Divine being, with an angelic vision. Randolph has always denied that description. He likes to use Wm Wordsworth's phrase, 'a man speaking to men' and is, dare I say it, acquainted with more of the variety and vagaries of human nature than ever Wordsworth was, who looked customarily inward.

Herbert Baulk came and spoke with great kindness to Bertha who, as before with me, said nothing, and stood a red-faced block.

We played Chess. I won.

JULY

This morning Bertha was found to be slipped away during the night, with all her possessions and some also of Jenny's, she claims, including a carpet-bag and a woollen shawl. Nothing belonging to this house appears to have been taken, though all the silver is out or ranged accessibly in drawers and cabinets. It may be she mistook the shawl, or that Jenny herself is mistaken.

Where can she have gone? What should best be done? Should I write to her Mother? There are arguments for and against this – she did not wish her Mother to be told of her condition, but may now simply have taken refuge there.

I gave Jenny one of my own shawls and one of our own travelling-cases. She was much pleased.

Perhaps Bertha is gone to the man who [passage crossed out illegibly]

Should we pursue her? She cannot have taken to the streets, as she is. If we find her, shall we appear retributive? That would not be my intention.

I have done wrong in her regard. I have behaved less than well.

Herbert Baulk is not a tactful man. But I knew that when I embarked on this course. I should have

JULY

Another bad day. I lay all day in bed with the curtains open, for I became superstitiously afraid of spending so long in a house with

231

drawn curtains. A dull sun shone through rolling mist and fog. At even it was replaced by a smaller duller moon on an inky sky. I was motionless all day, in one position. I had a haven of painlessness and torpor and every other twist and turn was agony. How many days do we spend lying still, waiting for them to end, so that we may sleep. I lay suspended almost as Snow White lay maybe, in the glass casket, alive but out of the weather, breathing but motionless. Outside, in the weather, men suffer heat and cold and fluctuating air.

When he returns, I must be quick and lively. It must be so.

Maud said,

'She could write. I didn't immediately see what you meant by baffling. And then, I think I did. On the evidence of that part of the journal – I couldn't form a very clear idea of what she was *like*. Or if I liked her. She tells things. Interesting things. But they don't make a whole picture.'

'Which of us do?' asked Beatrice.

'What happened to Bertha?'

'We never find out. She doesn't tell. Or even if she went after her.'

'It must have been *terrible* for Bertha. She – Ellen – doesn't seem to see ...'

'Doesn't she?'

'Oh, I don't know. She *describes* her clearly. Poor Bertha.'

'Dust and ashes,' Beatrice surprisingly said. 'Long ago. And the child, if it was born.'

'How frustrating, though. Not to know.'

'Professor Cropper found the jet brooch. The very one. It's in the Stant Collection. On sea-green moiré silk, he told me. I've seen a photograph.'

Maud ignored the brooch.

'Do you have any ideas about the hysterical letter-writer? Or does she vanish without trace, like Bertha?'

'There is no more about her. Nothing more.'

'Did she keep her letters?'

'Not all. Most. In bundles, in shoe-boxes. I've got them. Mostly fan-letters for him, as she says.'

'Could we look?'

'If you're interested. I have looked at them all, once or twice. I had an idea about writing an article about Victorian precursors of, as it were, fan clubs. But I found it rather sickly when I came to it.'

'Could I really see?'

Beatrice turned her impassive stare on Maud's eager ivory face, and read something there, if not precisely.

'Why not, I suppose . . .' she murmured, not moving. 'What reason why not?'

The shoe-box was made of tough black cardboard, cracking with dryness and bound with tape. Beatrice, sighing and sighing, undid this, and there they were, neatly bundled, letter upon letter. They sifted the dates, opened envelopes, pleas for charity, offers of secretarial help, flowing screeds of passionate admiration, written to Randolph and addressed to Ellen. Beatrice checked the date and came up with a screed at once agitated and artistically written, faintly Gothic. And there it was.

Dear Mrs Ash,

Please forgive the intrusion upon your most valuable time and attention. I am a gentlewoman, and at present totally unknown to you, but I have something to impart to you which closely concerns both of us and is in my case no less than a matter of life and death. Believe me I speak the cold truth, no more.

Oh how can I make you trust me? You must. May I trespass on your time and come to see you? I shall not need to stay long – but I have that to tell you – for which you may come to thank me – or not – but that is no matter – you must know –

I may be found at all times at the address which heads this letter. Believe me oh believe me, I wish to stand your friend.

> *Yours most sincerely*
> *Blanche Glover*

Maud closed her face and dropped her eyelids on what must be a glitter of pouncing. She said, trying to make her voice indifferent,

'This looks like it. Any more? This looks like the *second* letter she mentions. Is the first one there?'

Beatrice riffled.

'No. No more. At least – unless this is the same writing. It looks like the same paper. It's got no heading and no signature.'

You did wrong to keep my Evidence. If it was not mine, it is also not yours. I beg of you to consider more carefully and to think better of me. I know how I may have appeared to you. I chose my words ill. But what I said was true and urgent, as you will come to see.

Maud sat, holding this sheet of paper, in an agony of indecision. What Evidence had Ellen kept? And of what? A clandestine correspondence or a trip to the Yorkshire Coast with a solitary biologising poet? What had Ellen felt or understood? Had Blanche handed her the purloined manuscript of *Swammerdam*? How could she make copies of precisely *these* documents without alerting Beatrice, and with Beatrice, surely, Cropper and Blackadder? A kind of imperious will in her tapped at her like a hammer, and was interrupted in its coding of a cunning request by Beatrice's woolly voice.

'I don't know what you're up to, Dr Bailey. I don't know if I want to know. You came looking for something and you found it.'

'Yes,' said Maud in a whisper. She moved her long hands in a gesture of silence at the partition walls behind which lurked Blackadder and the Ash Factory.

Beatrice Nest's face was bland and patiently questioning.

'It isn't only my secret,' Maud hissed. 'Or I wouldn't have been disingenuous. I – I don't know *what* I've found, yet. I promise I'll tell you first when I do. I think I know what Blanche Glover told her. Well, one of two or three things it might have been.'

'Was it important?' asked the grey voice, with no indication of whether the 'importance' was scholarly, passionate or cosmic.

'I don't *know*. It might change our views of – of his work, I suppose, a bit.'

'What do you want of me?'

'A Xerox of those two letters. If it can be done, a copy of the Journal, between those dates. Not to tell Professor Cropper. Or Professor Blackadder. Yet. We discovered this ourselves –'

Beatrice Nest seemed to think for a longish time, her face propped in her hands.

'This – what you're so excited about – it won't – it won't expose her to ridicule – or – or misapprehension? I've become very concerned that she shouldn't be – exposed is the best word I suppose – *exposed*.'

'It isn't primarily to do with her.'

'That is not necessarily reassuring.' A maddening silence. 'I suppose I shall trust you. I suppose I shall.'

She walked briskly out through Blackadder's office, where Paola raised a languid hand; the Professor himself was not there. In the outer dark, in the corridor, however, a familiar Aran sweater whitened the murk, familiar gold hair shone.

'Surprise,' said Fergus Wolff. 'Surprise, ha?'

Maud drew herself up and made a dignified side-step.

'Wait a minute.'

'I'm in a hurry.'

'To do what? Pursue the labyrinthine coilings of the *Melusina*? Or to see Roland Michell?'

'Neither.'

'Then stay.'

'I can't.'

She stepped. He side-stepped. She stepped the other way. He was there. He put out a strong hand and clasped it like a handcuff on her wrist. She saw the egg-white bed.

'Don't be like that, Maud. I want to talk to you. I'm suffering terribly in about equal amounts of curiosity and jealousy. I can't *believe* you've got involved with sweet useless Roland and I can't *understand* what you're doing haunting the Crematorium here, unless you have.'

'Crematorium?'

'Ash Factory.' He was pulling on her arm while he talked so that her body and her briefcase were leaning towards his body, which put out its remembered flickers of electrification. 'I need to talk to you, Maud. Let me buy you a good meal. Let's just talk. You're the most intelligent woman I know. I miss you terribly, you know, I should have said that, too.'

'I can't. I'm busy. Let go, Fergus.'

'Tell me what's going on at least, go on, do. If you tell me I'll be fearfully discreet.'

'There's nothing to tell.'

'And if you don't tell me, I shall find out, and consider what I find out to be my own property, Maud.'

'Let go of my wrist.'

A large, black-uniformed, black-skinned woman appeared unsmiling behind them.

'Please read the notices. Silence at all times in the book corridors.'

Maud wrenched her wrist free and strode away. Fergus called after her 'I *warned* you', and could be seen going into the Ash Factory, followed by the black wardress, rattling chains of keys.

Two days later Roland and Maud met in Oodles, the vegetarian restaurant at the end of Museum Street. Maud had brought the collection of xeroxed sheets which Beatrice had given her. She had had another unnerving experience trying to telephone Roland to arrange this meeting; she was also troubled by an enthusiastic letter from Leonora Stern, who had been given a grant by the Tarrant Foundation to come to England, and wrote enthusiastically: 'next semester I shall be *with you*'.

They stood in a queue and bought tepidly microwaved spinach lasagne; they then took refuge in the underground part of the restaurant, hoping to avoid curious eyes. Roland read Ellen's journal and Blanche's letters. Maud watched him and then said,

'What do you think?'

'I think the only certain thing is that Blanche told Ellen something. Showed her the stolen letters, probably? I want to think Blanche did this because Christabel had gone to Yorkshire with Ash. It fits in beautifully. But it isn't proof.'

'I can't think how we could prove it.'

'I did have certain wild ideas. I thought of going through the poems – his and hers – written about then – with the idea that they might reveal something. I thought if I retraced his steps in Yorkshire – with the idea that she might have been there – and the poems in hand – I might get somewhere. We've already found one correlation no one could have thought of who wasn't *looking* for a connection. Randolph Ash wrote to his wife about a Hob who cured whooping-cough and Christabel wrote a tale about one. And then Ash relates his interest in drowned Yorkshire villages to the City of Is as well as to Lyell. People's minds do hook together —'

'They do.'

'One might find a cumulative series of such coincidences.'

'It would be interesting, anyway.'

'I even had a theory about water and fountains. I told you Ash's post-1860 poetry had this elemental streak — water and stones and earth and air. He mixes up geysers from Lyell with Norse myth and Greek mythical fountains. And Yorkshire waterfalls. And I wondered about the Fountain of Thirst in *Melusina*.'

'How?'

'Well, is there an echo here? This is out of *Ask to Embla*. It possibly links that fountain to the one in the Song of Songs, as well. Listen:

> We drank deep of the Fountain of Vaucluse
> And where the northern Force incessantly
> Stirs the still pool, were stirred. And shall those founts
> Which freely flowed to meet our thirsts, be sealed?'

Maud said 'Say that again.'

Roland said it again.

Maud said, 'Have you ever really felt your hackles rise? Because I just have. Prickles all down my spine and at the roots of my hair. You listen to this. This is what Raimondin says to Melusine after he is told she knows he has looked at her in her marble bath and broken the prohibition:

> Ah, Melusine, I have betrayed your faith.
> Is there no remedy? Must we two part?
> Shall our hearth's ash grow pale, and shall those founts
> Which freely flowed to meet our thirsts, be sealed?'

Roland said, 'Shall our hearth's *ash* grow pale.'

'The image of the hearth runs all through *Melusina*. She built castles and homes; the hearth is the home.'

'Which came first? His line or her line? There are problems about dating *Ask to Embla* — which we're obviously on the way to solving, among other things. It reads like a classic literary clue. She was a clever and hinting sort of woman. Look at those dolls.'

'Literary critics make natural detectives,' said Maud. 'You

know the theory that the classic detective story arose with the classic adultery novel – everyone wanted to know who was the Father, what was the origin, what is the secret?'

'We need,' said Roland, carefully, 'to do this together. I know his work, and you know hers. If we were both in Yorkshire –'

'This is all madness. We should tell Cropper and Blackadder and certainly Leonora and marshal our resources.'

'Is that what you want?'

'No. I want to – to – follow the – path. I feel taken over by this. I want to *know* what happened, and I want it to be me that finds out. I thought you were mad, when you came to Lincoln with your piece of stolen letter. Now I feel the same. It isn't professional greed. It's something more primitive.'

'Narrative curiosity –'

'Partly. Could you manage a few days' field research at Whit-suntide?'

'It might present difficulties. Things aren't easy at home. As you may have noticed. If you and I – went up there – it wouldn't be liked. It would be misconstrued.'

'I know, I understand. Fergus Wolff thinks. He thinks. He professes to believe – that you and I . . .'

'How dreadful –'

'He threatened me in the Library with finding out what we were up to. We must watch him.'

Roland considered Maud's embarrassment and did not ask what were her feelings about Fergus Wolff. That they were violent was clear. Equally he did not intend to discuss Val.

'People who are going off on real naughty weekends manage to find excuses,' he said. 'Put up smoke-screens. It happens all the time, I'm told. I don't see why I shouldn't think of something. Money's more of a problem.'

'What you need is a small research grant to look at something not too far away from Yorkshire and not too near either –'

'Ash did some work in York Minster Library –'

'Something like that.'

CHAPTER THIRTEEN

Three Ases wandered out from Ida plain
Where the Gods met in council, with clear brows
And joyous voices, knowing then no weight
Of sin, or the world's wryness. All was gleam
Of sun and moon well-wrought, and golden trees
With golden apples inside golden walls.
They stepped into the middle-garden, made
For men not made, drowsed in the lap of Time.

Round their divine bright faces, ceaselessly
Rushed the new air. Beneath their lovely feet
Rose the new grass, and leeks, untouched, uncropped
Green with the living Sap of that first Spring.

They came down to the shore
Where the salt breakers fell on the new sand
With roar unheard, and curling crest unseen
Like nothing else, for no man-mind was there
To name, or liken them, in any way.
They were themselves alone, and rose and fell
Changing-eternal, new, not knowing time
Which their succession measures for the mind.

And these three Ases were the sons of Bor
Who slew the Giant Ymir in his rage
And made of him the elements of earth,
Body and sweat and bones and curly hair,
Made soil and sea and hills and waving trees,
And his grey brains wandered the heavens as clouds.
These three were Odin, Father of the Gods,
Honir, his brother, also called the Bright,
The Wise and Thoughtful, and that third, the hot

Loki, the hearth-god, whose consuming fire
First warmed the world, then grown beyond the bounds
Of home and hearthstone, flamed in boundless greed
To turn the world, and Heav'n, to sifting ash.

Two senseless forms, on the wet shore o'the world
Lay at the tide's edge, and were water-lapped,
Rising a little with the creeping wave,
Then slipping back, with motion not their own.
Log-like they lay uprooted, simple forms
Of ash and alder, shorn of their green pride
But not quite dead perhaps, but nourishing
A kind of quickening shrunk back to the core
Of all the woody circles of their trunks.
(Circles of years not lived by the new wood
But sempiternal years, a present past
Stirred into being by the hand of time
As lines of water spired in the new pools.)

The new sun stood in the blue; her chariot's course
Not more than twice completed, who has since
Circled and run from dawn to dawn as Earth
Grows cool and cloudy in the calmer light,
Nor ever fails, nor swerves a pace from true
Till all·be swallowed in the final Fire.

Allfather in her heat felt his own force.
He said: shall these trunks live? and saw the life
The vegetable life, that sang i' th' quick.

Bright Honir said: if these could move and feel
And see and hear, the lines of leaping light
Would speak to ears and eyes. The garden's fruits
Would render life to life. This lovely world
Would be both known and loved, and so would live
An endless life in theirs, and they should hear
And speak its beauties, then first beautiful
When known to be so.

                Last he spoke, the dark
God of the hidden flames. He said, 'Hot blood
I give them, to make bright their countenance,
To move in them the passionate motion
Which draws them to each other, as the iron
Springs to the lodestone always. I give blood—

A human warmth, red with a human fire
A stream of vital sparks, which if preserved
Speaks each to each divinely, but which spilt
Is mortal ruin till the end of Time
For they are mortal.'

And so the laughing Gods, pleased with their work
Made man and woman of the senseless stumps
And called them Ask and Embla, for the ash
And alder of their woody origins.
Odin breathed in the soul, and bright Honir
Gave sense and understanding and the power
To stand and move. The quick-dark Loki last
Knitted the veins of circulating blood
And blew the spark of vital heat, as smiths
Stir fire with the bellows. So a sharp
And burning pain of apprehension
Stirred life in those who had been logs of peace
And thrilled along new channels, till it roared
In new-forged brain and ventricles of blood
And curling membranes of the ear and nose
And last, opened new eyes on a new world.

Now these first men were quite unmanned by light.
The first wet light, of the first days, that washed
Silver and gold the sand, gilded the sea
With liquid gold and silvered every crest
That crisped and curled and wrinkled into smooth.

What had lived by the whispering of the sap
Had feelingly discerned the shivering air
Known dark and light along the rugged bark
Or smoothest treeskin, kissed by warm and cool—
Now saw with eyes, waves of indifferent light
Pour on and over, arch and arch, a gold
And sunny wash, a rainbow fountain, shot
With glints of bright and streams of gleaming motes.

All this they more than saw and less than saw.
Then turning, saw those forms majestical
Wrought by the cunning of the watching gods,
White skins, blue-shadowed and blue-veined, with rose
And tawny gold inwoven, pearly-bright
Untouched unused, and breathing the bright air.

Those four eyes darkened by the burning Face
Of the bright lady of the sky, now saw
The milder circles of each other's gaze
Crowned with curls of glossy golden hair.

And as the steel-blue eyes of the first Man
Saw answering lights in Embla's lapis eyes
The red blood Loki set to spring in them
Flooded hot faces. Then he saw that she
Was like himself, yet other; then she saw
His smiling face, and by it, knew her own—
And so they stared and smiled, and the gods smiled
To see their goodly work, so fair begun
In recognition and in sympathy.

Then Ask stepped forward on the printless shore
And touched the woman's hand, who clasped fast his.
Speechless they walked away along the line
Of the sea's roaring, in their listening ears.
Behind them, first upon the level sand
A line of darkening prints, filling with salt,
First traces in the world, of life and time
And love, and mortal hope, and vanishing.

    Randolph Henry Ash, from *Ragnarök* II. 1 *et seq.*

The Hoff Lunn Spout hotel had existed in 1859, though there
was no mention of it in Ash's letters. He had stayed at The Cliff
in Scarborough, now demolished, and had had lodgings in Filey.
Maud had found the hotel in *The Good Food Guide*, where it
was recommended for 'Uncompromising fresh fish dishes, and
unremitting if unsmiling good service'. It was also cheap, and
Maud was worried about Roland.

It stood at the edge of the moorland, on the road from Robin
Hood's Bay to Whitby. It was long, low, and made of that grey
stone which to a northerner signifies reality, and to southerners,
used to warm bricks and a few curves and corners, can signify
unfriendliness. It had a slate roof and one row of white-sashed
windows. It stood in a car park, a largely empty expanse of
asphalt. Mrs Gaskell, who visited Whitby in 1859 to plan *Sylvia's
Lovers*, remarked that gardening was not a popular art in the
North, and that no attempt was made to plant flowers even on
the western or southern sides of the rough stone houses. In spring

the dry stone walls are briefly bright with aubretia, but in general, at places like the Hoff Lunn Spout, this absence of vegetation still prevails.

Maud drove Roland up from Lincoln in the little green car; they arrived in time for dinner. The place was kept by a huge handsome Viking woman, who watched incuriously as they carried packets of books up the stairs between the Public Bar and the Restaurant.

The Restaurant had recently been fitted with a maze of high, dim-lit cubicles in dark-stained wood. Roland and Maud met there and ordered what seemed to be a light meal: home-made vegetable soup, plaice with shrimps, and profiteroles. A younger Viking, substantial and serious, served them with all these things, which were good and hugely plentiful, the soup a thick casserole of roots and legumes, the fish an immense white sandwich of two plate-sized fillets containing a good half-pound of prawns between their solid flaps, the profiteroles the size of large tennis-balls, covered with a lake of bitter chocolate sauce. Maud and Roland exclaimed frequently about this gigantism; they were nervous of real conversation. They made a businesslike plan of action.

They had five days. They decided to go to the seaside places on the first two of these – Filey, Flamborough, Robin Hood's Bay, Whitby. Then they would retrace Ash's inland walks by rivers and waterfalls. And leave a day for what might come up.

Roland's bedroom had blue-sprigged rough wallpaper and a sloping roof. The floor was uneven and creaky; the door was old with a latch and sneck as well as a monumental keyhole. The bed was high, with a stained dark wooden head. Roland looked round this small private place and felt a moment of pure freedom. He was alone. Perhaps it had all been for this, to find a place where he could be alone? He slid into bed and began on his familiarisation with Christabel LaMotte. Maud had lent him Leonora Stern's book on *Motif and Matrix in the Poems of LaMotte*. He leafed through the chapter headings: 'From Venus Mount to the Barren Heath'; 'Female Landscapes and Unbroken Waters, Impenetrable Surfaces'; 'From the Fountain of Thirst to the Armorican Ocean-Skin':

And what surfaces of the earth do we women choose to celebrate, who have appeared typically in phallocentric texts as a penetrable hole, inviting or abhorrent, surrounded by, fringed with – something? Women writers and painters are seen to have created their own significantly evasive landscapes, with features which deceive or elude the penetrating gaze, tactile landscapes which do not privilege the dominant stare. The heroine takes pleasure in a world which is both bare and not pushy, which has small hillocks and rises, with tufts of scrub and gently prominent rocky parts which disguise sloping declivities, hidden clefts, not one but a multitude of hidden holes and openings through which life-giving waters bubble and enter reciprocally. Such external percepts, embodying inner visions, are George Eliot's Red Deeps, George Sand's winding occluded paths in Berry, Willa Cather's cañons, female-visioned female-enjoyed contours of Mother Earth. Cixous has remarked that many women experience visions of caves and fountains during the orgasmic pleasures of auto-eroticism and shared caresses. It is a landscape of touch and double-touch, for as Irigaray has showed us, all our deepest 'vision' begins with our self-stimulation, the touch and kiss of our two lower lips, our *double sex*. Women have noted that literary heroines commonly find their most intense pleasures alone in these secretive landscapes, hidden from view. I myself believe that the pleasure of the fall of waves on the shores is to be added to this delight, their regular breaking bearing a profound relation to the successive shivering delights of the female orgasm. There is a marine and salty female wave-water to be figured which is not, as Venus Anadyomene was, put together out of the crud of male semen scattered on the deep at the moment of the emasculation of Father Time by his Oedipal son. Such pleasure in the shapeless yet patterned succession of waters, in the formless yet formed sequence of waves on the shore, is essentially present in the art of Virginia Woolf and the form of her sentences, her utterance, themselves. I can only marvel at the instinctive delicacy and sensitivity of those female companions of Charlotte Brontë who turned aside when she first came face to face with the power of the sea at Filey, and waited peacefully until, her body trembling, her face flushed, her eyes wet, she was able to rejoin her companions and walk on with them.

The heroines of LaMotte's texts are typically watery beings. Dahud the matriarchal Sorceress-Queen rules a hidden kingdom below the unbroken waters of the Armoric Gulf. The Fairy

Melusina is in her primary and beneficent state a watery being. Like her magical mother, Pressine, she is first encountered by her husband-to-be at the Fontaine de Soif, which might be construed as either the Thirsty Fountain or The Fountain which satisfies Thirst. Although the second may seem 'logical', in the female world which is in-formed by illogic and structured by feeling and in-tuition, a sense can be perceived in which the Dry Fountain, the Thirsty Fountain, is the hard-to-access and primary signification. What does LaMotte tell us of the Fontaine de Soif?

Her poem draws extensively on the prose romance of the monk, Jean d'Arras, who tells us that the Fountain 'springs from a wild hillside, with great rocks above, and a beautiful meadow along a valley, after the high forest'. Melusine's mother is discovered by this fountain singing beautifully, 'more harmoniously than any siren, any fairy, any nymph ever sang'. They are perceived, that is, by the male view, as temptresses, allied with the seductive powers of Nature. LaMotte's fountain, by contrast, is inaccessible and concealed; the knight and his lost horse must descend and scramble to come to it and to the Fairy Melusina's 'small clear' voice 'singing to itself' which 'sings no more' when the man and beast disturb a stone on their damp descent. LaMotte's description of the ferns and foliage is Pre-Raphaelite in its precision and delicacy – the 'rounded' rocks are covered with a 'pelt' of 'mosses', 'worts', 'mints' and 'maidenhair' ferns. The fountain does not 'spring' but 'bubbles and seeps' up into the 'still and secret' pool, with its 'low mossy stone' surrounded by 'peaks and freshenings' of 'running and closing' waters.

This may all be read as a symbol of female language, which is partly suppressed, partly self-communing, dumb before the intrusive male and not able to speak out. The male fountain spurts and springs. Melusine's fountain has a *female* wetness, trickling out from its pool rather than rising confidently, thus mirroring those female secretions which are not inscribed in our daily use of language (*langue*, tongue) – the sputum, mucus, milk and bodily fluids of women who are silent for dryness.

Melusina, singing to herself on the brink of this mystic fountain, is a potent being of great authority who knows the beginnings and ends of things – and is, as has been pointed out, in her aspect of water-serpent, a complete being, capable of generating life, or meanings, on her own, without need for external help. The Italian scholar Silvia Veggetti Finzi sees Melusina's 'monstrous' body in this sense as a product of female auto-erotic fantasies of generation without copulation, which female desire, she says, has received very little expression in mythology. 'We find it most frequently in myths of origin as an expression of the chaos which precedes and justifies cosmic order. Of this kind is the Assyro-Babylonian myth of Ti'amat, or the myth of Tiresias, who saw the primordial reproduction of serpents and measured the superior quality (*plus-valore*) of female desire and the mythemes [*mitemi*] of the vegetable cycle of lettuce.'

Roland laid aside Leonora Stern with a small sigh. He had a vision of the land they were to explore, covered with sucking human orifices and knotted human body-hair. He did not like this vision, and yet, a child of his time, found it compelling, somehow guaranteed to be significant, as a geological survey of the oolite would not be. Sexuality was like thick smoked glass; everything took on the same blurred tint through it. He could not imagine a pool with stones and water.

He disposed himself for sleep. The sheets were white and felt slightly starched; he imagined that they smelled of fresh air and even the sea-salt. He moved down into their clean whiteness, scissoring his legs like a swimmer, abandoning himself to them, floating free. His unaccustomed muscles relaxed. He slept.

On the other side of the plaster-and-lath partition Maud closed *The Great Ventriloquist* with a snap. Like many biographies, she judged, this was as much about its author as its subject, and she did not find Mortimer Cropper's company pleasant. By extension, she found it hard to like Randolph Henry Ash, in Cropper's version. Part of her was still dismayed that Christabel LaMotte should have given in to whatever urgings or promptings Ash may have used. She preferred her own original vision of proud and particular independence, as Christabel, in the letters, had given some reason to think she did herself. She had not yet made a serious study of Ash's poems, with which she was reluctant to engage. Still, Cropper's account of the Yorkshire trip had been thorough:

On a bright June morning in 1859 the Filey bathing-women might have noticed a solitary figure striding firmly along the lone and level sands towards the Brigg, armed with the *impedimenta* of his new hobby, landing-net, flat basket, geologist's hammer, cold chisel, oyster-knife, paper-knife, chemists' phials and squat bottles and various mean-looking lengths of wire for stabbing and probing. He had even designed his own specimen box, made to be water-tight even in the post, an elegant lacquered metal case containing a close-fitting glass inner vessel, in which tiny creatures might be hermetically sealed in their own atmosphere. He carried also to be sure the sturdy *ash-plant* from which he was hardly to be parted, and which was, as I have already indicated, a part of his personal mythology, a solid metaphoric extension of his Self. (It is a matter of great regret to me that I have never been able to procure an authenticated examplar of this Wotan-stave for the Stant Collection.) He had been observed on earlier forays, stirring rock-pools at twilight with this staff, much in the manner of the Leech-gatherer, to observe the phosphorescence caused by those minute creatures, the Noctilucae, or Naked-Eye Medusas.

If, like many of his kind, pursuing a compulsive migration to the water's edge, he appeared more than a little ridiculous, a kind of gimcrack White Knight of the seashore, with his boots strung around his neck from their knotted laces, let us remember also, that like others of his kind, he was not harmless in his fashionable enthusiasm. The critic Edmund Gosse, that great pioneer of the modern art of biography and autobiography was the son of the tragically misguided naturalist, Philip Gosse, whose *Manual of Marine Zoology* was a *sine qua non* on such collecting expeditions. And Edmund Gosse believed he had observed during his lifetime a rape of an innocent Paradise, a slaughter amounting to genocide. He tells us:

> The ring of living beauty drawn about our shores was a very thin and fragile one. It had existed all those centuries solely in consequence of the indifference, the blissful ignorance of man. These rock-basins, fringed by corallines, filled with still water almost as pellucid as the upper air itself, thronged with beautiful sensitive forms of life – they exist no longer, they are all profaned, and emptied, and vulgarized. An army of 'collectors' has passed over them, and ravaged every corner of them. The fairy paradise has been violated, the exquisite product of centuries of natural selection has been crushed under the rough paw of well-meaning idle-minded curiosity.

Even so, not exempt from the blunderings of common men,

the poet in search as he put it of 'the origins of life and the nature of generation' was unwittingly, with his crashing boots covered with liquid india-rubber, as much as with his scalpel and killing-jar, dealing death to the creatures he found so beautiful, to the seashore whose pristine beauty he helped to wreck.

During his stay in the blustery North, then, Randolph spent his mornings collecting specimens which his indulgent landlady housed in various pie-dishes and 'other china receptacles' around his sitting-room. He wrote his wife that it was just as well she could not see the artificial rockpools amongst which he took his meals and in the afternoons worked with his microscope, for her orderly mind would never have tolerated his 'pregnant chaos'. He made a particular study of the sea anemone – which is abundant in various forms on that coast – thereby, as he himself acknow-ledged, doing no more than subscribe to a general mania which had overtaken the British, who were keeping the tiny creatures in various glass tanks and aquaria in thousands of respectable drawing-rooms around the land, their murky colours vying with the dusty colours of stuffed birds or pinned insects under glass domes.

Sages and spinster schoolmistresses, frock-coated clergymen and earnest workingmen at that time, all were murdering to dissect, parting and slicing, scraping and piercing tough and delic-ate tissues in an attempt by all possible means to get at the elusive stuff of Life itself. Anti-vivisection propaganda was widespread and vehement, and Randolph was aware of it, as he was also aware of the charges of cruelty that might be levelled at his enthusiastic operations with scalpel and microscope. He had the squeamishness and the resolution of his poet-nature; he did various precise experiments to prove that writhings which might be thought to be responses to pain in various primitive organisms in fact took place after death – long after his own dissection of the creature's heart and digestive system. He concluded that primitive organisms felt nothing we would call pain, and that hissing and shrinking were mere automatic responses. He might have con-tinued had he not come to this conclusion, as he was willing to concede that knowledge and science laid 'austere claims' on men.

He made a particular study of the reproductive system of his chosen life-forms. His interest in these matters dated back some time – the author of *Swammerdam* was well aware of the sig-nificance of the discovery of the ova of both human and insect worlds. He was much influenced by the work of the great anatomist, Richard Owen, on Parthenogenesis, or the reproduction of creatures by cell fission rather than by sexual congress. He conducted rigorous experiments himself on various hydras and plumed worms which could be got to bud new heads and segments all from the same tail, in a process known as gemmation. He was greatly interested in the way in which the lovely Medusa or transparent jellyfish were apparently unfertilised buds of certain Polyps. He busily sliced off the tentacles of hydra and lacerated polyps into fragments, each of which became a new creature. This phenomenon fascinated him because it seemed to him to indicate a continuity and interdependence of all life, which might perhaps assist in modifying or doing away with the notion of individual death, and thus deal with that great fear to which, as the certain promise of Heaven trembled and faded, he and his contemporaries were all hideously subject.

His friend Michelet was at this time working on *La Mer*, which appeared in 1860. In it the historian also tried to find in the sea the possibility of an eternal life which would overcome death. He describes his experiences in showing to a great chemist and subsequently to a great physiologist a beaker of what he called 'the *mucous* of the sea ... this whitish, viscous element'. The chemist replied that it was nothing other than life itself. The physiologist described a whole microcosmic drama:

We know no more about the constitution of water than we do about that of blood. What is most easily discerned, in the case of the seawater mucus, is that it is simultaneously an end and a beginning. Is it a product of the innumerable residues of death, who would yield them to life? That is without doubt a law; but in fact, in this marine world, of rapid absorption, most beings are absorbed live; they do not drag out a state of death, as occurs on the earth, where destructions are slower.

But life, without arriving at its supreme dissolution, moults or sheds, ceaselessly, exudes from itself all which is superfluous to it. In the case of us, terrestrial animals, the epidermis is shed incessantly. These moults which could be called a daily and partial death, fill the world of the seas with gelatinous richness from which newborn life profits momently. It finds, in suspension, the oily superabundance of this common exudation, the still animated particules, the still living liquids, which have no time to die. All this does not fall back into an inorganic state but rapidly enters new organisms. This is the most likely of all the hypotheses; if we abandon that, we find ourselves in extreme difficulties.

It can be understood why Ash wrote to this man at this time that he 'saw the inner meaning of Plato's teaching that the world was one huge animal'.

And what might a stringent modern psychoanalytic criticism make of all this feverish activity? To what needs in the individual psyche did this frenzy of dissection and 'generative' observation correspond?

It is my belief that at this point in time Randolph had reached what we crudely call a 'mid-life crisis', as had his century. He, the great psychologist, the great poetic student of individual lives and identities, saw that before him was nothing but decline and decay, that his individual being would not be extended by progeny, that men burst like bubbles. He turned away, like many, from individual sympathies with dying or dead men to universal sympathies with Life, Nature and the Universe. It was a kind of Romanticism reborn – gemmated, so to speak, from the old stock of Romanticism – but intertwined with the new mechanistic analysis and the new optimism not about the individual soul, but about the eternal divine harmony of the universe. Like Tennyson, Ash saw that Nature was red in tooth and claw. He responded by taking an interest in the life-continuing functions of the digestive functions of all forms, from the amoeba to the whale.

Maud decided she intuited something terrible about Cropper's imagination from all this. He had a peculiarly vicious version of reverse hagiography; the desire to cut his subject down to size. She indulged herself in a pleasant thought about the general ambiguity of the word 'subject' in this connection. Was Ash subject to Cropper's research methods and laws of thought? Whose subjectivity was being studied? Who was the subject of the sentences of the text, and how did Cropper and Ash fit into Lacan's perception that the grammatical subject of a statement differs from the subject, the 'I', who is the object discussed by that statement? Were these thoughts original, Maud wondered, and decided almost inevitably not, all the possible thoughts about literary subjectivity had recently and strenuously been explored.

Elsewhere in his chapter, almost inevitably, Cropper had quoted *Moby Dick*.

> Still deeper the meaning of that story of Narcissus who because he could not grasp the tormenting, mild image he saw in the fountain, plunged into it and was drowned. But that same image, we ourselves see in all rivers and oceans. It is the image of the ungraspable phantom of life; and this is the key to it all.

Narcissism, the unstable self, the fractured ego, Maud thought, who am I? A matrix for a susurration of texts and codes? It was both a pleasant and an unpleasant idea, this requirement that she think of herself as intermittent and partial. There was the question of the awkward body. The skin, the breath, the eyes, the hair, their history, which did seem to exist.

She stood by the uncurtained window and brushed her hair, looking up at the moon, which was full, and hearing a few faraway airy rushings off the North Sea.

Then she got into bed, and, with the same scissoring movement as Roland next door, swam down under the white sheets.

Semiotics nearly spoiled their first day. They drove out to Flamborough, in the little green car, following their certain predecessor and guide, Mortimer Cropper in his black Mercedes, his predecessor, Randolph Ash, and the hypothetical ghost, Christabel LaMotte. They walked out, in these footsteps, to Filey Brigg, not sure any more what they were looking for, feeling it impermissible simply to enjoy themselves. They paced well together, though they didn't notice that; both were energetic striders.

Cropper had written:

Randolph spent long hours poring over rock pools, deep and shallow, on the north side of the Brigg. He could be seen stirring the phosphorescent matter in them with his ashplant, and diligently collecting it in buckets, taking it home to study such microscopic animalcules as *Noctilucae* and Naked-eye *Medusae* 'which are indistinguishable to the naked eye from foam bubbles' but on inspection turned out to be 'globular masses of animated jelly with mobile tails'. Here too, he collected his sea-anemones (*Actiniae*) and bathed in the Emperor's Bath — a great, greenish rounded hollow in which a legendary Roman Emperor disported himself. Randolph's historical imagination, ever active, must have taken pleasure in this direct connection with the distant past of the region.

Roland found a sea anemone, the colour of a dark blood-blister, tucked under a pitted ledge above a layer of glistering gritty sand, pink and gold and bluish and black. It looked simple and ancient, and very new and shining. It was flourishing a vigorous crown of agitating and purposeful feelers, sifting and stirring the water. Its colour was like cornelian, like certain dark and ruddy ambers. Its stem or base or foot held the rock and stood sturdy.

Maud sat on a ledge above Roland's pool, her long legs tucked under her, *The Great Ventriloquist* open on her knee. She cited Cropper citing Ash:

> 'Imagine a glove expanded into a perfect cylinder by air, the thumb being removed and the fingers *encircling*, in two or three rows, the summit of the cylinder, while at the base the glove is closed by a flat surface of leather. If now on that disc which lies within the circle of fingers we press down the centre, and so force the elastic leather to *fold inwards*, and form a sort of sac suspended in a cylinder, we have by this means made a mouth and stomach . . .'

'A curious comparison,' said Roland.

'Gloves in LaMotte are always to do with secrecy and decorum. Covering things up. Also with Blanche Glover, of course.'

'Ash wrote a poem called *The Glove*. About a mediaeval Lady who gave one to a knight to wear as a favour. It was "milky-white with seed-pearls".'

'Cropper says here that Ash supposed wrongly that the ovaries of the *Actinia* were in the fingers of the glove . . .'

'I couldn't understand, as a little boy, *where* the knight wore the glove. Still can't, as a matter of fact.'

'Cropper goes on about how Ash meditated on his own name. That's interesting. Christabel certainly meditated on Glover. It produced some fine and disturbing poems.'

'Ash wrote a passage in *Ragnarök* about the time when the God Thor hid in a huge cave which turned out to be the little finger of a giant's glove. That was the giant who tricked him into trying to swallow the sea.'

'Or there's Henry James on Balzac, saying he wriggled his way into the constituted consciousness like fingers into a glove.'

'That's a phallic image.'

'Of course. So are all the others, in one way or another, I suppose. Not Blanche Glover, exactly.'

'The *Actinia*'s withdrawing. It doesn't like me poking it.'

The *Actinia* presented the appearance of a rubbery navel, out of which protruded two or three fleshy whiskers, in the process of being tucked away. Then it was there, a blood-dark, fleshy mound, surrounding a pinched hole.

'I read Leonora Stern's essay, "Venus Mount and Barren Heath".'

Maud hunted for an adjective to describe this work, rejected penetrating and settled on 'Very profound'.

'Of course it's profound. But. It worried me.'

'It was meant to.'

'No, not for that reason, not because I'm male. Because.

'Do you never have the sense that our metaphors *eat up* our world? I mean of course everything connects and connects – all the time – and I suppose one studies – I study – literature because all these connections seem both endlessly exciting and then in some sense dangerously powerful – as though we held a clue to the true nature of things? I mean, all those gloves, a minute ago, we were playing a professional game of hooks and eyes – mediaeval gloves, giants' gloves, Blanche Glover, Balzac's gloves, the sea-anemone's ovaries – and it all reduced like boiling jam to – human sexuality. Just as Leonora Stern makes the whole earth read as the female body – and language – all language. And all vegetation is pubic hair.'

Maud laughed, drily. Roland said,

'And then, really, what is it, what is this arcane power we have, when we see that everything is human sexuality? It's really *powerlessness.*'

'Impotence,' said Maud, leaning over, interested.

'I was avoiding that word, because that precisely *isn't the point*. We are so knowing. And all we've found out, is primitive sympathetic magic. Infantile polymorphous perversity. Everything relates to *us* and so we're imprisoned in ourselves – we can't see *things*. And we paint everything with this metaphor –'

'You are very cross with Leonora.'

'She's very good. But I don't want to see through her eyes. It isn't a matter of her gender and my gender. I just don't.'

Maud considered. She said, 'In every age, there must be truths people can't fight – whether or not they want to, whether or not they will go on being truths in the future. We live in the truth of what Freud discovered. Whether or not we like it. However we've modified it. We aren't really free to suppose – to imagine – he could possibly have been wrong about human nature. In particulars, surely – but not in the large plan –'

Roland wanted to ask: do you like that? He thought he had to suppose she did: her work was psychoanalytic, after all, this work on liminality and marginal beings. He said instead,

'It makes an interesting effort of imagination to think how they saw the world. What Ash saw when he stood on perhaps this ledge. He was interested in the anemone. In the origin of life. Also in the reason we were here.'

'They valued themselves. Once, they knew God valued them. Then they began to think there was no God, only blind forces. So they valued themselves, they loved themselves and attended to their natures –'

'And we don't?'

'At some point in history their self-value changed into – what worries you. A horrible over-simplification. It leaves out guilt, for a start. Now or then.'

She closed *The Great Ventriloquist* and leaned over the ledge on which she was curled, and extended a hand.

'Shall we move on?'

'Where? What are we looking for?'

'We'd better start looking for facts as well as images. I suggest Whitby, where the jet brooch was bought.'

My dearest Ellen,

I have found much that is curious in the town of Whitby, a prosperous fishing village at the mouth of the river Esk – it is a sloping town, crowding down in picturesque alleys or yards and flight after flight of stone stairs to the water – a terraced town, from the upper layers of which you seem to see, above a moving sphere of masts and smoking chimneys all about you, the town, the harbour, the ruined Abbey and the German Ocean.

The past lies all around, from the moorland graves and supposed Killing Pits of the Ancient Britons to the Roman occupation and the early days of Christian evangelism under St Hilda — the town in those days was called Streonshalh and what we are accustomed to think of as the Synod of Whitby, in 664, was of course the Synod of Streonshalh. I have meditated among calling gulls in the ruins of the Abbey and have seen older darker things — the tumuli or houes on the moors, and temples perhaps druidical, including the Bridestones, a row of uprights at Sleights, thought to be one side of an avenue of a stone circle, such as Stonehenge. Certain details may bring these long-vanished folk suddenly to life in the imagination. Such are the finding hereabouts of a heart-shaped ear-ring of jet in contact with the jaw-bone of a skeleton; and a number of large jet beads cut in angles, found with a similar inmate of a barrow, who had been deposited in the houe with the knees drawn upward to the chin.

There is a mythical story which accounts for the standing stones which appeals to my imagination, as suggesting the liveliness of ancient Gods in comparatively modern times. Whitby has its own local giant — a certain fearsome Wade, who with his wife Bell, was given to tossing about casual boulders on the moors. Wade and Bell were, like the Hrimthurse who built the wall of Asgard, or the fairy Melusina, builders of castles for ungrateful men — they are credited with the construction of the Roman Road across the moor to the delightful town of Pickering — a regular road, built of stones on a stratum of gravel or rubbish from the sandstone of the moor. I intend to walk this road, which is locally known as Wade's Causey, or Causeway, and was believed to have been built by Wade for the convenience of his wife Bell, who kept a giant cow on the moors, which she travelled to milk. One of the ribs of this monstrous ruminant was on show in Mulgrave Castle and was in fact the jawbone of a whale. The tumuli or houes on the moorland are heaps of boulders carried by the diligent Bell in her apron, whose strings occasionally broke. Charlton believes that Wade is simply a name for the ancient God Woden. Thor was certainly worshipped in Saxon times at the village of Thordisa which stood at the head of the Eastrow beck. So the human imagination mixes and adapts to its current preoccupations many ingredients into new wholes — it is essentially poetic — here are a Whale and Pickering Castle and the old Thunder God and the tombs of ancient Briton and Saxon chieftains and the military greed of the conquering Roman armies, all refashioned into a local giant and his dame — as the stones of the Roman road go to the construction of the dry stone walls, to the loss of archaeology and the preservation of our sheep — or as the huge boulder on Sleights Moor, thrown by Bell's giant child and dented by her iron ribcage — was broken up for road-mending — and I came along that road.

I have been visiting the local jet industry here, which flourishes and has produced work of a high standard of craftsmanship. I have sent you a piece — with a little poem to accompany it — with my great love, as always. I know you like well-made things; you would be truly delighted, for the most part, by the curious manufactures that go on here — adornments may be made from many things — ancient ammonite worms find new lives as polished brooches. I have been interested also by the reformation of fossil remains into elegant articles — a whole burnished tabletop will display the unthinkably ancient coils of long-dead snail-things, or the ferny stone leaves of primitive cycads as clear as the pressed flowers and ferns that inhabit your prayer-book. If there is a subject that is my own, my dear Ellen, as a writer I mean, it is the persistent shape-shifting life of things long-dead but not vanished. I should like to write something so perfectly fashioned that it should still be contemplated as those stone-impressed creatures are, after so long a time. Though I feel our durance on this earth may not equal theirs.

The jet, you know, was once alive too. 'Certain scientific thinkers have supposed it to be indurated petroleum or mineral pitch — but it is now generally accepted that its origins are ligneous — it is found in compressed masses, long and narrow — the outer surface always marked with longitudinal striae, like the grain of wood, and the transverse fracture which is conchoidal and has a resinous lustre, displays the annual growths in compressed elliptical zones.' I cite this description from Dr Young, though I have seen such raw lumps of jet in the working-sheds, yes, and held them in my hands, and been moved unspeakably by the traces of time — growing time long, long, unutterably long past — in their ellipses. They may be contaminated by an excess of siliceous matter in some cases — a craftsman carving a rose, or a serpent, or a pair of hands may suddenly come across a line or flaw of silex or flint in the material and be driven to desist. I have watched such craftsmen work — they are highly specialised workers — a carver may pass a brooch on to another who specialises in incising patterns — or gold or ivory or bone-carving may be joined to the jet.

All these new sights and discoveries, my dear, as you may imagine, have started off shoots of poetry in every direction. (I say shoots in Vaughan's sense, 'Bright shoots of everlastingness', where the word means simultaneously brightness of scintillation and flights of arrows, and growth of seeds of light — I wish you would despatch to me my Silex scintillans, for I have been *thinking much about his poetry and that stony metaphor since I have been working on the rocks here. When your jet brooch comes, I beg you will stroke it and watch how it electrically attracts scraps of hair and paper — it has its own magnetic life in it — and so has always been made use of in charms and white witchcraft and ancient medicines. I divagate without discipline — my mind runs all over — I have a poem I wish to write about modern discoveries of silex-coated twigs in ancient artesian wells, as described by Lyell.)*

Now let me know how you are — your health, your household doings, your reading —

Your loving husband
Randolph

Maud and Roland walked round Whitby harbour and up and down the narrow streets which radiated steeply from it. Where Randolph Ash had noticed busyness and prosperity these noticed general signs of unemployment and purposelessness. Few boats were in the harbour and those there were appeared to be battened down and chained up; no motor sounded, and no sail flapped. There was still a smell of coal smoke, but it carried, for them, different connotations.

The shop-fronts were old and full of romance. A fishmonger's slab was decorated with gaping skeletal shark-jaws and spiny monstrosities; a sweet-shop had all the old jars and pell-mell heaps of brightly-coloured sugary cubes and spheres and pellets. There were several jewellers specialising in jet. They stopped outside one of these: 'Hobbs and Bell, purveyors of Jet Ornaments'. It was tall and narrow; the window was like an upright box, along the sides of which were festooned rope upon rope of black and glistening beads, some with dangling lockets, some many-faceted, some glossily round. The front of the window was like a sea-chest of wave-tossed treasure, a dusty heap of brooches, bracelets, rings on cracked velvety cards, teaspoons, paperknives, inkwells and a variety of dim dead shells. It was the North, Roland thought, black as coal, solid, not always graceful craftsmanship, bright under dust.

'I wonder,' said Maud, 'if it would be a good idea to buy something for Leonora. She likes odd pieces of jewellery.'

'There's a brooch there — with forget-me-nots round the edge and clasped hands — that says FRIENDSHIP.'

'She'd like that—'

A very small woman appeared in the door of the box-shop. She wore a large apron covered with purple and grey florets, over a skinny black jumper. She had a small hard, brown-skinned face under white hair drawn into a bun. Her eyes were Viking blue and her mouth, when she opened it, contained apparently three teeth. She was puckered but wholesome, like an old apple, and the apron-dress was clean, though her stockings sagged at the ankles over thick black laced shoes.

'Come in, luv, and look around. There's plenty more inside. All good Whitby jet. I don't hold with no imitations. You won't find better.'

Inside the counter was another glass sarcophagus, inside which were tumbled more strings and pins and heavy bracelets.

'Anything you like the look of, I can easy get out for you.'

'That looks interesting.'

'That' was an oval locket with a vaguely classical carved figure, full-length, bending over a flowing urn.

'That's a Victorian mourning locket. Probably made by Thomas Andrews. He was jet-maker to the Queen. Those were good days for Whitby, after the Prince Consort died. They liked to be reminded of their dead in those days. Now it's out of sight, out of mind.'

Maud put the locket down. She asked to see the clasped-hand 'friendship' brooch, which the old woman reached in from the window. Roland was studying a card of brooches and rings made apparently from plaited and woven silks, some encircled by jet, some studded with pearls.

'This is pretty. Jet and pearls and silk.'

'Oh, not *silk*, sir. That's hair. That's another form of mourning brooch, with the hair. Look, these ones have 'IN MEMORIAM' round the frame. They cut it off at the death-bed. You could say they kept it alive.'

Roland peered through the glass at the interwoven strands of fine pale hair.

'They made all sorts of it, very ingenious. Look — here's a plaited watch-chain out of someone's long locks. And a bracelet with a pretty heart-shaped clasp, ever such delicate work, in dark hair.'

Roland took the thing, light and lifeless, apart from its gold clasp.

'Do you sell many of these?'

'Oh, now and then. Folk collect them, you know. Folk'll collect anything, given time. Butterflies. Collar-studs. Even my old flat-irons, as I used right up to 1960 when our Edith insisted on getting me an electric one, I had a man round, asking. And there's a lot of *work* in that bracelet, young man, a lot of care went into that. And solid gold, 18-carats, which was expensive for them times, when you got pinchbeck and such.'

Maud had a row of brooches laid out on the top of the counter.

'I can tell you know a good piece. Now, I've got a real good carved piece you won't see any more of – language of flowers, young man – clematis and gorse and heartsease – which is to say Mental Beauty and Enduring Affection and "I am always thinking of you". You should buy *that* for the young lady. Better than old hair.'

Roland made a demurring noise. The old woman leaned forward on her high stool and put out a hand to Maud's green scarf.

'Now *that*'s a good piece such as you won't come across easily – *that* looks to me like the best of the work out of Isaac Greenberg's Baxtergate undertaking – such as was sent all over Europe to Queens and Princesses. I'd dearly like a close look at that piece, mam, if you could –'

Maud put up her hands to her head, and hesitated between unpinning the brooch and pulling off the whole head-binding. Finally, awkwardly for her, she did both, putting the scarf on the counter, and then unpinning its carefully constructed folds and handing the large black knobby thing to the old woman, who trotted away to hold it up in the dusty light from the window.

Roland looked at Maud. The pale, pale hair in fine braids was wound round and round her head, startling white in this light that took the colour out of things and only caught gleams and glancings. She looked almost shockingly naked, like a denuded window-doll, he at first thought, and then, as she turned her supercilious face to him and he saw it changed, simply fragile and even vulnerable. He wanted to loosen the tightness and let the hair go. He felt a kind of sympathetic pain on his own skull-skin, so dragged and ruthlessly hair-pinned was hers. Both put their hands to their temple, as though he was her mirror.

The old woman came back and put Maud's brooch on the counter, switching on a dusty little Anglepoise to illuminate its darkness.

'I've never seen aught quite like this – though it's clear enough one of Isaac Greenberg's pieces, I reckon – there were a piece of his at t'Great Exhibition with corals and rocks on, though I've never seen a mermaid *and* the coral – with her little mirror and all. Where did you come by that, mam?'

'I suppose you might call it a family heirloom. I found it in the family button box when I was really quite young – we had a huge dressing-up box full of old buckles and buttons and bits and bobs – and it was just in there. I'm afraid nobody liked it much. My mother thought it was just hideous Victorian junk, she said. I suppose it *is* Victorian? I took it because it reminded me of the Little Mermaid.' She turned to Roland. 'And then lately of the Fairy Melusina, of course.'

'Oh, it's Victorian. I sh'd say it's earlier than the death of the Prince Consort in 1861 – there was more playful pieces before that – though always the sad ones predominated. Look at th' workmanship in that waving hair and the lifelikeness of the little tail-fins. What they could accomplish in them days. You wouldn't get work like that nowadays, not nowhere. It's forgotten and gone by.'

Roland had never closely approached Maud's brooch, which depicted indeed a little mermaid seated on a rock, her glossy black shoulders twisted towards the surface, modestly obviating any need to carve her little breasts. Her hair snaked down her back, and her tail snaked down the rock. The whole was enclosed in what he had taken to be twigs and now saw, through the old woman's eyes, to be branching coral.

He said to Maud, 'You inherited some of Christabel's books . . .'

'I know. I never thought. I mean, this brooch has always been there. I never thought to ask where it came from. It – it looks quite different in this shop. Among these other things. It was – it was a joke of mine.'

'Perhaps it was a joke of *his*.'

'Even if it was,' said Maud, thinking furiously, 'even if it was, it doesn't prove she was *here*. All it proves is, he bought brooches for two women at once...'

'It doesn't even prove that. She could have bought it for herself.'

'*If* she was here.'

'Or anywhere they were sold.'

'You should look after that piece,' the old woman put in. 'That's unique, I should say, that is.' She turned to Roland. 'Won't you have the flower-language piece, sir? It would be a real companion-piece to the little mermaid.'

'I'll take the FRIENDSHIP brooch,' said Maud quickly. 'For Leonora.'

Roland wanted badly to own something, anything, in this strange sooty stuff which Ash had touched and written about. He did not in fact want the ornate flower-piece and could think of no one to whom he might give it – these things were definitely not in Val's style, not in either of her styles, old or new. He found, in a green glass bowl on the counter, a pile of loose unrelated beads and chips which the old woman was selling at 75p each and sorted out for himself a little heap of these, some round, some flattened and elliptical, a hexagon, a highly polished satin cushion.

'Personal worry beads,' he told Maud. 'I do worry.'

'I noticed.'

Chapter Fourteen

> They say that women change: 'tis so: but you
> Are ever-constant in your changefulness,
> Like that still thread of falling river, one
> From source to last embrace in the still pool
> Ever-renewed and ever-moving on
> From first to last a myriad water-drops
> And you – I love you for it – are the *force*
> That moves and holds the form.

R. H. Ash, Ask to Embla, XIII

My dearest Ellen,

Today I varied my regimen of dissection and magnification by a long stride from foss to foss, or force to force, around the Dale of Goathland or Godeland – do you not admire the way we here see language in the making, in the alternative names, both accepted, for these things. These names were given by the ancient Vikings – the Danes settled these parts and embraced Christianity, whilst the wilder Norwegian pagans tried to invade from Ireland and the North – to meet defeat at Brunanburh. They left few traces of their 250 years of farming and fighting here – only words and names, which vanish and decay as W. Wordsworth has observed.

> *Mark! how all things swerve*
> *From their known course, or vanish like a dream;*
> *Another language spreads from coast to coast;*
> *Only perchance some melancholy Stream*
> *And some indignant Hills old names preserve,*
> *When laws, and creeds, and people all are lost!*

There are two constituent brooklets of the Mirk Esk, the Eller Beck and the Wheeldale Beck, which have their juncture at a place called Beck Holes – and along these Becks are many fine fosses — the Thomasine Foss, Water Ark and Walk Mill Fosses — and then the Nelly Ayre Foss and Malyan's Spout — a particularly impressive hundred-foot fall into the sylvan ravine. The effect of light and shade, both in the changing green of the pensile foliage and the depths of the pools, and in the racing clouds which bring dark, light and dark again, was particularly fine. I climbed up onto Glaisdale and Wheeldale moors — where these becks have their sources in small rills which bubble up amongst the heather and grit. The contrast between the cool dappled world of the little dales — and the shady caverns and pools into which the forces rush and hurry to be swallowed in quiet — and the open spaces where for dark mile upon mile nothing seems to stir and nothing sounds save a surprising harsh wailing cry of a bird — or a chipping sound of another — this contrast is so absolute and yet so natural — and the water running from one world to another — a man might think that here, in this rough north was, if not Paradise, the original earth — rocks, stones, trees, air, water — all so solid and immutable, apparently — and yet shifting and flowing and fleeting in the race of light and the driving cloaks of shadow, that alternately reveal and conceal, illuminate and smudge its contours. Here, dear Ellen, and not in the fat valleys of the south, one has a sense of the nearness of those remotest men whose blood and bones made our blood and bones and live still in them — Briton and Dane, Norseman and Roman — And of things infinitely more remote — creatures who once walked here when the earth was hot — Dr Buckland investigating the cave of Kirkdale in 1821 discovered a den of hyenas with bones of tiger, bear, wolf, probably lion and other carnivora, elephant, rhinoceros, horse, ox, and 3 species of deer as well as many of the rodentia and birds, consumed by the hyenas.

I cannot describe the air to you. It is like no other air. Our language was not designed to distinguish differences in air; it runs the risk of a meaningless lyricism or inexact metaphors — so I will not write of it in terms of wine or crystal, though both those things came into my mind. I have breathed the air of Mont Blanc — a chill light clean air that comes off the remote glaciers and has the purity of those snows, touched with the resin of pine and the hay of the high meadows. Thin air, as Shakespeare said, the air of vanishing things and refinements beyond apprehension by our senses. This Yorkshire air, the moorland air, that is, has no such glassy chill — it is all alive, on the move, like the waters that thread their way through the heath, as it does with them. It is visible air — you see it run in rivers and lines over the shoulders of bald stones — you see it rise in aery fountains and tremble over the heath when it is hot. And the scent of it — sharp, unforgettable — clean rain tossed and the ghost of ancient woodsmoke — and the cold clearness of brook water — and

something fine and subtle all of its own — oh, I cannot describe this air. it
expands a man's mind in his head, I do believe, and gives him extra senses he
knows nothing of, before coming on these heights and ranges . . .

There was more pleasure for Roland and Maud in their walk,
the next day, along the becks to the fosses. They walked out
from Goathland and saw the threads and glassy interrupted fans
of the Mallyan Spout; they scrambled along river paths above
the running peaty water, and crossed moorland, scrambling down
again to riversides. They found magical patches of greensward
between rocks, mown by the incessant attention of nibbling
sheep, surrounded by standing stones and mysterious clumps of
spotted purple foxgloves. Strange transparent insects whirred
past; dippers ran in the shallows; in one marshy place they disturbed whole groups of newly-shining young frogs which leaped
up in little showers of water under their feet. Over lunch, which
they ate in one of the grassy clearings near the Nelly Ayre
Foss, they discussed progress. Roland had been reading *Melusina*
in bed and was now convinced that Christabel had been in
Yorkshire.

'It *has* to be here. Where do people *think* it is? It's full of local
words from here, gills and riggs and ling. The air is from here.
Like in his letter. She talks about the air like summer colts playing
on the moors. That's a Yorkshire saying.'

'I suppose if it is no one has noticed it before because they
weren't looking. That is — her landscapes were always supposed
to be really Brittany, claiming to be Poitou, and heavily
influenced by Romantic local colour — the Brontës, Scott,
Wordsworth. Or symbolic.'

'Do *you* think she was here?'

'Oh yes. I feel certain. But I've no proof that will stand up.
The Hob. The Yorkshire words. Perhaps my brooch. What I
can't understand, still, is how he could write all those letters to
his wife — it makes me wonder —'

'Perhaps he did love his wife, too. He does say "when I come
back". He always meant to go back. And he did — we know that.
If Christabel was here, it wasn't a question of running away —'

'I wish we knew what it *was* a question of —'

'It was their business. It was private. I will say though, I feel

Melusina is very like some of Ash's poems – The rest of her work isn't at all. But *Melusina* sounds often as though he wrote it. To me. Not the subject matter. The style.'

'I don't want to think that. But I do see what you mean.'

The Thomason Foss is reached along a steep track from Beck Hole, a small hamlet in a fold of the moorland hills. They walked to it that way, rather than descending from the moors, so as to approach the pool below the fall. The weather was very lively and full of movement; huge white clouds sailed in a blue sky, above dry stone walls and woodland. Roland discovered on the surface of one of the walls, a series of shining silver mats which proved to be the openings of the lairs of tunnel spiders, who rushed out, waving fierce grasping arms and jaws, when even a thread of their structure was troubled by a straw. Towards the Foss the path descended steeply and they had to clamber among boulders. The water fell amongst a naturally cavernous circle of rocks and lowering brows, in which various saplings struggled for a precarious living; it was dark and smelled cold, and mossy, and weedy. Roland looked at the greenish-goldish-white rush of the fall for a time and then transferred his gaze to the outer edges of the troubled and turning pool. As he looked, the sun came out, and hit the pool, showing both the mirror-glitter from the surface, and various live and dead leaves and plants moving under it, caught as it were in a net of fat links of dappled light. He observed a curious natural phenomenon. *Inside* the cavern, and on the sides of the boulders in its mouth, what appeared to be flames of white light appeared to be striving and moving upwards. Wherever the refracted light off the water struck the uneven stone, wherever a fissure ran, upright or transverse, this same brightness poured and quivered along it, paleness instead of shadow, building a kind of visionary structure of non-existent fires and non-solid networks of thread inside it. He sat and watched for a time, squatting on a stone, until he lost his sense of time and space and his own precise location and saw the phantom flames as though they were the conscious centre. His contemplation was interrupted by Maud, who came and sat beside him.

'What's absorbing you?'

'The light. The fire. Look at that effect of light. Look how the whole cave roof is alight.'

Maud said, 'She saw this. I'm sure she saw this. Look at the beginning of *Melusina*.'

> Three elements combined to make the fourth.
> The sunlight made a pattern, through the air
> (Athwart ash-saplings rooted in the sparse
> Handfuls of peat in overhanging clefts)
> Of tessellation in the water's glaze:
> And where the water moved and shook itself
> Like rippling serpent-scales, the light ran on
> Under the liquid in a molten glow
> Of seeming links of chain-mail; but above
> The water and the light together made
> On the grey walls and roof of the dank cave
> A show of leaping flames, of creeping spires
> Of tongues of light that licked the granite ledge
> Cunningly flickered up along each cleft
> Each refractory roughness, creeping up
> Making, where shadows should have been, long threads
> And tapering cones and flame-like forms of white
> A fire which heated not, nor singed, nor fed
> On things material, but self-renewed
> Burnt on the cold stones not to be consumed
> And not consuming, made of light and stone
> A fountain of cold fire stirred by the force
> Of waterfall and rising spring at once
> With borrowed liveliness...

'She came here with him,' said Maud.

'Even this isn't proof. And if the sun hadn't struck out when it did I wouldn't have seen it. But it is proof, to me.'

'I've been reading his poems. *Ask to Embla*. They're good. He wasn't talking to himself. He was talking to *her* – Embla – Christabel or – Most love poetry is only talking to itself. I like those poems.'

'I'm glad you like something about him.'

'I've been trying to imagine him. Them. They must have been – in an extreme state. I was thinking last night – about what you said about our generation and sex. We see it everywhere. As

266

you say. We are very knowing. We know all sorts of other things, too – about how there isn't a unitary ego – how we're made up of conflicting, interacting systems of things – and I suppose we *believe* that? We know we are driven by desire, but we can't see it as they did, can we? We never say the word Love, do we – we know it's a suspect ideological construct – especially Romantic Love – so we have to make a real effort of imagination to know what it felt like to be them, here, believing in these things – Love – themselves – that what they did mattered –'

'I know. You know what Christabel says. "Outside our small safe place flies Mystery." I feel we've done away with that too – And desire, that we look into so carefully – I think all the *looking-into* has some very odd effects on the desire.'

'I think that, too.'

'Sometimes I feel,' said Roland carefully, 'that the best state is to be without desire. When I really look at myself –'

'If you have a self –'

'At my life, at the way it is – what I *really* want is to – to have nothing. An empty clean bed. I have this image of a clean empty bed in a clean empty room, where nothing is asked or to be asked. Some of that is to do with – my personal circumstances. But some of it's general. I think.'

'I know what you mean. No, that's a feeble thing to say. It's a much more powerful coincidence than that. That's what I think about, when I'm alone. How good it would be to have nothing. How good it would be to desire nothing. And the same image. An empty bed in an empty room. White.'

'White.'

'Exactly the same.'

'How strange.'

'Maybe we're symptomatic of whole flocks of exhausted scholars and theorists. Or maybe it's just us.'

'How funny – how very funny – that we should have come here, for this purpose, and sit here, and discover – *that* – about each other.'

They walked back in companionable silence, listening to birds and the movement of weather in trees and water. Over dinner that night they combed *Melusina* for more Yorkshire words. Roland said,

'There's a place on the map called the Boggle Hole. It's a nice word – I wondered – perhaps we could take a day off from *them*, get out of their story, go and look at something for ourselves. There's no Boggle Hole in Cropper or the Ash Letters – Just not to be caught up in anything?'

'Why not? The weather's improving. It's hot.'

'It wouldn't matter. I just want to look at something, with interest, and without layers of meaning. Something new.'

Something new, they had said. They had a perfect day for it. A day with the blue and gold good weather of anyone's primitive childhood expectations, when the new, brief memory tells itself that this is what is, and therefore was, and therefore will be. A good day to see a new place.

They took a simple picnic. Fresh brown bread, white Wensley-dale cheese, crimson radishes, yellow butter, scarlet tomatoes, round bright green Granny Smiths and a bottle of mineral water. They took no books.

The Boggle Hole is a cove tucked beneath cliffs, where a beck runs down across sand to the sea, from an old mill which is now a youth hostel. They walked down through flowering lanes. The high hedges were thick with dog-roses, mostly a clear pink, sometimes white, with yellow-gold centres dusty with yellow pollen. These roses were intricately and thickly entwined with rampant wild honeysuckle, trailing and weaving creamy flowers among the pink and gold. Neither of them had ever seen or smelled such extravagance of wildflowers in so small a space. The warm air brought the smell of the flowers in great gusts and lingering intense canopies. Both had expected one or two flowers at most, late modern survivors of thickets seen by Shakespeare or painted by Morris. But here was abundance, here was growth, here were banks of gleaming scented life.

There is not exactly a beach, under the cliff. There is a stretch of sand and then shelf after shelf of wet stone and ledges of rock-pools, stretching away to the sea. These ledges are brilliantly coloured: pink stone, silvery sand under water, violent green mossy weed, heavy clumps of rosy-fingered weeds among banks of olive and yellow bladderwrack. The cliffs themselves are grey and flaking. Roland and Maud noticed that the flat stones at their bases were threaded and etched with fossil plumes and tubes. There was a notice: please do not damage the cliffs; respect our heritage and preserve it for all of us. Ammonites and belemnites were on sale in Whitby. A young man with a hammer and a sack was nevertheless busy chipping away at the rock-face, from which coiled and rimmed circular forms protruded everywhere. A peculiarity of that beach is the proliferation of large rounded stones which lie about like the aftermath of a bombardment, cosmic or gigantic. These stones are not uniform in colour or size; they can be shiny black, sulphurous yellow, a kind of old potato blend of greenish waxy, sandy, white or shot with a kind of rosy quartz. Maud and Roland walked along with their heads down, saying to each other 'Look at this, look at this, look at this', distinguishing stones for a moment, with their attention, then letting these fall back into the mass-pattern, or random distribution, as new ones replaced them.

When they stopped and spread their picnic on a rock, they were able to look out, to take a large view. Roland took off his shoes; his feet were white on the sands like things come up out of blind dark. Maud sat on the rock in jeans and a short-sleeved shirt. Her arms were white and gold; white skin, glinting hairs. She poured Perrier water from its green flask, declaring its pure origin, Eau de Source; its bubbles winked in cardboard cups. The tide was out; the sea was far away. The moment had come for a personal conversation. Both felt this; both were mostly willing, but inhibited.

'Will you be sorry to go back?' Maud.

'Will you?'

'This is very good bread.' Then, 'I have the impression both of us will be sorry.'

'We shall have to decide what – if anything – to tell Blackadder and Cropper.'

'And Leonora. Who will be arriving. I am apprehensive about Leonora. She carries one away in the force of her enthusiasm.'

Roland could not quite imagine Leonora. He knew somehow that she was large and now imagined her suddenly like some classical goddess in draperies, pulling the fastidious Maud along by the hand. Two women, running. Leonora's writings made him imagine more than that. Two women...

He looked at separate Maud, in her jeans and white shirt under the sun. She still wore a scarf – not the silk turret now, but a crisp cotton one, green and white squares, tied under her hair in the nape of her neck.

'You will have to decide what to say to her.'

'Oh, I have decided. Nothing. Until at least you and I have reached some – end – or decision. It won't be easy. She is – she is – invasive. An expert in intimacy. She reduces my space. I'm not very good with that sort of thing. As we were saying. In a way.'

'Perhaps Sir George will make a move.'

'Perhaps.'

'I don't know what will happen to me when I get back. I've got no real job, as you know – only bits of sufferance teaching and the piecework on the edition. I depend on Blackadder. Who writes dull references about me, making me sound even duller. I can't tell him all this, either. But it's going to make it harder to just go on. And then there's Val.'

Maud was looking, not at him, but at an apple, which she was dividing into paper-thin wafers with a sharp knife, each with its half-moon of bright green rind, its paper-white crisp flesh, its shining dark seeds.

'I don't know about Val.'

'I've never talked about her. Better not. I feel I shouldn't. I've lived with her since I went to university. She's the breadwinner. I suppose I'm here partly on her money. She doesn't like her work – temping and things – but she does it. I owe her so much.'

'I see.'

'Only it doesn't work. Not for any good reason. But because of the – because – I have this vision of the white bed –'

Maud put a little fan of apple curves onto a paper plate and handed it to him.

'I know. I had this thing with Fergus. I expect you heard.'

'Yes.'

'I expect he told you. I had a bad time, with Fergus. We tormented each other. I hate that, I hate the noise, the distraction. I remembered something, thinking about what you said – about the sea anemone and the gloves and Leonora on Venus Mount. Yes. I remember Fergus had a long patch of lecturing me on Penisneid. He's one of those men who argues by increments of noise – so that as you open your mouth he says another, cleverer, louder thing. He used to quote Freud at me at six in the morning. *Analysis Terminable and Interminable.* He got up very early. He used to *prance around* the flat – with nothing on – quoting Freud saying that "at no point in one's analytic work does one suffer more from a suspicion that one has been preaching to the winds than when one is trying to persuade a woman to abandon her wish for a penis" – I don't think he – Freud – is right about that – but anyway – there was something intrinsically ridiculous about this silly shouting – before breakfast – letting it all hang out – I couldn't work. That was how it was. I – I felt battered. For no good reason.'

Roland looked at Maud to see if she might laugh and saw that she was smiling, an embarrassed, fierce smile, but a smile.

He laughed. Maud laughed. He said,

'It's exhausting. When everything's a deliberate political stance. Even if it's interesting.'

'Celibacy as the new volupté. The new indulgence.'

'If it is you should relax into it. Tell me – why do you always cover your hair?'

He thought for a moment he might have offended her, but she only looked down, and then answered with a kind of academic accuracy.

'It's to do with Fergus. With Fergus and with its colour. I used to wear it very short – sheared short. It's the wrong colour, you see, no one believes it's natural. I once got hissed at a conference, for dyeing it to please men. And then Fergus said, the shaved style was a cop-out, a concession, it made me look like a skull, he said. I should simply have it. So I grew it. But now it's grown, I put it away.'

'You shouldn't. You should let it out.'

'Why do you say that?'

'Because if anyone can't see it they think and think about it, they wonder what it's like, so you attract attention to it. Also because, because . . .'

'I see.'

He waited. Maud untied the head-square. The segments of the plaits were like streaked and polished oval stones, celandine yellow, straw-yellow, silvery yellow, glossy with constricted life. Roland was moved – not exactly with desire, but with an obscure emotion that was partly pity, for the rigorous constriction all that mass had undergone, to be so structured into repeating patterns. If he closed his eyes and squinted, the head against the sea was crowned with knobby horns.

'Life is so short,' said Roland. 'It has a right to breathe.'

And indeed his feeling was for the hair, a kind of captive creature. Maud pulled out a pin or two and the mass slipped, and then hung, still plaited, unbalanced on her neck.

'You are an odd man.'

'I'm not making a pass. You know that. I just wanted to see it let out once. I know you will know I'm telling the truth.'

'Yes, I do. That's what's so odd.'

She began slowly to undo, with unweaving fingers, the long, thick braids. Roland watched, intently. There was a final moment when six thick strands, twice three, lay still and formed over her shoulders. And then she put down her head and shook it from side to side, and the heavy hair flew up, and the air got into it. Her long neck bowed, she shook her head faster and faster, and Roland saw the light rush towards it and glitter on it, the whirling mass, and Maud inside it saw a moving sea of gold lines, waving, and closed her eyes and saw scarlet blood.

Roland felt as though something had been loosed in himself, that had been gripping him.

He said, 'That feels better.'

Maud pushed aside her hair and looked out at him, a little flushed.

'All right. That feels better.'

CHAPTER FIFTEEN

And is love then more
Than the *kick* galvanic
Or the thundering roar
Of *Ash* volcanic
Belched from some crater
Of earth-fire within?
Are we automata
Or Angel-kin?

R. H. Ash

The man and the woman sat opposite each other in the railway carriage. They had an appearance of quiet decorum; both had books open on their knees, to which they turned when the motion of the carriage permitted. He was indeed leaning lazily back into his corner, with crossed ankles, indicating a state of relaxation. She had her eyes for the most part cast demurely down at her book, though she would occasionally raise a pointed chin and look intently out at the changing countryside. An observer might have speculated for some time as to whether they were travelling together or separately, for their eyes rarely met, and when they did, remained guarded and expressionless. Such an observer might have concluded, after a considerable period of travelling, that the gentleman admired, or felt a considerable interest in, the lady. When she was most determinedly looking at her book, or the flashing fields and vanishing cattle, his eyes would rest on her, speculative or simply curious, it was very hard to tell.

He was a handsome man, with a flowing head of very dark brown hair, almost black but with russet lights in its waves, and a glossy beard, a little browner, the colour of horse-chestnuts. His brow was expansive, the organ of intellect well-developed, though he was equally well-endowed with the bumps of compassion and fellow-feeling. He had black brows, a little rough and craggy, under which very large dark eyes looked out at the world steadily enough, fearless but with something held in reserve. The nose was clearcut and the mouth firm and settled – a face, one might think, that knew itself and had a decided way of taking in the world. His book was Sir Charles Lyell's *Principles of Geology* which he took in, when he applied himself, with concentrated speed. His clothes were elegant without ostentation. The hypothetical observer might have been unable to decide whether his subject pursued an active or a contemplative life: he looked accustomed to decision, and yet also one who 'had thought long and deeply'.

The lady was dressed elegantly if not in the first flight of fashion; she wore a grey-striped muslin dress over which she had cast an Indian shawl with marine-blue and peacock paisleys on a dove-grey ground; she had a small grey silk bonnet, under the brim of which appeared a few white silk rosebuds. She was very fair, pale-skinned, with eyes, not unduly large, of a strange green colour which transmuted itself as the light varied. She was not exactly beautiful – her face was too long for perfection, and not in the first flush of youth, though the bones were well-cut and the mouth an elegant curve, no pouting rosebud. Her teeth were a little large for an exacting taste, but they were strong and white. It was hard to tell whether she was a married lady or a spinster, and hard too, to decide what her circumstances might be. Everything about her was both neat and tastefully chosen, breathing no hint of extravagance, but betraying no signs of poverty or skimping to the curious eye. Her white kid gloves were supple and showed no signs of wear. Her little feet, which appeared from time to time as the carriage movement displaced the large bell of her skirt, were encased in a gleaming pair of laced boots in emerald green leather. If she was aware of her travelling companion's interest, she showed no sign of it, unless it were that her eyes were studiously averted from his person, and that circumstance might have indicated only a proper modesty.

It was indeed only when they were well beyond York that the

question of their relationship might have been resolved, for the gentleman leaned forward and asked, very earnestly, if she was quite comfortable and not tired. And by then there were no other passengers, for the most part had changed trains, or reached their destination at York, and none was proceeding beyond Malton and Pickering, so that the two were alone in the carriage. She looked directly at him then, and said no, she was not in the least tired; she considered for a moment and added precisely that she was not in a state of mind that allowed of tiredness, she believed. Whereupon they did smile at each other, and he leaned forward and possessed himself of one of the little gloved hands, which lay still and then clasped his. There were matters, he said, that they had an urgent need to discuss before they arrived, things which they had had no time or peace to make clear in the haste and turmoil of setting off, things to which there was a degree of awkwardness attached, which he hoped, with resolution, they could overcome.

He had been planning this speech since they left King's Cross. He had been quite unable to imagine how he would say it, or how she would respond.

She said she was listening attentively. The little hand in his curled and crisped. He gripped it.

'We are travelling together,' he said. 'We decided – you decided – to come. What I do not know is whether you would wish – whether you would choose – to lodge and manage yourself separately from me after this point – or whether – or whether – you would wish to travel as my wife. It is a large step – It is attended with all sorts of inconvenience, hazard and – embarrassment. I have rooms reserved in Scarborough where a wife could well – find space. Or I could reserve other rooms – under some false name. Or you may not wish to take this step at all – you may wish to be lodged separately and respectably elsewhere. Forgive this baldness. I am truly trying to discover your wishes. We left in so exalted a state – I wish decisions could arise naturally – but you see how it is.'

'I want to be with you,' she said. 'I took a vast step. If it is taken, it is taken. I am quite happy to be called your wife, wherever you choose, for this time. That is what I had understood I – we – had decided.'

She spoke quickly and clearly; but the gloved hands, in their warm kid, turned and turned in his. He said, still in the quiet, dispassionate tone they had so far employed:

'You take my breath away. This is generosity –'

'This is necessity.'

'But you are not sad, you are not in doubt, you are not –'

'That doesn't come into it. This is necessity. You know that.' She turned her face away and looked out, through a stream of fine cinders, at the slow fields. 'I am afraid, of course. But that seems to be of no real importance. None of the old considerations – none of the old cares – seem to be of any importance. They are not tissue paper, but seem so.'

'You must not regret this, my dear.'

'And you must not speak nonsense. Of course I shall regret. So will you, will you not? But that, too, is of no importance at this time.'

They were silent, for a time. Then he said, choosing his words carefully,

'If you are to come with me as my wife – I hope you will accept this ring. It is a family ring – it belonged to my mother. It is a plain gold band, engraved with daisies.'

'I too have brought a ring. It belonged to a great-aunt, Sophie de Kercoz. It has a green stone – look – jade – a simple stone, with an engraved S.'

'You would prefer not to accept my ring?'

'I did not say that. I was giving proof of foresight and resolution. I shall be happy to wear your ring.'

He peeled off the little white glove, and pushed his ring over her fine one with its green stone, so that the two lay together. It fitted, though loosely. He would have liked to say something – with this ring I thee wed, with my body I thee worship – but these good and true words were doubly treacherous to two women. Their unspoken presence hung in the air. He seized the little hand and carried it to his lips. Then he sat back and turned the glove reflectively in his hands, pushing its soft leather pockets back into shape, one by one, smoothing their fine creases.

All the way from London, he had been violently confused by her real presence in the opposite inaccessible corner. For months he had been possessed by the imagination of her. She had been distant and closed away, a princess in a tower, and his imagination's work had been all to make her present, all of her, to his mind and senses, the quickness of her and the mystery, the whiteness of her, which was part of her extreme magnetism, and the green look of those piercing or occluded eyes. Her presence had been unimaginable, or more strictly, *only* to be imagined. Yet here she was, and he was engaged in observing the ways in which she resembled, or differed from, the woman he dreamed, or reached for in sleep, or would fight for.

As a young man he had been much struck by the story of Wordsworth and his solitary Highland girl; the poet had heard the enchanted singing, taken in exactly as much as he had needed for his own immortal verse, and had refused to hear more. He himself, he had discovered, was different. He was a poet greedy for information, for facts, for details. Nothing was too trivial to interest him; nothing was inconsiderable; he would, if he could, have mapped every ripple on a mudflat and its evidence of the invisible workings of wind and tide. So now his love for this woman, known intimately and not at all, was voracious for information. He learned her. He studied the pale loops of hair on her temples. Their sleek silver-gold seemed to him to have in it a tinge, a hint of greenness, not the copper-green of decay, but a pale sap-green of vegetable life, streaked into the hair like the silvery bark of young trees, or green shadows in green tresses of young hay. And her eyes were green, glass-green, malachite green, the cloudy green of seawater perturbed and carrying a weight of sand. The lashes over them silver, but thick enough to be visibly present. The face not kind. There was no kindness in the face. It was cut clean but not fine – strong-boned rather, so that temples and slanting cheeks were pronounced and solid-shadowed, the shadows bluish, which in imagination he always touched with green too, but it was not so.

If he loved the face, which was not kind, it was because it was clear and quick and sharp.

He saw, or thought he saw, how those qualities had been disguised or overlaid by more conventional casts of expression – an assumed modesty, an expedient patience, a disdain masking itself as calm. At her worst – oh, he saw her clearly, despite her possession of him – at her worst she would look down and sideways and smile demurely, and this smile would come near a mechanical simper, for it was an untruth, it was a convention, it was her brief constricted acknowledgement of the world's expectations. He had seen immediately, it seemed to him, what in essence she was, sitting at Crabb Robinson's breakfast table, listening to men disputing, thinking herself an unobserved observer. Most men, he judged, if they had seen the harshness and fierceness and absolutism, yes, absolutism, of that visage, would have stood back from her. She would have been destined to be loved only by timid weaklings, who would have secretly hoped she would punish or command them, or by simpletons, who supposed her chill look of delicate withdrawal to indicate a kind of female purity, which all desired, in those days, at least ostensibly. But he had known immediately that she was for him, she was to do with him, as she really was or could be, or in freedom might have been.

The lodgings were kept by a Mrs Cammish, a tall woman with the heavy-browed frown of the Northmen in the Bayeux Tapestry, who had also, in their long ships, settled this coast. She and her daughter carried up the quantities of baggage – hatboxes, tin trunks, collecting boxes, nets and writing-desks – a collection whose very bulk made the enterprise seem respectable. Left in the solidly furnished bedroom to take off their travelling clothes, they were struck dumb, and stood and stared. He held out his arms, and she came into them, saying however, 'Not now, not yet.' 'Not now, not yet,' he said agreeably, and felt her relax a little. He led her across to the window, which gave a good view, over the cliff, of the long sands and the grey sea.

'There,' he said. 'The German Sea. Like steel, with life in it.'

'I have often thought of visiting the Breton coast which is in some sense my home.'

'I have never seen that sea.'

'It is very changeable. Blue and clear one day and the next furiously dun and swollen with sand and everywhere sodden.'

'I – we – must go there too.'

'Ah, hush. This is enough. Maybe more than enough.'

They had their own dining-room, where Mrs Cammish served a huge meal that should have fed twelve, on plates rimmed with cobalt blue and spattered with fat pink rosebuds. There was a tureen of buttery soup, there was boiled hake and potatoes, there were cutlets and peas, there were arrowroot moulds and treacle tart. Christabel LaMotte pushed her food across her plate with her fork. Mrs Cammish told Ash that his lady was a bit peaky and clearly in need of sea air and good food. Christabel said, when they were alone again,

'It is no good. We eat like two small birds, in our house.'

He watched her remember her home, stricken for a moment, and said easily,

'You must not be intimidated by landladies. But she is right. You must enjoy the sea air.'

He watched her. He noted that she assumed no manners that might be thought wifely. She handed him nothing. She did not lean forward intimately, she did not defer. She watched him with her sharp look when she thought herself unobserved, but not with solicitude, nor yet with affection, nor yet with the greedy curiosity he could not suppress in himself. She watched him as a bird watches, the sort that is chained to a stand, some bright-plumed creature of tropical forests, some gold-eyed hawk from northern crags, wearing its jesses with what dignity it could muster, enduring man's presence with a still-savage hauteur, ruffling its feathers from time to time, to show both that it tended itself with respect, and that it was not quite comfortable. So she pushed back the wrists of her sleeves, so she held herself in her chair. He would change all that. He could change all that, he was tolerably certain. He *knew* her, he believed. He would teach her that she was not his possession, he would show her she was free, he would see her flash her wings. He said,

'I have an idea for a poem about necessity. As you said in the train. So seldom in a life do we feel that what we do is necessary in that sense – gripped by necessity – I suppose death must be like that. If it is given to us to know its approach, we must know we are now complete – do you see, my dear – without further awkward choices, or the possibility of lazy denial. Like balls rolling down a smooth slope.'

'With no possibility of return. Or like armies advancing, which could in fact turn back, but cannot believe it, have wrought themselves to a pitch of singleness of purpose–'

'You may turn back at any point, if–'

'I have said. I cannot.'

They walked by the sea. He watched their footprints, his in a straight line by the water's edge, hers snaking away and back, meeting his, wandering, meeting again. She did not take his arm, though once or twice, when they coincided, she took hold of it, and stepped along beside him rapidly for a time. They both walked very quickly. 'We walk well together,' he told her. 'Our paces suit.'

'I imagined that would be so.'

'And I. We know each other very well, in some ways.'

'And in others, not at all.'

'That can be remedied.'

'Not wholly,' she said, moving away again. A seagull shouted. There was a late sun, just going down. A wind ruffled the sea, which was green in places and grey in others. He walked calmly, in his private electric storm.

'Do they have selkies here?' she asked him.

'Seals? I think not. Further north, yes. And many legends, of seal-wives, seal-women, on the Northumberland coast, and in Scotland. Women from the sea, who come for a time and then must leave.'

'I have never seen seals.'

'I have seen them on the other side of this sea – when I was travelling in Scandinavia. They have human eyes, very liquid and intelligent, and sleek round bodies.'

'They are wild but kindly.'

'In the water they move like huge lithe fish. On land they have to creep and haul themselves, as though maimed.'

'I wrote a tale about a seal and woman. Metamorphoses interest me.'

He could not say to her, you will not leave me, like the seal-wives. Because she could and must.

'Metamorphoses,' he said, 'are our way of showing, in riddles, that we know we are part of the animal world.'

'You believe there is no essential difference between ourselves and a seal?'

'As to that, I don't know. There are immense numbers of similarities. Bones in hands and feet, even those uncouth flippers. Bones in skulls and vertebrae. We all begin as fish.'

'And our immortal souls?'

'There are creatures whose intelligence is hard to distinguish from what we call the soul.'

'Yours is lost, I think, from want of being valued and nourished.'

'I stand reproved.'

'No reproof was intended.'

The time came nearer. They returned to The Cliff and sat in their dining-room, to which a tea tray was brought. He poured the tea. She sat and watched him. He was like a blind man moving in a cluttered and unfamiliar room; half-sensed hazards made their presence felt. There were rules of courtesy for honeymoons which were passed on from father to son, or from friend to friend. As with the ring and wedding words, his purpose faltered, when he thought of them. This was no honeymoon, though it had the impenetrable respectability of one.

'Will you go up first, dear?' he said, and his voice, which he had kept light and kind through that long, extreme day, sounded grinding to him. She stood looking at him, strained but mocking, and smiled. 'If you wish,' she said, not submissively, not at all submissively, but with some amusement. She took a candle and left. He poured himself more tea – he would have given much for cognac, but Mrs Cammish had no concept of such things, and he himself had not thought to include it in his necessities. He did light a long thin cigarillo. He thought of his hopes and expectations and the absence of language for most of them. There were euphemisms, there were male group brutalities, there were books. He did not want above all, to think at this time of his own previous life, so he thought about books. He walked up and down by that sharp-smoky fire of seacoals and remembered Shakespeare's *Troilus*:

'What will it be
When that the wat'ry palate tastes indeed
Love's thrice-repured nectar?'

He thought of Honoré de Balzac, from whom he had learned much, some of it erroneous, some of it simply too *French* to be useful in the world he still lived in. The woman upstairs was part French and a reader. It might explain her lack of diffidence, her surprising matter-of-fact directness. Balzac's cynicism was always nevertheless romantic – such greed, such gusto. 'Le dégoût, c'est voir juste. Après la possession, l'amour voit juste chez les hommes.' Why should that be so? Why was disgust any clearer-eyed than desire? These things have their rhythms. He remembered, as a small boy, quite a small boy, just, though hardly, aware that he must willy-nilly become a man – he remembered reading *Roderick Random*, an English work, full of robust and genial disgust at the human condition and its failings, but with none of Balzac's fine dissection of mentalities. There had been a happy ending. At the end, the hero had been left at the bedroom door by the writer, and then let in, as a kind of *post scriptum*. And She – he forgot her name, some Celia or Sophia, some characterless embodiment of physical and spiritual perfection, or more accurately of the male imagination – She had appeared in a silk sack with her limbs glimmering through it, and had then lifted this over her head and had turned to hero and reader, and had left the rest, the promise, to them. This moment had been his touchstone. He had not known, as a little boy, what a Sack was, and still did not, and had had at best an inaccurate imagination of rosy limbs etc etc etc. But he had been stirred. He walked to and fro. And how, up there, did she see *him*, for whom she waited? He walked.

The staircase was very steep, polished and wooden, with a plum-red runner.Mrs Cammish's house was well kept. The wood smelled of beeswax and the brass carpet-fittings gleamed.

The bedroom was papered with trellises of monstrous roses on a cabbage-green ground. There was a dressing-table, a wardrobe, a curtained alcove, one armchair with upholstered arms and curly legs, and a huge brass bed on which several feather mattresses lay majestically, as though separating a princess from a pea. On top of all this she sat waiting, under a stiff white crocheted bedspread and a patchwork quilt, holding these high to her chest, peering over. No 'sack' here, but a high-necked white lawn nightdress, covered at neck and wrists with intricate goffering and pin-tucks and lacy edges, buttoned with a row of minute linen buttons. Her face was white and sharp and slightly gleaming in the candle-light, like bone. No hint of pink. And the hair. So fine, so pale, so much, crimped by its plaiting into springy zigzag tresses, clouding neck and shoulders, shining metallic in the candlelight, catching a hint, there it was, of green again, from the reflection of a large glazed cache-pot containing a vigorous sword-leafed fern. She watched him in silence.

She had not, as many women might have done, strewn the room or covered the surfaces with female things. On one chair stood a kind of trembling collapsed cage, the crinoline, with its steel hoops and straps. Under it, the small green boots. Not a hairbrush, not a bottle. He put down his candle with a sigh, and undressed briskly, out of its light, in the shadows. She watched him. When he looked up, he caught her eye. She might have lain with her face turned away, but did not.

When he took her in his arms, it was she who said, harshly, 'Are you afraid?'

'Not in the least, now,' he said. 'My selkie, my white lady, Christabel.'

That was the first of those long strange nights. She met him with passion, fierce as his own, and knowing too, for she exacted her pleasure from him, opened herself to it, clutched for it, with short animal cries. She stroked his hair and kissed his blind eyes, but made no more specific move to pleasure him, the male – nor did she come to that, all those nights. It was like holding Proteus, he thought at one point, as though she was liquid moving through his grasping fingers, as though she was waves of the sea rising all round him. How many many men have had that thought, he told himself, in how many many places, how many climates, how many rooms and cabins and caves, all supposing themselves swimmers in salt seas, with the waves rising, all supposing them-selves – no, knowing themselves – unique. Here, here, here, his head beat, his life had been leading him, it was all tending to this act, in this place, to this woman, white in the dark, to this moving and slippery silence, to this breathing end. 'Don't fight me,' he said once, and 'I *must*,' said she, intent, and he thought, 'No more speech', and held her down and caressed her till she cried out. Then he did speak again. 'You see, I know you,' and she answered breathless, 'Yes, I concede. You know.'

Much later, he came out of a half-sleep, imagined he heard the sea, which was just possible from there, and then was aware that she was weeping silently beside him. He put out an arm, and she pushed her face into his neck, a little awkwardly, not clinging, but pushing blindly to lose herself.

'What is it? My dear?'

'Ah, how can we bear it?'

'Bear what?'

'This. For so short a time. How can we sleep this time away?'

'We can be quiet together, and pretend – since it is only the beginning – that we have all the time in the world.'

'And every day we shall have less. And then none.'

'Would you rather, therefore, have had nothing at all?'

'No. This is where I have always been coming to. Since my time began. And when I go away from here, this will be the mid-point, to which everything ran, before, and *from* which everything will run. But now, my love we are here, we are *now*, and those other times are running elsewhere.'

'Poetic, but not comfortable doctrine.'

'You know, as I know, that good poetry is not comfortable, however. Let me hold you, this is our night, and only the first, and therefore the nearest infinite.'

He felt her face, hard and wet on his shoulder, and imagined the living skull, living bone, fed with threads and fine tubes of blue blood and inaccessible thoughts, running in her hidden cavities.

'You are safe with me.'

'I am not at all safe, with you. But I have no desire to be elsewhere.'

In the morning, washing, he found traces of blood on his thighs. He had thought, the ultimate things, she did *not* know, and here was ancient proof. He stood, sponge in hand, and puzzled over her. Such delicate skills, such informed desire, and yet a virgin. There were possibilities, of which the most obvious was to him slightly repugnant, and then, when he thought about it with determination, interesting, too. He could never ask. To show speculation, or even curiosity, would be to lose her. Then and there. He knew that, without thinking. It was like Melusina's prohibition, and no narrative bound him, unlike the unfortunate Raimondin, to exhibit indiscreet curiosity. He liked to know everything he could – even this – but he knew better than to be curious, he told himself, about things he could not hope to know. She must have bundled away the tell-tale white nightdress, too, in her luggage, for he never saw it again.

They were good days. She helped to prepare his specimens, and scrambled indomitably over rocks to obtain them. She sang like Goethe's sirens and Homer's from the rocks on Filey Brigg where Mrs Peabody and her family had been swept away. She marched indomitably over the moors, the crinoline cage and half her petticoats left behind, with the wind ruffling the pale hair. She sat intent beside a turf fire and watched an old woman cook pikelets on a griddle; she spoke little to strangers, it was he who enquired, who invited confidences and information, who learned them. She said, after he had held a countryman half an hour in talk, learning about the swivens, the burnt moorland and peat-cutting,

'You are in love with all the human race, Randolph Ash.'

'With you. And by extension, all creatures who remotely resemble you. Which is, all creatures, for we are all part of some divine organism I do believe, that breathes its own breath and lives a little here, and dies a little there, but is eternal. And you are a manifestation of its secret perfection. You are the life of things.'

'Oh no. I am a chilly mortal, as Mrs Cammish said yesterday morning, when I put on my shawl. It is you who are the life of things. You stand there and draw them into you. You turn your gaze on the dull and the insipid to make them shine. And ask them to stay, and they will not, so you find their vanishing of equal interest. I love that in you. Also I fear it. I need quiet and nothingness. I tell myself I should fade and glimmer if long in your hot light.'

He remembered most, when it was over, when time had run out, a day they had spent in a place called the Boggle Hole, where they had gone because they liked the word. She had taken delight in the uncompromising Northern words, which they had collected like stones, or spiny sea-creatures. Ugglebarnby. Jugger Howe. Howl Moor. She had made notes in her little notebooks of the female names of the Meres or standing stones they met on the moors. Fat Betty, the Nan Stone, Slavering Ciss. 'There is a terrible tale to be told,' she said, 'and a few bright guineas to be earned, of Slavering Ciss.' That too had been a good day, with blue and gold weather, a day that had put him in mind of the youth of the Creation.

They had come across summer meadows and down narrow lanes between tall hedges thick with dog-roses, intricately entwined with creamy honeysuckle, a tapestry from Paradise Garden, she said, and smelling so airily sweet, it put you in mind of Swedenborg's courts of heaven where the flowers had a language and colours and scents were correspondent forms of speech. They came down the lane from the Mill, into the closed cove, and the smell changed to the sharpness of salt, a fresh wind off the northern sea full of brine and turning fish-forms and floating weeds, running away to the northern ice. The tide was in, and they had to make their way tightly under the overhang of the cliff. He watched her move swiftly and surely along. Her arms were spread above her head, her strong small fingers gripping cracks and crannies, her tiny booted feet picking a sure way over the slippery shelves below. The stone was a peculiar gunmetal slate, striated and flaking, dull with no sheen, except where water dripped and seeped from above, bringing with it ruddy traces of earth. The layers of grey were full of the regularly rippled rounds of the colonies of ammonites that lay coiled in its substance, stony forms of life, living forms in stone. Her bright pale head, with its circling braids, seemed to repeat those forms. Her grey dress, with the winds loose in the skirts, blended almost into the grey of the stone. All along those multiplied fine ledges, all through those crazed and intricate fissures, ran hundreds of tiny hurrying spiderlike living things, coloured an intense vermilion. The bluish cast of the grey of the stone increased the brightness of the red. They were like thin lines of blood; they were like a web of intermittent flame. He saw her white hands like stars on the grey stone and he saw the red creatures run through and around them.

Most of all, he saw her waist, just where it narrowed, before the skirts spread. He remembered her nakedness as he knew it, and his hands around that narrowing. He thought of her momentarily as an hour-glass, containing time, which was caught in her like a thread of sand, of stone, of specks of life, of things that had lived and would live. She held his time, she contained his past and his future, both now cramped together, with such ferocity and such gentleness, into this small circumference. He remembered an odd linguistic fact – the word for waist in Italian is *vita*, is life – and this must be, he thought, to do with the navel, which is where our separate lives cast off, that umbilicus which poor Philip Gosse believed had had to be made by God for Adam as a kind of mythic sign of the eternal existence of the past and the future in all presents. He thought too of the Fairy Melusina, a woman *jusqu'au nombril, sino alla vita, usque ad umbilicum*, as far as the waist. This is my centre, he thought, here, at this place, at this time, in her, in that narrow place, where my desire has its end.

On that shore can be found round stones of many kinds of rocks, black basalt, various coloured granites, sandstones and quartz. She was delighted by these, she filled the picnic basket with a heavy nest of them, like ordnance balls, a soot-black, a sulphur-gold, a chalky grey, which under water revealed a whole dappling of the purest translucent pink. 'I shall take them home,' said she, 'and use them to prop doors and to weigh down the sheets of my huge poem, huge at least in mass of paper.'

'I shall carry them for you until then.'

'I can carry my own burdens. I must.'

'Not while I am here.'

'You will not be here – I shall not be here – much longer.'

'Let us not think of *time*.'

'We have reached Faust's non-plus. We say to every moment

'*Verweile doch, du bist so schön*', and if we are not immediately damned, the stars move still, time runs, the clock will strike. But it is open to us to regret each minute as it passes.'

'We shall be exhausted.'

' "And is not that a good state to end in? A man might die, though nothing else ailed him, only upon an extreme weariness of doing the same thing, over and over." '

'I can never tire of you – of this–'

'It is in the nature of the human frame to tire. Fortunately. Let us collude with necessity. Let us play with it.

> "And if we cannot make our sun
> Stand still, yet we will make him run."

'A poet after my own heart,' she said. 'Though not more beloved than George Herbert. Or Randolph Henry Ash.'

CHAPTER SIXTEEN

The Fairy Melusine
PROEM

And what was she, the Fairy Melusine?
Men say, at night, around the castle-keep
The black air ruffles neath the outstretched vans
Of a long flying worm, whose sinewy tail
And leather pinions beat the parted sky
Scudding with puddered clouds and black as soot,
And ever and again a shuddering cry
Mounts on the wind, a cry of pain and loss,
And whirls in the wind's screaming and is gone.

Men say, that to the Lords of Lusignan
On their death's day appointed comes a Thing,
Half sable serpent, half a mourning Queen
Crowned and thick-veilèd. Then they cross themselves
And make their peace with Heaven's blessed King
And with a cry of pain she vanishes,
Unable, so they say, to hear that Name,
Forever banished from the hope of Heaven.

The old nurse says, within the castle-keep
The innocent boys slept in each other's arms
To keep away the chill from hearts and limbs.
And in the dead of night a slender hand
Would part the hangings, and lift sleepy forms
To curl and suck the mother's milky breasts
As they had dreamed they did, and all the while
Warm tears in silence mingled with the milk
In dreaming mouths combining sweet and salt,
So that they smile for warmth, and weep for loss,

And waking, hope and fear to dream again.
So says the old nurse, and the boys grow strong.

Outside our small safe place flies Mystery.
We hear it howl adown the winds; we see
Its forces set great whirlpools on the spin
In the dark deeps, as a child sets a top
Idly in motion, whips it for a while
Then tires and lets it stagger. On grey walls
We see the indents of its viewless teeth.
We hear it snake beneath the forest floor
Weaving the lives and deaths of roots, the weft
And warp of pillar-boles and tracery
Of twigs and sighing sunkist canopies
Which sway and change, glow and decay and fall.
Inhuman Powers cross our little lives.
The whale's warm milk runs beneath icy seas.
Electric currents run from eye to eye
And pole to pole, magnetic messages
From out our Beings, through them, and beyond.
The whelk's foot grips; the waves pile fragments up
Smooth sands compacted, skull on shell on scrap
Of horny carapace on silex sparks
Sandstone and chalk and grit, and out of these
Sculpts dunes like dinosaurs and mammoth banks
And breaks them back to flying specks of stuff.
. . . .

I read, writ in the ancient chronicle
By John of Arras (who wrote for his Lord
To please and to instruct), 'King David said
The judgments of the Lord are like vast deeps
With neither wall nor bottom, where the soul
Spins in a place without foundation
Which comprehensively engulfs the mind
That cannot comprehend it.' The monk, John,
Humbly concludes the human soul should not
Use reason where it cannot stretch to work.
A reasonable man, says the good monk,
Must see that Aristotle told the truth
Who stated firmly that the world contained
Creatures invisible and visible
Both in their kind. He cited next St Paul

Who claimed the first Invisibles of the world
As witnesses to their Creator's Power,
Beyond the scope of men's inquiring mind
Save as revealed from time to time in Books
Writ by wise men, as guides to wandering wits.

And in the air, says the brave Monk, there fly
Things, Beings, Creatures, never seen by us
But very potent in their wandering world,
Crossing our heavy paths from time to time,
And such, he says, are faeries or Fates
Who Paracelsus said were Angels once
Now neither damn'd nor blessèd, simply tossed
Eternally between the solid earth
And Heav'n's closed golden gate . . .
Not good enough to save, spirits of air
Not evil neither, with no steadfast harm
In their intents, but simply volatile.

The Laws of Heaven run through the earth as poles
That twist and turn this Globe at His command
Or net (to change the metaphor) the skies
And seas and all the swaying, moving mass
In fine constraining meshes, beyond which
Matter slips not, and mind may never step
Save into vacant Horror and Despair
Forms of illusion only.

                   What are they
Who haunt our dreams and weaken our desires
And turn us from the solid face of things?
Sisters of Horror, or Heav'n's exiled queens
Reduced from spirit-power to fantasy?

The Angels of the Lord, from Heaven's Gate
March helmeted in gold and silver ranks
Thrones, Dominations, Princedoms, Virtues, Powers,
As quick as thought between desire and deed.
They are the instruments of Law and Grace.
Then who are those who wander indirect
Those whose desires mount precipice of Air
As easy as say wink, or plunge again
For pleasure of the terror in the cleft
Between the dark brow of a mounting cloud
And plain sky's opal ocean? Who are they

Whose soft hands cannot shift the fixèd chains
Of cause and law that bind the earth and sea
And ice and fire and flesh and blood and time?

When heavenly Eros lay at Psyche's side,
Her envious sisters said, the light of day
Would show a monstrous serpent was her Lord.
When she transgressed and held the trembling flame
Over the bed, the drops of wax fell fast
On love in perfect human form, who rose
In burning anger from his place and fled.

But let the Power take a female form
And 'tis the Power is punished. All men shrink
From dire Medusa and her writhing locks.
Who weeps for Scylla in her cave of bones,
Thrashing her tail and howling for her fate
With yelping hound-mouths, though she once was fair,
Loved by the sea-god for her | mystery,
Daughter of Hecate, beautiful as Night?
Who weeps the fall of Hydra's many heads?
The siren sings and sings, and virtuous men
Bind ears and eyes and sail resolved away
From all her pain that what she loves must die,
That her desire, though lovely in her song
Is mortal in her kiss to mortal men.
The feline Sphinx roamed free as air and smiled
In the dry desert at those foolish men
Who saw not that her crafted Riddle's clue
Was merely Man, bare man, no Mystery.
But when they found it out they spilt her blood
For her presumption and her Monstrous shape.
Man named Himself and thus assumed the Power
Over his Questioner, till then his Fate—
After, his Slave and victim.

And what was she, the Fairy Melusine?
Were these her kin, Echidna's gruesome brood,
Scaly devourers, or were those her kind
More kind, those rapid wanderers of the dark
Who in dreamlight, or twilight, or no light
Are lovely Mysteries and promise gifts—
Whiteladies, teasing dryads, shape-changers—
Like smiling clouds, or sparkling threads of streams

Bright monsters of the sea and of the sky
Who answer longing and who threaten not
But vanish in the light of rational day
Doomed by their own desire for human souls,
For settled hearths and fixèd human homes.

Shall I presume to tell the Fairy's tale?
Meddle with doom and magic in my song
Or venture out into the shadowland
Beyond the safe and solid? Shall I dare?
Help me Mnemosyne, thou Titaness,
Thou ancient one, daughter of Heaven and Earth,
Mother of Muses, who inhabit not
In flowery mount or crystal spring, but in
The dark and confin'd cavern of the skull—
O Memory, who holds the thread that links
My modern mind to those of ancient days
To the dark dreaming Origins of our race,
When visible and invisible alike
Lay quietly, O thou, the source of speech
Give me wise utterance and safe conduct
From hearthside storytelling into dark
Of outer air, and back again to sleep,
In Christian comfort, in a decent bed.

BOOK I

A draggled knight came riding o'er the moor.
Behind him fear, before him empty space.
His horse, besprent with blood, dispirited,
Came slowly on, and stumbled as he came,
Feeling the rider's slackness, and the reins
Slack too, against his sweat-streaked neck. The day
Drew in, and on the moor small shadows stirred
And ate the heather-roots, and flowed in tongues
Of seal-skin soft and sly insidious shape
Between the hill's clefts and the dark gill's mouth
Whither, for lack of will, they two were drawn.
For all the moor, immense, characterless
Shrubby and shapeless, stretched about their feet
Off'ring no point of hold, nor track to guide
Save witless wanderings of nibbling sheep.

Between the wild moor and the mother Sun

Is reciprocity of flash and frown.
When she is hid, the heather's knotted mat
Of purple bell-heather and pinker ling
Lies in an unreflective sullen gloom,
A rough black coat, indifferently cast o'er
The peat and grit and flints, extending on
As far as eye can see, to the high riggs.
But when she smiles, a thousand thousand lights
Gleam out from sprig and floret or from where
The white sand on the crow-stones in the peat
Glitters in tracery 'neath amber pools
Of shining rain, and all the moor is live
Basking and smiling up, as She smiles down.
And after rain, live vapours rise and play
Curvet and eddy over the live ling,
Current and counter-current, like a sea
Or, as the shepherds say, like summer colts
At play above a meadow, or like geese
Who skim the air and water in their flight.
So uniform, so various, is the Moor.

But he rode on, nor looked to right nor left
All lustreless, his first fine fury gone
With which he fled the boar-hunt and the death—
Death at his hand, and death at random dealt
To Aymeri, his kinsman and his Lord.
Defensive stroke working an unkind Fate
On him most kind, most genial and most brave
Whom most he loved and most he wished to spare.
Before his weary eyes a veil of blood
Beat, and his brain beat with its motion
Despair and die, for what is left to do?

Between two boulders bald the horse stepped down
Into a narrow track within a cleft
Whose flanks were wind-blown, clothed with juniper,
Bilberry and stunted thorn-trees. Water oozed
Out of the clammy rock-face, water brown
With juice of peat, and black with powdered soot
From ancient swidden. Neath the heavy hoofs
Broke little trains of stones which jounced a while
And clattered down into the brook beneath.
The stone struck chill. The cleft wound in and down.

How long he was descending, he knew not.
But in his blood-grief and extreme fatigue
He slowly knew that he had heard the sound
Of falling water for some small time past,
A wayward, windblown, rushing, chuckling sound,
An intermittent music, bubbling up.

And then he heard, within the water's voice
A melody more fluent and more strange,
A silver chant that wove its liquid length
Along the hurrying channel of the stream
And wound with that to twist one rope of sound,
Silver and stony. They went on and down
Steady and hearkening, and on either hand
The wet walls narrowed. Then, around a bend
There came an opening, and both horse and man
Stockstill, with humming ear and dazzled eye
Stared at a mystery.

A kind of hollowed chamber in the hill
Sheltered a still and secret pool, beneath
A frowning crag, whose rim was cleft to form
A lip for falling water, white with air
Like streaming needles of a shattered glass
Tossed as it turned, then smoothly combing down
Like one unending tress of silver-white
Holding its form beneath the basin's rim
By virtue of its force and of the air
Caught in its hurtling substance, spreading out
Like pale and solid livid ice beneath
The black and moss-green dappling of the pool.

A rounded rock stood low among the curl
Of dim-discernèd weeds, whose fronds were stirred
By many little springs that bubbled up
And seeped through coiling strands and stirred the plane
Of the dark water into dimpling life.
This rock was covered with a vivid pelt
Of emerald mosses, maidenhairs and mints
Dabbling dark crowns and sharply-scented stems
Amongst the water's peaks and freshenings.
The pensile foliage tumbled down the crag
To join the pennywort and tormentil
That wound below and wove a living mat

Dark green, but sparked with gold and amethyst.

And on the rock a lady sat and sang.
Sang to herself most clear and quietly
A small clear golden voice that seemed to run
Without the need to breathe or pause for thought,
Simple and endless as the moving fall,
Surprising as the springs that bubbled up
Now here, now there, among the coiling weeds.

As milky roses at the end of day
In some deserted bower seem still alight
With their own luminous pallor, so she cast
A softened brightness and a pearly light
On that wild place, in which she sate and sang.
She wore a shift of whitest silk, that stirred
With her song's breathing, and a girdle green
As emerald or wettest meadow-grass.
Her blue-veined feet played in the watery space
Slant in its prism-vision like white fish
Darting together. When she stretched them out
The water made her silver anklet-chains
Glancing with diamond-drops and lucid pearls
Which shone as bright as those about her neck
Carelessly cast, a priceless brilliant rope
Of sapphire, emerald, and opaline.

Her living hair was brighter than chill gold
With shoots of brightness running down its mass
And straying out to lighten the dun air
Like phosphorescent sparks off a pale sea,
And while she sang, she combed it with a comb
Wrought curiously of gold and ebony,
Seeming to plait each celandine-bright tress
With the spring's sound, the song's sound and the sound
Of its own living whisper, warm and light
So that he longed to touch it, longed to stretch
If but a finger out across the space
That stood between his blood-stained, stiffened self
And all this swaying supple brilliance,
Save that her face forbade.

                    It was a face
Queenly and calm, a carved face and strong

Nor curious, nor kindly, nor aloof,
But self-contained and singing to itself.
And as he met her eyes, she ceased her song
And made a silence, and it seemed to him
That in this silence all the murmuring ceased
Of leaves and water, and they two were there,
And all they did was look, no question,
No answer, neither frown nor smile, no move
Of lip or eye or brow or eyelid pale
But all one long look which consumed his soul
Into desire beyond the reach of hope
Beyond the touch of doubt or of despair,
So that he was one thing, and all he was,
The fears, the contradictions and the pains,
The reveller's pleasures and the sick man's whims,
All gone, forever gone, all burned away
Under the steady and essential gaze
Of this pale Creature in this quiet space.

A movement in the shadows made him ware
Of a gaunt hound that stood like a dark cloud
Rough-curled and smoky grey, with golden eyes
And patient noble face that snuffed the air
And heard and felt air's movements motionless,
Alert and motionless behind his dame.

Then Raimondin bethought him of his hunt
And of his crime, and of his later flight,
And bowed low in the saddle where he stood
And begged her, of her grace, to let him drink
The water of the fountain; he was faint
And sore with travelling, and needs must drink.
'My name is Raimondin of Lusignan
And where I go, and what I shall become
I know not, but I crave a place of rest,
A draught of water, for I choke on dust.'

Then said she, 'Raimondin of Lusignan
Both who you are, and what you may become—
What you have done, how you may save yourself
And prosper greatly, all these things, I know.
Therefore dismount, and take this cup from me,
This cup of clear spring water from the fount
Whose name is called La Fontaine de la Soif,

The Thirsty Fountain. Therefore, come and drink.

And she held out the cup, and he came down
And took it from her and drank deep therein.
All dazed with glamour was he, in her gaze.
She ministered unto his extreme need
And his face took the brightness of her glance
As dusty heather takes the tumbling rays
Of the sun's countenance and shines them back.
Now was he hers, if she should ask of him
Body or soul, he would have offered all.
And seeing this, at last, the Fairy smiled.

CHAPTER SEVENTEEN

James Blackadder composed a footnote. He was working on *Mummy Possest* (1863). He used a pen; he had never learned newer methods; Paola would transfer his script to the glimmering screen of the word-processor. The air smelled of metal, dust, metal-dust and burning plastic.

R. H. Ash attended at least two seances in the house of the famous medium, Mrs Hella Lees, who was an early specialist in materialisation, particularly of lost children, and in the touch of dead hands. Mrs Lees was never exposed as a fraud and is still thought of as a pioneer in this field by contemporary spiritualists. (See F. Podmore, *Modern Spiritualism*, 1902, vol. 2, pp. 134–9.) Whilst there can be no doubt that the poet went to the seances in a spirit of rational enquiry, rather than with any predisposition to believe what he saw, he records the medium's activities with sharp distaste and fear, rather than with simple contempt for chicanery. He also implicitly compares her activities – the *false* or *fictive* bringing to life of the dead, with his own poetic activities. For an account (somewhat lurid and imaginative) of these encounters see Cropper, *The Great Ventriloquist*, pp. 340–4. See also a curious feminist attack on Ash's choice of title by Dr Roanne Wicker, in the *Journal of the Sorcières*, March 1983. Dr Wicker objects to Ash's use of his title to castigate the 'intuitive female' actions of his speaker, Sybilla Silt (an obvious reference to Hella Lees). *Mummy Possest* is of course a quotation from John Donne, 'Love's Alchemy'. 'Hope not for minde in women; at their best/Sweetnesse and wit, they'are but *Mummy*, Possest.'

Blackadder looked at all this, and crossed out the adjective 'curious' before 'feminist attack'. He thought about crossing out 'somewhat lurid and imaginative' before Cropper's account of the seances. These superfluous adjectives were the traces of his own views, and therefore unnecessary. He contemplated crossing out the references to Cropper and Dr Wicker in their entirety. Much of his writing met this fate. It was set down, depersonalised, and then erased. Much of his time was spent deciding whether or not to erase things. He usually did.

A whitish figure slid round the end of his desk. It was Fergus Wolff, who sat down uninvited on the desk corner, and looked down, uninvited, at Blackadder's work. Blackadder put a hand over his writing.

'You should be up in the sun. It's lovely weather up there.'

'No doubt. The Oxford University Press is not concerned with the weather. Can I do anything for you?'

'I was looking for Roland Michell.'

'He's on holiday. He asked for a week off. He's never had one, that I can remember, when I come to think about it.'

'Did he say where he was going?'

'Not at all. North, I think he said. He was very vague.'

'Did he take Val?'

'I assumed so.'

'Did his new discovery lead anywhere?'

'New discovery?'

'He was quite chuffed at Christmas. Discovered a mystery letter or something, I thought he said. I may have been wrong.'

'I don't remember anything precisely of that kind. Unless you mean all those notes in the Vico. Nothing of great importance there, sadly. Humdrum notes.'

'This was personal. Something to do with Christabel LaMotte. He was quite excited. I sent him off to see Maud Bailey at Lincoln.'

'Feminists don't like Ash.'

'She's been seen down here, since. Maud Bailey.'

'I don't know of anything to do with LaMotte, offhand.'

'I was pretty sure Roland did. But it may have come to nothing. Or he'd have told you.'

'He probably would.'

'Exactly.'

*

Val was eating cornflakes. She ate very little else, at home. They were light, they were pleasant, they were comforting, and then after a day or two they were like cotton wool. Outside the back area, the roses were drifting down the steps, and the borders were bright with tiger lilies and moon daisies. London was hot: Val wanted to be anywhere else, out of the dust and cat piss. The doorbell rang. When she looked up, expecting perhaps Euan MacIntyre and a dinner invitation, she saw Fergus Wolff.

'Hello, my dearest. Is Roland in?'

'No. He's gone away.'

'What a pity. Can I come in? Where has he gone?'

'Somewhere in Lancashire or Yorkshire or Cumbria. Blackadder sent him to look at a book. He was a bit vague.'

'Have you a phone number? I need to get in touch with him rather urgently.'

'He said he'd leave one. I was out when he left. But he didn't. Or if he did, I haven't found it. And he hasn't phoned. He should be back on Wednesday.'

'I *see*.'

Fergus sat down on the old sofa and looked up at the irregular pools and peninsulas of staining on the ceiling.

'Does that strike you as a bit odd, my love, that he hasn't communicated?'

'I wasn't being all that nice to him.'

'I see.'

'I don't know *what* you see, Fergus. You always see a bit more than there is to see. What's up?'

'I just wondered — you don't happen to know where Maud Bailey is?'

'I *see*,' said Val. There was a silence. Then Val asked, 'Do *you* know where she is?'

'Not exactly. There's something going on that I don't understand. Yet, that is. I shall understand it quite soon.'

'She has called him here, once or twice. I wasn't very polite.'

'A pity. I should so like to know what's going on.'

'Perhaps it's to do with Randolph Henry.'

'It is. That's for definite. Though perhaps it has to do with Maud, too. She's a formidable woman.'

'They were away at Christmas, working on something.'

'He went to Lincoln to see her.'

'Well, sort of. They *both* went somewhere or other, to look at a manuscript. Honestly I've lost interest in all his footnotes and things and all those dead letters from dead people about missing trains and supporting Copyright Bills and all that stuff. Who wants to spend their life in the British Museum basement? It smells as bad as Mrs Jarvis's flat up there, full of cat piss. Who wants to spend their life reading old menus in cat piss?'

'Nobody. They want to spend their lives in lovely hotels at international conferences. You didn't bother to enquire *what* they were reading?'

'He didn't say. He knows I'm not interested.'

'So you don't know exactly where they went?'

'I did have a phone number. For emergencies. If the flat burned down. Or I couldn't pay the gas bill. In which case there was nothing *he* could do, of course. Some of us earn money in the enterprise culture and some of us don't.'

'There *may* be money in all this. You haven't still got the telephone number, have you, my love?'

Val went out into the hall, where the telephone stood at floor level, balanced on a heap of papers – old *Times Literary Supplements*, old book bills, cards with minicab numbers, cards offering discounts on OMO DAZ KODAK MUREX, invitations to Convocation and the ICA. She seemed to know her way around this, and after a moment turned over a Takeaway Indian bill at the bottom of the heap and found the number. No name. Only in Val's hand, 'Roland in Lincoln'.

'Could be Maud's number.'

'No. It's not. I know Maud's. Can I have that?'

'Why not? What do you want to do with it?'

'I don't know. I simply want to know what's going on. Do you see?'

'Perhaps it's Maud.'

'Perhaps. I have an interest in Maud. I want her to be happy.'

'Perhaps she's happy with Roland.'

'Not possible. He's not her sort at all. No *bite*, don't you agree?'

'I don't know. I don't make him happy.'

'Nor he you, by the looks of it. Come out to supper and forget him.'

'Why not?'
'Why not?'

'Hello, Bailey here.'
  'Bailey?'
  'Is that Dr Heath?'
  'No, it's not. I'm a friend of Roland Michell's. He was work-
ing . . . in the winter . . . I wondered if you knew where he . . .'
  'Not the slightest idea.'
  'Is he coming back?'
  'I shouldn't think so. No. No, he's not. Do you think you
could get off the line? I'm expecting the doctor.'
  'I'm so sorry to have troubled you. Have you seen Dr Bailey?
Dr Maud Bailey?'
  'No. I haven't. I don't plan to. We just want leaving in peace.
Goodbye.'
  'But their work went well?'
  'The fairy poet. I should think it did. They seemed pleased. I
haven't thought about it. I don't want to be disturbed. I'm a busy
man. My wife's unwell. Really very unwell. Please get off the
line.'
  'That would be Christabel LaMotte, the fairy poet?'
  'I don't know what you want to know, but I want you off my
line, *now*. If you don't go I'll – I'll – look here, my wife is ill, I'm
trying to call the doctor, you sodding fool. *Goodbye.*'
  'May I ring again?'
  'No point. *Goodbye.*'
  'Goodbye.'

Mortimer Cropper had lunched at L'Escargot with Hildebrand
Ash, the eldest son of Thomas, Baron Ash, who was a direct
descendant of that cousin of Randolph Ash who had been
ennobled under Gladstone. Lord Ash, the Methodist, was now
very old and frail. He had been civil enough to Cropper, but that
was as far as it went. He preferred Blackadder, whose gloomy
temperament and Scottish dryness pleased him. Also he was a
nationalist, and had deposited the Ash manuscripts he owned in
the British Library. Hildebrand was in his forties, balding,
gingery, cheerful and somewhat vacant. He had taken a fourth

at Oxford, in English, and had since worked in an undistinguished way in travel firms, garden publishing and various Heritage trusts. Cropper invited him out from time to time, and had discovered he had buried histrionic ambitions. They had formed a half-project, half-daydream of a high-powered tour of American universities, where Hildebrand would put on a display of Ash memorabilia, slides and readings, and lecture on the background of English society in the time of Ash. On this occasion Hildebrand said he was short of money and would really like to have a new source. Cropper asked about the health of Lord Ash and was told that he was very frail. They discussed possible venues and fees. They ate *magret de canard*, turbot and earthy new little turnips. Cropper grew paler and Hildebrand grew pinker as the meal proceeded. Hildebrand had visions of a rapt and respectful American audience, and Cropper had visions of new glass cases containing treasures he'd only been allowed to look at reverently: the Poet's Letter from the Queen, the Portable Writing-Desk, the ink-stained notebook of drafts of *Ask to Embla*, which the family had not parted with and displayed in the dining-room of their house at Ledbury.

After seeing Hildebrand Ash into a taxi, Cropper walked the streets of Soho, looking casually in at windows and illuminated stairmouths. Peepshow. Model. Young girls wanted. Live Sex NonStop. Come Up and Have Fun. Serious Instruction. His own tastes were precise, narrow, and somewhat specialist. He drifted, a fine black figure, from window to window, tasting the ghosts of good food and wine. He stopped momentarily, to observe an obscured glimpse of white twisted flesh placed to suggest to him that what he wanted might be within, after all – not much of a picture, mostly obscured by a quite different, bouncy, busty one, but he lived in a world of hints and flickering indications, it was enough. All the same, he thought, he would not go in, he would go home . . .

'Professor Cropper' – a voice said behind him.

'Ah,' said Cropper.

'Fergus Wolff. Do you remember me? I came up to you after your paper on the identity of the narrator in Ash's *Chidiock*

Tichbourne. A brilliant piece of deduction. Of course it was the executioner. You do remember?'

'I do indeed. With great pleasure. I have just been lunching with the son of the present Lord Ash, who will hopefully speak in Robert Dale Owen University on his family's holdings of Ash manuscripts. *Chidiock Tichbourne* is in the British Library, of course.'

'Of course. Are you going there? May I walk with you?'

'I shall be most happy.'

'I was interested to learn of Ash's connection with Christabel LaMotte.'

'LaMotte? Oh, yes. *Melusina*. There was a feminist sit-in, in the Fall of '79, demanding that the poem be taught in my nineteenth-century poetry course, instead of the *Idylls of the King*, or *Ragnarök*. As I remember, it was conceded. But then Women's Studies took it on, so I was released and we were able to restore *Ragnarök*. But that's hardly a connection. I don't believe I know of a real connection.'

'I thought some letters were discovered.'

'I should doubt that. I've never heard of any connection. Now, what *do* I know about Christabel LaMotte? There is something.'

'Roland Michell discovered something.'

Cropper stopped on the Greek Street pavement and caused two Chinese people to stop equally suddenly.

'Something?'

'I don't really know what. Yet. He thinks it's important.'

'And James Blackadder?'

'He doesn't seem to know.'

'You interest me, Dr Wolff.'

'I hope to, Professor.'

'Would you care for a cup of coffee?'

CHAPTER EIGHTEEN

Gloves lie together
Limp and calm
Finger to finger
Palm to palm
With whitest tissue
To embalm

In these quiet cases
White hands creep
With supple stretchings
Out of sleep
Fingers clasp fingers
Troth to keep

C. LaMotte

Maud sat in the Women's Studies Resource Centre, on an apple-green chair, at an orange table. She was going through the box-file which contained what little they possessed on the suicide of Blanche Glover. A newspaper report, a transcript of the Inquest, a copy of the note which had been found, weighed down by a granite stone, on the table at Bethany in Mount Ararat Road. There were also a few letters to an old pupil, daughter of an MP not unsympathetic to the cause of women. Maud inspected these meagre remains in the hope of finding some clue as to how Christabel LaMotte had spent the time between the Yorkshire journey and the inquest. So little remained of Blanche.

To whom it may concern:

What I do, I do in sound mind, whatever may be decided upon me, and after long and careful reflection. My reasons are simple and can be simply stated. First, poverty. I can afford no more paint and have sold so little work in the last months. I have left four truly pretty flower-pieces, wrapped, in the drawing room, of just the kind that Mr Cressy, upon Richmond Hill, has liked in the past, and hope he may offer enough for them to pay for my funeral, should that turn out to be practicable. I particularly wish *that this matter be not put to* MISS LAMOTTE's *charge, and so hope that Mr Cressy may oblige, otherwise I am at my wits' end.*

Second, and maybe more reprehensibly, pride. I cannot again demean myself to enter anyone's home as a governess. Such a life is hell on earth, even when families are kind, and I would rather not live than be a slave. Nor will I throw myself upon the Charity *of* MISS LAMOTTE, *who has her own obligations.*

Third, failure of ideals. I have tried, initially with MISS LAMOTTE, *and also alone in this little house, to live according to certain beliefs about the possibility, for independent single women, of living useful and fully human lives, in each other's company, and without recourse to help from the outside world, or men. We believed it was possible to live frugally, charitably, philosophically, artistically, and in* harmony *with each other and Nature. Regrettably, it was not. Either the world was too fiercely inimical to our experiment (which I believe it was) or we ourselves were insufficiently resourceful and strong-minded (which I believe was also so, in both cases, and from time to time). It is to be hoped that our first heady days of economic independence, and the work we leave behind us, may induce other stronger spirits to take up the task and try the experiment and not fail. Independent women must expect more of themselves, since neither men nor other more conventionally domesticated women will hope for anything, or expect any result other than utter failure.*

I have little to leave, and would like my few possessions to be disposed of as follows. This is not, because of the circumstances, a legally enforceable document, but I would hope that its reader or readers will treat it with as much respect as though it was.

My wardrobe I leave to our servant, Jane Summers, *to take whatever she will and distribute the rest as she sees fit. I take this opportunity of asking her to forgive me a little deception. I could only prevail upon her to leave me — despite my complete inability to pay her — by assuming a dissatisfaction I was very far from feeling. I had already taken the resolution I now carry out, and wanted her to have no direct responsibility for its consequences. That was my only reason for acting as I did. I am not skilled at dissimulation.*

The house is not in effect mine. It belongs to MISS LAMOTTE. *These chattels and furnishings inside it which we bought together with our savings belong more to her than to me, as the richer partner and I wish her to do with them what she will.*

I should like my Shakespeare, my Poems of Keats, and Poetical Works of Lord Tennyson to go to Miss Eliza Daunton, if she has a use for such battered and well-read volumes. We often read them together.

I have little jewellery, and that of no value, excepting my cross with the seed-pearls, which I shall wear tonight. My other trinkets may go to Jane, if she likes any of them, excepting the jet brooch of two hands clasped in Friendship, which was given to me by MISS LAMOTTE *and which I wish her to take back again.*

That is all I have of my own, except my work, which I firmly believe has value, though it is not at present wanted by many. There are twenty-seven paintings in the house at the present time, which are finished work, besides many sketches and drawings. Of these large works, two are the property of MISS LAMOTTE. *These are 'Christabel before Sir Leoline' and 'Merlin and Vivien'. I should like her to keep these works and hope she may wish to hang them in the room where she works, as she has done in the past, and that they may recall to her her happy times. If she finds this too painful, I charge her not to dispose of these paintings, either by gift or by sale, during her lifetime, and to make such provision for them in after time as I myself would have made. They are the best of me, as she well knows. Nothing endures for certain, but good art endures for a time, and I have wanted to be understood by those not yet born. By whom else, after all? The fate of my other works I leave equally in the hands of* MISS LAMOTTE *who has an artistic conscience. I should like them to stay together, if possible, until a taste may be created and a spirit of judgement may prevail where their true worth may be assessed. But I shall, in a little time, have forfeited my right to watch over them, and they must make their own dumb and fragile way.*

In a very little time I shall have left this house, where we have been so happy, never to return. I intend to emulate the author of the Vindication of the Rights of Women, *but, profiting by her example, I shall have sewn into the pockets of my mantle those large volcanic stones which* MISS LAMOTTE *had ranged upon her writing desk, hoping by that means to ensure that it is quick and certain.*

I do not believe that Death is the end. We have heard many marvels at the spiritual meetings of Mrs Lees and had ocular testimony of the painless survival of the departed, in a fairer world, on the other side. Because of this faith, I feel strong in the trust that my Maker will see and forgive all, and will make better use hereafter of my capacities — great and here unwanted and unused — for love and for creative Work. It has indeed been borne in upon me that here I am a superfluous creature. There I shall know and be known. In these later days where we peer in a darkling light through the dim Veil that divides us from those departed and gone before, I trust perhaps to speak, to forgive and be forgiven. Now may the Lord have mercy upon my poor soul and upon all our souls.

· *Blanche Glover, spinster.*

Maud shivered, as she always shivered, on reading this document. What had Christabel thought, when she read it? Where had Christabel been, and why had she gone, and where had Randolph Ash been, between July 1859 and the summer of 1860? There was no record, Roland said, of Ash not being at home. He had published nothing during 1860 and had written few letters — those there were were dated from Bloomsbury, as usual. LaMotte scholars had never found any satisfactory explanation for Christabel's apparent absence at the time of Blanche's death, and had worked on the supposition of a quarrel between the two women. This quarrel now looked quite different, Maud thought, without becoming clearer. She took up the newspaper cutting.

On the night of June 26th, in driving wind and rain, another unfortunate young woman plunged to a terrible death in the swollen waters of the Thames. The body was not recovered until June 28th, cast up a little below Putney Bridge at low tide, upon a gravel bank. Foul play is not suspected. Several large round stones were carefully sewn into the pockets of the unfortunate creature's clothing, which was genteel but not opulent. The deceased has been identified as a Miss Blanche Glover. She lived alone, in a house once shared with the Poetess, Miss Christabel LaMotte, whose whereabouts are not at present known, and have not been known for some time, according to the recently dismissed house-parlourmaid, Jane Summers. Police are seeking to find out Miss LaMotte's current place of residence. A message was left in Mount Ararat Road, sufficiently establishing the unfortunate Miss Glover's intention of doing away with herself.

The police had found Christabel for the Inquest. Where?

Steps sounded in a rush behind the partitions. A voice boomed. 'Surprise, surprise.' Maud, half-risen from her chair, was enveloped in large warm arms, in musky perfume, in soft spreading breasts.

'Darling, *darling* Maud. I thought, where will she be, and told myself, she'll be at work, when is she ever anywhere else for God's sake, so I came right in and here you are, just as I pictured you. Are you surprised? Are you real surprised?'

'Leonora, put me down, I can't breathe. Of course I'm surprised. I sort of felt you coming, across the Atlantic, like a warm front—'

'What a metaphor. I love the way you talk.'

'But I didn't think you'd have swept in here. Not today, anyway. I'm so happy.'

'Can you put me up for a night or two? Can I have a carrell in your archives? I always forget how pitifully tiny your space is here. It indicates a disrespect for Women's Studies, I guess, or is it just English university meanness? Can you read French, my darling? I've got things to show you.'

Maud, who was always afraid of the arrival of Leonora, was then always extraordinarily pleased, at least at first, to see her. Her friend's expansive presence more than filled the small Resource Centre. Leonora was a majestically large woman, in all directions. She dressed up to her size, and was clothed in a full skirt and long shirt-like loose jacket, all covered with orange and gold sunbursts or flowers. She had an olive skin, with a polished sheen on it, an imposing nose, a full mouth, with a hint of Africa in the lips, and a mass of thick black, waving hair, worn shoulder-length and alive with natural oils – the sort of hair that would clump and gather in the hands, not fly apart. She wore several barbaric, but obviously costly, necklaces of amber lumps and varied egg-shapes. Round her head was a yellow silk bandeau, a half-tribute to the Indian bands of her hippy days at the end of the Sixties. She originated in Baton Rouge and claimed both Creole and native Indian ancestry. Her maiden name had been Champion, which she said was French Creole. Stern was the name of her first husband, Nathaniel Stern, who was an assistant Professor at Princeton who had been a happily meticulous New Critic, and had totally failed to survive Leonora and the cut-throat ideological battles of structuralism, post-structuralism, Marxism, deconstruction and feminism. His little book on Harmony and Discord in *The Bostonians* had come at just the wrong time. Leonora had joined in the feminist attack on its approval of James's anxiety about the 'sentiment of sex' in Boston in 1860, and had gone off with a hippy poet, Saul Drucker, to live in a commune in New Mexico. Nathaniel Stern, an anxious, white, pointed little man, whom Maud had met at a conference in Ottawa, had tried to placate the feminists by embarking on a biography of Margaret Fuller Ossoli. Twenty years later he was still working on it, disapproved of by everyone, particularly the feminists. Leonora always referred to Nathaniel as the 'poor sap' but had kept his name, as it appeared on the cover of her first major opus, *No Place Like Home*, a study of the imagery of home-making in nineteenth-century women's fiction, written before Leonora's militant middle and later Lacanian phases. Saul Drucker was the father of Leonora's son, Danny, now seventeen. He had, Leonora said, a curly ginger beard and a positive pelt of ginger fur all over his torso and right down below his belly button to his pubes. This was all Maud knew about the appearance of Saul Drucker, whose poetry was full of fuck and crap and shit and come, and who had apparently been big enough to beat up Leonora from time to time, which could not have been easy. His most famous poem, *Millenarial Crawling*, described a kind of resurrection of men and serpents in Death Valley, with debts to Blake, Whitman and Ezekiel, and, Leonora said, far too much bad acid. 'Shouldn't it be "millennial"?' Maud had enquired, and Leonora had said, 'Not if it could be drawn out any longer, you do miss the point in a delightful way, you precise creature.' She referred to Drucker as 'meaty-man'. She had left him for an Indian woman professor of Anthropology, who had taught her yoga, vegetarianism, how to make multiple orgasms to the point of swooning, literally, and had filled her with sympathetic rage about suttee and the worship of the lingam. Saul Drucker now worked on a ranch in Montana – 'he doesn't beat up horses,' said Leonora – and had Danny with him. He had married again and his new wife was, Leonora said, devoted to Danny. After the professor there had been Marge, Brigitta, Pocahontas and Martina. 'I love 'em dearly,' Leonora would say, moving on, 'but I'm paranoid about home-making, I can't bear the feeling of sinking into cushions and sticking there, the world's too full of other marvellous creatures...'

'What are you doing?' she said now to Maud.

'Reading Blanche Glover's suicide note.'

'Why?'

'I do wonder where Christabel was, when she jumped.'

'If you can read French, I might be able to help. I've got this letter, from Ariane Le Minier, in Nantes. I'll show you.'

She took up the note.

'Poor old Blanche, what rage, what dignity, what a mess. Did any of the pictures ever turn up? They'd be fascinating. Documented lesbian feminist works.'

'None have ever been found. I suppose Christabel may have kept them all. Or burned them up in distress, we simply don't know.'

'Perhaps she took them all to that mock-castle with that nasty old man with the gun. I felt like stabbing him with the shears, the pig. They're probably *mouldering* in a glory-hole up there.'

Maud did not feel like pursuing the idea of Sir George, though Leonora's idea was a good, indeed a probable one. She said,

'How do you imagine the paintings, Leonora? Do you think they were any good?'

'I dreadfully want them to have been. She had the dedication. She was sure they were good. I imagine them all pale and tense, don't you, voluptuous but pale, lovely willowy creatures with heaving breasts and great masses of pre-Raphaelite hair. But if they were really original, we aren't going to be able to imagine them, until we find them, in the nature of the case.'

'She did one called "A Spirit-Wreath and Fair Spirit-Hands at a Seance of Hella Lees".'

'That doesn't sound very hopeful. But maybe the hands were as good as Dürer's, maybe the wreath looked like Fantin-Latour. Only in their own way, of course. Not derivative.'

'Do you think so?'

'No, but we should give her the benefit of the doubt. She was a sister.'

'She was.'

*

That night, they sat in Maud's flat and Maud translated Dr Le Minier's letter for Leonora, who said, 'I got the general *gist* of it OK but my French is primitive. What it is to have an English education.'

Maud had unthinkingly sat down in her usual place in the corner of her white sofa under the tall lamp, and Leonora had plumped down next to her, one arm along the sofa behind Maud's back, one buttock bumping Maud's when she bounced. Maud felt threatened and tense, and almost got up, once or twice, but was restrained by an exigent and unhelpful English sense of good manners. She was aware that Leonora knew exactly how she felt, and was amused.

The letter was possibly treasure-trove. Maud, by now slightly more skilled at dissimulation than Blanche Glover with Jane, read it out flatly as if it were a routine scholarly enquiry.

Dear Professor Stern,

I am a French student of women's writings, here in the University of Nantes.I have much admired your work on the structures of signification of certain women poets, above all Christabel LaMotte, who is interesting to me also, as half-Breton, and drawing very much on her Breton heritage of myth and legend to create a female world. May I say in particular how very just and inspiring I found your remarks on the sexualisation of the landscape elements in The Fairy Melusina.

I am told you are researching materials for a feminist life of LaMotte and I have come across something I think may perhaps be of interest to you. I am currently working on an almost unpublished writer, Sabine de Kercoz, who published a few poems in the 1860s including several sonnets in praise of George Sand, whom she never met, but for whose ideals and way of life she had conceived a passionate admiration. There are also four unpublished novels, Oriane, Aurélia, Les Tourments de Geneviève, and La Deuxième Dahud, which I am hoping to edit and bring out in the near future. It draws on the same legend of the Drowned City of Is as LaMotte's beautiful poem of that title.

As you may already know, Mlle de Kercoz was a relation, through her paternal grandmother, of Christabel LaMotte. What you may not know is that in the autumn of 1859 LaMotte appears to have visited her family in Fouesnant. My source is a letter from Sabine de Kercoz to her cousin, Solange, which is amongst the papers – unedited and I believe unexamined since they were deposited here in the University by a descendant of Sabine (who became Mme de Kergarouet in Pornic, and died in childbed in 1870). I enclose a transcript of the letter, and if you find it of interest, I shall of course be delighted to share with you any further informations I may obtain. Mes Hommages.

'Sorry about the clumsy translation, Leonora. Now for Sabine de Kercoz.'

Ma chère petite cousine,

Our long and tedious days here have been enlivened by the unexpected – at least unexpected by me – arrival of a distant cousin, a Miss LaMotte, residing in England, the daughter of Isidore LaMotte, who collected all the French Mythology and also the Breton tales and folk beliefs. Imagine my excitement – it turns out that this new cousin is a poetess, who has published many works, unfortunately in English, and is highly thought of in that country. She is unwell at present, and keeps her bed, having had a terrible journey from England in the recent storm, and having been forced to remain for almost twenty-four hours outside the harbour walls at St Malo because of a howling gale. And then the roads were almost impassable for flooding water and high winds all the time. She has a fire in her room, and is probably unaware how singular an honour this is, in this austere household.

I liked what I saw of her well enough. She is little and slender, with a very white face (maybe because of the sea) and rather large white teeth. She sat up to dinner on the first evening and said only a few words. I sat by her side and whispered to her that I had hopes of being a poet. She said, 'It is not the way to happiness, ma fille.' I said on the contrary, it was only when writing that I felt wholly living. She said, 'If that is so, fortunately or unfortunately, nothing I can say will dissuade you.'

The wind howled and howled that night, all on one wailing note, without remission, so that one ached, body and soul, for just a moment of silence, which did not ensue until the early hours of the morning, when I was woken from the – tohu-bohu – hurly-burly – by a sudden dropping of the wind, rather than the more usual way, of waking because of sounds. My new cousin did not appear to have slept, in the morning, and my father insisted she should retire to her room with a tisane of raspberry leaves.

I forgot to say that she has brought with her a large wolf-hound, who is called, if I heard correctly, 'the Dog Tray'. The poor animal has also suffered terribly in the storm, and will not come out from under the little table in Miss LaMotte's bedroom where he lies with his ears between his paws. My cousin

314

says that when the weather is better, he can run in the forest of Brocéliande,
which is his natural habitat . . .

'That sounds worth investigation,' said Leonora, when Maud
had finished. 'That's more or less what I guessed it said. I might
go over to Nantes – where is Nantes exactly? – and take a look
at what Dr Le Minier has got there. Except that I don't read old
French. You'll have to come with me, my darling. We could
have a fun time. LaMotte and sea food and Brocéliande, what do
you say?'

'That at some future date that will be lovely, but just now I've
got a paper to finish for the York Conference on Metaphor and
I've got into a horrible knot with it.'

'Tell. Two minds are better than one. What metaphor?'

Maud was at a loss. She had distracted Leonora from Christabel
temporarily, only to find herself jounced into discussing a paper
which was hardly forming in her mind and which was in fact
better left another month to grow in the dark on its own.

'It's vague yet. It's to do with Melusina and Medusa and
Freud's idea that the Medusa-head was a castration-fantasy, female
sexuality, feared, not desired.'

'Ah,' said Leonora, 'I must tell you about a letter I had from a
German about Goethe's *Faust*, where the chopped off heads of
the Hydra creep about the stage and think they are still something
or other – I've been paying attention to Goethe recently – the
ewig weibliche, the Mothers, all that, the witches, the sphinxes . . .'

Leonora talked on. She was never dull, if always breathless.
Maud began to feel safe as the conversation moved from Brittany
to Goethe, from Goethe to sexuality in general, and from the
general to the particular and the peculiar habits of Leonora's two
husbands which she was given to deploring, and very occasionally
celebrating, in a kind of vehement recitative. Maud always
thought that there was no more to be known than she herself
knew, about the quirks and foibles, the secret lusts and incon-
siderate failures, the smells and funny noises and ejaculations
verbal and seminal emitted by the poor sap and the meaty-man.
She was always proved wrong. Leonora was a kind of verbal
Cleopatra, creating appetite where most she satisfied, making an
endless pillow-book out of the new oratory of the couch.

'As for you,' Leonora suddenly said. 'What's the state of your own love-life? You haven't contributed much, this evening.'

'How could I have?'

'Touché. I do go on. But that suits you fine, you're all uptight about your own sexuality. You were hurt by that bastard, Fergus Wolff, but you shouldn't have gotten so *annihilated*, it's letting the side down. You should branch out. Try other sweet things.'

'You mean women. Just at the moment, I'm trying celibacy. I like it. Its only hazard is people who will proselytise for their own way of doing things. You should try it.'

'Oh, I did, for a month, back in the Fall. It was great at first. I got to be quite in love with myself, and then I thought I was unhealthily attached to me, and should give myself up. So I found Mary-Lou. It's much more thrilling bringing someone else off – more generous, Maud.'

'You see what I mean about proselytising. Give up, Leonora. I'm happy the way I am.'

'It's your choice,' said Leonora, equably. She added, 'I tried calling you before I flew out. No one knew where you were. Gone off in a car with a man, I was told by the Department.'

'Who? Who said that?'

'That would be telling. I hope you had a good time.'

Maud became like her namesake, icily regular, splendidly null. She said frostily,

'Yes, thank you,' and stared tightlipped and white into space.

'Point taken,' said Leonora. 'No trespassers. I'm glad there *is* someone.'

'There isn't.'

'oκ. There isn't.'

Leonora splashed a long time in Maud's bathroom and left it covered with little puddles of water, lidless bottles and several different spicy smells of unknown unguents. Maud put the lids back, mopped up the puddles, had a shower between curtains redolent of Opium or Poison, and had just climbed into her cool bed when Leonora appeared in the doorway, largely naked except for an exiguous and unbelted crimson silk dressing-gown.

'A good-night kiss,' Leonora said.

'I can't.'

'You can. It's easy.'

Leonora came to the bed and folded Maud into her bosom. Maud fought to get her nose free. Loose hands met Leonora's majestic belly and heavy breasts. She couldn't *push*, that was as bad as submitting. To her shame, she began to cry.

'What is it with you, Maud?'

'I told you. I'm off the whole thing. Right off. I did tell you.'

'I can relax you.'

'*You must be able to see you have exactly the opposite effect.* Go back to bed, Leonora. Please.'

Leonora made various rrr-ooof noises like a large dog or bear, and finally rolled away, laughing. 'Tomorrow is another day,' said Leonora. 'Sweet dreams, Princess.'

A kind of desperation overcame Maud. The bulk of Leonora lay on her sofa in her living-room, between her and her books. She noticed a kind of rigorous aching of her limbs, from tense confinement, which was reminiscent of the last terrible days of Fergus Wolff. She wanted to hear her own voice, saying something simple and to the point. She tried to think whom she wanted to speak to, and came up with Roland Michell, that other devotee of white and solitary beds. She did not look at her watch — it was late, but not so very late, not for scholars. She would let it ring, just a few times, and then, if he didn't answer, ring off quickly, so that if seriously disturbed he would never know by whom. She picked up the telephone by her bed and dialled the London number. She would tell him what? Not about Sabine de Kercoz, but just that there was something to tell. That she was not alone.

Two rings, three, four. The phone was lifted. A listening silence at the other end.

'Roland?'

'He's asleep. *Have you any idea what time it is?*'

'I'm sorry. I'm ringing from abroad.'

'That is Maud Bailey, isn't it?'

Maud was silent.

'Isn't it, isn't it, Maud Bailey? Why don't you leave us alone?'

Maud held the phone silently, listening to the angry voice. She looked up and saw Leonora in the doorway, gleaming black curls and red silk.

'I came to say I'm sorry and have you got anything for a headache?'

Maud put the phone down.

'Don't let me interrupt you.'

'There was nothing to interrupt.'

The next day, Maud telephoned Blackadder, which was a tactical error.

'Professor Blackadder?'

'Yes.'

'This is Maud Bailey, from the Lincoln Resource Centre for Women's Studies.'

'Oh yes.'

'I am trying to get in touch with Roland Michell, rather urgently.'

'I don't know why you should apply to *me*, Dr Bailey. I never see him these days.'

'I thought he—'

'He's been away recently. He's been in poor health since he came back. Or so I assume, since I don't see him.'

'I'm sorry.'

'I don't see why you should be. I take it you are not responsible for his — ailing state?'

'Perhaps, if you see him, you would tell him I called.'

'If I do, I will. Is there any other message?'

'Could you ask him to call me.'

'About what, Dr Bailey?'

'Tell him Professor Stern is here, from Tallahassee.'

'If I remember, if I see him, I'll tell him that.'

'Thank you.'

Maud and Leonora, coming out of a shop in Lincoln, were almost killed by a large car, reversing at great and silent speed. They were carrying hobby-horses, with velvet heads on solid broomsticks, beautifully made with flowing silken manes and wicked embroidered eyes. Leonora wanted them for various godchildren and said they looked English and magical. The driver of the reversing car, seeing the two women through smoke-blue glass, thought they looked bizarrely cultish, in flowing skirts and scarfed heads, brandishing their totemic beasts. He made an economical contemptuous gesture at the gutter. Leonora raised her hobby-horse and addressed him, jingling its bells, as slob, prick and maniac. Insulated from her imprecations he completed his manoeuvre, distressing a push-chair, a grandmother, two cyclists, an errand-boy and a Cortina, which had to reverse behind him the length of the street. Leonora copied down his number plate which was ANK 666. Neither Maud nor Leonora had met Mortimer Cropper. Their power-circle was different – different conferences, different libraries. Maud therefore felt no shadow of threat or apprehension as the Mercedes slid away through the narrow old streets for which it had not been designed.

If Cropper had known one of his cult-figures was Maud Bailey, he would not have stopped; he had registered Leonora's American voice without much interest. He was on another quest. In a short time the Mercedes was having difficulty with a hay-wain in the twisting little wold roads near Bag-Enderby. He faced out the haywagon, making it pull precariously into a hedge. He kept his window closed and his aseptic leather interior air-conditioned.

The entrance to the drive to Seal Court was festooned with notices – old and greenish, new and red on white. PRIVATE PROPERTY KEEP OUT. NO TRESPASSERS. DANGEROUS DOG. PROTECTED PROPERTY. ANY ACCIDENTS YOUR OWN RISK. Cropper drove in. In his experience signboard verbosity was a substitute for, not an indicator of, mantraps. He drove along the beech drive and into the courtyard where he stopped, engine humming, and considered his next move.

Sir George, with his shotgun, was seen to peer from the kitchen window and then to emerge from the door. Cropper sat in his car.

'Lost your way?'

Cropper wound down his grey window, and saw crumbling stones instead of steely film set. He looked about with a practised eye. Battlements eroded. Doors hung askew. Weeds in the stable-yard.

'Sir George Bailey?'

'Uh h-huh. Can I help you?'

Cropper emerged from his car and turned off the engine.

'May I give you my card? Professor Mortimer Cropper, of the Stant Collection, in Robert Dale Owen University, in Harmony City, New Mexico.'

'Some mistake.'

'Oh, I don't think so. I've come a long way, just to ask for a few moments of your time.'

'I'm a busy man. My wife's ill. What do you want?'

Cropper moved towards him and thought of asking if he could come in; Sir George raised his gun a little. Cropper stopped in the yard. He wore a loose and elegant black silk and wool jacket over charcoal grey flannels and a cream silk shirt. He was thin, he was sinewy; he bore a faint resemblance to the film Virginians, poised like cats in corrals, ready to jump this way or that, or to draw.

'I am, I think I may safely say, the leading expert in the world on Randolph Henry Ash. Sources have led me to believe that you may be in possession of some documentation by him – say a letter, say a draft of something–'

'Sources?'

'Roundabout sources. These things always become known, sooner or later. Now, Sir George, I represent – I curate – the largest collection of the manuscript writings of R. H. Ash in the world–'

'Look, Professor, I'm not interested. I don't know anything about this Ash and I don't propose to start–'

'My sources–'

'*And* I don't like English things being bought up by foreigners.'

'A document to do, perhaps, with your illustrious ancestress, Christabel LaMotte?'

'Not illustrious. Not my ancestress. Inaccurate on both counts. Go away.'

'If I could just come in for a moment or two and discuss the matter – simply to know for scholarly purposes what you might or might not have–'

'I don't want any more scholars in this house. I don't want any interference. I have work to do.'

'You don't deny that you have something–'

'I don't say anything. It's none of your business. Get off my land. Poor little fairy poet. Leave her alone.'

Sir George took a stolid step or two forwards. Cropper elegantly raised his elegant hands; his crocodile-skin belt shifted a little like a gun-belt on his lean hips.

'Don't shoot. I'll go. I never trouble the truly reluctant. Let me say this to you, though. Have you any idea of how much such a piece of writing – if it existed – would be worth?'

'Worth?'

'In money. In money, Sir George.'

A blank.

'For instance one letter from Ash – simply fixing a sitting with a portrait-painter – recently went for £500 at Sotheby's. Went to me, of course. It is our rather too frank boast that we don't have a library precept from the university budget, Sir George, we simply have a cheque book. Now if you had *more than one* letter – or a poem –'

'Go on then –'

'Say twelve long letters – or twenty little ones with not much in – you'd be handsomely into six figures and maybe more. Six figures in pounds sterling. I observe your splendid home needs a lot of upkeep.'

'Letters by the fairy poet?'

'By Randolph Henry Ash.'

Sir George's red brow creased with thought.

'And if you had these letters you'd take 'em off –'

'And preserve them in Harmony City and make them accessible to all scholars of all nations. They would join their fellows in perfect conditions – air pressure, humidity, light – our conditions of keeping and viewing are the best in the world.'

'English things should stay in England in my view.'

'Understandable. An admirable sentiment. But in these days of microfilm and photocopying – how relevant is sentiment?'

Sir George made one or two convulsive movements with the shotgun, perhaps a product of thought. Cropper, his keen eyes on Sir George's, kept his hands rather absurdly in the air, and smiled, a darkly vulpine smile, not anxious, but watchful.

'If you tell me, Sir George, that I am wholly mistaken in supposing you have discovered any significant new manuscripts –

any manuscripts at all – you must simply say so and I shall leave instantly. Though I hope you will take my card – it may be that a closer look at any old letters of Christabel LaMotte's – any old diaries, any old account books – may turn up something by Ash. If you are in any doubt about the nature of any manuscript at all, I should be only too happy to give an opinion – an unprejudiced opinion – as to its provenance and worth. And worth.'

'I don't know.' Sir George retreated into bull-faced squireish idiocy; Cropper could see his eyes calculating, and in that moment knew for certain that there was something, and that Sir George could lay his hands on it.

'May I hand you my card without being blasted?'

'I suppose so. I suppose you can. Mind you, I don't say it's any use, I don't say...'

'You say nothing. You are unprejudiced. I understand perfectly.'

The Mercedes slipped back through Lincoln faster than it had come out. Cropper considered, and rejected, the idea of calling on Maud Bailey at this point. He thought about Christabel LaMotte. Somewhere in the Stant Collection – for which he had a loving and near-photographic recall, once activated – was something about Christabel LaMotte. What was it?

Maud was crossing Lincoln Market Square between the stalls. She was bumped into, with a heavy thud, by Sir George, in an unexpected suit, tight and greenish-brown. He put out a hand and seized her sleeve.

'Do you know,' he cried loudly, 'young woman, do you know how much an electric wheelchair might cost? Or a stairlift, perhaps you can price that?'

'No,' said Maud.

'Perhaps you should find out. I've just been to see my solicitor, who has a low opinion of you, Maud Bailey, a low opinion.'

'I'm not sure what–'

'Don't look so mimsy and mild. Six-figures or more, that's what he said, that sly cowboy in his Merc. And you said never a word of that, oh no, butter wouldn't melt in your cold little mouth, would it?'

'You mean, the letters . . .'

'Norfolk Baileys have never given a damn about Seal Court. The old Sir George built it to spite them and in my opinion they'd be pleased to see it crack up as it will do pretty soon. But an *electric wheelchair*, young woman, you should have thought of that.'

Maud's mind whirled. A cowboy in a Merc, why not the National Health, what would become of the letters, where was blissfully ignorant Leonora, wandering between the market stalls selecting saucers?

'I'm sorry. I had no idea of their value. I knew they must have some, of course. I thought they should stay where they were. Where Christabel left them —'

'My Joan is alive. *She's* dead.'

'Of course. I see that.'

'Of course, I see that,' mimicking. 'No, you don't. My solicitor thinks you've got some idea of benefiting *yourself* — in your career, that is, or even selling them on. Relying on my ignorance, d'you see?'

'You've got it wrong.'

'I don't think so.'

Leonora emerged from between banked flowers darkly smelling and a rack of leather jackets embellished with death's-heads.

'Are you being harassed, darling?' she enquired. And then cried, 'Oh, it's the savage woodsman with the gun.'

'*You*,' said Sir George, purply. He was kneading and twisting Maud's sleeve. 'There are Americans cropping up everywhere. You're all in it together.'

'In what?' enquired Leonora. 'Is it a war? Is it an international incident? Are you being threatened, Maud?'

She advanced on Sir George, towering above him, flowing with generous indignation.

Maud, who prided herself on her rationality under stress, was trying to decide whether she most feared Sir George's rage or Leonora's inopportune discovery of the concealment of the letters. She decided Sir George was a lost cause, whereas Leonora, if hurt, or feeling betrayed, might be terrible. This did not help her to

think what to say. Leonora took hold of Sir George's wiry little
fist with her own long strong hands.

'Leave hold of my friend or I'll call the police.'

'It won't be you needing their services, it'll be me. Trespassers.
Thieves. Nasty vultures.'

'He means harpies, but he's not educated.'

'Leonora, *please.*'

'I'm waiting for an explanation, Miss Bailey.'

'Not here, not now, Oh please.'

'What does he want explaining, Maud?'

'Nothing important. Oh, surely you can see this isn't the
moment, Sir George?'

'I can indeed. Take your hands off me, you vulgar woman, *go
away.* I hope I never see either of you again.'

Sir George turned smartly, parted the small crowd that had
gathered, and hurried away.

Leonora said, 'What does he want explaining, Maud?'

'I'll tell you later.'

'You certainly will. I'm intrigued.'

Maud felt near to complete despair. She wished she was anywhere but here and now. She thought of Yorkshire, the white
light on the Thomasine Foss, the sulphurous stones and glimpsed
ammonites at the Boggle Hole.

A jingling warder, her black face severe, gestured at pale
Paola.

'Phone,' she said. 'For Ash editors.'

Paola followed the sound of keys and the solid jacketed hips
down carpeted tunnels to a telephone at a security point which the
Ash Factory was allowed, as a great favour, to use in emergency.

'Paola Fonseca.'

'Are you the editor of the Collected Poems of Randolph Henry
Ash?'

'His assistant.'

'I have been told I should speak to a Professor Blackadder. My
name is Byng. I am a solicitor. I am speaking on behalf of a client,
who would like to enquire about the – well – the market price
of certain – certain – possible manuscripts.'

'*Possible*, Mr Byng?'

'My client is very unclear. Are you sure I can't speak directly to Professor Blackadder?'

'I'll fetch him. It's a long walk. You must be patient.'

Blackadder spoke to Mr Byng. He came back to the Ash Factory white and sharp and in a state of highly irritated excitement.

'Some fool wants a valuation of an unspecified number of letters from Ash to an unspecified woman. I said, are there five or fifteen, or twenty. Byng said he didn't know, but was instructed to say in the region of fifty or so. Long ones, he said, not dentist's appointments and thank yous. Wouldn't name his client. I said how could I set a price on something potentially so important, sight unseen. I've always hated that phrase, haven't you, Paola, sight *unseen*, it's a tautology or something near, it simply means *unseen*, doesn't it? So Mr Byng says he believes there is already an offer in the region of six large figures. An English offer, I asked, and Byng said no, not necessarily. That sod Cropper has been there, wherever it is. I said, may I know where you're talking from, and he said Tuck Lane Chambers, Lincoln. I said, can I see the damn things, and Byng said his client was very opposed to being disturbed, very irascible. Now what do you make of that? I get the impression if I made a guesstimate of a generous kind, I might just be allowed a look. But if I do that, we'll never get the funds to back the guess, not if that sod Cropper's involved with his bottomless cheque book and Mr Byng's client is already asking questions about money and not about scholarly value.

'I tell you what, Paola, all this has something to do with the funny behaviour of Roland Michell and his visits to that Dr Bailey in Lincoln. Now what has young Roland been up to? Where, for that matter, is he? Wait till I get a word with him...'

'Roland?'

'No. Who is that. Is that Maud Bailey?'

'This is Paola Fonseca. I don't sound remotely like Maud Bailey. Val, I have to speak to Roland, it's urgent.'

'I'm not surprised, he doesn't go into the library any more, he sits here writing...'

'Is he there now?'

'Always so urgent, you and Maud Bailey.'

'What *is* this about Maud Bailey?'

'She's a telephone heavy breather.'

'Val, is he there? I'm in an open corridor, I can't hang on long, you know about these silly phones—'

'I'll get him.'

'Roland, this is Paola. You're in big trouble. Blackadder's in a fearful rage. He's looking for you.'

'He can't have looked far. I'm here. Getting on with my article.'

'You don't understand. Listen — I don't know if this means anything to you. He had a call from someone called Byng, wanting to price a collection of about fifty letters from Ash to a woman.'

'What woman?'

'Byng didn't say. Blackadder thinks he knows. He thinks you know too. He thinks you're up to things behind his back. He says you're treacherous — Roland, are you there?'

'Yes. I'm thinking. It's terribly nice of you to phone, Paola. I don't know why you bothered; but it's nice.'

'I hate noise, that's why.'

'Noise?'

'Uh-huh. If you come in he'll roar. And roar and roar. It makes me sick to the stomach. I hate shouting. Also, I'm quite fond of you.'

'That's nice of you. I hate shouting too. I hate Cropper. I hate the Ash Factory. I wish I was anywhere but here, I wish I could disappear off the face of the earth.'

'A fellowship in Auckland or Yerevan.'

'A hole in the ground, more like. Tell him you don't know where I am. And thanks.'

'Val seems cross.'

'That's endemic. That's one reason I hate shouting. It's mostly my fault.'

'Guard's coming back. I'm going. Look after yourself.'

'Thanks for everything.'

Roland went out. He felt wholly helpless and desperate. Telling himself that any intelligent man in his position should have foreseen these possible developments made things worse, not better. He had been emotionally wholly convinced that the letters would remain his private secret, until he chose to reveal it, until he knew the end of the story, until – until he knew what Randolph Ash would have wanted done. Val asked him where he was going, and he didn't answer. He went along Putney High Street in search of an unvandalised telephone box. He went into an Indian grocery and provided himself with a telephone card and a stack of change. He walked over Putney Bridge and into Fulham, where he found a cardphone box that had to be functioning because it had a long queue. He waited. Two people, a black man and a white woman, exhausted their cards. Another white woman played some complicated trick on the phone box with her car keys and talked interminably. Roland and his co-queuers looked at each other and began to circle the box like hyenas, threatening eye-contact and then occasionally slapping the glass with casual palms. When, finally, looking neither to right nor left, the woman flounced out, Roland's predecessors were courteously brief. He was not unhappy in the queue. No one knew where he was.

He got through.

'Maud?'

'She isn't available right now. Can I take a message?'

'No. It doesn't matter. I'm in a call box. When will she be back?'

'She isn't exactly away. She's bathing.'

'It's kind of urgent. There's a queue behind me.'

'MAUD. I was just calling her. Will you hang on please, until I see what she – MAUD.'

When would they tap on the glass?

'She's just coming. Who shall I say?'

'It doesn't matter. If she's coming.'

He imagined Maud, wet, in a white towel. Who was the American? Must be Leonora. Had Maud said anything to Leonora. Could she say anything to him, in front of Leonora . . . ?

'Hullo? Maud Bailey speaking.'

'Maud. At last. Maud. This is Roland. I'm in a call box. There are disasters –'

'Indeed there are. We've got to talk. Leonora, do you mind if I just take the phone to the bedroom? This call is sort of private.' A gap. A reconnection. 'Roland, Mortimer Cropper came.'

'A solicitor telephoned Blackadder.'

'Sir George made a horrid scene at me in Lincoln. About electric wheelchairs. He needs money.'

'It was his solicitor. Is he very cross?'

'Furious. It didn't help him seeing Leonora.'

'Have you told her?'

'No. But I can't go on without her guessing. Every day makes it worse.'

'They will see us in a bad light. Cropper, Blackadder, Leonora.'

'Listen – speaking of Leonora – she's found out the next stage. Christabel went to the family in Brittany. There was a cousin who wrote poems. A French scholar has them, she wrote to Leonora. She stayed some time. It might cover the suicide. No one knew where she was.'

'I wish no one knew where I was. I've actually run away from being sent for by Blackadder.'

'I tried to phone you. I don't know if she told you. It didn't sound as if she would. I don't even know what we are or were trying to do. How did we ever hope to keep it from C and B?'

'And Leonora. We didn't – after we knew all we could find out. We just needed time. It is our Quest.'

'I do know. That isn't how they're going to see it.'

'I wish I could disappear.'

'You keep saying that. So do I. Living with Leonora's bad enough, without Sir George and all that –'

'Is it really?' He found himself voluptuously discarding a vision of Leonora, whom he had never seen, unwrapping the imagined white towel. Maud lowered her voice.

'I keep thinking of what we said to each other, about empty beds, at the Foss.'

'So do I. And about the white light on the stone. And the sun at the Boggle Hole.'

'We knew where we were, there. We should just disappear. Like Christabel.'

'You mean, go to Brittany?'

'Not precisely. At least. After all. Why *not*?'

'I've got no money.'

'I have. And a car. And good French.'

'So is mine.'

'They wouldn't know where we were.'

'Not even Leonora?'

'Not if I lied to her. She thinks I've got a secret lover. She's got a romantic soul. It would be an awful lie, to go off with her information and betray her.'

'Does she know Cropper and Blackadder?'

'Not to speak to. Nor who you are. Not even your name.'

'Val might tell her.'

'I'll get her out of this flat. I'll get her invited away. Then if Val phones, no answer.'

'I am not a natural conspirator, Maud.'

'Nor am I.'

'I can't face going home. In case Blackadder . . . In case Val . . .'

'You must. You must go home and have a row, and get your passport secretly, and all the papers, and just move out. Into one of those little hotels in Bloomsbury.'

'Too near the BM.'

'Victoria then. I'll deal with Leonora and come there. I know one I used to stay in . . .'

CHAPTER NINETEEN

High howled the wind, the Ocean hurled
His mass of crested jet uncurled
Against the sea-wall and the tower
Where Dahud and her paramour
In shuttered silence, silky white
Lay side by side the live-long night.
The people ran about the street
Their fearful voice, their wet hands beat
Against the opposing steely door
All smoothly silent, as before.

Confusedly in Dahud's arm
He felt presentiment of harm
Raising his ears from her white skin
And heart's noise, to the people's din
And beyond them, the growling roar
Of angry Ocean at the door.

'Go to the window,' then said she,
'Tell me the movement of the sea
His colour and his strategy.'

'Lady, his waves are green as glass
The sky is jet, the small skiffs pass
From gulf to gulf like flying things
Soaked through, sucked down, with sodden wings.'

'Then come to me and my embrace—
I will press kisses on your face
Whose heat and sharpness shall occlude
The murmuring of the multitude
The rumble of the waters rude.'

Bewitched, he does her bidding, till
He hears a splashing at the sill
Of the tower's portal, and he cries,
'Lady, he comes, and we must rise.'

''Tis he must rise,' she answers fast,
'We are safe until the iron gate's past.
Go to the window, tell to me,
The pace and movement of the sea
His colour and his strategy.'

'Lady, his waves are livid pale
The sky is covered with a veil
Of flying foam, and drowning men
Cry from the crests and sink again.'

'Come and lie still within my arms,
What care we for these weak things' harms?
I can subdue him with my charms.'

Again he stirs, again he cries,
'The Ocean comes, and we must rise.'

'Go to the window, tell to me
The height and movement of the sea
His colour and his strategy.'

'Lady, his waves are black and boil
Like stinking pitch, like raging oil,
He mounts and mounts, his million jaws
Snatch at the tower with open maws
Fringèd with foam-teeth, curv'd and white
Shape-shifting monsters of the night
Now one, now myriad, open, high.
Lady, I cannot see the sky.
The stars are out, the waters race
Where the town was, over the place
Where steeple pointed, clock-tower smiled.
Now all is turbulent and wild.
There is a sound of grinding chains
The very tower sways and strains
He laughs with rage, flings his fist down.
Now rise up, lady, or we drown.'

Christabel LaMotte, *The City of Is*

They were closed in a cabin on the *Prince of Brittany*. It was night: they could hear the steady throb of the engines, and beyond and around them, the huge heavy rush of the sea. They were both faint with over-excitement. They had stood on deck and watched the lights of Portsmouth glare and dwindle. They had stood apart, not touching, though earlier, in London, full of obscure emotion, they had rushed into each other's arms. Now they sat side by side on the lower bunk and drank duty-free whisky and water from toothmugs.

'We must be mad,' said Roland.

'Of course we are mad. And bad. I lied shamelessly to Leonora. I've done worse – I nicked Ariane Le Minier's address when she wasn't looking. I'm as bad as Cropper and Blackadder. All scholars are a bit mad. All obsessions are dangerous. This one's got a bit out of hand. But the bliss of breathing sea air and not having to share my flat with Leonora for the next few weeks –'

It was odd to hear Maud Bailey talking wildly of madness and bliss.

'I think I've just lost everything I've ever had or cared about. My bit of job in the Ash Factory. Val. Which means my home because it's her home, she pays the rent. I should feel frightful. I probably shall. But at the moment I feel all – clear in the head – and *single*, if you know what I mean. I suppose it feels so good because of the sea. I'd just feel silly if I'd gone to earth in London.'

They were not touching. They were sitting amicably close and not touching.

'Oddly,' said Maud, 'if we were obsessed with each other, no one would think we were mad.'

'Val thinks we are obsessed with each other. She even said it was healthier than being obsessed with Randolph Ash.'

'Leonora thinks I've rushed away in response to a telephone call from a lover.'

Roland thought, all this giddy clear-headedness is dependent on our not being obsessed with each other.

He said, 'These are clean narrow white beds.'

'So they are. Do you prefer top or bottom?'

'I'm indifferent. And you?'

'I'll take the top.' She laughed. 'Leonora would say it's because of Lilith.'

'Why Lilith?'

'Lilith refused to take the inferior position. So Adam sent her away and she roamed the Arabian deserts and the dark beyond the pale. She's an avatar of Melusina.'

'I don't see that it matters, top or bottom,' Roland said stolidly, perfectly aware of the absurd range of this comment between mythography, sexual preference and distribution of bolted bunks. He felt happy. Everything was absurd and at one. He turned on the shower.

'Do you want a shower? It's salt.'

'So it is. A sea-water shower under the sea. We *are* under the sea, in this cabin? After you.'

The water hissed and pricked and calmed. Outside, the same water ran darkly, carved by the bulk of the huge craft, and beyond that supporting the rush and balance of unseen life, schools of porpoises and threatened singing dolphins, moving and darting masses of mackerel and whiting, the propulsive canopies of the medusa, the phosphorescent semen of herrings which Michelet, mixing his genders and functions as he had a habit of doing, called the sea of milk, *la mer de lait*. Roland lay peacefully on his inferior bunk, and thought of a magical sentence of Melville's about schools of – what was it exactly? – rushing beneath the pillow. He heard the shower-streams break and rattle on Maud's invisible body, which he imagined to himself gently and vaguely, without urgency or precision, white as milk, turning this way and that in the jets and the rising steam. He saw her ankles as she climbed the ladder, white and fine, in white cotton and an air of fern-scented powder and damp hair. He felt a great contentment, that she should be shelved there, invisible and inaccessible, but there. 'Sleep well,' she said, 'good night,' and he answered, the same. But for a long time he did not sleep, only lay wide-eyed in the dark, listening voluptuously for small creaks and rustles, sighings and shiftings, as she moved above him.

Maud had telephoned Ariane Le Minier, who was about to set out for a holiday in the South but had agreed to see them briefly. They drove peacefully to Nantes in good weather and met over lunch in a surprising restaurant, mysteriously and brilliantly decorated in fin de siècle Turkish tiles with pillars and jewelled stained glass. Ariane Le Minier was young, warm, and decisive, with ink-black hair carved into a precise geometric form, angled at the nape, across the brow. The two women liked each other; they shared a passionate precision in their approach to scholarship, and discussed liminality and the nature of Melusina's monstrous form as a 'transitional area', in Winnicott's terms – an imaginary construction that frees the woman from gender-identification. Roland said very little. It was his first French meal in France and he was overcome with precise sensuality, with sea food, with fresh bread, with sauces whose subtlety required and defied analysis.

Maud's task was delicate. She needed to be given access to Sabine de Kercoz's papers without exactly saying why and without explaining the relationship between her request and Leonora's absence. This seemed initially to be made more difficult by Ariane's incipient departure. The papers were locked away and access was not really possible in her absence. 'If I had known you were coming...'

'We didn't know ourselves. We turned out to have this small holiday. We thought of travelling through Brittany and seeing LaMotte's family home –'

'There is nothing to see, alas. It was burned down at the time of the First World War. But simply to see Finistère and the Bay of Audierne – under which Is traditionally lies – and the Baie des Trépassés – the Bay of the Dead –'

'Have you found out anything else about the visit LaMotte made in the autumn of 1859?'

'Ah. I have a surprise for you. Since I wrote to Professor Stern I have made a discovery – I have found a *journal intime* kept by Sabine de Kercoz which covers almost all LaMotte's visit. I think Sabine was imitating George Sand in keeping such a journal – and for that reason, wrote in French rather than in the Breton which might have seemed natural.'

'I cannot say how much I should like to see that –'

'I have a further surprise for you. I have made you a photocopy. To show to Professor Stern, and because I have such great admiration for your work on Melusina. And to make up for my absence and the closure of the archive. The photocopier is a great democratic invention. And we should share our information, should we not – it is a feminist principle, co-operation. I think you will be very surprised by the contents of this journal. I hope we may discuss their implications when you have read it. I shall say no more now. One should not spoil surprises.'

Maud expressed surprise and gratitude in some confusion. What Leonora would say was sharp in her mind. But curiosity and narrative greed were sharper.

The next day they drove through Brittany to the end of the earth, to Finistère. They drove through the forests of Paimpol and Brocéliande, and came to the quiet enclosed bay of Fouesnant, where they found a hotel at le Cap Coz, a hotel which combined the wind-battered ruggedness of the North with something dreamier and softer and more southern, which had a terrace and a palm tree, looking down through a copse of almost Mediterranean pines to a circling sandy bay and a blue-green sea. There, over the next three days, they read Sabine's journal. What they thought will be told later. This is what they read.

Sabine Lucrèce Charlotte de Kerçoz.
Journal Intime.
Begun, at the Manoir de Kernemet,

OCTOBER 13TH 1859.

The blank space of these white pages fills me with fear and desire. I could write anything I wished here, so how shall I decide where to begin? This is the book in which I shall make myself into a true writer; here I shall learn my craft, and here I shall record whatever of interest I may experience or discover. I have begged the notebook from my dear father, Raoul de Kercoz, who uses these bound volumes for his notes on folklore and his scientific observations. I began this writing task at the suggestion of my cousin, the poet, Christabel LaMotte, who said something that struck me most forcibly. 'A writer only becomes a true writer by practising his craft, by experimenting constantly with language, as a great artist may experiment with clay or oils until the medium becomes second nature, to be moulded however the artist may desire.' She said too, when I told her of my great desire to write, and the great absence in my daily existence of things of interest, events or passions, which might form the subject matter of poetry or fiction, that it was an essential discipline to write down whatever there was in my life to be noticed, however usual or dull it might seem to me. This daily recording, she said, would have two virtues. It would make my style flexible and my observation exact for when the time came – as it must in all lives – when something momentous should cry out – she said 'cry out' – to be told. And it would make me see that nothing was in fact dull in itself, nothing was without its own proper interest. Look, she said, at your own rainy orchard, your own terrible coastline, with the eyes of a stranger, with my eyes, and you will see that they are full of magic and sad but beautifully various colour. Consider the old pots and the simple strong platters in your kitchen with the eyes of a new Ver Meer come to make harmony of them with a little sunlight and shade. A writer cannot do this, but consider what a writer *can* do – always supposing the craft is sufficient.

I see I have written a page now, and all that is of value in it is the precepts of my cousin Christabel. That is only right – she is the most important person in my life at present, and moreover a shining example because she is both an acknowledged writer of some importance and a woman, thus a sign of hope, a leader, for all of us. I am not sure how much she relishes this role – indeed I think I know very little of what she inwardly thinks and feels. She treats me, in the gentlest way possible, as though she were a governess and I were a tiresome charge, full of enthusiasms, never still, hopelessly ignorant of life.

If she resembles a governess I am sure that she resembles the romantic Jane Eyre, so powerful, so passionate, so observant beneath her sober exterior.

The last two sentences cause me to think of a problem. Am I writing this for Christabel to see, as a kind of *devoir* – a writer's exercises – or even as a kind of intimate letter, for her to read alone, in moments of contemplation and withdrawal? Or am I writing it privately to myself, in an attempt to be wholly truthful with myself, for the sake of truth alone?

I know *she* would prefer the latter. So I shall lock away this volume – anyway during its earliest life – and write in it only what is meant for my eyes alone, and those of the Supreme Being (my father's deity, when he does not seem to believe in much older ones, Lug, Dagda, Taranis. Christabel has a strong but peculiarly English devotion to Jesus, which I do not wholly understand, nor is it clear to me what her allegiances are, Catholic or Protestant).

A lesson. Work written only for one pair of eyes, the writer's, loses some of its vitality, but *en revanche* gains a certain freedom, and rather to my surprise, adult quality. It loses its desire, female as well as infantile, to *charm*.

I shall begin this work by describing Kernemet as it is today, at this hour, four on a dark, autumnal, misty afternoon.

I have spent all my short life – which has at times felt very long and dragging to me – in this house. Christabel was surprised, she said, both by its beauty and by its simplicity. No, I will not say what Christabel said, I will record what I myself notice of what is so familiar that in moods of *ennui* I hardly see it.

Our house is built of granite, like most of the houses on this coast, long and low, with high pointed slate roofs and *pignons*. It stands in a courtyard surrounded by a high wall, to create a space of quiet inside the wind, as much as to keep out anything. Everything here is built to stand in the streaming winds and beating rain off the Atlantic. The slate is more often glistening with wet than not. I love it also in the summer, when it can shine in the heat. Our windows are deep, and high-arched, like church-windows. Our house has only four major rooms, two upstairs, two down, each with two deep windows, on two walls, to provide light in all weathers. Outside also is a turret, with a dovecot above, and a place for dogs below. Dog Tray, however, and my father's brach, Mirża, live indoors. Behind the house, sheltered from the Ocean, is the orchard, where I played as a child, which then seemed infinitely spacious and now is cramped. It too is walled with a wall of dry stones and huge sea cobbles which, the peasants say, 'spend' the wind, breaking its force among innumerable holes and crannies. In storms, when the wind is in that quarter, the whole wall sings, a stony song like a pebble beach. The whole of this country is full of the song of the wind. When it blows, the people plant their feet more firmly, and so to speak, sing into it, the men deepening their bass, the women raising their tones.

(That is not badly put. And having written it, I am now full of a kind of aesthetic love of my countrymen and of our wind. I would go on, if I were a poet, to write the poem of its keening. Or if I were a novelist I could go on to say that in sober truth its monotonous singing can drive you half mad for silence, in the long winter days, like a man thirsting in a desert. The psalms sing with praise of the cool shelter of rocks in the hot sun. We here are athirst for a drop or two of dry, bright silence.)

In the house, at this time, three people are sitting quietly in three rooms, writing. My cousin and I have the two upper rooms –

she has the one that was my mother's room, where my father has never wanted me to be (nor indeed, have I myself). From these upper rooms it is possible to see across the fields, to the edge of the cliff, and the moving surfaces of the sea. That is, on a bad day, it moves, it heaves. On a good day, it is only the light that appears to move. Is this so? I must check. Another point of interest.

My father has one of the rooms downstairs, which is at once his library and his bedroom. Three walls of his room are lined with books, and he constantly grieves over the terrible effect of the damp sea air on their pages and bindings. When I was a girl it was one of my tasks to polish the leather covers with a preservative mixture of beeswax and I know not what else – gum arabic? terebinth? – which he had devised himself to protect them. This I did instead of embroidery. I can mend a shirt, I have had, of necessity, to learn that, I can do good plain white sewing – but of the more delicate feminine skills I have none. I remember the sweet smell of the beeswax as pampered young ladies may remember rosewater and essence of violets. My hands were supple and shining with it. In those days we lived largely, the two of us, in that one room, with a good fire, and a kind of pottery stove as well.

My father has the old style of Breton box-bed, like a great cupboard, with its own stairs and ventilated door. My mother's bed had heavy velvet hangings with braid and embroidery. My father asked me to clean these two months ago; he did not say why; I formed the mad idea that he had some project of marrying me, and was preparing my mother's room as a bridal chamber. When we took down the hangings they were heavy with dust, and Gode made herself very ill with beating them out in the courtyard, her lungs were stuffed with a lifetime's (*my* lifetime's) spiderwebs and filth. And then, when they were beaten, they were nothing, all their substance was gone with their encrustation, so that huge rents and ragged tatters appeared everywhere. Then my father said, 'Your cousin from England is coming, and new bed furniture must be had somewhere.' I rode all day to Quimperlé, and asked Mme de Kerléon, who gave me a set in serviceable red linen, for which she had, she said, no foreseeable need. They are embroidered with a border of lilies and briar roses, which my cousin likes very well.

These box-beds, the wooden chambers within chambers, of Brittany, are said to have been devised as protection against wolves. There are still some wolves roaming the high ground and the moorland in this part of the world, or wandering through the forests of Paimpol and Brocéliande. In the past, in the villages and farmhouses, it is said, these beasts used to come into the houses and snatch and carry off the sleeping infants in their cots by the hearth. So the peasants and farmers, to make quite sure of their young ones, would close them inside the box-beds and make the door fast before going out to the fields. Gode says this protects them also against wandering pigs with indiscriminate snouts and greedy hens who go in and out of the cottages and are not particular about what they tear or stab, an eye or an ear, a tiny foot or hand.

Gode used to terrify me when I was small with these terrible stories. I was afraid of wolves, day and night, and of werewolves too, though I cannot say I have ever seen a wolf, nor certainly heard one, though Gode has held up a finger on snowy nights when *something* has howled, and has said, 'The wolves are coming closer; they are hungry.' In this misty land the borderline between myth, legend and fact is not decisive, my father says, as a stone arch might be between this world and another, but more like a series of moving veils or woven webs between one room and another. Wolves come; and there are men as bad as wolves; and there are sorcerers who believe they control such powers, and there is the peasant's faith in wolves and in the need to put solid doors between the child and all these dangers. In my childhood the fear of the wolves was hardly greater than the fear of being closed in, out of the light, into that box which resembled, at times a chest or shelf in a family vault as much as a safe retreat (a hermit's cave when I played at being Sir Lancelot, before I learned I was only a woman and must content myself with being Elaine aux Mains Blanches, who did nothing but suffer and complain and die). It was so dark in that bed, I cried for the light, unless I was very ill or unhappy, when I would curl up in a small ball, like a hedgehog or sleeping caterpillar, and lie still as death, or the time before birth, or between autumn and spring (the hedgehog) or the crawling state and the flying (the grub).

I am now making metaphors. Christabel says that Aristotle says that a good metaphor is the sign of true genius. This piece of writing has come a long way, from its formal beginning, back in time, inward in space, to my own beginnings in a box-bed, inside the chamber inside the manor inside the protecting wall.

I have much to learn about the organisation of my discourse. I wanted, when I was writing about my father's bed, both to describe my mother's bed, which followed on, and to construct a disquisition or digression on box-beds and the borderland between fact and fancy which also followed on. I have not been wholly successful – there are awkward gaps and hops in the sequence, like too-great holes in the drystone wall. But something is done, and how *interesting* it all is, seen as craftwork which can be bettered, or remade, or scrapped as an apprentice piece.

What comes next? My history. The family history. Lovers? I have none, I see no one, I have not only formed no attachment and rejected no offer, I have never been together with anyone who could be thought of in that light. My father seems to think it will all settle itself by some gentle and inevitable process 'when the right time comes', which he believes is still far off – I believe, already almost past and lost. I am twenty years old. I will not write of that. I cannot control my thoughts, and Christabel says that this journal must be free from 'the repetitious vapours and ecstatic sighing of commonplace girls with commonplace feelings'.

What is clear is that I have described the house, in part, but not the people. Tomorrow, I shall describe the people. 'Action, not character, is the essence of tragic drama,' Aristotle said. My father and cousin were disputing about Aristotle over dinner last night; I have rarely seen my father so lively. I think *inaction* is the essence of tragic drama, in the case of many modern women, but I did not venture upon this near-epigram, as they were disputing in Greek, which Christabel learned from her father, but I do not know. When I think of mediaeval princesses running their households during the Crusades, or prioresses running the life of great abbeys, or St Theresa as a little girl going out to fight evil, as George Sand's Jacques says, I think a kind of softness has overcome modern life. De Balzac says that the new occupations of men in cities, their work in businesses, have turned women into pretty and peripheral *toys*, all silk, perfume and full of the *fantaisies* and intrigues of the boudoir. I would like to *see* silk floss and experience the atmosphere of a boudoir – but I do not want to be a relative and passive being, anywhere. I want to live and love and write. Is this too much? Is this declaration vapouring?

THURSDAY OCTOBER 14TH

Today I said I should describe the characters. I find I am afraid, that is the *mot juste*, of describing my father. He has always been there and it has always been only he who was there. My mother is not my mother but one of his tales, which in childhood I could not tell from truth, although he always scrupulously insisted that I be truthful. My mother came from the South, she was born in Albi. 'She missed the sun,' he would say. I have a clear image of her deathbed. She called to see me, he told me, she was wild with agitation over what would become of me, in this rough land, with no mother to care for me. She cried and cried, her force was spent even for living, to see the child, and when I was brought, she was calm, she turned her white face to me and was calm, he says. He says that he promised to be father and mother to me, both, and she said he would do better to marry again, and he said no, that could never be, he was one of those who only love once. He has tried to be father and mother to me both, but poor good man, he has not much skill at the practical side of things – he is gentle enough and kind, it is not that. It is more that he cannot make practical decisions as a woman would. And that he has no knowledge of what I fear. Or desire. But he took me in his arms with infinite gentleness when I was an infant, I remember that, he kissed and comforted me, and read me tales.

I see one of my faults as a writer will be a tendency to rush off in all directions at once.

I am afraid to describe my father because what is between us is accepted and unspoken. I hear his breathing in the house at night, I should know immediately if it faltered or stopped. I should know, I think, if anything happened to him, even if I were a great distance away. And he would know if I were in danger, or sick, I know. He appears to be very abstracted, very bound up in his work, but he has a sixth sense, an inner ear, which hears me. When I was a tiny child he would attach me to his desk with a great band of linen, like a long rope, and I would run in and out of his room and the great room quite contentedly. He has a book with an old emblem of Christ and the Soul where the Soul runs free in the household on just such a linen tie; he says it gave him the idea. I have since read *Silas Marner*, the story of an old bachelor who attaches a foundling to his loom in the same way. I feel his anger and his love as gentle tugs on that limiting linen band, whenever I think too rebelliously, or ride too fast. I do not wish to try to write of him too objectively. I love him like the air and the hearthstones, the wind-twisted apple tree in the orchard and the sound of the sea.

De Balzac always describes his people's faces as though they were painted by the Dutch masters. A snail-curly nose, indicating sensuality, an eye which has red fibrils in the white, a bumped brow. I can't so describe my father's eyes, nor his hair, nor his stoop. He is too close. If you hold a book too close to your face in poor candlelight, the characters blur. So with my father. His father, the *philosophe*, the Republican, I remember in the days of my early infancy. He wore his iron-grey hair long, as the Breton nobility used to do, and put it up with a comb. He had a good shapely beard, whiter than the hair. And leather gauntlets, in which he went out to visit, or attend weddings or funerals. The people called him Benoit, even though he was the Baron de Kercoz, as they call my father Raoul. They ask their advice, on matters about which they have no particular knowledge, and matters of which they know nothing. We are a little like bees in the beehive; all will not go well unless they are informed or consulted.

When Christabel came, my emotions were confused, like the waves at high tide, some still advancing, some falling back. I have never really had a female friend or *confidante* – even my nurse and the house-servants are too old and respectful to fulfil the second function, though I love them dearly, especially Gode. So I was ablaze with hope. But also I have never shared my father or my home with another woman, and was afraid I should not like this, afraid of nameless interferences or criticism or at the least embarrassment.

Perhaps I still feel all these things.

How to describe Christabel? I see her now – she has been here exactly one month – so very differently from when she arrived. I shall try first to recapture that first impression. I am not writing for her eyes.

She came on the wings of a storm. (Is that too romantic? It does not give a sufficient idea of all the volume of wind and water that were thrown at our house during that terrible week. If you tried to open a shutter, or step outside the door, the weather met you like an implacable Creature, intent on breaking and overwhelming.)

She arrived in the courtyard when it was already dark. The wheels on the paving stones made a grinding and unsteady noise. The carriage advanced – even inside the yard wall – in little swaying bursts. The horses had their heads down, and their coats were streaming mud and salt-white. My father ran out with his *roquelaure* and a tarpaulin: the wind nearly wrenched the carriage door out of his hand. He held it open, and Yann put down the steps, and a grey ghost slipped out in the gloom, a huge beast, silent and hairy, making a kind of pale space on the dark. And then behind this very large beast, a very small woman, with a hood and mantle and a useless umbrella, all black. When she was down the steps, she stumbled and fell, into my father's arms. She said, in Breton, 'Sanctuary'. My father held her in his arms, and kissed her wet face – her eyes were closed – and said, 'You have a home here for as long as you desire.' I stood in the door, fighting to hold it steady against the blast, with huge stains of rainwater spreading on my skirts. And the great beast pressed himself against me, trembling and muddying me even further with his wet coat. My father carried her in, past me, and put her down in his own great chair, where she lay, half-fainting. I came forward and said I was her cousin Sabine, and she was welcome: she seemed hardly to see me. Later, my father and Yann between them supported her up the stairs, and we saw no more of her until dinner the next evening.

I do not think I can say I liked her, at first. If that is so, it is at least in part because she seemed not to like me. I think I am an affectionate being – I believe I would attach myself lovingly to whoever offered me a little warmth, a human welcome. But whilst my cousin Christabel showed herself full of a near-devotion to my father, she seemed to look on me – how shall I say? – a little coolly. She came down to dinner that first time in a dark-checked woollen dress, black and grey, with a voluminous fringed shawl, very handsome, in dark green with a black trim. She is not elegant, but studiously neat and carefully dressed, with a jet cross on a silk rope around her neck, and elegant little green boots. She wears a lace cap. I do not know her age. Maybe thirty-five. Her hair is a strange colour, silvery-fair, almost metallic in its sheen, a little like winter butter made from milk from cows fed on sunless hay, the gold bleached out. She wears it – not becomingly – in little bunches of curls over her ears.

Her little face is white and pointed. I have never seen anyone so white as she was, that first evening (she is not much better now). Even the inner curl of the nostril, even the pinched little lips, were white, or faintly touched with ivory. Her eyes are a strange pale green; she keeps them half-hidden. She keeps her mouth compressed too – she is thin-lipped – so that when she opens it one is surprised by the size and apparent strength of her large, very regular, teeth, which are distinctly ivory in colour.

We ate boiled fowl – my father has ordered the stock to be put aside to restore her strength. We ate round the table in the Great Hall – usually my father and I have our cheese, and bowl of milk, and bread, by the fire in his room. My father talked to us about Isidore LaMotte and his great collection of tales and legends. He then said to my cousin that he believed she too was a writer. 'Fame,' he said, 'travels very slowly from Great Britain to Finistère. You must forgive us if we see few modern books.'

'I write poetry,' she said, putting her handkerchief to her mouth, and frowning a little. She said, 'I am diligent and I hope a craftsman. I have no fame, I think, of a kind that would have brought me to your attention.'

'Cousin Christabel, I have a great desire to be a writer. I have always had this ambition–'

She said, in English,

'Many desire, but few or none succeed,' and then, in French, 'I would not recommend it as a way to a contented life.'

'I never thought of it in *that* way,' I said, stung.

My father said, 'Sabine, like yourself, has grown up in a strange world where leather and paper are as commonplace and essential as bread and cheese.'

'If I were a Good Fairy,' said Christabel, 'I would wish her a pretty face – which she has – and a capacity to take pleasure in the quotidian.'

'You wish me to be Martha, not Mary,' I cried, with some little fire.

'I did not say that,' she said. 'The opposition is false. Body and soul are not separable.' She put her little handkerchief to her lips again and frowned as though I had said something to hurt. 'As I know,' she said. 'As I know.'

Shortly after that, she asked to be excused, and went to her bedroom, where Gode had set a fire.

SUNDAY

The pleasures of writing are various. The language of reflection has its own pleasure and the language of narration quite a different one. This is an account of how I came to have, in some measure, the confidence of my cousin after all.

The storm continued unabated for three or four days. After that first dinner she came down no more, but kept her room, sitting in the deep alcove of her arched window, which is cut into the granite, and looking out at not much, the sodden orchard, the wall of pebbles, merging into a thick wall of mist, with rounded forms on it, like mist-pebbles. Gode said she ate too little, like a sick bird.

I went in and out of her room as much as I dared without seeming to intrude, to see if there was anything we could do to add to her comfort. I tried to tempt her with a fillet of sole, or a little beef jelly, made with wine, but she would eat only a bare spoonful or two. Sometimes when I came in after an hour or two she would not have moved from her earlier position, and I would feel I had returned indecently quickly, or that for her time did not exist as it did for me.

Once she said, 'I know I am a great trouble to you, ma cousine. I am unrewarding and sick and small-minded. You should let me sit here, and think of other things.'

'I want you to be comfortable and happy here,' I said.

She said, 'God did not endow me with very much capacity for being comfortable.'

I was hurt that, although I have been running this house almost since I was ten years old, my cousin deferred to my father in all practical matters and thanked *him* for acts of foresight or hospitality of which he would have been quite incapable, though full of good will.

The big dog too, refused to eat. He lay inside her room, with his nose to the door, flat on the ground, rising stiffly twice a day to be let out. I brought titbits for him too, which he refused. She watched me try to speak to him, passively at first, without encouraging me. I persisted. One day she said,

'He will not respond. He is very angry with me, for taking him away from his home, where he was happy, and reducing him to terror and sickness on that boat. He has a right to be angry, but I did not know a dog could bear a grudge for so long. They are believed to be foolishly forgiving and even Christian towards those creatures who pretend to "own" them. Now I think he means to die, to spite me for having uprooted him.'

'Oh no. It is very cruel of you to say that. The dog is unhappy, not spiteful.'

'It is I who am spiteful. I plague myself and others. And good Dog Tray who never harmed any creature.'

I said, 'When he comes downstairs, I will take him out in the orchard.'

'He will not come, I fear.'

'And if he does?'

'Then your patience and kindness will have wrought something with my gentle dog, if not with me. But I believe him to be a one-man dog, or I should not have brought him. I left him for a little, recently, and he refused to eat until I returned.'

I persisted, and little by little he came more willingly, did the tour of the yard, the stables, the orchard, made himself at home in the hall, left his post at her door and greeted me with a push of his great muzzle. One day he ate two bowls of chicken soup his mistress had rejected, and waved his great tail in pleasure thereafter. When she saw this, she said, sharply enough,

'I see I was mistaken about his exclusive loyalty too. I should have done better to leave him where he was. All the magic glades of Brocéliande are not worth a good run in Richmond Park to poor Dog Tray. And he might have given comfort—'

Here she broke off. I affected not to notice, for she was obviously in distress and not given to confidence. I said,

'When the good weather comes you and I may take him walking in Brocéliande. We may make an excursion to see the wilderness of the Pointe du Raz and the Baie des Trépassés.'

'When the good weather comes, who knows where we may be?'

'Will you leave us then?'

'Where would I go?'

That was no answer, as both of us well knew.

FRIDAY

Gode said, 'In ten days, she will feel strong.' I said, 'Have you been giving her herb-stew, Gode?' for Gode is a witch, as we all know. And Gode said, 'I offered. But she would not.' I said, 'I will tell her your potions do nothing but good.' And Gode said, 'Too late. She will be better by Wednesday week.' I told Christabel this, laughing, and she said nothing, and then asked what Gode could magic? I told her, warts and colic and childlessness and women's pains, coughs and accidental poisoning. She can set a limb and deliver a child, Gode can, and lay out a corpse and resuscitate the drowned. We all learn that here.

Christabel said, 'And she never kills what she cures?'

346

I said, 'No, not to my knowledge, she is very scrupulous and very clever, or very lucky. I would trust my life to Gode.'

Christabel said, '*Your* life would be a great trust.'

'Or any man's,' I said. She frightens me. I see her meaning, and she makes me afraid.

As Gode predicted, she grew stronger, and when in the beginning of November we had three or four clear days, as can happen on this chancy changing coast, I drove her and Dog Tray to see the sea, in the bay at Fouesnant. I thought she might run with me along the beach, or climb rocks, despite a chill wind. But she simply stood at the edge of the water, with her boots sinking into the wet sand, and her hands tucked into her sleeves for warmth, and listened to the breakers and the gulls crying, quite still, quite still. Her eyes were closed when I came up with her, and with every breaker her brows creased in a little frown. I had the fanciful idea that they were beating on her skull like blows, and that she was *enduring* the sound, for reasons of her own. I went away again – I have never met anyone who so gave the impression that normal acts of friendliness are a deadly intrusion.

TUESDAY

I was still determined that we should talk about writing together. I waited until one day she seemed relaxed and friendly; she had offered to help me to darn sheets, which she does much better than I do – she is a fine needlewoman. Then I said,

'Cousin Christabel, it is *true* that I have a great desire to be a writer.'

'If that is true, and if you have the gift, nothing I can say will change the outcome.'

'You know that cannot be true. That is a sentimental thing to say, cousin, forgive me. Much could prevent me. Solitude. The lack of sympathy. The lack of faith in myself. Your contempt.'

'My contempt?'

'You judge me in advance, as a silly girl, who wants she knows not what. You see your idea, not me.'

'And you are determined I shan't persist in that error. You have one of the gifts of the novelist at least, Sabine, you persist in undermining facile illusions. With courtesy and good humour. I stand corrected. Tell me then, what do you write? For I suppose you *do* write? It is a métier where the desire without the act is a destructive phantom.'

'I write what I can. Not what I should like to write but what I know. I would like to write the history of the feelings of a woman. A modern woman. But what do I know of that, in these granite walls somewhere between Merlin's thorny prison and the Age of Reason? So I write what I know best, the strange and the fantastic, my father's tales. I have written down the legend of Is, for instance.'

She said she would be happy to read my story of Is. She said she had written an English poem upon the same subject. I said I knew a little English, not much, and should be glad if she would teach me some. She said, 'I will try, of course. I am not a good teacher, I am not patient. But I will try.'

She said, 'Since I came here, I have not attempted to write anything, because I do not know what language to think in. I am like the Fairy Mélusine, the Sirens and the Mermaids, half-French, half-English and behind these languages the Breton and the Celt. Everything shifts shape, my thoughts included. My desire to write came from my father, who was not unlike your father. But the language in which I write – my *mother-tongue* exactly – is not his language, but my mother's. And my mother is not a spiritual woman, and her language is that of household minutiae and female fashion. And English is a language full of little blocks, and solid objects and quiddities and unrelated matters of fact, and observation. It is my first language. My father said that every human being needs a *native tongue*. He withdrew himself and spoke to me only in English, in my earliest years, he told me English tales and sang me English songs. Later I learned French, from him, and Breton.'

This was the first confidence she made to me, and it was a writer's confidence. At the time, I did not think so much about what she had said about language, as about the fact that her mother was alive, for she said she '*is* not a spiritual woman.' She was in great trouble, so much was clear, and had turned not to her mother, but to us – to my father, that is, for I do not think I counted for anything in her decision.

SATURDAY

She read my story of King Gradlon, the Princess Dahud, the horse Morvak, and the Ocean. She took it away on the evening of October 14th and returned it two days later, coming into my room and putting it into my hands brusquely, with a funny little smile. She said, 'Here is your tale. I have not marked it, but I have taken the liberty of writing one or two notes on a separate sheet.'

How shall I describe the happiness of being taken seriously? I could see in her face when she took the tale that she expected to find sentimental vapourings and rosy sighs. I knew she would not, but her certainty overwhelmed mine. I knew I must be found wanting, one way or another. And yet I knew that what I had written was *written*, that it had its *raison d'être*. So I waited her inevitable disdain with half my soul, and with the other knew that it ought not to be so.

I seized the paper from her hands. I ran through the notes. They were practical, they were intelligent, they acknowledged what I had tried to do.

What I had meant was to make of the wild Dahud an *embodiment* as it were of our desire for freedom, for autonomy, for our own proper passion, which women have, and which it seems, men fear. Dahud is the sorceress whom the Ocean loves and whose excesses cause the City of Is to be engulfed (by that same Ocean) and drowned. In one of my father's mythological recensions the editor says, 'In the legend of the City of Is may be felt, like the passing of a whirlwind, the terror of ancient pagan cults and the terror of the passion of the senses, let loose in women. And to these two terrors is added the third, that of the Ocean, which, in this drama, has the role of Nemesis and fate. Paganism, woman and the Ocean, these three desires and these three great fears of man, are mingled in this strange legend and come to a tempestuous and terrible end.'

On the other hand, my father says, the name Dahud, or Dahut, in ancient times, signified 'The good sorceress'. He says she must have been a pagan priestess, akin to an Icelandic saga, or one of the virgin priestesses of the Druids in the Ile de Sein. He says even that Ys, maybe, is the vestigial memory of an other world where women were powerful, before the coming of warriors and priests, a world like the Paradise of Avallon, the Floating Isles, or the Gaelic Síd, the Land of the Dead.

Why should desire and the senses be so terrifying in women? Who is this author, to say that these are the fears of man, by which he means the whole human race? He makes us witches, outcasts, *sorcières*, monsters . . .

I will copy out some of Christabel's phrases which particularly pleased me. I should in all honesty copy out also those criticisms she made of what was banal or overdone or clumsy – but these are engraved on my mind.

Some comments of Christabel LaMotte on *Dahud La Bonne Sorcière* by Sabine de Kercoz.

'You have found, by instinct or intelligence, a way which is not allegory nor yet *faux-naïf* to give significance and your own form of universality to this terrible tale. Your Dahud is both individual human being and symbolic truth. Other writers may see other truths in this tale. (I do.) But you do not pedantically exclude.

All old stories, my cousin, will bear telling and telling again in different ways. What is required is to keep alive, to polish, the simple clean forms of the tale which *must* be there – in this case the angry Ocean, the terrible leap of the horse, the fall of Dahud from the crupper, the engulfment etc etc. And yet to add something of yours, of the writer, which makes all these things seem new and first seen, without having been appropriated for private or personal ends. This you have done.'

FRIDAY

After the reading, things went better. I cannot recount all, and yet we are now nearly at the present time. I told my cousin what a great relief it had been to me to have my work read as my work, and by someone who knew how to value it. She said this experience was rare in any writer's life, and one would do better neither to expect nor to rely on it. I asked her if she had a *good* reader and she frowned a little and then said briskly, 'Two. Which is more than we may hope for. One too indulgent, but with intelligence of the heart. One, a poet – a better poet –' She was silent.

She was not angry, but she would say no more.

I think it must happen to men as well as to women, to know that strangers have made a false evaluation of what they may achieve, and to watch a change of tone, a change of language, a pervasive change of respect after their work has been judged to be worthwhile. But *how much more* for women, who are, as Christabel says, largely thought to be unable to write well, unlikely to try, and something like changelings or monsters when indeed they do succeed, and achieve something.

She is like Breton weather. When she smiles and makes sharp, clever little jokes, one cannot imagine her otherwise – as the coast here may smile and smile in the sun, and in the sheltered coves at Beg-Meil may grow round pines and even a date-palm which suggest the sunnier south, where I have never been. And the air may be soft and gentle, so that, like the peasant in Aesop's tale, one takes off one's heavy coat, one's armour, so to speak.

She is much better, as Gode said she would be. She and Dog Tray go for long walks together, and also with me, when I am invited or when she accepts my invitation. She insists also on taking part in the daily life of the household, and it is in the kitchen, or mending by the fire, that we have our closest talk. We talk much of the meanings of myths and legends. She is very desirous of seeing our Standing Stones, which are some way away, along the cliff – I have promised to go there with her. I told her that the village girls still dance round the menhir, dressed in white, to celebrate May Day – they move in two circles, one clockwise, one widdershins, and whoever slackens and tires so that she falls, or touches the stone in any way, is mercilessly cuffed and kicked by the others, who all set on her as a flock of gulls will attack an intruder, or one of their own weaklings. My father says this rite is a relic of ancient sacrifice, perhaps Druidic, that the fallen one is a kind of sacrificial scapegoat. He says the Stone is a male symbol, a phallos; and the women of the village go to it in the dark night and clasp it, or rub it with certain preparations (Gode knows but Father and I do not) to have strong sons, or to have their husbands return safely. My grandfather said the church spire was only this ancient stone in a metamorphic form – a slate column, he said, instead of granite, that was all – and the women huddled beneath it like white hens, as in earlier times they danced before the other. I did not quite like to hear that said and hesitated to repeat it to Christabel, for she has Christian belief of some kind certainly. But I did say it, for her mind is fearless, and she laughed, and said it was so, the Church had successfully taken in and absorbed, and partly overcome, the old pagan deities. It was now known that many little local saints are *genii loci*, Powers who inhabited a particular fount or tree.

She said also, 'So the girl who stumbles in the dance is also the Fallen Woman and the others stone her.'

'Not *stone*, I said, not now, only blows with the hands or feet.'

'Those are not the most cruel,' she said.

What is strange is that she seems to have no life anywhere but here. It is as though she had walked in out of that storm like some selkie or undine, streaming wet and seeking shelter. She writes no letters and never asks if any have come for her. I know – I am not foolish – that something must have happened to her, something terrible, I imagine, from which she fled. I ask her nothing about that, for it is so very clear that she does not wish to be asked. But occasionally I arouse her anger, without meaning to.

For instance, I asked her about the curious name of Dog Tray and she began to tell me that he had been named as a joke, for a line in Wm Shakespeare's *King Lear* – 'The little dogs and all – Tray, Blanche and Sweetheart, see they bark at me.' She said, 'He used to live in a house where there was a Blanche and where I was jokingly called Sweetheart–' and then she turned her face away and would say no more, as though she choked. Then she said, 'In the nursery rhyme, of Mother Hubbard, in some versions, the Dog who finds the cupboard bare is called Dog Tray. Maybe he was truly named for that old woman's dog, who found nothing but disappointment.'

NOVEMBER I TOUSSAINT

Today the storytelling begins. Everywhere in Brittany the story-telling begins at Toussaint, in the Black Month. It goes on through December, the Very Black month, as far as the Christmas story. There are storytellers everywhere. In our village, the people gather round the workbench of Bertrand, the shoemaker, or Yannick, the smith. They bring their work and warm each other with their comfortable presences – or with the heat of the forge – and hear the messengers in the dark that is thick outside their thick walls, the unexplained crack of wood, or flap of wings, or creaking at worst, of the axles of the bumpy cart of the Ankou.

My father made a habit of telling me tales, every night during the two Black Months. This year will be the same, except that Christabel is here. My father's audience is not as numerous as Bertrand's or Yannick's and to tell the truth, his tale-telling is not as dramatic as theirs, it has that scholarly courtesy which is part of him, a pernickety insistence on accuracy – no Pam! or Pouf! of demon or wolf-man. And yet he made me believe absolutely in the creatures of his myths and legends, over the years. He would open his tale of the Fontaine Baratoun, the Fontaine des Fées, in the magical forest of Brocéliande, with a scholarly register of all its possible names. I can recite the litany: Breselianda, Bercillant, Brucellier, Berthelieu, Berceliande, Brecheliant, Brecelieu, Brecilieu, Brocéliande. I can hear him say, pedantic and mysterious, 'The place shifts its name as it shifts its borders and the directions of its dark rides and wooded alleys – it cannot be pinned down or fixed, any more than can its invisible inhabitants and magical properties, but it is always there, and all these names indicate only one time or aspect of it...' Every winter, he tells the tale of Merlin and Vivien, always the same tale, never twice the same telling.

Christabel says her father too, told her tales in winter. She seems ready to be part of our fireside circle. What will she tell? Once we had a visitor who told a dead tale, a neat little political allegory with Louis Napoleon as ogre and France as his victim, and it was as though a net had drawn up a shoal of dull dead fish with loose scales, no one knew where to look, or how to smile.

But she is wise and partly Breton.

'I could a tale unfold,' she said to me in English, when I asked if she would tell (I know that is *Hamlet*, it is the speech of the revenant and much *à propos*).

Gode always joins us and tells of the year's trafficking between this world and *that*, the other side of the threshold, which at Toussaint may be crossed in both directions, by live men walking into that world, and by spies, or outposts, or messengers sent from There to our brief daylight.

TOUSSAINT, LATE AT NIGHT

My father told the tale of Merlin and Vivien. The two characters are never the same in successive years. Merlin is always old and wise, and clearsighted about his doom. Vivien is always beautiful, and various and dangerous. The end is always the same. So is the essence of the tale – the coming of the magician to the old Fairy Fountain, the invocation of the fay, their love beneath the hawthorns, the charming of the old man into telling her the spell which can erect round him a solid tower visible and tangible only to himself. But my father, within this framework, has many stories. Sometimes the fairy and the magician are true lovers, whose reality is only this dreamed chamber, which she, with his complicity, makes eternal stone of air. Sometimes he is old and tired and ready to lay down his burden and she is a tormenting daemon. Sometimes it is a battle of wits, in which she is all passionate emulation, a daemonic will to overcome him, and he wise beyond belief, and impotent with it. Tonight he was not so decrepit, nor yet so clever – he was ruefully courteous, knowing that her time had come, and ready to take pleasure in his eternal swoon, or dream or contemplation. The description of the Fairy Fountain, with its cold dark boiling rings was masterly. So were the flowers which strewed the lovers' bed – my father was lavish with imagined primroses and bluebells; he made birds sing in dark hollies and yews, so that I remembered my childhood life which was lived *in* tales, so that I saw flowers and fountains and hidden paths and figures of power and despised – no, diminished in my mind, the life of real things, the house, the orchard, Gode.

When he had finished she said in a very small sharp voice,

'You are an enchanter yourself, Cousin Raoul, you make lights and perfumes in the dark, and spent passions.'

He said, 'I spread my skills, as the old magician did for the young fairy.'

She said, 'You are not old.' She said, 'I remember my father told that tale.'

'It is everyone's tale.'

'And its meaning?'

Then I was angry with her, for we do not talk of meanings in this pedantic nineteenth-century way, on the Black Nights, we simply tell and hear and believe. I thought he would not answer her, but he said, thoughtfully and courteously enough,

'It is one of many tales that speak of fear of Woman, I believe. Of a male terror of the subjection of passion, maybe – of the sleep of reason under the rule of – what shall I call it – desire, intuition, imagination. But it is older than that – in its reconciling aspect, it is homage to the old female deities of the earth, who were displaced by the coming of Christianity. Just as Dahut was the Good Sorceress before she became a destroyer, so Vivien was one of the local divinities of streams and fountains – whom we still acknowledge, with our little shrines to who knows what Lady –'

'I have always read it differently.'

'How, cousin Christabel?'

'As a tale of female emulation of male power – she wanted not him but his magic – until she found that magic served only to enslave *him* – and then, where was she, with all her skills?'

'That is a perverse reading.'

'I have a painting –' she said, 'which portrays the moment of triumph – *so* – perhaps it is perverse.'

I said, 'Too much meaning is bad at Toussaint.'

'Reason must sleep,' said Christabel.

'The stories come before the meanings,' I said.

'As I said, reason must sleep,' she said again.

I do not believe all these *explanations*. They diminish. The idea of Woman is less than brilliant Vivien, and the idea of Merlin will not allegorise into male wisdom. He is Merlin.

NOVEMBER 2ND

Today Gode told tales of the Baie des Trépassés. I have promised Christabel that in the good weather we may make a day's excursion there. The name, she says, moves her. It is not so much the Bay of the Dead as the bay of those who have crossed the barrier which divides this world from *that*. My father says that the name may not derive from any such otherworldly connection, but simply be the name given to this apparently wide and smiling beach where the shattered pieces of ships and men are tossed up after breaking against the terrible reefs of the Pointe du Raz and the Pointe du Van. But he says also that the Bay was always thought of as one of those places on the earth – as with Virgil's grove of the Golden Bough, or Tam Lin's journey under the Hill – where two worlds cross. From here the dead, in ancient Celtic times, would be sent out on their last journey to the Ile de Sein, where the Druid priestesses would receive them (no man was allowed to set foot on their island). And there, according to some legends, they found a way to the Earthly Paradise, the land of golden apples in the midst of winds and storms and dark blades of water.

I can't write down Gode's way of telling things. My father has from time to time encouraged her to tell him tales which he has tried to take down verbatim, keeping the rhythms of her speech, adding nothing and taking nothing away. But the life goes out of her words on the page, no matter how faithful he is. He said once to me, after such an experiment, that he saw now why the ancient Druids believed that the spoken word was the breath of life and that writing was a form of death. I thought of this journal, at first, to see how I might best follow Christabel's advice and record accurately what I heard, but my very intention in some strange way took life from my listening and from Gode's telling, so I desisted, from courtesy and something more. (Yet the *interest* has its life, there *must* be a way of writing.)

So now. I have something to tell which is not to do with Gode's tale, though it was then that. Start again. Write it like a story, write it to *write* it – how wise I was to keep this journal for my eyes only. For now I can write to find out what I saw.

And turn a kind of pain to a kind of interest, a kind of curiosity, which is to be my salvation.

Gode's stories, even more than my father's, depend on the outer dark and the closeness, indoors, of tellers and listeners. Our great hall is bleak and bare enough in the daylight, it does not make for intimacy. But at night in the Black Month it is different. We have the logs burning in the great chimney – flaring and fitful in the beginning of the evening, with black spaces where the fire has not caught – but in the later part, glowing with scarlet and golden cinders in a thick warm blanket of grey ash under the burning wood. And the great leather backs of the chairs make a kind of wall against the cold other end of the room, and the light of the fire gilds all our faces and reddens white cuffs and collars. We have no oil-lamps during these evenings – we work by the light of the fire, such work as can be done in such moving shadows, knitting, snipping, plaiting. Gode will even bring a cake she is stirring, or a bowl of roasted chestnuts to be peeled. But when she tells, she will raise her hands, or throw back her head, or shake her shawl, and long tattered shadows race across the ceiling into the dark of the unseen half of the room, or huge faces with gaping mouths and monstrous noses and chins – our own, transfigured by the flames into witches and spectres. And Gode's telling is a play with all these things, with the firelight and the gesturing shadows and the streamers of light and dark – she brings all their movements together as I imagine the leader of an orchestra may. (I have never heard an orchestra. I have heard one or two ladylike harps and the fifes and drums at the Kermesse, but all these sublime sounds I read of, I have to imagine at best through the church organ.)

My father sat in his high chair at the side of the fire, with ruddy lights in his beard, which is not all grey, and Christabel sat close beside him, lower, into the dark, her hands busy with knitting. And Gode and I were on the other side of the circle.

Gode said:

'There was once a young sailor who had nothing but his courage and his bright eyes – but those were *very* bright – and the strength the gods gave him, which was sufficient.

'He was not a good match for any girl in the village, for he was thought to be rash as well as poor, but the young girls liked to see him go by, you can believe, and they liked most particularly to see him dance, with his long, long legs and his clever feet and his laughing mouth.

'And most of all one girl liked to see him, who was the miller's daughter, beautiful and stately and proud, with three deep velvet ribbons to her skirt, who would by no means let him see that she liked to see him, but looked sideways with glimpy eyes, when he was not watching. And so did many another. It is always so. Some are looked at, and some may whistle for an admiring glance till the devil pounces on them, for so the Holy Spirit makes, crooked or straight, and naught to be done about it.

'He came and went, the young man, for it was the long voyages he was drawn to, he went with the whales over the edge of the world and down to where the sea boils and the great fish move under it like drowned islands and the mermaids sing with their mirrors and their green scales and their winding hair, if tales are to be believed. He was first up the mast and sharpest with the harpoon but he made no money, for the profit was all the master's, and so he came and went.

'And when he came he sat in the square and told of what he had seen, and they all listened. And the miller's daughter came, all clean and proud and proper, and he saw her listening at the edge and said he would bring her a silk ribbon from the East, if she liked. And she would not say if she liked, yes or no, but he saw that she would.

'And he went again, and had the ribbon from a silk-merchant's daughter in one of those countries where the women are golden with hair like black silk, but they like to see a man dance with long, long legs, and clever feet and a laughing mouth. And he told the silk-merchant's daughter he would come again and brought back the ribbon, all laid up in a perfumed paper, and at the next village dance he gave it to the miller's daughter and said, "Here is your ribbon."

'And her heart banged in her side, you may believe, but she mastered it, and asked coolly how much she was to pay him for it. It was a lovely ribbon, a rainbow-coloured silk ribbon, such as had never been seen in these parts.

'And he was very angry at this insult to his gift, and said she must pay what it had cost her from whom he had it. And she said,

'"What was that?"

'And he said, "Sleepless nights till I come again."

'And she said, "The price is too high."

'And he said, "The price is set, you must pay."

'And she paid, you may believe, for he saw how it was with her, and a man hurt in his pride will take what he may, and he took, for she had seen him dance, and she was all twisted and turned in her mind and herself by his pride and his dancing.

'And he said, if he went away again, and found some future in any part of the world, would she wait till he came again and asked her father for her.

'And she said, "Long must I wait, and you with a woman waiting in every port, and a ribbon fluttering in every breeze on every quay, if I wait for you."

'And he said, "You will wait."

'And she would not say yes or no, she would wait or not wait.

'And he said, "You are a woman with a cursed temper, but I will come again and you will see."

'And after a time, the people saw that her beauty dimmed, and her step grew creeping, and she did not lift her head, and she grew heavy all over. And she took to waiting in the harbour, to see the ships come in, and though she asked after none, everyone knew well enough why she was there, and who it was she waited for. But she said nothing to anyone. Only she was seen up on the point, where the Lady Chapel is, praying, it must be thought, though none heard her prayers.

'And after more time, when many ships had come and gone, and others had been wrecked, and their men swallowed, but his had not been seen or heard of, the miller thought he heard an owl cry, or a cat miawl in his barn, but when he came there there was no one and nothing, only blood on the straw. So he called his daughter and she came, deathly-white, rubbing her eyes as if in sleep, and he said, "Here is blood on the straw," and she said, "I would thank you not to wake me from my good sleep to tell me the dog has killed a rat, or the cat eaten a mouse here in the barn."

'And they all saw she was white, but she stood upright, holding her candle, and they all went in again.

'And then the ship came home, over the line of sea and into the harbour, and the young man leaped to the shore to see if she was waiting, and she was not. Now he had seen her in his mind's eye, all round the globe, as clear as clear, waiting there, with her proud pretty face, and the coloured ribbon in the breeze, and his heart hardened, you will understand, that she had not come. But he did not ask after her, only kissed the girls and smiled and ran up the hill to his house.

'And by and by he saw a pale thin thing creeping along in the shadow of a wall, all slow and halting. And he did not know her at first. And she thought to creep past him like that, because she was so altered.

'He said, "You did not come."

'And she said, "I could not."

'And he said, "You are here in the street all the same."

'And she said, "I am not what I was."

'And he said, "What is that to me? But you did not come."

'And she said, "If it is nothing to you, it is much to me. Time has passed. What is past is past. I must go."

'And she did go.

'And that night he danced with Jeanne, the smith's daughter, who had fine white teeth and little plump hands like fat rosebuds.

'And the next day he went to seek the miller's daughter and found her in the chapel on the hill.

'He said, "Come down with me."

'And she said, "Do you hear little feet, little bare feet, dancing?"

'And he said, "No, I hear the sea on the shore, and the air running over the dry grass, and the weathercock grinding round in the wind."

'And she said, "All night they danced in my head, round this way and back that, so that I did not sleep."

'And he, "Come down with me."

'And she, "But can you not hear the dancer?"

'And so it went on for a week or a month, or two months, he dancing with Jeanne, and going up to the Chapel and getting only the one answer from the miller's daughter, and in the end he wearied, as rash and handsome men will, and said,

'"I have waited as you would not, come now, or I shall wait no more."

'And she, "How can I come if you cannot hear the little thing dancing?"

'And he said, "Stay with your little thing then, if you love it better than me."

'And she said not a word, but listened to the sea and the air and the weathercock, and he left her.

'And he married Jeanne the smith's daughter, and there was much dancing at the wedding, and the piper played, you may believe, and the drums hopped and rolled, and he skipped high with his long long legs and his clever feet and his laughing mouth and Jeanne was quite red with whirling and twirling, and outside the wind got up and the clouds swallowed the stars. But they went to bed in good spirits enough, full of good cider and closed their bed-doors against the weather and were snug and tumbled in feathers.

'And the miller's daughter came out in the street in her shift and bare feet, running this way and that, holding out her hands like a woman running after a strayed hen, calling "Wait a little, wait a little." And *some* claimed to have seen a tiny naked child dancing and prancing in front of her, round this way, back widdershins, signing with little pointy fingers and with its hair like a little mop of yellow fire. And *some* said there was nothing but a bit of blown dust whirling in the road, with a hair or two and a twig caught in it. And the miller's apprentice said he had heard little naked feet patting and slip-slapping in the loft for weeks before. And the old wives and the bright young men who know no better, said he had heard mice. But he said he had heard enough mice in his lifetime to know what was and was not mice, and he was generally credited with good sense.

'So the miller's daughter ran after the dancing thing, on through the streets and the square and up the hill to the chapel, tearing her shins on the brambles and always holding out her hands and calling out "Wait, oh wait." But the thing danced on and on, it was full of life, you may believe, it glittered and twisted and turned and stamped its tiny feet on the pebbles and the turf, and she struggled with the wind in her skirts and the dark in her face. And over the cliff went she, calling "Wait, wait," and so fell to her death on the needle-rocks below and they got her back at low tide, all bruised and broken, no beautiful sight at all, as you may understand.

'But when he came out into the street and saw it, he took her hand and said, "This is because I had no faith and would not believe in your little dancing thing. But now I hear it, plain as plain."

'And poor Jeanne had no joy of him from that day.

'And when Toussaint came he woke in his bed with a start and heard little hands that tapped, and little feet that stamped, all round the four sides of his bed, and shrill little voices calling in tongues he knew not, though he had travelled the globe.

'So he threw off the covers, and looked out, and there was the little thing, naked, and blue with cold yet rosy with heat so it seemed to him, like a sea fish and a summer flower, and it tossed its fiery head and danced away and he came after. And he came after and he came after, as far as the Baie des Trépassés and the night was clear but there was a veil of mist over the bay.

'And the long lines of the waves came in from the Ocean, one after another after another, and always another, and he could see the Dead, riding the crests of them, coming in from another world, thin and grey and holding out helpless arms, and tossing and calling in their high voices. And the dancing thing stamped and tossed on and on, and he came to a boat with its prow to the sea, and when he came into the boat he felt it was full of moving forms pressed closely together, brimming over but unseen.

'He said there were so many Dead, in the boat, on the crests of the waves, that he felt a panic of terror for being so crowded. For though they were all insubstantial so he could put his hand this way or that, yet they packed around him, and shrilled their wild cries on the waves, so many, so many, as though the wake of a ship would have not a flock of gulls calling after it, but the sky and the sea solid with feathers, and every feather a soul, so it was he said, after.

'And he said to the dancing child, "Shall we put to sea in this boat?"

'And the thing was still and would not answer.

'And he said, "So far I have come, and I am very greatly afraid, but if I may come to her, I will go on."

'And the little thing said, "Wait."

'And he thought of her among all the others out on the water, with her thin white face and her flat breast and her starved mouth, and he called after her "Wait", and her voice howled back like an echo,

'"Wait."

'And he stirred the air, that was full of things, with his arms, and shuffled his clever feet among the dust of the dead on the boards of that boat, but all was heavy, and would not move, and the waves went rolling past, one after another, after another, after another. Then he tried to jump in, he says, but could not. So he stood till dawn and felt them come and go and well in and draw back and heard their cries and the little thing that said,

' "Wait."

'And in the dawn of the next day he came back to the village a broken man. And he sat in the square with the old men, he in the best of his manhood, and his mouth slackened and his face fell away and mostly he said nothing, except "I can hear well enough" or otherwise "I wait", these two things only.

'And two or three or ten years ago he put up his head and said, "Do you not hear the little thing, dancing?" And they said no, but he went in, and made his bed businesslike, and called his neighbours and gave Jeanne the key to his seachest and stretched himself out, all thin as he was and wasted, and said, "In the end I waited longest, but now I hear it stamping, the little thing is impatient, though I have been patient enough." And at midnight he said, "Why, there you are, then", and so he died.

'And the room smelled of apple blossom and ripe apples together, Jeanne said. And Jeanne married the butcher and bore him four sons and two daughters, all of them lusty, but ill-disposed for dancing.'

No, I have not told it like Gode. I have missed out patterns of her voice and have put in a note of my own, a literary note I was trying to avoid, a kind of prettiness or portentousness which makes the difference between the tales of the Brothers Grimm and La Motte Fouqué's *Undine*.

I must write what I saw, and worse, if I can, what I thought. As Gode's story went on, I saw Christabel knit faster and faster, with her shining head bent over her work. And then after a time she laid her work by, and put her hand to her breast and to her head, as though she was hot, or had not enough air. Then I saw my father take that wandering little hand and hold it in his. (It is not so little, neither; *that* is a poeticism; it is a strong enough hand, nervous but capable.) And she let him hold it. And when the tale was over, he bent his head and kissed her hair. And she put up her other hand and clung to his.

We looked so like a family, round that fire. I have been used to thinking of my father as old, old. And of 'my cousin' Christabel as a young woman something of my own age, a friend, a confidante, an example.

But she is in truth much older than I am, if still nearer in age to me than to him. And he is not old. She told him his hair was not grey, that he was not old like Merlin.

I do not want it that way. I wanted her to stay, to be a friend, to be a companion.

Not to replace me. Not to replace my mother.

Those are distinct things. I have not aspired to my mother's place, but my place is what it is because she is not there. And I do not want another to have the care of my father, or the first right to hear his thoughts or his discoveries.

Or steal his kiss, write it, that is what I felt, or steal his kiss.

I did not offer to embrace him when we went to bed. And when he put out his arms, I went in and out of them quickly, stiff and dutiful. I did not look to see how he received this. I ran up to my room, and closed the door.

I must guard myself from behaving improperly. I have no right to resent a natural kindness, to fear an event he might think I should welcome, for I have complained often enough of the dull life we lead here.

A thief in the night, I want to cry, a thief in the night.

Better write no more.

NOVEMBER

My father takes much pleasure in her company these days. I remember when I was glad when she began to talk to him, for I thought then she would not go away and our household would be livelier. She asks him good questions, better than I do, or did, for her interest is newer and she brings him new information, different reading, her father's and her own. Whereas all my ideas – save those which are mine, and do not interest him for he would see them as trivial and female and *ungrateful* – all my ideas that would interest him are his own. And of late, before she came, I have not shown much interest in all this, the eternal mist and rain and the angry Ocean and Druids and dolmens and all those old magics. I wanted to know about Paris, and walk its streets in trousers and boots and an elegant jacket, like Mme Sand, free and not in the vapourising solitude. So maybe I failed him, thinking of myself and thinking – in part – that he had failed me, not seeing I might have other needs. He treats her with such respect, his voice comes to life when he tells her things. He said today it did him so much good to feel her interest in his ideas. Those were his very words. 'It does me so much good to feel you take an interest in these recondite matters.'

They talked over our midday meal about the intersection of this world and that other. He said, as he has often said, that in our part of Brittany – la Cornouaille, l'Armorique – there is a persistence of the ancient Celtic belief that death is simply a step – a passage – between two stages of a man's existence. That there are many stages, and this life is one, and that many worlds exist simultaneously, round and about each other, interpenetrating perhaps here and there. So that in uncertain areas – the dark of night, or sleep, or the curtain of spray where the solid earth meets the running Ocean, which is itself always a threshold of death for men who cross and recross it – messengers might hover between states. Such as Gode's little dancing thing. Or owls or those butterflies who have been known to be blown in off the salt wastes of the Atlantic.

He said that the Druid religion as he understood it had a mysticism of *the centre* – there was no linear time, no before and after – but a still centre – and the Happy Land of Síd – which their stone corridors imitated, pointed to.

Whereas for Christianity this life was all, as the life, was our testing-ground, and then there were Heaven and Hell, absolute.

But in Brittany a man could fall down a well and find himself in a summer land of apples. Or catch a fish-hook on the bell tower of a drowned church in another country.

'Or walk through the gate of a barrow into Avallon,' she said. She said,

'I have been asking myself whether the current interest in the spirit-world is an indication that the Celts have the right view of these matters. For Swedenborg went into the world of spirits and saw, he says, successive states of being, all being purified, all with their own homes and temples and libraries in their own kinds. And of late there have been many moved to seek apparent messages from the debatable lands beyond the veil that separates this world from the next. I have seen a few small unexplainable acts, myself. Spirit-wreaths brought by unseen hands, shining white, of unearthly beauty. Messages tapped painfully out by little hands that found this mode of communication infinitely clumsy for their now-refined nature, and yet persisted, out of love for those left behind. Music played by invisible hands on an accordion placed under a velvet pall out of reach of all. Moving lights.'

I said, 'I do not believe that these drawing-room tricks have anything to do with religion. Or with whatever it is that we hear in our streams and fountains here.'

She seemed surprised at my vehemence.

'That is because you make the mistake of supposing that spirits dislike vulgarity as much as you do. A spirit may speak to a peasant like Gode, because that is picturesque, she is surrounded by Romantic crags on the one hand and primitive enough huts and hearths on the other, and her house is lapped by real thick moral dark. But if there are spirits, I do not see why they are not everywhere, or may not be presumed to be so. You could argue that their voices may well be muffled by solid brick walls and thick plush furnishings and house-proud antimacassars. But the mahogany-polishers and the drapers' clerks are as much in need of salvation – as much desirous of assurance of an afterlife – as poets or peasants, in the last resort. When they were sure in their unthinking faiths – when the Church was a solid presence in their midst, the Spirit sat docile enough behind the altar rails and the Souls kept – on the whole – to the churchyard and the vicinity of their stones. But now they fear they may not be raised, that their lids may not be lifted, that heaven and hell were no more than faded drawings on a few old church walls, with wax angels and gruesome bogies – they ask, what *is* there? And if the man in shiny boots and gold watch-chain or the woman in bombazine and whalebone stays, with her crinoline hoop-lifter for crossing puddles – if these fat and tedious people *want* to hear spirits as Gode does, why may they not? The Gospel was preached to all men, and if we exist in successive states, the materialists among us must waken in this world and the next. Swedenborg saw them sweat unbelief and rage like heaps of glistening maggots.'

'You move too quickly for me to argue,' I said sullenly enough, 'But I have read about table-turning and spirit rappings in Papa's magazines and I say it sounds like conjuring tricks for the credulous.'

'You have read accounts by sceptics,' she said, all fire. 'Nothing is easier to mock.'

'I have read accounts by believers,' I said staunchly. 'I have recognised *credulity*.'

'Why are you so angry, Cousin Sabine?' said she.

'Because I have never heard you say what was silly before now,' I said, and that was true, though doubtless it was not why I was angry.

'One may conjure real daemons with drawing-room conjuring tricks,' said my father, meditatively.

I have always thought of myself as an affectionate being. I have complained of not having enough people to love, or make much of. I do think it is true to say I have had no experience of hatred until this time. I dislike the hatred, which seems to come from outside myself and take possession of me, like some great bird fixing its hooked beak in me, like some hungry thing with a hot pelt and angry eyes that look out of mine that leaves my better self, with her pleasant smile and her serviceableness, helpless. I fight and fight and no one seems to notice. They sit at table and exchange metaphysical theories and I sit there like a shape-changing witch, swelling with rage and shrinking with shame, and they see *nothing*. And *she* changes in my sight. I hate her smooth pale head and her greeny eyes and her shiny green feet beneath her skirts, as though she was some sort of serpent, hissing quietly like the pot in the hearth, but ready to strike when warmed by generosity. She has huge teeth like Baba Yaga or the wolf in the English tale who pretended to be a grandmother. He gives her *my* tasks when she asks him for employment, and salts the wound by saying 'Sabine was finding all this copying burdensome, it is good to have other so-skilled hands and eyes.' He strokes her hair as he passes her, the coil on her neck. She will bite him. She will.

At the time I write this I know I am absurd.

And when I write *that*, I know I am not.

Today I set out for a long walk along the cliff. It wasn't a good day for a walk, there were great solid patches of mist and spindrift – and quite a powerful wind. I took Dog Tray. I did not ask her if I might. I took pleasure in the idea that he will follow me anywhere now, although she said he was a dog who loved exclusively and once only. He loves me, I am sure, and his mood suits mine, for he is a sorrowful and reserved sort of beast, he makes his way purposefully in the weather, but he does not play, or smile, as some dogs do. His love is a sad offer of trustfulness.

She came after me. That has never happened. All those times when I hoped she might come or follow, she never came, unless I begged, or cajoled for her own good. But when I walk to escape

her, she comes running after, hurrying a little without wishing to
be seen to hurry, in her great cape and hood, with the silly
umbrella flapping and creaking in and out in the wind and of no
particular use at all. That is human nature, that people come after
you, willingly enough, provided only that you no longer love or
want them.

There is the walk which passes all the monuments – the Dolmen,
the fallen menhir, the little Lady Chapel with its granite image
on its granite table, not so different from the rough stone of the
first two, and probably made from part of one or the other.

She caught me up and said,

'Cousin Sabine, may I go with you?'

'As you will,' I said, with my hand on the dog's shoulder. 'As
you please, of course.'

We walked a little, and she said, 'I fear I have offended you in
some way?'

'Not in the least, not at all.'

'You have all been so kind to me, I have truly felt I have found
a sanctuary, a kind of home, here in my father's country.'

'My father and I are glad of that.'

'I do not feel *you* are glad. I have a sharp tongue and a thorny
exterior. If I have said anything –'

'You have not.'

'But I have intruded into your peace? Yet you did not seem
wholly satisfied with your peace – in the beginning.'

I could not speak. I quickened my step and the dog loped after.

'All that I touch,' she said, 'is damaged.'

'As to that, I know nothing, for you have told me nothing.'

It was she who was silent, then, for a time. I walked quicker
and quicker; it is my country, I am young and strong; she had
some difficulty in keeping up.

'I cannot tell,' she said, after a time. Not plaintively, that is
not her way, but sharply, almost impatiently. 'I cannot make
confidences. It is not in me. I keep to myself, I survive in that
way, only in that way.'

And that is not true, I wanted to say, but did not. You do not
treat my father as you treat me.

'Perhaps you do not trust women,' I said. 'That is your right.'

'I *have* trusted women –' she began, and did not finish. Then
'That did harm. Great harm.'

She sounded portentous, like a sibyl. I went quicker. She sighed after a little and said her side hurt her, she would go back. I asked if she needed to be accompanied. I asked in such a way that pride must make her refuse, as it did. I put a hand out to the hound, and willed him to stay, which he did. I watched her turn back with her hand to her side and her head down into the wind, toiling a little. I am young, I thought, and should have added 'and bad', but did not. I watched her go and smiled. Part of me would have given almost anything for things to have been as they were before, for her not to be melodramatic and pitiful, but all I did was smile and then stride on, because I am at least young and strong.

Note by Ariane Le Minier
Here there are some pages missing, and what *is* written becomes perfunctory and repetitive. I have not made photocopies of the rest of this month until the evening of Christmas. You may see this material if you wish.

CHRISTMAS NIGHT 1859

We all went to hear Mass at the church at midnight. My Father and I always go. My grandfather would not enter the church; his principles were republican and atheist. I am not sure that my father's religious beliefs would please the Curé, if he were to discuss them with him, which he does not. But he believes strongly in the continuance of the life of the community, the Breton people, which includes Christmas and all its meanings, old and new. *She* says she is a member of the Church of England in England, but that here the faith of her fathers is the Catholic faith, in its Breton form. I think that the Curé would be surprised to know what she thinks also, but he seems to welcome her into his church, and respects her isolation. She has been going up to the church more and more during Advent. She stands in the cold, looking at the work of the sculptor of the Calvary, the crude figures carved with such effort out of intractable granite. Ours has a good St Joseph, holding the ass, on the way to Bethlehem (our church is dedicated to St Joseph). My father spoke of how in our country the animals in the barns have speech on the night of the Nativity, when all the world is reconciled to its maker in primeval innocence, as it was in the days of the first Adam. She said, the Puritan Milton, on the contrary, makes the moment of the Nativity the moment of the death of Nature – at least, he calls on the old tradition that Greek travellers heard the shrines cry out on that night Weep, Weep, the great god Pan is dead. I said nothing. I watched him put his cloak round her shoulders and lead her up to our place in the front of the Church, and saw it, God help me, as a prefiguration of our life to come.

It is always so beautiful when the candles are lit to signify the new world, the new year, the new life. Our heavy little church is not unlike the cave where the birth of Jesus is so often pictured. The people knelt and prayed, shepherds and fishermen. I knelt too, and tried to turn my confused thoughts into some kind of charity and goodwill, to pray in my way. I prayed, as I always pray, that the people would understand the spirit in which my father keeps those festivals only that he considers universal – for him, the nativity is the winter solstice, the turning of the earth to the light. The Curé is afraid of him. He knows he should remonstrate, and dare not.

I saw that she was not kneeling, and then that she was lowering herself, after all, rather carefully, as though she felt faint. When we were seated again, after the candles were lit, I looked to see if she was well, and understood. She was leaning back, in the corner of the bench, with her head against a pillar and her eyes and lips tightly closed, wearily closed, but not patiently. She was shadowed, the church-shadows swallowed her, but I saw she was pale. She had her hands clasped under her bosom, and some trick of the twist of her body, some ancient protectiveness in those hands made me see clearly what she had concealed and what I, a good countrywoman and mistress of a household, should have understood long ago. I have seen too many women hold their hands *so* to be mistaken. Leaning like that, I could see how she is stout. She came to us for sanctuary indeed. Much, if not all, is explained.

Gode knows. She is quick-eyed and wise about these things.

My father knows, I think, he must have known for some time, if not before she came. What he feels is pity and protectiveness, I see it now, I have read sentiments that did not exist except in my own fevered imagination.

What shall I say or do?

Dec. 31

I see I shall dare to say nothing to her. I went up to her room in the afternoon, with a gift of barley sugar and a book I had borrowed in earlier times before I grew angry. I said to her,

'I am sorry to have been so disagreeable, Cousin. I have been misunderstanding things.'

'Indeed,' she said, not so agreeably. 'I am glad you find it to be a misunderstanding.'

'Oh, I know how things are, now,' I said. 'I wish to be good to you. To help you.'

'You know how things are now, do you?' she said slowly. 'You know how things are. Do we ever know that about a fellow-creature? Tell me then, Cousin Sabine, *how do you think things are with me?*'

And she stared at me with her white face and her pale eyes, defying me to speak. If I had, if I had uttered it, what could she have done or said? It is so, I know it. But I stammered, I did not know what I meant, I believed I had made her unhappy, and then, as she stared on, I burst into tears.

'Things are well enough with me,' she said. 'I am a grown woman, and you are a young girl, full of the fancies and instability of youth. I can look after myself. I do not desire help from *you*, Sabine. But I am glad you are no longer so full of rage. Rage hurts the spirit, as I know to my cost.'

I felt she knew all, all I had suspected and feared and resented. And that she did not choose to forgive me. And then I was angry again, in my turn, and went out still weeping. For she says she does not need help, but she does, she has already requested it, that is why she is here. What will become of her? Of us? Of the child? Shall I speak to my father? I still feel she is like Aesop's frozen serpent. A figure of speech may get hold of your imagination even when its appositeness is worn away. In which case which of us is the serpent? But she looked at me so coldly. I wonder if she is a little mad.

[LATE JAN]

Today I made up my mind to speak to my father about Cousin Christabel's state. I have thought of it once or twice, but something has always prevented me. Possibly a fear that he too may reprove me. But the silence lies between me and him. So I waited until she had gone away to the church – any practised eye could tell her condition by now, for sure. She is too little in stature to disguise it.

I went in to my father and said very quickly, before I could be deflected from my purpose, 'I wish to talk to you about Christabel.'

'I have noticed, with regret, that you seem to show her less affection than you did.'

'As to that, I do not think she wants my affection. I misunderstood. I thought she was growing so close to you that I – that there was no space left for me.'

'That was most unjust. Both to her and to me.'

'I know now, for I have seen, father, I have seen her condition, which is unmistakable. I was blind, but now I see.'

He turned his face away to the window and said, 'I do not think we should speak of that.'

'You mean, you do not think I should.'

'I do not think we should.'

'But what is to become of her? Of the child? Are they to stay here always? I am the mistress of this house, I wish to know, I need to know. And I wish to *help*, Father, I wish to help Christabel.'

'The best way to help her seems to be by maintaining silence.'

He sounded puzzled. I said, 'Well, if you know what she intends, I am content, I will be quiet and say no more. I only wish to help.'

'Ah, my dear,' he said, 'I know no more than you do, of what she intends. I am as much in the dark as you are. I offered a home, as she requested – "for some time" was all she said in her letter. But she has not allowed me to speak of – the reason for her need. Indeed, it was Gode who enlightened me, very early. It may be that she will turn to Gode, when the time comes. She is our kin – we offered sanctuary.'

'She must speak of her trouble,' I said.

'I have tried,' he said. 'She turns it all aside. As though she wished to deny her state, even to herself.'

FEBRUARY

I have noticed that I have lost pleasure in this journal. For some time now it has been neither writer's exercise nor record of my world, only a narrative of jealousy and bafflement and resentment. I have noticed that writing such things down does not exorcise them, only gives them solid life, as the witch's wax dolls take on vitality when she warms them into shape before pricking them. I did not start this journal to be a confidante for my spying on another's private pain. Also I am afraid that it might be read, by accident, and misconstrued. So, for all these reasons, and as a kind of spiritual discipline, I shall give it up for the time being.

I am witnessing something so strange, so strange I must write about it, though I said I would not, in order to help myself to understand. My cousin is now so big, so ripe, so heavy, it must be soon, and yet she has allowed no word of discussion of her condition or her expectations. And she has us all under some spell, for no one of us dare take her to task, or bring into the open, to be spoken of, what is already in full view and yet hidden. My father says he has several times tried to make her speak of it, and has always been unable. He wants to tell her that the child is welcome, it is, as she is, our kin, whatever its origins, and we will care for it and see it is well brought up and wants for nothing. But he says he cannot speak, and this for two reasons. One, that she *daunts* him, she prohibits him absolutely with her eye and manner from opening the subject, and though he knows he is morally required to do so he cannot. The second is that he is truly afraid that she is mad. That she is somehow fatally split in two, and that she has not let her conscience and public self know what is about to happen to her. And although he feels she *must* be prepared he fears also to set about it wrongly and shock her into complete alienation and frenzy and despair, and perhaps kill both. He heaps little loving-kindnesses upon her, and she accepts all, gracefully, like some princess, as a kind of due, and talks to him of Morgan le Fay, Plotinus, Abelard and Pelagius as one rendering courteous payment for favours. Her mind is clearer than ever. She is quick and razor-sharp and witty. My poor father feels, as I do, a growing sense of madness in himself, to be driven by courtesy and what was once a pleasure into these elaborate disputations and recensions and recitations, when what should be talked of is solid flesh and practical provisions.

I said to him, she is not so unknowing, for her clothes have been let out, around the waist, under the arms, with firm enough lines of stitching, with intelligent care. He said he doubted but that was Gode's work, and we resolved that if we had neither courage nor hardness enough to confront Christabel we would at least find out what Gode knew, whether she had been privileged, as was possible, even probable, with any confidence. But Gode said no, the needlework was not hers, and Mademoiselle had always turned the conversation, as though she had misunderstood, when Gode had offered help. 'She drinks my tisanes, but as though she did it indulgently to please me,' Gode said. Gode said she had known cases like it, of women who had resolutely refused to know their state and yet had been brought to bed as sweetly and easily as any heifer in the barn. And others, she said, more gloomily, who had broken themselves up fighting, and so killed either or both, mother and child. Gode thinks we may leave it to her – she will know by certain sure signs when the time is come, and will give my cousin drinks to calm her, and then bring her to her senses all practically at the last. I think Gode has the measure of most men or women, at least where they are most animal and instinctive, but not at all certainly of my cousin Christabel.

I have considered writing her a letter, setting out our fears and knowledge, on the grounds that she reads easier than she speaks, and could reflect alone upon these careful words. But I cannot conceive how to cast such a letter, or how she would respond.

TUESDAY

During all this late time she has been very good to me, in her way, discussing this and that, asking to see my work, embroidering me, in secret, a little case for my scissors, a pretty thing with a peacock on it in blue and green silks, all eyes. But I cannot love her as I did, because she is not open, because she withholds what matters, because she makes me, with her pride or her madness, live a lie.

Today we were able to be in the orchard, under the cherry blossom, talking of poetry, and she brushed falling petals off her full skirt with apparent unconcern. She talked of *Melusina* and the nature of epic. She wants to write a Fairy Epic, she says, not grounded in historical truth, but in poetic and imaginative truth – like Spenser's *Faerie Queene*, or Ariosto, where the soul is free of the restraints of history and fact. She says Romance is a proper form for women. She says Romance is a land where women can be free to express their true natures, as in the Ile de Sein or Síd, though not in this world.

She said, in Romance, women's two natures can be reconciled. I asked, which two natures, and she said, men saw women as double beings, enchantresses and demons or innocent angels.

'Are all women double?' I asked her.

'I did not say that,' she said. 'I said all men see women as double. Who knows what Melusina was in her freedom with no eyes on her?'

She spoke of the fishtail and asked me if I knew Hans Andersen's story of the Little Mermaid who had her fishtail cleft to please

373

her Prince, and became dumb, and was not moreover wanted by him. 'The fishtail was her freedom,' she said. 'She felt, with her legs, that she was walking on knives.'

I said I had terrible dreams of walking on knives since reading that tale, and that pleased her.

And so she talked on, of the pains of Melusina and the Little Mermaid; and of her own pain to come, nothing.

Now I am clever enough to recognise a figure of speech or a parable, I hope, and I see that it could well be thought that she was telling me, in her own riddling way, of the pains of womanhood. All I can say, is that at the time it did not feel so. No, her voice flashed, with all the assurance of her needle when she sews, fabricating a pretty pattern. And under the dress I swear I saw *that* move, which was not her, and was not acknowledged by all her brightness.

APRIL 30

I can't sleep. I shall take the gift she gave me and *write* then, write what she has done.

We have been looking for her for two days. She went out yesterday morning to walk up to the church, as she has increasingly done over these last weeks. It turns out that the villagers have seen her, standing they say for long periods, and tracing the history of the life and death of the Virgin round the base of the Calvary, leaning against it to catch breath, tracing the little figures with her fingers 'like a blind woman' one said, 'like a carver' another said. And she has spent hours in the church praying too, or sitting quietly, that we knew, that all of us knew, we and the people, with her head covered with a black shawl and her hands clenched in her lap. They saw her yesterday, as usual, go in. No one saw her come out, but she must have come out.

We didn't begin to look until dinner-time. Gode came and stood in my father's room and said, 'I should take out the horse and trap, Monsieur, for the young woman is not back, and her time was near.'

And our minds filled with terrible pictures of my cousin fallen and in pain, perhaps in a ditch or a field, or maybe a barn. So we took out the horse and trap, and drove all along the roads, between the stone walls, looking into hollows and isolated huts, calling sometimes, but not often, for we felt a sort of shame, for ourselves that we had lost her, for her that she had strayed, in the state she was in. This was a horrid time, for all of us I know, for me most certainly. Every inch was painful – I think *uncertainty* is maybe more painful than any other emotion, it both drives one on and disappoints and paralyses, so that we went on in a mounting kind of suffocation and bursting. Every large dark patch – a gorse bush with a rag caught on it, an abandoned worm-eaten barrel – were objects of terrible hope and fear. We climbed up to the Lady Chapel and peered in through the mouth of the Dolmen, and saw nothing. And so we went on until it grew dark, and then my father said, 'Heaven forbid she has fallen over the cliff.'

'Perhaps she is with one of the village people,' I said.

'They would have told me,' said my Father. 'They would have sent for me.'

Then we decided to search the shore – we constructed great torches, as we do for times when boats are driven on the coast and there are survivors, or wreckage, to be picked up. Yannick built a small fire and my father and I ran from cove to cove, calling and waving our torches. Once I heard a crying sound, but it was only a disturbed gull's nest. We went on like that, without food, without respite, under the moon, until after midnight, and then my father said we must go home, news might have come in our absence. I said, surely not, they would have sent to find us, and my father said, they are too few to tend a sick woman and fetch us from here. So we went home with a sort of half-hope, but there was nothing and no one, except Gode, who had been conjuring the smoke, and said nothing would be known before the morrow.

Today we aroused the neighbourhood. My Father, his pride and his hat in his hand, knocked at all the doors and asked if anyone had knowledge of her – and all denied it, though it was established that she had been in the Church in the morning. The peasants came out and searched the fields and lanes again. My father went to see the Curé. He does not like to see the Curé, who is not an educated man, and embarrasses both himself and my father by knowing that he should try to argue with my father's religious views, which he must see as most irreligious. For he dare not argue – he would lose and he would lose respect in the neighbourhood, if it were known that he had interfered with M. de Kercoz, however much in the interest of his immortal soul.

The Curé said, 'I am sure Le Bon Dieu has good care of her.'

My father said, 'But have you *seen* her, mon père?'

The Curé said, 'I saw her in church this morning.'

My father thinks the Curé may know where she is. For he did

not offer to come out and join the searchers, as he should surely have done, if his mind had been unquiet? But then again, the Curé is fat and closed up in his fat, and unimaginative and stupid and might well have simply supposed that the searching was being adequately done by the young and agile. I said, 'How should the Curé know?' And my father said, 'She might have asked him for help.'

I could not imagine how anyone could ask the Curé for help, let alone in such a circumstance. He has staring eyes and a blubber mouth and lives for his stomach. But my father said, 'He visits the Convent of St Anne, on the road into Quimperlé, where the Bishop has made provision for the care of cast-out and fallen women.'

'He could not send her *there*,' I said. 'It is an unhappy place.'

Yannick's sister's friend, Malle, was brought to bed there, when her parents cast her off and no one claimed her child, for no one, it was said, could be certain whose it was. Malle claimed that the nuns pinched her and made her do penance of foul scrubbing and carrying all sorts of dirt, when she was barely delivered. The child died, Malle said. She went into service as a housemaid in Quimper, with a chandler's wife, who beat her unmercifully, and did not live long.

'Perhaps Christabel asked to go there,' my father said.

'Why should she do that?'

'Why should she do anything she has done? And where is she, for we have searched and searched? And no one has been cast up from the sea.'

I said we could at least ask the nuns. My father will drive down to the Convent tomorrow.

I feel sick at heart. I am afraid for her, and angry too, and sorry for my father, a good man burdened with grief and anxiety and shame. For now we all know, that unless she has had an accident, she has run away from our offer of shelter. Or else they suppose we cast her out, which is also a disgrace, as we never should.

But perhaps she is lying dead in some cave, or on the shore of some cove we cannot climb to. Tomorrow I will go out again. I cannot sleep.

MAY 1ST

Today my Father drove to the convent and back. The Mother Superior gave him wine, he says, and said no one answering Christabel's name or description had been brought to the convent that week. She said she would pray for the young woman. My father asked to be told if she found her way there. 'As to that,' said the nun, 'that depends on what the woman herself says, seeking sanctuary.'

'I wish her to know that we offer her, her and her child, a home with us, and care for as long as she requires it,' my father said.

And the nun: 'I am sure she must already know that, wherever she is. Perhaps she cannot come to you, in her trouble. Perhaps she will not, for shame, or for other reasons.'

My father tried to tell the nun about Christabel's mad obstinacy in silence, but she became, apparently, brusque and impatient, and turned him away. He did not like the nun, who, he says, enjoyed her power over him. He is much set back and depressed.

MAY 8TH

She is back. We were at table, my father and I, sadly enough, going over yet again our talk of where we might have looked, or whether she went away in the two carts or the innkeeper's trap that went through the village on that fateful day, when we heard wheels in the courtyard. And before we were up, there she was in the doorway. This second sight of her – a revenant in broad day – was more terribly strange than her first coming in the night and the storm. She is thin and frail, and she has pulled in her clothes with a great heavy leather belt. She is as white as bone, and all her bones seem to have dispossessed her flesh, she is all sharp edges and knobs, as though the skeleton were trying to get out. And she has cut off her hair. That is, all the little curls and coils are gone – she has a kind of cap of dull pale spikes, like dead straw. And her eyes look pale and dead out of deep hollows.

My father ran to her, and would have put his arms tenderly round her, but she put up a bony hand and pushed him back. She said,

'I am quite well, thank you. I can stand on my own feet.'

And so, with great care, and with what I can only call a proud creeping, she made her way, infinitely slowly, but always upright, to the side of the fire and sat down. My father asked if we should not carry her upstairs, and she said no, and repeated 'I am quite well, thank you.' But she accepted a glass of wine and some bread and some milk, and drank and ate almost greedily. And we sat round, open-mouthed, and ready to ask a thousand questions, and she said:

'Do not ask, I beg you. I have no right to ask favours. I have abused your kindness, as you must see it, though I had no choice. I shall not abuse it much longer. Please ask *nothing*.'

How can I write what we feel? She forbids all normal feeling, all ordinary human warmth and communication. Does she mean, that is, does she fear or expect, to *die* here, when she talks of not abusing our kindness much longer? Is she mad, or is she very clever and secret, is she working out a plan she has always had, since her coming here? Will she stay, will she go?

Where is the child? We are all in an agony of curiosity, which she has cleverly, or desperately turned against us, making it seem a kind of sin, prohibiting all normal solicitude and questioning. Is it live or dead? Boy or girl? What does she mean to do?

I will write here, for I am ashamed, and yet it is an interesting part of human nature, that it is impossible to love where there is such lack of openness. I feel a kind of terrible pity when I see her *thus*, with her bony face and cropped head and imagine her pain. But I cannot imagine it well, because she forbids it, and in a strange way her prohibition turns my concern into a kind of anger.

MAY 9TH

Gode said, if you take the shirt of a little child and float it on the surface of the *feuteun ar hazellou*, the fairy fountain, you may see if the child will grow to be lusty, or if it will be weak or die. For if the wind fills the arms of the shirt, and if the body of it swells and moves across the water, the child will live and flourish. But if the shirt is limp, and takes water, and sinks, the child will die.

My father said, 'Since we have neither child nor shirt, this divination is not much use.'

She made no little shirts, during those months, only pretty pen-cases and my scissor-case, and the mending of sheets.

She stays in her room mostly. Gode says she is not fevered, nor in decline, but very weak.

Last night I had a nightmare. We were by the side of a great pool, very black, with a surface like jet, lumpy, with a sheen on it. We were surrounded by hollies, a thick hedge of them – when I was a girl, we used to pick the leaves, and prick our fingers ever so slightly from thorn to thorn, moving around the circumference, 'Il m'aime, il ne m'aime pas.' I taught this to Christabel, who said holly was better for this game of chance, which in England is played with the petals of daisies, which they tear off, one by one.

In my dream I was afraid of the holly. I feared it as one automatically fears snakebite, if something rustles in the undergrowth.

In my dream we were several women by the edge of the water – as in many dreams it was not possible to see *how* many – I was aware of some behind my shoulders crowding me. Gode was launching a small parcel – at one point this was all swaddled and wrapped, like pictures of the hiding of Moses among the bulrushes. At another point it was a stiff little nightshirt, all pleated, which sailed out into the centre of the pool – there were no ripples – and then raised its empty arms and struggled with the air, and tried to heave itself out of the thick water, which swallowed it very slowly, more like mud or jelly than water, more like liquid stone, and all the time the thing twisted and waved its – so to speak – hands, for it clearly had *no* hands.

It is clear enough what all this is about. But the vision changes my sense of the shape of events. When I ask myself, now, what became of the child, I see the black obsidian pool, and the lively white shirt going down.

MAY 10TH

A letter came today for my father from M. Michelet, and enclosed in it one for Christabel. She took it composedly enough, as though she had been expecting it, and then when she saw it properly, caught her breath and put it aside, unopened. My Father says M. Michelet writes that it is sent by a friend, upon a hope rather than a certainty that Miss LaMotte might be with us. He asks us to return it to him, if she is not here, and it goes undelivered. All day she did not open it. I do not know when or if she did.

Note to Maud Bailey from Ariane Le Minier.

Dear Professor Bailey,

Here the journal ends, and the notebook almost ends. It is possible that Sabine de K. took it up in another book; if so, it has not yet been found.

I made up my mind not to tell you much of its content, as I wished you, perhaps a little childishly, to have the narrative shock and pleasure that I had from discovering it. When I return from the Cévennes we must compare notes, you and I and Professor Stern.

I was certainly under the impression that students of LaMotte believe her to have lived a secluded life, in a happy lesbian relationship with Blanche Glover. Do you know of any lover or possible lover who might have been the father of this child? The question imposes itself — was the suicide of Blanche connected to the history related in this text? Perhaps you can enlighten me?

I should also tell you that I have made efforts of my own to discover whether the child survived. The convent of St Anne was the obvious place to look, and I have been there and have convinced myself that there is no trace of LaMotte in their somewhat scanty records. (Much was cleared out under a zealous Mother Superior in the 1920s who believed dusty papers were an unnecessary waste of space and nothing to do with the timeless mission of the sisterhood.)

I still suspect the curé, if only because there is no one else, and I cannot quite believe the child was born and murdered in a barn. I imagine it may well not have survived, however.

I enclose a few English poems and parts of poems I found among Sabine's things. I have no access to any specimen of LaMotte's handwriting, but I think they may be hers, and confirm the view that all was not well?

Sabine's story after these events is part happy, part sad. She published the three novels I wrote of, of which La Deuxième Dahud *is much the most interesting, and depicts a heroine of powerful will and passions, an imperious mesmeric presence, and a scorn of the conventional female virtues. She is drowned in a boating accident, after having destroyed the peace of two households, and whilst pregnant with a child whose father may be her meek husband or her Byronic lover, who drowns with her. The strength of the novel is its use of Breton mythology to deepen its themes and construct its imaginary order.*

She married in 1863, after a prolonged battle with her father to be allowed to meet possible partis. *The M. de Kergarouet she married was a dull and melancholic person, considerably older than she was, who became obsessively devoted to her, and died of grief, it was said, a year after she died in her third child-bed. She bore two daughters, neither of whom survived into adolescence.*

I hope all this has been of interest to you, and that we may compare our findings at leisure at some later date.

May I say finally, as I hoped to be able to say during our brief meeting, how much I admire your work on liminality. I think from that point of view too, you will find poor Sabine's journal interesting. La Bretagne is full of the mythology of crossing-places and thresholds, as she says.

Mes amitiés
Ariane Le Minier

A page of scraps of poems. Sent by Ariane Le Minier to Maud
Bailey.

Our Lady – bearing – Pain
She bore what the Cross bears
She bears and bears again –
As the Stone – bears – its scars

The Hammer broke her out
Of rough Rock's ancient – Sleep –
And chiselled her about
With stars that weep – that weep –

The Pain inscribed in Rock –
The Pain he bears – she Bore
She hears the Poor Frame Crack –
And knows – He'll – come – no More –

It came all so still
The little Thing –
And would not stay –
Our Questioning –

A heavy Breath
One two and three –
And then the lapsed
Eternity –

A Lapis Flesh
The Crimson – Gone –
It came as still
As any Stone –

My subject is Spilt Milk.
A white Disfigurement
A quiet creeping Sleek
Of squandered Nourishment

Others in heavy Vase
Raise darkly scented Wine –
This warm and squirted White
In solid Pot – was mine –

And now a paradox
A bleaching blot, a stain
Of pure and innocent white
It goes to Earth again –

Which smelled of summer Hay
Of crunching Cow – Divine –
Of warm flanks and of love
More quiet, more still – than mine –

It runs on table top
It drips onto the Ground
We hear its liquid Lapse
Wet on soft dust its sound.

We run with milk and blood
What we would give we spill
The hungry mouths are raised
We spill we fail to fill

This cannot be restored
This flow cannot redeem
This white's not wiped away
Though blanched we seem

Howe'er I wipe and wipe
Howe'er I frantic – scour
The ghost of my spilled milk
Makes my Air sour.

CHAPTER TWENTY

I press my palms on
Window's white cross
Is that Your dark Form
Beyond the glass?

How do they come who haunt us
In gown or plumey hat
Or white marbling nakedness
Frozen – is it – That?

Their remembrances haunt us
A trick of a wrist
Loved then – automatic–
Caught at and kist

Gone now to what melting
Of flesh and bone
Infinite Graces
Bundled – in One

Do not walk lonely
Out in the cold
I will come to you
Naked and bold

And your sharp fingers
Featly might pick
Flesh from my moist bones
Touch at the quick –

My warm your cold's food–
Your chill breath my air
When our white mouths meet
It mingles – there–

C. LaMotte

Ordinarily, Mortimer Cropper would not have minded how long it took to wear down Sir George. In the end he would have been there, sitting inside the dilapidated mock-castle, listening to the little woes of the invalid wife (whom he had not met but imagined vividly, he had a vivid imagination; it was, well-regulated of course, his major asset in his craft). And at night he would have turned over the delectable letters, one by one, searching out their hints and secrets, passing them across the bright recording eye of his black box.

But now, because of James Blackadder, there was no time for patience and finesse. He must have those papers. He felt real pangs, a kind of famishing.

He gave his lecture, 'The Art of a Biographer', in a fashionable City church whose Vicar liked people to come, and eclectically made sure they did, with guitars, faith-healing, anti-racist rallies, vigils for peace and passionate debates on the camel and the eye of the needle, and sexuality in the shadow of Aids. He had persuaded the Vicar, whom he had met at an episcopal tea party, that biography was just as much a spiritual hunger of modern man as sex or political activity. Look at the sales, he had urged, look at the column space in the Sundays, people need to know how other people lived, it helps them to live, it's human. A form of religion, said the Vicar. A form of ancestor worship, said Cropper. Or more. What are the Gospels but a series of varying attempts at the art of biography?

He saw that the lecture, already scheduled, could be used. He wrote discreet letters to various academies, friendly and inimical. He rang up the Press and said that a major discovery was to be unveiled. He interested the directors of some of the new American banks and financial institutions that were expanding in the City. He invited Sir George, who did not reply, and the solicitor, Toby Byng, who said it would be very interesting. He invited Beatrice Nest, and saved her a front-row seat. He invited Blackadder, not because he thought he would come, but because he liked to imagine Blackadder's annoyance at receiving the invitation at all. He invited the US Ambassador. He invited the radio and the television.

*

Cropper loved lecturing. He was not of the old school, who fix the audience with a mesmeric eye and a melodious voice. He was a hi-tech lecturer, a magician of white screens and light-beams, sound-effects and magnifications. He filled the church with projectors and transparent cages of promptings which helped him, like President Reagan, to orchestrate with impromptu naturalness a highly complicated presentation.

The lecture, in the dark of the church, was accompanied by a series of brilliant images on the double screens. Huge oil-portraits, jewel-bright magnified miniatures, early photographs of bearded sages among broken arches of Gothic cathedrals, were juxtaposed with visions of the light and space of Robert Dale Owen University, of the sparkling sheen of the glass pyramid that housed the Stant Collection, of the brilliant little boxes which preserved the tresses of Randolph's and Ellen's woven hair, Ellen's cushion embroidered with lemon-trees, the jet brooch of York roses on its cushion of green velvet. From time to time, as if by accident, the animated shadow of Cropper's aquiline head would be thrown, as if in silhouette, across these luminous objects. On one of these occasions he would laugh, apologise, and say half-seriously, carefully scripted, *there* you see the biographer, a component of the picture, a moving shadow, not to be forgotten among the things he works with. It was in Ash's time that the intuition of historians became a respectable, even an essential object of intellectual attention. The historian is an indissoluble part of his history, as the poet is of his poem, as the shadowy biographer is of his subject's life...

At this point in the lecture Cropper had himself lit again, briefly. He spoke with careful simplicity.

'Of course, what we all hope for and at the same time fear, is some major discovery that will confirm, or disprove, or change at the least, a lifetime's work. A lost Shakespeare play. The vanished works of Aeschylus. Such a discovery was made recently when a collection of letters from Wordsworth to his wife were found in a trunk in an attic. Scholars had said that Wordsworth's only passion was his sister. They had confidently called his wife dull, and unimportant. Yet here, after all those years of marriage, were these letters, full of sexual passion on both parts. History has had to be rewritten. Scholars have taken humble pleasure in rewriting it.

'I have to make known to you that an event of similar magnitude has just taken place in the field in which I have the honour to work, the field of Randolph Henry Ash. Letters have been discovered between him and the woman poet, Christabel LaMotte, that are going to electrify – to *upheave* – the relevant associated fields. I cannot quote these letters – I have seen only a small few at this time. I can only express the hope that they may be freely made available to all scholars of all nations, for it is in the interest of international communication, free movement of ideas and intellectual property that they be most widely accessible.'

The finale of Cropper's lecture was a product of his passion. The truth was, he had come to love the bright transparencies of the things he had acquired, almost as much as the things themselves. When he thought of Ash's snuff-box, he thought, not of the weight of it in his hand, the cold metal warming in his own dry palm, but also now of the enamelled cover magnified on the screen. Ash had never seen such gilded birds of Paradise, such blooming grapes, such deep red roses, though all their colours had been fresher in his time. He had never seen the sheen on the pearly rim as the light touched it through Cropper's projector. At the end of the lecture, Cropper would present this object in hologram, floating in the church like a miraculously levitated object.

'Look,' he would say, 'at the museum of the future. The Russians are already stocking their museums, not with sculptures or ceramics, nor with copies in fibreglass or plaster, but with these constructions of light. Everything can be everywhere, our culture can be, is, worldwide. The original objects must be preserved where the air is best, where breath cannot harm them, as the cave-paintings at Lascaux have been damaged by those who came to marvel at them. With modern technology, mere possession of the relics of the past is of little importance. All that *is* of importance is that those entrusted with the care of these fragile and fading things should have the requisite skills – and resources – to prolong their life indefinitely, and to send their representations, fresh, vivid, even, as you have seen, *more* vivid than in the flesh, so to speak, journeying round the world.'

At the end of his lecture, Cropper would take out Ash's large gold watch, and check with it his own perfect timing: 50 minutes 22 seconds, this time. He had given up his naive youthful practice of publicly claiming the watch, with a little joke about continuity, Ash's time and Cropper's. For although the watch had been purchased with his own funds, it was arguable that by his own arguments it should be stowed away safely in the Stant cabinets. He had wondered once, about juxtaposing it, in his, its owner's hand, with a hologram of itself. But he saw that his emotions, which were violent, about Ash's watch, were private, not to be confused with his public appeals. For he believed the watch had come to him, that it had been meant to come to him, that he had and held something of R. H. Ash. It ticked near his heart. He would have liked to be a poet. He put it on the edge of the pulpit, to time his responses while he took questions, and it beat away cheerfully, whilst the Press took hold of the *Unknown Sex Life of Eminent Victorians*.

Meanwhile he followed up his vague memory that there had been mention of Christabel LaMotte in the papers of his ancestress, Priscilla Penn Cropper. He telephoned Harmony City and asked for a search to be done of P. P. Cropper's correspondence, which he had routinely copied into his computer archives. This produced, by Fax the next day, the following letter.

Dear Mrs Cropper,

I am sensible of yr kind Interest in me – across all the wild wastes – shrieking gulls and tossing Ice – of the Atlantic. Indeed it is as strange a thing – that You – in your pleasantly Hot desert – should have knowledge of my small struggles – as that the Telegraph should utter imperatives of Arrest, or sale of Men and Commodities – from Continent's Rim to Rim. But we live in a time of Change – I am told. Miss Judge, whose elegant Mind is habituated to the Gusts of the Invisible Powers, received an Intuition last night that the Veil of Flesh and Sense shall be rent away – there shall be no more Hesitation or gentle knocking on the Portal – but the Cherubim, the Living Creatures, shall walk the Earth, connected to us. And this she perceives as she perceives Matter of Fact — the moonlight and firelight in her quiet room — the cat — all sparks of electricity and Rays of starting hairs — coming in out of the Garden.

You say — you are told — that I have some Power — as a Medium. Indeed it is not so. I see not nor hear much that delights and pleasantly — Exhausts — the sensitive Motor — of Mrs Lees. I have seen Wonders worked by Her. I have heard Twangling Instruments — all diffused through the Air, now here, now there, and in all places at once. I have seen Spirit hands of great beauty, and felt them Warm my own, and melt, or Evaporate in my clasp. I have seen Mrs Lees Crowned with Stars, a true Persephone, a light in Darkness. I have seen also a cake of Violet soap go spiralling like an angry Bird above our heads and heard it utter a strange Hum. But I have no — Skill — it is not skill — I have no Attraction, I Magnetise no vanished beings — they come not — Mrs Lees says they will, and I have Faith.

· I have, it seems, a power of Scrying. I see Creatures — Animate and Inanimate — or Intricate Scenes — I have tried the Crystal Ball and also a Pool of Ink in a Dish — wherein I have seen these things: a Woman sewing, her face turned away, a great Gold Fish, whose every scale could be reckoned, an ormolu Clock I later — a week or more — first saw in its Solid Presence on the shelf of Mrs Nassau Senior — a suffocating Mass — of Feathers. These things begin — as points of Light — they cloud and thicken — and are present as it were solid.

You ask, as to my Faith. I do not know. I know true Faith when I meet it — as George Herbert who spoke daily to his Lord — chiding him for harshness it may be as:

> O that thou shouldst give dust a tongue
> To crie to thee
> And then not heare it crying!

But in his poem 'Faith' he does speak — of the Grave — and beyond — in great security.

> What though my bodie runne to dust?
> Faith cleaves unto it, counting ev'ry grain
> With an exact and most particular trust
> Reserving all for flesh again.

With what bodies, think you, with what corporeal nature come they, who crowd against our windows and are made solid in our thick air? Are they the bodies of the Resurrection? Are they, as Olivia Judge believes, manifest in temporary withdrawal of both Matter and Kinetic Force from the indomitable *medium? What do we clasp if we are granted the unspeakable Grace — of Clasping — again? Orient and immortal wheat, Mrs Cropper, incorruptible — or the simulacra of our Fallen Flesh?*

Dust falls from us daily as we walk, dust of us, lives a little in the air and is Trodden — we sweep away — Parts of Ourselves — and shall all these — jots and omicra — cohaere? O we die daily — and there — is it all reckoned and gathered, husks restored to gloss and bloom?

Flowers full — full of Scent — on our Tables — wet with the asperges — of this world — or that? But they wither and die, like any other. I have a Wreath — all brown now — of white rosebuds — will it bloom again — there?

And then I would ask of you, if you are wise, why those who come from, from that world — those visitants, those Revenants, those Loved Ones — why are they all so Singly and Singularly Cheerful in their mode of address? For we are taught that there is eternal progression — perfection by degrees — no sudden Bliss. Why may we not hear the Voices of Righteous Anger? We are guilty towards Them, we have Betrayed — for our own good — should they not Chide and be Terrible?

What constraint of Flesh or decorum renders them, I would inquire, so uniformly Saccharine, Mrs Cropper? Is there in our sad Age no wholesome Wrath, divine or human? As for me, I strangely hunger to hear — not assurances of Peace and Sanctification — but the True Human Voice — of wounds — and woe — and Pain — that I might share it — if it might be — as I should share it — as I would share All — with those I loved — in my earthly Life —

But I run on — maybe incomprehensibly. I have a Desire. I will not tell you what it is, for I am adamant I shall tell none — until — I have — the Substance of it.

A crumb, Mrs Cropper, of living dust, in my hand. A crumb. So far denied . . .

> Your friend, in thought,
> C. LaMotte

Cropper decided that this letter showed strong symptoms of derangement. He left its interpretation aside for the moment. It gave him a pang of pure hunting pleasure. He was on the scent. It was in the house of Miss Olivia Judge, at a seance of Mrs Lees, that Randolph Henry Ash had carried out what he had once, in a letter to Ruskin, called 'my Gaza exploit', a name by which the episode was generally known in scholarly circles since Cropper, in *The Great Ventriloquist*, had used it as a chapter heading. In fact this letter was Ash's only reference to the episode, which had presumably given rise to his poem, *Mummy Possest*. Cropper took down his copy of *The Great Ventriloquist* and looked up his reference:

I do not think you should allow yourself to be taken in by these ghouls and goblins who *play with* our most sacred fears and hopes, in the desire, often enough simply to enliven the humdrum with a *frisson*, or to compose, conduct and orchestrate as it were the vulnerable passions of the bereaved and the desperate. I do not deny that *human* and *inhuman* things are maybe made manifest at such times – tricksy little goblins may walk and tap and tremble inkwells – men and women in the dark may hallucinate, as is well known in the case of the sick or the wounded. We have all, my dear friend, an infinite capacity to be deceived by desire, to hear what we long to hear, to see what we incessantly form to our own eye or ear as gone and lost – this is a *near-universal* human feeling – easy to play upon, as it is most highly-strung and unstable.

I was at a seance, a week back, where I made myself *unpopular* to the point of hissing and scratching – by catching at a floating wreath which dropped wet drops on my brow, and finding I was clutching the hand of the medium – one Mrs Hella Lees, who, when not transported, is a sombre enough Roman-looking matron, with a pallid face and dark shadows under liquid blackish eyes – but who can twist and howl and thrash with her arms when the spirits lay hold on her, greatly facilitating the withdrawal of a few fingers from the precautionary hands that clasp hers on the table. We sat in the dark – moony light through the curtains, a glow in the hearth from a dying fire – and saw much the usual things, I suppose, hands appearing (with long trailing muslinish *drapes* over their joins) above the far edge of the table, a fall of hothouse flowers from the air, the shuffling advance of an armchair from a corner, and the patting of our knees and ankles by something *fleshy* and certainly warm. And winds in our hair and floating phosphorous lights, you may imagine.

I am convinced as I may be that we are all being practised upon – I will not say by a simple fraud – but by someone who lives by such practising. So I put up my arms, and fished and *pulled*, and down came the house of cards, as far as I am concerned, with a veritable clattering to the ground of travelling fire-irons and thudding of books and tablelegs and dissonant chords on the concealed accordions and clack of the tongue of the handbell – all, I *have no doubt*, connected to the person of Mrs Lees by a Lilliputian cat's-cradle of invisible threads. I have been much abused, since, for my Gaza exploit, and indeed called to task for a kind of mental destruction of spirit-matter and sensitive souls. A great bull in a china shop, I felt myself to be, amongst all the floating gauze and tinkling cymbals and soft perfumes. But *if it were so*, if the departed spirits were called back – what good does it do? Were we meant to spend our days sitting and peering into the edge of the shadows? Much is said of the experiences of Sophia Cotterell, who is said to have held her dead baby on her knee for a quarter of an hour whilst its hands patted its father's cheeks. If this is fraud, playing on a mother's harrowed feelings, it is wickedness indeed. But *if it is not* – and if the soft loading of the knee be not a goblin or a product of the imagination – does it not still make us tremble with a kind of sick distaste, to see such frenzied dwelling in the dark . . . ?

In any case, here was trickery . . .

Cropper thought fast. What if LaMotte, who seemed to be at the house of Olivia Judge, had also been present at the Gaza Exploit? An account of this seance existed also in *The Shadowy Portal*, the autobiographical reminiscences of Mrs Lees. As was her custom, Mrs Lees had protected the names of her clients and the private nature of the messages they had received. There had been twelve people at the seance, of whom three had retired into an inner room to receive particular communications, as the spirit guides had instructed through Mrs Lees. It was clear from Priscilla Cropper's correspondence that Olivia Judge, an active promoter of many good causes, had at that time housed a group of female searchers after enlightenment, in her house in Twickenham. Priscilla Cropper had been in regular communion with Mrs Judge, who sent her regular accounts of the marvels evinced by Mrs Lees, as well as of the progress of other good causes, meetings, for spiritual healing and Fourierist doctrine, the emancipation of women and the proscription of strong drink.

The group in Twickenham was known as the Vestal Lights, a name which Cropper thought to be an affectionate term used among its members, rather than anything more formal. It might be that Christabel LaMotte had joined the Vestal Lights. Cropper was catching up on the biography of LaMotte, hampered by lack of access to the Lincoln papers, and by an incapacity to read the Lacanian riddles in which feminist speculations were couched. He was at this stage unaware of the lost year of LaMotte's life, and not fully apprised of the circumstances of the death of Blanche Glover. He went to the London Library, at the top of which is an excellent shelf of spiritualist writings, and asked for *The Shadowy Portal*, which was out to another reader. He tried the British Library whose copy had been, he was informed by a polite note, destroyed by enemy action. He sent off to Harmony City for a microfilm, and waited.

James Blackadder, with none of Cropper's gusto, was picking his way through the London Library's *Shadowy Portal*. He too had begun in total ignorance of the movements of Christabel LaMotte, and lacked Cropper's certain knowledge of any connection between LaMotte and Hella Lees in 1861. But he had picked up an earlier reference to Mrs Lees in a letter Sir George had tried to intrigue him with, and he was engaged in a thorough re-reading of Ash's known work and life round the crucial months of 1859. He had read an article on *Actiniae*, or sea anemones, without enlightenment, and had noticed an absence of information about Ash in early 1860. He had reread *Mummy Possest* which he had always thought anomalous in its hostility to its female protagonist and by extension to women in general. He asked himself now if this hitherto unexplained burst of bitterness was connected to the poet's feelings about Christabel LaMotte. Or, of course, his wife.

The *Shadowy Portal* was a rich violet in colour, with gilded leaves and an embossed design on its cover, of a gilded dove, bearing a wreath, emerging from a keyhole-shaped black space. Inside, glued to the frontispiece, inside a frame of Puginesque arches, was a photograph of the medium, oval in shape. It showed a dark-skirted woman, seated at a table, her heavily beringed hands clasped on her lap, her beaded front hung with jet necklaces and a heavy funereal locket. Her hair, which hung about her face, was black and glossy, her nose aquiline and her mouth large. Her eyes, under heavy black brows, were deepset, and, as Ash had said, shadowed. It was a powerful face, strong-boned and fleshy together.

Blackadder leafed through the introductory matter. Mrs Lees came from a Yorkshire family with Quaker connections and had 'seen' grey strangers in an early Quaker Meeting, where she was accustomed to seeing threads and clouds of odylic light run about the heads and shoulders of the Elders. On visiting a pauper hospital, at the age of twelve, with her mother, she had observed thick clouds of dove-grey or purplish light hovering above the forms of the sick, and had been able accurately to predict who would die and who would recover. She had become entranced in a Meeting and had given an oration in Hebrew, a language of which she knew nothing. She had provoked winds in closed rooms, and had seen her dead grandmother perched on the end of her bed, singing and smiling. Rapping, table-shifting and written messages on slates had followed, and a career as a private medium. She had also had some success as a public speaker of Spiritual Discourses, under the control of her spirit guides, who were mostly a Red Indian girl called Cherry (an affectionate abbreviation of Cherokee) and a dead Scottish professor of chemistry, one William Morton, who had had a hard passage working out the debris of his spiritual scepticism before he realised his true nature and his mission to aid and inform those mortals still in the flesh. Some of these Discourses, on such topics as 'Spiritualism and Materialism', 'Physical Manifestation and Spectral Light', or 'Standing on the Threshold' were appended to the volume of reminiscences. These discourses, whatever their ostensible subject, all had a certain sameness – possibly the effect of trance – related to 'that protoplasm of human speech flavoured with mild cosmic emotion' which Podmore discovered in the 'dead level' style and sentiment of another inspired speaker.

Ash's Gaza Exploit had raised her to an unusual pitch of unforgiving wrath.

Sometimes you may hear a positive person say 'The spirits are never able to perform in my presence.' Very likely – very likely indeed! But it should be no boast. If it is a fact, it is almost a disgraceful one. The fact that any human beings can take with them an element of such positiveness, a scepticism of such power, that it may overcome the influence of a mind disembodied, is certainly not to the credit of the individual. A positive mind entering a circle or seance for the investigation of spiritualism is like introducing a ray of light into the dark compartment of the photographer when not wanted; or like taking up a seed from under the ground to see if it be growing; or like any other violent intervention in the processes of nature.

A positive mind may well say, 'Why can the spirits not show themselves in the light of day as well as in the dark?' Professor Morton's reply to this is that we see how many natural processes are subject to fluctuations in light and dark. The leaves of a plant do not produce 'oxygen' without *sunlight*, and Professor Draper has recently shown that the relative powers of different rays to decompose carbon move through the spectrum thus: yellow, green, orange, red, blue, indigo, violet. Now the spirits have steadily indicated that their materialisation is best effected in those rays which are at the blue and indigo and violet end of the spectrum. If a seance could be lit by a violet ray from a prism we might see marvels. I have found that a small quantity of indigo light from a thick pane of glass over a lantern allows our spirit friends marvellous freedom to bring us gifts of a solid kind, or to make themselves airy forms, for a time, from the substance of the *medium* and of the gases and solids present in the room. They cannot work in harsh light, and past centuries have known this by experiment. Do not ghosts appear at twilight, and the Celtic races meet the messengers of the dead in what they call the Black Month?

Now, a positive mind often brings with it a cloud of odylic fire of a disagreeable red or yellow colour, flaming and angry, which the medium and any other sensitive person may perceive. Or such a person may emit a kind of chill – like the cold rays from the fingers of Jack Frost – which may penetrate the atmosphere and prevent the aura, or the spiritual matter, from accumulating. I feel such freezing presences as a blow in my lungs, even before the cutaneous surface is aware of them. All exosmose action ceases, and the consequence is, there is no atmosphere out of which the spirit can produce manifestations.

Perhaps the most terrible example of the effects of such a presence on the delicate operations of spirit communication is the damage wreaked by the self-regarding behaviour of the poet, Randolph Ash, at a seance I held at Miss Olivia Judge's house, in the days when that group of marvellously sensitive women, the Vestal Lights, were gathered together under her roof for the purpose of sustained enquiry into spiritual Truth. Miss Judge has a beautiful house, Yew Tree Lodge, in Twickenham, near the river, and many marvellous things have happened there, many gatherings of the living and the departed, many signs and supremely comforting sounds and utterances. Elementals from the water play on her lawns and can be heard laughing at her window in the twilight. Her guests have been distinguished men and women: Lord Lytton, Mr Trollope, Lord and Lady Cotterell, Miss Christabel LaMotte, Dr Carpenter, Mrs de Morgan, Mrs Nassau Senior.

At the date I speak of, we were engaged in a series of profoundly illuminating talks with our spirit friends and guides, and many marvels had been vouchsafed to us. It was made known to me, I think by Lord Lytton, that Mr Ash was greatly desirous of attending a seance. When I demurred – for it is often harmful to disrupt a circle which is working well together – I was told that Mr Ash had experienced a recent loss, and was in great need of spiritual consolation and comfort. I was still doubtful, but the case was forcefully pleaded and I agreed. It was a condition on Mr Ash's part, that no one should know in advance of his identity or purpose in coming, so that, he said, he should not impinge on the naturalness of the circle. I agreed to this condition.

It is not too much to say that upon Mr Ash's entry into Miss Judge's drawing-room I felt a *blast* of sceptical cold in my face and a kind of choking fog in my throat. Miss Judge asked me if I felt quite well and I said I believed I felt a chill coming on. Mr Ash shook my hand nervously, and the electricity of his touch revealed a paradox to me – beneath the congealed ice of his scepticism burned a spiritual sensitivity and force of unusual power. He said to me in a jocular tone, 'So it is you who calls spirits from the vasty deep?' I told him, 'You should not mock. I have no power to summon spirits. I am their instrument; they speak through me, or not, as they please, not as I please.' He said, 'They speak to me too, through the medium of language.'

He looked about him nervously and did not address the rest of the assembled company, which included seven ladies and four gentlemen, as well as myself. Of the Vestal Lights, all were present, as at all the previous sittings, to wit, Miss Judge, Miss Neve, Miss LaMotte and Mrs Furry.

We sat around the table in near darkness, as was our custom.

Mr Ash was not next to me, but on the right of the gentleman beside me – as was our practice, we all clasped hands. I felt still the weight of cold in my lungs and throat, and had to cough repeatedly, so much so that Miss Judge asked if I were ill. I said I was prepared to try if our friends would speak, but I feared they would not, as the atmosphere was inhospitable. After a time I felt a terrible coldness creeping up my legs and my frame began to tremble greatly. Many trances are preceded by a moment of nausea and giddiness, but the trance into which I now fell was preceded by the shaking of approaching death, and Mr Ritter on my right remarked that my poor hands were as cold as stones. I have no more conscious memory of the events of that seance, but Miss Judge kept notes which I reproduce *as they stand*:

Mrs Lees shook all over and a strange raucous voice cried out, 'Do not force me.' We asked if it was Cherry and were told, 'No, no, she will not come.' We asked who it was again and were told 'Nobodaddy' with a horrible laugh. Miss Neve said the undeveloped spirits must be playing tricks on us. Then there was a violent cracking and rapping, and several of us felt our skirts lifted and our knees patted by spirit hands. Mrs Furry asked if Adeline, her baby daughter, was present. The horrible voice cried out, 'There is no child'. It then added, 'Curiosity killed the cat' and other silly phrases. A large book, from the table beside Mrs Lees, was flung across the room amidst laughter.

Miss Neve said that perhaps there was a hostile presence in the room. One of the other ladies present, who had never before displayed any skill as a medium, began to weep and laugh, crying out in German 'Ich bin der Geist, der stets verneint.' A voice spoke through Mrs Lees saying 'Remember the stones.' Someone present cried out 'Where are you?' and for answer we all heard the sound of flowing water and waves, with marvellous distinctness. I asked if there was a particular spirit present who wished to speak to one of our company. The answer came back through Mrs Lees, that yes, there was present a spirit who had had great difficulty in making itself known but might speak if anyone who felt themselves addressed were to follow the medium into the inner room. As she spoke, a marvellously sweet voice said, 'I bring gifts of reconciliation,' and a white hand was seen hovering above the table, carrying a marvellous white wreath, with the dew still fresh upon it, and surrounded by a crown of silvery lights. The medium slowly rose to go into the inner room, and two of the ladies, both much moved, and indeed sobbing, rose to follow her, when Mr Ash cried out, 'Oh, you shall not escape me', and snatched at the air, crying out 'Lights! Lights!' The medium collapsed in a dead faint, and another lady fell back in her chair and was soon seen, when the lights were put on, to be without consciousness. Mr Ash was clutching the medium's wrist, which he claimed had been transporting the wreath, though how *that* could be, considering where it fell, and where the 'gentleman' and the medium were found, defies understanding.

Now here was chaos, and considerable danger, all caused by Mr Ash's impulsive and destructive acts. Two delicate organisations disturbed – my own and that of the other lady, who was experiencing her first trance in these desperate circumstances. And the poet seemed quite unaware of the harm he might do to a disembodied mind attempting, heroically and with critical effort, to *materialise* itself in a new and experimental form. Miss Judge records that I myself lay with a chill and livid face, uttering deep groans. The poet meanwhile compounded his act of folly by releasing my wrist and rushing to the side of the other lady, seizing her by the shoulders, despite urgent assurances from the other Vestal Lights, that it was dangerous to disturb or startle a person so entranced. He was, they tell me, calling out in an uncontrolled and frantic manner, 'Where is the child? Tell me what they have done with the child?' I understood at the time that Mr Ash was enquiring after the spirit of a departed child of his own, but I am told that this could not be the case, as Mr Ash is childless. At this point a voice spoke through my lips, saying 'Whose were the stones?'

The other lady became very ill, very pale, her breathing irregular, her pulse weak and fluttering. Miss Judge asked Mr Ash to leave, which he refused to do, saying that he wanted an answer, and that he had been 'practised upon'. I came to my senses at this point and saw him; he looked most horrid and uncontrolled, with veins standing on his brow, and a most *thunderous* expression. All round him was a fiery mass of dull red actinic light, seething with hostile energies.

He seemed to me in that moment a *demon* and I asked, weakly, that he should be requested to leave. At the same time two of the Vestal Lights bore away the unconscious body of our friend. This lady *did not recover consciousness* for two whole days, to the great distress of the company, and when she did, seemed unable to speak and unwilling to eat or drink, so great was the shock to her delicate form of the terrible acts which had taken place.

Mr Ash nevertheless took it upon himself to communicate, *as a matter of fact*, to various persons, that he had detected 'cheating' at the seance, at which he represented his own position as that of a detached observer. He was far from that, very far, as I hope the account of Miss Judge, as well as my own, will bear witness. When he later wrote his cleverly insinuating poem, *Mummy Possest*, he was taken by the general public as a champion of *reason* against knavery. Happy are they who have been persecuted for truth's sake – I suppose we must say – but there is no harder blow to bear than *indirect malice*, bred I am sure of impotent disappointment, for Mr Ash's whole manner was that of a *seeker* betrayed by his own positivism into the frustration of any communication he might have received.

And for my pain, and that of the other afflicted lady, not a thought, not a flicker of regard!!

Blackadder had written to every public body he could think of who might be concerned with the Ash–LaMotte correspondence. He had lobbied the Reviewing Committee on the Export of Works of Art, and had requested an interview with the Minister for the Arts, which had resulted in a dialogue with an aggressive and not wholly gentlemanly civil servant, who had said that the Minister was fully apprised of the importance of the discovery, but did not believe that it warranted interfering with Market Forces. It might be possible to allocate some small sum from the National Heritage Trust. It was felt that Professor Blackadder might attempt to match this sum from private sponsorship or public appeal. If the retention of these old letters in this country is truly in the national interest, this young man appeared to be saying, with his vulpine smile and slight snarl, then Market Forces will ensure that the papers are kept in this country without any artificial aid from the state. He added, as he saw Blackadder to the lift, through corridors smelling faintly of brussels sprouts and blackboard dusters, like forgotten schools, that he had had to do Randolph Henry Ash for his A-Level, and hadn't been able to make head or tail of him. 'They did go on so, don't you think, those Victorian poets, they took themselves so horribly seriously?' he said, pushing the lift button, summoning it from the depths. As it creaked up, Blackadder said, 'That's not the worst thing a human being can do, take himself seriously.' 'So pompous, don't you think?' returned the young man, smoothly impervious, closing the professor into his box.

Blackadder, who had been immersed in *Mummy Possest* and the reminiscences of Hella Lees, felt grimly that Market Forces were invisible winds and odylic currents quite as wild and unpredictable as any interrupted by Ash's Gaza Exploit. He also felt that Mortimer Cropper had a direct line to infinitely more powerful Market Forces than he himself, in the lower depths of the Museum. He had heard about Cropper's sermon-lecture, invoking these. He was gloomily considering his next move, when he was telephoned by a television journalist, Shushila Patel, who had an occasional five minutes on the Arts on *Events in Depth*, a late-night news analysis programme. Ms Patel had taken against Cropper because he represented capitalist and cultural imperialism. She had asked around and had been told that James Blackadder was the expert to have on her programme.

At first Blackadder was quietly but fiercely excited at the idea of putting the power of television behind his cause. He was not a broadcasting academic; he had never written a review outside a learned journal, had never spoken on the radio. He made sheafs of notes, as he would do on a conference paper, on Ash, on LaMotte, on National Art Treasures, on the effect of the discovery of the letters on the wrong interpretations advanced in *The Great Ventriloquist*. It did not occur to him to ask if Cropper would be present in person; he envisaged the broadcast as a kind of potted lecture. As it approached he began to feel a chill of apprehension. He watched the television and observed politicians, surgeons, planners and policemen being sternly and volubly interrupted by hostile interviewers. He woke sweating from nightmares in which he was required to sit his Finals again at a moment's notice and with new papers on Commonwealth Literature and post-Derridean strategies of non-interpretation, or in which he was asked in a machine-gun stutter of rapid questions, what Randolph Ash had to say about Social Security cuts, the Brixton riots and the destruction of the ozone.

They sent a car for him, a Mercedes driven by a chauffeur with a patrician accent who looked as though Blackadder's mackintosh would dirty his clean cushions. This did not prepare Blackadder for the rabbit-warren of dusty cubicles and agitated young women in which he found himself on arrival. He sat bemused on a moquette bucket-couch, dating from the mid-1950s, staring at a water-cooler and clutching his copy of the Oxford Standard Ash. He was given a plastic cup of unpleasant tea, and told to wait for Ms Patel, who finally arrived, carrying a clipboard of yellow paper, and sat down beside him. She was extremely beautiful, fine-boned, with her black silk hair in a complicated knot and her neck decorated with a fine silver and turquoise lacy necklace. She wore a peacock blue sari, decorated with silver flowers, and she smelled of something lightly exotic, sandalwood, cinnamon? She smiled on Blackadder and made him feel, briefly, wholly welcome and desired. She then became businesslike, fetching out her pad and saying,

'Well, what's important about Randolph Henry Ash?'

Blackadder had an incoherent vision of his own life's work, a fine line here, a philosophical joke tracked down there, a sense of the shape of many men's interwoven thought, none of which would go bluntly into words. He said,

'He understood the nineteenth-century loss of religious faith. He wrote about history – he understood history – he saw what the new ideas about development had done to the human idea of time. He's a central figure in the tradition of English poetry. You can't understand the twentieth century without understanding him.'

Ms Patel looked politely baffled. She said, 'I'm afraid I never heard of him until I got onto this story. I did a literature course in my degree, but it was in modern American literature and Post-colonial English. So tell me why we should still care about Randolph Henry Ash?'

'If we care about history at all –'

'*English* history –'

'Not English. He wrote about Jewish history, and Roman, and

Italian, and German, and prehistoric, and – English of course–'

Why must the English now always apologise?

'He wanted to understand how individual people at any particular time saw the shape of their lives – from their beliefs to their pots and pans–'

'Individualism. I see. So why should we want to keep this correspondence in this country?'

'Because it may illuminate his ideas – I've seen some of the letters – he writes about the story of Lazarus – he was very interested in Lazarus – and about nature study, the development of organisms–'

'Lazarus,' repeated Ms Patel, blankly.

Blackadder looked rather wildly about his dimly-lit, porridge-coloured box. He was getting claustrophobia. He was wholly unfitted for one-sentence claims on behalf of Ash. He could not detach himself from Ash enough to see what was not known. Ms Patel looked a little despondent. She said, 'We've got time for three questions and a quickie to finish on. How about my asking you what is Randolph Ash's importance to our society now?'

Blackadder heard himself say, 'He thought carefully and didn't make up his mind in a hurry. He believed knowledge mattered–'

'Sorry, I don't understand–'

The door opened. A bright female voice said, 'I've brought your other speaker. This is right, isn't it, this is the last item on *Events in Depth*? This is Professor Leonora Stern.'

Leonora was resplendent and barbaric in a scarlet silk shirt and trousers, faintly Oriental, faintly Peruvian, with woven rainbow-coloured borders. Her black hair flowed on her shoulders, her wrists and ears and visible bosom were hung with suns and stars of gold. She shone in the small space by the water-cooler and emitted pulses of florid and musky scent.

'I expect you know Professor Stern,' said Ms Patel. 'She's the expert on Christabel LaMotte.'

'I was staying in Maud Bailey's apartment,' said Leonora. 'And they called her, and got me, that's how it was. I'm glad to know you, Professor. We've got things to discuss.'

'I've been asking Professor Blackadder a few questions about the importance of Randolph Ash,' said Ms Patel. 'I'd like to ask you the same questions about Christabel LaMotte.'

'Go ahead,' said Leonora, expansively.

Blackadder watched with a mixture of fine distaste, technical admiration and sheer trepidation as Leonora built up a memorable thumb-nail miniature Christabel. Great neglected poet, little lady with sharp eyes and a sharp pen, great and unflinching analyses of female sexuality, of lesbian sexuality, of the importance of the trivial... 'Good,' said Ms Patel. 'Excellent, a major discovery, isn't it? And I shall ask you at the end, what is the importance of this discovery – don't answer now. It's time to go to make-up, or almost. I'll see you in the studio in about half an hour.'

Left alone with Leonora, Blackadder was apprehensive. Leonora plumped down beside him, her thigh touching his, and took his copy of Ash from him, without asking.

'Better read this now, I guess. I've never gone much for Randolph Henry. Too male. Long-winded. Old hat—'

'No.'

'Obviously not. I tell you what, a lot of us are going to have to eat our words when this all gets out in the open, a whole lot of us. I should put this book away, Professor. Uh-hunh. I guess we've got *three minutes* to make out the importance of all this stuff to the great greedy public and that don't include illustrations. No, you've got to make out your Mr Ash to be the sexiest property in town. You've got to get them by the balls, Professor. Make 'em cry. Think what you got to say and get it said whatever that pretty creature out there tries to get you to say. If you get me—'

'Oh yes. I – get you.'

'*One* thing you'll get said in the time, and that's your lot, Professor.'

'I see that. Mmn. One thing—'

'One *sexy* thing, Professor.'

In Make-up, Blackadder and Leonora lay back together, side by side. He submitted to powder-puffs and paintbrush, thinking of the hands of morticians, watching the fine grey cobwebs round his eyes being blocked out by a fine brushload of Max Factor

Creme Puff. Leonora had her head back but spoke on, indifferently, to him and the girl.

'I like a lot of colour at the edge of the lids there — load it on, I can take it, I've got huge features and striking colouring, I can carry it off OK — as I was saying, Professor, you and I have to have a serious talk. I guess you're as keen as I am to know the whereabouts of Maud Bailey, hunh? That's great, how about some of that thundery dark pink under the brow here — and I'd like a manslaying scarlet lipstick, which on reflection I'll get out of my own bag, you have to be careful with communal body fluids these days, in the nicest possible way, of course — as I say, Professor, or as I didn't say, I've got a pretty good idea about where that young woman's gone — and your researcher with her — I showed her the way — have you got any of those metallic spangles you can dust on here and there, ma'am, I like to strike the odd shaft of light across the screen, show that the scholarly world's got its glitter... Red in tooth and claw I am now, Professor, but calm yourself, I'm not out to get *you*. I'm out to strike a blow for Christabel and a punch in the guts of that bastard Mortimer Cropper, who wouldn't have Christabel on his course and threatened to sue a dear friend of mine for defamation, he really did. I guess all this makes him look a bit of a fool?'

'Not really. These things happen.'

'Well you got to *say* it makes him look a fool, if you want to keep those papers, don't you?'

Shushila sat between her guests and smiled. Blackadder watched the cameras and felt like a dusty barman. Dusty grey between these two peacocks, dusty with face-powder — he could smell himself — under the hot light. The moment before the broadcast seemed eternal, and then suddenly, like a sprint race, they were all talking very rapidly and as suddenly silent again. He had only the vaguest recollection of what had been said. The two women, like gaudy parrots, talking about female sexuality and its symbols when repressed, the Fairy Melusina and the danger of the female, LaMotte and the love that dared not speak its name, Leonora's huge surprise when it seemed that Christabel might have loved a man. And his own voice: 'Randolph Henry Ash was one of the great love poets in our language. *Ask to Embla* is one of the great

403

poems of true sexual passion. No one has ever really known whom those poems were written for. In my view the explanation advanced in the standard biography always looked unconvincing and silly. Now we know who it was — we've discovered Ash's Dark Lady. It's the kind of discovery scholars dream of. The letters have got to stay in our country — they're part of our national story.'

And Shushila: 'You won't agree with *that*, Professor Stern? Being an American?'

And Leonora: 'I think the letters should be in the British Library. We can all have microfilms and photocopies, the problems are only sentimental. And I'd like Christabel to have honour in her own country, and Professor Blackadder here, who's the greatest living Ash scholar, to have charge of the correspondence. I'm not acquisitive, Shushila — all I want is a chance to write the best critique of these letters once they're available. The days of cultural imperialism are over, I'm glad to say . . .'

Afterwards Leonora took his arm. 'I'll buy you a drink,' she said. 'You need one, I guess. So do I. You did fine, Professor, better than I thought.'

'It was your influence,' Blackadder said. 'What I said was an awful travesty. I apologise, Dr Stern. I didn't mean to imply that you influenced me to travesty, I meant that you influenced me enough to make me articulate *at all* —'

'I know what you meant. I bet you like malt whisky, you're a Scot.'

They found themselves in a dim and beery bar, where Leonora shone like a Christmas tree.

'Now, let me tell you where I think Maud Bailey is . . .'

CHAPTER TWENTY-ONE

Mummy Possest

Look, Geraldine, into the stones of fire
I spread my hands out on the velvet cloth —
Come closer, child, if you would learn to scry
And read the hieroglyphics of my rings!
See, how the stones glow on the milky skin —
Beryl and emerald and chrysoprase —
The gifts of lords and ladies, which I prize
Not for their cost, but for their mystic sense
The subtle silent speech of Mother Earth.

Your hands, like mine, are sweetly soft and white.
I touch your fingers, and the electric spark
Springs twixt our skins — you sense it? Good. Now see
The shifting lights move on the stones and see
If any vision show itself to you
As, it may be, a mystic Face, all flushed
With floating radiance of actinic light,
Or, it may be, the interlacing boughs
Of God's unearthly Orchard of Desire.
What do you see? A spider-web of light?
That's a beginning. Soon the lines will form
The blessed showings of the Spirit World.
Lights are Intelligences in our minds, whose force
We no more comprehend than here, in these
Glittering jewels, we can say how rose
Or sapphire blue or emerald steady shines,
Or what makes all the brilliant colours glow
Along the throat of the Arabian bird,
Whilst here, in milder air, her neck is grey

Or in the Polar void a brilliant white.
Thus in God's Garden the stones speak and shine.
Here we may read their silences, or scry
Eternal forms in earthly blocks of light.

Take up the crystal ball, sweet Geraldine.
Gaze on the sphere. Observe how left and right,
Above, below, reverse themselves in this
And in its depth a glittering chamber lies
Like a drowned world with downward-pointing flames,
This room in miniature, all widdershins.
Look steadily, and you will see all shift
Under the veils of spirit vision, see
What is not *here*, but comes from o'er the bourn.
My face, reversed, shall bathe in rosy fronds
As in her rocky cave, *Actinia*
The sea-anemone, puts out a cloud
Of hidden halo of odylic force—
And after mine, you shall see other Forms
In other lights, come swimming into view,
You shall, I swear it. Still be patient.
The force is fitful, and the vital spark
Which kindles in the Medium and lights
Conductive channels for the venturesome
Friends in the Spirit, leaps and dies again
Like Will-o-the-Wisps, or marsh-lights flickering.

I have called you here to teach you certain things.
You made a good beginning, all agreed.
Last Sunday's trance was deep and absolute.
I held your fainting form against my breast
Whilst spirits jostled at those pretty lips
To speak their pure consoling speech, though *some*
Forced through their vileness that your innocence
Could never in its waking hours have framed
In thought or word. To these I cried 'Avaunt!'
And fought them off, and in my listening ear
I heard the spirit voices bell-like sing
That you were chosen as their crystal cup
Their bright translucent Vessel, where ev'n I
With all my weary wisdom, might drink deep
A draught of power, and sweetness to refresh.

I mean that now I choose you to conduct

My seances with me, my partner sweet,
My Helper now, and in some future time
Who knows, a Seeress of Power yourself.

You know the ladies who will come tonight.
The Baroness is exigent. She mourns
A fat pug dog, who gambols in the Fields,
The flowery fields Beyond, and can be heard
To yap in satisfaction, as it used.
Beware of Mr Holm. He is a Judge,
In whom the injurious Sprite of scepticism
Dies hard, and rears his head, once laid to rest,
At any sight or sound that's untoward.
Most promising – that is, in spiritual terms –
Most heart-torn, and most sorrowing, is the young
Countess of Claregrove, who has lost her child,
Her only son, a year since, when he was
Scarce more than lisping Babe of two years' growth
Snatched by a fever in a summer Tour.
His small voice has been heard in broken sounds –
He makes, he says, perpetual daisy-chains
In wondrous meadows – but she weeps and weeps,
And will not be consoled, and takes with her
Where'er she goes, a lock of his bright hair
Cut from his marble brow as he lay cold.
More than all else she longs to touch his hand,
To kiss his little cheek, to know he *is*
And was not claimed by Chaos and the Dark.
I tell you this because – I tell you this –
In fine, I tell you this, because I must
Explain how we, to whom the Spirits speak
Eke out their wayward signals and the gifts
Vouchsafed from time to time of sight and touch
And otherworldly hearing, with our own –
How shall I say? – manifestations
We fabricate to demonstrate their Truth.

Sometimes, 'tis true, our Visitors ring Bells,
Lights dance about the room, and heavenly Hands
Touch mortal flesh. Sometimes there are Apports –
Glasses of flowery wine, or fragrant wreaths,
Or snapping Lobsters from the ocean Deep.
Sometimes the Power falters and is dumb.

Yet on these blank days, when my aching frame
Is lumpish flesh of flesh and no voice sounds—
The anxious Seekers gather with their Cares,
Griefs unassuaged, and incredulities—
And I have asked the Spirits and been taught
A way of *helping out*, to improvise
Display and substitute the mysteries
And thus console the sad, and thus confound
The savage sceptics with a visible Proof.

White gloves and gossamer threads move and amaze
As disembodied hands do; angel-wreaths
Descend on finest threads from chandeliers.
And what one Medium may do, my sweet,
Two may improve on almost endlessly.
Your figure is so fairy-fine, my Love,
Could, at a pinch, glide between these two screens?
Your little hands in kidskin could take hold
In teasing mode, of sceptical male knees
Or stir a crinoline, or brush a beard
With a hint of wholesome perfume, could they not?

What's that you say? You do not like to lie?
I hope you may remember who you are
And what you were, a pretty parlour-maid
Whose mistress did not like her prettiness
Or soulful stare at the young man o' the house.
Who helped you then, I ask you, gave you home
And home's essential comforts, bread and clothes,
Discovered talents in you quite unguessed,
Cosseted you and turned your soulfulness
To use both spiritual and lucrative?
You are grateful? So I should suppose. Well then,
Let Gratitude hold ope the door to Trust!

Our small deceptions are a form of Art
Which has its simple and its high degree
As women know, who lavish on wax dolls
The skills and the desires that large-souled men
Save up for marble Cherubs, or who sew
On lowly cushions thickets of bright flowers
Which done in oils were marvelled at on walls
Of ducal halls or city galleries.
You call these spirit *mises en scène* a lie.

I call it artfulness, or simply Art,
A Tale, a Story, that may hide a Truth
As wonder-tales do, even in the Best Book.

Consider this. Arts have their Medium —
Coloratura, tempera, or stone.
Through medium of paint the Ideal Form
Of the Eternal Mother shows herself
(Though modelled maybe on some worthless wench
No better than she should be, we may guess).
Through medium of language the great Poets
Keep constant the Ideal, as Beatrice
Speaks still to us, though Dante's flesh is dust.
So through the Medium of this poor flesh
With sweats and groanings, nauseas and cries
Of animal anguish, the sublimest Souls
Make themselves known to those who sit and wait.
And through this self-same flesh, they urge the skills
That light the phosphor-matches, knot the threads
Or lift the heavy chair from off the rug.

The spirits weave them flesh and robes of air,
Of air and matter of my grosser breath
Whose warmth brushes thy brow in this my kiss —
And if one night they neither come nor weave —
Why you and I may make their motions felt
With subtle fingers and the self-same breath
Lifting the more corporeal veils of flesh . . .
You catch my meaning?

One night the flute is filled with spirit breath
Swooningly sweet. The next, my breath, or thine,
Tutored by them, must body forth their sound
Since they neglect to whistle, but the notes
The self-same notes breathe still the self-same sigh
Of sweet regret and sweeter hope to come —
Art tells a truth, sweet girl, though all her tales
Are lies i'the law-court, or the chemist's phial —
We must be artful for the spirit's truth
In which we're tutored by them, d'you see?

You must not stare at me with fair large eyes
Full of a question and a glittering tear.
Drink up this cordial glass of wildflower wine —

'Twill settle you – come near – compose yourself
And fix your eyes on mine, your hand in mine,
And feel us breathe together. So. When first
I mesmerised you, and your youthful soul
Opened itself to mine, as morning flowers
Open their cups to the warm Sun, I knew
You were a being set apart, a Soul
Responsive to my powers, and ductile too.
Look up into my eyes, I say. You see
The love of a good woman there, whate'er
The spirit lords may else reveal, my dear.
Draw in the influence fearlessly. Now drowse
And calm your pulses, whilst my stronger arm
Supports your softnesses. Here, Geraldine.
My love is merciless to do you good.

Know you not that we Women have no Power
In the cold world of objects Reason rules,
Where all is measured and mechanical?
There we are chattels, baubles, property,
Flowers pent in vases with our roots sliced off,
To shine a day and perish. But you see,
Here in this secret room, all curtained round
With vaguest softnesses, all dimly lit
With flickerings and twinklings, where all shapes
Are indistinct, all sounds ambiguous,
Here we have Power, here the Irrational,
The Intuition of the Unseen Powers
Speaks to our women's nerves, galvanic threads
Which gather up, interpret and transmit
The unseen Powers and their hidden Will.
This is *our* negative world, where the Unseen,
Unheard, Impalpable, and Unconfined
Speak to and through *us* – it is *we* who hear,
Our natures that receive their thrilling force.
Come into this reversed world, Geraldine,
Where power flows upwards, as in the glass ball,
Where left is right, and clocks go widdershins,
And women sit enthroned and wear the robes,
The wreaths of scented roses and the crowns,
The jewels in our hair, the sardonyx,
The moonstones and the rubies and the pearls,

The royal stones, where we are priestesses
And powerful Queens, and all swims with our Will.

All mages have been tricksters. We are no
More and no less than all High Priests have been
Holding the masses to the faith with shows
Of firework and magic to impress
With symbols of Heaven's brightness those dull eyes
Which won't conceive our meanings from our speech.
You are calmer now. That's good. That's good. I stroke
The blue veins in your arms with my ringed hands
And power flows from me to you. You feel
The benefit of it. You are calm. Quite calm.

You call yourself my Slave. Not so, my dear.
Avoid extravagance of phrase or tone
If you would taste success in this new Sphere.
You are my Pupil and my dear, dear friend,
You are, who knows, the next Sybilla Silt,
But now you must be decorous and show
Deference to the ladies, gentle tact
To the rough male-folk, bring them cups of tea
And smile, and listen, for we need to know
All that their innocent gossiping reveals.

Here, as you see, the gauze lies hid, and here,
The flowers to let fall, and here the gloves
Ready to make the airy passes with.

I need your help with Lady Claregrove's son.
She is almost mad to feel his touch, and grasp
The tiny fingers. If the room is dark –
And you creep – *so* – and rest your elbow – *so* –
Briefly – and touch her cheek – your fingers are
Most exquisitely dimpling and fine.
What's that you say? How can it do her hurt?
Her will to Faith's a good, and our small tricks
Our genial deceptions, strengthen *that*,
And so are good too, in their harmless way.
Here is a lock of hair – the housemaid's hair –
As golden as her son's, and just as fine –
Which at some aptest moment you let fall
You understand me – in her lap – or on
Her clutching fingers – that will do such good –

411

Will give such Happiness that you and I
May grow and prosper in its lovely warmth.
We shall have gifts and she her moment's hope,
Nay more, her certainty . . .

Caetera desunt

CHAPTER TWENTY-TWO

Val was in the stand at Newmarket, watching the empty track, straining her ears for the sound of the hooves, seeing the small bunch of dust and regular surging turn into a stream of shining muscle and brilliant silk, and then come past in a flash, bay, grey, chestnut, bay, so much waiting for so short a time of thundering life. And then the release of tension, the sweat-streaked beasts with flaring nostrils, the people congratulating or shrugging.

'Who won?' she said to Euan MacIntyre. 'It was so quick, I didn't see.' Though she had cried out with the rest.

'We won,' said Euan. 'He won, The Reverberator. He was great.'

Val flung her arms around Euan's neck.

'We can have a celebration,' said Euan. '25–1, not bad, we knew he would come good.'

'I bet on him,' said Val. 'To win. I put some money on White Nights, each way, because its name was nice, but I bet on him to win.'

'There,' said Euan.'You see I've cheered you up. Nothing like a gamble and a bit of action.'

'You didn't tell me it was so beautiful,' said Val.

It was a good day, an English day, palely sunny, with patches of mist out at the edges of vision, out at the invisible end of the track, where the horses gathered.

Val had had the idea that racecourses were like the betting shops of her childhood, smelling of beer and fag ends and, it seemed to her, sawdust and male piss.

And this was grass and clean air and a sense of cheerfulness, and the dancing lovely creatures.

'I don't know if the others are here,' said Euan. 'Want to look?'

Euan was part of a syndicate, two solicitors, two stockbrokers, who each owned a part of The Reverberator.

They made their way round to the winner's enclosure, where the horse stood and quivered under his rug, a bright bay with white stockings, streaked black with sweat, which rose from him in steam and joined the mist. He smelled marvellous, Val thought, he smelled of hay and health and effort which was – loose, which was free, was natural. She breathed his smell and he ruffled his nostrils and tossed his head.

Euan had talked to the jockey and trainer. He came back to Val with another young man, whom he introduced to her as Toby Byng, one of the partners. Toby Byng was thinner than Euan, with a freckled face and a small amount of curly fair hair, over his ears only. His bald patch was like a pink tonsure. He wore cavalry twill and affected an elegant waistcoat, a flash of dandified peacock under his town and country tweed jacket. He had a soft smile, briefly incoherent with pleasure, because of the horse.

'I'll buy you dinner,' he said to Euan.

'No, no, I'll buy you. Or at least, could we crack a bottle of champagne, now, because I've got other plans for tonight.'

The three of them wandered off, amiably, and bought champagne, and smoked salmon, and lobster salad. Val had not done anything that was simply designed for pleasure, she thought, since she could remember, unless you counted a film, or a pub-evening.

She looked at her programme.

'The horses' names are jokes. White Nights, by Dostoevsky out of Carroll's Alice.'

'We are literate,' said Euan. 'Whatever your sort might think. Look at The Reverberator. His sire was James the Scot, and his dam was Rock Drill – I think the idea was that drills reverberate and Henry James, the American, wrote a story or something called The Reverberator. A horse's name has to contain an allusion to the names of both its parents.'

'They are poems,' said Val, who felt increasingly full of pale gold goodwill and champagne.

'Val is interested in literature,' said Euan to Toby, having patently tried to think of a way of explaining Val that didn't include Roland.

'I'm by way of being a literary solicitor,' said Toby. 'Which isn't my line at all, I don't mind telling you. I've got involved in the most ferocious wrangle about a correspondence between dead poets that someone's just discovered. The Americans have offered my client huge sums for the manuscripts. But the English have got onto it, and are trying to have the whole lot declared of national importance, and stop the export. They seem to hate each other. I've had them both in the office. The Englishman says it will change the face of international scholarship. They only get to see specimen letters at a time – my client's a cranky old sod, he's not letting the whole collection out of his hands . . . And now the Press have got onto it. I've had TV journalists and gossip columnists phoning in. The English professor's gone to see the Minister for the Arts.'

'Love-letters?' said Euan.

'Oh yes. *Complicated* love-letters. They wrote a lot, in those days.'

'Which poets?' said Val.

'Randolph Henry Ash, whom we did at school, and I never made head nor tail of, and a woman I'd never heard of. Christabel LaMotte.'

'In Lincolnshire,' said Val.

'Oh yes. I live in Lincoln. You know about it?'

'Dr Maud Bailey?'

'Ah yes. They all want to see *her*. But she's disappeared. On holiday, no doubt. It's the summer vacation. Scholars do go away. She found them –'

'I used to live with an Ash scholar,' said Val, and stopped, wholly disconcerted by her own automatic past tense.

Euan put his hand over hers, and poured more champagne.

He said, 'If they are *letters*, there must be a complicated question of ownership and copyright.'

'Professor Blackadder has called in Lord Ash. He seems to own the copyrights on most of the Ash papers. But the American – Professor Cropper – has got the manuscripts of almost all the letters in his library – and he's the editor of the big edition of letters – so his claim makes sense. The Baileys seem to own the manuscripts themselves. Maud Bailey seems to have found them. Christabel was an old spinster who died in the room where the letters were found – hidden away in a doll's cot or something – Our client is very sore that he wasn't told – by Maud B – what they were *worth*–'

'Perhaps she didn't know.'

'Perhaps. They'd be quite glad, all of them, if she came back.'

'I shouldn't think she will,' said Val, looking at Euan. 'I should think she's got reasons for staying away.'

'All sorts of reasons,' said Euan.

Val had never ascribed Roland's sudden disappearance to anything other than a desire to be with Maud Bailey. She had, in a moment of rage, telephoned Maud's flat, only to be told by a rich American voice that Maud was away. When asked where, the voice said with a mixture of amusement and rancour, 'I am not privileged to know that.' Val had complained to Euan, who had said, 'But you didn't *want* him, did you, it was over?' Val had cried, 'How do you know that?' and Euan had said, 'Because I've been watching you and assessing the evidence for weeks now, it's my job.'

So here she was, staying with Euan, in the house by the stables. In the cool of the evening they walked round the yard, so well-swept, so orderly, with the large-eyed long heads peering out over the stable doors, and inclining gracefully to accept apples, with wrinkling soft lips and huge, inoffensive, vegetarian teeth. The low brick house was covered with climbing roses and wistaria. It was the sort of house where breakfast was kidneys, bacon, mushrooms, or kedgeree in silver dishes. The bedroom was designed, and full of cream and rose-coloured chintz, frothing around solid old furniture. Val and Euan made love in a kind of cavern of rosy light, and looked out of the open window onto the dark shadows and subdued night-scent of real roses.

Val looked down at the naked length of Euan MacIntyre. He was like his horse in reverse. All the central part of his body was pale – ranging from buff to very white. But his extremities were brown, as The Reverberator's were white. And he had the same face. Val laughed.

'Oh Love, be fed with apples while you may,' she said.

'What?'

'It's a poem. It's Robert Graves. I love Robert Graves. He stirs me up.'

'Go on, then.' He made her say it twice, and then recited it himself.

> 'Walk between dark and dark – a shining space
> With the grave's narrowness, though not its peace.'

'I like that,' said Euan MacIntyre.

'I didn't think –'

'You didn't think yuppies liked poetry. Don't be vulgar and simplistic, dear Val.'

'I'm sorry. I don't know – more to the point – why you like *me*.'

'We work together, don't we? In bed?'

'Oh yes –'

'One knows that sort of thing. And I wanted to see you smile. You were torturing a lovely face into an expression of permanent disappointment, and soon it would have been too late.'

'An act of charity.' Half in the Putney Val's voice.

'Don't be silly.'

But he had always loved mending things. Broken models, stray kittens, grounded kites.

'Look, Euan, I'm no good at being happy, I shall mess you up.'

'That depends on me. On me too, that is. O love, be fed with apples while you may.'

CHAPTER TWENTY-THREE

The irruption, or interruption, occurred at the Baie des Trépassés. It was one of Brittany's smiling days. They stood amongst the sand-dunes and watched the wide waves crawling in quietly from the Atlantic. The sea wove amber-sandy lights in its grey-green. The air was milk-warm, and smelled of salt, and warm sand, and distant sharp leaves, heather or juniper or pine.

'Would it be so magical, or sinister, without its name?' Maud asked. 'It looks bland and sunny.'

'If you knew about the currents you might find it dangerous. If you were a sailor.'

'It says in the *Guide Vert* that its name comes from a corruption of "boe an aon" (baie du ruisseau) into "boe an anaon" (baie des âmes en peine). It says that the City of Is was traditionally in those marshes at the river-mouth. Trépassés, trespassed, passed, past. Names accrue meaning. We came because of the name.'

Roland touched her hand, which took hold of his.

They were standing in a fold of the dunes. They heard, from beyond the next sandhill, a loud transatlantic cry, rich and strange.

'And that must be the Ile de Sein, right out there, I've always dreamed of seeing that place, where the nine terrible virgins lived who were called Seines or Sénas or Sènes after the island, which is *Sein*, which is a fantastically suggestive and polysemous word, suggesting the divinity of the female body, for the French use *sein* you know to mean both breasts and womb, the female sexual organs, and from that it has also come to mean a fishing-net

418

which holds fish and a bellying sail which holds wind, these women could control tempests, and attract sailors into their nets like the sirens, and they built this funeral temple for the dead druids — a dolmen I suppose it was, another female form, and whilst they constructed it there were all sorts of taboos about not touching the earth, not letting the stones *fall* to the earth, for it was feared the sun or the earth would pollute them or be polluted by them, just like the mistletoe, which can only be gathered without touching the earth. It has often been thought that Dahud Queen of Is was the child of one of these sorceresses, and when she became Queen of the Drowned City she became Marie-Morgane, a kind of siren or mermaid who drew men to their death, and it is thought she was a relic of a matriarchy as the Senes were, in their floating island. Have you read Christabel's *Drowned City*?'

'No,' said a male voice. 'It is an omission I must rectify.'

'Leonora,' said Maud.
'And Blackadder,' said Roland.

The two could be seen advancing towards the sea. Leonora's hair was loose, and as she came out of the shelter of the dunes, was lifted in dark snaking ringlets, by the small sea-wind. She wore a Greek sun-dress in very fine cotton, a swirl of tiny pleats, scarlet patterned with silver moons, held by a wide silver band of cloth above her ample breasts, exposing shoulders dark gold with the glare of no English sun. Her large and shapely feet were naked, and her toe-nails painted alternately scarlet and silver. As she advanced, the wind fluttered the pleats. She held up her arms, with a musical chime of catching bracelets. Behind her came James Blackadder, in heavy shoes and a dark parka over dark creased trousers.

'Over there must be Nantucket, and the soft green breast of the New World.'

'Fitzgerald can hardly have been talking about druidesses.'

'But he made the Earthly Paradise a woman.'

'A disappointing one.'

'Of course.'

★

Maud said, 'They must have got together and worked out where we were.'

Roland said, 'If they got *here*, they must have seen Ariane.'

Maud said, 'And read the journal. If Leonora wanted to find Ariane, she would have. And I take it Blackadder reads French.'

'They must be pretty mad with us. Tricking them, taking advantage, they're bound to think.'

'Do you think we should go and confront them? Or be confronted?'

'Do you?'

Maud put out both her hands and he took them.

She said, 'I think we should, and I think we *can't*. I think we must go. Quickly.'

'Where?'

'Back, probably.'

'Unenchanted?' said Roland.

'Are we enchanted? I suppose we must start *thinking* again, some time.'

'Not yet,' he said quickly.

'No, not yet.'

They drove silently back to their hotel. Turning out of its car park, as they came in, was a large black Mercedes. Because its windows were darkened, Maud could not see, as it passed by, whether Cropper had observed her at the wheel, or not. In any case, the Mercedes did not slacken its speed, but vanished, in the direction they had come from.

The hotel proprietress said, 'An American gentleman has been asking if you were here. He says he will dine here this evening.'

'We've done nothing wrong,' said Roland, in English.

'No one said we had. He wants to buy what we know, or find out if we know any more. He wants the letters. He wants to *have* the story–'

'I don't think we can stop him.'

'We can *not help* him, can't we? If we leave, now this minute. Do you think he saw Ariane?'

'He might be following Leonora. And Blackadder.'

'They can fight it out. They can find out the end of the story.

I feel it's bad, I feel I – at the moment I feel I – don't want to know. Later, perhaps.'

'We can go home, *now*. Pack our bags and go home.'

'We must.'

They had been in Brittany three weeks. They had supposed, when they made their precipitate flight, that they would spend such time as they stole, decorously in the university library at Nantes. Instead, they had found themselves, owing to the closure of the library and the absence of Ariane Le Minier, on holiday, on holiday together, and for the second time that summer. They had separate rooms – with the requisite white beds – but there was no doubt that there was a marital, or honeymooning aspect to their lingering. Both of them were profoundly confused and very ambivalent about this. Someone like Fergus Wolff would have known how to take advantage of this state of affairs, and would have assumed that it was natural for, indeed incumbent upon, him to take advantage. But Maud would not again willingly have gone anywhere with Fergus. And she had more than willingly set out with Roland. They had run away together, and were sharply aware of the usual connotations of this act. They spoke peacefully, and with a kind of parody of ancient married agreement of 'we' or 'us'. 'Shall we go to Pont-Aven?' one would placidly ask, and the other would answer, 'We might try to see the crucifix that was the original of Gauguin's Christ Jaune.' They did not, however, discuss this use of the pronoun, although both thought about it.

Somewhere in the locked-away letters, Ash had referred to the plot or fate which seemed to hold or drive the dead lovers. Roland thought, partly with precise postmodernist pleasure, and partly with a real element of superstitious dread, that he and Maud were being driven by a plot or fate that seemed, at least possibly, to be not their plot or fate but that of those others. And it is probable that there is an element of superstitious dread in any self-referring, self-reflexive, inturned postmodernist mirror-game or plot-coil that recognises that it has got out of hand, that connections proliferate apparently at random, that is to say, with equal verisimilitude, apparently in response to some ferocious ordering principle, not controlled by conscious intention, which would of course, being a good postmodernist intention, *require* the aleatory or the multivalent or the 'free', but structuring, but controlling, but driving, to some – to what? – end. Coherence and closure are deep human desires that are presently unfashionable. But they are always both frightening and enchantingly desirable. 'Falling in love', characteristically, combs the appearances of the world, and of the particular lover's history, out of a random tangle and into a coherent plot. Roland was troubled by the idea that the opposite might be true. Finding themselves in a plot, they might suppose it appropriate to behave as though it was that sort of plot. And that would be to compromise some kind of integrity they had set out with.

So they continued to discuss, almost exclusively, the problems of those dead. They sat over buckwheat pancakes in Pont-Aven, and drank cider from cool earthenware pitchers and asked the difficult questions.

What became of the child?

How or why, in what state of ignorance or knowledge, had Blanche been abandoned? How had Ash and LaMotte parted? Did Ash know of the possible child?

The letter returning the letters to Christabel was undated. When had that been sent? Had there been more contact? A long affair, an immediate rupture?

Maud was muted and saddened by the poems Ariane had enclosed. She interpreted the second to mean that the child had been born dead, and the 'spilt milk' poem to be an evidence of a terrible guilt, on Christabel's part, at the fate, whatever it was, of the infant.

'Milk hurts,' Maud said. 'A woman with milk who can't feed a child, is in pain.'

In terms of Christabel, she too discussed the parodying of plots.

'She wrote a lot about Goethe's *Faust* round about then. It's a regular motif, the innocent infanticide, in European literature at that time. Gretchen, Hetty Sorrel, Wordsworth's Martha in "The Thorn". Despairing women with dead babies.'

'We don't *know* it was dead.'

'I can't help thinking, if it was not destined to die, why did she run away? She had gone there for sanctuary. Why didn't she stay where she was safe?'

'She meant no one to know what happened.'

'There's an ancient taboo on seeing childbirth. Early versions of the Melusina myth have childbirth instead of the bath.'

'Repeating patterns. Again.'

They discussed also the future of the project, that is, of the research, without knowing where to go next. Back to Nantes was an obvious step, and they condoned their lingering on this ground. Maud said Christabel had stayed with friends in London in the early 1860s – she was unaware of the connection with the Vestal Lights. Roland remembered a glancing reference to the Pointe du Raz in Ash – '*tristis usque ad mortem*', Ash had said it was – but that was no guarantee he had come there.

Beyond the future of the project, Roland was worried about his own future. He would have been in a panic if he had allowed himself to think, but the dreamy days, the pearly light alternating with the hot blue, and something else, made it possible to leave thinking in abeyance. Things did not look good. He had simply walked out on Blackadder. He had done the same to Val, who was, he considered, unforgiving and dependent in equal proportion – he would have to go back to be berated, and then how could he leave, where would he go, how should he live?

Things had changed between them nevertheless. They were children of a time and culture which mistrusted love, 'in love', romantic love, romance *in toto*, and which nevertheless in revenge proliferated sexual language, linguistic sexuality, analysis, dissection, deconstruction, exposure. They were theoretically knowing: they knew about phallocracy and penisneid, punctuation, puncturing and penetration, about polymorphous and polysemous perversity, orality, good and bad breasts, clitoral tumescence, vesicle persecution, the fluids, the solids, the metaphors for these, the systems of desire and damage, infantile greed and oppression and transgression, the iconography of the cervix and the imagery of the expanding and contracting Body, desired, attacked, consumed, feared.

They took to silence. They touched each other without comment and without progression. A hand on a hand, a clothed arm, resting on an arm. An ankle overlapping an ankle, as they sat on a beach, and not removed.

One night they fell asleep, side by side, on Maud's bed, where they had been sharing a glass of Calvados. He slept curled against her back, a dark comma against her pale elegant phrase.

They did not speak of this, but silently negotiated another such night. It was important to both of them that the touching should not proceed to any kind of fierceness or deliberate embrace. They felt that in some way this stately peacefulness of unacknowledged contact gave back their sense of their separate lives inside their separate skins. Speech, the kind of speech they knew, would have undone it. On days when the sea-mist closed them in a sudden milk-white cocoon with no perspectives they lay lazily together all day behind heavy white lace curtains on the white bed, not stirring, not speaking.

Neither was quite sure how much, or what, all this meant to the other.

Neither dared ask.

Roland had learned to see himself, theoretically, as a crossing-place for a number of systems, all loosely connected. He had been trained to see his idea of his 'self' as an illusion, to be replaced by a discontinuous machinery and electrical message-network of various desires, ideological beliefs and responses, language-forms and hormones and pheromones. Mostly he liked this. He had no desire for any strenuous Romantic self-assertion. Nor did he desire to know *who* Maud essentially was. But he wondered, much of the time, what their mute pleasure in each other might lead to, anything or nothing, would it just go, as it had just come, or would it change, could it change?

He thought of the Princess on her glass hill, of Maud's faintly contemptuous look at their first meeting. In the real world – that was, for one should not privilege one world above another, in the social world to which they must both return from these white nights and sunny days – there was little real connection between them. Maud was a beautiful woman such as he had no claim to possess. She had a secure job and an international reputation. Moreover, in some dark and outdated English social system of class, which he did not believe in, but felt obscurely working and gripping him, Maud was County, and he was urban lower-middle-class, in some places more, in some places less acceptable than Maud, but in almost all incompatible.

All *that* was the plot of a Romance. He was in a Romance, a vulgar and a high Romance simultaneously, a Romance was one of the systems that controlled him, as the expectations of Romance control almost everyone in the Western world, for better or worse, at some point or another.

He supposed the Romance must give way to social realism, even if the aesthetic temper of the time was against it.

In any case, since Blackadder and Leonora and Cropper had come, it had changed from Quest, a good romantic form, into Chase and Race, two other equally valid ones.

During his stay he had become addicted to a pale, chilled, slightly sweet pudding called Îles Flottantes, which consisted of a white island of foam floating in a creamy yellow pool of vanilla custard, haunted by the ghost, no more, of sweetness. As he and Maud packed hurriedly, and turned the car towards the Channel, he thought how much he would regret this, how the taste would fade and diminish in his memory.

Blackadder saw the Mercedes when he and Leonora came back to the hotel in the evening. He was feeling strained. Ariane had indeed given Leonora a photocopy of Sabine's journal, which he had attempted to translate for her, with a fair degree of success. He had been pulled along, initially, by the sheer force of her presence, and her insistence that Roland and Maud had snuck off together to steal a scholarly march on both of them. He had suggested, when they were possessed of the journal, that they should come home and order a good translation and pursue their investigations. Leonora, who had asked Ariane a lot of questions about Roland and Maud, was concerned that they were 'on to something' and should be tracked across Finistère. If the weather had been bad Blackadder might yet have insisted on returning to his burrow, the tools of his trade, his typewriter, his telephone. But the temptress sun shone, and he ate a couple of good meals and said that now he was here, he would come to look at Kernemet and its surroundings.

Leonora drove. Her driving had panache and swoop, but was not comfortable. He sat beside her, wondering how he had got talked into all this. Her perfume filled the car, which was a hired Renault. It was a perfume of musk and sandalwood and something sharp which affected Blackadder in contradictory ways. He believed he found it suffocating. Underneath he sensed something else, a promise of darkness, thickness, flesh. He looked down once or twice at Leonora's naked expanse of shoulders and bound breasts. Her skin, close up, had very fine wrinkles all over its dark gold, wrinkles not of old age but of a mixture of earlier softening and sun-toughening. He found these moving.

'I don't understand Maud,' Leonora was saying. 'I can't figure out why she dashed off without a word to *me*, since that letter was mine after all, if property comes into it, which between friends I didn't think it did, and we *were* friends, we'd pooled our ideas and written joint papers, all those things. Perhaps your Roland Michell is some kind of macho boss-man. It doesn't figure.'

'He's not. He's not forceful. It's his major failing.'

'It must be love.'

'That doesn't explain Ariane Le Minier.'

'It sure doesn't. What a turn-up. Not only a lesbian but a Fallen Woman and Unmarried Mother. Every archetype. I guess this is the hotel. Where they seemed to be staying. Maybe they're back now.'

She began to turn into the hotel car park, only to find her way blocked by the Mercedes, which appeared to be backing awkwardly across the gateposts.

'Fuck off,' said Leonora. 'Fuck off, asshole.'

'Oh dear,' said Blackadder. 'That's Cropper.'

'Well he'll have to fuck off. He's obstructing the gateway,' said Leonora magisterially, hooting several times with great vigour. The Mercedes went backwards and forwards, part of a series of precise adjustments designed to insert it into a parking-space that would just, but barely, contain it. Leonora rolled down the window and cried out,

'Listen, you bastard. I don't have all night. I'll be through in a second. Just hold off, can you?'

The Mercedes advanced and retreated.

Leonora advanced into the gateway.

The Mercedes pulled across it.

'For Chrissake, clear the entrance, you prick,' shouted Leonora.

The Mercedes retreated a little, slanting itself further.

Leonora put her foot firmly on the accelerator. Blackadder heard a reverberating clang and felt a jar along his spine. Leonora swore again and put the Renault into reverse. There was a sound and a sensation of tearing metal. The bumpers were locked and the two cars, like two bulls with crumpled horns, locked together. Leonora continued to reverse. Blackadder said nervously, 'No, stop.' The sound of the Mercedes' angry purr ceased abruptly. The dark window rolled down and Cropper put out his head. He said,

'Arrêtez s'il vous plaît. Nous nous abîmons. Veuillez croire que je n'ai jamais rencontré de pires façons sur les routes françaises. Une telle manque de politesse—'

Leonora swung open her door and shot out a naked leg.

'We speak good American,' she said. 'You arrogant pig. I remember you from Lincoln. You nearly killed me in Lincoln.'

'Hello, Mort,' said Blackadder.

'Ah,' said Cropper. 'James. You have damaged my car.'

'*I* damaged it,' said Leonora.'Owing to your bad manners and lack of signals.'

'This is Professor Stern, Mortimer,' said Blackadder.'From Tallahassee. The editor of Christabel LaMotte.'

'In search of Bailey and Michell.'

'Exactly.'

'They've checked out. Three hours back. No one knows what they did here. Or where they went.'

Blackadder said, 'If you put your back to your bumper, Mortimer, and I sit on ours, we might disengage them by joggling and swaying.'

'It will never be the same,' said Cropper.

'Are you staying here?' said Leonora. 'We could discuss it over a drink. I don't know what the insurance on this car hire runs to.'

It was not a pleasant dinner. Cropper was more put out than Blackadder had seen him, by the damage to his car, or by the flight of Roland and Maud, or by the presence of Leonora. He ordered lavishly, a huge platter of *fruits de mer* to start with, a mound of shells and whiskers and stony carapaces, surrounded by seaweed on a metal pedestal, followed by a huge boiled sea-spider or araignée, a hot angry scarlet, crusted with bumps and armoured crestings, waving a multiplication of feelers. He was provided with an armoury of implements for this feast, like a mediaeval torture chamber, pincers and grippers, prods and corkscrew skewers.

Blackadder ate hake abstemiously. Leonora ate lobster and talked about Kernemet.

'So sad, only the foundations and the orchard wall, nothing left. The menhir's still there but the house is quite gone. Do you know what happened to LaMotte after she came here, Professor Cropper?'

'No. There are some letters in America in my possession, which describe her whereabouts in 1861. But about the time you speak of, the end of 1860, no. But I shall find out.'

He wielded a claw-cracker and a serpent-tongued pick. The heap of debris on his plate was higher than the original creatures had been, every sweet white morsel extracted.

'I intend to have those letters if I can,' he said. 'And I intend to find out the rest.'

'The rest?'

'What became of their child. What they concealed from us. *I intend to know.*'

'It may lie concealed forever in the grave,' said Blackadder, raising his glass to the fierce and melancholy face across the table. 'May I propose a toast? Randolph Henry Ash and Christabel LaMotte. May they rest in peace.'

Cropper raised his glass.

'I'll drink to that. But I shall find out.'

They parted at the foot of the stairs. Cropper bowed to Blackadder and Leonora and took himself off. Leonora put a hand on Blackadder's arm.

'He's kinda scarey, so intense, he takes it all personally. As though they did it to deceive him. Personally.'

'So they probably did. Among others. Shakespeare foresaw him, writing that curse.'

'I'm glad I scraped his great hearse. Do you want to come up with me? I feel all sad, we could comfort each other. It makes me sentimental, the sea and the sun.'

'It's nice of you, but no thank you. I'm touched and grateful and glad you brought me here – I shall probably regret it forever – but better not. I'm not –' he wanted to say 'up to it' or 'in your class' or simply 'strong enough', but all those sounded vaguely insulting.

'Not to worry. Pity to complicate a good working relationship, hunh?'

She kissed him good night, with considerable force, and strode away.

The next day, they were driving quietly along a side road, having decided to make a small detour and take in the chapel with Gauguin's wooden Christ, when they heard behind them a strange and fearsome sound. It combined a cough with a regular rhythmic thump followed by a scraping wheeze. It was like a beast in pain, or a creaking cart with an uneven wheel. It was the Mercedes with a crushed mudguard and an obviously damaged fan-belt, which overtook them, grinding, at the next junction. Its driver was again invisible, its wound painfully prominent.

'Horrid,' said Leonora. 'Sinister.'

'Cropper is the Ankou,' said Blackadder, with sudden wit.

'Of course he is,' said Leonora. 'We should have known that.'

'He won't catch Bailey and Michell at that rate.'

'Nor shall we.'

'There isn't much point to catching them, I suppose, really. We could have a picnic.'

'Let's do that.'

---◦→ ◉ →◦---

CHAPTER TWENTY-FOUR

Maud sat at her desk in Lincoln and copied out a useful passage of Freud for her paper on metaphor:

> It is only when a person is completely in love that the main quota of libido is transferred on to the object and the object to some extent takes the place of the ego.

She wrote: 'Of course ego, id and super-ego, indeed the libido itself, are metaphorical hypostasisations of what must be seen as'.
She crossed out 'seen' and wrote 'could be felt as'.
Both were metaphors. She wrote: 'could be explained as events in an undifferentiated body of experience'.
Body was a metaphor. She had written 'experience' twice, which was ugly. 'Event' was possibly a metaphor, too.

She was wholly aware of Roland, sitting behind her on the floor, wearing a white towelling dressing-gown, leaning up against the white sofa on which he had slept during his first visit, and on which he slept now. She felt the fuzz of his soft black hair, starting up above his brow, with imaginary fingers. She felt his frown between her eyes. He felt his occupation was gone; she felt his feeling. He felt he was *lurking*.
If he went out of the room it would be grey and empty.
If he did *not* go out of it, how could she concentrate?

It was October. Her term had begun. He had not gone back to Blackadder. He had not gone back to his own flat, except once, after repeated telephone calls that failed to rouse Val, to make sure she was not dead. There had been a large notice, propped against an empty milk bottle: GONE AWAY FOR SOME DAYS.

He was writing lists of words. He was writing lists of words that resisted arrangement into the sentences of literary criticism or theory. He had hopes – more, intimations of imminence – of writing poems, but so far had got no further than lists. These were, however, compulsive and desperately important. He didn't know whether Maud understood – *saw* – their importance, or thought they were silly. He was wholly aware of Maud. He could feel her feeling that he felt his occupation was gone, and that he was *lurking*.

He wrote: blood, clay, terracotta, carnation.

He wrote: blond, burning bush, scattering.

He annotated this, "scattering as in Donne, 'extreme and scattering bright', nothing to do with scattergraphs."

He wrote: anemone, coral, coal, hair, hairs, nail, nails, fur, owl, isinglass, scarab.

He rejected wooden, point, link, and other ambivalent words, also blot and blank, though all these sprang (another word he hesitated over) to mind. He was uncertain about the place of verbs in this primitive language. Spring, springs, springes, sprung, sprang.

Arrow, bough (not branch, not root), leaf-mould, water, sky.

Vocabularies are crossing circles and loops. We are defined by the lines we choose to cross or to be confined by.

He said, 'I'll go out, so you can think.'
    'No need.'
    'I'd better. Can I buy anything?'
    'No. It's seen to.'
    'I could get a job, a job in a bar or a hospital or something.'
    'Take time to think.'
    'There isn't much time.'
    'One can make time.'
    'I feel I'm simply lurking.'

'I know. Things will change.'

'I don't know.'

The telephone rang.

'Is that Dr Bailey?'

'Yes.'

'Is Roland Michell there?'

'It's for you.'

'Who?'

'Young, male and well-bred. Who is that, please?'

'You won't know me. My name is Euan MacIntyre. I'm a solicitor. I wanted to talk to you – not to Roland – or at least Roland will be very welcome, I've got things to say to him, too. But I've got something interesting to communicate to *you*.'

Maud covered the mouthpiece and communicated this to Roland.

'How about dinner in the White Hart at say seven-thirty tonight? Both of you.'

'We'd better,' said Roland.

'Thank you very much,' said Maud. 'We'd love to.'

'I don't know about *love*,' said Roland.

They went into the bar in the White Hart that evening with some apprehension. It was the first time they had gone out publicly as a couple, if that was what they were. Maud was dressed in bluebell blue, her hair well-anchored, gleaming. Roland looked at her with love and despair. He had nothing in the world but Maud – no home, no job, no future – and these very negatives made it impossible that Maud would long go on taking him seriously or desiring his presence.

Three people were waiting for them. Euan MacIntyre in a charcoal suit and a golden shirt, Val, shining in a putty-coloured glossy suit over a plum-coloured shirt, and a third person, tweedy and fluffy-haired about his bald patch, whom Euan introduced as 'Toby Byng. We both own a leg of a horse. He's a solicitor.'

'I know,' said Maud. 'Sir George's solicitor.'

'That's not why he's here, or not exactly why.'

Roland stared at sleek Val, who had the shine of really expensive and well-made clothes, and more important and unmistakable, the glistening self-pleasure of sexual happiness. She had had her hair done in a new way – short, soft, shaped, rising when she tossed her head and settling back to perfection. She was all muted violets and shot-silk dove-colours, all balanced and pretty, stockings, high shoes, padded shoulders, painted mouth. He said, instinctively,

'You look *happy*, Val.'

'I decided I could be.'

'I've been looking for you. I rang and rang. To see if you were all right.'

'It wasn't necessary. I thought if you could vanish, I could. So I did.'

'I'm glad.'

'I'm going to marry Euan.'

'I'm glad.'

'I hope not *altogether* glad.'

'Of course not. But you look –'

'And you. Are you happy?'

'In some ways. In others, I'm in a mess.'

'The rent's paid until the first week in October. This week, that is.'

'Not that sort of mess. At least –'

'Euan has had an idea about the real mess, about Randolph and Christabel.'

They sat at a corner-table with a pink cloth and stiff pink napkins, in a large dining-room, with glittering crystal chandeliers and panelled walls. There was an autumn posy on the table: dusty pink asters, mauve chrysanthemums, a few freesias. Euan ordered champagne and they settled down to smoked salmon, pheasant with trimmings, Stilton and lemon soufflé. Roland found his pheasant tough. The bread sauce reminded him of his mother's Christmas cooking. They talked about the weather in an English way and little currents of sexual anxiety ran round the table, also in an English way. Roland could see Val summing up Maud as beautiful and cold; he could see Maud studying Val, and judging himself in relation to Val, but he had no idea what judgment she had formed. He could see that both women responded to Euan's friendliness and enthusiasm. Euan made everyone laugh and Val

433

gleamed with pride and happiness and Maud relaxed into a smile. They drank good burgundy, and laughed more freely. Maud and Toby Byng turned out to have childhood friends in common. Euan and Maud talked about hunting. Roland felt peripheral, a watcher. He asked Toby Byng how Joan Bailey was, and was told that she'd had a long spell in hospital but was now out.

'Mortimer Cropper has led Sir George to believe that the proceeds from the sale of the correspondence – at least if it's sold to *him* – will rebuild Seal Court and provide Lady Bailey with the latest technology.'

'That's good for someone,' said Roland, 'at least.'

Euan leaned across the table.

'That was what we wanted to discuss. Good for whom?'

He turned to Maud.

'Who owns the copyright in Christabel LaMotte's poems and stories?'

'We do. My family. We think. The papers have been deposited in the Women's Studies Resource Centre at Lincoln where I work. That is, the manuscripts of *Melusina*, the *City of Is*, the two books of fairy tales and a lot of scattered lyrics. We don't have many letters at all – we bought Blanche Glover's journal in a Sotheby's sale – quite secretly, no one realised its importance. There isn't that much money in women's studies yet. Of course, once the works are in print they go out of copyright after fifty years as anything else does.'

'Has it occurred to you that you might be the owner of the copyright in Christabel's half of the correspondence?'

'It has, but I don't think so. I don't think there was a Will or anything. What happened was – when Christabel died in 1890 her sister Sophia sent a whole package to her daughter, May, who was my great-great-grandmother – she would have been about thirty, my great-grandfather was born in 1880 and May was married in 1878. There was some unpleasantness – the then Sir George didn't believe in the marriage of first cousins, which this was. And the families didn't get on. So Sophia sent these papers with a covering letter – I don't remember it exactly, but something like "My dearest May, I have to convey some very sad news to you, which is that my dearest sister, Christabel, died very suddenly last night. She has often expressed the wish that you should have her papers and poems – you are my only daughter, and she believed strongly in the importance of handing things on through the female line. So I have sent what I could find – I do not know how much value or lasting interest they may have – but hope you will keep them safely, as she at least believed and other authorities have said, that she was a better poet than has yet been generally acknowledged."

'She said that if she felt she could travel for the funeral her presence would be a comfort – but she (Sophia) knew that my great-great-grandmother had had trouble with the birth of her last child and was much preoccupied. There's no evidence that she went. She kept the things but there's no evidence that she took any interest in them.'

'That has had to wait for you,' said Euan.

'I suppose so. Yes. But as to the *ownership* – it's even possible that what I have got might turn out to belong to Sir George if Christabel died intestate . . . I can't see Cropper and Co acknowledging any moral right I may have.'

Euan said, 'That's more or less what I thought. I got Val to tell me what she knew –'

'Not much,' said Val.

'Enough, about Cropper and Co. So I got my good friend Toby to poke about in all the old deedboxes his firm holds. This worries him – he's *Sir George's* family solicitor. In fact, he can't go any further in this matter. But he – we – found something we feel you should see – we shall – you will, but I *hope* you'll consent to let me act for you – we shall have to think very carefully about how to proceed. But anyway, in my professional view, there is no doubt about whose the letters are. I've brought a Xerox. God bless the Xerox machine. I've verified the signature in your women's studies place while you were away. What do you think?'

Maud took the single Xerox sheet.

Dictated to my sister, Sophia Bailey, May 1st 1890, I being too weak to write clearly. I wish Sophia to have my money, and my furniture and china. If Jane Summers from Richmond is alive she should have something to remember me by, and £60. All my books and papers, and my copyrights, to go to Maia Thomasine

Bailey in the hope that in the fulness of time she may become interested in poetry. Signed Christabel LaMotte, in the presence of Lucy Tuck, lady's maid, and William Marchmont, gardener.

Euan said, 'It was folded up in a heap of Sophia's accounts. It's clear from these that she found Jane Summers and paid her the bequest. And kept the bit of paper. I imagine she felt she'd done all that was necessary – carried out her sister's intentions – and simply put the bit of paper away.'

Maud said, 'Does that make the letters mine?'

'The copyright in unpublished letters is the property of the writer of the letters. The physical letters themselves are the property of the recipient. Unless returned, as these were.'

'You mean, his letters from her were returned?'

'Exactly. I believe – well, Toby says – that they contain a letter from him saying that he returns the letters to her possession.'

'So – if you are right – all the letters are my property, and the copyright in her letters is mine.'

'Exactly. It isn't cut and dried. It's open to be disputed. Sir George could dispute it and probably should. That document isn't a proper Will, it's not registered at Somerset House, there are all sorts of loopholes and chinks for contesting it. But my own opinion is, that you should be able to prove your title to the whole collection, his and hers. What is the problem is how we should proceed whilst protecting the interests of Toby here, whose position is ethically very dicey. How may this document come to light without his agency?'

Toby said, 'If Sir George disputes your claim you could spend the whole proceeds on legal fees –'

'Like *Bleak House*,' said Val.

'Exactly,' said Euan. 'He *might* settle. What we need now is a way for this to come to light without Toby deliberately finding it – I think I'll have to devise a story which makes him my victim – I could persuade him to show me some of the papers in a trumped-up search – and then spring a surprise on him –'

'Piratical,' said Val, adoring.

'If you would consider my acting for you –'

'You won't make a lot of money,' said Maud. 'If the papers are mine, they will go in the Women's Resource Centre.'

'Understood. I'm not in it for the money. For the drama, the curiosity, you know? Though I think you should consider that you may *have* to sell – not to Cropper but to the British Library or somewhere acceptable – to pay off Sir George.'

Roland said, 'Lady Bailey was good to us. She could do with the wheelchair.'

Maud said, 'The Women's Resource Centre has been *disgracefully* underfunded since its inception –'

'If all those papers were in the British Library, you could have microfilms and funding and a wheelchair –'

Maud looked at him with a fighting look.

'If those papers were in the Resource Centre they'd *attract* funding –'

'Maud –'

'George Bailey has been extremely unpleasant to me – and to Leonora –'

'He loves his wife,' said Roland. 'And his woods.'

'So he does,' said Toby Byng.

'I don't think,' said Val, 'we should start fighting over what we – you, that is, haven't got yet. I think we should take it step by step. I think we should drink to Euan, who thought up all this, and think of a next step.'

'I've got one or two more ideas,' said Euan. 'But they need a bit of thought and research.'

'You think I'm being greedy,' said Maud, when they were at home.

'No, I don't. How could I?'

'I can feel you disapproving of me.'

'You're quite mistaken. What right have I to disapprove?'

'That means you do. Do you think I should tell Euan to go away?'

'That's up to you.'

'Roland.'

'It has very little to do with me.'

That was the problem. He felt marginal. Marginal to her family, her feminism, her ease with her social peers. There were a great many circles here, all of which he was outside. He had begun this – what should it be called – this investigation – and had lost everything – whilst handing to Maud the materials with which she could improve her own lot immeasurably – job, future, Christabel, money . . . he hated eating dinners he could not have paid for. He hated living off Maud.

Maud said, 'We can't quarrel now – after everything we've –'

He was about to say they were not quarrelling, when the telephone rang.

The voice was female, trembling, and very agitated.

'I wish to speak to Dr Bailey.'

'This is Maud Bailey, speaking.'

'Yes. Well. Yes. Oh dear. I have thought and thought about whether I should ring you – you may think I am mad, or you may think I am simply bad – or presumptuous – I don't know – I could only think of you – and I have sat and thought about it all evening and I only see now how *late* it is to be ringing anyone, I must have lost all sense of time, I should perhaps ring back tomorrow, that might be better only it might be too late, well, not perhaps *tomorrow*, but very soon, if I'm right – it was only that you seemed *concerned*, you see, you did seem to *care* –'

'Please – who is that speaking?'

'Oh dear, yes. I *never* initiate telephone calls. I am terrified of the telephone. This is Beatrice Nest. On behalf of Ellen Ash. No, not exactly on behalf – except that I do feel – I do feel – that it is for her that I am –'

'What has happened, Dr Nest?'

'I'm sorry. Let me try to settle down and speak clearly. I did try to ring you earlier, Dr Bailey, but there was no answer. I didn't really expect you to answer this call, either, that is why I am so flustered and taken off my guard. Yes.'

'I do understand.'

'It is about Mortimer Cropper. He has been here – well not here, I'm at home now of course, in Mortlake, but into my room in the Museum, he has been *there* several times, looking very particularly at *certain sections* of the journal –'

'About Blanche Glover's visit?'

'No, no, about the funeral of Randolph Ash. And today he brought young Hildebrand Ash – well he isn't so young, he's quite *old*, and certainly fat, but younger than Lord Ash himself, of course – perhaps you don't know that Hildebrand Ash will succeed Lord Ash if he dies, when he dies, and he *isn't well*, James Blackadder says, he certainly doesn't answer letters at all – not that I write often, there is no real need, but when I do he doesn't answer–'

'Dr Nest–'

'I know. Are you *sure* you wouldn't rather I rang back tomorrow?'

'No. I mean yes. I am sure. I am consumed with curiosity.'

'I overheard them talking to each other. They believed I had gone – well, out of the room. Dr Bailey, I am *absolutely certain* that Professor Cropper means to disturb – to *dig up* – the Ashes. The grave in Hodershall. He and Hildebrand Ash together. He wants to find out what is in the box.'

'What box?' said Maud.

Beatrice Nest, with much circumlocution and breathiness explained what box.

'He has been saying for years it should be dug up. Lord Ash wouldn't countenance it, and anyway you have to have a Faculty from the Bishop to disturb an interment, you know, and he could never get one, but he says Hildebrand Ash has a *moral right* to the box and he himself has a – a right – because he – he – has done so much for Randolph Ash – he says he – I heard him say – "Why not behave like the thieves who took *Impression at Sunrise*, why not take it and think of a plausible way to account for whatever we find later?" – I heard him–'

'Have you spoken to Professor Blackadder?'

'No.'

'Don't you think you should?'

'He dislikes me. He dislikes everyone, but he dislikes me more than most. He might say I was mad, or he might think it was *my* fault that Mortimer Cropper had formed this dreadful plan – he hates Cropper too – I don't think he would listen. I am sick of small humiliations. You talked to me sensibly, you *understood*

439

Ellen Ash, you will see how this must be stopped for her sake.'
She continued:

'I would have tried to tell Roland Michell, but he's disappeared.
What do you think I should do? What can be done?'

'Roland is here, Dr Nest. Perhaps we should come to London.
We can't really call the police —'

'What could we *possibly* say to them?'

'Exactly. Do you know the Vicar at the Church where the
grave is?'

'Mr Drax. He doesn't like scholars. Or students. Or Randolph
Ash, I think.'

'Everybody concerned with this business seems to be very
prickly.'

'And Ash himself was such a *generous* man,' said Dr Nest, not
refuting this judgment.

'Let us hope he sees off Mortimer Cropper. Perhaps we should
go and see him?'

'I don't know. I don't know what to do.'

'Let me consult. I'll call you back tomorrow.'

'Please — Dr Bailey — hurry.'

Maud was excited. She told Roland they must go to London,
and suggested that they consult Euan MacIntyre about Cropper's
possible courses of action and how to foil them. Roland said that
this was a good plan, which it was, in its way, though it increased
his own sense of unreal isolation. He lay awake at night, alone in
the white bed, and worried. Something which had been kept
secret had gone. He and Maud had felt impelled to keep the
'research' secret, and whilst it was secret they had silently shared
it and each other. Now it was out in the light of common day
he saw it somehow diminished by the excited curiosity of Euan
and Toby as much as by the hot desire and rage of Cropper and
Blackadder. Euan's charm and enthusiasm had not only smoothed
the resentment and sullenness out of Val's face but had somehow
brought a brightness and recklessness to Maud herself. He fancied
she spoke more freely to Euan and Toby than she had done to
him. He fancied Val took pleasure in taking over the pursuit.
He remembered his earliest impression of Maud — managerial,
arrogant, critical. She had once belonged to Fergus. Their own

strange silent games were the product of chance, of a brief artificial solitude, of secrecy. They could not survive in the open. He did not even know if he wanted them to. He looked for his own primary thought, and said to himself that before Maud came he had had Randolph Ash and his words, and now even that, that above all, had been changed and taken from him.

He said nothing of all this to Maud, who appeared to notice nothing.

Euan, consulted the next day, was also excited. They would *all* go to London, he said, and talk to Miss Nest, and have a council of war. Perhaps they could follow Cropper around and catch him *in flagrante delicto*. The law was subtly different as to the disturbance of interments in burial grounds and alternatively cemeteries. Hodershall sounded like an Anglican graveyard that would qualify as a burial ground. He and Val would go in the Porsche and meet up with Roland and Maud. Why didn't they come to his pad and telephone Dr Nest from there? He had a flat in the Barbican, very comfortable. Toby must stay and mind his deedboxes and Sir George's interests.

Maud said, 'I might stay with my aunt Lettice. She's an old lady in Cadogan Square. Would you like to come?'

'I think I shall stay in the Putney flat.'

'Shall I come with you?'

'No.'

It was not the sort of place for her, with its dingy chintz and feline smell. And it was overlaid with memories of his life with Val, with his thesis. He didn't want Maud there. 'I need to think a few things out. About the future. What I am going *to do*. About the flat, how to pay the rent, or perhaps not to. I could do with a night on my own.'

Maud said, 'Is anything wrong?'

'*I have to think my life out.*'

'I'm sorry. You *could* come to my aunt's—'

'Don't worry. I'd like to stay alone, that one night.'

CHAPTER TWENTY-FIVE

Ellen Ash's Journal

NOVEMBER 25TH 1889

I write this sitting at His desk at two in the morning. I cannot sleep and he sleeps his last sleep in the coffin, quite still, and his soul gone away. I sit among his possessions – now mine or no one's – and think that his life, his presence, departs more slowly from these inanimate than from him, who was once animate and is now, I cannot write it, I should not have started writing. My dear, I sit here and write, to whom but thee? I feel better here amongst thy things – the pen is reluctant to form 'thee', 'thy', there is no one there, and yet here is still a presence.

Here is an unfinished letter. There are the microscope, the slides, a book with a marker, and – oh, my dear – uncut leaves. I fear sleep, I fear what dreams may come, Randolph, and so I sit here and write.

When he was lying there he said, 'Burn what they should not see,' and I said, 'Yes', I promised. At such times, it seems, a kind of dreadful energy comes, to do things quickly, before action becomes impossible. He hated the new vulgarity of *contemporary* biography, the ransacking of Dickens's desk for his most trivial memoranda, Forster's unspeakable intrusions into the private pains and concealments of the Carlyles. He said often to me, burn what is alive for us with the life of our memory, and let no one else make idle curios or lies of it. I remember being much struck with Harriet Martineau, in her autobiography, saying that to print private letters was a form of treachery – as though one should tell the intimate talk of two friends with their feet on the fender, on winter nights. I have made a fire here, and burned some things. I shall burn more. He shall not be picked by vultures.

There are things I cannot burn. Nor ever I think look at again. There are things here that are not mine, that I could not be a party to burning. And there are our dear letters, from all those foolish years of separation. What can I do? I cannot leave them to be buried with me. Trust may be betrayed. I shall lay these things to rest with him now, to await my coming. Let the earth take them.

Mortimer Cropper: *The Great Ventriloquist* 1964, Chapter 26, 'After Life's fitful fever', pp. 449 *et seq.*

A committee was hastily constituted to see whether it might not be possible to inter the great man in Westminster Abbey. Lord Leighton went to see the Dean, who was understood to have some doubts about Randolph Ash's religious beliefs. The poet's widow, who had watched devoted and sleepless by his bedside during his last illness, wrote to both Lord Leighton and the Dean to say that it was her wish, as she was sure that it had been her husband's, that he should lie in the quiet country churchyard of St Thomas's Church at Hodershall on the edge of the North Downs, where her sister Faith's husband was Vicar, and where she hoped to lie herself. Accordingly a great number of fashionable and literary personages made their way through the leafy lanes of Downland, on a dripping English November day, when yellow leaves were pashed into mud by the hooves of the horses and the sun was red and low in the sky.[22] The pall-bearers were Leighton, Hallam Tennyson, Sir Rowland Michaels and the painter, Robert Brunant.[23] When the coffin had been lowered into the clay, covered with huge white wreaths, Ellen laid upon it a box, containing 'our letters and other mementoes' which were 'too dear to burn, too precious ever to expose to the public view'.[24] Then the grave was filled up with flowers and the mourners turned away, leaving the last sad acts to the spades of the sextons, who engulfed both the ebony casket and the fragile flowers with the local mixture of chalk, flint and clay.[25] The young Edmund Meredith, Ellen's nephew, carried away from the grave's edge a cluster of violets which he carefully pressed and kept among the leaves of his Shakespeare.[26]

In later months, Ellen Ash caused a simple black headstone to be set up, with a carving of an ash tree, showing the spread of both the crown and the roots, such as he would occasionally playfully draw beside his signature in some of his letters.[27] Beneath it was carved Ash's own translation of Cardinal Bembo's epitaph for Raphael, which is carved around Raphael's tomb in the Pantheon, and appeared in Ash's poem about the painting of the Stanze in the Vatican, *The Sacred and the Profane*.

> Here lies that Man, who, whilst he was in Breath
> Made our great Mother tremble that her skill
> Was overmastered, who now, by his Death,
> Fears her own Powers may grow forever still.[28]

Beneath this is written

> This stone is dedicated to Randolph Henry Ash, a great poet and a true and kind husband, by his sorrowing widow and wife of more than 40 years, Ellen Christiana Ash, in the hope that 'one short sleep past, we wake eternally'[29] where there is no more parting.

Later critics have expressed amusement or scorn at the 'bathos'[30] of comparing this prolific Victorian poet to the great Raphael, though both, in the early part of this century, were out of favour. It is perhaps more surprising that there is no contemporary record either of disapproval that the Stone should have no mention of the Christian faith, or possibly, conversely, admiration for the tact with which Ellen had avoided this. What her choice of citation does is to link her husband, through his own poem and Raphael and Bembo, to the whole ambiguous Renaissance tradition, exemplified in the circular Pantheon, a Christian church which was originally in the form of a classical temple. It is not to be supposed that these thoughts were necessarily in her mind, although they may have discussed these matters together.

We cannot avoid speculating about what was contained in the box which was buried with Randolph Ash, and was observed to be still intact when his widow's casket was lowered beside him four years later.[31] Ellen Ash shared her generation's prudery and squeamishness about the publication of private papers. The claim is frequently made – not least by Ellen herself[32] – that Randolph participated in these scruples. Fortunately for us he left no testamentary indications to this effect, and even more fortunately for us, his widow's carrying out of his supposed injunctions was patchy and haphazard. We do not know what invaluable evidence is lost to us, but we have seen, in these pages, the ample richness of what remains. Nevertheless we cannot help wishing that those who disturbed his rest in 1893 had seen fit at least to open the hidden box, survey it and record for posterity what it contained. Such decisions to destroy, to hide, the records of an exemplary life are made in the heat of life, or more often in the grip of immediate *post-mortem* despair, and have little to do with the measured judgment, and desire for full and calm knowledge, which succeed these perturbations. Even Rossetti thought better of burying his poems with his tragic wife and had to demean himself and her in disinterring them. I think often of what Freud said about the relations of our primitive forebears to the dead, who could be seen ambivalently as demons and ghosts, or as revered ancestors:

'The fact that demons are always regarded as the spirits of those who have died *recently* shows better than anything the influence of mourning on the origin of belief in demons. Mourning has a quite specific psychical task to perform: its function is to detach the survivors' memories and hopes from the dead. When this has been achieved, the pain grows less and with it the remorse and self-reproaches and consequently the fear of the demon as well. And the same spirits who to begin with were feared as demons may now expect to meet with friendlier treatment; they are revered as ancestors and appeals are made to them for help.'[33]

Might we not argue, in extenuation of our desire to behold what is hidden, that those whose disapproval made demons of them to their nearest and dearest, are now our beloved ancestors, whose relics we would cherish in the light of day?

[22] Recorded by Swinburne in a letter to Theodore Watts-Dunton. A. C. Swinburne, *Collected Letters*, vol V, p. 280. Swinburne's poem, 'The Old Ygdrasil and the Churchyard Yew', is supposed to have been inspired by his emotions on the passing of R. H. Ash.

[23] Reported in *The Times*, November 30th 1889. The reporter remarked 'several comely young maidens, in floods of unembarrassed tears and a large gathering of respectful working men, beside the Literary Lions.'

[24] Ellen Ash, in a letter to Edith Wharton, December 20th 1889, reprinted in *The Letters of R. H. Ash* ed. Cropper, vol. 8, p. 384. A similar expression of her intention occurs in an unpublished passage of her Journal, written two nights after the poet's death. The Journal is shortly (1967) to appear, edited by Dr Beatrice Nest, of Prince Albert College, London University.

[25] I have spent long hours walking in this countryside, and have observed the way the earth characteristically lies in layers, and throws up the dark

flints embedded in the white chalk, which shine in the ploughed fields like snow.

26 This Shakespeare, and those violets, repose now in the Stant Collection in Robert Dale Owen University, where they are preserved.

27 See, for instance, the letter to Tennyson, in the Stant Collection (August 24th 1859) which is wholly bordered by a series of such formalised trees, the roots and branches intermingling, not unlike a William Morris repeating pattern. Stant MS no 146093a.

28 The Latin is *Ille hic est Raphael timuit quo sospite vinci rerum magna parens et moriente mori.*

29 John Donne, 'Death be not Proud', *Divine Poems*, ed. Helen Gardner, p. 9.

30 An irritable comment of F. R. Leavis in *Scrutiny*, vol. XIII, pp. 130–31 'That the Victorians took Randolph Ash seriously as a poet is sufficiently evinced by the seriousness of their obituary panegyrics, which claimed, like his bathetic tombstone, supplied by his wife, that he was the equal of Shakespeare, Milton, Rembrandt, Raphael and Racine.'

31 Recorded by Patience Meredith in a letter to her sister Faith, now in the possession of Marianne Wormald, great-granddaughter of Edmund Meredith.

32 See above, note 24, and in the unpublished Journal, November 25th 1889.

33 Sigmund Freud, *Totem and Taboo*, *Works* (Standard edn 1955), vol. 13, pp. 65–6.

NOVEMBER 27TH 1889

The old woman trod softly along the dark corridors, and climbed the stairs, standing in uncertainty on various landings. From the back – we are going to see her clearly now – from the back and in the shadow, she might still have been any age. She wore a velvet dressing-gown, and soft embroidered slippers. She carried herself upright and without creaking, though her body was comfortably fleshed out. Her hair hung in a long pale plait between her shoulders; in the light of her candle, it could have been palest gold, though it was creamy white, a soft brown turned.

She listened to the house. Her sister Patience was sleeping in the best spare room, and somewhere on the second floor her nephew George, now an aspiring young barrister, slept too.

In his own bedroom, his hands crossed, his eyes closed, Randolph Henry Ash lay still, his soft white hair framed by quilted satin, his head pillowed on embroidered silk.

When she found she could not sleep, she had gone to him, opened his door quietly, quietly, and stood, looking down, taking in the change. Immediately after death, he had looked like himself, gentled and calmed after the struggle, resting. Now he was gone away, there was no one there, only an increasingly carved and bony simulacrum, the yellowing skin stretched taut over peaks of bone, the eyes sunk, the jaw sharp.

She looked at these changes, murmured a prayer into the blanket of silence, and said to the thing on the bed, 'Where are you?'

The whole house smelled, as it did every night, of extinguished coal fires, cold grates, old smoke.

She went into her own little writing-room, where her escritoire was covered with letters of condolence, to be answered, and the list of those invited to tomorrow's funeral, checked. She took her journal out of her drawer, and one or two other papers, looked irresolutely at the heap, and slipped out again, listening to sleep and death.

She went up another flight, towards the top of the house, where Randolph's workroom was, from which it had been the business of her life to exclude everyone, anyone, even herself. His curtains were open. Light from a gas-lamp came in, and light from a full moon too, swimming silvery. There was the ghost of the smell of his tobacco. Heaps of books on his desk, from before that last illness. The feeling of him working was still in that room. She sat down at his writing-table, putting the candle in front of her, and felt, not better, that was the wrong thought, but less desolate, as though whatever was still present here was less gaunt and terrible than what slept, or lay as still as stone, down there.

She had his watch in her dressing-gown pocket, with the few papers she had brought up. She took it out and looked at it. Three. Three in the last morning he would be in the house.

She looked around at the glass-fronted bookcases, vaguely reflecting multiplied flames back at her. She opened a drawer or two, in the desk, and found sheafs of paper, in his hand, in others'; how was she to judge and decide the fate of all this?

Along one wall was his botanical and zoological collection. Microscopes in their wooden cases, hinged and latched. Slides, drawings, specimens. The Wardian cases containing sealed worlds

447

of plant life, misted with their own breath, the elegantly panelled marine aquarium, with its weeds, its *Actinia* and starfish, against which M. Manet had painted the poet amongst his ferns, suggesting a world perhaps of primaeval vegetable swamp or foreshore. All this must go. She would consult his friends at the Science Museum as to a suitable home for it. Maybe it should be donated to an appropriate educational institution – a Working Men's club, a school of some kind. There had been, she remembered, his special airtight specimen box, glass-lined and sealed. She found it where it was kept; he was orderly in his habits. It would be ideal for her purpose.

There was a decision to be made and tomorrow would be too late.

He was a man who had never really had a serious illness, until this last one. And that was long-drawn-out; he had been confined to his bed for the last three months, with both of them knowing what was coming, though not when, nor how fast. They had both, during those months, lived in that one room, his bedroom. She had been close to him at all times, adjusting his air or his pillow, towards the end helping him to feed, reading to him when even the lightest book became too heavy. She thought she could feel his needs and discomforts, without words. The pain too, there was a sense in which she had shared the pain. She had sat quietly beside him, holding the papery white hand, and felt his life ebb, day by day. Not his intelligence. At the beginning there had been a feverish piece of time in which, for some reason, he had become obsessed by the poems of John Donne, had recited them to the ceiling, in a voice both resonant and beautiful, puffing away the fronds of beard from his mouth. When he couldn't find a line he called, 'Ellen, Ellen, quickly, I am lost', and she had had to riffle and seek.

'What would I do without you, my dear? Here we are at the end, close together. You are a great comfort. We have been happy.'

'We have been happy,' she would say, and it was so. They were happy even then, in the way they had always been happy, sitting close, saying little, looking at the same things, together.

She would come into the room and hear the voice:

> Dull sublunary lovers' love
> (Whose soul is sense) cannot admit
> Absence, because it doth remove
> Those things which elemented it.

He carried out his dying in style. She watched him working it out, fighting the pain, the nausea, the fear, in order to have something to say to her that she would remember later, with warmth, with honour. Some of the things he said were said as endings. 'I see why Swammerdam longed for the quiet dark.' Or, 'I tried to write justly, to see what I could from where I was.' Or, for her, 'Forty-one years with no anger. I do not think that many husbands and wives can say as much.'

She wrote these things down, not for what they were, though they were good things to say, but because they reminded her of his face turned towards hers, the intelligent eyes under the damp creased brow, the frail grip of the once-strong fingers. 'Do you remember – dear – when you sat – like a water-nixie on that stone – on that stone in the weeds at the – the name's gone – don't tell me – the poet's fountain – the fountain – the Fontaine de Vaucluse. You sat in the sun.'

'I was afraid. It was all rushing.'

'You did not look – afraid.'

Most of what they shared, after all, after all was done, was silence.

'It was all a question of silence,' she said aloud to him, in his work-room, where she could no longer expect any answer, neither anger nor understanding.

She laid out the objects involved in her decision. A packet of letters, tied with faded violet ribbons. A bracelet of hair she had worked, from his hair and her own, over those last months, which now she meant to bury with him. His watch. An unfinished letter, undated, in his own hand, which she had earlier found in his desk. A letter to herself, in a spidery hand.

A sealed envelope.

Trembling slightly, she took up the letter to herself, which had come a month ago.

Dear Mrs Ash,

I believe my name will not be strange to you — that you know something of me — I cannot imagine you cannot — though if by chance my letter is an absolute surprise I ask your pardon. I ask your pardon, however things may be, for intruding on you at this time.

I am told Mr Ash is ill. Indeed the papers report so, and make no concealment of the gravity of his state. I am reliably told that he may not live long, though of course I ask your pardon again if I am in error, as I may be, as I must hope to be.

I have writ down some things I find I wish, after all, that he should know. I am in a state of considerable doubt as to the wisdom of putting myself forward at this time — do I write for my own absolution or for him — I cannot know. I am in your hands, in this matter. I must trust to your judgment, your generosity, your goodwill.

We are two old women now, and my fires at least are out and have long been out.

I know nothing of you, for the best of reasons, that nothing has been said to me, at any time.

I have writ down, for his eyes only, some things — I find I cannot say, what things — and have sealed the letter. If you wish to read it, it is in your hands, though I must hope, if it can be, that he will read the letter, and decide.

And if he cannot or will not read it … oh, Mrs Ash, I am in your hands again, do with my hostage as you see fit, and have the right.

I have done great harm though I meant none to you, as God is my witness, and I hope I have done none — to you that is, or nothing irretrievable.

I find I shall be grateful for a Line from you — of forgiveness — of pity — of anger, if you must — will you — go so far?

I live in a Turret like an old Witch, and make verses nobody wants.

If in the goodness of your heart, you would tell me what becomes of him — I shall praise God for you.

I am in your hands.

                                                        Yours
                                              Christabel LaMotte

So for the last month of his life she had carried these two letters, hers and that sealed one, in her pocket, like a knife. In and out of his room, in and out of their time together.

She brought him posies she had arranged. Winter jasmine, Christmas roses, hothouse violets.

'*Helleborus niger*. Why are green petals so mysterious – Ellen? Do you remember – when we read Goethe – metamorphoses of plants – all is one – leaves – petals –'

'That was the year you wrote about Lazarus.'

'Ah, Lazarus. *Etiam si mortuus fuerit* . . . Do you think – in your heart of hearts – we continue – after?'

She bowed her head and looked for the truth.

'We are promised – men are so wonderful, so singular – we cannot be lost – for nothing. I don't know, Randolph, I don't know.'

'If there is nothing – I shall not – feel the cold. But put me in the open air, my dear – I don't want – to be shut in the Abbey. Out in the earth, in the air. Yes?'

'Don't cry, Ellen. It cannot be helped. I am not sorry. I have not – done nothing, you know. I have lived –'

Outside his bedroom, she wrote letters in her head.

'I cannot give him your letter, he is calm and almost happy, how can I disturb his peace of mind at this time?'

'You must understand that I have *always known* of your –' How to find a word? Relationship, liaison, love?

'You must understand that my husband told me, long ago, freely and truthfully, of his feeling for you, and that the matter, having been understood between us, was set aside as something past and understood.'

Too much repetition of 'understood'. But better.

'I am grateful to you for your assurance that you *know nothing of me*. I might reciprocate truthfully by saying that *I know nothing essential of you* – only a few bare necessary facts – and that my husband loved you, that he said he loved you.'

One old woman to another. Who described herself as a Witch in a turret.

'How can you ask this of me, how can you break up this short time I have with him, the life *we* have, of small kindnesses and unspoken ties, how can you menace my last days, for they are mine too, *he is my happiness*, which I am about to lose forever, can you not understand that, I cannot give him your letter.'

She wrote down nothing.

She sat beside him, weaving their hair together, pinning it to a band of black silk. At her throat, the brooch he had sent from Whitby, the white roses of York carved in black jet. The white, or whitish, hairs, on the dark ground.

'A bracelet of bright hair – about the bone. When my grave is broken up again – ha, Ellen? Always – that poem – thought of that poem– as ours, yours and mine – yes.'   .

It was one of his bad days. He had moments of clarity, and then he could be seen to wander, his mind wandering – where?

'Odd thing – sleep. You go – all over. Fields. Gardens. Other worlds. You can be – in another state – in sleep.'
   'Yes, dear. We don't know much about our lives, really. About what we know.'
   'Summer fields – just in a – twinkling of an eyelid – I saw her. I should have – looked after her. How could I? I could only – hurt her –
   'What are you doing?'
   'Making a bracelet. Out of our hair.'
   'In my watch. Her hair. Tell her.'
   'Tell her what?'
   'I forget.'
   His eyes closed.

The hair was in the watch. A very long, very fine, plaited chain of very pale gold hair. She had it on the desk before her. It was tied with pale-blue cotton, neatly.

'You must understand that I have *always known*, that my

husband told me, long ago, freely and truthfully, of his feelings for you ...'

And if she did write that, it would be no more and no less than the truth, but it would not ring true, it would not convey the truth of the way it had been, of the silence in the telling, the silences that extended before and after it, always the silences.

They had sat by the library fire, in the autumn of 1859. There had been chrysanthemums on the table, and coppery beech leaves and some strangely changing bracken, fawn and crimson and gold. And that had been the time of his glass vivariums, the time of the silkworms, which had to be kept warm, and so were in this warmest room, drab little buff moths, and their fat rough little cocoons on bare twigs, his study of metamorphosis. She was copying out *Swammerdam* and he was walking to and fro, watching her work, thinking.

'Stop writing for a moment, Ellen. I have something I must tell you.'

She remembered the rush of her own feelings. Like silk in the throat, like nails in her veins, the desire not to be told, not to hear.

'You need not –'

'I must. We have always been truthful with each other, whatever else, Ellen. You are my dear, dear wife, and I love you.'

'But,' she said. 'Such sayings always lead on to but.'

'For the last year perhaps I have been in love with another woman. I could say it was a sort of madness. A possession, as by daemons. A kind of blinding. At first it was only letters – and then – in Yorkshire – I was not alone.'

'I know.'

There had been a silence.

She repeated, 'I know.'

He said 'How long?' his proud crest fallen.

'Not so long. Nor through anything you did or said, that I saw. I was told. I had a visitor. I have something to restore to you.'

She had hidden the first *Swammerdam* in her swing-table, and now brought it out, in its envelope, addressed to Miss LaMotte, Bethany, Mount Ararat Road, Richmond.

She told him, 'The passage about the Mundane Egg in this version is superior, I think, to what we have here.'

More silence.

'If I had not told you – about this – about Miss LaMotte – would you have restored this to me?'

'I don't know. I think not. How could I? But you have told me.'

'Miss Glover gave you this?'

'She wrote twice, and came here.'

'She said nothing hurtful to you, Ellen?'

The poor mad white-faced woman, in her neat, worn boots, pacing and pacing, in all those skirts they had all worn then, clasping and unclasping her little dove-grey hands. Behind her steel-framed glasses she had had very bright blue eyes, glassy blue. And the reddish hair, and a few orange patches of freckling on the chalky skin.

'We were so happy, Mrs Ash, we were all in all to each other, we were innocent.'

'I can do nothing about your happiness.'

'Your own happiness is ruined, is a lie, I am telling you.'

'Please leave my house.'

'You could help me if you chose.'

'Please leave my house.'

'She said very little. She was venomous and distraught. I asked her to go away. She gave me the poem – as evidence – and asked for it back. I told her she should be ashamed to steal.'

'I do not know what to say, Ellen. I do not expect to see her – Miss LaMotte again. We were agreed that – that this one summer must see the end – of – the end. And even if that were not so – she has vanished, she has gone away –'

She had heard the pain in that, had noted it, had said nothing.

'I cannot explain, Ellen, but I can tell you –'

'No more. No more. We will not speak of it again.'

'You must be angry – distressed –'

'I don't know. Not angry. I don't want to know any more. Let us not talk of it again. Randolph – it is not *between us*.'

Had she done well, or ill? She had done what was in her nature, which was profoundly implicated in not knowing, in silence, in avoidance, she said to herself, in harsher moments.

She had never read his letters. She had never, that is, gone through his papers out of curiosity, idle or directed, she had never even sorted or pigeon-holed. She had answered letters for him, letters from readers, admirers, translators, loving women who had never met him.

One day, during that last month, she went upstairs, her two letters, open and unopened, in her pocket, and looked through his desk. This filled her with a superstitious bodily fear. His workroom had a cold light, in the daytime, because of a skylight, which now at night showed a few stars and a running smoky cloud, but on that day had been clear blue and blank.

So many scraps of poetry. So many heaps of ends of leaves of paper. She pushed away the thought that she would be responsible for all this. She was not, now. Not yet.

When she found the unfinished letter, it was as though she had been guided to it. It was tucked away, at the back of a drawer full of bills and invitations, and should have taken hours to find and not the few minutes in fact needed.

My dear,

I write each year, round about All Souls, because I must, although I know – I was about to say, although I know that you will not answer, although I know no such thing with certainty; I must hope; you may remember, or forget, it is all one, enough to feel able to write to me, to enlighten me a little, to take away some of the black weight I labour under.

I ask your forgiveness freely for some things, of which I stand accused, both by your silence, your obdurate silence, and by my own conscience. I ask forgiveness for my rashness and precipitance in hurrying to Kernemet, on the suppositious chance that you might be there, and without ascertaining whether or not I had your permission to go there. I ask your forgiveness, above all, for the degree of duplicity with which, on my return, I insinuated myself into the confidence of Mrs Lees, and so disastrously surprised you. You have punished me since, as you must know, I am punished daily.

But have you sufficiently considered the state of mind which drove me to these actions? I feel I stand accused, also, by your actions, of having loved you at all, as though my love was an act of brutal forcing, as though I were a heartless ravisher out of some trumpery Romance, from whom you had to flee, despoiled and ruined. Yet if you examine your memories truthfully – if you can be truthful – you must know that it was not so – think over what we did together and ask, where was the cruelty, where the coercion, where, Christabel, the lack of love and respect for you, alike as woman and as intellectual being? That we could not honourably continue as lovers after that summer was, I think, agreed by both – but was this a reason for a sudden pulling down of a dark blanket, nay, a curtain of sheet steel, between one day and the next? I loved you entirely then; I will not say now, I love you, for that would indeed be romance, and a matter at best of hope – we are both psychologists of no mean order – love goes out, you know, like a candle in one of Humphry Davy's jars, if not fed with air to breathe, if deliberately starved and stifled. Yet

> Now if thou wouldst, when all have given him over,
> From death to life, thou might'st him yet recover.

And perhaps I say that only for the pleasure of the aptness in quoting. That would have made you smile. Ah, Christabel, Christabel, I force out these careful sentences, asking for your consideration, and remember that we heard each other's thoughts, so quick, so quick, that there was no need of ending speeches –

There is something I must know and you know what that is. I say 'I must know' and sound peremptory. But I am in your hands and must beg you to tell me. What became of my child? Did he live? How can I ask, not knowing? How can I not ask, not knowing? I spoke at length to your cousin Sabine who told me what all at Kernemet knew – which was the fact only – no certainty of outcome –

You must know I went there, to Brittany, in love, and care, and anxiety, for you, for your health – I went eager to care for you, to make all well as far as could be – Why did you turn away from me? Out of pride, out of fear, out of independence, out of sudden hatred, at the injustice of the different fates of men and women?

Yet a man who knows he has or had a child and does not know more deserves a little pity.

How can I say this? Whatever became of that child, *I say in advance, whatever it is, I shall understand, if I may only know, the worst is already imagined and put behind me — so to speak —*

You see, I cannot write it, so I cannot post you these letters, I end by writing others, less direct, more glancing, which you do not answer, my dear demon, my tormentor . . . I am prohibited.

How can I ever forget that terrible sentence cried out at the ghastly spirit-summoning.

'You have made a murderess of me,' was said, blaming me, and cannot be unsaid; I hear it daily.

'There is no child' came through that silly woman's mouth, in a great groan, in what mixture of cunning, involuntary exclamation, genuine telepathy, how can I tell? I tell you Christabel — you who will never read this letter, like so many others, for it has passed the limit of possible communication — I tell you, what with disgust, and terror, and responsibility, and the coiling vestiges of love gripping my heart, I was like to have made a murderer of myself in good earnest —

She took this letter gingerly by its corner, now, as though it were a stunned biting creature, wasp or scorpion. She made a little fire in Randolph's attic grate, and burned the letter, turning it with the poker until it was black flakes. She took the sealed letter and turned it over, thinking of adding it, but allowed the flames to die down. She was quite sure that neither he nor she would have wanted his own letter to persist; nor would Christabel LaMotte, with its implicit accusations — of what? Better not to think.

She made a little fire, for warmth, with wood and a few coals, and huddled over it in her nightgown, waiting for the light to catch and the warmth to rise.

My life, she thought, has been built round a lie, a house to hold a lie.

She had always believed, stolidly, doggedly, that her avoidances, her approximations, her whole *charade* as she at times saw it, were, if not justified, at least held in check, neutralised, by her rigorous requirement that she be truthful with herself.

Randolph had been complicit. She had no idea how the story of their lives looked to him. It was not a matter they discussed.

But if she did not *know*, and occasionally look at, the truth, she had a sense that she was standing on shifting shale, sliding down into some pit.

She thought of her sense of the unspoken truths of things in terms of a most beautiful passage from Sir Charles Lyell's *Principles of Geology*, which she had read out one evening to Randolph, who had been excited by the passage immediately preceding it, about the Plutonian theory of the formation of rocks.

She had written it down.

It is the total distinctness, therefore, of crystalline formations, such as granite, hornblendeschist, and the rest, from every substance of which the origin is familiar to us, that constitutes their claim to be regarded as the effects of causes now in action in the subterranean regions. They belong not to an order which has passed away; they are not the monuments of a primeval period, bearing inscribed upon them in obsolete characters the words and phrases of a dead language; but they teach us that part of the living language of nature, which we cannot learn by our daily intercourse with what passes on the habitable surface.

Ellen liked the idea of these hard, crystalline things, which were formed in intense heat, beneath the 'habitable surface' of the earth and were not primeval monuments but 'part of the living language of nature'.

I am no ordinary or hysterical self-deceiver, she more or less said to herself. I keep faith with the fire and the crystals, I do not pretend the habitable surface *is all* and so I am not a destroyer nor cast into outer darkness.

A few flames made their sinuous way upwards. She remembered her honeymoon, as she did, from time to time, and deliberately.

She did not remember it in words. There were no words attached to it, that was part of the horror. She had never spoken of it to anyone, not even to Randolph, precisely not to Randolph.

She remembered it in images. A window, in the South, all hung about with vines and creepers, with the hot summer sun fading.

The nightdress embroidered for these nights, white cambric, all spattered with lovers' knots and forget-me-nots and roses, white on white.

A thin white animal, herself, trembling.

A complex thing, the naked male, curly hairs and shining wet, at once bovine and dolphin-like, its scent feral and overwhelming.

A large hand, held out in kindness, not once, but many times, slapped away, pushed away, slapped away.

A running creature, crouching and cowering in the corner of the room, its teeth chattering, its veins clamped in spasms, its breath shallow and fluttering. Herself.

A respite, generously agreed, glasses of golden wine, a few days of Edenic picnics, a laughing woman perched on a rock in pale blue poplin skirts, a handsome man in his whiskers, lifting her, quoting Petrarch.

An attempt. A hand not pushed away. Tendons like steel, teeth in pain, clenched, clenched.

The approach, the locked gateway, the panic, the whimpering flight.

Not once, but over and over and over.

When did he begin to know that however gentle he was, however patient, it was no good, it would never be any good?

She did not like to remember his face in those days, but did, for truthfulness, the puzzled brow, the questioning tender look, the largeness of it, convicted of its brutality, rejected in its closeness.

The eagerness, the terrible love, with which she had made it up to him, his abstinence, making him a thousand small comforts, cakes and titbits. She became his slave. Quivering at every word. *He had accepted her love.*

She had loved him for it.

He had loved her.

She turned over Christabel's letter.

She howled. 'What shall I be without you?' She put her hand over her mouth. If they came, her time to reflect was gone or lost. She had lied to them too, to her sisters, implied a lie in her bashful assertions that they were supremely happy, that they had simply had no good fortune with children . . .

That other woman was in one sense his true wife. Mother, at least briefly, of his child, it seemed.

She found she did not want to know what was in the letter. That, too, was better simply avoided. Not known, not spoken about, not an instrument of useless torture, as it would be if seen, whether its contents were good or bad.

She took the black japanned specimen box, with its oiled silk pocket in its glass lining, and put the letter in it. She added the hair bracelet – here, in white age, they were intertwined – and curled the long, thick thread – it was no more – of the blonde plait from his watch, inside the bracelet. She put in the tied bundles of their love-letters.

A young girl of twenty-four should not be made to wait for marriage until she is thirty-six and her flowering long over.

She remembered from the days of the Close, seeing herself once, naked, in a cheval glass. She must have been barely eighteen. Little high breasts, with warm brown circles. A skin like live ivory and long hair like silk. A princess.

Dearest Ellen,

I cannot get out of my mind – as indeed, how should I wish to, whose most ardent desire is to be possessed entirely by the pure thought of you – I cannot get out of my mind the entire picture of you, sitting in your white dress among the rosy teacups, with all the garden flowers, the hollyhocks, the delphiniums, the larkspur, burning crimson and blue and royal purple behind you, and only emphasising your lovely whiteness. And you smiled at me so kindly today, under your white hat with its palest pink ribbons. I remember every bunch of little bows, I remember every gentle ruffle, indeed it is a shame I am not a painter, but only an aspiring poet, or you should see how I treasure every smallest detail.

As I shall treasure – until death, theirs alas, and not mine, not for centuries yet, for I need a very long lifetime to love and cherish you, and must spend another such lifetime, alas proleptically, waiting for the right to do so – I shall treasure, I say, those flowers you gave me, which are before me as I write, in a very fine blue glass vase. I love the white roses most — they are not open yet — I have decades of their time, days at least of my own longer and most impatient duration in which to enjoy them. They are not a simple colour, you know, although they look it. They contain snow, and cream, and ivory, all quite distinct. Also at their heart they are still green — with newness, with hope, with that fine cool vegetable blood which will flush a little, when they open. (Did you know that the old painters gave an ivory glow to a rich skin by painting on a green base — it is a paradox of optics, strange and delightful.)

I lift them to my face and admire them. They are mildly fragrant, with a promise of richness. I push my enquiring nose in amongst them — not to hurt or derange their beautiful scrolling — I can be patient — each day they will unfold a little — one day I will bury my face in their white warmth — Did you ever play that childhood game with the huge opium poppy buds — we did — we would fold back the calyx and the tightly packed silk skirts, one by one — all crumpled — and so the poor flaunting scarlet thing would droop and die — such prying is best left to Nature and her hot sun, which opens them soon enough.

I have composed over 70 lines today, mindful of your injunctions to be busy, and avoid distraction. I am writing about the pyre of Balder — and his wife, Nanna's grief for him — and Hermodur's brave and fruitless journey to the Underworld to have him released by the goddess Hel — it is all most violently interesting, dear Ellen, an account of the human mind imagining and inventing a human story to account for the great and beautiful and terrible limiting facts of — existence — the rising and vanishing of the golden Sun, the coming of blossom (Nanna) in the Spring — her shrivelling in the Winter — the recalcitrance of dark (the goddess Thöck who refused to mourn for Balder, who was no use to her, she said, living or dead). And is not this the subject for great modern poetry as much as for the mythy speculations of our forefathers?

But I would rather be sitting in a certain garden — in a certain Close — among green and white roses — with a certain — decidedly a certain — young lady in white with a grave brow and a sudden sunny smile —

Ellen read no more. They could go with him. And wait for her.

She thought of putting the jet brooch he had sent from Whitby into the box, but decided against it. She would wear it at her throat, when they drove out to Hodershall.

She put more coal and more pieces of wood on the fire, and made a brave little blaze, by the side of which she sat down to manufacture the carefully edited, the carefully *strained* (the metaphor was one of jelly-making) truth of her journal. She would decide later what to do with *that*. It was both a defence against, and a bait for, the gathering of ghouls and vultures.

And why were the letters so carefully put up then, in their sealed enclosure? Could she read them, where she was going, could he? This last house was no house, why not leave them open to the things that tunnelled in the clay, the mites and blind worms, things that chewed with invisible mouths, and cleansed and annihilated?

I want them to have a *sort of duration*, she said to herself. A demi-eternity.

And if the ghouls dig them up again?

Then justice will perhaps be done to *her* when I am not here to see it.

She thought, one day, not now, not yet, I will put pen to paper and write to *her*, and tell her, tell her, what?

Tell her he died peacefully.

Tell her?

And the crystalline forms, the granite, the hornblende-schist, shone darkly with the idea that she would not write, that the Protean letter would form and reform, in her head, that it might become too late, too late for decency, absolutely too late. The other woman might die, she herself might die, they were both old and progressing towards it.

In the morning she would pull on her black gloves, and pick up the black box, and a spray of those white scentless hothouse roses that were all over the house, and set out on his last blind journey.

I am in your hands.

CHAPTER TWENTY-SIX

Since riddles are the order of our day
Come here, my love, and I will tell thee one.

There is a place to which all Poets come
Some having sought it long, some unawares,
Some having battled monsters, some asleep
Who chance upon the path in thickest dream,
Some lost in mythy mazes, some direct
From fear of death, or lust of life or thought
And some who lost themselves in Arcady...

These things are there. The garden and the tree
The serpent at its root, the fruit of gold
The woman in the shadow of the boughs
The running water and the grassy space.

They are and were there. At the old world's rim
In the Hesperidean grove, the fruit
Glowed golden on eternal boughs, and there
The dragon Ladon crisped his jewelled crest
Scraped a gold claw and showed a silver tooth
And dozed and waited through eternity
Until the tricksy hero, Herakles
Came to his dispossession and the theft.

Far otherwise, among the northern ice
In a high frozen fastness, in the waste
Of jagged ice-teeth and tall glassy spikes
Hidden from demons of the frost and mist
Freya's walled garden, with its orchard green
With summery frothing leaves and bright with fruit
Lay where the Ases came to eat the warm

Apples of everlasting youth and strength.
Close by, the World Ash rose from out the dark,
Thrusting his roots into the cavern where
Nidhogg the dark coiled with his forking tongue
And gnawed the roots of life that still renewed.
And there too were the water and the lawns,
The fount of Urd, where past and future mixed
All colours and no colour, glassy still
Or ominously turbulent and twined.

And are these places shadows of one Place?
Those trees of one Tree? And the mythic beast
A creature from the caverns of men's minds,
Or from a time when lizards walked the earth
On heavy legs as large as trees, or sprang
From bank to bank in swampy primal creeks
Where no man's foot had trod . . .?
Was he a dark Lord whom we dispossessed?
Or did our minds frame him to name ourselves
Our fierceness and our guile, our jealous grasp
At the bright stem of life, our wounded pride?

The first men named this place and named the world.
They made the words for it: garden and tree
Dragon or snake and woman, grass and gold
And apples. They made names and poetry.
The things *were* what they named and made them. Next
They mixed the names and made a metaphor
Or truth, or visible truth, apples of gold.
The golden apples brought a rush of words
The silvery water and the horrent scales
Upon the serpentining beast, the leaves
All green and shining on the curving boughs
(The serpentining boughs) that called to mind
The lovely gestures of the woman's arms
Her curving arms, her serpentining arms,
The forest wove a fence of its dark boughs
For the green grass and made a sacred place
Where the gold globes of fruit, like minor suns
Shone in their shadowy caverns made of leaves
So all was more and more distinct, and all
Was intertwined and serpentining, and
Parts of one whole, they saw, the later men

Who saw connections between shining things
And next saw movements (snatch and steal and stab)
And consequential stories where the Tree
Once stood in solitude and steady shone.

We see it and we make it, oh my dear.
People the place with creatures of our mind,
With lamias and dryads, melusines
And firedrakes, sparking, sliding, wreathing on,
We make commotion there and mystery
Hunger and grief and joy and tragedy.
We add and take away, we complicate
And multiply the foliage and the birds –
Place birds of paradise upon the boughs,
Make the stream run with blood and then run clear,
O'er grit of precious stones, diamonds and pearls
And emerald green and sapphires and anon
Wash these away and leave the pleasant sand
Holding the traces of the water's flow
As it has done since time began, we say.

I see the Tree all rugged-thick with bulk
Of corky bark about its knotted base.
You see it like a silver pillar, straight
With breathing skin for bark, and graceful arms.
The place is at the centre of a maze
Where men have died in thorny culs-de-sac.
The place is in a desert where men die
From thirst in sight of it, nor know they see
The true place, who have stumbled through a glare
Of mirage upon mirage, vanishing
Like melting ice, in the hot sun, or foam
Breaking at tide's edge, on the sifting beach.

All these are true and none. The place is there
Is what we name it, and is not. It *is*.

Randolph Henry Ash, from '*The Garden of Proserpina*'

As Roland was going down the area steps, a large woman in an
apron leaned over the railings.

'There isn't nobody there any more, luv.'

'I live here.'

'Oh yes? And where was you when they took her off, after

two days lying in pain under the letter-box too faint to squeak? It was me as noticed the milk-bottles and informed the Social Services. They took 'er off to Queen Mary's.'

'I was staying with friends in Lincoln. You mean Mrs Irving?'

'Yah. 'Ad a stroke and broke 'er 'ip. I 'ope they 'aven't cut off the electric. They do sometimes.'

'I'm only back –' Roland began, before Londoner's caution overtook him, and the thought of loitering burglars. 'I'm only back until I can find another flat,' he said carefully.

'Watch out for cats.'

'Cats?'

'When they come to take 'er off, they all come spitting and hissing out and ran off into the street. They make a nuisance of themselves, messing in the area, thieving in the bins. I telephoned the RSPCA to come and put them down. They say they'll look into it. I don't *think* there's any shut in the house. They come out like bugs shaken out of a blanket. A dozen or more.'

'Oh dear.'

'You can smell them.'

He could. It was the old smell of failure and sourness, with a fresh intensity to it.

Inside, it was, as always, dark. He turned on the hall light, which did work, and discovered he was standing on a heap of unopened letters, addressed to him, mostly limp and damp. He gathered them up, and moved through the flat, putting on lights. It was early evening; the area windows were dark periwinkle blue. Outside a cat mewed and another, further away, uttered a brief howl.

He said aloud, 'Listen to the silence.' The silence gathered thickly round his voice, so that he wondered, after all, if he had really spoken.

In the hall, in the light, the Manet portrait sprang out at him. The solid-shadowed head, the sharply thoughtful face, looking out, past him, with its expression eternally curious and composed. The light in Roland's hall caught the photographed painted light in the shiny thickness of the crystal ball. It illuminated the hints and traces of reflected light on the glass-contained jungle-ferns and watery sea-depth behind the head. Manet must have come close and peered at the light which made the life of those long-dead eyes.

Opposite, the print of the G. F. Watts's Ash rose silver-haired from its blackly shadowed trunk, the folded emptiness of the hinted frock-coat, and stared, prophetic perhaps, beautiful certainly, fiercely alert, like an ancient hawk at the solid and sensuous being opposite.

They were recognisably the same man and yet utterly different, years apart, visions apart. Yet recognisably the same.

Roland had once seen them as parts of himself. How much they had been that, to him, he only now understood, when he saw them as wholly distant and separate, not an angle, not a bone, not a white speck of illumination comprehensible by him or to do with him.

He put the stove on in the hall, and the gas-fire in the living-room, and sat down on the bed to read his letters. One was from Blackadder, which he put immediately at the bottom of the heap. Some were bills and some were postcards from holidaying friends. There were also what appeared to be answers to his last routine set of job-applications. They had foreign stamps. Hong Kong, Amsterdam, Barcelona.

Dear Dr Michell,

I am happy to tell you that the Board of Studies in English has recommended that we offer you a post as lecturer in English in the University of Hong Kong. The post is tenable initially for a period of two years after which a review will take place....

The salary is....

I hope very much that you will feel able to accept this offer. May I say how very much I admired your paper, 'Line by Line', on R. H. Ash, which you sent with your application. I hope to have the chance of discussing it with you.

We should be glad of an early reply, as there was very strong competition for the post. We have tried to telephone, but there has been no answer.

Dear Dr Michell,

We are happy to tell you that your application for an assistant lectureship at the Free University of Amsterdam has been successful. The appointment is to begin in October 1988: it is understood that you will learn Dutch within two years of taking up your post, though the majority of your teaching will be in English.

A prompt reply would be appreciated. Professor de Groot has asked me to tell you that he thinks very highly of your paper, 'Line by Line', on R. H. Ash's vocabulary....

Dear Dr Michell,

It is with great pleasure that I write to inform you that your application for the post of Lecturer in the Autonomous University of Barcelona has been successful, and that you are offered the position with effect from January 1988. We are particularly keen to strengthen our teaching in the nineteenth century, and your paper on R. H. Ash was very much admired....

Roland was so used to the pervasive sense of failure that he was unprepared for the blood-rush of success. He breathed differently. The dingy little room humped around in his vision briefly and settled at a different distance, an object of interest, not of choking confinement. He reread his letters. The world opened. He imagined aeroplanes and a cabin on the ferry from Harwich to the Hook, the sleeper from the Gare d'Austerlitz to Madrid. He imagined canals and Rembrandt, Mediterranean oranges, Gaudí and Picasso, junks and skyscrapers, a glimpse of hidden China and the sun on the Pacific. He thought of 'Line by Line' with a great rush of the first excitement with which he had first mapped it out. The gloomy self-disparagement inspired in him by Maud's theoretic certainties and sharpnesses vanished like smoke. Three professors had particularly admired it. How true it was that one needed to be seen by others to be sure of one's own existence. Nothing in what he had written had changed and everything had changed. Quickly, before his courage went, he opened Blackadder's letter.

Dear Roland,

I am somewhat concerned to have heard nothing from you for some considerable time. I hope you will feel able to tell me about the Ash-LaMotte correspondence in due course. You may even care to know what steps have been taken to preserve it for 'the Nation'. You may not; your proceedings in this matter are hard for me to understand.

I am writing now, however, not on account of this, nor because of your

unexplained absence from the British Library, but because I have had urgent
telephone calls from Professor de Groot in Amsterdam, Professor Liu in Hong
Kong and Professor Valverde in Barcelona, all of whom are anxious to appoint
you. I would not wish you to lose these chances. I have assured them that you
will reply as soon as you return, and that you are available. But I need
instruction as to your plans in order to know how to protect your interests.

I hope you are not ill.

Yours
James Blackadder.

After a moment's needled irritation, in which he heard the
whole of this message in Blackadder's most sarcastic Scots, Roland
realised that this was quite possibly a very generous letter –
certainly kinder than he deserved. Unless it contained a hidden
Machiavellian plan to re-establish contact and then savage him?
This seemed unlikely; the threatening and repressive demon in
the BM basement seemed in this new light partly a figment of
his own subjected imagination. Blackadder had held his fate in
his hands and had seemed not to care to help. Now Roland could
be free of him – and he was actively helping, not hindering, that
freedom. Roland thought over the whole thing. Why had he run
away? Partly because of Maud – the discovery had been half hers,
neither of them could have shared with anyone else without
betraying the other. He decided not to think about Maud. Not
yet, not here, not in this context.

He began restlessly to walk about the flat. He thought of tele-
phoning Maud to tell her about his letters and then decided
against it. He needed to be alone and to think.

He became aware of a strange sound in the flat – a kind of sawing
and scraping, as though someone was trying to force his way in.
It stopped and then started again. Roland listened. The scraping
was accompanied by a strange intermittent moaning cry. After a
moment's fear, he worked out that the cats were scratching at
the matting outside his front door. In the garden, a full-throated
feline howl rose and was answered from the area. He wondered
idly how many they were and what would become of them.

He thought about Randolph Henry Ash. The pursuit of the

letters had distanced him from Ash as they had come closer to Ash's life. In the days of his innocence Roland had been, not a hunter but a reader, and had felt superior to Mortimer Cropper, and in some sense equal to Ash, or anyway related to Ash, who had written for him to read intelligently, as best he could. Ash had not written the letters for Roland or for anyone else but Christabel LaMotte. Roland's find had turned out to be a sort of loss. He took the draft letters out of their safe place, inside a file on his desk marked *Notes on Aeneid VI*, and read them again.

'Since our extraordinary conversation I have thought of nothing else.'

'Since our pleasant and unexpected conversation I have thought of little else.'

He remembered the day those dark leaves had flown out of R. H. Ash's Vico. He remembered looking up Vico's Proserpine. He remembered he had been reading Ash's *Golden Apples* and had been looking for a connection between Vico's Proserpina and Ash's version of her in that poem. He took down his Ash from the shelf, sat at his desk, and read.

It is possible for a writer to make, or remake at least, for a reader, the primary pleasures of eating, or drinking, or looking on, or sex. Novels have their obligatory tour-de-force, the green-flecked gold omelette *aux fines herbes*, melting into buttery formlessness and tasting of summer, or the creamy human haunch, firm and warm, curved back to reveal a hot hollow, a crisping hair or two, the glimpsed sex. They do not habitually elaborate on the equally intense pleasure of reading. There are obvious reasons for this, the most obvious being the regressive nature of the pleasure, a *mise-en-abîme* even, where words draw attention to the power and delight of words, and so *ad infinitum*, thus making the imagination experience something papery and dry, narcissistic and yet disagreeably distanced, without the immediacy of sexual moisture or the scented garnet glow of good burgundy. And yet, natures such as Roland's are at their most alert and heady when reading is violently yet steadily alive. (What an amazing word 'heady' is, *en passant*, suggesting both acute sensuous alertness and its opposite, the pleasure of the brain as opposed to the viscera – though each is implicated in the other, as we know very well, with both, when they are working.)

Think of this, as Roland thought of it, rereading 'The Garden of Proserpina' for perhaps the twelfth, or maybe even the twentieth time, a poem he 'knew' in the sense that he had already experienced all its words, in their order, and also out of order, in memory, in selective quotation or misquotation – in the sense also, that he could predict, at times even recite, those words which were next to come, or more remotely approaching, the place where his mind rested, like clawed bird feet on twig. Think of this – that the writer wrote alone, and the reader read alone, and they were alone with each other. True, the writer may have been alone also with Spenser's golden apples in the *Faerie Queene*, Proserpina's garden, glistering bright among the place's ashes and cinders, may have seen in his mind's eye, apple of his eye, the golden fruit of the Primavera, may have seen Paradise Lost, in the garden where Eve recalled Pomona and Proserpina. He was alone when he wrote and he was not alone then, all these voices sang, the same words, golden apples, different words in different places, an Irish castle, an unseen cottage, elastic-walled and grey round blind eyes.

There are readings – of the same text – that are dutiful, readings that map and dissect, readings that hear a rustling of unheard sounds, that count grey little pronouns for pleasure or instruction and for a time do not hear golden or apples. There are personal readings, that snatch for personal meanings, I am full of love, or disgust, or fear, I scan for love, or disgust, or fear. There are – believe it – impersonal readings – where the mind's eye sees the lines move onwards and the mind's ear hears them sing and sing.

Now and then there are readings which make the hairs on the neck, the non-existent pelt, stand on end and tremble, when every word burns and shines hard and clear and infinite and exact, like stones of fire, like points of stars in the dark – readings when the knowledge that we *shall know* the writing differently or better or satisfactorily, runs ahead of any capacity to say what we know, or how. In these readings, a sense that the text has appeared to be wholly new, never before seen, is followed, almost immediately, by the sense that it was *always there*, that we the readers, knew it was always there, and have *always known* it was as it was, though we have now for the first time recognised, become fully cognisant of, our knowledge.

Roland read, or reread, *The Golden Apples*, as though the words were living creatures or stones of fire. He saw the tree, the fruit, the fountain, the woman, the grass, the serpent, single and multifarious in form. He heard Ash's voice, certainly his voice, his own unmistakable voice, and he heard the language moving around, weaving its own patterns, beyond the reach of any single human, writer or reader. He heard Vico saying that the first men were poets and the first words were names that were also things, and he heard his own strange, necessary meaningless *lists*, made in Lincoln, and saw what they were. He saw too that Christabel was the Muse and Proserpina and that she was not, and this seemed to be so interesting and *apt*, once he had understood it, that he laughed aloud. Ash had started him on this quest and he had found the clue he had started with, and all was cast off, the letter, the letters, Vico, the apples, his list.

'In the garden they howled, they lifted their voices and howled with hunger and desolation.'

Over his desk the little print of the photograph of Randolph Ash's death mask was ambiguous. You could read it either way; as though you were looking into a hollow mould, as though the planes of the cheeks and forehead, the blank eyes and the broad brow were sculpted and looking out. You were inside – behind those closed eyes like an actor, masked: you were outside, looking at closure, if not finality. The frontispiece of his book was a photograph of Ash on his death-bed, the abundant white hair, the look of fatigue caught at a transient moment between the semblance of life and the set of death. These dead men, and Manet's wary, intelligent sensualist and Watts's prophet were all one – though also they were Manet and Watts – and the words too were one, the tree, the woman, the water, the grass, the snake and the golden apples. He had always seen these aspects as part of himself, of Roland Michell, he had lived with them. He remembered talking to Maud about modern theories of the incoherent self, which was made up of conflicting systems of beliefs, desires, languages and molecules. All and none of these were Ash and yet he knew, if he did not encompass, Ash. He touched the letters, which Ash had touched, over which Ash's hand had moved, urgent and tentative, reforming and rejecting his own words. He looked at the still fiery traces of the poem.

What Ash said – not to him specifically, there was no privileged communication, though it was he who happened to be there, at that time, to understand it – was that the lists were the important thing, the words that named things, the language of poetry.

He had been taught that language was essentially inadequate, that it could never speak what was there, that it only spoke itself.

He thought about the death mask. He could and could not say that the mask and the man were dead. What had happened to him was that the ways in which it *could* be said had become more interesting than the idea that it could not.

He felt hugely hungry. On the way to fetch himself a tin of sweetcorn he heard the cats again, crying, scraping at his door. He found a heap of tins of pilchards and sardines – he and Val had lived frugally, these were a staple. He opened one of these and put it into a saucer, put it down inside the entrance to the flat and opened the door. Faces looked up at him, triangular sleek black faces, golden-eyed, owlish whiskered faces, tiger-striped, a smoke-grey kitten and a heavy orange Tom. He put down his saucer and called, as he had heard the old woman call. For a moment they hesitated there, heads on one side, and he watched their nostrils spread and snuff the oil on the air. Then they came past him in a rush, on their bellies, and the food was gone, two heads, snatching and gulping, a battle of legs and sinuous bodies, a long cry of the disappointed. He opened more tins, and put down a row of saucers. Soft feet hurried down the area steps, white needle teeth tore at the fish flesh, satisfied fur coiled and purred around his ankles, setting off little electric sparks. He watched them. Fifteen cats. They looked up at him, clear green glass eyes, tawny eyes, yellow and amber eyes, their pupils narrowing to slits in the light of his hall.

*

He thought there was no reason why he should not go out into the garden. He went back through the basement, pursued by several padding beasts, and pulled open the forbidden bolts, against the grittiness of the rust. He had to move heaps of papers away from the door. (Val had said they were a fire hazard.) The central lock was a Yale, which he turned, propping the door open. The night air came in, cold and damp and earthy, and the cats came out with him, running ahead. He went up the stone steps, and round the wall, beyond the extent of his confined view, and stood in the narrow garden, under the trees.

It had been a wet October; the lawn was covered with damp leaves, although some of the trees were still green. They held up their complicated arms, black against the pink haze of street lighting which lay over, rather than mixing with, the black of the space beyond. In his imagination, when he could not get into the garden, it had seemed a large space of breathing leaves and real earth. Now he was out, it seemed smaller, but still mysterious, because of the earth, in which things were growing. He could see the espaliered peaches on the red bricks of the serpentining wall which had once bounded General Fairfax's Putney estate. He walked over and touched the wall, the baked bricks put up sturdily then, and still solid now. Andrew Marvell had been Fairfax's secretary and had written poems in Fairfax's gardens. Roland was not sure why he felt so happy. Was it the letters, was it Ash's poem, was it the opening of his future, was it simply being alone, which was something he needed ferociously from time to time and lately had missed? He walked along the path, inside the wall, to the end of the garden, where a couple of fruit trees obscured the view of the garden beyond. He looked back at the gaunt house, across the lawn. The cats were coming after him. Their snaking bodies wove in and out of the shadows of the trees on the grass, now glossy in the light, now velvet black in the dark. Their eyes shone fitfully and intermittently, hollow reddish balls, with a bluish spark at the centre, green-streaked curves on the dark that glittered and were gone. He was so pleased to see them, he stood with a silly smile on his face. He thought of the years of their dank smell, the dripping cave he had lived in, and felt, now he was going – for that was certain, he was going away – simply friendly towards them. Tomorrow he would have to think how to arrange for their survival. Tonight, he began to think of words, words came from some well in him, lists of words that arranged themselves into poems, 'The Death Mask', 'The Fairfax Wall', 'A Number of Cats'. He could hear, or feel, or even almost see, the patterns made by a voice he didn't yet know, but which was his own. The poems were not careful observations, nor yet incantations, nor yet reflections on life and death, though they had elements of all these. He added another, 'Cats' Cradle', as he saw he had things to say which he could say about the way shapes came and made themselves. Tomorrow he would buy a new notebook and write them down. Tonight he would write down enough, the mnemonics.

He had time to feel the strangeness of before and after; an hour ago there had been no poems, and now they came like rain and were real.

CHAPTER TWENTY-SEVEN

In certain moods we eat our lives away
In fast successive greed; we must have more
Although that *more* depletes our little stock
Of time and peace remaining. We are driven
By endings as by hunger. We *must know*
How it comes out, the shape o' the whole, the thread
Whose links are weak or solid, intricate
Or boldly welded in great clumsy loops
Of primitive workmanship. We feel our way
Along the links and we cannot let go
Of this bright chain of curiosity
Which is become our fetter. So it drags
Us through our time – 'And *then*, and *then*, and *then*',
Towards our figured consummation.
And we must have the knife, the dart, the noose,
The last embrace, the golden wedding ring
The trump of battle or the deathbed rasp
Although we know and must know, they're all one,
Finis, The End, the one consummate shock
That ends all shocks and us. Do we desire
We prancing, cogitating, nervous lives
Movement's cessation or a maw crammed full
Of sweetest certainty, though with that bliss
We cease as in his thrilling bridal dance
The male wasp finds the bliss and swift surcease
Of his small time i' the air.

                              Randolph Henry Ash.

The Mortlake conference was held in an unlikely atmosphere of
gaiety and conspiracy. It was held in Beatrice Nest's house, at her

invitation. (Mortlake was agreed, conspiratorially, to be beyond the beam of Mortimer Cropper's attention.) Beatrice made onion and cream tart, green salad and chocolate mousse, as she had once done for her graduate students. The tarts and mousse looked delicious, and Beatrice was happy. Concentrating on the matter in hand, the threat from Mortimer Cropper, she ignored the currents of tension between her guests, the things not being said, the things substituted for what was not being said.

Maud arrived first, looking severe and preoccupied, her green silk scarf again wound round her head and pinned with the jet mermaid. She stood in one corner, considering the silver-framed photograph of Randolph Henry Ash that stood, where those of father or lover might have stood, on Beatrice's little secretaire. It was not a photograph of the late silvered sage, but an early one, with a mass of dark hair and an almost piratical look. Maud automatically began to analyse it semiotically; the solid silver arabesques of the frame, the choice of image, the fact that the sitter apparently met the onlooker's eye, the still nineteenth-century pre-snapshot stare. The fact that the photograph was of the poet, not of his wife.

Maud was followed by Val and Euan MacIntyre. Beatrice did not quite understand this grouping. She had met Val from time to time, sullenly staring from the edge of the working group in the Ash Factory. She noted Val's new, slightly defiant radiance, but with scholarly single-mindedness did not attempt to account for it. Euan complimented her on her presence of mind in over-hearing and reporting Mortimer Cropper's intentions, and pro-nounced the whole business to be very exciting, which, combined with the success of the tart and mousse, further changed Beatrice's mood, which had initially been alarm and a sense of oppression.

Val and Euan were followed by Roland, who said nothing to Maud and began a long conversation with Val about the arrangements for feeding a horde of savage cats and the making of telephone calls to the Animal Welfare. Beatrice did not hear the silence between Roland and Maud, and was of course not aware that Roland was not telling anyone at all about Hong Kong, Barcelona and Amsterdam.

Beatrice herself had telephoned Blackadder, saying in a matter-of-fact way that she had made contact with Dr Bailey and Roland

Michell and that they wanted to meet to discuss the Ash-LaMotte correspondence and something she had overheard Professor Cropper saying. When she opened the door to this final member of the group, he presented her, with a look of mingled embarrassment and amusement, to Professor Leonora Stern. Leonora was resplendent in a purple hooded woollen cape, fringed with black silk braid, which covered a kind of scarlet Russian tunic, in heavy silk, over wide black Chinese trousers. Leonora said to Beatrice, 'I hope you don't mind me coming. I promise not to harass anyone, but I have my own scholarly interest in all this.' Beatrice could feel her own round face failing to achieve a welcoming smile. Leonora said, 'Oh, please. I'll keep as quiet as a mouse. I can swear in advance I'm not out to snatch any manuscript, covertly or openly. I only want to *read* the damn things.'

Blackadder said, 'I think Professor Stern may be of material help to us.'

Beatrice held open the door and they climbed the narrow stairs to the little first-floor drawing-room. Beatrice naturally noticed a certain complicated silence surrounding Blackadder's nod of recognition directed at Roland, but she failed altogether to read the omissions of information or accusation in the long dramatic embrace between Leonora and Maud.

They sat around the edges of the room in armchairs and kitchen chairs with plates on their knees. Euan MacIntyre opened the discussion by saying that he thought he should explain his own presence, which was that of a kind of legal adviser to Maud, who was in his opinion certainly the heir to the ownership of the LaMotte letters, and almost certainly of the manuscripts of the Ash letters, though not of the copyright in these, which was vested in the heirs of Randolph Ash.

'Letters are the property of the recipient – as physical entities – but the copyright remains with the sender. In the case of these letters, it is clear that Christabel LaMotte requested the return of her letters to her possession, and that Randolph Ash willingly complied. Roland and Maud, who have seen the whole correspondence, are quite clear on this. I have legal proof – a Will, signed and witnessed, of Christabel LaMotte, leaving *all* her

478

manuscripts to Maia Thomasine Bailey, who was Maud's great-great-great-grandmother. The true heir would, I suppose, be Maud's father, who is still living, but he has already made a gift of what manuscripts came to his ancestress, at the time of this bequest, to Maud, who has deposited them in the Women's Resource Centre at Lincoln. Maud has not told him yet of my discovery, and does not think he has taken any interest in the press reports of Professor Cropper's large offers of money to Sir George Bailey, who believes himself to be the owner of the letters. Maud thinks, however, that there is almost no likelihood that her father would want to sell to the Stant Foundation, given her interest in the retention of the documents in this country.

'I should perhaps add, in case any of you are thinking about the copyright law, that the ownership of copyright is protected *from the moment of publication* for the author's lifetime plus fifty years, or in the case of posthumous publication, for fifty years from the date of publication. This correspondence is unpublished, and therefore the copyright remains the property of the heirs of the original writers of the letters. As I have said, manuscripts belong to recipients, copyright to the senders of letters. It is not clear what Lord Ash would wish to happen, but from what Dr Nest has to tell us, it appears that Cropper has induced Hildebrand Ash to promise him both letters and copyright.'

Blackadder said, 'He is an infuriating person and an unscrupulous operator, but his edition is thorough and scrupulously researched, and it would be churlish in my view not to permit publication of these letters in the standard edition. I suppose if the letters remained in this country it would be theoretically possible to refuse him access to them, and theoretically possible for Hildebrand Ash to refuse anyone else permission to edit them, thus producing an impasse. There is, of course, Lord Ash himself. He might allow an early British edition which would protect the copyright, before allowing access to Cropper. Do you foresee protracted legal disputes with Sir George Bailey, Mr MacIntyre?'

'Given his pugnacity, and his actual, *de facto possession* of the letters, yes, I do.'

'Lord Ash is very ill.'

'So I understand.'

'May I ask, Dr Bailey – if you do find yourself in possession of the manuscripts of the whole correspondence – what you would intend doing with them?'

'I think it's premature to say where they should be, and I also feel a kind of superstitious fear of it – the letters aren't mine, and may never be. *If* they were – if they are – I should want them to stay in this country. I should naturally like LaMotte's letters to be in the Women's Resource Centre – which isn't very secure, but the rest of her things – that came from my family – are already there. On the other hand I don't want – I feel, having read them – the letters should stay together. They belong together. It's not only that they need to be read consecutively to make any sense – they – they are part of each other.'

She looked quickly at Roland, on this, and away, fixing her eye on the photograph of Ash, which was beyond him, between him and Val.

'If you sold them to the British Library,' said Blackadder, 'you could benefit the Resource Centre in other ways.'

Leonora said, 'If scholars came from all over the world to the Centre, *that* would benefit it.'

Roland said, 'I wish Lady Bailey *could* have a new electric wheelchair.'

Everyone suddenly turned their attention to him.

'She was good to us. And she's ill.'

Maud flushed to her hairline.

'I had thought of that myself,' she said, with a touch of anger. 'If the letters *are* mine – if I sell half or all to the British Library – we could help with the wheelchair.'

'He'd probably throw it back at you,' said Roland.

'Do you want me to *give* him the manuscripts?'

'No. Just to find a way –'

Blackadder looked at the developing quarrel between the two original researchers.

'I should like to know,' he said, 'how you came across the correspondence in the first place.'

Everyone looked at Maud, who looked at Roland.

This was the moment of truth. Also the moment of dispossession, or perhaps the word was exorcism.

'I was reading Vico,' he said. 'Ash's copy of Michelet's translation of Vico. In the London Library. And all these papers sprang out. Stationery bills, Latin notes, letters, invitations. I told Professor Blackadder, of course. But I didn't tell him I found – I found two drafts of a beginning of a letter to a woman – it didn't say who – but it was after he went to breakfast with Crabb Robinson – so I did some research – and found Christabel LaMotte. So I went to see Maud, who was suggested to me – oh yes, by Fergus Wolff – I didn't know of the family connection, or anything – and she showed me Blanche Glover's journal – and then we began to wonder about whether there was anything at Seal Court – we went past just to *look* at it – and met Lady Bailey – and were shown Christabel's turret – and Maud remembered a poem about dolls keeping a secret, and investigated a doll's bed – it was still in her room – and there it was – there *they* were, the letters – hidden in a cavity under the mattress . . .'

'And Lady Bailey took to Roland, who saved her life, he forgot to tell you, and said he might come back and *look* at the letters and advise – so we went at Christmas –'

'And we read them first and took notes –'

'And Roland worked out that LaMotte might have gone to Yorkshire with Ash on his zoological expedition in 1859 –'

'So we went up there and found – a lot of *textual* evidence in both poets that perhaps both were there – Yorkshire phrases and landscapes in *Melusina* – the same line in both poets – we think she was certainly there –'

'And then we found out that LaMotte had been in Brittany in the lost year before the suicide of Blanche Glover –'

'Ah yes, so you did,' said Leonora.

Maud said, 'I was very wrong, Leonora. I took your letter from Ariane Le Minier and went without telling you – because the secret wasn't mine but also Ash's – and Roland's – or so it felt at the time. Anyway, Dr Le Minier gave us a copy of Sabine de Kercoz's journal, and it became clear that a child had been born there – which can't be traced –'

'And then you came, and Professor Cropper, and we came home,' said Roland briefly.

'And Euan appeared as if by magic with the Will –'

'I know Sir George's lawyer, we share a horse,' said Euan to the great puzzlement of Beatrice.

'It seems clear,' said Blackadder, 'that *Mummy Possest* is directed at *LaMotte's* association with Hella Lees, and that *LaMotte* was present at the seance which Ash infamously interrupted, and I would *conjecture* that Ash believed that LaMotte was trying to speak to her dead child in the seance, which if it was *his* child, would have angered him immensely.'

'And I know,' said Leonora, 'because I have a good friend and sister-feminist who works in the offices of the Stant Collection, that Cropper has been reading faxes of letters containing great guilt from LaMotte to his spiritualist-socialist-feminist-mesmerist great-great-grandma, Priscilla Penn Cropper.'

'Which brings us,' said Blackadder, 'to two, no three, final questions.

'One: what became of the child, alive or dead?

'Two: what is Cropper trying to find out? On what basis of knowledge?

'And three: what became of the original letters?'

Everyone looked at Roland again. He brought out his wallet and unfolded the letters from their safe place inside it.

He said, 'I took them. I don't know why. I never meant to – to *keep* them forever. I don't know what possessed me to do it – it seemed so easy, and they seemed to be my find – I mean, as no one else had touched them, since he put them away in Vico, as bookmarks or whatever. I'll have to give them back. Whose are they?'

Euan said, 'If the book was a gift or bequest to the London Library, they probably belong to it. The copyright belongs to Lord Ash.'

Blackadder said, 'If you give them to me, I guarantee they can go back to the Library with no questions asked, of you, anyway.'

Roland stood up and walked across the room, and handed the letters to Blackadder, who could be seen to be unable to resist reading them then and there, to turn the paper lovingly, possessively, recognising the writing.

'You have been very resourceful,' he said drily, to Roland.

'One thing led to another.'

'Indeed.'

'And all's well that ends well,' said Euan. 'This feels like the ending of a Shakespearean comedy — who's the chappie that comes down on a swing at the end of *As You Like It*?'

'Hymen,' said Blackadder, smiling slightly.

'Or like the unmasking at the end of a detective story. I've always wanted to be Albert Campion, myself. We still haven't tackled our villain. I suggest Dr Nest tells us what she overheard.'

'Well,' said Beatrice, 'they came to look at the end of Ellen's journal, that is, not the *end*, but her description of *his* end, and the mention of that box that Professor Cropper has always been so interested in, the one that was seen to be intact when Ellen herself was buried, you know the one. And I went out to the Ladies' Room — it was a day when no one else was there, Professor Blackadder, no one was in your part of the office *at all* — and as you know, it's a terribly long walk, to the cloakrooms and back — so when I came, they weren't expecting me, and I heard Professor Cropper say — this isn't verbatim but I do have a good verbal memory and I was very shocked — he said, "It could remain quite secret for several years, a secret between the two of us, and then when you have inherited it would *appear*, we could come upon it — you could *find* it — and I would purchase it from you — all above board." And Hildebrand Ash said, "Morally it's mine, isn't it, whatever the Vicar says?" And Cropper said, "Yes, but the Vicar's a most obstructive person, and there are all sorts of silly English laws about disturbing burials and needing a Faculty from the Bishop and I don't think we can afford to risk all that." And Hildebrand Ash said again, "It's my own property." And Professor Cropper said it belonged both to Hildebrand and to the world, and that he himself would be a "discreet custodian". And Hildebrand said it would be a Hallowe'en adventure, and Professor Cropper said severely that it would have to be a very serious professional undertaking, and soon, as he was due back in New Mexico . . .

'And then I thought I should cough, or something, in case they noticed me standing in the shadow. So I took a lot of steps backward and *advanced more noisily*, so to speak.'

'I believe he is capable of grave robbery,' said Blackadder, tight-lipped.

'I know he is,' said Leonora Stern. 'There are all sorts of rumours, in the States. Things that have disappeared from glass cabinets in little local collections, you know, curios of particular interest, Edgar Allan Poe's pawned tie-pin, a note from Melville to Hawthorne, that sort of thing. A friend of mine had almost persuaded a descendant of a friend of Margaret Fuller's to sell a letter about her meeting with English writers in Florence, before her fatal voyage – *full* of feminist interest – and Cropper turned up, and offered a blank cheque, and was refused. So the next day, when they went to look for the MS, it had gone. It was never traced. But *we* think he's like those mythical millionaires who pay thieves to get them *the* Mona Lisa and *the* Potato Eaters –'

'He feels they *are* really his, perhaps,' said Roland, 'because he loves them most.'

'A kind way of putting it,' said Blackadder, turning the original Ash letter in his hand. 'So we are to assume a private, inaccessible inner cabinet of curios that he turns over, and breathes in at the dead of night, things no one ever sees –'

'So the rumour goes,' said Leonora. 'You know how it is with rumours. They waft, they burgeon. But I think this one has some foundation. I know for a fact that the Fuller story is true.'

'How are we to stop him?' said Blackadder. 'Tell the police? Complain to Robert Dale Owen University? Confront him? He'd brush off the last two, and the first is a bit ridiculous – they've not got the men to mount guard at a grave for the next few months. If we put him off now, he'll just give up graciously and try later. We can't get him deported.'

Euan said, 'I've rung his hotel, and Hildebrand's house in the country, and found out a few things. I pretended to be their lawyer, in a hurry with important information, and got told where they really were. Which is, The Old Rowan Tree pub, on the North Downs, near, but not very near, Hodershall. Both of them. That's very significant.'

'We should alert Drax, the vicar,' said Blackadder. 'Though that's not much use, he hates *all* Ash scholars and poetic trippers.'

'*I* think,' said Euan. 'This may sound melodramatic and toujours Mr Campion, but I do really think, that we have to catch him in the act and take whatever – it – is *from* him.'

A pleased murmur ran around the room. Beatrice said,

'We can catch him in the act before he desecrates the grave.'

'In theory, in theory,' said Euan. 'In practice, we may need to safeguard whatever there is, if there is anything.'

'Do you think he thinks,' asked Val, 'that the end of the story is there in that box? Because there's no reason why it should be. There could be anything or nothing, in that box.'

'We know that. He knows that. But these letters have made us all look — in some ways — a little silly, in our summing-up of lives on the evidence we had. None of Ash's post-1859 poems is uncontaminated by this affair — we shall need to reassess *everything* — the reasons for his animus against the spiritualists is a case in point.'

'And LaMotte,' said Leonora, 'has always been cited as a lesbian-feminist poet. Which she was, but not exclusively, it appears.'

'And *Melusina*,' said Maud, 'appears very different if the early landscapes are seen as partly Yorkshire. I've been rereading. No use of the word "ash" may be presumed to be innocent.'

Euan said, 'How are we going to foil the body-snatchers, which I take to be the main purpose of our meeting?'

Blackadder said doubtfully, 'I suppose I could invoke Lord Ash.'

'I have a better idea. I think we set spies and *watch him.*'

'How?'

'I think if Dr Nest is right he must be going to dig *soon*. And I think if two of us stay in the same pub — two he doesn't know at all — we can alert the others — or if necessary confront him alone, follow him to the churchyard, stop his car with a legal-looking piece of paper — we shall have to play it by ear. Val and I could go. I've got a bit of holiday. And you, I believe, Professor Blackadder, have an order preventing the export of Ash's papers until the Heritage Advisory Board has decided what to do —'

'If he could be stopped from disturbing their rest,' said Beatrice.

'I do wonder,' said Blackadder, 'what is or was in that box.'

'And for whom it was put there,' said Maud.

'She leads you on and baffles you,' said Beatrice. 'She wants you to know and not to know. She took care to write down that the box was there. And she buried it.'

Val and Euan left first, hand in hand. Roland looked at Maud, who was immediately engaged by Leonora in an intense conversation and a series of demonstratively forgiving hugs. He found himself leaving with Blackadder. They walked along the pavement together.

'I've behaved badly. I'm sorry.'

'It's understandable, I believe.'

'I felt possessed. I had to know.'

'Did ye hear about the posts ye've been offered?'

'I don't know what to do.'

'You've got mebbe a week's grace. I've spoken to them all. Sung your praises.'

'That was kind.'

'Your work is good. I liked that piece, "Line by Line". A thorough piece of work. I've got funding for a full-time research fellowship, on Ash. If you're interested. A spin-off, I believe you'd call it, from the screen appearance I made. A Scottish philanthropic trust run by a lawyer who turns out to be obsessed with Ash.'

'I can't decide what to do. I'm not even sure I want to stay in academic life.'

'Well, as I said, you've got a week. Drop by, if you feel like discussing the pros and cons.'

'Thanks. I'll think a bit, and then I will.'

CHAPTER TWENTY-EIGHT

The Rowan Tree Inn stands about a mile outside Hodershall, in the shelter of a curve of the North Downs. It was built of flint and slate in the eighteenth century, and is long and low, under a mossy slate roof. It fronts a meandering road, now modernised and widened, which cuts across largely bare downland; across the road, a further mile up a long grassy track, is the Hodershall Parish Church, built in the twelfth century, squat and stony, also under a slate roof, with an unassuming tower and a weathercock in the shape of a flying dragon. These two buildings stand apart from Hodershall village, behind the arm of the down. The Rowan Tree has twelve bedrooms, five along the main road front, and seven more in a modern annexe, built in the same local stones, behind the original building. It has an orchard, with tables and wooden swings for summer visitors. It is mentioned in all the Good Food guides.

On October 15th it had few visitors. The weather was warm for the time of year – the trees still had their leaves – but very wet. Five of the bedrooms were taken, two of them by Mortimer Cropper and Hildebrand Ash. Cropper had the best bedroom, over the solidly handsome front door, looking out to the track to the church. Hildebrand Ash was next to him. They had been there a week, and had gone for long tramps along the Downs in all weathers, well-protected with high boots, waxed jackets and portable parkas. Mortimer Cropper said, once or twice in the bar, which was panelled and dark, with shining gold hints of brass and dark green shades on its discreet lights, that he was thinking of buying a home in the district, a place in which to settle and write for part of the year. He visited various house agents and looked at various estates. He was knowledgeable about forestry and interested in organic farming.

On the fourteenth, Ash and Cropper went into Leatherhead and visited the offices of Densher and Winterbourne. They stopped at a garden centre on their way out of the town and purchased – for cash – various heavy-duty spades and forks and a pickaxe which they stowed in the boot of the Mercedes. On the afternoon of the fourteenth, they took a walk to the church, which was, as usual, locked against vandals, and wandered round the churchyard, looking at the gravestones. There was a notice at the entrance to the little graveyard, which was fenced with crumbling iron railings; the notice informed them that this parish, the parish of St Thomas, was part of a group of three parishes, of which the Reverend Percy Drax was Vicar. Holy Eucharist and Morning Prayer were held there on the first Sunday of every month; Evensong on the last.

'I don't know this Drax,' said Hildebrand Ash.

'A most unpleasant person,' said Mortimer Cropper. 'The Schenectady Poetry Fellowship made a presentation to this Church of an inkwell Ash had used on his American tour, and some of his books he had signed for American admirers, with his photograph pasted in. They presented a glass case as well, to display the treasures; Mr Drax has sited it in a *most obscure* corner and covered it with a dusty baize pall and absolutely no external indication of its nature, so that it is entirely missed by the casual visitor ...'

'Who can't get in anyway,' said Hildebrand Ash.

'Precisely. And this Drax is very hostile to being asked for keys by Ash scholars and admirers who wish to pay their respects. He says – he has written to me in letters – that the church is God's house, not Randolph Henry Ash's mausoleum. *I* see no contradiction.'

'You could buy the things back.'

'I could. I have offered substantial donations to him even for the loan of the objects. The books are already represented in the Stant Collection, but the inkwell is unique. He replies that unfortunately it is not in the terms of the gift that the objects may be disposed of. He is not interested in ways of altering the terms of the gift. He is positively surly.'

'We could take them too,' said Hildebrand. 'While we were at it.'

He laughed, and Mortimer Cropper frowned.

'I am not a common thief,' he said severely. 'It is only that box – whose contents we may only guess at – the thought of it decaying in the ground until such time as we acquire the legal right to exhume it – the thought of *perhaps never knowing* –'

'The value –'

'The value is partly the value *I* set on it.'

'Which is high,' said Hildebrand, with a question.

'Which is high even if it contains nothing,' said Cropper. 'For my peace of mind. But it will *not* contain nothing. I know.'

They took a turn or two about the churchyard. Everything was quiet, English and dripping. The graves were mostly nineteenth-century with some earlier and a few later. The grave of Randolph and Ellen was at one edge of the churchyard, in the shelter of a kind of grassy knoll, or mound, on which grew an ancient cedar and an even older yew, screening the quiet corner from the eyes of anyone on the path to the church door. The railings were just beyond the grave and beyond them a field, closely-cropped, of down grass, containing a few stolid sheep and a little stream, bisecting it. Someone had already been digging; green turfs were neatly stacked against the rails. Hildebrand counted thirteen.

'One for the head and a double row for the length of the ... I could do that. I can cut turfs, I take an interest in our lawn. Are you thinking of trying to leave it so it looks undisturbed?'

Cropper thought. 'We could try that. Put it all back real neatly and strow it with old leaves and things, and hope it grows back before anyone notices who might think twice. We should try that.'

'We could set up a diversion. Leave a trail of false clues so it looked as if we were Satanists, practising a black mass or something.' Hildebrand gave another snort and long high chuckle of solitary laugher. Cropper looked at his heavy pink face and felt twinges of fastidious distaste. He was going to have to spend much more of his time than would be pleasant in this banal creature's company.

'Our best hope is that nobody notices. Anything else is *bad* – if anyone notices at all that the grave has been disturbed, they will also notice our presence here quite likely. And put two and two together. Then we just fake it out. If we find the box and take it away, no one can *prove* it ever existed, even if they dig again and have a look. Which they won't. Drax won't let them. But our best hope – I repeat – is to be unobtrusive.'

On their way out of the churchyard they passed two other visitors, a man and a woman, green-clad in quilted jackets and wellingtons against the pervasive rain, blending into the background in an English way. They were examining the sculpted heads of laughing cherubs or baby angels on two tall leaning stones; the little creatures rested their dimpled feet on footstool skulls. 'Morning,' said Hildebrand, in his county English voice, and 'Morning' they replied, in the same tone. Nobody met anyone else's eye; it was very English.

On the fifteenth Cropper and Hildebrand dined together in the restaurant, which was panelled like the bar, and had a cheerful log fire burning in the stone fireplace. Cropper and Hildebrand were to one side of this; a young couple, who had attention only for each other, and who were holding hands across the table, had the other. Cracking oil portraits of eighteenth-century parsons and squires, half-obscured and blackened by candle-smoke and thickened varnish, stared down heavily from the panels. They ate by candlelight, salmon mousse in lobster sauce, pheasant with all the trimmings, Stilton, sorbet *cassis maison*. Cropper savoured it all with regret. He was not going to be able to come back here for some considerable time, and he had enjoyed his visits to this part of the world. He liked the Rowan Tree Inn; it had romantically uneven floors, paved on the ground floor, creaking under carpets above; its corridors were so low and narrow that he was forced to stoop his tall head. The water made strange thumping and hawking sounds, which he treasured as he treasured, with equal love, the endless silver flow in his streamlined, gold-tapped bathroom in New Mexico. Both were good of their kind, snug, cramped, ancient smoky England, and the dry sun, the glass, the airy steel, the expansiveness of New Mexico. His blood was running, he was excited, as he always was when truly on the move, when his mind hung, like the moon, over his trajectory from one earth-mass to another, when he was neither here nor there. Only this time, more than ever. He had spent the time before dinner in his room, running through exercises and routines, limbering up, contorting his muscles, swaying and twisting and punching and coercing his body into suppleness. He liked that. He looked good, still. He stood in front of a cheval glass in his special exercise clothes, long black pants and towelling sweater. He resembled his piratical ancestors, or a film version of them, his silvery hair romantically dishevelled on his brow.

Hildebrand said, 'And tomorrow, USA, here we come. I've never been, you know. Only seen it on telly. You'll have to teach me about giving lectures.'

Cropper thought that perhaps he could, or should have done it all entirely alone. But then it would have been absolute theft, absolute intrusion, whereas this way, he was only speeding up a natural process, buying from Hildebrand what would have been his in any case, later, a very little later, if he was to be believed about Lord Ash's state of health.

'Where have you parked the Merc?' said Hildebrand.

'Tell me about your –' said Cropper, casting about for a safe topic of conversation. 'Tell me about your gardening, about your lawn.'

'How did you know about my lawn?'

'You told me. Never mind why, now. What sort of garden do you have?'

Hildebrand began a long description. Cropper looked round the dining-room. The honeymoon couple had their heads together over their table. The man, smoothly handsome, in what Cropper recognised as a Christian Dior wool and cashmere jacket in dark peacock, took their joined hands to his mouth and kissed the inside of the girl's wrists. She wore an ivory silk shirt, displaying an amethyst necklace on a smooth throat, above a purple skirt. She caressed her partner's hair, evidently in that obsessive and compulsive state that excludes, for brief periods of human lives, all consciousness of other observers.

'How late shall we have to leave it?' said Hildebrand.

'We won't discuss that here,' said Cropper. 'Tell me about – about –'

'Have you told them we're checking out?'

'I paid them for tomorrow night.'

'It's a good night. Nice and quiet. Good moon.'

On the way up to their bedrooms they crossed the young couple, both coming out of the wooden telephone cubicle in the hall. Mortimer Cropper inclined his head. Hildebrand said 'Goo' night.'

'Good night,' said the couple, together.

'We're going to bed early,' said Hildebrand. 'Done in with the exercise.'

The girl smiled and took hold of her companion's arm.

'So are we. Going to bed. Good night. Sleep well.'

Cropper waited until one o'clock to go out. Everything was quiet. The fire still smoked. The air was heavily still. He had parked the Mercedes by the car park gate; there was no problem about getting back to the hotel as the room-keys all had Yale keys attached for the front door. The great car purred away smoothly, across the road, up the track to the church. Cropper parked it under a tree by the church gate, and got out storm lanterns and his newly purchased implements from the boot. It was raining a little; the ground underfoot was wet and slippery. He and Hildebrand made their way in the dark to the Ashes' grave. 'Look,' said Hildebrand, standing in a patch of moonlight between the church and the knoll with the yew and the cedar. A huge white owl circled the church tower, unhurried, powerful and entirely silent, intent on its own business.

'Spooky,' said Hildebrand Ash.

'A beautiful creature,' said Mortimer Cropper, somehow identifying his own excitement, his own sense of potency and certainty in his muscles and mind with the measured wing beat, the easy, easy floating. Above the owl, the dragon moved a little, this way, that way, creaking, desisting, catching a desultory air movement.

They had to move fast. It was a lot of work, potentially, for two men, before daylight. They cut and stacked turf. Hildebrand said, panting, 'Do you have any idea whereabouts it might be?' and Cropper realised that although he had indeed a *very precise* idea, that the thing lay somewhere about the heart of the larger-than-mansize space of the plot of land, this idea had been nurtured in his own hot imagination; he had seen the scene of the box's reinterment so often, so often in his mind's eye, that he had invented the place. But not for nothing was he the descendant of spiritualists and Shakers. He gave weight to intuition. 'We'll start at the head,' he said, 'and excavate a decent depth, and progress towards the feet in an orderly way.'

They dug. They threw up an increasing mound, a mixture of clay and flints, chopped ends of roots, small bones of vole and bird, stones, sifted pebbles. Hildebrand grunted as he worked, his bald head glinting in the moonlight. Cropper swung his spade with a kind of joy. He felt he was over some border of the permissible and everything was just fine. He was not a grey old scholar, smelling of the lamp, sitting on his fundament. He was *doing*, he would find, it was his destiny. He poised his sharp spade above the earth and struck and struck with a terrible glee, slicing, penetrating the sloppy and the resistant. He took off his jacket, and felt the rain on his back with pleasure, and his own sweat trickling between his shoulder-blades and down his breast, with joy. He struck, he struck, he struck. 'Steady on,' said Hildebrand, and 'Keep going,' hissed Cropper, pulling with his bare hands at a long snake of the yew's root system, getting out his heavy knife to cut it.

'It is here. I know it is here.'

'Go steady. We don't want to disturb the – disturb – if we can help it.'

'No. We shouldn't have to. Keep at it.'

A wind was getting up. It flapped a little: one or two of the churchyard trees creaked and groaned. A sudden gust lifted Cropper's discarded jacket briefly from the stone where it hung, and dropped it to the earth. Cropper thought, as he had not precisely thought so far, that at the bottom of the pit he was excavating, lay Randolph Ash and his wife Ellen, or what was left of them. The storm-light showed only slice-marks of their spades and raw, cold-smelling soil. Cropper snuffed the air. Something seemed to move and swing and sway in it, as if ready to slap at him. He felt for a moment, very purely, a *presence*, not of someone, but of some mobile *thing*, and for a moment rested dully on his spade, forbidden. In that moment, the great storm hit Sussex. A long tongue of wind howled past, a wall of air banged at Hildebrand, who sat down suddenly in the clay, winded. Cropper began to dig again. A kind of dull howling and whistling began, and then a chorus of groans, and creaking sighs, the trees, protesting. A tile spun off the church roof. Cropper opened his mouth and shut it again. The wind moved in the graveyard like a creature from another dimension, trapped and screaming. The branches of the yew and cedar gesticulated desperately.

Cropper went on digging. 'I will,' he said. 'I *will*.'

He told Hildebrand to go on, but Hildebrand couldn't hear and wasn't looking; he was sitting in the mud next to a gravestone, clutching the neck of his jacket, fighting the air that had worked its way inside.

Cropper dug. Hildebrand began to crawl slowly round the rim of Cropper's excavation. The very bases of the yew and the cedar began to shift, to move laterally and to complain.

Hildebrand pulled at Cropper's sleeve.

'Stop. Go in. This is – beyond the limit. Not safe. Shelter.' Horizontal rain whipped and sliced the flesh of his cheeks.

'Not now,' said Cropper, poising his spade like a divining rod, and struck again.

He hit metal. He got down to the earth and scrabbled with his hands. It came up – an oblong thing, covered with corrosion, a nugget recognisably shaped. He sat down, on the adjacent stone, clutching it.

The wind prised at the church roof and flung off a few more tiles. The trees cried out and swung. Cropper pushed at the box with useless fingers, chipped at a corner with a knife. The wind took his hair and turned it in mad spirals round his head. Hildebrand Ash had his hands over his ears. He edged closer and cried in Cropper's ear,

'This? It?'

'Right. Size. Yes. This is It.'

'What now?'

Cropper gestured at the hole.

'Fill that. I'll put my box in the trunk of the car –'

He set out across the churchyard. The air was full of noises. There was a whining, ripping noise which he saw was the sound of the trees along the track and in the hedgerow whipping to and fro, tossing their crowns of trailing twigs from earth to sky to earth. More tiles cut the air with a sound of their own, and hit the ground, or gravestones, with keen crashing explosions. Cropper hurried on, bearing his box, his face smeared with flying leaves and with streaks of sap. Nevertheless, as he went, he fingered his find, seeking, and touching, the edge of the box's rim. As he struggled with the gate to the churchyard, which danced dementedly on its hinges, bucked under his hand and so saved him, he heard a sound of something rising and bursting in the earth, as he had seen oil gushers do in Texas, and mixed with this another sound, tearing, straining, creaking so horridly loudly that its creaks were an outcry. Around his very feet the earth quaked and moved; he sat down; there was a sound of rending and a great mass of grey descended before his eyes like a tumbling hill, accompanied by the sweeping sound of a whole mass of leaves and fine branches whipping the moving air. The final sound of all these – except the original rushing which persisted – was a mixture of drums, cymbals, and theatrical thundersheet. His nostrils were full of wet soil and sap and gasoline fumes. A tree had fallen directly across the Mercedes. His car was gone, and his path back to the inn was barred, by one tree at least, possibly by many.

He came back towards Ash's grave, pushing against a howling tide of air, hearing other trees crash all around. As he came to the knoll and turned his storm lantern on it, he saw the yew tree throw up its arms and a huge gaping white mouth appear briefly in the reddish trunk, close to the thick base of the tree, which leaned giddily over, and went on cracking slowly, slowly, descending in a burst of needle-leaves, and finally snapping and shuddering to rest across the grave, obscuring it utterly. He could now go neither forwards nor backwards. He cried out 'Hildebrand!' and his own voice seemed to curl uselessly back like smoke in his face. Was he safer nearer the church? Could he get there? Where was Hildebrand? There was a momentary lull and he called again.

Hildebrand called out, 'Help. Help. Where are you?'

Another voice said, 'Here, by the church. Hang on.'

Peering between the branches of the yew, Cropper saw Hildebrand crawling along the grass between the graves towards the church. Waiting for him was a dark figure with a flashlight, whose beam was swung in his direction.

'Professor Cropper?' said this being, in a clear, authoritative male voice. 'Are you all right?'

'I seem to be trapped by trees.'

'We can get you out, I expect. Have you got the box?'

'What box?' said Cropper.

'Yes, he has,' said Hildebrand, 'Oh, get us out of here, this is ghastly, I can't take any more.'

There was a crackling sound, like the electric forces that played at Hella Lees's seances. The figure spoke to the air.

'Yes, he's here. Yes, he's got it. We're all cut off by trees. Are you OK?'

Crackle, crackle.

Cropper decided to run for it. He turned back. It must be possible to circumnavigate the tree in the track – except that there seemed to be other trees, a hedge, a huge scaly barrier reared where none had been.

'It's no good,' the figure incredibly said. 'You're surrounded. And there's a tree on your Mercedes.'

Cropper spun round, and the beam of the other's flashlight revealed, peering through the branches, like bizarre flowers or fruit, wet and white, Roland Michell, Maud Bailey, Leonora Stern, James Blackadder, and with streaming white woolly hair descended, like some witch or prophetess, a transfigured Beatrice Nest.

It took them an hour and a half to scramble back on foot to the Rowan Tree Inn. The Londoners, who had set out in two cars from Mortlake before the storm, but had begun to see its effects before they set out for the church, had brought a small saw from Blackadder's Peugeot, as well as the walkie-talkie with which Euan had equipped them. Armed with this, and Cropper's shovels, they scrambled and climbed over and under fallen columns and sighing vegetation, holding out hands to help, pushing, pulling, until they arrived at the road and saw festoons of cable and dark windows. The power was cut. Cropper let them all in to the Inn, still clutching the box. In the hall already were a crew of stranded lorry drivers, motor cyclists and a couple of firemen. The landlord was moving round the hall with candles in bottles. Huge pans of water were boiling on the kitchen Aga. At no other time would the incursion of so many wet, dirty scholars in the small hours have been taken with such casual and unquestioning calm. Pots of coffee and hot milk – and, at Euan's suggestion, a bottle of brandy – were taken up to Cropper's room, where his captors accompanied him. Dressing-gowns and spare sweaters were found for all, amongst Cropper's bags and Hildebrand's brand-new luggage. It was all so unreal, and the sense of communal survival was so powerful that they sat stupidly good, smiling weakly, damp and chill. Neither Cropper nor the others, curiously, could find force to be angry or even indignant. The box sat between candles, on the table in the window, rusty and earthy and wet. The women, all three clothed in pyjamas – Maud in Cropper's black silk, Leonora in his scarlet cotton, and Beatrice in peppermint and white stripes belonging to Hildebrand, sat side by side on the bed. Val and Euan had their own clothes and represented normality. Blackadder wore a sweater and cotton trousers of Hildebrand's. Euan said,

'I've *always* wanted to say, "You are surrounded".'

'You said it very well,' said Cropper. 'I don't know you, but I've seen you. In the restaurant.'

'And at the Garden Centre, and Densher and Winterbourne, and the churchyard yesterday, yes. I'm Euan MacIntyre. Dr Bailey's lawyer. I believe I can prove she is the legal owner of the manuscripts of the letters – both sides – at present in the possession of Sir George Bailey.'

'This box, however, is nothing to do with her.'

'It will be *mine*,' said Hildebrand.

'Unless you had a Faculty from the Bishop, and permission from Mr Drax and permission from Lord Ash, it was feloniously obtained by disturbing a burial, and I can take it from you, and take you into custody as a citizen's arrest. Moreover, Professor Blackadder has a letter forbidding the export of the contents until their status as national heritage treasures has been ascertained.'

'I see,' said Mortimer Cropper. 'There may, of course, be nothing in there. Or merest dust. Might we – conjointly – examine the contents? Since we are unable to leave this place, or each other's company?'

'It shouldn't be disturbed,' said Beatrice. 'It should be put back.'

She looked round the group and saw no support. Mortimer Cropper said, 'If you believed that, you could have made your citizen's arrest before I found it.'

Blackadder said, 'That is perfectly true.'

Leonora said, 'Why did she leave it to be found, if she didn't entertain the thought of it? Why wasn't it clasped to her bosom – or his?'

Maud said, 'We need the end of the story.'

'There is no guarantee that *that* is what we shall find,' said Blackadder.

'But we *must look*,' said Maud.

Cropper produced a can of oil, and rubbed the oil round the join, working it with his knife, flaking off particles of rust. After a long few moments, he inserted the knife point under the join and pushed. The lid sprang off, revealing Randolph Ash's glass specimen container, cloudy and stained, but intact. Cropper lifted the lid of this too, slipping his knife round it, neatly, neatly, and took out the contents. An oiled silk bag contained: a hair bracelet, with a silver clasp of two hands joining: a blue envelope containing a long thread of very finely plaited pale hair: another oiled silk package which proved to contain a thick bundle of letters tied with ribbon: and a long envelope, once white, sealed, inscribed in brown letters: *To: Randolph Henry Ash, under cover.*

Cropper ruffled the large packet of letters and said, 'Their love letters. As she said.' He looked at the sealed letter and handed it to Maud. Maud looked at the handwriting and said,

'I *think* . . . I'm nearly sure . . .'

Euan said, 'If it's unopened the question of ownership becomes very interesting. Is it the property of the sender – if it wasn't received – or the property of the addressee, since it lies unopened in his grave?'

Cropper, before anyone could think of any reason why not, took the envelope, slipped his knife under the seal, and opened it. Inside were a letter and a photograph. The photograph was stained at the edges and covered with silvery dashes like a storm of hailstones or white blossom, and with circles of dark sooty markings, like the infestations of mirrors, but behind and through all this glimmered the ghostly figure of a bride, holding a bouquet of lilies and roses, looking out from a mass of veiling and a heavy crown of flowers.

Leonora said, 'Miss Havisham. The Bride of Corinth.'

Maud said slowly, 'No, no, I begin to see —'

Euan said 'Do you? I thought so. Read the letter. You know the writing.'

'Shall I?'

So, in that hotel room, to that strange gathering of disparate seekers and hunters, Christabel LaMotte's letter to Randolph Ash was read aloud, by candlelight, with the wind howling past, and the panes of the windows rattling with the little blows of flying debris as it raced on and on, over the downs.

My dear — my dear —

They tell me you are very ill. I do ill to disturb your peace at this time, with unseasonable memories — but I find I have — after all — a thing which I must tell you. You will say, it should have been told twenty-eight years ago — or never — and so maybe it should — but I could or would not. And now I think of you continuously, also I pray for you, and I know — I have known for these many years — that I have done you wrong.

You have a daughter, who is well, and married, and the mother of a beautiful boy. I send you her picture. You will see — she is beautiful — and resembles, I like to think, both her parents, neither of whom she knows to be her parent.

So much is — if not easy to indite — at least simple. But the history? With such a truth, I owe you also its history — or owe myself, it may be — I have sinned against you — but for causes —

All History is hard facts — and something else — passion and colour lent by men. I will tell you — at least — the facts.

When we two parted I knew — but not with certain proof — that the consequences would be — what they were. We agreed — on that last black day — to leave, to leave each other and never for a moment look back. And I meant to keep my side of it for pride's sake and for yours, whatever might come. So I made arrangements — you would not believe how I calculated and schemed — I found a place to go — (which you later discovered, I know) where I should make no one but myself responsible for our fate — hers and mine — And then I consulted the one possible helper — my sister Sophie — who arranged to help me in a lie more appropriate to a Romance than to my previous quiet life — but Necessity sharpens the wits and fortifies resolution — and so our daughter was born in Brittany, in the Convent, and carried to England, where Sophie took her and brought her up as her own, as we had agreed. And I will say that Sophie has loved and cherished her as well as anyone not her true mother might do. She has run free in English fields and married a cousin (no cousin, of course, truly seen) in Norfolk, and is a Squire's wife, and comely.

And I came here — not long after you and I met for the last time — as it turns out — at Mrs Lees's seance, where you were so angry, so wrathful — and so was I too, for you tore away the dressings from my spirit's wounds, and I thought, as women will, you might suffer a little with my good will, for the greater part of suffering in this world is ours — we bear it. When I said to you — you have made a murderess of me — I spoke of poor Blanche, whose terrible end torments me daily. But I saw you thought I spoke as Gretchen might to Faust. And I thought — with a cold little malice born of my then extreme sickness of body and mind — let him think so, then, if he knows me so little, let him wear himself away, thinking so. Women in childbirth cry out exceedingly against the author as they see it of their misfortunes, for whom a moment's passion may have no lasting reminder, no monstrous catastrophe of body or of soul — so I thought then — I am calmer now. I am old now.

Oh, my dear, here I sit, an old witch in a turret, writing my verses by licence of my boorish brother-in-law, a hanger-on as I had never meant to be, of my sister's good fortune (in the pecuniary sense) and I write to you, as if it was yesterday, of all that rage like iron bands burning round my breast, of the spite and the love (for you, for my sweet Maia, for poor Blanche too). But it is not yesterday, and you are very ill. I wish you may be well, Randolph, and I send you my blessing, and I ask yours, and your forgiveness, if it may be. For I knew and must have known that you have a generous heart and would have cared for us — for me and for Maia — but I had a secret fear — here it all tumbles out, after all — but Truth is best, now — is it not? — I was afraid, you see, that you would wish to take her, you and your wife, for your very own — and she was mine, I bore her — I could not let her go — and so I hid her from you — and you from her, for she would have loved you, there is a space in her life forever, which is yours. ~~Oh, what have I done?~~

And here I might stop, or might have stopped a few lines back, with my proper request for forgiveness. I write under cover to your wife — who may read this, or do as she pleases with it — I am in her hands — but it is so dangerously sweet to speak out, after all these years — I trust myself to her and your goodwill — This is in some sort my Testament. I have had few friends in my life, and of those friends two only whom I trusted – Blanche – and you – and both I loved too well and one died terribly, hating me and you. But now I am old I regret most of all not those few sharp sweet days of passion – which might have been almost anyone's passion, it seems, for all passions run the same course to the same end, or so it now seems to me being old – I regret, I would say, had I not grown garrulously digressive – our old letters, of poetry and other things, our trusting minds which recognised each the other. Did you ever read, I wonder, one of the few poor exemplars sold of The Fairy Melusina and think – I knew her once – or as you most truly might – 'Without me this Tale might not have come to the Telling'? I owe you Melusina and Maia both, and I have paid no debts. (I think she will not die, my Melusina, some discerning reader will save her?)

I have been Melusina these thirty years. I have so to speak flown about and about the battlements of this stronghold crying on the wind of my need to see and feed and comfort my child, who knew me not. She was a happy soul – a sunny creature, simple in her affections and marvellously direct in her nature. She loved her adoptive parents most deeply – Sir George too, who had not a drop of her blood in his beef-veins, but was entranced by her prettiness and good nature, which was as well for her and me.

Me she did not love. To whom can I say this but to you? She sees me as a sorcière, a spinster in a fairy tale, looking at her with glittering eye and waiting for her to prick her poor little finger and stumble into the brute sleep of adult truth. And if my eye glittered with tears she saw them not. No, I will go on, I fill her with a sort of fear, a sort of revulsion – she feels, rightly, a too-much in my concern for her – but misreads that, which is most natural, as something unnatural.

You will think – if the shock of what I have had to tell you has left you any power to care or to think about my narrow world – that a romancer such as I (or a true dramatist, such as you) would not be able to keep such a secret for nigh on thirty years (think, Randolph, thirty years), without bringing about some peripeteia, some dénouement, some secret hinting or open scene of revelation. Ah, but if you were here, you would see how I dare not. For her sake, for she is so happy. For mine, in that I fear – I fear the possible horror in her fair eyes. If I told her – that – and she stepped back? And then I swore to Sophie that it should be a condition of her kindness that it was absolute and irrevocable – and without Sophie's goodwill there would have been no home and no support for her.

She laughed and played like Coleridge's limber elf 'Singing, dancing to itself' – do you remember our letters of Christabel? She cared nothing for books, nothing. I wrote her small tales, and they were bound and printed, and I gave them to her, and she smiled sweetly and thanked me, and put them by. I never saw her read them for pleasure. She loved to ride, and to do archery, and played boys' games with her (so-called) brothers ... and in the end married a visiting cousin she had tumbled in haystacks with as a tiny staggering little thing of five. I wanted her to have an untroubled life and so she did – but it is not mine, I am not of it, I am the spinster aunt who is not loved....

So I am punished, in some sort, for keeping her from you.

Do you remember how I wrote to you of the riddle of the egg? As an eidolon of my solitude and self-possession which you threatened whether you would or no? And destroyed, my dear, meaning me nothing but good, I do believe and know. I wonder – if I had kept to my closed castle, behind my motte-and-bailey defences – should I have been a great poet – as you are? I wonder – was my spirit rebuked by yours – as Caesar's was by Antony – or was I enlarged by your generosity as you intended? These things are all mixed and mingled – and we loved each other – for each other – only it was in the end for Maia (who will have nothing of her 'strange name' and is called plain May, which becomes her).

I have been so angry for so long – with all of us, with you, with Blanche, with my poor self. And now near the end 'in calm of mind all passion spent' I think of you again with clear love. I have been reading Samson Agonistes and came upon the dragon I always thought you were – as I was the 'tame villatic fowl' –

> His fiery virtue roused
> From under ashes into sudden flame
> And as an evening dragon came
> Assailant on the perched roosts
> And nests in order ranged
> Of tame villatic fowl –

Is not that fine? Did we not – did you not flame, and I catch fire? Shall we survive and rise from our ashes? Like Milton's Phoenix?

> that self-begotten bird
> In the Arabian woods embossed
> That no second knows nor third
> And lay erewhile a holocaust,
> From out her ashy womb now teemed
> Revives, reflourishes, then vigorous most
> When most unactive deemed

502

And though her body die, her fame survives
A secular bird, ages of lives.

I would rather have lived alone, so, if you would have the truth. But since that might not be – and is granted to almost none – I thank God for you – if there must be a Dragon – that He was You –

I must give up this writing. One more thing. Your grandson (and mine, most strange). His name is Walter and he chants verses to the amazement of his stable- and furrow-besotted parents. I have taught him much of the Ancient Mariner: *he recites the passage of the blessing of the snakes, and the vision of the glittering eye of the ocean cast up to the moon, most feelingly, and his own eyes are bright with it. He is a strong boy, and* will live.

I must close. If you are able or willing – please send me a sign that you have read this. I dare not ask, if you forgive.

                               Christabel LaMotte

There was silence. Maud's voice had begun clear, expressionless, like matt glass, and had ended with suppressed feeling.

Leonora said, 'Wow!'

Cropper said, 'I knew it. I knew it was something *vast –*'

Hildebrand said, 'I don't understand –'

Euan said, 'Unfortunately illegitimate children couldn't inherit at that time. Or you, Maud, would be the outright owner of the whole mass of documents. I *suspected* something like this might be the case. Victorian families often looked after bastards in this way, hiding them in legitimate families to give them a decent chance –'

Blackadder said, 'How strange for you, Maud, to turn out to be descended from both – how strangely appropriate to have been exploring all along the myth – no the truth – of your own origins.'

Everyone looked at Maud, who sat looking at the photograph.

She said, 'I have seen this before. We have one. She was my great-great-great-grandmother.'

Beatrice Nest was in tears. They rose to her eyes and flashed and fell. Maud put out a hand.

'Beatrice –'

'I'm sorry to be so silly. It's just so terrible to think – he can't ever have read it, can he? She wrote all that for no one. She must have waited for an answer – and none can have come –'

Maud said, 'You know Ellen. Why do you think she put it in the box – with her own love-letters –'

'And their hair,' said Leonora. 'And Christabel's hair, it must be, the blonde –'

Beatrice said,

'She didn't know what to do, perhaps. She didn't give it to him, and she didn't read it – I can imagine that – she just put it away –'

'For Maud,' said Blackadder. 'As it turns out. She preserved it, for Maud.'

Everyone looked at Maud, who sat whitely, looking at the picture, holding the manuscript.

Maud said, 'I can't go on thinking. I must sleep. I'm exhausted. We shall think of all this in the morning. I don't know why it's such a shock. But.' She turned to Roland. 'Help me find a bedroom to sleep in. All these papers should go to Professor Blackadder, for safe-keeping. I'd like to keep the photograph, just tonight, if I may.'

Roland and Maud sat side by side on the edge of a four-poster bed, hung about with William Morris golden lilies. They looked at the photograph of Maia's wedding-day, in the light of a candle, held in a silver chamber-candlestick. Because it was hard to see, their heads were close together, dark and pale, so that they could smell each other's hair, still full of the smells of the storm, rain and troubled clay and crushed and flying leafage. And underneath that, their own particular, separate human warmths.

Maia Bailey smiled up at them serenely. They read her face now in the light of Christabel's letter, and thus saw it, amongst all its silvery spangles and shine of ageing, as a happy confident face, wearing its thick wreath with a certain ease, and feeling pleasure, not drama, in the occasion.

'She looks like Christabel,' said Maud. 'You can see it.'

'She looks like you,' said Roland. He added, 'She looks like Randolph Ash, too. The width of the brow. The width of the mouth. The end of the eyebrows, there.'

'So I look like Randolph Henry Ash.'

Roland touched her face. 'I would never have seen it. But yes. The same things. Here, at the corner of the eyebrow. There, at the edge of the mouth. Now I have seen it, I shall always see it.'

'I don't quite like it. There's something unnaturally *determined* about it all. Daemonic. I feel they have taken me over.'

'One always feels like that about ancestors. Even very humble ones, if one has the luck to know them.'

He stroked her wet hair, gently, absently.

Maud said, 'What next?'

'How do you mean, what next?'

'What happens next? To us?'

'*You* will have a lot of legal problems. And a lot of editing to do. I – I have made some plans.'

'I thought – we might edit the letters together, you and I?'

'That's generous, but not necessary. You turn out to be a central figure in this story. I only got into it by stealing, in the first place. I've learned a lot.'

'What have you learned?'

'Oh – something from Ash and Vico. About poetic language. I'm – I – I have things I have to write.'

'You seem angry with me. I don't understand why.'

'No, I'm not. That is, yes, I have been. You have your certainties. Literary theory. Feminism. A sort of social ease, it comes out with Euan, a world you belong in. I haven't got anything. Or hadn't. And I grew – attached to you. I know male pride is out of date and unimportant, but it mattered.'

Maud said 'I feel –' and stopped.

'You feel?'

He looked at her. Her face was like carved marble in the candlelight. Icily regular, splendidly null, as he had often said to himself.

He said, 'I haven't told you. I've got three jobs. Hong Kong, Barcelona, Amsterdam. The world is all before me. I shan't be here, you see, to edit the letters. They aren't to do with me.'

Maud said, 'I feel –'

'*What?*' said Roland.

'When I feel – anything – I go cold all over. I freeze. I can't – speak out. I'm – I'm – not good at relationships.'

She was shivering. She still looked – it was a trick of her lovely features – cool and a little contemptuous. Roland said,

'Why do you go cold?' He kept his voice gentle.

'I – I've *analysed* it. Because I have the sort of good looks I have. People treat you as a kind of *possession* if you have a certain sort of good looks. Not lively, but sort of clear-cut and –'

'Beautiful.'

'Yes, why not. You can become a property or an idol. I don't want that. It kept happening.'

'It needn't.'

'Even you – drew back – when we met. I expect that, now. I use it.'

'Yes. But you don't want –`do you – to be alone always. Or do you?'

'I feel as she did. I keep my defences up because I must go on *doing my work*. I know how she felt about her unbroken egg. Her self-possession, her autonomy. I don't want to think of that going. You understand?'

'Oh yes.'

'I write about liminality. Thresholds. Bastions. Fortresses.'

'Invasion. Irruption.'

'Of course.'

'It's not my scene. I have my own solitude.'

'I know. You – you would never – blur the edges messily –'

'Superimpose –'

'No, that's why I –'

'Feel safe with me –'

'Oh no. Oh no. I love you. I think I'd rather I didn't.'

'I love you,' said Roland. 'It isn't convenient. Not now I've acquired a future. But that's how it is. In the worst way. All the things we – we grew up not believing in. Total obsession, night and day. When I see you, you look *alive* and everything else – fades. All that.'

'Icily regular, splendidly null.'

'How did you know I used to think that?'

'Everyone always does. Fergus did. Does.'

'Fergus is a devourer. I haven't got much to offer. But I could let you be, I could –'

'In Hong Kong, Barcelona and Amsterdam?'

'Well, certainly, if I was there. I wouldn't threaten your autonomy.'

'Or be here to love me,' said Maud, 'Oh, love is terrible, it is a *wrecker* –'

'It can be quite cunning.' said Roland. 'We could think of a way – a modern way – Amsterdam isn't far –'

Cold hand met cold hand.

'Let's get into bed,' said Roland. 'We can work it out.'

'I'm afraid of that too.'

'What a coward you are after all. I'll take care of you, Maud.'

So they took off their unaccustomed clothes, Cropper's multi-coloured lendings, and climbed naked inside the curtains and into the depths of the feather bed and blew out the candle. And very slowly and with infinite gentle delays and delicate diversions and variations of indirect assault Roland finally, to use an outdated phrase, entered and took possession of all her white coolness that grew warm against him, so that there seemed to be no boundaries, and he heard, towards dawn, from a long way off, her clear voice crying out, uninhibited, unashamed, in pleasure and triumph.

In the morning, the whole world had a strange new smell. It was the smell of the aftermath, a green smell, a smell of shredded leaves and oozing resin, of crushed wood and splashed sap, a tart smell, which bore some relation to the smell of bitten apples. It was the smell of death and destruction and it smelled fresh and lively and hopeful.

--◦◦❦◦◦--

POSTSCRIPT 1868

There are things which happen and leave no discernible trace, are not spoken or written of, though it would be very wrong to say that subsequent events go on indifferently, all the same, as though such things had never been.

Two people met, on a hot May day, and never later mentioned their meeting. This is how it was.

There was a meadow full of young hay, and all the summer flowers in great abundance. Blue cornflowers, scarlet poppies, gold buttercups, a veil of speedwells, an intricate carpet of daisies where the grass was shorter, scabious, yellow snapdragons, bacon and egg plant, pale milkmaids, purple heartsease, scarlet pimpernel and white shepherd's purse, and round this field a high bordering hedge of Queen Anne's lace and foxgloves, and above that dogroses, palely shining in a thorny hedge, honeysuckle all creamy and sweet-smelling, rambling threads of bryony and the dark stars of deadly nightshade. It was abundant, it seemed as though it must go on shining forever. The grasses had an enamelled gloss and were connected by diamond-threads of light. The larks sang, and the thrushes, and the blackbirds, sweet and clear, and there were butterflies everywhere, blue, sulphur, copper, and fragile white, dipping from flower to flower, from clover to vetch to larkspur, seeing their own guiding visions of invisible violet pentagrams and spiralling coils of petal-light.

There was a child, swinging on a gate, wearing a butcher-blue dress and a white pinafore, humming to herself and making a daisy-chain.

There was a man, tall, bearded, his face in shadow under a wide-brimmed hat, a wanderer coming up the lane, between high hedges, with an ashplant in his hand and the look of a walker.

He stopped to speak to the child who smiled and answered cheerfully, without ceasing her creaking swinging to and fro. He asked where he was, and the name of the house in the narrow valley below, which he knew, in fact, very well, and so went on to ask her name, which she told him was May. She had another name, she said, which she did not like. He said perhaps that might come to change, names grew and diminished as time ran on: he would like to know her long name. So she said, swinging more busily, that her name was Maia Thomasine Bailey, and that her father and mother lived in the house down there, and that she had two brothers. He told her that Maia was the mother of Hermes, thief, artist and psychopomp; and that he knew a waterfall called Thomasine. She had known a pony called Hermes, she said, fast as the *wind*, she could tell him, and she had never heard of a waterfall with a name like Thomasine.

He said, 'I think I know your mother. You have a true look of your mother.'

'No one else says that. *I* think I look like my father. My father is strong and kind and takes me riding like the *wind*.'

'I think you have a look of your father too,' he said then, and put his arms around her waist, very matter-of-fact and brief, so as not to frighten her, and lifted her down onto his side. They sat there on a hummock and talked, in a cloud of butterflies, as he remembered it with absolute clarity, and she remembered it more and more vaguely, as the century ran on. Beetles ran about their feet, jet and emerald. She told him about her pleasant life, her amusements, her ambitions. He said, 'You seem extraordinarily happy,' and she said, 'Oh yes, I am, I am.' And then he sat quietly for a moment or two, and she asked him if he could make daisy chains.

'I will make you a crown,' he said. 'A crown for a May Queen. But you must give me something, in exchange.'

'I haven't got anything to give.'

'Oh, just a lock of hair – a very fine one – to remember you by.'

'Like a fairy story.'

'Just so.'

So he made her a crown, on a base of pliant twigs from the coppiced hedge, and wove in it green fronds and trails of all colours, ivy and ferns, silvery grasses and the starry leaves of bryony, the wild clematis. And he studded it with roses and honeysuckle and fringed it with belladonna ('but you know that you must never *eat* this,' he said and she replied scornfully that she knew *all* about what she must not eat, she had been told often enough).

'There,' he said, crowning the little pale head. 'Full beautiful, a fairy's child. Or like Proserpine. Do you know

> "that fair field
> Of Enna, where Proserpine gathering flowers,
> Herself a fairer flower, by gloomy Dis
> Was gathered, which cost Ceres all that pain
> To seek her through the world"?'

She looked at him, proud and still a little scornful, holding her head steady under its burden.

'I have an aunt who is always telling me poems like that. But I don't like poetry.'

He took out a little pair of pocket scissors, and cut, very gently, a long lock from the buttercup-gold floss which fell about her shoulders in a great cloud.

'Here,' she said, 'I'll plait it for you, to keep it tidily.'

Whilst her little fingers worked, and her face frowned over her work, he said,

'I am sorry you don't like poetry, as I am a poet.'

'Oh, I like *you*,' she hastened to say, 'You make lovely things and don't fuss —'

She held out the finished plait, which he wound in a fine coil, and put into the back of his watch.

'Tell your aunt,' he said, 'that you met a poet, who was looking for the Belle Dame Sans Merci, and who met you instead, and who sends her his compliments, and will not disturb her, and is on his way to fresh woods and pastures new.'

'I'll try to remember,' she said, steadying her crown.

So he kissed her, always matter-of-fact, so as not to frighten her, and went on his way.

And on the way home, she met her brothers, and there was a rough-and-tumble, and the lovely crown was broken, and she forgot the message, which was never delivered.

1990: LITERARY EVENTS

April – Pulitzer Prize for Fiction announced:
The Mambo Kings Play Songs of Love – Oscar Hijuelos

September – Booker Prize shortlist announced:
An Awfully Big Adventure – Beryl Bainbridge
Possession – A.S. Byatt
The Gate of Angels – Penelope Fitzgerald
Amongst Women – John McGahern
Lies of Silence – Brian Moore
Solomon Gursky Was Here – Mordecai Richler

October – Booker Prize winner announced:
Possession by A.S. Byatt

Upon winning the Booker Prize, A.S. Byatt announced that she
now had the money she needed to build her longed-for
swimming pool in Provence.

October – Nobel Prize for Literature goes to Octavio Paz
(Mexico)

November – Roald Dahl dies aged 74 (b. 1916)

The biggest selling hardback fiction title in the USA is
The Plains of Passage by Jean M. Auel. The biggest selling
hardback non-fiction title of the year is *A Life on the Road* by
Charles Kuralt

Other bestselling titles:
Clear and Present Danger – Tom Clancy
Jurassic Park – Michael Crichton
Four Past Midnight – Stephen King
The Buddha of Suburbia – Hanif Kureishi
The Bourne Ultimatum – Robert Ludlum
The Black Book – Orhan Pamuk

1990: WORLD EVENTS

The Cold War ends

7 January – The Leaning Tower of Pisa is closed due to safety concerns

11 February – Apartheid in South Africa ends and Nelson Mandela is released from prison after 27 years

13 February–3 October – German reunification is agreed and East and West Germany become a single nation

March – Protests and riots against the poll tax in Britain

15 March – Mikhail Gorbachev is voted as the first Executive President of the Soviet Union

20 April – The Hubble Space Telescope is launched

17 May – The World Health Organisation removes homosexuality from its list of diseases

8 July – West Germany beat Argentina 1–0 in the FIFA World Cup final, held in Italy after England lose to the Germans on penalties in the semi finals

2 August – Iraq invades Kuwait, leading to the Gulf War

24 August – Brian Keenan, a Northern Irish writer, is released after being held hostage for nearly five years in Lebanon

28 September – *Have I Got News For You* first broadcast

1 November – Mary Robinson becomes the first female President of Ireland

12 November – Tim Berners-Lee publishes a formal proposal for the World Wide Web and the first web page is written

28 November – Margaret Thatcher resigns as Prime Minister and is succeeded by John Major

2 December – Helmut Kohl wins the first free all-German elections since 1932

9 December – Slobodan Milošević becomes President of Serbia

Home Alone is the highest grossing film of the year; *Dances With Wolves* wins the Best Picture at the Academy Awards; the UK's biggest selling single of the year is *Unchained Melody* by the Righteous Brothers; the biggest selling album of the year is *But Seriously* by Phil Collins

Deaths:
Sammy Davis, Jr. (b. 1925)
Greta Garbo (b. 1905)

www.vintage-books.co.uk